FROM THE PAGES OF *GREAT AMERICAN SHORT STORIES: FROM HAWTHORNE TO HEMINGWAY*

"By the sympathy of your human hearts for sin, ye shall scent out all the places—whether in church, bed-chamber, street, field, or forest—where crime has been committed, and shall exult to behold the whole earth one stain of guilt, one mighty blood-spot."

(from Hawthorne's "Young Goodman Brown," page 17)

I had been passing alone, on horseback, through a singularly dreary tract of country, and at length found myself, as the shades of evening drew on, within view of the melancholy House of Usher.

(from Poe's "The Fall of the House of Usher," page 72)

At first, Bartleby did an extraordinary quantity of writing. As if long famishing for something to copy, he seemed to gorge himself on my documents. There was no pause for digestion. He ran a day and night line, copying by sunlight and by candlelight. I should have been quite delighted with his application, had he been cheerfully industrious. But he wrote on silently, palely, mechanically.

(from Melville's "Bartleby the Scrivener," page 116)

A man stood upon a railroad bridge in northern Alabama, looking down into the swift water twenty feet below. The man's hands were behind his back, the wrists bound with a cord. A rope closely encircled his neck.

(from Bierce's "An Occurrence at Owl Creek Bridge," page 151)

Conscious as I am of a deep aversion to stories of a painful nature, I have often asked myself whether, in the events here set forth, the element of pain is stronger than that of joy.

(from James's "My Friend Bingham," page 161)

"I never wanted for pa'tridges or gray squer'ls while he was to home. He's been a great wand'rer, I expect, and he's no hand to write letters. There, I don't blame him, I'd ha' seen the world myself if it had been so I could." (from Jewett's "A White Heron," page 229)

"We people of mixed blood are ground between the upper and the nether millstone. Our fate lies between absorption by the white race and extinction in the black. The one doesn't want us yet, but may take us in time. The other would welcome us, but it would be for us a backward step."

(from Chesnutt's "The Wife of His Youth," page 288)

"I ain't attempting," says he, "to decry the celebrated moral aspect of parental affection, but we're dealing with humans, and it ain't human for anybody to give up two thousand dollars for that forty-pound chunk of freckled wildcat. I'm willing to take a chance at fifteen hundred dollars. You can charge the difference up to me."

(from O. Henry's "The Ransom of Red Chief," page 342)

"It feels uncommonly queer to have enough cash to pay one's bills. I'd have sold my soul for it a few years ago!"

(from Wharton's "The Other Two," page 356)

He cherished the flame carefully and awkwardly. It meant life, and it must not perish.

(from London's "To Build a Fire," page 431)

The story of Wing Biddlebaum is a story of hands. Their restless activity, like unto the beating of the wings of an imprisoned bird, had given him his name. (from Anderson's "Hands," page 437)

"Isn't love any fun?"

(from Hemingway's "The End of Something," page 518)

GREAT AMERICAN SHORT STORIES

FROM HAWTHORNE TO HEMINGWAY

Edited with an Introduction
by Corinne Demas

George Stade
Consulting Editorial Director

BARNES & NOBLE CLASSICS
NEW YORK

Barnes & Noble Classics
New York

Published by Barnes & Noble Books
122 Fifth Avenue
New York, NY 10011

www.barnesandnoble.com/classics

Published in 2004 by Barnes & Noble Classics with new Introduction, Biographical Sketches of the Authors, and For Further Reading.

Great American Short Stories: from Hawthorne to Hemingway
ISBN-13: 978-1-59308-338-0
ISBN-10: 1-59308-338-6
LC Control Number 2004110468

Produced and published in conjunction with:
Fine Creative Media, Inc.
322 Eighth Avenue
New York, NY 10001
Michael J. Fine, President and Publisher

Printed in the United States of America

QM

9 10

TABLE OF CONTENTS

INTRODUCTION

When Edgar Allan Poe first described his conception of an ideal "prose tale" he could hardly have imagined that his vision would be guiding the genre of the short story for the next century and a half. His definition was not a rigid formula—like the rules for a sonnet, for instance—but rather a prototype for success. He outlined the qualities that he believed made a short story succeed, rather than set an immutable standard, and his insights influenced all the short-story writers who followed him.

Poe's influential discourse on the short story was part of a critical review that he wrote about Nathaniel Hawthorne's collection *Twice Told Tales* in *Graham's Magazine* in May 1842. The elements of the short story that he centers on in his critique are unity and length, and the necessary connection between the two.

> In almost all classes of composition, the unity of effect or impression is a point of the greatest importance. It is clear, moreover, that this unity cannot be thoroughly preserved in productions whose perusal cannot be completed at one sitting (see p. 524 of this edition).

The concept of the "single sitting," as Poe presents it, is not a mere erudite hypothesis, but a tangible, practical one.

> The ordinary novel is objectionable, from its length. . . . As it cannot be read at one sitting, it deprives itself, of course, of the immense force derivable from *totality*. Worldly interests intervening during the pauses of perusal, modify, annul, or counteract, in a greater or less degree, the impressions of the book. But simple cessation in reading, would, of itself, be sufficient to destroy the true unity. In the brief tale, however, the author is enabled to carry out the fullness of his

> intention, be it what it may. During the hour of perusal the soul of the reader is at the writer's control. There are no external or extrinsic influences—resulting from weariness or interruption (p. 525).

With a short story a reader can be totally immersed from start to finish without once having to abandon the fictional world until the story is over. Poe describes the kind of ideal hold a short-story writer can exert on a reader, and it's not surprising that he would take full advantage of it in his own fiction. It's not just the reader's mind that a short-story writer can engage, suggests Poe, but the reader's soul.

In his review, Poe writes: "Mr. Hawthorne's distinctive trait is invention, creation, imagination, originality—a trait which, in the literature of fiction, is positively worth all the rest" (p. 527). Certainly what Poe valued most in this other, contemporary writer was one of his own particular gifts. Poe's short story "The Mask of the Red Death" was published for the first time in the same issue of *Graham's Magazine* as his review. It was an issue that brought together, then, these first two great American short-story writers, and it was the moment that we might well think of as the launching of the genre. It's important to remember that Poe and Hawthorne preceded the European short-story masters Anton Chekhov and Guy de Maupassant by several decades.

Over the years, the short story has strained against its own definition, but that, of course, is what healthy genres do. If writers cease actively questioning and testing the definition, then that genre is probably no longer particularly vital (take the epic poem, for example). Whenever you have a literary definition that prescribes certain limits, it inspires a particular kind of creativity. Writing is an intellectual pursuit, and the mind of the short-story writer is engaged in a kind of contest: Given the limitations of the genre—which in the case of the short story is its length—what can be accomplished?

It is this question that can be the most enlightening for anyone who's interested in the history of the short story. If the short story is attempting to capture the essence of something important and do it on a small scale, then concision and selection are going to be key. How writers select and compress their material will be determined by the decade when they are writing as well as their individual stylistic taste.

We can get an overview of the development of the short story from its first American beginnings to its twentieth-century incarnation by juxtaposing Hawthorne and Ernest Hemingway. When we place their work side by side, we can appreciate the degree of transformation. It's not, of course, as if the history of the short story in America follows a simple or predictable chronology. (It does, however, parallel a similar development in the history of the novel.) What we can observe is the general shift in both the choice of subject matter and the way it is presented. And, of course, the alteration in prose style reflects the transition that took place in language itself, from the more formal and elaborate language of the mid-nineteenth century to the more informal, leaner language after the turn of the twentieth century.

In "Rappaccini's Daughter," Hawthorne's prose is as lush as the vegetation in Rappaccini's poisonous garden:

> In the midst, by the shattered fountain, grew the magnificent shrub, with its purple gems clustering all over it; they glowed in the air, and gleamed back again out of the depths of the pool, which thus seemed to overflow with colored radiance from the rich reflection that was steeped in it (p. 44).

Hemingway's prose is bare and terse, and the few descriptive details in "The End of Something" stand out, dramatically. When Hemingway makes use of an image, like the description of minnows jumping when the trout feed, it's notable for its clarity and precision: "They sprinkled the surface like a handful of shot thrown into the water" (p. 516).

A significant difference between Hawthorne's stories and Hemingway's is their scope. Nineteenth-century short stories, in general, cover more time and territory; twentieth-century stories focus on a shorter period of time, a more abbreviated view. The size of the canvas determines, in part, each author's task. Hawthorne uses his narrator to summarize his characters' situations, and his story evolves over time. "Rappaccini's Daughter" covers weeks. Hemingway selects a moment in the lives of his characters, and from that glimpse his reader is left to infer the larger situation. "The End of

Something" covers only a few hours. Hawthorne's narrator shapes the story from start to finish before our eyes, while Hemingway's narrator describes the setting, briefly, at the start, then leaves it up to the dialogue to carry the story. It's more, though, than a distinction between "telling" and "showing." The narrator in "Rappaccini's Daughter" is audience-aware. To lend a tone of veracity to the story, as was a convention of the time, Hawthorne appeals directly to the reader: "If the reader be inclined to judge for himself, we refer him to certain black-letter tracts on both sides, preserved in the medical department of the University of Padua" (p. 43). In "The End of Something" the reader is dropped into a fictional world and left there as almost a voyeur, quite ignored by the narrator.

Hawthorne makes use of allegory and fantasy in "Young Goodman Brown," "The Birthmark," and "Rappaccini's Daughter," as he does in many of his stories. His themes are laid right out for the reader. Hemingway's themes are more recondite. "The End of Something," as with all of the Nick Adams stories in Hemingway's collection *In Our Time,* is totally grounded in the realm of realism. At first it seems as if Hawthorne is grappling with grander issues—good and evil, the quest for perfection—while Hemingway is content to focus on more mundane matters, like the breakup of an affair. Yet Hemingway's stories are often deceptively simple. He is equally interested in exploring the range and depth of human emotion, and though morality is not a topic that he takes on directly (as Hawthorne does, for instance, in "Young Goodman Brown") it's an underlying concern.

Both "Rappaccini's Daughter" and "The End of Something" deal with the relationship between a young man and a young woman, and both stories raise questions about the nature and longevity of love. Hawthorne's narrator approaches the subject directly:

> Oh, how stubbornly does love—or even that cunning semblance of love which flourishes in the imagination, but strikes no depth of root into the heart—how stubbornly does it hold its faith, until the moment come, when it is doomed to vanish into thin mist! (p. 54).

Hemingway touches on the subject of love only briefly, in the dialogue. Nick tells Marjorie, "It isn't fun any more. Not any of it." And in answer to her question "Isn't love any fun?" he answers simply, "No" (p. 518).

Beatrice and Giovanni in "Rappaccini's Daughter," like the ill-fated couples Aylmer and Georgiana in "The Birthmark" and Faith and Young Goodman Brown in "Young Goodman Brown," are tools of the allegory. We're not expected to test their credibility. Marjorie and Nick in "The End of Something" are, in contrast, so painfully real that the story seems to be almost incidental to them.

To our modern sensibilities, the end of "Rappaccini's Daughter"—with Beatrice, the victim of her scientist father's "perverted wisdom," dying at the feet of her lover and father—is undeniably melodramatic. Yet Hawthorne's story is saved from bathos because its impact comes not from its plot but from the psychological inquiry that surrounds it.

While Hawthorne brought his skills as a fiction writer to a longer genre, the novel (he's probably best known for *The Scarlet Letter*), Poe, in his fiction, remained faithful to the short story. What he called "the immense force of totality" is certainly characteristic of his work, and Poe accomplished that totality by utilizing many of the same techniques that he refined as a poet. "In the whole composition," wrote Poe in his famous review, "there should be no word written, of which the tendency, direct or indirect, is not to the one preestablished design" (p. 526). Every word in Poe's stories is carefully selected, and the imagery is craftily woven into the plot.

In "The Fall of the House of Usher" the mood of the story is established in the opening sentence:

> During the whole of a dull, dark, and soundless day in the autumn of the year, when the clouds hung oppressively low in the heavens, I had been passing alone, on horseback, through a singularly dreary tract of country, and at length found myself, as the shades of evening drew on, within view of the melancholy House of Usher (p. 72).

Poe gives us not only a visual description of a landscape but works upon our ear as well. The alliterative word choice in the first line—"during," "dull," "dark," and "day"—helps create the sense of those "oppressively low" clouds. Throughout the story Poe sustains his tone, building the terror and horror until the dramatic and symbolic end of the story, when the narrator flees in a storm, and the "melancholy" house and its corpses are reclaimed by the landscape.

Poe uses a first-person narrator in all three of the stories in this anthology, and each narrator is specifically designed to serve the tale. The narrator in "The Fall of the House of Usher" presents himself as the reliable outsider, and it's his perception of the horror that makes it vivid for us. In "The Purloined Letter" the narrator is also a reliable voice, an instrument for the story within the story, which is told, through dialogue, by Poe's perspicacious detective, Dupin. It's in "The Cask of Amontillado" that Poe's use of a first-person narrator is at its most powerful, for although the narrator apprises us of his bias and animus at the start of the story—"The thousand injuries of Fortunato I had borne as I best could, but when he ventured upon insult, I vowed revenge" (p. 65)—the extent of his unreliability grows until his full madness and criminality is revealed at the end.

"The Purloined Letter" is the third of Poe's trilogy of tales of ratiocination—what we now call the detective story—featuring Dupin. It's unlike the others ("The Murders in the Rue Morgue" and "The Mystery of Marie Roget") and the majority of Poe's other stories in that it involves neither death nor terror. Because of the story's relatively unsensational subject matter, we can appreciate the intellectual tour de force, in contrast to "The Murders in the Rue Morgue," in which the bizarre and gruesome image of a vicious orangutan decapitating one victim and choking another rather overshadows the cleverness of the deduction. In "The Purloined Letter" we even see a sparkle of Poe's humor, when the prefect of police says of the suspect, "He is a poet, which I take to be only one remove from a fool" (p. 95).

In "The Cask of Amontillado," published in 1846, four years after his review of Hawthorne's work appeared, Poe's genius is at its peak. In this story the setting is as vivid as it is in "The Fall of the House of Usher," and the plot is as suspenseful and clever as that of "The Purloined Letter." The narrator, Montresor, coolly relates his murderous scheme, recalling precise details, although we learn that he is distanced from the event by fifty years—or at least that is what he tells us. Poe's setting for this story is a wine cellar that doubles as a crypt, where the bones lie "promiscuously upon the earth," as if they have been involved in untoward behavior even after death (p. 69). Yet he sets his story during carnival season so he can have an excuse to clad the victim, Fortunato, in a jester's costume, which adds poignancy to the final scene, where what we hear from him is "only a jingling of the bells" (p. 71) on his cap. Fortunato is a fool, of course, because he is gullible. "He had a weak point. . . . He prided himself on his connoisseurship in wine" (p. 65), and it's his pride that makes him vulnerable to Montresor's cunning treachery. But who doesn't have a weak point? Who isn't foolish?

Poe's control in this story is unsurpassed. Although our suspicions have been aroused at the outset, we are only a step ahead of the doomed (and ironically named) Fortunato as he is lured down the path to his chilling end. Unlike Lady Marian, in the gothic "The Fall of the House of Usher," he will not be able to claw his way out of his sealed tomb. "The Cask of Amontillado" stays just enough within the boundaries of realism to keep us in the grip of the story without providing the comforting awareness that it is artifice, the kind of intellectual distancing from the human experience of evil that allegory and fantasy provide.

Herman Melville's first person narrator in "Bartleby the Scrivener" is quick to establish his reliability early in the story. He is not only an "unambitious lawyer" (p. 110) but insists, "All who know me consider me an eminently *safe* man" (p. 110). Yet the narrative that he relates, in spite of its bland beginning, grows increasingly strange. Though Melville encourages us to trust the narrator's voice and sanity, we find ourselves on uncertain ground. The story seems realistic at the outset yet slyly shifts into symbolism as resonant as Hawthorne's. Melville's Bartleby, a copyist in the lawyer's office, is introduced to us as "pallidly neat, pitiably respectable, incurably forlorn!" (p. 115). It's the word "forlorn" that's unexpected because it's so emotionally raw. Initially, Bartleby is the quintessential clerk, copying out legal documents, an occupation a fiction writer like Melville would find to be particularly soulless. Though Bartleby sustains himself on a meager amount of food, the narrator reports that "he seemed to gorge himself on my documents" (p. 116). Yet when asked to do even the smallest task that is beyond the precise "legal" terms of his employment, he replies, "I would prefer not to"

(p. 117). His passive resistance confounds the narrator. Eventually Bartleby's preference to abstain extends to his job itself, and subsequently to the larger job of carrying on his existence. Though the narrator attributes Bartleby's ultimately self-destructive behavior to an "innate and incurable disorder" (p. 126), it's clear there's also a perverse wisdom to Bartleby, who seems to comprehend the pointlessness of human existence.

Bartleby, in his supreme isolation, is unfathomably unknowable. Melville has detailed his behavior, but left the "why" behind it unanswered, and the story throbs with possible interpretations. In a postscript at the end, we're told a rumor that Bartleby had once been employed by the Dead Letter Department, sorting the cartloads of mail that never reached its destination and that was relegated to being burned. It was a job that could not help but inspire "hopelessness" (p. 144). In these letters, Melville encapsulates the whole of human futility and misery, fate thwarting the best of intentions:

> Sometimes from out the folded paper the pale clerk takes a ring—the finger it was meant for, perhaps, molders in the grave; a bank note sent in swiftest charity—he whom it would relieve nor eats nor hungers any more; pardon for those who died despairing; hope for those who died unhoping; good tidings for those who died stifled by unrelieved calamities. On errands of life, these letters speed to death (p. 144).

The story ends with a simple cry: "Ah, Bartleby! Ah, humanity!" (p. 144). Melville's character carries his symbolic burdens, yet he remains poignantly real.

Melville had become friends with Nathaniel Hawthorne in 1850, and when Melville's novel *Moby-Dick* was published in 1851, he dedicated it to Hawthorne "in token of my admiration for his genius." As Poe had done a few years before him, Melville recognized and extolled Hawthorne's unique talents. In an article Melville wrote before meeting Hawthorne (it appeared in *Literary World* in August 1850; see "For Further Reading"), he calls *Twice-Told Tales* and *The Scarlet Letter* "excellent" but reserves his rapturous—and he did wax eloquent!—praise for Hawthorne's short-story collection *Mosses from an Old Manse,* which includes the three stories selected here. He concludes "that whatever Nathaniel Hawthorne may hereafter write, *The Mosses from an Old Manse* will be ultimately accounted his masterpiece."

It's no surprise that "Bartleby the Scrivener," which was first published in 1853, two years after *Moby-Dick* (it appeared in his short story collection *Piazza Tales* in 1856), shows Hawthorne's influence. Melville speaks of his debt to Hawthorne in his essay: "I feel that this Hawthorne has dropped germinous seeds into my soul. He expands and deepens down, the more I contemplate him; and further, and further, shoots his strong New England roots into the hot soil of my Southern soul." More precisely, Melville writes that "it is that blackness in Hawthorne . . . that so fixes and fascinates me." We can see Bartleby walking in the footsteps of Hawthorne's character Goodman Brown.

Melville compares Hawthorne to Shakespeare in his article but goes to great length to emphasize the importance of Hawthorne as an American writer. Melville addresses his readers as "my countrymen" and calls Hawthorne "an excellent author, of your own flesh and blood," but his appeal is more than simple chauvinism. Melville sees in Hawthorne not only a new approach to fiction but one that he labels as characteristically American. It is significant that the modern short story has as its birthplace this young nation, that its first great artists—Hawthorne, Poe, Melville, and Samuel Langhorne Clemens (Mark Twain)—were all American. The vitality of a country still discovering itself inspired freedom of thought and expression. Fortuitously, there was a flourishing of literary journals—tailor-made for works of short fiction—and an audience ready to appreciate the originality and ingenuity of a newly hewn genre.

Twain's story "The Notorious Jumping Frog of Calaveras County" most closely links the short story with its early roots in the oral tradition. The oral story was a flexible form, adapted by itinerant storytellers to the particular culture of their audience. Though the plot was predictable and the characters stereotypes, the storyteller shaped it, providing the details, the style, and the tone. The storyteller was, by default, the narrator, as well as the dramatic voice for all the characters in the story.

Twain, himself a mesmerizing lecturer, understood the power of the oral tale, and he drew on its vitality in his written stories. The first-person narrator in "The Notorious Jumping Frog of Calaveras County" introduces the story, and then relinquishes it to a character, Simon Wheeler, a storyteller within the story, who tells a tale about a gambler named Jim Smiley and his champion frog. This double layering gives Simon Wheeler's colloquial voice authenticity, and the seeming casualness of the telling and the undramatic ending are part of Twain's calculated artlessness. Sam Wheeler's monologue seems so alive we can almost hear him breathing on the page.

Henry James's narrator in "My Friend Bingham" is more refined than Twain's. While "The Notorious Jumping Frog of Calaveras County" seems to spill out effortlessly, James's story feels studied and cerebral. James, who was himself a major influence on the short-story writers who came after him, was greatly influenced by Hawthorne. In his book on Hawthorne, published in 1879, James praises Hawthorne for "the element of simple genius, the quality of imagination." (*Hawthorne,* p. 56). In particular, he cites "Rappaccini's Daughter" as one of Hawthorne's "little masterpieces . . . the highest point that Hawthorne reached in this direction" (*Hawthorne,* p. 55). Hawthorne's influence is certainly evident in James's story "The Beast in the Jungle."

James wrote in his journal (August 27, 1901) about the germ of this story: a "small notion that comes to me of a man haunted by the fear, more and more, throughout life, that *something will happen to him*: he doesn't quite know what" (*The Notebooks of Henry James,* p. 311). The small notion grew, and like many of James's stories it expanded into a narrative that certainly strained against Poe's ideal of the limited length of a short story. Although the magazine market for the short story was flourishing at this time, James was finding it difficult to place his longer stories. What began for him as a short story often grew into a novella (*nouvelle*), and his novellas grew into novels. In one of his prefaces James described Poe's ideal length as "too little room to turn around" (*The Art of the Novel,* p. 179).

In "The Beast in the Jungle," James's character Marcher is a man obsessed with his conviction that "something or other lay in wait for him, amid the twists and the turns of the months and years, like a crouching beast in the jungle" (p. 195). May Bartram's lifelong, patient fidelity to the self-centered Marcher and his idée fixe makes her seem an even more tragic character than the haunted Marcher, but James cunningly turns things around for us at the end. May Bartram, James shows us, at least had lived, because she had loved Marcher, whereas Marcher had missed out: "No passion had ever touched him" (p. 224). The beast James has conjured up is a beast that could have stalked a Hawthorne short story. Marcher "had been the man of his time, *the* man, to whom nothing on earth was to have happened" (p. 224).

In "My Friend Bingham" a great deal happens to George Bingham, the major character in the story: He accidentally shoots and kills a child, then marries the child's widowed mother. But the story is not so much about the events as about the question the narrator, who calls himself "a cordial observer," puts to the reader about the story: whether "the element of pain is stronger than that of joy" (p. 161). James has taken the most dramatic of plots and shifted the emphasis to an intellectual inquiry. In this, he's demonstrated the significant characteristic of the modern short story, and the element that distinguishes it from the oral tale and the earliest written tales. What Hawthorne and Poe achieved, and what James so well exemplifies, is the development of the short story from a recital of events that characters experience to a psychological investigation beyond those events into the minds and hearts of those characters, a basic shift from the "what" to the "why." It's not the plot that matters as much as the characters themselves, and they matter because they are human. In the American short-story writers who follow, this is the defining factor, though each of these writers will shape the short story according to his or her style and taste.

Edith Wharton, a disciple of James, perfected the short story as social satire. In "The Other Two," she portrays a recently married man, Waythorn, who must come to terms with his wife Alice's past—in particular, her previous two husbands. The nuances of class distinction emerge from Wharton's brilliantly selected details. Alice's first husband, Haskett, is acutely aware of his social place. "In the library he [Waythorn] found Haskett occupying a chair in his usual provisional way. Waythorn always felt grateful to him for not leaning back" (p. 365). Waythorn views Haskett with moral superiority:

> It was grotesquely uppermost in Waythorn's mind that Haskett had worn a made-up tie attached with an elastic. Why should that ridiculous detail symbolize the whole man? Waythorn was exasperated by his own paltriness, but the fact of the tie expanded, forced itself on him, became as it were the key to Alice's past (p. 358).

Wharton uses the tie not only to point out the absurd conventions of upper-class New York society but to delve into the intricacies of her character's mind. The tie is an interesting note in itself, but it is more interesting as a clue to Waythorn's character.

As the American short story moves from allegory to realism, the specific setting of the story takes on more importance. "The Other Two" is a story of a particular time and place. Wharton stages the final scene—in which Alice has orchestrated the coming together of all three of her husbands in a haze of cigar smoke—in Waythorn's library in their New York town house.

Sarah Orne Jewett's rural settings on the Maine coast are dramatically different from Wharton's New York. The Byfleet Poorhouse, where "The Flight of Betsey Lane" takes place, is a world away from Waythorn's library. But for both authors the setting is not only a vehicle to reveal the lives of their characters, but a life force of the story itself. Although the stories are specific and accurate in their historical moment—"The Flight of Betsey Lane" involves Betsey's trip to the Philadelphia Centennial in 1876, for instance—they are no less universal.

In Jewett's story "A White Heron," setting, character, and theme are closely intertwined. In this description of the landscape we begin to see the spiritual connection between the little girl, Sylvia, and the heron:

> . . . she knew that strange white bird, and had once stolen softly near where it stood in some bright green swamp grass, away over at the other side of the woods. There was an open place where the sunshine always seemed strangely yellow and hot, where tall, nodding rushes grew. . . . Not far beyond were the salt marshes and beyond those was the sea, the sea which Sylvia wondered and dreamed about, but never had looked upon, though its great voice could often be heard above the noise of the woods on stormy nights (p. 230).

Jewett's unlikely heroine, Sylvia, may not have the sophistication to decode the culture beyond her limited rural sphere, but she has the moral clarity of the innocent. The ornithologist who intrudes upon her world is charismatic, yet "Sylvia would have liked him vastly better without his gun; she could not understand why he killed the very birds he seemed to like so much" (p. 231).

Sylvia rises at daybreak to climb a great pine tree, symbolically "the last of its generation," to see if she can spot the heron and locate its nest and claim the ornithologist's monetary prize. Sylvia not only spots the bird but the sea itself. The narrator reaches into the story and appeals to the character—"And wait! wait! do not move a foot or a finger, little girl"—and Jewett intensifies the moment by switching to the present tense: "She knows his secret now, the wild, light, slender bird that floats and wavers, and goes back like an arrow presently to his home in the green world beneath" (p. 234). And again, at the end of the story, when Sylvia struggles with her moral dilemma and ends up choosing a different reward from the one of pleasing the young man and earning the promised money, Jewett once more makes use of the present tense: "The murmur of the pine's green branches is in her ears, she remembers how the white heron came flying through the golden air and how they watched the sea and the morning together, and Sylvia cannot speak; she cannot tell the heron's secret and give its life away" (p. 235). It is a virtuosic technical feat, a move that brings the American short story into the modern area.

Willa Cather recognized Jewett's particular genius. In her preface to Jewett's collection *The Country of the Pointed Firs,* she describes the stories as "living things caught in the open, with light and freedom and air-spaces about them. They melt into the land and the life of the land until they are not stories at all, but life itself." Cather praises Jewett's ability to see her country "as it was" and to capture the local voices: her "tactful handling of this native language of the waterside and countryside, never overdone, never pushed a shade too far."

The setting Willa Cather is best known for is the Nebraska prairie of her girlhood, but her short story "Paul's Case" is set in Pittsburgh, where she worked as a journalist and high-school teacher. The teachers she portrays in the story are unable to understand

Paul and are "humiliated to have felt so vindictive toward a mere boy" (p. 450). Cather gives the reader sufficient reason to forgive them, though, and it's not so much Paul as his situation that finally draws our sympathy for him. Here it's the descriptive details of the setting that give the story its emotional impact: "the cold bathroom with the grimy zinc tub, the cracked mirror, the dripping spigots; his father, at the top of the stairs, his hairy legs sticking out from his nightshirt, his feet thrust into carpet slippers" (p. 454). The contrast between Paul's bleak home on Cordelia Street and the aesthetically perfect life he is able to buy for himself—replete with "the flowers, the white linen, the many-colored wine glasses, the gay toilettes of the women, the low popping of corks, the undulating repetitions of the *Blue Danube*" (p. 462)—compels us to feel charitable toward Paul's attempt to change himself into "the kind of boy he had always wanted to be" (p. 461). If Paul's demise at the end of the story seems melodramatic to a contemporary sensibility, as naturalistic stories of the period so often do now, Paul's "case" is no less moving, and Cather's suggestion "It was a losing game in the end, it seemed, this revolt against the homilies by which the world is run" (p. 467) is no less true.

In Stephen Crane's stories we can see several notable developments in the modern short story and recognize the elements that Ernest Hemingway was to emulate. Crane wrote a journalistic account of the same event he relates in his story "The Open Boat." In the fictional version he employs a third-person narrator to tell the story and maintains the clean directness of a journalistic approach, a prose style that Hemingway (himself a journalist) embraced, as well as the reliance on straight dialogue that became a Hemingway trademark. In a discussion of literature in his nonfiction travel account *The Green Hills of Africa,* Hemingway singles out James, Twain, and Crane as the best American writers, but it's Crane's stylistic influence that we can most readily observe in his own work. "The Open Boat" and "The Blue Hotel" were the stories Hemingway most admired.

"The Open Boat" begins in medias res. The shipwreck has occurred off-stage, before the story begins, and we are dropped into the dinghy with the four survivors: the wounded captain, the cook, the oiler, and the correspondent (drawn from Crane himself). The opening line—"None of them knew the color of the sky" (p. 368)—is brief and simple, yet it is brilliantly designed. The entire situation of the story is established here: We have characters so intent on what is at eye level that they can't afford to look up. What they are watching—what we will be watching throughout the story—is the sea, the adversary. The sentence is composed of only nine, short words; all monosyllables except for the word "color." Crane gives emphasis to this word so that in the third sentence it can expand: "These waves were of the hue of slate, save for the tops, which were of foaming white, and all of the men knew the colors of the sea" (p. 368).

"The Open Boat" is a story as visual as a Winslow Homer seascape, but Crane appeals to our other senses—tactile and auditory—as well. "The spray, when it dashed uproariously over the side, made the voyagers shrink and swear like men who were being branded" (p. 380). Against the background voice of the sea we hear the voices of the men: the plea of the exhausted man rowing, "Will you spell me?" (a refrain that runs through the story); the sections of dialogue; and the interior monologue "If I am going to be drowned . . . why . . . was I allowed to come thus far" (p. 381). In some parts Crane strips the dialogue of even its tag lines—as Hemingway does in "The End of Something"—to give it added verisimilitude. Point of view is suspended here, and the reader is brought right on stage:

> "There comes something up the beach."
> "What the devil is that thing?"
> "Why, it looks like a boat."
> "Why, certainly, it's a boat."
> "No; it's on wheels."
> "Yes, so it is. Well, that must be the life-boat. They drag them along shore on a wagon."
> "That's the life-boat, sure."
> "No, by God, it's—it's an omnibus."
> "I tell you it's a life-boat."
> "It is not! It's an omnibus. I can see it plain. See? One of these big hotel omnibuses" (p. 379).

Crane elevates the story of "The Open Boat" beyond the dramatic event to make it a story about the comradeship among the men, but then he takes it one step beyond, to an illustration about the power of fiction itself. The correspondent remembers a poem about a soldier dying in Algiers that he had learned as a child. At the time, that death had been "less to him than the breaking of a pencil's point" (p. 385). But now, himself a victim of the indifference of nature, the correspondent finds himself engaged. The situation described in the poem becomes brutally real to him. He sees this soldier's "pale left hand was upon his chest in an attempt to thwart the going of his life," and he is "moved by a profound and perfectly impersonal comprehension" (p. 385). This is exactly what Crane wants from his reader at the end of his story. He wants us to see and be moved by the oiler: "a still and dripping shape" who was "carried slowly up the beach" to the "sinister hospitality of the grave" (p. 391).

"The Blue Hotel," like "The Open Boat," begins with a visual description that centers on color. It's not any blue, but "a light blue, a shade that is on the legs of a kind of heron, causing the bird to declare its position against any background" (p. 392). The blueness of the hotel is striking against the dull Nebraska background, and Crane intensifies the image by adding a snowstorm. The four card players in "The Blue Hotel" are brought together by the storm, as the men in the open boat are brought together by the sea. But in this story the enemy is not the outside elements, but the discord among the men. Although the dialogue in the story is as grounded in the colloquial idiom as Twain's, the story has a strangely surreal quality, and we're not exactly sure what to make of the character of the Swede, whose paranoid fear that he will be killed comes to pass; the gambler who carries out the deed; or the blue hotel itself. Discussing the murder months later, the character called "The Easterner" says about the unpredictable course of events: "A thousand things might have happened" (p. 418). And that, of course, is the nature of the short story. It illustrates what did happen but suggests all the surrounding possibilities.

Jack London's story "To Build a Fire" involves the reader in the same kind of suspense as Crane's "The Open Boat." It, too, is a story about a struggle—mental as well as physical—for survival in a hostile environment. Because "To Build a Fire" is about a single character, a man who remains nameless, there's no dialogue to relieve the narrative, and this absence of dialogue reinforces the sense of the silence and isolation of the setting. London uses a third-person narrator similar to Crane's, and here the detachment of the observer's voice makes the character's situation seem even more pathetic. The reader is placed in the position of voyeur, helplessly watching the character as he becomes less and less able to perform the necessary tasks to keep himself from freezing to death. London's prose is spare and precise, and the man's labors are followed with meticulous detail:

> After some manipulation he managed to get the bunch between the heels of his mittened hands. In this fashion he carried it to his mouth. The ice crackled and snapped when by a violent effort he opened his mouth. He drew the lower jaw in, curled the upper lip out of the way, and scraped the bunch with his upper teeth in order to separate a match. He succeeded in getting one, which he dropped on his lap. He was no better off. He could not pick it up. Then he devised a way. He picked it up in his teeth and scratched it on his leg (p. 430).

Jack London and Sherwood Anderson were born in the same year, 1876, and we can think of them as a skilled and diverse pair of literary artists who helped shape the short story in the twentieth-century. Sherwood Anderson's fiction, like Crane's, was a major influence on Hemingway, though the lessons from each were significantly different. "Hands" and "The Untold Lie" are both part of Anderson's celebrated collection of interrelated stories, *Winesburg, Ohio*. Hemingway's "The End of Something" is part of his collection of interrelated stories *In Our Time*. Both collections are built around a common character and setting.

The stories in *Winesburg, Ohio* are slender tales, gently told. The narrator of "The Untold Lie" is given an informal, conversational voice: "This is not the story of Windpeter Winters nor yet of his son Hal who worked on the Wills farm with Ray Pearson. It is Ray's story. It will, however, be necessary to talk a little of young Hal so that you will get into the spirit of it" (p. 443). Anderson's short story may have the flavor of an oral tale, but plot is the least important element, in contrast to the stories of William Sydney Porter

(O. Henry), which are noted for their clever plots and surprise endings—"The Gift of the Magi" is perhaps the best known. In Anderson, not only is plot subordinated to character and theme, as it is, for instance, in Henry James's "My Friend Bingham," but often it's barely evident. Anderson's unconventional interpretation of what a short story could be redefined the genre.

In "The Untold Lie" two farmhands, Ray and Hal, share an unexpected moment of revelation, when Hal asks Ray's advice about marrying a woman whom he's made pregnant. "There they stood in the big empty field with the quiet corn shocks standing in rows behind them and the red and yellow hills in the distance, and from being just two indifferent workmen they had become all alive to each other" (p. 444). This moment (what James Joyce called an "epiphany") is all that Anderson's story requires. Ray later throws off his torn overcoat—a perfect symbol of the burdens of his family life—and runs across the field. "As he ran he shouted a protest against his life, against all life, against everything that makes life ugly" (p. 446). But there are no easy answers, no single truth in Anderson's story. Ray reclaims his overcoat, but Anderson keeps the story rich with meanings by denying the narrator omniscience at this moment; the narrator does not tell us what Ray is thinking, he merely suggests a possibility: "Some memory of pleasant evenings spent with the thin-legged children in the tumble-down house by the creek must have come into his mind" (p. 447). Anderson closes his story with Ray's own statement of ambivalence: "It's just as well. Whatever I told him would have been a lie," and then has the setting claim his character: "His form also disappeared into the darkness of the fields" (p. 447).

F. Scott Fitzgerald, like Edith Wharton, was adept at capturing a particular period and sector of American life. When Fitzgerald's character Bernice has her tonsorial adventure in "Bernice Bobs Her Hair," we know he's writing about more than a haircut; the story is about the emergence of the flapper of the Jazz Age, with a new style and a new morality. We smile at Bernice when she turns plucky and seeks her revenge against her cousin Marjorie—who'd trapped her into the haircut—by snipping off Marjorie's pigtails, but rarely in Fitzgerald stories are triumphs so neat.

Like Edith Wharton, Fitzgerald zoomed in on the nuances of social class. His great appeal is his ability to get beneath the surface glitz and expose the flaws and sadnesses of the world he portrays. His stories convey the sense of the moment at the same time that they explore the characters' universal vulnerabilities.

In "Winter Dreams," when Dexter Green makes his fortune and returns to the golf course where he was once a lowly caddy, he looks at the caddies there and tries "to catch a gleam or gesture that would remind him of himself, that would lessen the gap which lay between his present and his past" (p. 498). Yet what Fitzgerald shows us in the story is how much Dexter is still part of that past. He loves the desirable and "unprincipled" Judy Jones, who was born to the society he had to work to attain, though he knows that even if she claims to want him for the moment, he can never, finally, have her. At the end of the story Dexter realizes that his loss is more significant than this one woman, whose unsettling beauty has faded with time: "The dream was gone" (p. 514). Fitzgerald allows his narrator the luxury of elaborating on the theme, and his language is imagistic and romantic:

> For he had gone away and he could never go back any more. The gates were closed, the sun was gone down, and there was no beauty but the gray beauty of steel that withstands all time. Even the grief he could have borne was left behind in the country of illusion, of youth, of the richness of life, where his winter dreams had flourished (p. 514).

Fitzgerald's narrator in "Winter Dreams" appeals directly to the reader, as Anderson's does in "The Untold Lie," so that the structure of the story is there, on the surface. The narrator calls attention to the reading process, for example, reminding the reader: "This story is not his biography, remember, although things creep into it which have nothing to do with those dreams he had when he was young" (p. 512). This fictional self-awareness is a particularly useful technique in a story that grapples with its themes so deliberately.

The modern short story takes on subjects of heightened emotion, but each great writer working in the realistic mode employs a special strategy for keeping melodrama and sentimentality at bay. Hemingway's strategy is spareness and understatement; his themes are only hinted at. In "The End of Something," when Marjorie leaves the scene, Nick isn't alone long before his friend Bill appears.

> "Did she go all right?" Bill said.
> "Yes," Nick said, lying, his face on the blanket.
> "Have a scene?"
> "No, there wasn't any scene."
> "How do you feel?"
> "Oh, go away, Bill! Go away for a while."
> Bill selected a sandwich from the lunch basket and walked over to have a look at the rods (pp. 518–519).

There's very little text here, yet so much is conveyed. We can infer that Bill knew in advance about Nick's plan to end things with Marjorie. We know how Nick is feeling, though he doesn't answer Bill's question. We know Bill's attitude from his two, small actions. We realize that Bill has been lying in wait during the course of the whole story, ready to reclaim the fishing rods that Marjorie surrendered. The story that had seemed to be about a couple ending their relationship becomes a more complex story about Nick's divided loyalties—all this accomplished with extraordinary verbal economy.

Like Hawthorne and Poe a century before them, Fitzgerald and Hemingway were the major influences on the generation of short-story writers who came after them. They offered contrasting stylistic approaches to the short story, and although a deluge of imitators followed them, the very best short-story writers learned from them but cultivated styles of their own.

The American short story has proved to be a sturdy and elastic genre, as vigorous today as it was 150 years ago. It's been refined and recast, expanded and condensed, yet the core elements that Poe put his finger on—the unity, the "single sitting," the length—still resonate. Although we may talk about the "development" of the American short story and trace how the modern story derives from its predecessors, the early examples still speak to us with freshness and energy. All the stories here take their revered place in the history of the genre, but each radiates the very qualities that Poe spoke of: invention, creation, imagination, and originality. Each casts its own, enduring spell.

Corinne Demas is a professor of English at Mount Holyoke College and a fiction editor of the *Massachusetts Review.* A graduate of Tufts University, she has a Ph.D. in English and Comparative Literature from Columbia University. She is the author of two collections of short stories, *What We Save for Last* and *Daffodils or the Death of Love;* two novels, *The Same River Twice* and *If Ever I Return Again;* a memoir, *Eleven Stories High: Growing Up in Stuyvesant Town, 1948–1968;* and numerous books for children. She has published more than fifty short stories in a variety of magazines and literary journals. (Her publications before 2000 are under the name Corinne Demas Bliss.) Her awards include two National Endowment for the Arts Creative Writing Fellowships and an Andrew W. Mellon Foundation Fellowship. She is the winner of a Lawrence Foundation Prize, the University of Missouri Press's Breakthrough Contest, and a PEN Syndicated Fiction Competition, and she has been a finalist for the Massachusetts Book Award.

EDITOR'S NOTE

Selecting stories for an anthology is a daunting task, and I feel regret for the many deserving authors who aren't represented here and the many fine stories I wasn't able to include. Because one aim of this collection is to give readers a sense of the development of the American short story, I tried to focus on authors who would best document its history, and who had the greatest role in the shaping of the genre. The stories I selected are ones that not only engaged me when I first read them, but that retained a richness after many readings and, in some cases, extensive seminar discussion.

I'd like readers to see this anthology not as a complete offering, but rather as a sampling of the enormous wealth of American short fiction that is there, waiting to be discovered.

Acknowledgments

I'm grateful to my colleagues at Mount Holyoke College and the numerous individuals who helped with this project. In particular, I want to thank: Lois Brown, John Clayton, Leah Glasser, Betsy Hartmann, Roger King, Karen Osborn, Robert Redick, Artemis Demas Roehrig, Michelle Stephens, Jane Yolen, and especially Elaine von Bruns and my husband, Matthew Roehrig.

—Corinne Demas, October 2003

GREAT AMERICAN SHORT STORIES

CONTENTS

NATHANIEL HAWTHORNE

Young Goodman Brown

YOUNG GOODMAN BROWN CAME forth, at sunset, into the street of Salem village, but put his head back, after crossing the threshold, to exchange a parting kiss with his young wife. And Faith, as the wife was aptly named, thrust her own pretty head into the street, letting the wind play with the pink ribbons of her cap, while she called to Goodman Brown.

'Dearest heart,' whispered she, softly and rather sadly, when her lips were close to his ear, 'pr'y thee, put off your journey until sunrise, and sleep in your own bed to-night. A lone woman is troubled with such dreams and such thoughts, that she's afeard of herself, sometimes. Pray, tarry with me this night, dear husband, of all nights in the year!'

'My love and my Faith,' replied young Goodman Brown, 'of all nights in the year, this one night must I tarry away from thee. My journey, as thou callest it, forth and back again, must needs be done 'twixt now and sunrise. What, my sweet, pretty wife, dost thou doubt me already, and we but three months married!'

'Then, God bless you!' said Faith, with the pink ribbons, 'and may you find all well, when you come back.'

'Amen!' cried Goodman Brown. 'Say thy prayers, dear Faith, and go to bed at dusk, and no harm will come to thee.'

So they parted; and the young man pursued his way, until, being about to turn the corner by the meeting-house, he looked back, and saw the head of Faith still peeping after him, with a melancholy air, in spite of her pink ribbons.

'Poor little Faith!' thought he, for his heart smote him. 'What a wretch am I, to leave her on such an errand! She talks of dreams, too. Methought, as she spoke, there was trouble in her face, as if a dream had warned her what work is to be done to-night. But, no, no! 'twould kill her to think it. Well; she's a blessed angel on earth; and after this one night, I'll cling to her skirts and follow her to Heaven.'

With this excellent resolve for the future, Goodman Brown felt himself justified in making more haste on his present evil purpose. He had taken a dreary road, darkened by all the gloomiest trees of the forest; which barely stood aside to let the narrow path creep through, and closed immediately behind. It was all as lonely as could be; and there is this peculiarity in such a solitude, that the traveller knows not who may be concealed by the innumerable trunks and the thick boughs overhead; so that, with lonely footsteps, he may yet be passing through an unseen multitude.

'There may be a devilish Indian behind every tree,' said Goodman Brown, to himself; and he glanced fearfully behind him, as he added, 'What if the devil himself should be at my very elbow!'

His head being turned back, he passed a crook of the road, and looking forward again, beheld the figure of a man, in grave and decent attire, seated at the foot of an old tree. He arose, at Goodman Brown's approach, and walked onward, side by side with him.

'You are late, Goodman Brown,' said he. 'The clock of the Old South was striking as I came through Boston; and that is full fifteen minutes agone.'

'Faith kept me back awhile,' replied the young man, with a tremor in his voice, caused by the sudden appearance of his companion, though not wholly unexpected.

It was now deep dusk in the forest, and deepest in that part of it where these two were journeying. As nearly as could be discerned, the second traveller was about fifty years old, apparently in the same rank of life as Goodman Brown, and bearing a considerable resemblance to him, though perhaps more in expression than features. Still, they might have been taken for father and son. And yet, though the elder person was as simply clad as the younger, and as simple in manner too, he had an indescribable air of one who knew the world, and would not have felt abashed at the governor's dinner-table, or in King William's court, were it possible that his affairs should call him thither. But the only thing about him, that could be fixed upon as remarkable, was his staff, which bore the likeness of a great black snake, so curiously wrought, that it might almost be seen to twist and wriggle itself, like a living serpent. This, of course, must have been an ocular deception, assisted by the uncertain light.

'Come, Goodman Brown!' cried his fellow-traveller, 'this is a dull pace for the beginning of a journey. Take my staff, if you are so soon weary.'

'Friend,' said the other, exchanging his slow pace for a full stop, 'having kept covenant by meeting thee here, it is my purpose now to return whence I came. I have scruples, touching the matter thou wot'st of.'

'Sayest thou so?' replied he of the serpent, smiling apart. 'Let us walk on, nevertheless, reasoning as we go, and if I convince thee not, thou shalt turn back. We are but a little way in the forest, yet.'

'Too far, too far!' exclaimed the goodman, unconsciously resuming his walk. 'My father never went into the woods on such an errand, nor his father before him. We have been a race of honest men and good Christians, since the days of the martyrs. And shall I be the first of the name of Brown, that ever took this path, and kept—'

'Such company, thou wouldst say,' observed the elder person, interpreting his pause. 'Well said, Goodman Brown! I have been as well acquainted with your family as with ever a one among the Puritans; and that's no trifle to say. I helped your grandfather, the constable, when he lashed the Quaker woman so smartly through the streets of Salem. And it was I that brought your father a pitch-pine knot, kindled at my own hearth, to set fire to an Indian village, in King Philip's war. They were my good friends, both; and many a pleasant walk have we had along this path, and returned merrily after midnight. I would fain be friends with you, for their sake.'

'If it be as thou sayest,' replied Goodman Brown, 'I marvel they never spoke of these matters. Or, verily, I marvel not, seeing that the least rumor of the sort would have driven them from New-England. We are a people of prayer, and good works, to boot, and abide no such wickedness.'

'Wickedness or not,' said the traveller with the twisted staff, 'I have a very general acquaintance here in New-England. The deacons of many a church have drunk the communion wine with me;

the selectmen, of divers towns, make me their chairman; and a majority of the Great and General Court are firm supporters of my interest. The governor and I, too—but these are state-secrets.'

'Can this be so!' cried Goodman Brown, with a stare of amazement at his undisturbed companion. 'Howbeit, I have nothing to do with the governor and council; they have their own ways, and are no rule for a simple husbandman, like me. But, were I to go on with thee, how should I meet the eye of that good old man, our minister, at Salem village? Oh, his voice would make me tremble, both Sabbath-day and lecture-day!'

Thus far, the elder traveller had listened with due gravity, but now burst into a fit of irrepressible mirth, shaking himself so violently, that his snake-like staff actually seemed to wriggle in sympathy.

'Ha! ha! ha!' shouted he, again and again; then composing himself, 'Well, go on, Goodman Brown, go on; but pr'y thee, don't kill me with laughing!'

'Well, then, to end the matter at once,' said Goodman Brown, considerably nettled, 'there is my wife, Faith. It would break her dear little heart; and I'd rather break my own!'

'Nay, if that be the case,' answered the other, 'e'en go thy ways, Goodman Brown. I would not, for twenty old women like the one hobbling before us, that Faith should come to any harm.'

As he spoke, he pointed his staff at a female figure on the path, in whom Goodman Brown recognized a very pious and exemplary dame, who had taught him his catechism, in youth, and was still his moral and spiritual adviser, jointly with the minister and Deacon Gookin.

'A marvel, truly, that Goody Cloyse should be so far in the wilderness, at night-fall!' said he. 'But, with your leave, friend, I shall take a cut through the woods, until we have left this Christian woman behind. Being a stranger to you, she might ask whom I was consorting with, and whither I was going.'

'Be it so,' said his fellow-traveller. 'Betake you to the woods, and let me keep the path.'

Accordingly, the young man turned aside, but took care to watch his companion, who advanced softly along the road, until he had come within a staff's length of the old dame. She, meanwhile, was making the best of her way, with singular speed for so aged a woman, and mumbling some indistinct words, a prayer, doubtless, as she went. The traveller put forth his staff, and touched her withered neck with what seemed the serpent's tail.

'The devil!' screamed the pious old lady.

'Then Goody Cloyse knows her old friend?' observed the traveller, confronting her, and leaning on his writhing stick.

'Ah, forsooth, and is it your worship, indeed?' cried the good dame. 'Yea, truly is it, and in the very image of my old gossip, Goodman Brown, the grandfather of the silly fellow that now is. But—would your worship believe it?—my broomstick hath strangely disappeared, stolen, as I suspect, by that unhanged witch, Goody Cory, and that, too, when I was all anointed with the juice of smallage and cinque-foil and wolf's-bane—'

'Mingled with fine wheat and the fat of a new-born babe,' said the shape of old Goodman Brown.

'Ah, your worship knows the receipt,' cried the old lady, cackling aloud. 'So, as I was saying, being all ready for the meeting, and no horse to ride on, I made up my mind to foot it; for they tell me, there is a nice young man to be taken into communion to-night. But now your good worship will lend me your arm, and we shall be there in a twinkling.'

'That can hardly be,' answered her friend. 'I may not spare you my arm, Goody Cloyse, but here is my staff, if you will.'

So saying, he threw it down at her feet, where, perhaps, it assumed life, being one of the rods which its owner had formerly lent to the Egyptian Magi. Of this fact, however, Goodman Brown could not take cognizance. He had cast up his eyes in astonishment, and looking down again, beheld neither Goody Cloyse nor the serpentine staff, but his fellow-traveller alone, who waited for him as calmly as if nothing had happened.

'That old woman taught me my catechism!' said the young man; and there was a world of meaning in this simple comment.

They continued to walk onward, while the elder traveller exhorted his companion to make good speed and persevere in the path, discoursing so aptly, that his arguments seemed rather to spring up in the bosom of his auditor, than to be suggested by himself. As they went, he plucked a branch of maple, to serve for a walking-stick, and began to strip it of the twigs and little boughs, which were wet with evening dew. The moment his fingers touched them, they became strangely withered and dried up, as with a week's sunshine. Thus the pair proceeded, at a good free pace, until suddenly, in a gloomy hollow of the road, Goodman Brown sat himself down on the stump of a tree, and refused to go any farther.

'Friend,' said he, stubbornly, 'my mind is made up. Not another step will I budge on this errand. What if a wretched old woman do choose to go to the devil, when I thought she was going to Heaven! Is that any reason why I should quit my dear Faith, and go after her?'

'You will think better of this, by-and-by,' said his acquaintance, composedly. 'Sit here and rest yourself awhile; and when you feel like moving again, there is my staff to help you along.'

Without more words, he threw his companion the maple stick, and was as speedily out of sight, as if he had vanished into the deepening gloom. The young man sat a few moments, by the road-side, applauding himself greatly, and thinking with how clear a conscience he should meet the minister, in his morning-walk, nor shrink from the eye of good old Deacon Gookin. And what calm sleep would be his, that very night, which was to have been spent so wickedly, but purely and sweetly now, in the arms of Faith! Amidst these pleasant and praiseworthy meditations, Goodman Brown heard the tramp of horses along the road, and deemed it advisable to conceal himself within the verge of the forest, conscious of the guilty purpose that had brought him thither, though now so happily turned from it.

On came the hoof-tramps and the voices of the riders, two grave old voices, conversing soberly as they drew near. These mingled sounds appeared to pass along the road, within a few yards of the young man's hiding-place; but owing, doubtless, to the depth of the gloom, at that particular spot, neither the travellers nor their steeds were visible. Though their figures brushed the small boughs by the way-side, it could not be seen that they intercepted, even for a moment, the faint gleam from the strip of bright sky, athwart which they must have passed. Goodman Brown alternately crouched and stood on tip-toe, pulling aside the branches, and thrusting forth his head as far as he durst, without discerning so much as a shadow. It vexed him the more, because he could have sworn, were such a thing possible, that he recognized the voices of the minister and Deacon Gookin, jogging along quietly, as they were wont to do, when bound to some ordination or ecclesiastical council. While yet within hearing, one of the riders stopped to pluck a switch.

'Of the two, reverend Sir,' said the voice like the deacon's, 'I had rather miss an ordination-dinner than to-night's meeting. They tell me that some of our community are to be here from Falmouth and beyond, and others from Connecticut and Rhode-Island; besides several of the Indian powows, who, after their fashion, know almost as much deviltry as the best of us. Moreover, there is a goodly young woman to be taken into communion.'

'Mighty well, Deacon Gookin!' replied the solemn old tones of the minister. 'Spur up, or we shall be late. Nothing can be done, you know, until I get on the ground.'

The hoofs clattered again, and the voices, talking so strangely in the empty air, passed on through the forest, where no church had ever been gathered, nor solitary Christian prayed. Whither, then, could these holy men be journeying, so deep into the heathen wilderness? Young Goodman Brown caught hold of a tree, for support, being ready to sink down on the ground, faint and overburthened with the heavy sickness of his heart. He looked up to the sky, doubting whether there really was a Heaven above him. Yet, there was the blue arch, and the stars brightening in it.

'With Heaven above, and Faith below, I will yet stand firm against the devil!' cried Goodman Brown.

While he still gazed upward, into the deep arch of the firmament, and had lifted his hands to pray, a cloud, though no wind was stirring, hurried across the zenith, and hid the brightening stars. The blue sky was still visible, except directly overhead, where this black mass of cloud was sweeping swiftly northward. Aloft in the air, as if from the depths of the cloud, came a confused and doubtful sound of voices. Once, the listener fancied that he could distinguish the accents of town's-people of his own, men and women, both pious and ungodly, many of whom he had met at the communion-table, and had seen others rioting at the tavern. The next moment, so indistinct were the sounds, he doubted whether he had heard aught but the murmur of the old forest, whispering without a wind. Then came a stronger swell of those familiar tones, heard daily in the sunshine, at Salem village, but never, until now, from a cloud of night. There was one voice, of a young woman, uttering lamentations, yet with an uncertain sorrow, and entreating for some favor, which, perhaps, it would grieve her to obtain. And all the unseen multitude, both saints and sinners, seemed to encourage her onward.

'Faith!' shouted Goodman Brown, in a voice of agony and desperation; and the echoes of the forest mocked him, crying—'Faith! Faith!' as if bewildered wretches were seeking her, all through the wilderness.

The cry of grief, rage, and terror, was yet piercing the night, when the unhappy husband held his breath for a response. There was a scream, drowned immediately in a louder murmur of voices, fading into far-off laughter, as the dark cloud swept away, leaving the clear and silent sky above Goodman Brown. But something fluttered lightly down through the air, and caught on the branch of a tree. The young man seized it, and beheld a pink ribbon.

'My Faith is gone!' cried he, after one stupefied moment. 'There is no good on earth; and sin is but a name. Come, devil! for to thee is this world given.'

And maddened with despair, so that he laughed loud and long, did Goodman Brown grasp his staff and set forth again, at such a rate, that he seemed to fly along the forest-path, rather than to walk or run. The road grew wilder and drearier, and more faintly traced, and vanished at length, leaving him in the heart of the dark wilderness, still rushing onward, with the instinct that guides mortal man to evil. The whole forest was peopled with frightful sounds; the creaking of the trees, the howling of wild beasts, and the yell of Indians; while, sometimes, the wind tolled like a distant church-bell, and sometimes gave a broad roar around the traveller, as if all Nature were laughing him to scorn. But he was himself the chief horror of the scene, and shrank not from its other horrors.

'Ha! ha! ha!' roared Goodman Brown, when the wind laughed at him. 'Let us hear which will laugh loudest! Think not to frighten me with your deviltry! Come witch, come wizard, come Indian powow, come devil himself! and here comes Goodman Brown. You may as well fear him as he fear you!'

In truth, all through the haunted forest, there could be nothing more frightful than the figure of Goodman Brown. On he flew, among the black pines, brandishing his staff with frenzied gestures, now giving vent to an inspiration of horrid blasphemy, and now shouting forth such laughter, as set all the echoes of the forest laughing like demons around him. The fiend in his own shape is less hideous, than when he rages in the breast of man. Thus sped the demoniac on his course, until, quivering among the trees, he saw a red light before him, as when the felled trunks and branches of a clearing have been set on fire, and throw up their lurid blaze against the sky, at the hour of midnight. He paused, in a lull of the tempest that had driven him onward, and heard the swell of what seemed a hymn, rolling solemnly from a distance, with the weight of many voices. He knew the tune; it was a familiar one in the choir of the village meeting-house. The verse died heavily away, and was lengthened by a chorus, not of human voices, but of all the sounds of the benighted wilderness, pealing in awful harmony together. Goodman Brown cried out; and his cry was lost to his own ear, by its unison with the cry of the desert.

In the interval of silence, he stole forward, until the light glared full upon his eyes. At one extremity of an open space, hemmed in by the dark wall of the forest, arose a rock, bearing some rude, natural resemblance either to an altar or a pulpit, and surrounded by four blazing pines, their tops aflame, their stems untouched, like candles at an evening meeting. The mass of foliage, that had overgrown the summit of the rock, was all on fire, blazing high into the night, and fitfully illuminating the whole field. Each pendent twig and leafy festoon was in a blaze. As the red light arose and fell, a numerous congregation alternately shone forth, then disappeared in shadow, and again grew, as it were, out of the darkness, peopling the heart of the solitary woods at once.

'A grave and dark-clad company!' quoth Goodman Brown.

In truth, they were such. Among them, quivering to-and-fro, between gloom and splendor, appeared faces that would be seen, next day, at the council-board of the province, and others which, Sabbath after Sabbath, looked devoutly heavenward, and benignantly over the crowded pews, from the holiest pulpits in the land. Some affirm that the lady of the governor was there. At least, there were high dames well known to her, and wives of honored husbands, and widows, a great multitude, and ancient maidens, all of excellent repute, and fair young girls, who trembled, lest their mothers should espy them. Either the sudden gleams of light, flashing over the obscure field, bedazzled Goodman Brown, or he recognized a score of the church-members of Salem village, famous for their especial sanctity. Good old Deacon Gookin had arrived, and waited at the skirts of that venerable saint, his revered pastor. But, irreverently consorting with these grave, reputable, and pious people, these elders of the church, these chaste dames and dewy virgins, there were men of dissolute lives and women of spotted fame, wretches given over to all mean and filthy vice, and suspected even of horrid crimes. It was strange to see, that the good shrank not from the wicked, nor were the sinners abashed by the saints. Scattered, also, among their pale-faced enemies, were the Indian priests, or powows, who had often scared their native forest with more hideous incantations than any known to English witchcraft.

'But, where is Faith?' thought Goodman Brown; and, as hope came into his heart, he trembled.

Another verse of the hymn arose, a slow and mournful strain, such as the pious love, but joined to words which expressed all that our nature can conceive of sin, and darkly hinted at far more. Unfathomable to mere mortals is the lore of fiends. Verse after verse was sung, and still the chorus of the desert swelled between, like the deepest tone of a mighty organ. And, with the final peal of that dreadful anthem, there came a sound, as if the roaring wind, the rushing streams, the howling beasts, and every other voice of the unconverted wilderness, were mingling and according with the voice of guilty man, in homage to the prince of all. The four blazing pines threw up a loftier flame, and obscurely discovered shapes and visages of horror on the smoke-wreaths, above the impious assembly. At the same moment, the fire on the rock shot redly forth, and formed a glowing arch above its base, where now appeared a figure. With reverence be it spoken, the figure bore no slight similitude, both in garb and manner, to some grave divine of the New-England churches.

'Bring forth the converts!' cried a voice, that echoed through the field and rolled into the forest.

At the word, Goodman Brown stept forth from the shadow of

the trees, and approached the congregation, with whom he felt a loathful brotherhood, by the sympathy of all that was wicked in his heart. He could have well nigh sworn, that the shape of his own dead father beckoned him to advance, looking downward from a smoke-wreath, while a woman, with dim features of despair, threw out her hand to warn him back. Was it his mother? But he had no power to retreat one step, nor to resist, even in thought, when the minister and good old Deacon Gookin seized his arms, and led him to the blazing rock. Thither came also the slender form of a veiled female, led between Goody Cloyse, that pious teacher of the catechism, and Martha Carrier, who had received the devil's promise to be queen of hell. A rampant hag was she! And there stood the proselytes, beneath the canopy of fire.

'Welcome, my children,' said the dark figure, 'to the communion of your race! Ye have found, thus young, your nature and your destiny. My children, look behind you!'

They turned; and flashing forth, as it were, in a sheet of flame, the fiend-worshippers were seen; the smile of welcome gleamed darkly on every visage.

'There,' resumed the sable form, 'are all whom ye have reverenced from youth. Ye deemed them holier than yourselves, and shrank from your own sin, contrasting it with their lives of righteousness, and prayerful aspirations heavenward. Yet, here are they all, in my worshipping assembly! This night it shall be granted you to know their secret deeds; how hoary-bearded elders of the church have whispered wanton words to the young maids of their households; how many a woman, eager for widow's weeds, has given her husband a drink at bed-time, and let him sleep his last sleep in her bosom; how beardless youths have made haste to inherit their fathers' wealth; and how fair damsels—blush not, sweet ones!—have dug little graves in the garden, and bidden me, the sole guest, to an infant's funeral. By the sympathy of your human hearts for sin, ye shall scent out all the places—whether in church, bed-chamber, street, field, or forest—where crime has been committed, and shall exult to behold the whole earth one stain of guilt, one mighty blood-spot. Far more than this! It shall be yours to penetrate, in every bosom, the deep mystery of sin, the fountain of all wicked arts, and which inexhaustibly supplies more evil impulses than human power—than my power, at its utmost!—can make manifest in deeds. And now, my children, look upon each other.'

They did so; and, by the blaze of the hell-kindled torches, the wretched man beheld his Faith, and the wife her husband, trembling before that unhallowed altar.

'Lo! there ye stand, my children,' said the figure, in a deep and solemn tone, almost sad, with its despairing awfulness, as if his once angelic nature could yet mourn for our miserable race. 'Depending upon one another's hearts, ye had still hoped, that virtue were not all a dream. Now are ye undeceived! Evil is the nature of mankind. Evil must be your only happiness. Welcome, again, my children, to the communion of your race!'

'Welcome!' repeated the fiend-worshippers, in one cry of despair and triumph.

And there they stood, the only pair, as it seemed, who were yet hesitating on the verge of wickedness, in this dark world. A basin was hollowed, naturally, in the rock. Did it contain water, reddened by the lurid light? or was it blood? or, perchance, a liquid flame? Herein did the Shape of Evil dip his hand, and prepare to lay the mark of baptism upon their foreheads, that they might be partakers of the mystery of sin, more conscious of the secret guilt of others, both in deed and thought, than they could now be of their own. The husband cast one look at his pale wife, and Faith at him. What polluted wretches would the next glance shew them to each other, shuddering alike at what they disclosed and what they saw!

'Faith! Faith!' cried the husband. 'Look up to Heaven, and resist the Wicked One!'

Whether Faith obeyed, he knew not. Hardly had he spoken, when he found himself amid calm night and solitude, listening to a roar of the wind, which died heavily away through the forest. He staggered against the rock and felt it chill and damp, while a hanging twig, that had been all on fire, besprinkled his cheek with the coldest dew.

The next morning, young Goodman Brown came slowly into the street of Salem village, staring around him like a bewildered man. The good old minister was taking a walk along the grave-yard, to get an appetite for breakfast and meditate his sermon, and bestowed a blessing, as he passed, on Goodman Brown. He shrank from the venerable saint, as if to avoid an anathema. Old Deacon Gookin was at domestic worship, and the holy words of his prayer were heard through the open window. 'What God doth the wizard pray to?' quoth Goodman Brown. Goody Cloyse, that excellent old Christian, stood in the early sunshine, at her own lattice, catechising a little girl, who had brought her a pint of morning's milk. Goodman Brown snatched away the child, as from the grasp of the fiend himself. Turning the corner by the meeting-house, he spied the head of Faith, with the pink ribbons, gazing anxiously forth, and bursting into such joy at sight of him, that she skipt along the street, and almost kissed her husband before the whole village. But, Goodman Brown looked sternly and sadly into her face, and passed on without a greeting.

Had Goodman Brown fallen asleep in the forest, and only dreamed a wild dream of a witch-meeting?

Be it so, if you will. But, alas! it was a dream of evil omen for young Goodman Brown. A stern, a sad, a darkly meditative, a distrustful, if not a desperate man, did he become, from the night of that fearful dream. On the Sabbath-day, when the congregation were singing a holy psalm, he could not listen, because an anthem of sin rushed loudly upon his ear, and drowned all the blessed strain. When the minister spoke from the pulpit, with power and fervid eloquence, and, with his hand on the open Bible, of the sacred truths of our religion, and of saint-like lives and triumphant deaths, and of future bliss or misery unutterable, then did Goodman Brown turn pale, dreading, lest the roof should thunder down upon the gray blasphemer and his hearers. Often, awakening suddenly at midnight, he shrank from the bosom of Faith, and at morning or eventide, when the family knelt down at prayer, he scowled, and muttered to himself, and gazed sternly at his wife, and turned away. And when he had lived long, and was borne to his grave, a hoary corpse, followed by Faith, an aged woman, and children and grand-children, a goodly procession, besides neighbors, not a few, they carved no hopeful verse upon his tomb-stone; for his dying hour was gloom.

NATHANIEL HAWTHORNE

The Birthmark

IN THE LATTER PART of the last century there lived a man of science, an eminent proficient in every branch of natural philosophy, who not long before our story opens had made experience of a spiritual affinity more attractive than any chemical one. He had left his laboratory to the care of an assistant, cleared his fine countenance from the furnace smoke, washed the stain of acids from his fingers, and persuaded a beautiful woman to become his wife. In those days when the comparatively recent discovery of electricity and other kindred mysteries of Nature seemed to open paths into the region of miracle, it was not unusual for the love of science to rival the love of woman in its depth and absorbing energy. The higher intellect, the imagination, the spirit, and even the heart might all find their congenial aliment in pursuits which, as some of their ardent votaries believed, would ascend from one step of powerful intelligence to another, until the philosopher should lay his hand on the secret of creative force and perhaps make new worlds for himself. We know not whether Aylmer possessed this degree of faith in man's ultimate control over Nature. He had devoted himself, however, too unreservedly to scientific studies ever to be weaned from them by any second passion. His love for his young wife might prove the stronger of the two; but it could only be by intertwining itself with his love of science, and uniting the strength of the latter to his own.

Such a union accordingly took place, and was attended with truly remarkable consequences and a deeply impressive moral. One day, very soon after their marriage, Aylmer sat gazing at his wife with a trouble in his countenance that grew stronger until he spoke.

'Georgiana,' said he, 'has it never occurred to you that the mark upon your cheek might be removed?'

'No, indeed,' said she, smiling; but perceiving the seriousness of his manner, she blushed deeply. 'To tell you the truth it has been so often called a charm that I was simple enough to imagine it might be so.'

'Ah, upon another face perhaps it might,' replied her husband; 'but never on yours. No, dearest Georgiana, you came so nearly perfect from the hand of Nature that this slightest possible defect, which we hesitate whether to term a defect or a beauty, shocks me, as being the visible mark of earthly imperfection.'

'Shocks you, my husband!' cried Georgiana, deeply hurt; at first reddening with momentary anger, but then bursting into tears. 'Then why did you take me from my mother's side? You cannot love what shocks you!'

To explain this conversation it must be mentioned that in the centre of Georgiana's left cheek there was a singular mark, deeply interwoven, as it were, with the texture and substance of her face. In the usual state of her complexion—a healthy though delicate bloom—the mark wore a tint of deeper crimson, which imperfectly defined its shape amid the surrounding rosiness. When she blushed it gradually became more indistinct, and finally vanished amid the triumphant rush of blood that bathed the whole cheek with its brilliant glow. But if any shifting motion caused her to turn pale there was the mark again, a crimson stain upon the snow, in what Aylmer sometimes deemed an almost fearful distinctness. Its shape bore not a little similarity to the human hand, though of the smallest pygmy size. Georgiana's lovers were wont to say that some fairy at her birth hour had laid her tiny hand upon the infant's cheek, and left this impress there in token of the magic endowments that were to give her such sway over all hearts. Many a desperate swain would have risked life for the privilege of pressing his lips to the mysterious hand. It must not be concealed, however, that the impression wrought by this fairy sign manual varied exceedingly, according to the difference of temperament in the beholders. Some fastidious persons—but they were exclusively of her own sex—affirmed that the bloody hand, as they chose to call it, quite destroyed the effect of Georgiana's beauty, and rendered her countenance even hideous. But it would be as reasonable to say that one of those small blue stains which sometimes occur in the purest statuary marble would convert the Eve of Powers to a monster. Masculine observers, if the birthmark did not heighten their admiration, contented themselves with wishing it away, that the world might possess one living specimen of ideal loveliness without the semblance of a flaw. After his marriage,—for he thought little or nothing of the matter before,—Aylmer discovered that this was the case with himself.

Had she been less beautiful,—if Envy's self could have found aught else to sneer at,—he might have felt his affection heightened by the prettiness of this mimic hand, now vaguely portrayed, now lost, now stealing forth again and glimmering to and fro with every pulse of emotion that throbbed within her heart; but seeing her otherwise so perfect, he found this one defect grow more and more intolerable with every moment of their united lives. It was the fatal flaw of humanity which Nature, in one shape or another, stamps ineffaceably on all her productions, either to imply that they are temporary and finite, or that their perfection must be wrought by toil and pain. The crimson hand expressed the ineludible gripe in which mortality clutches the highest and purest of earthly mould, degrading them into kindred with the lowest, and even with the very brutes, like whom their visible frames return to dust. In this manner, selecting it as the symbol of his wife's liability to sin, sorrow, decay, and death, Aylmer's sombre imagination was not long in rendering the birthmark a frightful object, causing him more trouble and horror than ever Georgiana's beauty, whether of soul or sense, had given him delight.

At all the seasons which should have been their happiest, he invariably and without intending it, nay, in spite of a purpose to the contrary, reverted to this one disastrous topic. Trifling as it at first appeared, it so connected itself with innumerable trains of thought and modes of feeling that it became the central point of all. With the morning twilight Aylmer opened his eyes upon his wife's face and recognized the symbol of imperfection; and when they sat together at the evening hearth his eyes wandered stealthily to her cheek, and beheld, flickering with the blaze of the wood fire, the spectral hand that wrote mortality where he would fain have worshipped.

Georgiana soon learned to shudder at his gaze. It needed but a glance with the peculiar expression that his face often wore to change the roses of her cheek into a deathlike paleness, amid which the crimson hand was brought strongly out, like a bas-relief of ruby on the whitest marble.

Late one night when the lights were growing dim, so as hardly to betray the stain on the poor wife's cheek, she herself, for the first time, voluntarily took up the subject.

'Do you remember, my dear Aylmer,' said she, with a feeble attempt at a smile, 'have you any recollection of a dream last night about this odious hand?'

'None! none whatever!' replied Aylmer, starting; but then he added, in a dry, cold tone, affected for the sake of concealing the real depth of his emotion, 'I might well dream of it; for before I fell asleep it had taken a pretty firm hold of my fancy.'

'And you did dream of it?' continued Georgiana, hastily; for she dreaded lest a gush of tears should interrupt what she had to say. 'A terrible dream! I wonder that you can forget it. Is it possible to forget this one expression?—"It is in her heart now; we must have it out!" Reflect, my husband; for by all means I would have you recall that dream.'

The mind is in a sad state when Sleep, the all-involving, cannot confine her spectres within the dim region of her sway, but suffers them to break forth, affrighting this actual life with secrets that perchance belong to a deeper one. Aylmer now remembered his dream. He had fancied himself with his servant Aminadab, attempting an operation for the removal of the birthmark; but the deeper went the knife, the deeper sank the hand, until at length its tiny grasp appeared to have caught hold of Georgiana's heart; whence, however, her husband was inexorably resolved to cut or wrench it away.

When the dream had shaped itself perfectly in his memory, Aylmer sat in his wife's presence with a guilty feeling. Truth often finds its way to the mind close muffled in robes of sleep, and then speaks with uncompromising directness of matters in regard to which we practise an unconscious self-deception during our waking moments. Until now he had not been aware of the tyrannizing influence acquired by one idea over his mind, and of the lengths which he might find in his heart to go for the sake of giving himself peace.

'Aylmer,' resumed Georgiana, solemnly, 'I know not what may be the cost to both of us to rid me of this fatal birthmark. Perhaps its removal may cause cureless deformity; or it may be the stain goes as deep as life itself. Again: do we know that there is a possibility, on any terms, of unclasping the firm gripe of this little hand which was laid upon me before I came into the world?'

'Dearest Georgiana, I have spent much thought upon the subject,' hastily interrupted Aylmer. 'I am convinced of the perfect practicability of its removal.'

'If there be the remotest possibility of it,' continued Georgiana, 'let the attempt be made at whatever risk. Danger is nothing to me; for life, while this hateful mark makes me the object of your horror and disgust,—life is a burden which I would fling down with joy. Either remove this dreadful hand, or take my wretched life! You have deep science. All the world bears witness of it. You have achieved great wonders. Cannot you remove this little, little mark, which I cover with the tips of two small fingers? Is this beyond your power, for the sake of your own peace, and to save your poor wife from madness?'

'Noblest, dearest, tenderest wife,' cried Aylmer, rapturously, 'doubt not my power. I have already given this matter the deepest thought—thought which might almost have enlightened me to create a being less perfect than yourself. Georgiana, you have led me deeper than ever into the heart of science. I feel myself fully competent to render this dear cheek as faultless as its fellow; and then, most beloved, what will be my triumph when I shall have corrected what Nature left imperfect in her fairest work! Even Pygmalion, when his sculptured woman assumed life, felt not greater ecstasy than mine will be.'

'It is resolved, then,' said Georgiana, faintly smiling. 'And, Aylmer, spare me not, though you should find the birthmark take refuge in my heart at last.'

Her husband tenderly kissed her cheek—her right cheek—not that which bore the impress of the crimson hand.

The next day Aylmer apprised his wife of a plan that he had formed whereby he might have opportunity for the intense thought and constant watchfulness which the proposed operation would require; while Georgiana, likewise, would enjoy the perfect repose essential to its success. They were to seclude themselves in the extensive apartments occupied by Aylmer as a laboratory, and where, during his toilsome youth, he had made discoveries in the elemental powers of Nature that had roused the admiration of all the learned societies in Europe. Seated calmly in this laboratory, the pale philosopher had investigated the secrets of the highest cloud region and of the profoundest mines; he had satisfied himself of the causes that kindled and kept alive the fires of the volcano; and had explained the mystery of fountains, and how it is that they gush forth, some so bright and pure, and others with such rich medicinal virtues, from the dark bosom of the earth. Here, too, at an earlier period, he had studied the wonders of the human frame, and attempted to fathom the very process by which Nature assimilates all her precious influences from earth and air, and from the spiritual world, to create and foster man, her masterpiece. The latter pursuit, however, Aylmer had long laid aside in unwilling recognition of the truth—against which all seekers sooner or later stumble—that our great creative Mother, while she amuses us with apparently working in the broadest sunshine, is yet severely careful to keep her own secrets, and, in spite of her pretended openness, shows us nothing but results. She permits us, indeed, to mar, but seldom to mend, and, like a jealous patentee, on no account to make. Now, however, Aylmer resumed these half-forgotten investigations; not, of course, with such hopes or wishes as first suggested them; but because they involved much physiological truth and lay in the path of his proposed scheme for the treatment of Georgiana.

As he led her over the threshold of the laboratory, Georgiana was cold and tremulous. Aylmer looked cheerfully into her face, with intent to reassure her, but was so startled with the intense glow of the birthmark upon the whiteness of her cheek that he could not restrain a strong convulsive shudder. His wife fainted.

'Aminadab! Aminadab!' shouted Aylmer, stamping violently on the floor.

Forthwith there issued from an inner apartment a man of low stature, but bulky frame, with shaggy hair hanging about his visage, which was grimed with the vapors of the furnace. This personage had been Aylmer's underworker during his whole scientific career, and was admirably fitted for that office by his great mechanical readiness, and the skill with which, while incapable of comprehending a single principle, he executed all the details of his master's experiments. With his vast strength, his shaggy hair, his smoky aspect, and the indescribable earthiness that incrusted him, he seemed to represent man's physical nature; while Aylmer's slender figure, and pale, intellectual face, were no less apt a type of the spiritual element.

'Throw open the door of the boudoir, Aminadab,' said Aylmer, 'and burn a pastil.'

'Yes, master,' answered Aminadab, looking intently at the lifeless form of Georgiana; and then he muttered to himself, 'If she were my wife, I'd never part with that birthmark.'

When Georgiana recovered consciousness she found herself breathing an atmosphere of penetrating fragrance, the gentle potency of which had recalled her from her deathlike faintness. The scene around her looked like enchantment. Aylmer had converted those smoky, dingy, sombre rooms, where he had spent his brightest years in recondite pursuits, into a series of beautiful apartments not unfit to be the secluded abode of a lovely woman. The walls were hung with gorgeous curtains, which imparted the combination of grandeur and grace that no other species of adornment can achieve; and as they fell from the ceiling to the floor, their rich and ponderous folds, concealing all angles and straight lines, appeared to shut in the scene from infinite space. For aught Georgiana knew, it might be a pavilion among the clouds. And Aylmer, excluding the sunshine, which would have interfered with his chemical processes, had supplied its place with perfumed lamps, emitting flames of various hue, but all uniting in a soft, impurpled radiance. He now knelt by his wife's side, watching her earnestly, but without alarm; for he was confident in his science, and felt that he could draw a magic circle round her within which no evil might intrude.

'Where am I? Ah, I remember,' said Georgiana, faintly; and she placed her hand over her cheek to hide the terrible mark from her husband's eyes.

'Fear not, dearest!' exclaimed he. 'Do not shrink from me! Believe me, Georgiana, I even rejoice in this single imperfection, since it will be such a rapture to remove it.'

'Oh, spare me!' sadly replied his wife. 'Pray do not look at it again. I never can forget that convulsive shudder.'

In order to soothe Georgiana, and, as it were, to release her mind from the burden of actual things, Aylmer now put in practice some of the light and playful secrets which science had taught him among its profounder lore. Airy figures, absolutely bodiless ideas, and forms of unsubstantial beauty came and danced before her, imprinting their momentary footsteps on beams of light. Though she had some indistinct idea of the method of these optical phenomena, still the illusion was almost perfect enough to warrant the belief that her husband possessed sway over the spiritual world. Then again, when she felt a wish to look forth from her seclusion, immediately, as if her thoughts were answered, the procession of external existence flitted across a screen. The scenery and the figures of actual life were perfectly represented, but with that bewitching, yet indescribable difference which always makes a picture, an image, or a shadow so much more attractive than the original. When wearied of this, Aylmer bade her cast her eyes upon a vessel containing a quantity of earth. She did so, with little interest at first; but was soon startled to perceive the germ of a plant shooting upward from the soil. Then came the slender stalk; the leaves gradually unfolded themselves; and amid them was a perfect and lovely flower.

'It is magical!' cried Georgiana. 'I dare not touch it.'

'Nay, pluck it,' answered Aylmer,—'pluck it, and inhale its brief perfume while you may. The flower will wither in a few moments and leave nothing save its brown seed vessels; but thence may be perpetuated a race as ephemeral as itself.'

But Georgiana had no sooner touched the flower than the whole plant suffered a blight, its leaves turning coal-black as if by the agency of fire.

'There was too powerful a stimulus,' said Aylmer, thoughtfully.

To make up for this abortive experiment, he proposed to take her portrait by a scientific process of his own invention. It was to be effected by rays of light striking upon a polished plate of metal. Georgiana assented; but, on looking at the result, was affrighted to find the features of the portrait blurred and indefinable; while the minute figure of a hand appeared where the cheek should have been. Aylmer snatched the metallic plate and threw it into a jar of corrosive acid.

Soon, however, he forgot these mortifying failures. In the intervals of study and chemical experiment he came to her flushed and exhausted, but seemed invigorated by her presence, and spoke in glowing language of the resources of his art. He gave a history of the long dynasty of the alchemists, who spent so many ages in quest of the universal solvent by which the golden principle might be elicited from all things vile and base. Aylmer appeared to believe that, by the plainest scientific logic, it was altogether within the limits of possibility to discover this long-sought medium; 'but,' he added, 'a philosopher who should go deep enough to acquire the power would attain too lofty a wisdom to stoop to the exercise of it.' Not less singular were his opinions in regard to the elixir vitae. He more than intimated that it was at his option to concoct a liquid that should prolong life for years, perhaps interminably; but that it would produce a discord in Nature which all the world, and chiefly the quaffer of the immortal nostrum, would find cause to curse.

'Aylmer, are you in earnest?' asked Georgiana, looking at him with amazement and fear. 'It is terrible to possess such power, or even to dream of possessing it.'

'Oh, do not tremble, my love,' said her husband. 'I would not wrong either you or myself by working such inharmonious effects upon our lives; but I would have you consider how trifling, in comparison, is the skill requisite to remove this little hand.'

At the mention of the birthmark, Georgiana, as usual, shrank as if a red-hot iron had touched her cheek.

Again Aylmer applied himself to his labors. She could hear his voice in the distant furnace room giving directions to Aminadab, whose harsh, uncouth, misshapen tones were audible in response, more like the grunt or growl of a brute than human speech. After hours of absence, Aylmer reappeared and proposed that she should now examine his cabinet of chemical products and natural treasures of the earth. Among the former he showed her a small vial, in which, he remarked, was contained a gentle yet most powerful fragrance, capable of impregnating all the breezes that blow across a kingdom. They were of inestimable value, the contents of that little vial; and, as he said so, he threw some of the perfume into the air and filled the room with piercing and invigorating delight.

'And what is this?' asked Georgiana, pointing to a small crystal globe containing a gold-colored liquid. 'It is so beautiful to the eye that I could imagine it the elixir of life.'

'In one sense it is,' replied Aylmer; 'or, rather, the elixir of immortality. It is the most precious poison that ever was concocted in this world. By its aid I could apportion the lifetime of any mortal at whom you might point your finger. The strength of the dose would determine whether he were to linger out years, or drop dead in the midst of a breath. No king on his guarded throne could keep his life if I, in my private station, should deem that the welfare of millions justified me in depriving him of it.'

'Why do you keep such a terrific drug?' inquired Georgiana in horror.

'Do not mistrust me, dearest,' said her husband, smiling; 'its virtuous potency is yet greater than its harmful one. But see! here is a powerful cosmetic. With a few drops of this in a vase of water, freckles may be washed away as easily as the hands are cleansed. A stronger infusion would take the blood out of the cheek, and leave the rosiest beauty a pale ghost.'

'Is it with this lotion that you intend to bathe my cheek?' asked Georgiana, anxiously.

'Oh, no,' hastily replied her husband; 'this is merely superficial. Your case demands a remedy that shall go deeper.'

In his interviews with Georgiana, Aylmer generally made minute inquiries as to her sensations and whether the confinement of the rooms and the temperature of the atmosphere agreed with her. These questions had such a particular drift that Georgiana began to conjecture that she was already subjected to certain physical influences, either breathed in with the fragrant air or taken with her food. She fancied likewise, but it might be altogether fancy, that there was a stirring up of her system—a strange, indefinite sensation creeping through her veins, and tingling, half painfully, half pleasurably, at her heart. Still, whenever she dared to look into the mirror, there she beheld herself pale as a white rose and with the crimson birthmark stamped upon her cheek. Not even Aylmer now hated it so much as she.

To dispel the tedium of the hours which her husband found it necessary to devote to the processes of combination and analysis, Georgiana turned over the volumes of his scientific library. In many dark old tomes she met with chapters full of romance and poetry. They were the works of the philosophers of the middle ages, such as

Albertus Magnus, Cornelius Agrippa, Paracelsus, and the famous friar who created the prophetic Brazen Head. All these antique naturalists stood in advance of their centuries, yet were imbued with some of their credulity, and therefore were believed, and perhaps imagined themselves to have acquired from the investigation of Nature a power above Nature, and from physics a sway over the spiritual world. Hardly less curious and imaginative were the early volumes of the Transactions of the Royal Society, in which the members, knowing little of the limits of natural possibility, were continually recording wonders or proposing methods whereby wonders might be wrought.

But to Georgiana the most engrossing volume was a large folio from her husband's own hand, in which he had recorded every experiment of his scientific career, its original aim, the methods adopted for its development, and its final success or failure, with the circumstances to which either event was attributable. The book, in truth, was both the history and emblem of his ardent, ambitious, imaginative, yet practical and laborious life. He handled physical details as if there were nothing beyond them; yet spiritualized them all, and redeemed himself from materialism by his strong and eager aspiration towards the infinite. In his grasp the veriest clod of earth assumed a soul. Georgiana, as she read, reverenced Aylmer and loved him more profoundly than ever, but with a less entire dependence on his judgment than heretofore. Much as he had accomplished, she could not but observe that his most splendid successes were almost invariably failures, if compared with the ideal at which he aimed. His brightest diamonds were the merest pebbles, and felt to be so by himself, in comparison with the inestimable gems which lay hidden beyond his reach. The volume, rich with achievements that had won renown for its author, was yet as melancholy a record as ever mortal hand had penned. It was the sad confession and continual exemplification of the shortcomings of the composite man, the spirit burdened with clay and working in matter, and of the despair that assails the higher nature at finding itself so miserably thwarted by the earthly part. Perhaps every man of genius in whatever sphere might recognize the image of his own experience in Aylmer's journal.

So deeply did these reflections affect Georgiana that she laid her face upon the open volume and burst into tears. In this situation she was found by her husband.

'It is dangerous to read in a sorcerer's books,' said he, with a smile, though his countenance was uneasy and displeased. 'Georgiana, there are pages in that volume which I can scarcely glance over and keep my senses. Take heed lest it prove as detrimental to you.'

'It has made me worship you more than ever,' said she.

'Ah, wait for this one success,' rejoined he, 'then worship me if you will. I shall deem myself hardly unworthy of it. But come, I have sought you for the luxury of your voice. Sing to me, dearest.'

So she poured out the liquid music of her voice to quench the thirst of his spirit. He then took his leave with a boyish exuberance of gayety, assuring her that her seclusion would endure but a little longer, and that the result was already certain. Scarcely had he departed when Georgiana felt irresistibly impelled to follow him. She had forgotten to inform Aylmer of a symptom which for two or three hours past had begun to excite her attention. It was a sensation in the fatal birthmark, not painful, but which induced a restlessness throughout her system. Hastening after her husband, she intruded for the first time into the laboratory.

The first thing that struck her eye was the furnace, that hot and feverish worker, with the intense glow of its fire, which by the quantities of soot clustered above it seemed to have been burning for ages. There was a distilling apparatus in full operation. Around the room were retorts, tubes, cylinders, crucibles, and other apparatus of chemical research. An electrical machine stood ready for immediate use. The atmosphere felt oppressively close, and was tainted with gaseous odors which had been tormented forth by the processes of science. The severe and homely simplicity of the apartment, with its naked walls and brick pavement, looked strange, accustomed as Georgiana had become to the fantastic elegance of her boudoir. But what chiefly, indeed almost solely, drew her attention, was the aspect of Aylmer himself.

He was pale as death, anxious and absorbed, and hung over the furnace as if it depended upon his utmost watchfulness whether the liquid which it was distilling should be the draught of immortal happiness or misery. How different from the sanguine and joyous mien that he had assumed for Georgiana's encouragement!

'Carefully now, Aminadab; carefully, thou human machine; carefully, thou man of clay!' muttered Aylmer, more to himself than his assistant. 'Now, if there be a thought too much or too little, it is all over.'

'Ho! ho!' mumbled Aminadab. 'Look, master! look!'

Aylmer raised his eyes hastily, and at first reddened, then grew paler than ever, on beholding Georgiana. He rushed towards her and seized her arm with a gripe that left the print of his fingers upon it.

'Why do you come hither? Have you no trust in your husband?' cried he, impetuously. 'Would you throw the blight of that fatal birth-mark over my labors? It is not well done. Go, prying woman, go!'

'Nay, Aylmer,' said Georgiana with the firmness of which she possessed no stinted endowment, 'it is not you that have a right to complain. You mistrust your wife; you have concealed the anxiety with which you watch the development of this experiment. Think not so unworthily of me, my husband. Tell me all the risk we run, and fear not that I shall shrink; for my share in it is far less than your own.'

'No, no, Georgiana!' said Aylmer, impatiently, 'it must not be.'

'I submit,' replied she calmly. 'And, Aylmer, I shall quaff whatever draught you bring me; but it will be on the same principle that would induce me to take a dose of poison if offered by your hand.'

'My noble wife,' said Aylmer, deeply moved, 'I knew not the height and depth of your nature until now. Nothing shall be concealed. Know, then, that this crimson hand, superficial as it seems, has clutched its grasp into your being with a strength of which I had no previous conception. I have already administered agents powerful enough to do aught except to change your entire physical system. Only one thing remains to be tried. If that fail us we are ruined.'

'Why did you hesitate to tell me this?' asked she.

'Because, Georgiana,' said Aylmer, in a low voice, 'there is danger.'

'Danger? There is but one danger—that this horrible stigma shall be left upon my cheek!' cried Georgiana. 'Remove it, remove it, whatever be the cost, or we shall both go mad!'

'Heaven knows your words are too true,' said Aylmer, sadly. 'And now, dearest, return to your boudoir. In a little while all will be tested.'

He conducted her back and took leave of her with a solemn tenderness which spoke far more than his words how much was now at stake. After his departure Georgiana became rapt in musings. She considered the character of Aylmer, and did it completer justice than at any previous moment. Her heart exulted, while it trembled, at his honorable love—so pure and lofty that it would accept nothing less than perfection nor miserably make itself contented with an earthlier nature than he had dreamed of. She felt how much more precious was such a sentiment than that meaner kind which would have borne with the imperfection for her sake, and have been guilty of treason to holy love by degrading its perfect idea to the level of the actual; and with her whole spirit she prayed that, for a single moment, she might satisfy his highest and deepest conception. Longer than one moment she well knew it could not be; for his spirit was ever on the march, ever ascending, and each instant required something that was beyond the scope of the instant before.

The sound of her husband's footsteps aroused her. He bore a crystal goblet containing a liquor colorless as water, but bright enough to be the draught of immortality. Aylmer was pale; but it seemed rather the consequence of a highly-wrought state of mind and tension of spirit than of fear or doubt.

'The concoction of the draught has been perfect,' said he, in answer to Georgiana's look. 'Unless all my science have deceived me, it cannot fail.'

'Save on your account, my dearest Aylmer,' observed his wife, 'I might wish to put off this birthmark of mortality by relinquishing mortality itself in preference to any other mode. Life is but a sad possession to those who have attained precisely the degree of moral advancement at which I stand. Were I weaker and blinder it might be happiness. Were I stronger, it might be endured hopefully. But, being what I find myself, methinks I am of all mortals the most fit to die.'

'You are fit for heaven without tasting death!' replied her husband. 'But why do we speak of dying? The draught cannot fail. Behold its effect upon this plant.'

On the window seat there stood a geranium diseased with yellow blotches, which had overspread all its leaves. Aylmer poured a small quantity of the liquid upon the soil in which it grew. In a little time, when the roots of the plant had taken up the moisture, the unsightly blotches began to be extinguished in a living verdure.

'There needed no proof,' said Georgiana, quietly. 'Give me the goblet. I joyfully stake all upon your word.'

'Drink, then, thou lofty creature!' exclaimed Aylmer, with fervid admiration. 'There is no taint of imperfection on thy spirit. Thy sensible frame, too, shall soon be all perfect.'

She quaffed the liquid and returned the goblet to his hand.

'It is grateful,' said she with a placid smile. 'Methinks it is like water from a heavenly fountain, for it contains I know not what of unobtrusive fragrance and deliciousness. It allays a feverish thirst that had parched me for many days. Now, dearest, let me sleep. My earthly senses are closing over my spirit like the leaves around the heart of a rose at sunset.'

She spoke the last words with a gentle reluctance, as if it required almost more energy than she could command to pronounce the faint and lingering syllables. Scarcely had they loitered through her lips ere she was lost in slumber. Aylmer sat by her side, watching her aspect with the emotions proper to a man the whole value of whose existence was involved in the process now to be tested. Mingled with this mood, however, was the philosophic investigation characteristic of the man of science. Not the minutest symptom escaped him. A heightened flush of the cheek, a slight irregularity of breath, a quiver of the eyelid, a hardly perceptible tremor through the frame,—such were the details which, as the moments passed, he wrote down in his folio volume. Intense thought had set its stamp upon every previous page of that volume, but the thoughts of years were all concentrated upon the last.

While thus employed, he failed not to gaze often at the fatal hand, and not without a shudder. Yet once, by a strange and unaccountable impulse, he pressed it with his lips. His spirit recoiled, however, in the very act; and Georgiana, out of the midst of her deep sleep, moved uneasily and murmured as if in remonstrance. Again Aylmer resumed his watch. Nor was it without avail. The crimson hand, which at first had been strongly visible upon the marble paleness of Georgiana's cheek, now grew more faintly outlined. She remained not less pale than ever; but the birthmark, with every breath that came and went, lost somewhat of its former distinctness. Its presence had been awful; its departure was more awful still. Watch the stain of the rainbow fading out of the sky, and you will know how that mysterious symbol passed away.

'By Heaven! it is well-nigh gone!' said Aylmer to himself, in almost irrepressible ecstasy. 'I can scarcely trace it now. Success! success! And now it is like the faintest rose color. The lightest flush of blood across her cheek would overcome it. But she is so pale!'

He drew aside the window curtain and suffered the light of natural day to fall into the room and rest upon her cheek. At the same time he heard a gross, hoarse chuckle, which he had long known as his servant Aminadab's expression of delight.

'Ah, clod! ah, earthly mass!' cried Aylmer, laughing in a sort of frenzy, 'you have served me well! Matter and spirit—earth and heaven—have both done their part in this! Laugh, thing of the senses! You have earned the right to laugh.'

These exclamations broke Georgiana's sleep. She slowly unclosed her eyes and gazed into the mirror which her husband had arranged for that purpose. A faint smile flitted over her lips when she recognized how barely perceptible was now that crimson hand which had once blazed forth with such disastrous brilliancy as to scare away all their happiness. But then her eyes sought Aylmer's face with a trouble and anxiety that he could by no means account for.

'My poor Aylmer!' murmured she.

'Poor? Nay, richest, happiest, most favored!' exclaimed he. 'My peerless bride, it is successful! You are perfect!'

'My poor Aylmer,' she repeated, with a more than human tenderness, 'you have aimed loftily; you have done nobly. Do not repent that with so high and pure a feeling, you have rejected the best the earth could offer. Aylmer, dearest Aylmer, I am dying!'

Alas! it was too true! The fatal hand had grappled with the mystery of life, and was the bond by which an angelic spirit kept itself in union with a mortal frame. As the last crimson tint of the birthmark—that sole token of human imperfection—faded from her cheek, the parting breath of the now perfect woman passed into the atmosphere, and her soul, lingering a moment near her husband, took its heavenward flight. Then a hoarse, chuckling laugh was heard again! Thus ever does the gross fatality of earth exult in its invariable triumph over the immortal essence which, in this dim sphere of half development, demands the completeness of a higher state. Yet, had Aylmer reached a profounder wisdom, he need not thus have flung away the happiness which would have woven his mortal life of the selfsame texture with the celestial. The momentary circumstance was too strong for him; he failed to look beyond the shadowy scope of time, and, living once for all in eternity, to find the perfect future in the present.

NATHANIEL HAWTHORNE

Rappaccini's Daughter

A YOUNG MAN, NAMED Giovanni Guasconti, came, very long ago, from the more southern region of Italy, to pursue his studies at the University of Padua. Giovanni, who had but a scanty supply of gold ducats in his pocket, took lodgings in a high and gloomy chamber of an old edifice, which looked not unworthy to have been the palace of a Paduan noble, and which, in fact, exhibited over its entrance the armorial bearings of a family long since extinct. The young stranger, who was not unstudied in the great poem of his country, recollected that one of the ancestors of this family, and perhaps an occupant of this very mansion, had been pictured by Dante as a partaker of the immortal agonies of his Inferno. These reminiscences and associations, together with the tendency to heart-break natural to a young man for the first time out of his native sphere, caused Giovanni to sigh heavily, as he looked around the desolate and ill-furnished apartment.

"Holy Virgin, Signor," cried old dame Lisabetta, who, won by the youth's remarkable beauty of person, was kindly endeavoring to give the chamber a habitable air, "what a sigh was that to come out of a young man's heart! Do you find this old mansion gloomy? For the love of heaven, then, put your head out of the window, and you will see as bright sunshine as you have left in Naples."

Guasconti mechanically did as the old woman advised, but could not quite agree with her that the Paduan sunshine was as cheerful as that of southern Italy. Such as it was, however, it fell upon a garden beneath the window, and expended its fostering influences on a variety of plants, which seemed to have been cultivated with exceeding care.

"Does this garden belong to the house?" asked Giovanni.

"Heaven forbid, Signor!—unless it were fruitful of better pot-herbs than any that grow there now," answered old Lisabetta. "No; that garden is cultivated by the own hands of Signor Giacomo Rappaccini, the famous Doctor, who, I warrant him, has been heard of as far as Naples. It is said that he distils these plants into medicines that are as potent as a charm. Oftentimes you may see the Signor Doctor at work, and perchance the Signora his daughter, too, gathering the strange flowers that grow in the garden."

The old woman had now done what she could for the aspect of the chamber, and, commending the young man to the protection of the saints, took her departure.

Giovanni still found no better occupation than to look down into the garden beneath his window. From its appearance, he judged it to be one of those botanic gardens, which were of earlier date in Padua than elsewhere in Italy, or in the world. Or, not improbably, it might once have been the pleasure-place of an opulent family; for there was the ruin of a marble fountain in the centre, sculptured with rare art, but so wofully shattered that it was impossible to trace the original design from the chaos of remaining fragments. The water, however, continued to gush and sparkle into the sunbeams as cheerfully as ever. A little gurgling sound ascended to the young man's window, and made him feel as if the fountain were an immortal spirit, that sung its song unceasingly, and without heeding the vicissitudes around it; while one century embodied it in marble, and another scattered the perishable garniture on the soil. All about the pool into which the water subsided, grew various plants, that seemed to require a plentiful supply of moisture for the nourishment of gigantic leaves, and, in some instances, flowers gorgeously magnificent. There was one shrub in particular, set in a marble vase in the midst of the pool, that bore a profusion of purple blossoms, each of which had the lustre and richness of a gem; and the whole together made a show so resplendent that it seemed enough to illuminate the garden, even had there been no sunshine. Every portion of the soil was peopled with plants and herbs, which, if less beautiful, still bore tokens of assiduous care; as if all had their individual virtues, known to the scientific mind that fostered them. Some were placed in urns, rich with old carving, and others in common garden-pots; some crept serpent-like along the ground, or climbed on high, using whatever means of ascent was offered them. One plant had wreathed itself round a statue of Vertumnus, which was thus quite veiled and shrouded in a drapery of hanging foliage, so happily arranged that it might have served a sculptor for a study.

While Giovanni stood at the window, he heard a rustling behind a screen of leaves, and became aware that a person was at work in the garden. His figure soon emerged into view, and showed itself to be that of no common laborer, but a tall, emaciated, sallow, and sickly-looking man, dressed in a scholar's garb of black. He was beyond the middle term of life, with grey hair, a thin grey beard, and a face singularly marked with intellect and cultivation, but which could never, even in his more youthful days, have expressed much warmth of heart.

Nothing could exceed the intentness with which this scientific gardener examined every shrub which grew in his path; it seemed as if he was looking into their inmost nature, making observations in regard to their creative essence, and discovering why one leaf grew in this shape, and another in that, and wherefore such and such flowers differed among themselves in hue and perfume. Nevertheless, in spite of this deep intelligence on his part, there was no approach to intimacy between himself and these vegetable existences. On the contrary, he avoided their actual touch, or the direct inhaling of their odors, with a caution that impressed Giovanni most disagreeably; for the man's demeanor was that of one walking among malignant influences, such as savage beasts, or deadly snakes, or evil spirits, which, should he allow them one moment of license, would wreak upon him some terrible fatality. It was strangely frightful to the young man's imagination, to see this air of insecurity in a person cultivating a garden, that most simple and innocent of human toils, and which had been alike the joy and labor of the unfallen parents of the race. Was this garden, then, the Eden of the present world?—and this man, with such a perception of harm in what his own hands caused to grow, was he the Adam?

The distrustful gardener, while plucking away the dead leaves or pruning the too luxuriant growth of the shrubs, defended his hands with a pair of thick gloves. Nor were these his only armor. When, in his walk through the garden, he came to the magnificent plant that hung its purple gems beside the marble fountain, he placed a kind of mask over his mouth and nostrils, as if all this beauty did but conceal a deadlier malice. But finding his task still too dangerous, he drew back, removed the mask, and called loudly, but in the infirm voice of a person affected with inward disease:

"Beatrice!—Beatrice!"

"Here am I, my father! What would you?" cried a rich and youthful voice from the window of the opposite house; a voice as rich as a tropical sunset, and which made Giovanni, though he knew not why, think of deep hues of purple or crimson, and of perfumes heavily delectable.—"Are you in the garden?"

"Yes, Beatrice," answered the gardener, "and I need your help."

Soon there emerged from under a sculptured portal the figure of a young girl, arrayed with as much richness of taste as the most splendid of the flowers, beautiful as the day, and with a bloom so deep and vivid that one shade more would have been too much. She looked redundant with life, health, and energy; all of which attributes were bound down and compressed, as it were, and girdled tensely, in their luxuriance, by her virgin zone. Yet Giovanni's fancy must have grown morbid, while he looked down into the garden; for the impression which the fair stranger made upon him was as if here were another flower, the human sister of those vegetable ones, as beautiful as they—more beautiful than the richest of them—but still to be touched only with a glove, nor to be approached without a mask. As Beatrice came down the garden path, it was observable that she handled and inhaled the odor of several of the plants, which her father had most sedulously avoided.

"Here, Beatrice," said the latter,—"see how many needful offices require to be done to our chief treasure. Yet, shattered as I am, my life might pay the penalty of approaching it so closely as circumstances demand. Henceforth, I fear, this plant must be consigned to your sole charge."

"And gladly will I undertake it," cried again the rich tones of the young lady, as she bent towards the magnificent plant, and opened her arms as if to embrace it. "Yes, my sister, my splendor, it shall be Beatrice's task to nurse and serve thee; and thou shalt reward her with thy kisses and perfumed breath, which to her is as the breath of life!"

Then, with all the tenderness in her manner that was so strikingly expressed in her words, she busied herself with such attentions as the plant seemed to require; and Giovanni, at his lofty window, rubbed his eyes, and almost doubted whether it were a girl tending her favorite flower, or one sister performing the duties of affection to another. The scene soon terminated. Whether Doctor Rappaccini had finished his labors in the garden, or that his watchful eye had caught the stranger's face, he now took his daughter's arm and retired. Night was already closing in; oppressive exhalations seemed to proceed from the plants, and steal upward past the open window; and Giovanni, closing the lattice, went to his couch, and dreamed of a rich flower and beautiful girl. Flower and maiden were different and yet the same, and fraught with some strange peril in either shape.

But there is an influence in the light of morning that tends to rectify whatever errors of fancy, or even of judgment, we may have incurred during the sun's decline, or among the shadows of the night, or in the less wholesome glow of moonshine. Giovanni's first movement on starting from sleep, was to throw open the window, and gaze down into the garden which his dreams had made so fertile of mysteries. He was surprised, and a little ashamed, to find how real and matter-of-fact an affair it proved to be, in the first rays of the sun, which gilded the dew-drops that hung upon leaf and blossom, and, while giving a brighter beauty to each rare flower, brought everything within the limits of ordinary experience. The young man rejoiced, that, in the heart of the barren city, he had the privilege of overlooking this spot of lovely and luxuriant vegetation. It would serve, he said to himself, as a symbolic language, to keep him in communion with Nature. Neither the sickly and thought-worn Doctor Giacomo Rappaccini, it is true, nor his brilliant daughter, were now visible; so that Giovanni could not determine how much of the singularity which he attributed to both, was due to their own qualities, and how much to his wonder-working fancy. But he was inclined to take a most rational view of the whole matter.

In the course of the day, he paid his respects to Signor Pietro Baglioni, professor of medicine in the University, a physician of eminent repute, to whom Giovanni had brought a letter of introduction. The Professor was an elderly personage, apparently of genial nature, and habits that might almost be called jovial; he kept the young man to dinner, and made himself very agreeable by the freedom and liveliness of his conversation, especially when warmed by a flask or two of Tuscan wine. Giovanni, conceiving that men of science, inhabitants of the same city, must needs be on familiar terms with one another, took an opportunity to mention the name of Doctor Rappaccini. But the Professor did not respond with so much cordiality as he had anticipated.

"Ill would it become a teacher of the divine art of medicine," said Professor Pietro Baglioni, in answer to a question of Giovanni, "to withhold due and well-considered praise of a physician so eminently skilled as Rappaccini. But, on the other hand, I should answer it but scantily to my conscience, were I to permit a worthy youth like yourself, Signor Giovanni, the son of an ancient friend, to imbibe erroneous ideas respecting a man who might hereafter chance to hold your life and death in his hands. The truth is, our worshipful Doctor Rappaccini has as much science as any member of the faculty—with perhaps one single exception—in Padua, or all Italy. But there are certain grave objections to his professional character."

"And what are they?" asked the young man.

"Has my friend Giovanni any disease of body or heart, that he is so inquisitive about physicians?" said the Professor, with a smile. "But as for Rappaccini, it is said of him—and I, who know the man well, can answer for its truth—that he cares infinitely more for science than for mankind. His patients are interesting to him only as subjects for some new experiment. He would sacrifice human life, his own among the rest, or whatever else was dearest to him, for the sake of adding so much as a grain of mustard-seed to the great heap of his accumulated knowledge."

"Methinks he is an awful man, indeed," remarked Guasconti, mentally recalling the cold and purely intellectual aspect of Rappaccini. "And yet, worshipful Professor, is it not a noble spirit? Are there many men capable of so spiritual a love of science?"

"God forbid," answered the Professor, somewhat testily—"at least, unless they take sounder views of the healing art than those adopted by Rappaccini. It is his theory, that all medicinal virtues are comprised within those substances which we term vegetable poisons. These he cultivates with his own hands, and is said even to have produced new varieties of poison, more horribly deleterious than Nature, without the assistance of this learned person, would ever have plagued the world withal. That the Signor Doctor does less mischief than might be expected, with such dangerous substances, is undeniable. Now and then, it must be owned, he has effected—or seemed to effect—a marvellous cure. But, to tell you my private mind, Signor Giovanni, he should receive little credit for such instances of success—they being probably the work of chance—but should be held strictly accountable for his failures, which may justly be considered his own work."

The youth might have taken Baglioni's opinions with many grains of allowance, had he known that there was a professional warfare of long continuance between him and Doctor Rappaccini, in which the latter was generally thought to have gained the advantage. If the reader be inclined to judge for himself, we refer him to certain black-letter tracts on both sides, preserved in the medical department of the University of Padua.

"I know not, most learned Professor," returned Giovanni, after musing on what had been said of Rappaccini's exclusive zeal for science—"I know not how dearly this physician may love his art; but surely there is one object more dear to him. He has a daughter."

"Aha!" cried the Professor with a laugh. "So now our friend Giovanni's secret is out. You have heard of this daughter, whom all the young men in Padua are wild about, though not half a dozen have ever had the good hap to see her face. I know little of the Signora Beatrice, save that Rappaccini is said to have instructed her deeply in his science, and that, young and beautiful as fame reports her, she is already qualified to fill a professor's chair. Perchance her father destines her for mine! Other absurd rumors there be, not worth talking about, or listening to. So now, Signor Giovanni, drink off your glass of Lacryma."

Guasconti returned to his lodgings somewhat heated with the wine he had quaffed, and which caused his brain to swim with strange fantasies in reference to Doctor Rappaccini and the beautiful Beatrice. On his way, happening to pass by a florist's, he bought a fresh bouquet of flowers.

Ascending to his chamber, he seated himself near the window, but within the shadow thrown by the depth of the wall, so that he could look down into the garden with little risk of being discovered. All beneath his eye was a solitude. The strange plants were basking in the sunshine, and now and then nodding gently to one another, as if in acknowledgment of sympathy and kindred. In the midst, by the shattered fountain, grew the magnificent shrub, with its purple gems clustering all over it; they glowed in the air, and gleamed back again out of the depths of the pool, which thus seemed to overflow with colored radiance from the rich reflection that was steeped in it. At first, as we have said, the garden was a solitude. Soon, however,—as Giovanni had half-hoped, half-feared, would be the case,—a figure appeared beneath the antique sculptured portal, and came down between the rows of plants, inhaling their various perfumes, as if she were one of those beings of old classic fable, that lived upon sweet odors. On again beholding Beatrice, the young man was even startled to perceive how much her beauty exceeded his recollection of it; so brilliant, so vivid was its character, that she glowed amid the sunlight, and, as Giovanni whispered to himself, positively illuminated the more shadowy intervals of the garden path. Her face being now more revealed than on the former occasion, he was struck by its expression of simplicity and sweetness; qualities that had not entered into his idea of her character, and which made him ask anew, what manner of mortal she might be. Nor did he fail again to observe, or imagine, an analogy between the beautiful girl and the gorgeous shrub that hung its gem-like flowers over the fountain; a resemblance which Beatrice seemed to have indulged a fantastic humor in heightening, both by the arrangement of her dress and the selection of its hues.

Approaching the shrub, she threw open her arms, as with a passionate ardor, and drew its branches into an intimate embrace; so intimate, that her features were hidden in its leafy bosom, and her glistening ringlets all intermingled with the flowers.

"Give me thy breath, my sister," exclaimed Beatrice; "for I am faint with common air! And give me this flower of thine, which I separate with gentlest fingers from the stem, and place it close beside my heart."

With these words, the beautiful daughter of Rappaccini plucked one of the richest blossoms of the shrub, and was about to fasten it in her bosom. But now, unless Giovanni's draughts of wine had bewildered his senses, a singular incident occurred. A small orange-colored reptile, of the lizard or chameleon species, chanced to be creeping along the path, just at the feet of Beatrice. It appeared to Giovanni—but, at the distance from which he gazed, he could scarcely have seen anything so minute—it appeared to him, however, that a drop or two of moisture from the broken stem of the flower descended upon the lizard's head. For an instant, the reptile contorted itself violently, and then lay motionless in the sunshine. Beatrice observed this remarkable phenomenon, and crossed herself, sadly, but without surprise; nor did she therefore hesitate to arrange the fatal flower in her bosom. There it blushed, and almost glimmered with the dazzling effect of a precious stone, adding to her dress and aspect the one appropriate charm, which nothing else in the world could have supplied. But Giovanni, out of the shadow of his window, bent forward and shrank back, and murmured and trembled.

"Am I awake? Have I my senses?" said he to himself. "What is this being?—beautiful, shall I call her?—or inexpressibly terrible?"

Beatrice now strayed carelessly through the garden, approaching closer beneath Giovanni's window, so that he was compelled to thrust his head quite out of its concealment in order to gratify the intense and painful curiosity which she excited. At this moment, there came a beautiful insect over the garden wall; it had perhaps wandered through the city and found no flowers nor verdure among those antique haunts of men, until the heavy perfumes of Doctor Rappaccini's shrubs had lured it from afar. Without alighting on the flowers, this winged brightness seemed to be attracted by Beatrice, and lingered in the air and fluttered about her head. Now, here it could not be but that Giovanni Guasconti's eyes deceived him. Be that as it might, he fancied that while Beatrice was gazing at the insect with childish delight, it grew faint and fell at her feet;—its bright wings shivered; it was dead—from no cause that he could discern, unless it were the atmosphere of her breath. Again Beatrice crossed herself and sighed heavily, as she bent over the dead insect.

An impulsive movement of Giovanni drew her eyes to the window. There she beheld the beautiful head of the young man—rather a Grecian than an Italian head, with fair, regular features, and a glistening of gold among his ringlets—gazing down upon her like a being that hovered in midair. Scarcely knowing what he did, Giovanni threw down the bouquet which he had hitherto held in his hand.

"Signora," said he, "there are pure and healthful flowers. Wear them for the sake of Giovanni Guasconti!"

"Thanks, Signor," replied Beatrice, with her rich voice, that came forth as it were like a gush of music; and with a mirthful expression half childish and half woman-like. "I accept your gift, and would fain recompense it with this precious purple flower; but if I toss it into the air, it will not reach you. So Signor Guasconti must even content himself with my thanks."

She lifted the bouquet from the ground, and then as if inwardly ashamed at having stepped aside from her maidenly reserve to respond to a stranger's greeting, passed swiftly homeward through the garden. But, few as the moments were, it seemed to Giovanni when she was on the point of vanishing beneath the sculptured portal, that his beautiful bouquet was already beginning to wither in her grasp. It was an idle thought; there could be no possibility of distinguishing a faded flower from a fresh one at so great a distance.

For many days after this incident, the young man avoided the window that looked into Doctor Rappaccini's garden, as if something ugly and monstrous would have blasted his eyesight, had he been betrayed into a glance. He felt conscious of having put himself, to a certain extent, within the influence of an unintelligible power, by the communication which he had opened with Beatrice. The wisest course would have been, if his heart were in any real danger, to quit his lodgings and Padua itself, at once; the next wiser, to have accustomed himself, as far as possible, to the familiar and day-light view of Beatrice; thus bringing her rigidly and systematically within the limits of ordinary experience. Least of all, while avoiding her sight, ought Giovanni to have remained so near this extraordinary being, that the proximity and possibility even of intercourse, should give a kind of substance and reality to the wild vagaries which his imagination ran riot continually in producing. Guasconti had not a deep heart—or at all events, its depths were not sounded now—but he had a quick fancy, and an ardent southern temperament, which rose every instant to a higher fever-pitch. Whether or no Beatrice possessed those terrible attributes—that fatal breath—the affinity with those so beautiful and deadly flowers—which were indicated by what Giovanni had witnessed, she had at least instilled a fierce and subtle poison into his system. It was not love, although her rich beauty was a madness to him; nor horror, even while he fancied her spirit to be imbued with the same baneful essence that seemed to pervade her physical frame; but a wild offspring of both love and horror that had each parent in it, and burned like one and shivered like the other. Giovanni knew not what to dread; still less did he know what to hope; yet hope and dread kept a continual warfare in his breast, alternately vanquishing one another and starting up afresh to renew the contest. Blessed are all simple emotions, be they dark or bright! It is the lurid intermixture of the two that produces the illuminating blaze of the infernal regions.

Sometimes he endeavored to assuage the fever of his spirit by a rapid walk through the streets of Padua, or beyond its gates; his footsteps kept time with the throbbings of his brain, so that the walk was apt to accelerate itself to a race. One day, he found himself arrested; his arm was seized by a portly personage who had turned back on recognizing the young man, and expended much breath in overtaking him.

"Signor Giovanni!—stay, my young friend!" cried he. "Have you forgotten me? That might well be the case, if I were as much altered as yourself."

It was Baglioni, whom Giovanni had avoided, ever since their first meeting, from a doubt that the Professor's sagacity would look too deeply into his secrets. Endeavoring to recover himself, he stared forth wildly from his inner world into the outer one, and spoke like a man in a dream:

"Yes; I am Giovanni Guasconti. You are Professor Pietro Baglioni. Now let me pass!"

"Not yet—not yet, Signor Giovanni Guasconti," said the Professor, smiling, but at the same time scrutinizing the youth with an earnest glance.—"What; did I grow up side by side with your father, and shall his son pass me like a stranger, in these old streets of Padua? Stand still, Signor Giovanni; for we must have a word or two, before we part."

"Speedily, then, most worshipful Professor, speedily!" said Giovanni, with feverish impatience. "Does not your worship see that I am in haste?"

Now, while he was speaking, there came a man in black along the street, stooping and moving feebly, like a person in inferior health. His face was all overspread with a most sickly and sallow hue, but yet so pervaded with an expression of piercing and active intellect, that an observer might easily have overlooked the merely physical attributes, and have seen only this wonderful energy. As he passed, this person exchanged a cold and distant salutation with Baglioni, but fixed his eyes upon Giovanni with an intentness that seemed to bring out whatever was within him worthy of notice. Nevertheless, there was a peculiar quietness in the look, as if taking merely a speculative, not a human, interest in the young man.

"It is Doctor Rappaccini!" whispered the Professor, when the stranger had passed.—"Has he ever seen your face before?"

"Not that I know," answered Giovanni, starting at the name.

"He *has* seen you!—he must have seen you!" said Baglioni, hastily. "For some purpose or other, this man of science is making a study of you. I know that look of his! It is the same that coldly illuminates his face, as he bends over a bird, a mouse, or a butterfly, which, in pursuance of some experiment, he has killed by the perfume of a flower;—a look as deep as Nature itself, but without Nature's warmth of love. Signor Giovanni, I will stake my life upon it, you are the subject of one of Rappaccini's experiments!"

"Will you make a fool of me?" cried Giovanni, passionately. "*That,* Signor Professor, were an untoward experiment."

"Patience, patience!" replied the imperturbable Professor.—"I tell thee, my poor Giovanni, that Rappaccini has a scientific interest in thee. Thou hast fallen into fearful hands! And the Signora Beatrice? What part does she act in this mystery?"

But Guasconti, finding Baglioni's pertinacity intolerable, here broke away, and was gone before the Professor could again seize his arm. He looked after the young man intently, and shook his head.

"This must not be," said Baglioni to himself. "The youth is the son of my old friend, and shall not come to any harm from which the arcana of medical science can preserve him. Besides, it is too insufferable an impertinence in Rappaccini, thus to snatch the lad out of my own hands, as I may say, and make use of him for his infernal experiments. This daughter of his! It shall be looked to. Perchance, most learned Rappaccini, I may foil you where you little dream of it!"

Meanwhile, Giovanni had pursued a circuitous route, and at length found himself at the door of his lodgings. As he crossed the threshold, he was met by old Lisabetta, who smirked and smiled, and was evidently desirous to attract his attention; vainly, however, as the ebullition of his feelings had momentarily subsided into a cold and dull vacuity. He turned his eyes full upon the withered face that was puckering itself into a smile, but seemed to behold it not. The old dame, therefore, laid her grasp upon his cloak.

"Signor!—Signor!" whispered she, still with a smile over the whole breadth of her visage, so that it looked not unlike a grotesque carving in wood, darkened by centuries—"Listen, Signor! There is a private entrance into the garden!"

"What do you say?" exclaimed Giovanni, turning quickly about, as if an inanimate thing should start into feverish life.—"A private entrance into Doctor Rappaccini's garden!"

"Hush! hush!—not so loud!" whispered Lisabetta, putting her hand over his mouth. "Yes; into the worshipful Doctor's garden, where you may see all his fine shrubbery. Many a young man in Padua would give gold to be admitted among those flowers."

Giovanni put a piece of gold into her hand.

"Show me the way," said he.

A surmise, probably excited by his conversation with Baglioni, crossed his mind, that this interposition of old Lisabetta might perchance be connected with the intrigue, whatever were its nature, in which the Professor seemed to suppose that Doctor Rappaccini was involving him. But such a suspicion, though it disturbed Giovanni, was inadequate to restrain him. The instant that he was aware of the possibility of approaching Beatrice, it seemed an absolute necessity of his existence to do so. It mattered not whether she were angel or demon; he was irrevocably within her sphere, and must obey the law that whirled him onward, in ever lessening circles, towards a result which he did not attempt to foreshadow. And yet, strange to say, there came across him a sudden doubt, whether this intense interest on his part were not delusory—whether it were really of so deep and positive a nature as to justify him in now thrusting himself into an incalculable position—whether it were not merely the fantasy of a young man's brain, only slightly, or not at all, connected with his heart!

He paused—hesitated—turned half about—but again went on. His withered guide led him along several obscure passages, and finally undid a door, through which, as it was opened, there came the sight and sound of rustling leaves, with the broken sunshine glimmering among them. Giovanni stepped forth, and forcing himself through the entanglement of a shrub that wreathed its tendrils over the hidden entrance, he stood beneath his own window, in the open area of Doctor Rappaccini's garden.

How often is it the case, that, when impossibilities have come to pass, and dreams have condensed their misty substance into tangible realities, we find ourselves calm, and even coldly self-possessed, amid circumstances which it would have been a delirium of joy or agony to anticipate! Fate delights to thwart us thus. Passion will choose his own time to rush upon the scene, and lingers sluggishly behind, when an appropriate adjustment of events would seem to summon his appearance. So was it now with Giovanni. Day after day, his pulses had throbbed with feverish blood, at the improbable idea of an interview with Beatrice, and of standing with her, face to face, in this very garden, basking in the Oriental sunshine of her beauty, and snatching from her full gaze the mystery which he deemed the riddle of his own existence. But now there was a singular and untimely equanimity within his breast. He threw a glance around the garden to discover if Beatrice or her father were present, and perceiving that he was alone, began a critical observation of the plants.

The aspect of one and all of them dissatisfied him; their gorgeousness seemed fierce, passionate, and even unnatural. There was hardly an individual shrub which a wanderer, straying by himself through a forest, would not have been startled to find growing wild, as if an unearthly face had glared at him out of the thicket. Several, also, would have shocked a delicate instinct by an appearance of artificialness, indicating that there had been such commixture, and, as it were, adultery of various vegetable species, that the production was no longer of God's making, but the monstrous offspring of man's depraved fancy, glowing with only an evil mockery of beauty. They were probably the result of experiment, which, in one or two cases, had succeeded in mingling plants individually lovely into a compound possessing the questionable and ominous character that distinguished the whole growth of the garden. In fine, Giovanni recognized but two or three plants in the collection, and those of a kind that he well knew to be poisonous. While busy with these contemplations, he heard the rustling of a silken garment, and turning, beheld Beatrice emerging from beneath the sculptured portal.

Giovanni had not considered with himself what should be his deportment; whether he should apologize for his intrusion into the garden, or assume that he was there with the privity, at least, if not by the desire, of Doctor Rappaccini or his daughter. But Beatrice's manner placed him at his ease, though leaving him still in doubt by what agency he had gained admittance. She came lightly along the path, and met him near the broken fountain. There was surprise in her face, but brightened by a simple and kind expression of pleasure.

"You are a connoisseur in flowers, Signor," said Beatrice with a smile, alluding to the bouquet which he had flung her from the window. "It is no marvel, therefore, if the sight of my father's rare collection has tempted you to take a nearer view. If he were here, he could tell you many strange and interesting facts as to the nature and habits of these shrubs, for he has spent a life-time in such studies, and this garden is his world."

"And yourself, lady"—observed Giovanni—"if fame says true—you, likewise, are deeply skilled in the virtues indicated by these rich blossoms, and these spicy perfumes. Would you deign to be my instructress, I should prove an apter scholar than if taught by Signor Rappaccini himself."

"Are there such idle rumors?" asked Beatrice, with the music of a pleasant laugh. "Do people say that I am skilled in my father's science of plants? What a jest is there! No; though I have grown up among these flowers, I know no more of them than their hues and perfume; and sometimes, methinks I would fain rid myself of even that small knowledge. There are many flowers here, and those not the least brilliant, that shock and offend me, when they meet my eye. But, pray, Signor, do not believe these stories about my science. Believe nothing of me save what you see with your own eyes."

"And must I believe all that I have seen with my own eyes?" asked Giovanni pointedly, while the recollection of former scenes made him shrink. "No, Signora, you demand too little of me. Bid me believe nothing, save what comes from your own lips."

It would appear that Beatrice understood him. There came a

deep flush to her cheek; but she looked full into Giovanni's eyes, and responded to his gaze of uneasy suspicion with a queen-like haughtiness.

"I do so bid you, Signor!" she replied. "Forget whatever you may have fancied in regard to me. If true to the outward senses, still it may be false in its essence. But the words of Beatrice Rappaccini's lips are true from the depths of the heart outward. Those you may believe!"

A fervor glowed in her whole aspect, and beamed upon Giovanni's consciousness like the light of truth itself. But while she spoke, there was a fragrance in the atmosphere around her, rich and delightful, though evanescent, yet which the young man, from an indefinable reluctance, scarcely dared to draw into his lungs. It might be the odor of the flowers. Could it be Beatrice's breath, which thus embalmed her words with a strange richness, as if by steeping them in her heart? A faintness passed like a shadow over Giovanni, and flitted away; he seemed to gaze through the beautiful girl's eyes into her transparent soul, and felt no more doubt or fear.

The tinge of passion that had colored Beatrice's manner vanished; she became gay, and appeared to derive a pure delight from her communion with the youth, not unlike what the maiden of a lonely island might have felt, conversing with a voyager from the civilized world. Evidently her experience of life had been confined within the limits of that garden. She talked now about matters as simple as the day-light or summer-clouds, and now asked questions in reference to the city, or Giovanni's distant home, his friends, his mother, and his sisters; questions indicating such seclusion, and such lack of familiarity with modes and forms, that Giovanni responded as if to an infant. Her spirit gushed out before him like a fresh rill, that was just catching its first glimpse of the sunlight, and wondering at the reflections of earth and sky which were flung into its bosom. There came thoughts, too, from a deep source, and fantasies of a gem-like brilliancy, as if diamonds and rubies sparkled upward among the bubbles of the fountain. Ever and anon, there gleamed across the young man's mind a sense of wonder, that he should be walking side by side with the being who had so wrought upon his imagination—whom he had idealized in such hues of terror—in whom he had positively witnessed such manifestations of dreadful attributes—that he should be conversing with Beatrice like a brother, and should find her so human and so maiden-like. But such reflections were only momentary; the effect of her character was too real, not to make itself familiar at once.

In this free intercourse, they had strayed through the garden, and now, after many turns among its avenues, were come to the shattered fountain, beside which grew the magnificent shrub with its treasury of glowing blossoms. A fragrance was diffused from it, which Giovanni recognized as identical with that which he had attributed to Beatrice's breath, but incomparably more powerful. As her eyes fell upon it, Giovanni beheld her press her hand to her bosom, as if her heart were throbbing suddenly and painfully.

"For the first time in my life," murmured she, addressing the shrub, "I had forgotten thee!"

"I remember, Signora," said Giovanni, "that you once promised to reward me with one of these living gems for the bouquet, which I had the happy boldness to fling to your feet. Permit me now to pluck it as a memorial of this interview."

He made a step towards the shrub, with extended hand. But Beatrice darted forward, uttering a shriek that went through his heart like a dagger. She caught his hand, and drew it back with the whole force of her slender figure. Giovanni felt her touch thrilling through his fibres.

"Touch it not!" exclaimed she, in a voice of agony. "Not for thy life! It is fatal!"

Then, hiding her face, she fled from him, and vanished beneath the sculptured portal. As Giovanni followed her with his eyes, he beheld the emaciated figure and pale intelligence of Doctor Rappaccini, who had been watching the scene, he knew not how long, within the shadow of the entrance.

No sooner was Guasconti alone in his chamber, than the image of Beatrice came back to his passionate musings, invested with all the witchery that had been gathering around it ever since his first glimpse of her, and now likewise imbued with a tender warmth of girlish womanhood. She was human: her nature was endowed with all gentle and feminine qualities; she was worthiest to be worshipped; she was capable, surely, on her part, of the height and heroism of love. Those tokens, which he had hitherto considered as proofs of a frightful peculiarity in her physical and moral system, were now either forgotten, or, by the subtle sophistry of passion, transmuted into a golden crown of enchantment, rendering Beatrice the more admirable, by so much as she was the more unique. Whatever had looked ugly, was now beautiful; or, if incapable of such a change, it stole away and hid itself among those shapeless half-ideas, which throng the dim region beyond the daylight of our perfect consciousness. Thus did he spend the night, nor fell asleep, until the dawn had begun to awake the slumbering flowers in Doctor Rappaccini's garden, whither Giovanni's dreams doubtless led him. Up rose the sun in his due season, and flinging his beams upon the young man's eyelids, awoke him to a sense of pain. When thoroughly aroused, he became sensible of a burning and tingling agony in his hand—in his right hand—the very hand which Beatrice had grasped in her own, when he was on the point of plucking one of the gem-like flowers. On the back of that hand there was now a purple print, like that of four small fingers, and the likeness of a slender thumb upon his wrist.

Oh, how stubbornly does love—or even that cunning semblance of love which flourishes in the imagination, but strikes no depth of root into the heart—how stubbornly does it hold its faith, until the moment come, when it is doomed to vanish into thin mist! Giovanni wrapt a handkerchief about his hand, and wondered what evil thing had stung him, and soon forgot his pain in a reverie of Beatrice.

After the first interview, a second was in the inevitable course of what we call fate. A third; a fourth; and a meeting with Beatrice in the garden was no longer an incident in Giovanni's daily life, but the whole space in which he might be said to live; for the anticipation and memory of that ecstatic hour made up the remainder. Nor was it otherwise with the daughter of Rappaccini. She watched for the youth's appearance, and flew to his side with confidence as unreserved as if they had been playmates from early infancy—as if they were such playmates still. If, by any unwonted chance, he failed to come at the appointed moment, she stood beneath the window, and sent up the rich sweetness of her tones to float around him in his chamber, and echo and reverberate throughout his heart—"Giovanni! Giovanni! Why tarriest thou? Come down!"—And down he hastened into that Eden of poisonous flowers.

But, with all this intimate familiarity, there was still a reserve in

Beatrice's demeanor, so rigidly and invariably sustained, that the idea of infringing it scarcely occurred to his imagination. By all appreciable signs, they loved; they had looked love, with eyes that conveyed the holy secret from the depths of one soul into the depths of the other, as if it were too sacred to be whispered by the way; they had even spoken love, in those gushes of passion when their spirits darted forth in articulated breath, like tongues of long-hidden flame; and yet there had been no seal of lips, no clasp of hands, nor any slightest caress, such as love claims and hallows. He had never touched one of the gleaming ringlets of her hair; her garment—so marked was the physical barrier between them—had never been waved against him by a breeze. On the few occasions when Giovanni had seemed tempted to overstep the limit, Beatrice grew so sad, so stern, and withal wore such a look of desolate separation, shuddering at itself, that not a spoken word was requisite to repel him. At such times, he was startled at the horrible suspicions that rose, monster-like, out of the caverns of his heart, and stared him in the face; his love grew thin and faint as the morning-mist; his doubts alone had substance. But when Beatrice's face brightened again, after the momentary shadow, she was transformed at once from the mysterious, questionable being, whom he had watched with so much awe and horror; she was now the beautiful and unsophisticated girl, whom he felt that his spirit knew with a certainty beyond all other knowledge.

A considerable time had now passed since Giovanni's last meeting with Baglioni. One morning, however, he was disagreeably surprised by a visit from the Professor, whom he had scarcely thought of for whole weeks, and would willingly have forgotten still longer. Given up, as he had long been, to a pervading excitement, he could tolerate no companions, except upon condition of their perfect sympathy with his present state of feeling. Such sympathy was not to be expected from Professor Baglioni.

The visitor chatted carelessly, for a few moments, about the gossip of the city and the University, and then took up another topic.

"I have been reading an old classic author lately," said he, "and met with a story that strangely interested me. Possibly you may remember it. It is of an Indian prince, who sent a beautiful woman as a present to Alexander the Great. She was as lovely as the dawn, and gorgeous as the sunset; but what especially distinguished her was a certain rich perfume in her breath—richer than a garden of Persian roses. Alexander, as was natural to a youthful conqueror, fell in love at first sight with this magnificent stranger. But a certain sage physician, happening to be present, discovered a terrible secret in regard to her."

"And what was that?" asked Giovanni, turning his eyes downward to avoid those of the Professor.

"That this lovely woman," continued Baglioni, with emphasis, "had been nourished with poisons from her birth upward, until her whole nature was so imbued with them, that she herself had become the deadliest poison in existence. Poison was her element of life. With that rich perfume of her breath, she blasted the very air. Her love would have been poison!—her embrace death! Is not this a marvelous tale?"

"A childish fable," answered Giovanni, nervously starting from his chair. "I marvel how your worship finds time to read such nonsense, among your graver studies."

"By the bye," said the Professor, looking uneasily about him, "what singular fragrance is this in your apartment? Is it the perfume of your gloves? It is faint, but delicious, and yet, after all, by no means agreeable. Were I to breathe it long, methinks it would make me ill. It is like the breath of a flower—but I see no flowers in the chamber."

"Nor are there any," replied Giovanni, who had turned pale as the Professor spoke; "nor, I think, is there any fragrance, except in your worship's imagination. Odors, being a sort of element combined of the sensual and the spiritual, are apt to deceive us in this manner. The recollection of a perfume—the bare idea of it—may easily be mistaken for a present reality."

"Aye; but my sober imagination does not often play such tricks," said Baglioni; "and were I to fancy any kind of odor, it would be that of some vile apothecary drug, wherewith my fingers are likely enough to be imbued. Our worshipful friend Rappaccini, as I have heard, tinctures his medicaments with odors richer than those of Araby. Doubtless, likewise, the fair and learned Signora Beatrice would minister to her patients with draughts as sweet as a maiden's breath. But wo to him that sips them!"

Giovanni's face evinced many contending emotions. The tone in which the Professor alluded to the pure and lovely daughter of Rappaccini was a torture to his soul; and yet, the intimation of a view of her character, opposite to his own, gave instantaneous distinctness to a thousand dim suspicions, which now grinned at him like so many demons. But he strove hard to quell them, and to respond to Baglioni with a true lover's perfect faith.

"Signor Professor," said he, "you were my father's friend—perchance, too, it is your purpose to act a friendly part towards his son. I would fain feel nothing towards you, save respect and deference. But I pray you to observe, Signor, that there is one subject on which we must not speak. You know not the Signora Beatrice. You cannot, therefore, estimate the wrong—the blasphemy, I may even say—that is offered to her character by a light or injurious word."

"Giovanni!—my poor Giovanni!" answered the Professor, with a calm expression of pity, "I know this wretched girl far better than yourself. You shall hear the truth in respect to the poisoner Rappaccini, and his poisonous daughter. Yes; poisonous as she is beautiful! Listen; for even should you do violence to my grey hairs, it shall not silence me. That old fable of the Indian woman has become a truth, by the deep and deadly science of Rappaccini, and in the person of the lovely Beatrice!"

Giovanni groaned and hid his face.

"Her father," continued Baglioni, "was not restrained by natural affection from offering up his child, in this horrible manner, as the victim of his insane zeal for science. For—let us do him justice—he is as true a man of science as ever distilled his own heart in an alembic. What, then, will be your fate? Beyond a doubt, you are selected as the material of some new experiment. Perhaps the result is to be death—perhaps a fate more awful still! Rappaccini, with what he calls the interest of science before his eyes, will hesitate at nothing."

"It is a dream!" muttered Giovanni to himself, "surely it is a dream!"

"But," resumed the Professor, "be of good cheer, son of my friend! It is not yet too late for the rescue. Possibly, we may even succeed in bringing back this miserable child within the limits of ordinary nature, from which her father's madness has estranged her. Behold this little silver vase! It was wrought by the hands of the renowned Benvenuto Cellini, and is well worthy to be a love-gift to the fairest dame in Italy. But its contents are invaluable. One little sip of this antidote would have rendered the most virulent poisons of the Borgias innocuous. Doubt not that it will be as efficacious against those of Rappaccini. Bestow the vase, and the precious liquid within it, on your Beatrice, and hopefully await the result."

Baglioni laid a small, exquisitely wrought silver phial on the table, and withdrew, leaving what he had said to produce its effect upon the young man's mind.

"We will thwart Rappaccini yet!" thought he, chuckling to himself, as he descended the stairs. "But, let us confess the truth of him, he is a wonderful man!—a wonderful man indeed! A vile empiric, however, in his practice, and therefore not to be tolerated by those who respect the good old rules of the medical profession!"

Throughout Giovanni's whole acquaintance with Beatrice, he had occasionally, as we have said, been haunted by dark surmises as to her character. Yet, so thoroughly had she made herself felt by him as a simple, natural, most affectionate and guileless creature, that the image now held up by Professor Baglioni, looked as strange and incredible, as if it were not in accordance with his own original conception. True, there were ugly recollections connected with his first glimpses of the beautiful girl; he could not quite forget the bouquet that withered in her grasp, and the insect that perished amid the sunny air, by no ostensible agency, save the fragrance of her breath. These incidents, however, dissolving in the pure light of her character, had no longer the efficacy of facts, but were acknowledged as mistaken fantasies, by whatever testimony of the senses they might appear to be substantiated. There is something truer and more real, than what we can see with the eyes, and touch with the finger. On such better evidence, had Giovanni founded his confidence in Beatrice, though rather by the necessary force of her high attributes, than by any deep and generous faith, on his part. But, now, his spirit was incapable of sustaining itself at the height to which the early enthusiasm of passion had exalted it; he fell down, grovelling among earthly doubts, and defiled therewith the pure whiteness of Beatrice's image. Not that he gave her up; he did but distrust. He resolved to institute some decisive test that should satisfy him, once for all, whether there were those dreadful peculiarities in her physical nature, which could not be supposed to exist without some corresponding monstrosity of soul. His eyes, gazing down afar, might have deceived him as to the lizard, the insect, and the flowers. But if he could witness, at the distance of a few paces, the sudden blight of one fresh and healthful flower in Beatrice's hand, there would be room for no further question. With this idea, he hastened to the florist's, and purchased a bouquet that was still gemmed with the morning dew-drops.

It was now the customary hour of his daily interview with Beatrice. Before descending into the garden, Giovanni failed not to look at his figure in the mirror; a vanity to be expected in a beautiful young man, yet, as displaying itself at that troubled and feverish moment, the token of a certain shallowness of feeling and insincerity of character. He did gaze, however, and said to himself, that his features had never before possessed so rich a grace, nor his eyes such vivacity, nor his cheeks so warm a hue of superabundant life.

"At least," thought he, "her poison has not yet insinuated itself into my system. I am no flower to perish in her grasp!"

With that thought, he turned his eyes on the bouquet, which he had never once laid aside from his hand. A thrill of indefinable horror shot through his frame, on perceiving that those dewy flowers were already beginning to droop; they wore the aspect of things that had been fresh and lovely, yesterday. Giovanni grew white as marble, and stood motionless before the mirror, staring at his own reflection there, as at the likeness of something frightful. He remembered Baglioni's remark about the fragrance that seemed to pervade the chamber. It must have been the poison in his breath! Then he shuddered—shuddered at himself! Recovering from his stupor, he began to watch, with curious eye, a spider that was busily at work, hanging its web from the antique cornice of the apartment, crossing and re-crossing the artful system of interwoven lines, as vigorous and active a spider as ever dangled from an old ceiling. Giovanni bent towards the insect, and emitted a deep, long breath. The spider suddenly ceased its toil; the web vibrated with a tremor originating in the body of the small artizan. Again Giovanni sent forth a breath, deeper, longer, and imbued with a venomous feeling out of his heart; he knew not whether he were wicked or only desperate. The spider made a convulsive gripe with his limbs, and hung dead across the window.

"Accursed! Accursed!" muttered Giovanni, addressing himself. "Hast thou grown so poisonous, that this deadly insect perishes by thy breath?"

At that moment, a rich, sweet voice came floating up from the garden:—

"Giovanni! Giovanni! It is past the hour! Why tarriest thou! Come down!"

"Yes," muttered Giovanni again. "She is the only being whom my breath may not slay! Would that it might!"

He rushed down, and in an instant, was standing before the bright and loving eyes of Beatrice. A moment ago, his wrath and despair had been so fierce that he could have desired nothing so much as to wither her by a glance. But, with her actual presence, there came influences which had too real an existence to be at once shaken off; recollections of the delicate and benign power of her feminine nature, which had so often enveloped him in a religious calm; recollections of many a holy and passionate outgush of her heart, when the pure fountain had been unsealed from its depths, and made visible in its transparency to his mental eye; recollections which, had Giovanni known how to estimate them, would have assured him that all this ugly mystery was but an earthly illusion, and that, whatever mist of evil might seem to have gathered over her, the real Beatrice was a heavenly angel. Incapable as he was of such high faith, still her presence had not utterly lost its magic. Giovanni's rage was quelled into an aspect of sullen insensibility. Beatrice, with a quick spiritual sense, immediately felt that there was a gulf of blackness between them, which neither he nor she could pass. They walked on together, sad and silent, and came thus to the marble fountain, and to its pool of water on the ground, in the midst of which grew the shrub that bore gem-like blossoms. Giovanni was affrighted at the eager enjoyment—the appetite, as it were—with which he found himself inhaling the fragrance of the flowers.

"Beatrice," asked he abruptly, "whence came this shrub?"

"My father created it," answered she, with simplicity.

"Created it! created it!" repeated Giovanni. "What mean you, Beatrice?"

"He is a man fearfully acquainted with the secrets of nature," replied Beatrice; "and, at the hour when I first drew breath, this plant sprang from the soil, the offspring of his science, of his intellect, while I was but his earthly child. Approach it not!" continued she, observing with terror that Giovanni was drawing nearer to the shrub. "It has qualities that you little dream of. But I, dearest Giovanni,—I grew up and blossomed with the plant, and was nourished with its breath. It was my sister, and I loved it with a human affection: for—alas! hast thou not suspected it? there was an awful doom."

Here Giovanni frowned so darkly upon her that Beatrice paused and trembled. But her faith in his tenderness reassured her, and made her blush that she had doubted for an instant.

"There was an awful doom," she continued,—"the effect of my father's fatal love of science—which estranged me from all society of my kind. Until Heaven sent thee, dearest Giovanni, Oh! how lonely was thy poor Beatrice!"

"Was it a hard doom?" asked Giovanni, fixing his eyes upon her.

"Only of late have I known how hard it was," answered she tenderly. "Oh, yes; but my heart was torpid, and therefore quiet."

Giovanni's rage broke forth from his sullen gloom like a lightning-flash out of a dark cloud.

"Accursed one!" cried he, with venomous scorn and anger. "And finding thy solitude wearisome, thou hast severed me, likewise, from all the warmth of life, and enticed me into thy region of unspeakable horror!"

"Giovanni!" exclaimed Beatrice, turning her large bright eyes upon his face. The force of his words had not found its way into her mind; she was merely thunder-struck.

"Yes, poisonous thing!" repeated Giovanni, beside himself with passion. "Thou hast done it! Thou hast blasted me! Thou hast filled my veins with poison! Thou hast made me as hateful, as ugly, as loathsome and deadly a creature as thyself,—a world's wonder of hideous monstrosity! Now—if our breath be happily as fatal to ourselves as to all others—let us join our lips in one kiss of unutterable hatred, and so die!"

"What has befallen me?" murmured Beatrice, with a low moan out of her heart. "Holy Virgin pity me, a poor heart-broken child!"

"Thou! Dost thou pray?" cried Giovanni, still with the same fiendish scorn. "Thy very prayers, as they come from thy lips, taint the atmosphere with death. Yes, yes; let us pray! Let us to church, and dip our fingers in the holy water at the portal! They that come after us will perish as by a pestilence. Let us sign crosses in the air! It will be scattering curses abroad in the likeness of holy symbols!"

"Giovanni," said Beatrice calmly, for her grief was beyond passion, "why dost thou join thyself with me thus in those terrible words? I, it is true, am the horrible thing thou namest me. But thou!—what hast thou to do, save with one other shudder at my hideous misery, to go forth out of the garden and mingle with thy race, and forget that there ever crawled on earth such a monster as poor Beatrice?"

"Dost thou pretend ignorance?" asked Giovanni, scowling upon her. "Behold! This power have I gained from the pure daughter of Rappaccini!"

There was a swarm of summer-insects flitting through the air, in search of the food promised by the flower-odors of the fatal garden. They circled round Giovanni's head, and were evidently attracted towards him by the same influence which had drawn them, for an instant, within the sphere of several of the shrubs. He sent forth a breath among them, and smiled bitterly at Beatrice, as at least a score of the insects fell dead upon the ground.

"I see it! I see it!" shrieked Beatrice. "It is my father's fatal science! No, no, Giovanni; it was not I! Never, never! I dreamed only to love thee, and be with thee a little time, and so to let thee pass away, leaving but thine image in mine heart. For, Giovanni—believe it—though my body be nourished with poison, my spirit is God's creature, and craves love as its daily food. But my father!—he has united us in this fearful sympathy. Yes; spurn me!—tread upon me!—kill me! Oh, what is death, after such words as thine? But it was not I! Not for a world of bliss would I have done it!"

Giovanni's passion had exhausted itself in its outburst from his lips. There now came across him a sense, mournful, and not without tenderness, of the intimate and peculiar relationship between Beatrice and himself. They stood, as it were, in an utter solitude, which would be made none the less solitary by the densest throng of human life. Ought not, then, the desert of humanity around them to press this insulated pair closer together? If they should be cruel to one another, who was there to be kind to them? Besides, thought

Giovanni, might there not still be a hope of his returning within the limits of ordinary nature, and leading Beatrice—the redeemed Beatrice—by the hand? Oh, weak, and selfish, and unworthy spirit, that could dream of an earthly union and earthly happiness as possible, after such deep love had been so bitterly wronged as was Beatrice's love by Giovanni's blighting words! No, no; there could be no such hope. She must pass heavily, with that broken heart, across the borders of Time—she must bathe her hurts in some fount of Paradise, and forget her grief in the light of immortality—and *there* be well!

But Giovanni did not know it.

"Dear Beatrice," said he, approaching her, while she shrank away, as always at his approach, but now with a different impulse—"dearest Beatrice, our fate is not yet so desperate. Behold! There is a medicine, potent, as a wise physician has assured me, and almost divine in its efficacy. It is composed of ingredients the most opposite to those by which thy awful father has brought this calamity upon thee and me. It is distilled of blessed herbs. Shall we not quaff it together, and thus be purified from evil?"

"Give it me!" said Beatrice, extending her hand to receive the little silver phial which Giovanni took from his bosom. She added, with a peculiar emphasis: "I will drink—but do thou await the result."

She put Baglioni's antidote to her lips; and, at the same moment, the figure of Rappaccini emerged from the portal, and came slowly towards the marble fountain. As he drew near, the pale man of science seemed to gaze with a triumphant expression at the beautiful youth and maiden, as might an artist who should spend his life in achieving a picture or a group of statuary, and finally be satisfied with his success. He paused—his bent form grew erect with conscious power, he spread out his hands over them, in the attitude of a father imploring a blessing upon his children. But those were the same hands that had thrown poison into the stream of their lives! Giovanni trembled. Beatrice shuddered nervously, and pressed her hand upon her heart.

"My daughter," said Rappaccini, "thou art no longer lonely in the world! Pluck one of those precious gems from thy sister shrub, and bid thy bridegroom wear it in his bosom. It will not harm him now! My science, and the sympathy between thee and him, have so wrought within his system, that he now stands apart from common men, as thou dost, daughter of my pride and triumph, from ordinary women. Pass on, then, through the world, most dear to one another, and dreadful to all besides!"

"My father," said Beatrice, feebly—and still, as she spoke, she kept her hand upon her heart—"wherefore didst thou inflict this miserable doom upon thy child?"

"Miserable!" exclaimed Rappaccini. "What mean you, foolish girl? Dost thou deem it misery to be endowed with marvellous gifts, against which no power nor strength could avail an enemy? Misery, to be able to quell the mightiest with a breath? Misery, to be as terrible as thou art beautiful? Wouldst thou, then, have preferred the condition of a weak woman, exposed to all evil, and capable of none?"

"I would fain have been loved, nor feared," murmured Beatrice, sinking down upon the ground.—"But now it matters not; I am going, father, where the evil, which thou hast striven to mingle with my being, will pass away like a dream—like the fragrance of these poisonous flowers, which will no longer taint my breath among the flowers of Eden. Farewell, Giovanni! Thy words of hatred are like lead within my heart—but they, too, will fall away as I ascend. Oh, was there not, from the first, more poison in thy nature than in mine?"

To Beatrice—so radically had her earthly part been wrought upon by Rappaccini's skill—as poison had been life, so the powerful antidote was death. And thus the poor victim of man's ingenuity and of thwarted nature, and of the fatality that attends all such efforts of perverted wisdom, perished there, at the feet of her father and Giovanni. Just at that moment, Professor Pietro Baglioni looked forth from the window, and called loudly, in a tone of triumph mixed with horror, to the thunder-stricken man of science:

"Rappaccini! Rappaccini! And is *this* the upshot of your experiment?"

EDGAR ALLAN POE

The Cask of Amontillado

THE THOUSAND INJURIES OF Fortunato I had borne as I best could, but when he ventured upon insult, I vowed revenge. You, who so well know the nature of my soul, will not suppose, however, that I gave utterance to a threat. *At length* I would be avenged; this was a point definitely settled—but the very definitiveness with which it was resolved, precluded the idea of risk. I must not only punish, but punish with impunity. A wrong is unredressed when retribution overtakes its redresser. It is equally unredressed when the avenger fails to make himself felt as such to him who has done the wrong.

It must be understood that neither by word nor deed had I given Fortunato cause to doubt my good will. I continued as was my wont, to smile in his face, and he did not perceive that my smile *now* was at the thought of his immolation.

He had a weak point—this Fortunato—although in other regards he was a man to be respected and even feared. He prided himself on his connoisseurship in wine. Few Italians have the true virtuoso spirit. For the most part their enthusiasm is adapted to suit the time and opportunity—to practice imposture upon the British and Austrian *millionaires*. In painting and gemmary Fortunato, like his country men, was a quack—but in the matter of old wines he was sincere. In this respect I did not differ from him materially: I was skilful in the Italian vintages myself, and bought largely whenever I could.

It was about dusk, one evening during the supreme madness of the carnival season, that I encountered my friend. He accosted me with excessive warmth, for he had been drinking much. The man wore motley. He had on a tight-fitting partistriped dress, and his head was surmounted by the conical cap and bells. I was so pleased to see him, that I thought I should never have done wringing his hand.

I said to him: "My dear Fortunato, you are luckily met. How remarkably well you are looking to-day! But I have received a pipe of what passes for Amontillado, and I have my doubts."

"How?" said he. "Amontillado? A pipe? Impossible! And in the middle of the carnival!"

"I have my doubts," I replied; "and I was silly enough to pay the full Amontillado price without consulting you in the matter. You were not to be found, and I was fearful of losing a bargain."

"Amontillado!"

"I have my doubts."

"Amontillado!"

"And I must satisfy them."

"Amontillado!"

"As you are engaged, I am on my way to Luchesi. If any one has a critical turn, it is he. He will tell me—"

"Luchesi cannot tell Amontillado from Sherry."

"And yet some fools will have it that his taste is a match for your own."

"Come, let us go."

"Whither?"

"To your vaults."

"My friend, no; I will not impose upon your good nature. I perceive you have an engagement. Luchesi——"

"I have no engagement;—come."

"My friend, no. It is not the engagement, but the severe cold with which I perceive you are afflicted. The vaults are insufferably damp. They are encrusted with nitre."

"Let us go, nevertheless. The cold is merely nothing. Amontillado! You have been imposed upon. And as for Luchesi, he cannot distinguish Sherry from Amontillado."

Thus speaking, Fortunato possessed himself of my arm. Putting on a mask of black silk, and drawing a *roquelaire* closely about my person, I suffered him to hurry me to my palazzo.

There were no attendants at home; they had absconded to make merry in honor of the time. I had told them that I should not return until the morning, and had given them explicit orders not to stir from the house. These orders were sufficient, I well knew, to insure their immediate disappearance, one and all, as soon as my back was turned.

I took from their sconces two flambeaux, and giving one to Fortunato, bowed him through several suites of rooms to the archway that led into the vaults. I passed down a long and winding staircase, requesting him to be cautious as he followed. We came at length to the foot of the descent, and stood together on the damp ground of the catacombs of the Montresors.

The gait of my friend was unsteady, and the bells upon his cap jingled as he strode.

"The pipe?" said he.

"It is farther on," said I; "but observe the white web-work which gleams from these cavern walls."

He turned toward me, and looked into my eyes with two filmy orbs that distilled the rheum of intoxication.

"Nitre?" he asked, at length.

"Nitre," I replied. "How long have you had that cough?"

"Ugh! ugh! ugh!—ugh! ugh! ugh!—ugh! ugh! ugh!—ugh! ugh! ugh!—ugh! ugh! ugh!"

My poor friend found it impossible to reply for many minutes.

"It is nothing," he said, at last.

"Come," I said, with decision, "we will go back; your health is precious. You are rich, respected, admired, beloved; you are happy, as once I was. You are a man to be missed. For me it is no matter. We will go back; you will be ill, and I cannot be responsible. Besides, there is Luchesi——"

"Enough," he said; "the cough is a mere nothing; it will not kill me. I shall not die of a cough."

"True—true," I replied; "and, indeed, I had no intention of alarming you unnecessarily—but you should use all proper caution. A draught of this Medoc will defend us from the damps."

Here I knocked off the neck of a bottle which I drew from a long row of its fellows that lay upon the mould.

"Drink," I said, presenting him the wine.

He raised it to his lips with a leer. He paused and nodded to me familiarly, while his bells jingled.

"I drink," he said, "to the buried that repose around us."

"And I to your long life."

He again took my arm, and we proceeded.

"These vaults," he said, "are extensive."

"The Montresors," I replied, "were a great and numerous family."

"I forget your arms."

"A huge human foot d'or, in a field azure; the foot crushes a serpent rampant whose fangs are imbedded in the heel."

"And the motto?"

"Nemo me impune lacessit."

"Good!" he said.

The wine sparkled in his eyes and the bells jingled. My own fancy grew warm with the Medoc. We had passed through walls of piled bones, with casks and puncheons intermingling, into the inmost recesses of the catacombs. I paused again, and this time I made bold to seize Fortunato by an arm above the elbow.

"The nitre!" I said; "see, it increases. It hangs like moss upon the vaults. We are below the river's bed. The drops of moisture trickle among the bones. Come, we will go back ere it is too late. Your cough——"

"It is nothing," he said; "let us go on. But first, another draught of the Medoc."

I broke and reached him a flagon of De Grave. He emptied it at a breath. His eyes flashed with a fierce light. He laughed and threw the bottle upward with a gesticulation I did not understand.

I looked at him in surprise. He repeated the movement—a grotesque one.

"You do not comprehend?" he said.

"Not I," I replied.

"Then you are not of the brotherhood."

"How?"

"You are not of the masons."

"Yes, yes," I said; "yes, yes."

"You? Impossible! A mason?"

"A mason," I replied.

"A sign," he said.

"It is this," I answered, producing a trowel from beneath the folds of my *roquelaire*.

"You jest," he exclaimed, recoiling a few paces. "But let us proceed to the Amontillado."

"Be it so," I said, replacing the tool beneath the cloak, and again offering him my arm. He leaned upon it heavily. We continued our route in search of the Amontillado. We passed through a range of low arches, descended, passed on, and descending again, arrived at a deep crypt, in which the foulness of the air caused our flambeaux rather to glow than flame.

At the most remote end of the crypt there appeared another less spacious. Its walls had been lined with human remains, piled to the vault overhead, in the fashion of the great catacombs of Paris. Three sides of this interior crypt were still ornamented in this manner. From the fourth the bones had been thrown down, and lay promiscuously upon the earth, forming at one point a mound of some size. Within the wall thus exposed by the displacing of the bones, we perceived a still interior recess, in depth about four feet, in width three, in height six or seven. It seemed to have been constructed for no especial use within itself, but formed merely the interval between two of the colossal supports of the roof of the catacombs, and was backed by one of their circumscribing walls of solid granite.

It was in vain that Fortunato, uplifting his dull torch, endeavored to pry into the depth of the recess. Its termination the feeble light did not enable us to see.

"Proceed," I said; "herein is the Amontillado. As for Luchesi——"

"He is an ignoramus," interrupted my friend, as he stepped unsteadily forward, while I followed immediately at his heels. In an instant he had reached the extremity of the niche, and finding his progress arrested by the rock, stood stupidly bewildered. A moment more and I had fettered him to the granite. In its surface were two iron staples, distant from each other about two feet, horizontally. From one of these depended a short chain, from the other a padlock. Throwing the links about his waist, it was but the work of a few seconds to secure it. He was too much astounded to resist. Withdrawing the key I stepped back from the recess.

"Pass your hand," I said, "over the wall; you cannot help feeling the nitre. Indeed it is *very* damp. Once more let me *implore* you to return. No? Then I must positively leave you. But I must first render you all the little attentions in my power."

"The Amontillado!" ejaculated my friend, not yet recovered from his astonishment.

"True," I replied; "the Amontillado."

As I said these words I busied myself among the pile of bones of which I have before spoken. Throwing them aside, I soon uncovered a quantity of building stone and mortar. With these materials and with the aid of my trowel, I began vigorously to wall up the entrance of the niche.

I had scarcely laid the first tier of the masonry when I discovered that the intoxication of Fortunato had in a great measure worn off. The earliest indication I had of this was a low moaning cry from the depth of the recess. It was *not* the cry of a drunken man. There was then a long and obstinate silence. I laid the second tier, and the third, and the fourth; and then I heard the furious vibrations of the chain. The noise lasted for several minutes, during which, that I might hearken to it with the more satisfaction, I ceased my labors and sat down upon the bones. When at last the clanking subsided, I resumed the trowel, and finished without interruption the fifth, the sixth, and the seventh tier. The wall was now nearly upon a level with my breast. I again paused, and holding the flambeaux over the mason-work, threw a few feeble rays upon the figure within.

A succession of loud and shrill screams, bursting suddenly from the throat of the chained form, seemed to thrust me violently back. For a brief moment I hesitated—I trembled. Unsheathing my rapier, I began to grope with it about the recess; but the thought of an instant reassured me. I placed my hand upon the solid fabric of the catacombs, and felt satisfied. I reapproached the wall. I replied to the yells of him who clamored. I re-echoed—I aided—I surpassed them in volume and in strength. I did this, and the clamorer grew still.

It was now midnight, and my task was drawing to a close. I had completed the eighth, the ninth, and the tenth tier. I had finished a portion of the last and the eleventh; there remained but a single stone to be fitted and plastered in. I struggled with its weight; I placed it partially in its destined position. But now there came from out the niche a low laugh that erected the hairs upon my head. It was succeeded by a sad voice, which I had difficulty in recognizing as that of the noble Fortunato. The voice said—

"Ha! ha! ha!—he! he!—a very good joke indeed—an excellent jest. We will have many a rich laugh about it at the palazzo—he! he! he!——over our wine—he! he! he!"

"The Amontillado!" I said.

"He! he! he!—he! he! he!—yes, the Amontillado. But is it not getting late? Will not they be awaiting us at the palazzo, the Lady Fortunato and the rest? Let us be gone."

"Yes," I said, "let us be gone."

"For the love of God, Montresor!"

"Yes," I said, "for the love of God!"

But to these words I hearkened in vain for a reply. I grew impatient. I called aloud;

"Fortunato!"

No answer. I called again;

"Fortunato!"

No answer still. I thrust a torch through the remaining aperture and let it fall within. There came forth in return only a jingling of the bells. My heart grew sick—on account of the dampness of the catacombs. I hastened to make an end of my labor. I forced the last stone into its position; I plastered it up. Against the new masonry I re-erected the old rampart of bones. For the half of a century no mortal has disturbed them. *In pace requiescat!*

EDGAR ALLAN POE

The Fall of the House of Usher

Son coeur est un luth suspendu;
Sitôt qu'on le touche il résonne.

DE BÉRANGER

DURING THE WHOLE OF a dull, dark, and soundless day in the autumn of the year, when the clouds hung oppressively low in the heavens, I had been passing alone, on horseback, through a singularly dreary tract of country, and at length found myself, as the shades of evening drew on, within view of the melancholy House of Usher. I know not how it was—but, with the first glimpse of the building, a sense of insufferable gloom pervaded my spirit. I say insufferable; for the feeling was unrelieved by any of that half-pleasurable, because poetic, sentiment with which the mind usually receives even the sternest natural images of the desolate or terrible. I looked upon the scene before me—upon the mere house, and the simple landscape features of the domain—upon the bleak walls—upon the vacant eye-like windows—upon a few rank sedges—and upon a few white trunks of decayed trees—with an utter depression of soul, which I can compare to no earthly sensation more properly than to the after-dream of the reveller upon opium—the bitter lapse into every-day life—the hideous dropping off of the veil. There was an iciness, a sinking, a sickening of the heart—an unredeemed dreariness of thought which no goading of the imagination could torture into aught of the sublime. What was it—I paused to think—what was it that so unnerved me in the contemplation of the House of Usher? It was a mystery all insoluble; nor could I grapple with the shadowy fancies that crowded upon me as I pondered. I was forced to fall back upon the unsatisfactory conclusion, that while, beyond doubt, there *are* combinations of very simple natural objects which have the power of thus affecting us, still the analysis of this power lies among considerations beyond our depth. It was possible, I reflected, that a mere different arrangement of the particulars of the scene, of the details of the picture, would be sufficient to modify, or perhaps to annihilate its capacity for sorrowful impression; and, acting upon this idea, I reined my horse to the precipitous brink of a black and lurid tarn that lay in unruffled lustre by the dwelling, and gazed down—but with a shudder even more thrilling than before—upon the remodelled and inverted images of the gray sedge, and the ghastly tree-stems, and the vacant and eye-like windows.

Nevertheless, in this mansion of gloom I now proposed to myself a sojourn of some weeks. Its proprietor, Roderick Usher, had been one of my boon companions in boyhood; but many years had elapsed since our last meeting. A letter, however, had lately reached me in a distant part of the country—a letter from him—which, in its wildly importunate nature, had admitted of no other than a personal reply. The MS. gave evidence of nervous agitation. The writer spoke of acute bodily illness—of a mental disorder which oppressed him—and of an earnest desire to see me, as his best and indeed his only personal friend, with a view of attempting, by the cheerfulness of my society, some alleviation of his malady. It was the manner in which all this, and much more, was said—it was the apparent *heart* that went with his request—which allowed me no room for hesitation; and I accordingly obeyed forthwith what I still considered a very singular summons.

Although, as boys, we had been even intimate associates, yet I really knew little of my friend. His reserve had been always excessive and habitual. I was aware, however, that his very ancient family had been noted, time out of mind, for a peculiar sensibility of temperament, displaying itself, through long ages, in many works of exalted art, and manifested, of late, in repeated deeds of munificent yet unobtrusive charity, as well as in a passionate devotion to the intricacies, perhaps even more than to the orthodox and easily recognizable beauties, of musical science. I had learned, too, the very remarkable fact, that the stem of the Usher race, all time-honored as it was, had put forth, at no period, any enduring branch; in other words, that the entire family lay in the direct line of descent, and had always, with very trifling and very temporary variations, so lain. It was this deficiency, I considered, while running over in thought the perfect keeping of the character of the premises with the accredited character of the people, and while speculating upon the possible influence which the one, in the long lapse of centuries, might have exercised upon the other—it was this deficiency, perhaps of collateral issue, and the consequent undeviating transmission, from sire to son, of the patrimony with the name, which had, at length, so identified the two as to merge the original title of the estate in the quaint and equivocal appellation of the "House of Usher"—an appellation which seemed to include, in the minds of the peasantry who used it, both the family and the family mansion.

I have said that the sole effect of my somewhat childish experiment—that of looking down within the tarn—had been to deepen the first singular impression. There can be no doubt that the consciousness of the rapid increase of my superstition—for why should I not so term it?—served mainly to accelerate the increase itself. Such, I have long known, is the paradoxical law of all sentiments having terror as a basis. And it might have been for this reason only, that, when I again uplifted my eyes to the house itself, from its image in the pool, there grew in my mind a strange fancy—a fancy so ridiculous, indeed, that I but mention it to show the vivid force of the sensations which oppressed me. I had so worked upon my imagination as really to believe that about the whole mansion and domain there hung an atmosphere peculiar to themselves and their immediate vicinity—an atmosphere which had no affinity with the air of heaven, but which had reeked up from the decayed trees, and the gray wall, and the silent tarn—a pestilent and mystic vapor, dull, sluggish, faintly discernible and leaden-hued.

Shaking off from my spirit what *must* have been a dream, I scanned more narrowly the real aspect of the building. Its principal feature seemed to be that of an excessive antiquity. The discoloration of ages had been great. Minute fungi overspread the whole exterior, hanging in a fine tangled web-work from the eaves. Yet all this was apart from any extraordinary dilapidation. No portion of the masonry had fallen; and there appeared to be a wild inconsistency between its still perfect adaptation of parts, and the crumbling condition of the individual stones. In this there was much that reminded me of the specious totality of old woodwork which has rotted for long years in some neglected vault, with no disturbance from the breath of the external air. Beyond this indication of extensive decay, however, the fabric gave little token of instability. Perhaps the eye of a scrutinizing observer might have discovered a barely perceptible fissure, which, extending from the roof of the building in front, made its way down the wall in a zig-zag direction, until it became lost in the sullen waters of the tarn.

Noticing these things, I rode over a short causeway to the house. A servant in waiting took my horse, and I entered the Gothic archway of the hall. A valet, of stealthy step, then conducted me, in silence, through many dark and intricate passages in my progress to the *studio* of his master. Much that I encountered on the way contributed, I know not how, to heighten the vague sentiments of which I have already spoken. While the objects around me—while the carvings of the ceilings, the sombre tapestries of the walls, the ebon blackness of the floors, and the phantasmagoric armorial trophies which rattled as I strode, were but matters to which, or to such as which, I had been accustomed from my infancy—while I hesitated not to acknowledge how familiar was all this—I still wondered to find how unfamiliar were the fancies which ordinary images were stirring up. On one of the staircases, I met the physician of the family. His countenance, I thought, wore a mingled expression of low cunning and perplexity. He accosted me with trepidation and passed on. The valet now threw open a door and ushered me into the presence of his master.

The room in which I found myself was very large and lofty. The windows were long, narrow, and pointed, and at so vast a distance from the black oaken floor as to be altogether inaccessible from within. Feeble gleams of encrimsoned light made their way through the trellised panes, and served to render sufficiently distinct the more prominent objects around; the eye, however, struggled in vain to reach the remoter angles of the chamber, or the recesses of the vaulted and fretted ceiling. Dark draperies hung upon the walls. The general furniture was profuse, comfortless, antique, and tattered. Many books and musical instruments lay scattered about, but failed to give any vitality to the scene. I felt that I breathed an atmosphere of sorrow. An air of stern, deep, and irredeemable gloom hung over and pervaded all.

Upon my entrance, Usher arose from a sofa on which he had been lying at full length, and greeted me with a vivacious warmth which had much in it, I at first thought, of an overdone cordiality—of the constrained effort of the *ennuyé* man of the world. A glance, however, at his countenance convinced me of his perfect sincerity. We sat down; and for some moments, while he spoke not, I gazed upon him with a feeling half of pity, half of awe. Surely, man had never before so terribly altered, in so brief a period, as had Roderick Usher! It was with difficulty that I could bring myself to admit the identity of the wan being before me with the companion of my early boyhood. Yet the character of his face had been at all times remarkable. A cadaverousness of complexion; an eye large, liquid, and luminous beyond comparison; lips somewhat thin and very pallid, but of a surpassingly beautiful curve; a nose of a delicate Hebrew model, but with a breadth of nostril unusual in similar formations; a finely moulded chin, speaking, in its want of prominence, of a want of moral energy; hair of a more than web-like softness and tenuity;—these features, with an inordinate expansion above the regions of the temple, made up altogether a countenance not easily to be forgotten. And now in the mere exaggeration of the prevailing character of these features, and of the expression they were wont to convey, lay so much of change that I doubted to whom I spoke. The now ghastly pallor of the skin, and the now miraculous lustre of the eye, above all things startled and even awed me. The silken hair, too, had been suffered to grow all unheeded, and as, in its wild gossamer texture, it floated rather than fell about the face, I could not, even with effort, connect its Arabesque expression with any idea of simple humanity.

In the manner of my friend I was at once struck with an incoherence—an inconsistency; and I soon found this to arise from a series of feeble and futile struggles to overcome an habitual trepidancy—an excessive nervous agitation. For something of this nature I had indeed been prepared, no less by his letter than by reminiscences of certain boyish traits, and by conclusions deduced from his peculiar physical conformation and temperament. His action was alternately vivacious and sullen. His voice varied rapidly from a tremulous indecision (when the animal spirits seemed utterly in abeyance) to that species of energetic concision—that abrupt, weighty, un-hurried, and hollow-sounding enunciation—that leaden, self-balanced, and perfectly modulated gutteral utterance, which may be observed in the lost drunkard, or the irreclaimable eater of opium, during the periods of his most intense excitement.

It was thus that he spoke of the object of my visit, of his earnest desire to see me, and of the solace he expected me to afford him. He entered, at some length, into what he conceived to be the nature of his malady. It was, he said, a constitutional and a family evil and one for which he despaired to find a remedy—a mere nervous affection, he immediately added, which would undoubtedly soon pass off. It displayed itself in a host of unnatural sensation. Some of these, as he detailed them, interested and bewildered me; although, perhaps, the terms and the general manner of their narration had their weight. He suffered much from a morbid acuteness of the senses; the most insipid food was alone endurable; he could wear only garments of certain texture; the odors of all flowers were oppressive; his eyes were tortured by even a faint light; and there were but peculiar sounds, and these from stringed instruments, which did not inspire him with horror.

To an anomalous species of terror I found him a bounden slave. "I shall perish," said he, "I *must* perish in this deplorable folly. Thus, thus, and not otherwise, shall I be lost. I dread the events of the future, not in themselves, but in their results. I shudder at the thought of any, even the most trivial, incident, which may operate upon this intolerable agitation of soul. I have, indeed, no abhorrence of danger, except in its absolute effect—in terror. In this unnerved, in this pitiable, condition I feel that the period will sooner or later arrive when I must abandon life and reason together, in some struggle with the grim phantasm, FEAR."

I learned, moreover, at intervals, and through broken and equivocal hints, another singular feature of his mental condition. He was enchained by certain superstitious impressions in regard to the dwelling which he tenanted, and whence, for many years, he had never ventured forth—in regard to an influence whose supposititious force was conveyed in terms too shadowy here to be restated—an influence which some peculiarities in the mere form and substance of his family mansion had, by dint of long sufferance, he said, obtained over his spirit—an effect which the *physique* of the gray walls and turrets, and of the dim tarn into which they all looked down, had at length, brought about upon the *morale* of his existence.

He admitted, however, although with hesitation, that much of the peculiar gloom which thus afflicted him could he traced to a more natural and far more palpable origin—to the severe and long-continued illness—indeed to the evidently approaching dissolution—of a tenderly beloved sister, his sole companion for long years, his last and only relative on earth. "Her decease," he said, with a bitterness which I can never forget, "would leave him (him, the hopeless and the frail) the last of the ancient race of the Ushers." While he spoke, the lady Madeline (for so was she called) passed through a remote portion of the apartment, and, without having noticed my presence, disappeared. I regarded her with an utter astonishment not unmingled with dread; and yet I found it impossible to account for such feelings. A sensation of stupor oppressed me as my eyes followed her retreating steps. When a door, at length, closed upon her, my glance sought instinctively and eagerly the countenance of the brother; but he had buried his face in his hands, and I could only perceive that a far more than ordinary wanness had overspread the emaciated fingers through which trickled many passionate tears.

The disease of the lady Madeline had long baffled the skill of her physicians. A settled apathy, a gradual wasting away of the person, and frequent although transient affections of a partially cataleptical character were the unusual diagnosis. Hitherto she had steadily borne up against the pressure of her malady, and had not betaken herself finally to bed; but on the closing in of the evening of my arrival at the house, she succumbed (as her brother told me at night with inexpressible agitation) to the prostrating power of the destroyer; and I learned that the glimpse I had obtained of her person would thus probably be the last I should obtain—that the lady, at least while living, would be seen by me no more.

For several days ensuing, her name was unmentioned by either Usher or myself; and during this period I was busied in earnest endeavors to alleviate the melancholy of my friend. We painted and read together, or I listened, as if in a dream, to the wild improvisations of his speaking guitar. And thus, as a closer and still closer intimacy admitted me more unreservedly into the recesses of his spirit, the more bitterly did I perceive the futility of all attempt at cheering a mind from which darkness, as if an inherent positive quality, poured forth upon all objects of the moral and physical universe in one unceasing radiation of gloom.

I shall ever bear about me a memory of the many solemn hours I thus spent alone with the master of the House of Usher. Yet I should fail in any attempt to convey an idea of the exact character of the studies, or of the occupations, in which he involved me, or led me the way. An excited and highly distempered ideality threw a sulphureous lustre over all. His long improvised dirges will ring forever in my ears. Among other things, I hold painfully in mind a certain singular perversion and amplification of the wild air of the last waltz of Von Weber. From the paintings over which his elaborate fancy brooded, and which grew, touch by touch, into vaguenesses at which I shuddered the more thrillingly, because I shuddered knowing not why—from these paintings (vivid as their images now are before me) I would in vain endeavor to educe more than a small portion which should lie within the compass of merely written words. By the utter simplicity, by the nakedness of his designs, he arrested and overawed attention. If ever mortal painted an idea, that mortal was Roderick Usher. For me at least, in the circumstances then surrounding me, there arose out of the pure abstractions which the hypochondriac contrived to throw upon his canvass, an intensity of intolerable awe, no shadow of which felt I ever yet in the contemplation of the certainly glowing yet too concrete reveries of Fuseli.

One of the phantasmagoric conceptions of my friend, partaking not so rigidly of the spirit of abstraction, may be shadowed forth, although feebly, in words. A small picture presented the interior of an immensely long and rectangular vault or tunnel, with low walls, smooth, white and without interruption or device. Certain accessory points of the design served well to convey the idea that this excavation lay at an exceeding depth below the surface of the earth. No outlet was observed in any portion of its vast extent, and no torch or other artificial source of light was discernible; yet a flood of intense rays rolled throughout, and bathed the whole in a ghastly and inappropriate splendor.

I have just spoken of that morbid condition of the auditory nerve which rendered all music intolerable to the sufferer, with the exception of certain effects of stringed instruments. It was, perhaps, the narrow limits to which he thus confined himself upon the guitar which gave birth, in great measure, to the fantastic character of his performances. But the fervid *facility* of his *impromptus* could not be so accounted for. They must have been, and were, in the notes, as well as in the words of his wild fantasias (for he not unfrequently accompanied himself with rhymed verbal improvisations), the result of that intense mental collectedness and concentration to which I have previously alluded as observable only in particular moments of the highest artificial excitement. The words of one of these rhapsodies I have easily remembered. I was, perhaps, the more forcibly impressed with it as he gave it because, in the under or mystic current of its meaning, I fancied that I perceived, and for the first time, a full consciousness on the part of Usher of the tottering of his lofty reason upon her throne. The verses, which were entitled "The Haunted Palace," ran very nearly, if not accurately, thus:—

I

In the greenest of our valleys,
By good angels tenanted,
Once a fair and stately palace—
Radiant palace—reared its head.
In the monarch Thought's dominion—
It stood there!
Never seraph spread a pinion
Over fabric half so fair.

II

Banners yellow, glorious, golden,
On its roof did float and flow
(This—all this—was in the olden
Time long ago)
And every gentle air that dallied,
In that sweet day,
Along the ramparts plumed and pallid,
A winged odor went away.

III

Wanderers in that happy valley
    Through two luminous windows saw
Spirits moving musically
    To a lute's well-tunéd law;
Round about a throne, where sitting
    (Porphyrogene!)
In state his glory well befitting,
    The ruler of the realm was seen.

IV

And all with pearl and ruby glowing
    Was the fair palace door,
Through which came flowing, flowing, flowing
    And sparkling evermore,
A troop of Echoes whose sweet duty
    Was but to sing,
In voices of surpassing beauty,
    The wit and wisdom of their king.

V

But evil things, in robes of sorrow,
    Assailed the monarch's high estate;
(Ah, let us mourn, for never morrow
    Shall dawn upon him, desolate!)
And, round about his home, the glory
    That blushed and bloomed
Is but a dim-remembered story
    Of the old time entombed.

VI

And travellers now within that valley,
    Through the red-litten windows see
Vast forms that move fantastically
    To a discordant melody;

While, like a rapid ghastly river,
Through the pale door,
A hideous throng rush out forever,
And laugh—but smile no more.

I well remember that suggestions arising from this ballad led us into a train of thought wherein there became manifest an opinion of Usher's which I mention not so much on account of its novelty (for other men have thought thus), as on account of the pertinacity with which he maintained it. This opinion, in its general form, was that of the sentience of all vegetable things. But, in his disordered fancy the idea had assumed a more daring character, and trespassed, under certain conditions, upon the kingdom of inorganization. I lack words to express the full extent, or the earnest *abandon* of his persuasion. The belief, however, was connected (as I have previously hinted) with the gray stones of the home of his forefathers. The conditions of the sentience had been here, he imagined, fulfilled in the method of collocation of these stones—in the order of their arrangement, as well as in that of the many *fungi* which overspread them, and of the decayed trees which stood around—above all, in the long undisturbed endurance of this arrangement, and in its reduplication in the still waters of the tarn. Its evidence—the evidence of the sentience—was to be seen, he said (and I here started as he spoke), in the gradual yet certain condensation of an atmosphere of their own about the waters and the walls. The result was discoverable, he added, in that silent yet importunate and terrible influence which for centuries had moulded the destinies of his family, and which made *him* what I now saw him—what he was. Such opinions need no comment, and I will make none.

Our books—the books which, for years, had formed no small portion of the mental existence of the invalid—were, as might be supposed, in strict keeping with this character of phantasm. We pored together over such works as the "Ververt et Chartreuse" of Gresset; the "Belphegor" of Machiavelli; the "Heaven and Hell" of Swendenborg; the "Subterranean Voyage of Nicholas Klimm" by Holberg; the "Chiromancy" of Robert Flud, of Jean D'Indaginé and of De la Chambre; the "Journey into the Blue Distance" of Tieck;

and the "City of the Sun" of Campanella. One favorite volume was a small octavo edition of the "Directorium Inquisitorium," by the Dominican Eymeric de Gironne; and there were passages in Pomponius Mela, about the old African Satyrs and Œgipans, over which Usher would sit dreaming for hours. His chief delight, however, was found in the perusal of an exceedingly rare and curious book in quarto Gothic—the manual of a forgotten church—the *Vigiliæ Mortuorum scundum Chorum Ecclesiœ Maguntinœ.*

I could not help thinking of the wild ritual of this work, and of its probable influence upon the hypochondriac, when, one evening, having informed me abruptly that the lady Madeline was no more, he stated his intention of preserving her corpse for a fortnight (previously to its final interment), in one of the numerous vaults within the main walls of the building. The worldly reason, however, assigned for this singular proceeding, was one which I did not feel at liberty to dispute. The brother had been led to his resolution (so he told me) by consideration of the unusual character of the malady of the deceased, of certain obstrusive and eager inquiries on the part of her medical men, and of the remote and exposed situation of the burial-ground of the family. I will not deny that when I called to mind the sinister countenance of the person whom I met upon the staircase, on the day of my arrival at the house, I had no desire to oppose what I regarded as at best but a harmless, and by no means an unnatural precaution.

At the request of Usher, I personally aided him in the arrangements for the temporary entombment. The body having been encoffined, we two alone bore it to its rest. The vault in which we placed it (and which had been so long unopened that our torches, half smothered in its oppressive atmosphere, gave us little opportunity for investigation) was small, damp, and entirely without means of admission for light; lying, at great depth, immediately beneath that portion of the building in which was my own sleeping apartment. It had been used, apparently, in remote feudal times, for the worst purposes of a don-jon-keep, and, in later days, as a place of deposit for powder, or some other highly combustible substance, as a portion of its floor, and the whole interior of a long archway through which we reached it, were carefully sheathed with copper. The door, of massive iron, had been, also, similarly protected. Its immense weight caused an unusually sharp, grating sound, as it moved upon its hinges.

Having deposited our mournful burden upon tressels within this region of horror, we partially turned aside the yet unscrewed lid of the coffin, and looked upon the face of the tenant. A striking similitude between the brother and sister now first arrested my attention; and Usher, divining, perhaps, my thoughts, murmured out some few words from which I learned that the deceased and himself had been twins, and that sympathies of a scarcely intelligible nature had always existed between them. Our glances, however, rested not long upon the dead—for we could not regard her unawed. The disease which had thus entombed the lady in the maturity of youth, had left, as usual in all maladies of a strictly cataleptical character, the mockery of a faint blush upon the bosom and the face, and that suspiciously lingering smile upon the lip which is so terrible in death. We replaced and screwed down the lid, and, having secured the door of iron, made our way, with toil, into the scarcely less gloomy apartments of the upper portion of the house.

And now, some days of bitter grief having elapsed, an observable change came over the features of the mental disorder of my friend. His ordinary manner had vanished. His ordinary occupations were neglected or forgotten. He roamed from chamber to chamber with hurried, unequal, and objectless step. The pallor of his countenance had assumed, if possible, a more ghastly hue—but the luminousness of his eye had utterly gone out. The once occasional huskiness of his tone was heard no more; and a tremulous quaver, as if of extreme terror, habitually characterized his utterance. There were times, indeed, when I thought his unceasingly agitated mind was laboring with some oppressive secret, to divulge which he struggled for the necessary courage. At times, again, I was obliged to resolve all into the mere inexplicable vagaries of madness, for I beheld him gazing upon vacancy for long hours, in an attitude of the profoundest attention, as if listening to some imaginary sound. It was no wonder that his condition terrified—that it infected me. I felt creeping upon me, by slow yet uncertain degrees, the wild influences of his own fantastic yet impressive superstitions.

It was, especially, upon retiring to bed late in the night of the seventh or eighth day after the placing of the lady Madeline within the don-jon, that I experienced the full power of such feelings. Sleep came not near my couch—while the hours waned and waned away. I struggled to reason off the nervousness which had dominion over me. I endeavored to believe that much, if not all of what I felt, was due to the bewildering influence of the gloomy furniture of the room—of the dark and tattered draperies, which, tortured into motion by the breath of a rising tempest, swayed fitfully to and fro upon the walls, and rustled uneasily about the decorations of the bed. But my efforts were fruitless. An irrepressible tremor gradually pervaded my frame; and, at length, there sat upon my very heart an incubus of utterly causeless alarm. Shaking this off with a gasp and a struggle, I uplifted myself upon the pillows, and, peering earnestly within the intense darkness of the chamber, hearkened—I know not why, except that an instinctive spirit prompted me—to certain low and indefinite sounds which came, through the pauses of the storm, at long intervals, I knew not whence. Overpowered by an intense sentiment of horror, unaccountable yet unendurable, I threw on my clothes with haste (for I felt that I should sleep no more during the night), and endeavored to arouse myself from the pitiable condition into which I had fallen by pacing rapidly to and fro through the apartment.

I had taken but few turns in this manner, when a light step on an adjoining staircase arrested my attention. I presently recognized it as that of Usher. In an instant afterward he rapped, with a gentle touch, at my door, and entered, bearing a lamp. His countenance was, as usual, cadaverously wan—but, moreover, there was a species of mad hilarity in his eyes—an evidently restrained *hysteria* in his whole demeanor. His air appalled me—but any thing was preferable to the solitude which I had so long endured, and I even welcomed his presence as a relief.

"And you have not seen it?" he said abruptly, after having stared about him for some moments in silence—"you have not then seen it?—but, stay! you shall." Thus speaking, and having carefully shaded his lamp, he hurried to one of the casements, and threw it freely open to the storm.

The impetuous fury of the entering gust nearly lifted us from our feet. It was, indeed, a tempestuous yet sternly beautiful night, and one wildly singular in its terror and its beauty. A whirlwind had apparently collected its force in our vicinity; for there were frequent and violent alterations in the direction of the wind; and the exceeding density of the clouds (which hung so low as to press upon the turrets of the house) did not prevent our perceiving the life-like velocity with which they flew careering from all points against each other, without passing away into the distance. I say that even their exceeding density did not prevent our perceiving this—yet we had no glimpse of the moon or stars, nor was there any flashing forth of the lightning. But the under surfaces of the huge masses of agitated vapor, as well as all terrestrial objects immediately around us, were glowing in the unnatural light of a faintly luminous and distinctly visible gaseous exhalation which hung about and enshrouded the mansion.

"You must not—you shall not behold this!" said I, shuddering, to Usher, as I led him, with a gentle violence, from the window to a seat. "These appearances, which bewilder you, are merely electrical phenomena not uncommon—or it may be that they have their ghastly origin in the rank miasma of the tarn. Let us close this casement;—the air is chilling and dangerous to your frame. Here is one of your favorite romances. I will read, and you shall listen:—and so we will pass away this terrible night together."

The antique volume which I had taken up was the "Mad Trist" of Sir Launcelot Canning; but I had called it a favorite of Usher's more in sad jest than in earnest; for, in truth, there is little in its uncouth and unimaginative prolixity which could have had interest for the lofty and spiritual ideality of my friend. It was, however, the only book immediately at hand; and I indulged a vague hope that the excitement which now agitated the hypochondriac, might find relief (for the history of mental disorder is full of similar anomalies) even in the extremeness of the folly which I should read. Could I have judged, indeed, by the wild over-strained air of vivacity with which he hearkened, or apparently hearkened, to the words of the tale, I might well have congratulated myself upon the success of my design.

I had arrived at that well-known portion of the story where Ethelred, the hero of the Trist, having sought in vain for peaceable admission into the dwelling of the hermit, proceeds to make good an entrance by force. Here, it will be remembered, the words of the narrative run thus:

"And Ethelred, who was by nature of a doughty heart, and who was now mighty withal, on account of the powerfulness of the wine which he had drunken, waited no longer to hold parley with the hermit, who, in sooth, was of an obstinate and maliceful turn, but feeling the rain upon his shoulders, and fearing the rising of the tempest, uplifted his mace outright, and, with blows, made quickly room in the plankings of the door for his gauntleted hand; and now pulling therewith sturdily, he so cracked, and ripped, and tore all asunder, that the noise of the dry and hollow-sounding wood alarumed and reverberated throughout the forest."

At the termination of this sentence I started and, for a moment, paused; for it appeared to me (although I at once concluded that my excited fancy had deceived me)—it appeared to me that, from some very remote portion of the mansion, there came, indistinctly to my ears, which might have been, in its exact similarity of character, the echo (but a stifled and dull one certainly) of the very cracking and ripping sound which Sir Launcelot had so particularly described. It was, beyond doubt, the coincidence alone which had arrested my attention; for, amid the rattling of the sashes of the casements, and the ordinary commingled noises of the still increasing storm, the sound, itself, had nothing, surely, which should have interested or disturbed me. I continued the story:

"But the good champion Ethelred, now entering within the door, was sore enraged and amazed to perceive no signal of the maliceful hermit, but, in the stead thereof, a dragon of a scaly and prodigious demeanor, and of a fiery tongue, which sate in guard before a palace of gold, with a floor of silver; and upon the wall there hung a shield of shining brass with this legend enwritten—

> Who entereth herein, a conqueror hath bin;
> Who slayeth the dragon, the shield he shall win.

And Ethelred uplifted his mace, and struck upon the head of the dragon, which fell before him, and gave up his pesty breath, with a shriek so horrid and harsh, and withal so piercing, that Ethelred had fain to close his ears with his hands against the dreadful noise of it, the like whereof was never before heard."

Here again I paused abruptly, and now with a feeling of wild amazement—for there could be no doubt whatever that, in this instance, I did actually hear (although from what direction it proceeded I found it impossible to say) a low and apparently distant, but harsh, protracted, and most unusual screaming or grating sound—the exact counterpart of what my fancy had already conjured up for the dragon's unnatural shriek as described by the romancer.

Oppressed, as I certainly was, upon the extraordinary coincidence, by a thousand conflicting sensations, in which wonder and extreme terror were predominant, I still retained sufficient presence of mind to avoid exciting, by an observation, the sensitive nervousness of my companion. I was by no means certain that he had noticed the sounds in question; although, assuredly, a strange alteration had, during the last few minutes, taken place in his demeanor. From a position fronting my own, he had gradually brought round his chair, so as to sit with his face to the door of the chamber; and thus I could but partially perceive his features, although I saw that his lips trembled as if he were murmuring inaudibly. His head had dropped upon his breast—yet I knew that he was not asleep, from the wide and rigid opening of the eye as I caught a glance of it in profile. The motion of his body, too, was at variance with this idea—for he rocked from side to side with a gentle yet constant and uniform sway. Having rapidly taken notice of all this, I resumed the narrative of Sir Launcelot, which thus proceeded:

"And now, the champion, having escaped from the terrible fury of the dragon, bethinking himself of the brazen shield, and of the breaking up of the enchantment which was upon it, removed the carcass from out of the way before him, and approached valorously over the silver pavement of the castle to where the shield was upon the wall; which in sooth tarried not for his full coming, but fell down at his feet upon the silver floor, with a mighty great and terrible ringing sound."

No sooner had these syllables passed my lips, than—as if a shield of brass had indeed, at the moment, fallen heavily upon a floor of silver—I became aware of a distinct, hollow, metallic, and clangorous, yet apparently muffled, reverberation. Completely unnerved, I leaped to my feet; but the measured rocking movement of Usher was undisturbed. I rushed to the chair in which he sat. His eyes were bent fixedly before him, and throughout his whole countenance there reigned a stony rigidity. But, as I placed my hand upon his shoulder, there came a strong shudder over his whole person; a sickly smile quivered about his lips; and I saw that he spoke in a low, hurried, and gibbering murmur, as if unconscious of my presence. Bending closely over him I at length drank in the hideous import of his words.

"Not hear it?—yes, I hear it, and have heard it. Long—long—long—many minutes, many hours, many days, have I heard it—yet I dared not—oh, pity me, miserable wretch that I am!—I dared not—I *dared* not speak! *We have put her living in the tomb!* Said I not that my senses were acute? I *now* tell you that I heard her first feeble movement in the hollow coffin. I heard them—many, many days ago—yet I dared not—*I dared not speak!* And now—to-night—Ethelred—ha! ha!—the breaking of the hermit's door, and the death-cry of the dragon, and the clangor of the shield—say, rather, the rending of her coffin, and the grating of the iron hinges of her prison, and her struggles within the coppered archway of the vault! Oh! whither shall I fly? Will she not be here anon? Is she not hurrying to upbraid me for my haste? Have I not heard her footstep on the stair? Do I not distinguish that heavy and horrible beating of her heart? Madman!"—here he sprang furiously to his feet, and shrieked out his syllables, as if in the effort he were giving up his soul—*"Madman! I tell you that she now stands without the door!"*

As if in the superhuman energy of his utterance there had been found the potency of a spell, the huge antique panels to which the speaker pointed threw slowly back, upon the instant, their ponderous and ebony jaws. It was the work of the rushing gust—but then without those doors there *did* stand the lofty and enshrouded figure of the lady Madeline of Usher. There was blood upon her white robes, and the evidence of some bitter struggle upon every portion of her emaciated frame. For a moment she remained trembling and reeling to and fro upon the threshold—then, with a low moaning cry, fell heavily inward upon the person of her brother, and in her violent and now final death-agonies, bore him to the floor a corpse, and a victim to the terrors he had anticipated.

From that chamber, and from that mansion, I fled aghast. The storm was still abroad in all its wrath as I found myself crossing the old causeway. Suddenly there shot along the path a wild light, and I turned to see whence a gleam so unusual could have issued; for the vast house and its shadows were alone behind me. The radiance was that of the full, setting, and blood-red moon, which now shone vividly through that once barely-discernible fissure, of which I have before spoken as extending from the roof of the building, in a zig-zag direction, to the base. While I gazed, this fissure rapidly widened—there came a fierce breath of the whirlwind—the entire orb of the satellite burst at once upon my sight—my brain reeled as I saw the mighty walls rushing asunder—there was a long tumultuous shouting sound like the voice of a thousand waters—and the deep and dank tarn at my feet closed sullenly and silently over the fragments of the *"House of Usher."*

EDGAR ALLAN POE

The Purloined Letter

Nil sapientiae odiosius acumine nimio.

SENECA.

AT PARIS, JUST AFTER dark one gusty evening in the autumn of 18—, I was enjoying the twofold luxury of meditation and a meerschaum, in company with my friend, C. Auguste Dupin, in his little back library, or book-closet, *au troisième,* No. 33 *Rue Dunôt, Faubourg St. Germain.* For one hour at least we had maintained a profound silence; while each, to any casual observer, might have seemed intently and exclusively occupied with the curling eddies of smoke that oppressed the atmosphere of the chamber. For myself, however, I was mentally discussing certain topics which had formed matter for conversation between us at an earlier period of the evening; I mean the affair of the Rue Morgue, and the mystery attending the murder of Marie Rogêt. I looked upon it, therefore, as something of a coincidence, when the door of our apartment was thrown open and admitted our old acquaintance, Monsieur G——, the Prefect of the Parisian police.

We gave him a hearty welcome; for there was nearly half as much of the entertaining as of the contemptible about the man, and we had not seen him for several years. We had been sitting in the dark, and Dupin now arose for the purpose of lighting a lamp, but sat down again, without doing so, upon G.'s saying that he had called to consult us, or rather to ask the opinion of my friend, about some official business which had occasioned a great deal of trouble.

"If it is any point requiring reflection," observed Dupin, as he forebore to enkindle the wick, "we shall examine it to better purpose in the dark."

"That is another of your odd notions," said the Prefect, who had the fashion of calling every thing "odd" that was beyond his comprehension, and thus lived amid an absolute legion of "oddities."

"Very true," said Dupin, as he supplied his visitor with a pipe, and rolled toward him a comfortable chair.

"And what is the difficulty now?" I asked. "Nothing more in the assassination way I hope?"

"Oh, no; nothing of that nature. The fact is, the business is *very* simple indeed, and I make no doubt that we can manage it sufficiently well ourselves; but then I thought Dupin would like to hear the details of it, because it is so excessively *odd.*"

"Simple and odd," said Dupin.

"Why, yes; and not exactly that either. The fact is, we have all been a good deal puzzled because the affair *is* so simple, and yet baffles us altogether."

"Perhaps it is the very simplicity of the thing which puts you at fault," said my friend.

"What nonsense you *do* talk!" replied the Prefect, laughing heartily.

"Perhaps the mystery is a little *too* plain," said Dupin.

"Oh, good heavens! who ever heard of such an idea?"

"A little *too* self-evident."

"Ha! ha! ha!—ha! ha! ha!—ho! ho! ho!" roared our visitor, profoundly amused, "oh, Dupin, you will be the death of me yet!"

"And what, after all, *is* the matter on hand?" I asked.

"Why, I will tell you," replied the Prefect, as he gave a long, steady, and contemplative puff, and settled himself in his chair. "I will tell you in a few words; but, before I begin, let me caution you that this is an affair demanding the greatest secrecy, and that I should most probably lose the position I now hold, were it known that I confided it to any one."

"Proceed," said I.

"Or not," said Dupin.

"Well, then; I have received personal information, from a very high quarter, that a certain document of the last importance has been purloined from the royal apartments. The individual who purloined it is known; this beyond a doubt; he was seen to take it. It is known, also, that it still remains in his possession."

"How is this known?" asked Dupin.

"It is clearly inferred," replied the Prefect, "from the nature of the document, and from the non-appearance of certain results which would at once arise from its passing *out* of the robber's possession;—that is to say, from his employing it as he must design in the end to employ it."

"Be a little more explicit," I said.

"Well, I may venture so far as to say that the paper gives its holder a certain power in a certain quarter where such power is immensely valuable." The Prefect was fond of the cant of diplomacy.

"Still I do not quite understand," said Dupin.

"No? Well; the disclosure of the document to a third person, who shall be nameless, would bring in question the honor of a personage of most exalted station; and this fact gives the holder of the document an ascendancy over the illustrious personage whose honor and peace are so jeopardized."

"But this ascendancy," I interposed, "would depend upon the robber's knowledge of the loser's knowledge of the robber. Who would dare—"

"The thief," said G., "is the Minister D——, who dares all things, those unbecoming as well as those becoming a man. The method of the theft was not less ingenious than bold. The document in question—a letter, to be frank—had been received by the personage robbed while alone in the royal *boudoir*. During its perusal she was suddenly interrupted by the entrance of the other exalted personage from whom especially it was her wish to conceal it. After a hurried and vain endeavor to thrust it in a drawer, she was forced to place it, open as it was, upon a table. The address, however, was uppermost, and, the contents thus unexposed, the letter escaped notice. At this juncture enters the Minister D——. His lynx eye immediately perceives the paper, recognizes the handwriting of the address, observes the confusion of the personage addressed, and fathoms her secret. After some business transactions, hurried through in his ordinary manner, he produces a letter somewhat similar to the one in question, opens it, pretends to read it, and then places it in close juxtaposition to the other. Again he converses, for some fifteen minutes, upon the public affairs. At length, in taking leave, he takes also from the table the letter to which he had no claim. Its rightful owner saw, but, of course, dared not call attention to the act, in the presence of the third personage who stood at her elbow. The minister decamped; leaving his own letter—one of no importance—upon the table."

"Here, then," said Dupin to me, "you have precisely what you demand to make the ascendancy complete—the robber's knowledge of the loser's knowledge of the robber."

"Yes," replied the Prefect; "and the power thus attained has, for some months past, been wielded, for political purposes, to a very dangerous extent. The personage robbed is more thoroughly convinced, every day, of the necessity of reclaiming her letter. But this, of course, cannot be done openly. In fine, driven to despair, she has committed the matter to me."

"Than whom," said Dupin, amid a perfect whirlwind of smoke, "no more sagacious agent could, I suppose, be desired, or even imagined."

"You flatter me," replied the Prefect; "but it is possible that some such opinion may have been entertained."

"It is clear," said I, "as you observe, that the letter is still in the possession of the minister; since it is this possession, and not any employment of the letter, which bestows the power. With the employment the power departs."

"True," said G.; "and upon this conviction I proceeded. My first care was to make thorough search of the minister's hotel; and here my chief embarrassment lay in the necessity of searching without his knowledge. Beyond all things, I have been warned of the danger which would result from giving him reason to suspect our design."

"But," said I, "you are quite *au fait* in these investigations. The Parisian police have done this thing often before."

"Oh, yes; and for this reason I did not despair. The habits of the minister gave me, too, a great advantage. He is frequently absent from home all night. His servants are by no means numerous. They sleep at a distance from their master's apartment, and, being chiefly Neapolitans, are readily made drunk. I have keys, as you know, with which I can open any chamber or cabinet in Paris. For three months a night has not passed, during the greater part of which I have not been engaged, personally, in ransacking the D—— Hotel. My honor is interested, and, to mention a great secret, the reward is enormous. So I did not abandon the search until I had become fully satisfied that the thief is a more astute man than myself. I fancy that I have investigated every nook and corner of the premises in which it is possible that the paper can be concealed."

"But is it not possible," I suggested, "that although the letter may be in possession of the minister, as it unquestionably is, he may have concealed it elsewhere than upon his own premises?"

"This is barely possible," said Dupin. "The present peculiar condition of affairs at court, and especially of those intrigues in which D—— is known to be involved, would render the instant availability of the document—its susceptibility of being produced at a moment's notice—a point of nearly equal importance with its possession."

"Its susceptibility of being produced?" said I.

"That is to say, of being *destroyed*," said Dupin.

"True," I observed; "the paper is clearly then upon the premises. As for its being upon the person of the minister, we may consider that as out of the question."

"Entirely," said the Prefect. "He has been twice waylaid, as if by footpads, and his person rigorously searched under my own inspection."

"You might have spared yourself this trouble," said Dupin. "D——, I presume, is not altogether a fool, and, if not, must have anticipated these waylayings, as a matter of course."

"Not *altogether* a fool," said G., "but then he is a poet, which I take to be only one remove from a fool."

"True," said Dupin, after a long and thoughtful whiff from his meerschaum, "although I have been guilty of certain doggerel myself."

"Suppose you detail," said I, "the particulars of your search."

"Why, the fact is, we took our time, and we searched *everywhere*. I have had long experience in these affairs. I took the entire building, room by room; devoting the nights of a whole week to each. We examined, first, the furniture of each apartment. We opened every possible drawer; and I presume you know that, to a properly trained police agent, such a thing as a *'secret'* drawer is impossible. Any man is a dolt who permits a 'secret' drawer to escape him in a search of this kind. The thing is *so* plain. There is a certain amount of bulk—of space—to be accounted for in every cabinet. Then we have accurate rules. The fiftieth part of a line could not escape us. After the cabinets we took the chairs. The cushions we probed with the fine long needles you have seen me employ. From the tables we removed the tops."

"Why so?"

"Sometimes the top of a table, or other similarly arranged piece of furniture, is removed by the person wishing to conceal an article; then the leg is excavated, the article deposited within the cavity, and the top replaced. The bottoms and tops of bedposts are employed in the same way."

"But could not the cavity be detected by sounding?" I asked.

"By no means, if, when the article is deposited, a sufficient wadding of cotton be placed around it. Besides, in our case, we were obliged to proceed without noise."

"But you could not have removed—you could not have taken to pieces *all* articles of furniture in which it would have been possible to make a deposit in the manner you mention. A letter may be compressed into a thin spiral roll, not differing much in shape or bulk from a large knitting-needle, and in this form it might be inserted into the rung of a chair, for example. You did not take to pieces all the chairs?"

"Certainly not; but we did better—we examined the rungs of every chair in the hotel, and, indeed, the jointings of every description of furniture, by the aid of a most powerful microscope. Had there been any traces of recent disturbance we should not have failed to detect it instantly. A single grain of gimlet-dust, for example, would have been as obvious as an apple. Any disorder in the gluing—any unusual gaping in the joints—would have sufficed to insure detection."

"I presume you looked to the mirrors, between the boards and the plates, and you probed the beds and the bedclothes, as well as the curtains and carpets."

"That of course; and when we had absolutely completed every particle of the furniture in this way, then we examined the house itself. We divided its entire surface into compartments, which we numbered, so that none might be missed; then we scrutinized each individual square inch throughout the premises, including the two houses immediately adjoining, with the microscope, as before."

"The two houses adjoining!" I exclaimed; "you must have had a great deal of trouble."

"We had; but the reward offered is prodigious."

"You include the *grounds* about the houses?"

"All the grounds are paved with brick. They gave us comparatively little trouble. We examined the moss between the bricks, and found it undisturbed."

"You looked among D——'s papers, of course, and into the books of the library?"

"Certainly; we opened every package and parcel; we not only opened every book, but we turned over every leaf in each volume, not contenting ourselves with a mere shake, according to the fashion of some of our police officers. We also measured the thickness of every book-*cover,* with the most accurate admeasurement, and applied to each the most jealous scrutiny of the microscope. Had any of the bindings been recently meddled with, it would have been utterly impossible that the fact should have escaped observation. Some five or six volumes, just from the hands of the binder, we carefully probed, longitudinally, with the needles."

"You explored the floors beneath the carpets?"

"Beyond doubt. We removed every carpet, and examined the boards with the microscope."

"And the paper on the walls?"

"Yes."

"You looked into the cellars?"

"We did."

"Then," I said, "you have been making a miscalculation, and the letter is *not* upon the premises, as you suppose."

"I fear you are right there," said the Prefect. "And now, Dupin, what would you advise me to do?"

"To make a thorough research of the premises."

"That is absolutely needless," replied G——. "I am not more sure that I breathe than I am that the letter is not at the hotel."

"I have no better advice to give you," said Dupin. "You have, of course, an accurate description of the letter?"

"Oh, yes!"—And here the Prefect, producing a memorandum-book, proceeded to read aloud a minute account of the internal, and especially of the external appearance of the missing document. Soon after finishing the perusal of this description, he took his departure, more entirely depressed in spirits than I had ever known the good gentleman before.

In about a month afterward he paid us another visit, and found us occupied very nearly as before. He took a pipe and a chair and entered into some ordinary conversation. At length I said:

"Well, but G——, what of the purloined letter? I presume you have at last made up your mind that there is no such thing as over-reaching the Minister?"

"Confound him, say I—yes; I made the re-examination, however, as Dupin suggested—but it was all labor lost, as I knew it would be."

"How much was the reward offered, did you say?" asked Dupin.

"Why, a very great deal—a *very* liberal reward—I don't like to say how much, precisely; but one thing I *will* say, that I wouldn't mind giving my individual check for fifty thousand francs to any one who could obtain me that letter. The fact is, it is becoming of more and more importance every day; and the reward has been lately doubled. If it were trebled, however, I could do no more than I have done."

"Why, yes," said Dupin, drawlingly between the whiffs of his meerschaum. "I really—think, G——, you have not exerted yourself—to the utmost in this matter. You might—do a little more, I think, eh?"

"How?—in what way?"

"Why—puff, puff—you might—puff, puff—employ counsel in the matter, eh?—puff, puff, puff. Do you remember the story they tell of Abernethy?"

"No; hang Abernethy!"

"To be sure! hang him and welcome. But, once upon a time, a certain rich miser conceived the design of sponging upon this Abernethy for a medical opinion. Getting up, for this purpose, an ordinary conversation in a private company, he insinuated his case to the physician, as that of an imaginary individual.

"'We will suppose,' said the miser, 'that his symptoms are such and such; now, doctor, what would *you* have directed him to take?'

"'Take!' said Abernethy, 'why, take *advice,* to be sure.'"

"But," said the Prefect, a little discomposed, "I am *perfectly* willing to take advice, and to pay for it. I would *really* give fifty thousand francs to any one who would aid me in the matter."

"In that case," replied Dupin, opening a drawer, and producing a check-book, "you may as well fill me up a check for the amount mentioned. When you have signed it, I will hand you the letter."

I was astounded. The Prefect appeared absolutely thunder-stricken. For some minutes he remained speechless and motionless, looking incredulously at my friend with open mouth, and eyes that seemed starting from their sockets; then apparently recovering himself in some measure, he seized a pen, and after several pauses and vacant stares, finally filled up and signed a check for fifty thousand francs, and handed it across the table to Dupin. The latter examined it carefully and deposited it in his pocket-book; then, unlocking an *escritoire,* took thence a letter and gave it to the Prefect. This functionary grasped it in a perfect agony of joy, opened it with a trembling hand, cast a rapid glance at its contents, and then scrambling and struggling to the door, rushed at length unceremoniously from the room and from the house, without having uttered a syllable since Dupin had requested him to fill up the check.

When he had gone, my friend entered into some explanations.

"The Parisian police," he said, "are exceedingly able in their way. They are persevering, ingenious, cunning, and thoroughly versed in the knowledge which their duties seem chiefly to demand. Thus, when G—— detailed to us his mode of searching the premises at the Hotel D——, I felt entire confidence in his having made a satisfactory investigation—so far as his labors extended."

"So far as his labors extended?" said I.

"Yes," said Dupin. "The measures adopted were not only the best of their kind, but carried out to absolute perfection. Had the letter been deposited within the range of their search, these fellows would, beyond a question, have found it."

I merely laughed—but he seemed quite serious in all that he said.

"The measures then," he continued, "were good in their kind, and well executed; their defect lay in their being inapplicable to the case and to the man. A certain set of highly ingenious resources are, with the Prefect, a sort of Procrustean bed, to which he forcibly adapts his designs. But he perpetually errs by being too deep or too shallow for the matter in hand; and many a schoolboy is a better reasoner than he. I knew one about eight years of age, whose success at guessing in the game of 'even and odd' attracted universal admiration. This game is simple, and is played with marbles. One player holds in his hand a number of these toys, and demands of another whether that number is even or odd. If the guess is right, the guesser wins one; if wrong, he loses one. The boy to whom I allude won all the marbles of the school. Of course he had some principle of guessing; and this lay in mere observation and admeasurement of the astuteness of his opponents. For example, an arrant simpleton is his opponent, and, holding up his closed hand, asks, 'Are they even or odd?' Our schoolboy replies, 'Odd,' and loses; but upon the second trial he wins, for he then says to himself: 'The simpleton had them even upon the first trial, and his amount of cunning is just sufficient to make him have them odd upon the second; I will therefore guess odd';—he guesses odd, and wins. Now, with a simpleton a degree above the first, he would have reasoned thus: 'This fellow finds that in the first instance I guessed odd, and, in the second, he will propose to himself, upon the first impulse, a simple variation from even to odd, as did the first simpleton; but then a second thought will suggest that this is too simple a variation, and finally he will decide upon putting it even as before. I will therefore guess even';—he guesses even, and wins. Now this mode of reasoning in the schoolboy, whom his fellows termed 'lucky,'—what, in its last analysis, is it?"

"It is merely," I said, "an identification of the reasoner's intellect with that of his opponent."

"It is," said Dupin; "and, upon inquiring of the boy by what means he effected the *thorough* identification in which his success consisted, I received answer as follows: 'When I wish to find out how wise, or how stupid, or how good, or how wicked is any one, or what are his thoughts at the moment, I fashion the expression of my face, as accurately as possible, in accordance with the expression of his, and then wait to see what thoughts or sentiments arise in my mind or heart, as if to match or correspond with the expression.' This response of the schoolboy lies at the bottom of all the spurious profundity which has been attributed to Rochefoucault, to La Bougive, to Machiavelli, and to Campanella."

"And the identification," I said, "of the reasoner's intellect with that of his opponent, depends, if I understand you aright, upon the accuracy with which the opponent's intellect is admeasured."

"For its practical value it depends upon this," replied Dupin; "and the Prefect and his cohort fail so frequently, first by default of his identification, and, secondly, by ill-admeasurement, or rather through non-admeasurement, of the intellect with which they are engaged. They consider only their *own* ideas of ingenuity; and, in searching for anything hidden advert only to the modes in which *they* would have hidden it. They are right in this much—that their own ingenuity is a faithful representative of that of *the mass;* but when the cunning of the individual felon is diverse in character from their own, the felon foils them, of course. This always happens when it is above their own, and very usually when it is below. They have no variation of principle in their investigations; at best, when urged by some unusual emergency—by some extraordinary reward—they extend or exaggerate their old modes of *practice,* without touching their principles. What, for example, in this case of D——, has been done to vary the principle of action? What is all this boring, and probing, and sounding, and scrutinizing with the microscope, and dividing the surface of the building into registered square inches—what is it all but an exaggeration *of the application* of the one principle or set of principles of search, which are based upon the one set of notions regarding human ingenuity, to which the Prefect, in the long routine of his duty, has been accustomed? Do you not see he has taken it for granted that *all* men proceed to conceal a letter—not exactly in a gimlet-hole bored in a chair-leg, but, at least, in *some* out-of-the-way hole or corner suggested by the same tenor of thought which would urge a man to secrete a letter in a gimlet-hole bored in a chair-leg? And do you not see also that such *recherchés* nooks for concealment are adapted only for ordinary occasions, and would be adopted only by ordinary intellects; for, in all cases of concealment, a disposal of the article concealed—a disposal of it in this *recherché* manner,—is in the very first instance, presumable and presumed; and thus its discovery depends, not at all upon the acumen, but altogether upon the mere care, patience, and determination of the seekers; and where the case is of importance—or, what amounts to the same thing in the political eyes, when the reward is of magnitude,—the qualities in question have *never* been known to fail. You will now understand what I meant in suggesting that, had the purloined letter been hidden anywhere within the limits of the Prefect's examination—in other words, had the principle of its concealment been comprehended within the principles of the Prefect—its discovery would have been a matter altogether beyond question. This functionary, however, has been thoroughly mystified; and the remote source of his defeat lies in the supposition that the Minister is a fool, because he has acquired renown as a poet. All fools are poets; this the Prefect feels; and he is merely guilty of a *non distributio medii* in thence inferring that all poets are fools."

"But is this really the poet?" I asked. "There are two brothers, I know; and both have attained reputation in letters. The minister I believe has written learnedly on the Differential Calculus. He is a mathematician, and no poet."

"You are mistaken; I know him well; he is both. As poet *and* mathematician, he would reason well; as mere mathematician, he could not have reasoned at all, and thus would have been at the mercy of the Prefect."

"You surprise me," I said, "by these opinions, which have been contradicted by the voice of the world. You do not mean to set at naught the well-digested idea of centuries. The mathematical reason has long been regarded as *the* reason *par excellence.*"

" '*Il y a parier,*' " replied Dupin, quoting from Chamfort, " '*que toute idée publique, toute convention reçue, est une sottise, car elle a convenue au plus grand nombre.*' The mathematicians, I grant you, have done their best to promulgate the popular error to which you allude, and which is none the less an error for its promulgation as truth. With an art worthy a better cause, for example, they have insinuated the term 'analysis' into application to algebra. The French are the originators of this particular deception; but if a term is of any importance—if words derive any value from applicability—then 'analysis' conveys 'algebra' about as much as, in Latin, '*ambitus*' implies 'ambition,' '*religio*' 'religion,' or '*homines honesti*' a set of *honorable* men."

"You have a quarrel on hand, I see," said I, "with some of the algebraists of Paris; but proceed."

"I dispute the availability, and thus the value, of that reason which is cultivated in any especial form other than the abstractly logical. I dispute, in particular, the reason educed by mathematical study. The mathematics are the science of form and quantity; mathematical reasoning is merely logic applied to observation upon form and quantity. The great error lies in supposing that even the truths of what is called *pure* algebra are abstract or general truths. And this error is so egregious that I am confounded at the universality with which it has been received. Mathematical axioms are *not* axioms; of general truth. What is true of *relation*—of form and quantity—is often grossly false in regard to morals, for example. In this latter science it is very usually *un*true that the aggregated parts are equal to the whole. In chemistry also the axiom fails. In the consideration of motive it fails; for two motives, each of a given value, have not, necessarily, a value when united, equal to the sum of their values apart. There are numerous other mathematical truths which are only truths within the limits of *relation*. But the mathematician argues from his *finite truths,* through habit, as if they were of an absolutely general applicability—as the world indeed imagines them to be. Bryant, in his very learned 'Mythology,' mentions an analogous source of error, when he says that 'although the Pagan fables are not believed, yet we forget ourselves continually, and make inferences from them as existing realities.' With the algebraists, however, who are Pagans themselves, the 'Pagan fables' *are* believed, and the inferences are made, not so much through lapse of memory as through an unaccountable addling of the brains. In short, I never yet encountered the mere mathematician who could be trusted out of equal roots, or one who did not clandestinely hold it as a point of his faith that $x^2 + px$ was absolutely and unconditionally equal to q. Say to one of these gentlemen, by way of experiment, if you please, that you believe occasions may occur where $x^2 + px$ is not altogether equal to q, and, having made him understand what you mean, get out of his reach as speedily as convenient, for, beyond doubt, he will endeavor to knock you down.

"I mean to say," continued Dupin, while I merely laughed at his last observations, "that if the Minister had been no more than a mathematician, the Prefect would have been under no necessity of giving me this check. I knew him, however, as both mathematician and poet, and my measures were adapted to his capacity, with reference to the circumstances by which he was surrounded. I knew him as a courtier, too, and as a bold *intriguant.* Such a man, I considered, could not fail to be aware of the ordinary political modes of action. He could not have failed to anticipate—and events have proved that he did not fail to anticipate—the waylayings to which he was subjected. He must have foreseen, I reflected, the secret investigations of his premises. His frequent absences from home at night, which were hailed by the Prefect as certain aids to his success, I regarded only as *ruses,* to afford opportunity for thorough search to the police, and thus the sooner to impress them with the conviction to which G——, in fact, did finally arrive—the conviction that the letter was not upon the premises. I felt, also, that the whole train of thought, which I was at some pains in detailing to you just now, concerning the invariable principle of political action in searches for articles concealed—I felt that this whole train of thought would necessarily pass through the mind of the Minister. It would imperatively lead him to despise all the ordinary *nooks* of concealment. *He* could not, I reflected, be so weak as not to see that the most intricate and remote recess of his hotel would be as open as his commonest closets to the eyes, to the probes, to the gimlets, and to the microscopes of the Prefect. I saw, in fine, that he would be driven, as a matter of course, to *simplicity,* if not deliberately induced to it as a matter of choice. You will remember, perhaps, how desperately the Prefect laughed when I suggested, upon our first interview, that it was just possible this mystery troubled him so much on account of its being so *very* self-evident."

"Yes," said I, "I remember his merriment well. I really thought he would have fallen into convulsions."

"The material world," continued Dupin, "abounds with very strict analogies to the immaterial; and thus some color of truth has been given to the rhetorical dogma, that metaphor, or simile, may be made to strengthen an argument as well as to embellish a description. The principle of the *vis inertiæ,* for example, seems to be identical in physics and metaphysics. It is not more true in the former, that a large body is with more difficulty set in motion than a smaller one, and that its subsequent *momentum* is commensurate with this difficulty, than it is, in the latter, that intellects of the vaster capacity, while more forcible, more constant, and more eventful in their movements than those of inferior grade, are yet the less readily moved, and more embarrassed, and full of hesitation in the first few steps of their progress. Again: have you ever noticed which of the street signs, over the shop doors, are the most attractive of attention?"

"I have never given the matter a thought," I said.

"There is a game of puzzles," he resumed, "which is played upon a map. One party playing requires another to find a given word—the name of town, river, state, or empire—any word, in short, upon the motley and perplexed surface of the chart. A novice in the game generally seeks to embarrass his opponents by giving them the most minutely lettered names; but the adept selects such words as stretch, in large characters, from one end of the chart to the other. These, like the over-largely lettered signs and placards of the street, escape observation by dint of being excessively obvious; and here the physical oversight is precisely analogous with the moral inapprehension by which the intellect suffers to pass unnoticed those considerations which are too obtrusively and too palpably self-evident. But this is a point, it appears, somewhat above or beneath the understanding of the Prefect. He never once thought it probable, or possible, that the Minister had deposited the letter immediately beneath the nose of the whole world by way of best preventing any portion of that world from perceiving it.

"But the more I reflected upon the daring, dashing, and discriminating ingenuity of D——; upon the fact that the document must always have been *at hand,* if he intended to use it to good purpose; and upon the decisive evidence, obtained by the Prefect, that it was not hidden within the limits of that dignitary's ordinary search—the more satisfied I became that, to conceal this letter, the Minister had resorted to the comprehensive and sagacious expedient of not attempting to conceal it at all.

"Full of these ideas, I prepared myself with a pair of green spectacles, and called one fine morning quite by accident, at the Ministerial hotel. I found D—— at home, yawning, lounging, and dawdling, as usual, and pretending to be in the last extremity of *ennui.* He is, perhaps, the most really energetic human being now alive—but that is only when nobody sees him.

"To be even with him, I complained of my weak eyes, and lamented the necessity of the spectacles, under cover of which I cautiously and thoroughly surveyed the apartment, while seemingly intent only upon the conversation of my host.

"I paid especial attention to a large writing-table near which he sat, and upon which lay confusedly, some miscellaneous letters and other papers, with one or two musical instruments and a few books. Here, however, after a long and very deliberate scrutiny, I saw nothing to excite particular suspicion.

"At length my eyes, in going the circuit of the room, fell upon a trumpery filigree card-rack of pasteboard, that hung dangling by a dirty blue ribbon, from a little brass knob just beneath the middle of the mantel-piece. In this rack, which had three or four compartments, were five or six visiting cards and a solitary letter. This last was much soiled and crumpled. It was torn nearly in two, across the middle—as if a design, in the first instance, to tear it entirely up as worthless, had been altered or stayed in the second. It had a large black seal, bearing the D—— cipher *very* conspicuously, and was addressed, in a diminutive female hand, to D——, the minister, himself. It was thrust carelessly, and even, as it seemed, contemptuously, into one of the upper divisions of the rack.

"No sooner had I glanced at this letter than I concluded it to be that of which I was in search. To be sure, it was, to all appearance, radically different from the one of which the Prefect had read us so minutely a description. Here the seal was large and black, with the D—— cipher; there it was small and red, with the ducal arms of the S—— family. Here, the address, to the Minister, was diminutive and feminine; there the superscription, to a certain royal personage, was markedly bold and decided; the size alone formed a point of correspondence. But, then, the *radicalness* of these differences, which was excessive; the dirt; the soiled and torn condition of the paper, so inconsistent with the *true* methodical habits of D——, and so suggestive of a design to delude the beholder into an idea of the worthlessness of the document;—these things, together with the hyperobtrusive situation of this document, full in the view of every visitor, and thus exactly in accordance with the conclusions to which I had previously arrived; these things, I say, were strongly corroborative of suspicion, in one who came with the intention to suspect.

"I protracted my visit as long as possible, and, while I maintained a most animated discussion with the Minister, upon a topic which I knew well had never failed to interest and excite him, I kept my attention really riveted upon the letter. In this examination, I committed to memory its external appearance and arrangement in the rack;

and also fell, at length, upon a discovery which set at rest whatever trivial doubt I might have entertained. In scrutinizing the edges of the paper, I observed them to be more *chafed* than seemed necessary. They presented the *broken* appearance which is manifested when a stiff paper, having been once folded and pressed with a folder, is re-folded in a reversed direction, in the same creases or edges which had formed the original fold. This discovery was sufficient. It was clear to me that the letter had been turned as a glove, inside out, re-directed and re-sealed. I bade the Minister good-morning, and took my departure at once, leaving a gold snuff-box upon the table.

"The next morning I called for the snuff-box, when we resumed, quite eagerly, the conversation of the preceding day. While thus engaged, however, a loud report, as if of a pistol, was heard immediately beneath the windows of the hotel, and was succeeded by a series of fearful screams, and the shoutings of a mob. D—— rushed to a casement, threw it open, and looked out. In the meantime I stepped to the card-rack, took the letter, put it in my pocket, and replaced it by a *fac-simile,* (so far as regards externals) which I had carefully prepared at my lodgings—imitating the D—— cipher, very readily, by means of a seal formed of bread.

"The disturbance in the street had been occasioned by the frantic behavior of a man with a musket. He had fired it among a crowd of women and children. It proved, however, to have been without ball, and the fellow was suffered to go his way as a lunatic or a drunkard. When he had gone, D—— came from the window, whither I had followed him immediately upon securing the object in view. Soon afterward I bade him farewell. The pretended lunatic was a man in my own pay."

"But what purpose had you," I asked, "in replacing the letter by a *fac-simile*? Would it not have been better at the first visit, to have seized it openly, and departed?"

"D——," replied Dupin, "is a desperate man, and a man of nerve. His hotel, too, is not without attendants devoted to his interests. Had I made the wild attempt you suggest, I might never have left the Ministerial presence alive. The good people of Paris might have heard of me no more. But I had an object apart from these considerations. You know my political prepossessions. In this matter, I act as a partisan of the lady concerned. For eighteen months the

Minister has had her in his power. She has now him in hers—since, being unaware that the letter is not in his possession, he will proceed with his exactions as if it was. Thus will he inevitably commit himself, at once, to his political destruction. His downfall, too, will not be more precipitate than awkward. It is all very well to talk about the *facilis descensus Averni;* but in all kinds of climbing, as Catalani said of singing, it is far more easy to get up than to come down. In the present instance I have no sympathy—at least no pity—for him who descends. He is that *monstrum horrendum,* an unprincipled man of genius. I confess, however, that I should like very well to know the precise character of his thoughts, when, being defied by her whom the Prefect terms 'a certain personage,' he is reduced to opening the letter which I left for him in the card-rack."

"How? did you put any thing particular in it?"

"Why—it did not seem altogether right to leave the interior blank—that would have been insulting. D——, at Vienna once, did me an evil turn, which I told him, quite good-humoredly, that I should remember. So, as I knew he would feel some curiosity in regard to the identity of the person who had outwitted him, I thought it a pity not to give him a clew. He is well acquainted with my MS., and I just copied into the middle of the blank sheet the words—

> ——Un dessein si funeste,
> S'il n'est digne d' Atrée, est digne de Thyeste.

They are to be found in Crébillon's 'Atrée.'"

HERMAN MELVILLE

Bartleby the Scrivener

I AM A RATHER elderly man. The nature of my avocations for the last thirty years has brought me into more than ordinary contact with what would seem an interesting and somewhat singular set of men, of whom, as yet, nothing that I know of has ever been written—I mean the law-copyists, or scriveners. I have known very many of them, professionally and privately, and, if I pleased, could relate divers histories at which good-natured gentlemen might smile and sentimental souls might weep. But I waive the biographies of all other scriveners for a few passages in the life of Bartleby, who was a scrivener, the strangest I ever saw or heard of. While of other law-copyists I might write the complete life, of Bartleby nothing of that sort can be done. I believe that no materials exist for a full and satisfactory biography of this man. It is an irreparable loss to literature. Bartleby was one of those beings of whom nothing is ascertainable except from the original sources, and, in his case, those are very small. What my own astonished eyes saw of Bartleby, *that* is all I know of him, except, indeed, one vague report, which will appear in the sequel.

Ere introducing the scrivener as he first appeared to me, it is fit I make some mention of myself, my employees, my business, my chambers and general surroundings, because some such description is indispensable to an adequate understanding of the chief character about to be presented. *Imprimis:* I am a man who, from his youth upwards, has been filled with a profound conviction that the easiest way of life is the best. Hence, though I belong to a profession proverbially energetic and nervous even to turbulence at times, yet nothing of that sort have I ever suffered to invade my peace. I am one of those unambitious lawyers who never addresses a jury or in any way draws down public applause, but, in the cool tranquillity of a snug retreat, do a snug business among rich men's bonds, and mortgages, and title deeds. All who know me consider me an eminently *safe* man. The late John Jacob Astor, a personage little given to poetic enthusiasm, had no hesitation in pronouncing my first grand point to be prudence, my next, method. I do not speak it in vanity, but simply record the fact that I was not unemployed in my profession by the late John Jacob Astor, a name which, I admit, I love to repeat, for it hath a rounded and orbicular sound to it, and rings like unto bullion. I will freely add that I was not insensible to the late John Jacob Astor's good opinion.

Some time prior to the period at which this little history begins my avocations had been largely increased. The good old office, now extinct in the State of New York, of a Master in Chancery, had been conferred upon me. It was not a very arduous office, but very pleasantly remunerative. I seldom lose my temper, much more seldom indulge in dangerous indignation at wrongs and outrages, but I must be permitted to be rash here and declare that I consider the sudden and violent abrogation of the office of Master in Chancery, by the new Constitution, as a——premature act, inasmuch as I had counted upon a life lease of the profits, whereas I only received those of a few short years. But this is by the way.

My chambers were upstairs at No. —— Wall Street. At one end they looked upon the white wall of the interior of a spacious skylight shaft, penetrating the building from top to bottom.

This view might have been considered rather tame than otherwise, deficient in what landscape painters call "life." But, if so, the view from the other end of my chambers offered at least a contrast, if nothing more. In that direction, my windows commanded an unobstructed view of a lofty brick wall, black by age and everlasting shade, which wall required no spyglass to bring out its lurking beauties, but, for the benefit of all nearsighted spectators, was pushed up to within ten feet of my windowpanes. Owing to the great height of the surrounding buildings, and my chambers' being on the second floor, the interval between this wall and mine not a little resembled a huge square cistern.

At the period just preceding the advent of Bartleby, I had two persons as copyists in my employment, and a promising lad as an office boy. First, Turkey; second, Nippers; third, Ginger Nut. These may seem names the like of which are not usually found in the Directory. In truth, they were nicknames, mutually conferred upon each other by my three clerks, and were deemed expressive of their respective persons or characters. Turkey was a short, pursy Englishman, of about my own age—that is, somewhere not far from sixty. In the morning, one might say, his face was of a fine florid hue, but after twelve o'clock, meridian—his dinner hour—it blazed like a grate full of Christmas coals; and continued blazing—but, as it were, with a gradual wane—till six o'clock, P.M., or thereabouts; after which I saw no more of the proprietor of the face, which, gaining its meridian with the sun, seemed to set with it, to rise, culminate, and decline the following day, with the like regularity and undiminished glory. There are many singular coincidences I have known in the course of my life, not the least among which was the fact, that, exactly when Turkey displayed his fullest beams from his red and radiant countenance, just then, too, at that critical moment, began the daily period when I considered his business capacities as seriously disturbed for the remainder of the twenty-four hours. Not that he was absolutely idle or averse to business then; far from it. The difficulty was, he was apt to be altogether too energetic. There was a strange, inflamed, flurried, flighty recklessness of activity about him. He would be incautious in dipping his pen into his inkstand. All his blots upon my documents were dropped there after twelve o'clock, meridian. Indeed, not only would he be reckless and sadly given to making blots in the afternoon, but some days he went further and was rather noisy. At such times, too, his face flamed with augmented blazonry, as if cannel coal had been heaped on anthracite. He made an unpleasant racket with his chair; spilled his sandbox; in mending his pens, impatiently split them all to pieces and threw them on the floor in a sudden passion; stood up and leaned over his table, boxing his papers about in a most indecorous manner, very sad to behold in an elderly man like him. Nevertheless, as he was in many ways a most valuable person to me, and all the time before twelve o'clock, meridian, was the quickest, steadiest creature, too, accomplishing a great deal of work in a style not easily to be matched—for these reasons I was willing to overlook his eccentricities, though indeed, occasionally, I remonstrated with him. I did this very gently, however, because, though the civilest, nay, the blandest and most reverential of men in the morning, yet, in the afternoon he was disposed, upon provocation, to be slightly rash with his tongue—in fact, insolent. Now, valuing his morning services as I did, and resolved not to lose them—yet, at the same time, made uncomfortable by his inflamed ways after twelve o'clock—and being a man of peace, unwilling by my admonitions to call forth unseemly retorts from him, I took upon me one Saturday noon (he was always worse on Saturdays) to hint to him, very kindly, that perhaps, now that he was growing old, it might be well to abridge his labors; in short, he need not come to my chambers after twelve o'clock, but, dinner over, had best go home to his lodgings and rest himself till teatime. But no; he insisted upon his afternoon devotions. His countenance became intolerably fervid, as he oratorically assured me—gesticulating with a long ruler at the other end of the room—that if his services in the morning were useful, how indispensable, then, in the afternoon?

"With submission, sir," said Turkey, on this occasion, "I consider myself your right-hand man. In the morning I but marshal and deploy my columns, but in the afternoon I put myself at their head, and gallantly charge the foe, thus"—and he made a violent thrust with the ruler.

"But the blots, Turkey," intimated I.

"True; but, with submission, sir, behold these hairs! I am getting old. Surely, sir, a blot or two of a warm afternoon is not to be severely urged against gray hairs. Old age—even if it blot the page—is honorable. With submission, sir, we *both* are getting old."

This appeal to my fellow feeling was hardly to be resisted. At all events, I saw that go he would not. So I made up my mind to let him stay, resolving, nevertheless, to see to it that, during the afternoon, he had to do with my less important papers.

Nippers, the second on my list, was a whiskered, sallow, and upon the whole rather piratical-looking young man of about five and twenty. I always deemed him the victim of two evil powers—ambition and indigestion. The ambition was evinced by a certain impatience of the duties of a mere copyist, an unwarrantable usurpation of strictly professional affairs, such as the original drawing up of legal documents. The indigestion seemed betokened in an occasional nervous testiness and grinning irritability, causing the teeth to audibly grind together over mistakes committed in copying; unnecessary maledictions, hissed rather than spoken, in the heat of business; and especially by a continual discontent with the height of the table where he worked. Though of a very ingenious mechanical turn, Nippers could never get this table to suit him. He put chips under it, blocks of various sorts, bits of pasteboard, and at last went so far as to attempt an exquisite adjustment by final pieces of folded blotting paper. But no invention would answer. If, for the sake of easing his back, he brought the table lid at a sharp angle well up towards his chin, and wrote there like a man using the steep roof of a Dutch house for his desk, then he declared that it stopped the circulation in his arms. If now he lowered the table to his waistbands and stooped over it in writing, then there was a sore aching in his back. In short, the truth of the matter was Nippers knew not what he wanted. Or, if he wanted anything, it was to be rid of a scrivener's table altogether. Among the manifestations of his diseased ambition was a fondness he had for receiving visits from certain ambiguous-looking fellows in seedy coats, whom he called his clients. Indeed, I was aware that not only was he, at times, considerable of a ward politician, but he occasionally did a little business at the Justices' courts, and was not unknown on the steps of the Tombs. I have good reason to believe, however, that one individual who called upon him at my chambers, and who, with a grand air, he insisted was his client, was no other than a dun, and the alleged title deed, a bill. But, with all his failings, and the annoyances he caused me, Nippers, like his compatriot Turkey, was a very useful man to me; wrote a neat, swift hand; and, when he chose, was not deficient in a gentlemanly sort of deportment. Added to this, he always dressed in a gentlemanly sort of way, and so, incidentally, reflected credit upon my chambers. Whereas, with respect to Turkey, I had much ado to keep him from being a reproach to me. His clothes were apt to look oily, and smell of eating houses. He wore his pantaloons very loose and baggy in summer. His coats were execrable, his hat not to be handled. But while the hat was a thing of indifference to me, inasmuch as his natural civility and deference, as a dependent Englishman, always led him to doff it the moment he entered the room, yet his coat was another matter. Concerning his coats, I reasoned with him, but with no effect. The truth was, I suppose, that a man with so small an income could not afford to sport such a lustrous face and a lustrous coat at one and the same time. As Nippers once observed, Turkey's money went chiefly for red ink. One winter day, I presented Turkey with a highly respectable-looking coat of my own—a padded gray coat of a most comfortable warmth, and which buttoned straight up from the knee to the neck. I thought Turkey would appreciate the favor and abate his rashness and obstreperousness of afternoons. But no; I verily believe that buttoning himself up in so downy and blanket-like a coat had a pernicious effect upon him—upon the same principle that too much oats are bad for horses. In fact, precisely as a rash, restive horse is said to feel his oats, so Turkey felt his coat. It made him insolent. He was a man whom prosperity harmed.

Though, concerning the self-indulgent habits of Turkey, I had my own private surmises, yet, touching Nippers, I was well persuaded that, whatever might be his faults in other respects, he was, at least, a temperate young man. But indeed, nature herself seemed to have been his vintner, and, at his birth, charged him so thoroughly with an irritable, brandylike disposition that all subsequent potations were needless. When I consider how, amid the stillness of my chambers, Nippers would sometimes impatiently rise from his seat, and, stooping over his table, spread his arms wide apart, seize the whole desk, and move it, and jerk it, with a grim, grinding motion on the floor, as if the table were a perverse voluntary agent, intent on thwarting and vexing him, I plainly perceive that, for Nippers, brandy-and-water were altogether superfluous.

It was fortunate for me that, owing to its peculiar cause—indigestion—the irritability and consequent nervousness of Nippers were mainly observable in the morning, while in the afternoon he was comparatively mild. So that, Turkey's paroxysms only coming on about twelve o'clock, I never had to do with their eccentricities at one time. Their fits relieved each other, like guards. When Nippers's was on, Turkey's was off; and vice versa. This was a good natural arrangement, under the circumstances.

Ginger Nut, the third on my list, was a lad some twelve years old. His father was a carman, ambitious of seeing his son on the bench instead of a cart before he died. So he sent him to my office, as student at law, errand boy, cleaner and sweeper, at the rate of one dollar a week. He had a little desk to himself, but he did not use it much. Upon inspection, the drawer exhibited a great array of the shells of various sorts of nuts. Indeed, to this quick-witted youth, the whole noble science of the law was contained in a nutshell. Not the least among the employments of Ginger Nut, as well as one which he discharged with the most alacrity, was his duty as cake and apple purveyor for Turkey and Nippers. Copying law papers being proverbially a dry, husky sort of business, my two scriveners were fain to moisten their mouths very often with Spitzenbergs, to be had at the numerous stalls nigh the Custom House and Post Office. Also, they sent Ginger Nut very frequently for that peculiar cake—small, flat, round, and very spicy—after which he had been named by them. Of a cold morning, when business was but dull, Turkey would gobble up scores of these cakes, as if they were mere wafers—indeed, they sell them at the rate of six or eight for a penny—the scrape of his pen blending with the crunching of the crisp particles in his mouth. Of all the fiery afternoon blunders and flurried rashnesses of Turkey was his once moistening a ginger cake between his lips and clapping it on to a mortage for a seal. I came within an ace of dismissing him then. But he mollified me by making an Oriental bow, and saying:

"With submission, sir, it was generous of me to find you in stationery on my own account."

Now my original business—that of a conveyancer and title hunter, and drawer-up of recondite documents of all sorts—was considerably increased by receiving the Master's office. There was now great work for scriveners. Not only must I push the clerks already with me, but I must have additional help.

In answer to my advertisement, a motionless young man one morning stood upon my office threshold, the door being open, for it was summer. I can see that figure now—pallidly neat, pitiably respectable, incurably forlorn! It was Bartleby.

After a few words touching his qualifications, I engaged him, glad to have among my corps of copyists a man of so singularly sedate an aspect, which I thought might operate beneficially upon the flighty temper of Turkey and the fiery one of Nippers.

I should have stated before that ground-glass folding doors divided my premises into two parts, one of which was occupied by my scriveners, the other by myself. According to my humor, I threw open these doors or closed them. I resolved to assign Bartleby a corner by the folding doors, but on my side of them, so as to have this quiet man within easy call, in case any trifling thing was to be done. I placed his desk close up to a small side window in that part of the room, a window which originally had afforded a lateral view of certain grimy back yards and bricks, but which, owing to subsequent erections, commanded at present no view at all, though it gave some light. Within three feet of the panes was a wall, and the light came down from far above, between two lofty buildings, as from a very small opening in a dome. Still further to a satisfactory arrangement, I procured a high green folding screen, which might entirely isolate Bartleby from my sight, though not remove him from my voice. And thus, in a manner, privacy and society were conjoined.

At first, Bartleby did an extraordinary quantity of writing. As if long famishing for something to copy, he seemed to gorge himself on my documents. There was no pause for digestion. He ran a day and night line, copying by sunlight and by candlelight. I should have been quite delighted with his application, had he been cheerfully industrious. But he wrote on silently, palely, mechanically.

It is, of course, an indispensable part of a scrivener's business to verify the accuracy of his copy, word by word. Where there are two or more scriveners in an office, they assist each other in this examination, one reading from the copy, the other holding the original. It is a very dull, wearisome, and lethargic affair. I can readily imagine that, to some sanguine temperaments, it would be altogether intolerable. For example, I cannot credit that the mettlesome poet, Byron, would have contentedly sat down with Bartleby to examine a law document of, say five hundred pages, closely written in a crimpy hand.

Now and then, in the haste of business, it had been my habit to assist in comparing some brief document myself, calling Turkey or Nippers for this purpose. One object I had in placing Bartleby so handy to me behind the screen was to avail myself of his services on such trivial occasions. It was on the third day, I think, of his being with me, and before any necessity had arisen for having his own writing examined, that, being much hurried to complete a small affair I had in hand, I abruptly called to Bartleby. In my haste and natural expectancy of instant compliance, I sat with my head bent over the original on my desk, and my right hand sideways, and somewhat nervously extended with the copy, so that, immediately upon emerging from his retreat, Bartleby might snatch it and proceed to business without the least delay.

In this very attitude did I sit when I called to him, rapidly stating what it was I wanted him to do—namely, to examine a small paper with me. Imagine my surprise, nay, my consternation, when, without moving from his privacy, Bartleby, in a singularly mild, firm voice, replied, "I would prefer not to."

I sat awhile in perfect silence, rallying my stunned faculties. Immediately it occurred to me that my ears had deceived me, or Bartleby had entirely misunderstood my meaning. I repeated my request in the clearest tone I could assume; but in quite as clear a one came the previous reply, "I would prefer not to."

"Prefer not to," echoed I, rising in high excitement, and crossing the room with a stride. "What do you mean? Are you moon-struck? I want you to help me compare this sheet here—take it," and I thrust it towards him.

"I would prefer not to," said he.

I looked at him steadfastly. His face was leanly composed; his gray eyes dimly calm. Not a wrinkle of agitation rippled him. Had there been the least uneasiness, anger, impatience or impertinence in his manner; in other words, had there been anything ordinarily human about him, doubtless I should have violently dismissed him from the premises. But as it was I should have as soon thought of turning my pale plaster-of-Paris bust of Cicero out of doors. I stood gazing at him awhile, as he went on with his own writing, and then reseated myself at my desk. This is very strange, thought I. What had one best do? But my business hurried me. I concluded to forget the matter for the present, reserving it for my future leisure. So calling Nippers from the other room, the paper was speedily examined.

A few days after this, Bartleby concluded four lengthy documents, being quadruplicates of a week's testimony taken before me in my High Court of Chancery. It became necessary to examine them. It was an important suit, and great accuracy was imperative. Having all things arranged, I called Turkey, Nippers and Ginger Nut, from the next room, meaning to place the four copies in the hands of my four clerks, while I should read from the original.

Accordingly, Turkey, Nippers, and Ginger Nut had taken their seats in a row, each with his document in his hand, when I called to Bartleby to join this interesting group.

"Bartleby! quick, I am waiting."

I heard a slow scrape of his chair legs on the uncarpeted floor, and soon he appeared standing at the entrance of his hermitage.

"What is wanted?" said he, mildly.

"The copies, the copies," said I, hurriedly. "We are going to examine them. There"—and I held towards him the fourth quadruplicate.

"I would prefer not to," he said, and gently disappeared behind the screen.

For a few moments I was turned into a pillar of salt, standing at the head of my seated column of clerks. Recovering myself, I advanced towards the screen and demanded the reason for such extraordinary conduct.

"*Why* do you refuse?"

"I would prefer not to."

With any other man I should have flown outright into a dreadful passion, scorned all further words, and thrust him ignominiously from my presence. But there was something about Bartleby that not only strangely disarmed me, but, in a wonderful manner, touched and disconcerted me. I began to reason with him.

"These are your own copies we are about to examine. It is labor saving to you, because one examination will answer for your four papers. It is common usage. Every copyist is bound to help examine his copy. Is it not so? Will you not speak? Answer!"

"I prefer not to," he replied in a flutelike tone. It seemed to me that, while I had been addressing him, he carefully revolved every statement that I made; fully comprehended the meaning; could not gainsay the irresistible conclusion; but, at the same time, some paramount consideration prevailed with him to reply as he did.

"You are decided, then, not to comply with my request—a request made according to common usage and common sense?"

He briefly gave me to understand that on that point my judgment was sound. Yes: his decision was irreversible.

It is seldom the case that, when a man is browbeaten in some unprecedented and violently unreasonable way, he begins to stagger in his own plainest faith. He begins, as it were, vaguely to surmise that, wonderful as it may be, all the justice and all the reason is on the other side. Accordingly, if any disinterested persons are present, he turns to them for some reinforcement for his own faltering mind.

"Turkey," said I, "what do you think of this? Am I not right?"

"With submission, sir," said Turkey, in his blandest tone, "I think that you are."

"Nippers," said I, "what do *you* think of it?"

"I think I should kick him out of the office."

(The reader of nice perceptions, will here perceive that, it being morning, Turkey's answer is couched in polite and tranquil terms, but Nippers replies in ill-tempered ones. Or, to repeat a previous sentence, Nippers's ugly mood was on duty, and Turkey's off.)

"Ginger Nut," said I, willing to enlist the smallest suffrage in my behalf, "what do *you* think of it?"

"I think, sir, he's a little *luny,*" replied Ginger Nut, with a grin.

"You hear what they say," said I, turning towards the screen, "come forth and do your duty."

But he vouchsafed no reply. I pondered a moment in sore perplexity. But once more business hurried me. I determined again to postpone the consideration of this dilemma to my future leisure. With a little trouble we made out to examine the papers without Bartleby, though at every page or two Turkey deferentially dropped his opinion that this proceeding was quite out of the common; while Nippers, twitching in his chair with a dyspeptic nervousness, ground out between his set teeth occasional hissing maledictions against the stubborn oaf behind the screen. And for his (Nippers's) part, this was the first and the last time he would do another man's business without pay.

Meanwhile Bartleby sat in his hermitage, oblivious to everything but his own peculiar business there.

Some days passed, the scrivener being employed upon another lengthy work. His late remarkable conduct led me to regard his ways narrowly. I observed that he never went to dinner; indeed, that he never went anywhere. As yet I had never, of my personal knowledge, known him to be outside of my office. He was a perpetual sentry in the corner. At about eleven o'clock, though, in the morning, I noticed that Ginger Nut would advance towards the opening in

Bartleby's screen, as if silently beckoned thither by a gesture invisible to me where I sat. The boy would then leave the office jingling a few pence, and reappear with a handful of gingernuts, which he delivered in the hermitage, receiving two of the cakes for his trouble.

He lives, then, on gingernuts, thought I; never eats a dinner, properly speaking; he must be a vegetarian, then; but no, he never eats even vegetables, he eats nothing but gingernuts. My mind then ran on in reveries concerning the probable effects upon the human constitution of living entirely on gingernuts. Gingernuts are so called because they contain ginger as one of their peculiar constituents, and the final flavoring one. Now, what was ginger? A hot, spicy thing. Was Bartleby hot and spicy? Not at all. Ginger, then, had no effect upon Bartleby. Probably he preferred it should have none.

Nothing so aggravates an earnest person as a passive resistance. If the individual so resisted be of a not inhumane temper, and the resisting one perfectly harmless in his passivity, then, in the better moods of the former, he will endeavor charitably to construe to his imagination what proves impossible to be solved by his judgment. Even so, for the most part, I regarded Bartleby and his ways. Poor fellow! thought I, he means no mischief; it is plain he intends no insolence; his aspect sufficiently evinces that his eccentricities are involuntary. He is useful to me. I can get along with him. If I turn him away, the chances are he will fall in with some less indulgent employer, and then he will be rudely treated, and perhaps driven forth miserably to starve. Yes. Here I can cheaply purchase a delicious self-approval. To befriend Bartleby, to humor him in his strange willfulness, will cost me little or nothing, while I lay up in my soul what will eventually prove a sweet morsel for my conscience. But this mood was not invariable with me. The passiveness of Bartleby sometimes irritated me. I felt strangely goaded on to encounter him in new opposition—to elicit some angry spark from him answerable to my own. But, indeed, I might as well have essayed to strike fire with my knuckles against a bit of Windsor soap. But one afternoon the evil impulse in me mastered me, and the following little scene ensued:

"Bartleby," said I, "when those papers are all copied, I will compare them with you."

"I would prefer not to."

"How? Surely you do not mean to persist in that mulish vagary?"

No answer.

I threw open the folding doors near by, and, turning upon Turkey and Nippers, exclaimed:

"Bartleby a second time says he won't examine his papers. What do you think of it, Turkey?"

It was afternoon, be it remembered. Turkey sat glowing like a brass boiler, his bald head steaming, his hands reeling among his blotted papers.

"Think of it?" roared Turkey. "I think I'll just step behind his screen and black his eyes for him!"

So saying, Turkey rose to his feet and threw his arms into a pugilistic position. He was hurrying away to make good his promise when I detained him, alarmed at the effect of incautiously rousing Turkey's combativeness after dinner.

"Sit down, Turkey," said I, "and hear what Nippers has to say. What do you think of it, Nippers? Would I not be justified in immediately dismissing Bartleby?"

"Excuse me, that is for you to decide, sir. I think his conduct quite unusual, and indeed, unjust, as regards Turkey and myself. But it may only be a passing whim."

"Ah," exclaimed I, "you have strangely changed your mind, then—you speak very gently of him now."

"All beer," cried Turkey; "gentleness is effects of beer—Nippers and I dined together today. You see how gentle *I* am, sir. Shall I go and black his eyes?"

"You refer to Bartleby, I suppose. No, not today, Turkey," I replied; "pray, put up your fists."

I closed the doors and again advanced towards Bartleby. I felt additional incentives tempting me to my fate. I burned to be rebelled against again. I remembered that Bartleby never left the office.

"Bartleby," said I, "Ginger Nut is away; just step around to the Post Office, won't you? (it was but a three minutes' walk), and see if there is anything for me."

"I would prefer not to."

"You *will* not?"

"I *prefer* not."

I staggered to my desk and sat there in a deep study. My blind inveteracy returned. Was there any other thing in which I could procure myself to be ignominiously repulsed by this lean, penniless wight?—my hired clerk? What added thing is there, perfectly reasonable, that he will be sure to refuse to do?

"Bartleby!"

No answer.

"Bartleby," in a louder tone.

No answer.

"Bartleby," I roared.

Like a very ghost, agreeably to the laws of magical invocation, at the third summons he appeared at the entrance of his hermitage.

"Go to the next room, and tell Nippers to come to me."

"I prefer not to," he respectfully and slowly said, and mildly disappeared.

"Very good, Bartleby," said I, in a quiet sort of serenely severe self-possessed tone, intimating the unalterable purpose of some terrible retribution very close at hand. At the moment I half intended something of the kind. But upon the whole, as it was drawing towards my dinner hour, I thought it best to put on my hat and walk home for the day, suffering much from perplexity and distress of mind.

Shall I acknowledge it? The conclusion of this whole business was that it soon became a fixed fact of my chambers, that a pale young scrivener by the name of Bartleby had a desk there; that he copied for me at the usual rate of four cents a folio (one hundred words); but he was permanently exempt from examining the work done by him, that duty being transferred to Turkey and Nippers, out of compliment, doubtless, to their superior acuteness; moreover, said Bartleby was never, on any account, to be dispatched on the most trivial errand of any sort; and that even if entreated to take upon him such a matter, it was generally understood that he would "prefer not to"—in other words, that he would refuse point-blank.

As days passed on, I became considerably reconciled to Bartleby. His steadiness, his freedom from all dissipation, his incessant industry (except when he chose to throw himself into a standing reverie behind his screen), his great stillness, his unalterableness of demeanor under all circumstances, made him a valuable acquisition.

One prime thing was this—*he was always there*—first in the morning, continually through the day, and the last at night. I had a singular confidence in his honesty. I felt my most precious papers perfectly safe in his hands. Sometimes, to be sure, I could not, for the very soul of me, avoid falling into sudden spasmodic passions with him. For it was exceeding difficult to bear in mind all the time those strange peculiarities, privileges, and unheard-of exemptions, forming the tacit stipulations on Bartleby's part under which he remained in my office. Now and then, in the eagerness of dispatching pressing business, I would inadvertently summon Bartleby, in a short, rapid tone, to put his finger, say, on the incipient tie of a bit of red tape with which I was about compressing some papers. Of course, from behind the screen the usual answer, "I prefer not to," was sure to come; and then, how could a human creature, with the common infirmities of our nature, refrain from bitterly exclaiming upon such perverseness—such unreasonableness. However, every added repulse of this sort which I received only tended to lessen the probability of my repeating the inadvertence.

Here it must be said that, according to the custom of most legal gentlemen occupying chambers in densely populated law buildings, there were several keys to my door. One was kept by a woman residing in the attic, which person weekly scrubbed and daily swept and dusted my apartments. Another was kept by Turkey for convenience' sake. The third I sometimes carried in my own pocket. The fourth I knew not who had.

Now, one Sunday morning I happened to go to Trinity Church, to hear a celebrated preacher, and finding myself rather early on the ground I thought I would walk round to my chambers for a while. Luckily I had my key with me, but upon applying it to the lock, I found it resisted by something inserted from the inside. Quite surprised, I called out, when to my consternation a key was turned from within, and, thrusting his lean visage at me, and holding the door ajar, the apparition of Bartleby appeared, in his shirt sleeves, and otherwise in a strangely tattered *déshabillé*, saying quietly that he was sorry, but he was deeply engaged just then, and—preferred not admitting me at present. In a brief word or two, he moreover added, that perhaps I had better walk about the block two or three times, and by that time he would probably have concluded his affairs.

Now, the utterly unsurmised appearance of Bartleby, tenanting my law chambers of a Sunday morning, with his cadaverously gentlemanly *nonchalance*, yet withal firm and self-possessed, had such a strange effect upon me that incontinently I slunk away from my own door and did as desired. But not without sundry twinges of impotent rebellion against the mild effrontery of this unaccountable scrivener. Indeed, it was his wonderful mildness, chiefly, which not only disarmed me but unmanned me, as it were. For I consider that one, for the time, is sort of unmanned when he tranquilly permits his hired clerk to dictate to him and order him away from his own premises. Furthermore, I was full of uneasiness as to what Bartleby could possibly be doing in my office in his shirt sleeves, and in an otherwise dismantled condition, of a Sunday morning. Was anything amiss going on? Nay, that was out of the question. It was not to be thought of for a moment that Bartleby was an immoral person. But what could he be doing there?—copying? Nay again, whatever might be his eccentricities, Bartleby was an eminently decorous person. He would be the last man to sit down to his desk in any state approaching to nudity. Besides, it was Sunday; and there was something about Bartleby that forbade the supposition that he would by any secular occupation violate the proprieties of the day.

Nevertheless, my mind was not pacified, and, full of a restless curiosity, at last I returned to the door. Without hindrance I inserted my key, opened it, and entered. Bartleby was not to be seen. I looked round anxiously, peeped behind his screen, but it was very plain that he was gone. Upon more closely examining the place, I surmised that for an indefinite period Bartleby must have ate, dressed, and slept in my office, and that, too, without plate, mirror, or bed. The cushioned seat of a rickety old sofa in one corner bore that faint impress of a lean, reclining form. Rolled away under his desk I found a blanket; under the empty grate, a blacking box and brush; on a chair, a tin basin, with soap and a ragged towel; in a newspaper a few crumbs of gingernuts and a morsel of cheese. Yes, thought I, it is evident enough that Bartleby has been making his home here, keeping bachelor's hall all by himself. Immediately then the thought came sweeping across me, what miserable friendliness and loneliness are here revealed. His poverty is great, but his solitude, how horrible! Think of it. Of a Sunday, Wall Street is deserted as Petra, and every night of every day it is an emptiness. This building, too, which of weekdays hums with industry and life, at nightfall echoes with sheer vacancy, and all through Sunday is forlorn. And here Bartleby makes his home, sole spectator of a solitude which he has seen all populous—a sort of innocent and transformed Marius brooding among the ruins of Carthage!

For the first time in my life a feeling of overpowering stinging melancholy seized me. Before, I had never experienced aught but a not unpleasing sadness. The bond of a common humanity now drew me irresistibly to gloom. A fraternal melancholy! For both I and Bartleby were sons of Adam. I remembered the bright silks and sparkling faces I had seen that day, in gala trim, swanlike sailing down the Mississippi of Broadway; and I contrasted them with the pallid copyist, and thought to myself, Ah, happiness courts the light, so we deem the world is gay, but misery hides aloof, so we deem that misery there is none. These sad fancyings—chimeras, doubtless, of a sick and silly brain—led on to other and more special thoughts, concerning the eccentricities of Bartleby. Presentiments of strange discoveries hovered round me. The scrivener's pale form appeared to me laid out, among uncaring strangers in its shivering winding sheet.

Suddenly I was attracted by Bartleby's closed desk, the key in open sight left in the lock.

I mean no mischief, seek the gratification of no heartless curiosity, thought I; besides, the desk is mine, and its contents, too, so I will make bold to look within. Everything was methodically arranged, the papers smoothly placed. The pigeon-holes were deep, and, removing the files of documents, I groped into their recesses. Presently I felt something there, and dragged it out. It was an old bandanna handkerchief, heavy and knotted. I opened it, and saw it was a savings bank.

I now recalled all the quiet mysteries which I had noted in the man. I remembered that he never spoke but to answer; that, though at intervals he had considerable time to himself, yet I had never seen him reading—no, not even a newspaper; that for long periods he would stand looking out, at his pale window behind the screen, upon the dead brick wall; I was quite sure he never visited any refectory or eating house, while his pale face clearly indicated that he never drank beer like Turkey, or tea and coffee even, like other men;

that he never went anywhere in particular that I could learn; never went out for a walk, unless, indeed, that was the case at present; that he had declined telling who he was, or whence he came, or whether he had any relatives in the world; that though so thin and pale, he never complained of ill health. And more than all I remembered a certain unconscious air of pallid—how shall I call it?—of pallid haughtiness, say, or rather an austere reserve about him, which had positively awed me into my tame compliance with his eccentricities, when I had feared to ask him to do the slightest incidental thing for me, even though I might know, from his long-continued motionlessness, that behind his screen he must be standing in one of those dead-wall reveries of his.

Revolving all these things, and coupling them with the recently discovered fact that he made my office his constant abiding place and home, and not forgetful of his morbid moodiness—revolving all these things, a prudential feeling began to steal over me. My first emotions had been those of pure melancholy and sincerest pity; but just in proportion as the forlornness of Bartleby grew and grew to my imagination, did that same melancholy merge into fear, that pity into repulsion. So true it is, and so terrible too, that up to a certain point the thought or sight of misery enlists our best affections; but, in certain special cases, beyond that point it does not. They err who would assert that invariably this is owing to the inherent selfishness of the human heart. It rather proceeds from a certain hopelessness of remedying excessive and organic ill. To a sensitive being, pity is not seldom pain. And when at last it is perceived that such pity cannot lead to effectual succor, common sense bids the soul be rid of it. What I saw that morning persuaded me that the scrivener was the victim of innate and incurable disorder. I might give alms to his body, but his body did not pain him—it was his soul that suffered, and his soul I could not reach.

I did not accomplish the purpose of going to Trinity Church that morning. Somehow, the things I had seen disqualified me for the time from churchgoing. I walked homeward, thinking what I would do with Bartleby. Finally, I resolved upon this—I would put certain calm questions to him the next morning, touching his history, etc., and if he declined to answer them openly and unreservedly (and I supposed he would prefer not), then to give him a twenty-dollar bill over and above whatever I might owe him, and tell him his services were no longer required; but that if in any other way I could assist him, I would be happy to do so, especially if he desired to return to his native place, wherever that might be, I would willingly help to defray the expenses. Moreover, if, after reaching home, he found himself at any time in want of aid, a letter from him would be sure of a reply.

The next morning came.

"Bartleby," said I, gently calling to him behind his screen.

No reply.

"Bartleby," said I, in a still gentler tone, "come here; I am not going to ask you to do anything you would prefer not to do—I simply wish to speak to you."

Upon this he noiselessly slid into view.

"Will you tell me, Bartleby, where you were born?"

"I would prefer not to."

"Will you tell me *anything* about yourself?"

"I would prefer not to."

"But what reasonable objection can you have to speak to me? I feel friendly towards you."

He did not look at me while I spoke, but kept his glance fixed upon my bust of Cicero, which, as I then sat, was directly behind me, some six inches above my head.

"What is your answer, Bartleby," said I, after waiting a considerable time for a reply, during which his countenance remained immovable, only there was the faintest conceivable tremor of the white attenuated mouth.

"At present I prefer to give no answer," he said, and retired into his hermitage.

It was rather weak in me I confess, but his manner, on this occasion, nettled me. Not only did there seem to lurk in it a certain calm disdain, but his perverseness seemed ungrateful, considering the undeniable good usage and indulgence he had received from me.

Again I sat ruminating what I should do. Mortified as I was at his behavior, and resolved as I had been to dismiss him when I entered my office, nevertheless I strangely felt something superstitious knocking at my heart, and forbidding me to carry out my purpose, and denouncing me for a villain if I dared to breathe one bitter word against this forlornest of mankind. At last, familiarly drawing my chair behind his screen, I sat down and said: "Bartleby, never mind, then, about revealing your history; but let me entreat you, as a friend, to comply as far as may be with the usages of this office. Say now, you will help to examine papers tomorrow or next day: in short, say now, that in a day or two you will begin to be a little reasonable:—say so, Bartleby."

"At present I would prefer not to be a little reasonable," was his mildly cadaverous reply.

Just then the folding doors opened and Nippers approached. He seemed suffering from an unusually bad night's rest, induced by severer indigestion than common. He overheard those final words of Bartleby.

"*Prefer not,* eh?" gritted Nippers—"I'd *prefer* him, if I were you, sir," addressing me—"I'd *prefer* him; I'd give him preferences, the stubborn mule! What is it, sir, pray, that he *prefers* not to do now?"

Bartleby moved not a limb.

"Mr. Nippers," said I, "I'd prefer that you would withdraw for the present."

Somehow, of late, I had got into the way of involuntarily using this word "prefer" upon all sorts of not exactly suitable occasions. And I trembled to think that my contact with the scrivener had already and seriously affected me in a mental way. And what further and deeper aberration might it not yet produce? This apprehension had not been without efficacy in determining me to summary measures.

As Nippers, looking very sour and sulky, was departing, Turkey blandly and deferentially approached.

"With submission, sir," said he, "yesterday I was thinking about Bartleby here, and I think that if he would but prefer to take a quart of good ale every day, it would do much towards mending him, and enabling him to assist in examining his papers."

"So you have got the word, too," said I, slightly excited.

"With submission, what word, sir?" asked Turkey, respectfully crowding himself into the contracted space behind the screen, and by so doing making me jostle the scrivener. "What word, sir?"

"I would prefer to be left alone here," said Bartleby, as if offended at being mobbed in his privacy.

"*That's* the word, Turkey," said I—"*that's* it."

"Oh, *prefer*? oh yes—queer word. I never use it myself. But, sir, as I was saying, if he would but prefer——"

"Turkey," interrupted I, "you will please withdraw."

"Oh certainly, sir, if you prefer that I should."

As he opened the folding door to retire, Nippers at his desk caught a glimpse of me, and asked whether I would prefer to have a certain paper copied on blue paper or white. He did not in the least roguishly accent the word prefer. It was plain that it involuntarily rolled from his tongue. I thought to myself, surely I must get rid of a demented man, who already has in some degree turned the tongues, if not the heads, of myself and clerks. But I thought it prudent not to break the dismission at once.

The next day I noticed that Bartleby did nothing but stand at his window in his dead-wall reverie. Upon asking him why he did not write, he said that he had decided upon doing no more writing.

"Why, how now? what next?" exclaimed I, "do no more writing?"

"No more."

"And what is the reason?"

"Do you not see the reason for yourself?" he indifferently replied.

I looked steadfastly at him, and perceived that his eyes looked dull and glazed. Instantly it occurred to me that his unexampled diligence in copying by his dim window for the first few weeks of his stay with me might have temporarily impaired his vision.

I was touched. I said something in condolence with him, I hinted that of course he did wisely in abstaining from writing for a while; and urged him to embrace that opportunity of taking wholesome exercise in the open air. This, however, he did not do. A few days after this, my other clerks being absent, and being in a great hurry to dispatch certain letters by the mail, I thought that, having nothing else earthly to do, Bartleby would surely be less inflexible than usual, and carry these letters to the Post Office. But he blankly declined. So, much to my inconvenience, I went myself.

Still added days went by. Whether Bartleby's eyes improved or not, I could not say. To all appearance, I thought they did. But when I asked him if they did, he vouchsafed no answer. At all events, he would do no copying. At last, in reply to my urgings, he informed me that he had permanently given up copying.

"What!" exclaimed I; "suppose your eyes should get entirely well—better than ever before—would you not copy then?"

"I have given up copying," he answered, and slid aside.

He remained as ever, a fixture in my chamber. Nay—if that were possible—he became still more of a fixture than before. What was to be done? He would do nothing in the office; why should he stay there? In plain fact, he had now become a millstone to me, not only useless as a necklace, but afflictive to bear. Yet I was sorry for him. I speak less than truth when I say that, on his own account, he occasioned me uneasiness. If he would but have named a single relative or friend, I would instantly have written and urged their taking the poor fellow away to some convenient retreat. But he seemed alone, absolutely alone in the universe. A bit of wreck in the mid-Atlantic. At length, necessities connected with my business tyrannized over all other considerations. Decently as I could, I told Bartleby that in six days' time he must unconditionally leave the office. I warned him to take measures, in the interval, for procuring some other abode. I offered to assist him in this endeavor, if he himself would but take the first step towards a removal. "And when you finally quit me, Bartleby," added I, "I shall see that you go not away entirely unprovided. Six days from this hour, remember."

At the expiration of that period, I peeped behind the screen, and lo! Bartleby was there.

I buttoned up my coat, balanced myself, advanced slowly towards him, touched his shoulder, and said, "The time has come; you must quit this place; I am sorry for you; here is money; but you must go."

"I would prefer not," he replied, with his back still towards me.

"You *must*."

He remained silent.

Now I had an unbounded confidence in this man's common honesty. He had frequently restored to me sixpences and shillings carelessly dropped upon the floor, for I am apt to be very reckless in such shirt-button affairs. The proceeding, then, which followed will not be deemed extraordinary.

"Bartleby," said I, "I owe you twelve dollars on account; here are thirty-two; the odd twenty are yours—Will you take it?" and I handed the bills towards him.

But he made no motion.

"I will leave them here, then," putting them under a weight on the table. Then taking my hat and cane and going to the door, I tranquilly turned and added—"After you have removed your things from these offices, Bartleby, you will of course lock the door—since everyone is now gone for the day but you—and if you please, slip your key underneath the mat, so that I may have it in the morning. I shall not see you again; so good-bye to you. If, hereafter, in your new place of abode, I can be of any service to you, do not fail to advise me by letter. Good-bye, Bartleby, and fare you well."

But he answered not a word; like the last column of some ruined temple, he remained standing mute and solitary in the middle of the otherwise deserted room.

As I walked home in a pensive mood, my vanity got the better of my pity. I could not but highly plume myself on my masterly management in getting rid of Bartleby. Masterly I call it, and such it must appear to any dispassionate thinker. The beauty of my procedure seemed to consist in its perfect quietness. There was no vulgar bullying, no bravado of any sort, no choleric hectoring and striding to and fro across the apartment, jerking out vehement commands for Bartleby to bundle himself off with his beggarly traps. Nothing of the kind. Without loudly bidding Bartleby depart—as an inferior genius might have done—I *assumed* the ground that depart he must, and upon that assumption built all I had to say. The more I thought over my procedure, the more I was charmed with it. Nevertheless, next morning, upon awakening, I had my doubts—I had somehow slept off the fumes of vanity. One of the coolest and wisest hours a man has is just after he awakes in the morning. My procedure seemed as sagacious as ever—but only in theory. How it would prove in practice—there was the rub. It was truly a beautiful thought to have assumed Bartleby's departure; but, after all, that assumption was simply my own, and none of Bartleby's. The great point was, not whether I had assumed that he would quit me, but whether he would prefer so to do. He was more a man of preferences than assumptions.

After breakfast, I walked downtown, arguing the probabilities pro and con. One moment I thought it would prove a miserable failure, and Bartleby would be found all alive at my office as usual; the next moment it seemed certain that I should find his chair empty.

And so I kept veering about. At the corner of Broadway and Canal Street, I saw quite an excited group of people standing in earnest conversation.

"I'll take odds he doesn't," said a voice as I passed.

"Doesn't go?—done!" said I, "put up your money."

I was instinctively putting my hand in my pocket to produce my own, when I remembered that this was an election day. The words I had overheard bore no reference to Bartleby but to the success or nonsuccess of some candidate for the mayoralty. In my intent frame of mind, I had, as it were, imagined that all Broadway shared in my excitement, and were debating the same question with me. I passed on, very thankful that the uproar of the street screened my momentary absent-mindedness.

As I had intended, I was earlier than usual at my office door. I stood listening for a moment. All was still. He must be gone. I tried the knob. The door was locked. Yes, my procedure had worked to a charm; he indeed must be vanished. Yet a certain melancholy mixed with this: I was almost sorry for my brilliant success. I was fumbling under the door mat for the key, which Bartleby was to have left there for me, when accidentally my knee knocked against a panel, producing a summoning sound, and in response a voice came to me from within—"Not yet; I am occupied."

It was Bartleby.

I was thunderstruck. For an instant I stood like the man who, pipe in mouth, was killed one cloudless afternoon long ago in Virginia by summer lightning; at his own warm open window he was killed, and remained leaning out there upon the dreamy afternoon, till someone touched him, when he fell.

"Not gone!" I murmured at last. But again obeying that wondrous ascendancy which the inscrutable scrivener had over me, and from which ascendancy, for all my chafing, I could not completely escape, I slowly went downstairs and out into the street, and while walking round the block considered what I should next do in this unheard-of perplexity. Turn the man out by an actual thrusting I could not; to drive him away by calling him hard names would not do; calling in the police was an unpleasant idea; and yet, permit him to enjoy his cadaverous triumph over me—this, too, I could not think of. What was to be done? or, if nothing could be done, was there anything further that I could *assume* in the matter? Yes, as before I had prospectively assumed that Bartleby would depart, so now I might retrospectively assume that departed he was. In the legitimate carrying out of this assumption I might enter my office in a great hurry, and, pretending not to see Bartleby at all, walk straight against him as if he were air. Such a proceeding would in a singular degree have the appearance of a home thrust. It was hardly possible that Bartleby could withstand such an application of the doctrine of assumptions. But upon second thoughts the success of the plan seemed rather dubious. I resolved to argue the matter over with him again.

"Bartleby," said I, entering the office, with a quietly severe expression, "I am seriously displeased. I am pained, Bartley. I had thought better of you. I had imagined you of such a gentlemanly organization that in any delicate dilemma a slight hint would suffice—in short, an assumption. But it appears I am deceived. Why," I added, unaffectedly starting, "you have not even touched that money yet," pointing to it, just where I had left it the evening previous.

He answered nothing.

"Will you, or will you not, quit me?" I now demanded in a sudden passion, advancing close to him.

"I would prefer *not* to quit you," he replied, gently emphasizing the *not.*

"What earthly right have you to stay here? Do you pay any rent? Do you pay my taxes? Or is this property yours?"

He answered nothing.

"Are you ready to go on and write now? Are your eyes recovered? Could you copy a small paper for me this morning? or help examine a few lines? or step round to the Post Office? In a word, will you do anything at all to give a coloring to your refusal to depart the premises?"

He silently retired into his hermitage.

I was now in such a state of nervous resentment that I thought it but prudent to check myself at present from further demonstrations. Bartleby and I were alone. I remembered the tragedy of the unfortunate Adams and the still more unfortunate Colt in the solitary office of the latter; and how poor Colt, being dreadfully incensed by Adams, and imprudently permitting himself to get wildly excited, was at unawares hurried into his fatal act—an act which certainly no man could possibly deplore more than the actor himself. Often it had occurred to me in my ponderings upon the subject that had that altercation taken place in the public street, or at a private residence, it would not have terminated as it did. It was the circumstance of being alone in a solitary office, upstairs, of a building entirely unhallowed by humanizing domestic associations—an uncarpeted office, doubtless, of a dusty, haggard sort of appearance—this it must have been which greatly helped to enhance the irritable desperation of the hapless Colt.

But when this old Adam of resentment rose in me and tempted me concerning Bartleby, I grappled him and threw him. How? Why, simply by recalling the divine injunction: "A new commandment give I unto you, that ye love one another." Yes, this it was that saved me. Aside from higher considerations, charity often operates as a vastly wise and prudent principle—a great safeguard to its possessor. Men have committed murder for jealousy's sake, and anger's sake, and hatred's sake, and selfishness' sake, and spiritual pride's sake; but no man that ever I heard of ever committed a diabolical murder for sweet charity's sake. Mere self-interest, then, if no better motive can be enlisted, should, especially with high-tempered men, prompt all beings to charity and philanthropy. At any rate, upon the occasion in question, I strove to drown my exasperated feelings towards the scrivener by benevolently construing his conduct. Poor fellow, poor fellow! thought I, he don't mean anything, and besides, he has seen hard times, and ought to be indulged.

I endeavored, also, immediately to occupy myself, and at the same time to comfort my despondency. I tried to fancy that in the course of the morning, at such time as might prove agreeable to him, Bartleby, of his own free accord, would emerge from his hermitage and take up some decided line of march in the direction of the door. But no. Half-past twelve o'clock came; Turkey began to glow in the face, overturn his inkstand, and become generally obstreperous; Nippers abated down into quietude and courtesy; Ginger Nut munched his noon apple; and Bartleby remained standing at his window in one of his profoundest dead-wall reveries. Will it be credited? Ought I to acknowledge it? That afternoon I left the office without saying one further word to him.

Some days now passed during which, at leisure intervals, I looked a little into "Edwards on the Will," and "Priestley on Necessity." Under the circumstances, those books induced a salutary feeling. Gradually I slid into the persuasion that these troubles of mine touching the scrivener had been all predestinated from eternity, and Bartleby was billeted upon me for some mysterious purpose of an all-wise Providence, which it was not for a mere mortal like me to fathom. Yes, Bartleby, stay there behind your screen, thought I; I shall persecute you no more; you are harmless and noiseless as any of these old chairs; in short, I never feel so private as when I know you are here. At last I see it, I feel it; I penetrate to the predestinated purpose of my life. I am content. Others may have loftier parts to enact, but my mission in this world, Bartleby, is to furnish you with office room for such period as you may see fit to remain.

I believe that this wise and blessed frame of mind would have continued with me had it not been for the unsolicited and uncharitable remarks obtruded upon me by my professional friends who visited the rooms. But thus it often is that the constant friction of illiberal minds wears out at last the best resolves of the more generous. Though, to be sure, when I reflected upon it it was not strange that people entering my office should be struck by the peculiar aspect of the unaccountable Bartleby, and so be tempted to throw out some sinister observations concerning him. Sometimes an attorney having business with me, and calling at my office, and finding no one but the scrivener there, would undertake to obtain some sort of precise information from him touching my whereabouts; but without heeding his idle talk, Bartleby would remain standing immovable in the middle of the room. So, after comtemplating him in that position for a time, the attorney would depart no wiser than he came.

Also, when a reference was going on, and the room full of lawyers and witnesses, and business driving fast, some deeply-occupied legal gentleman present, seeing Bartleby wholly unemployed, would request him to run round to his (the legal gentleman's) office and fetch some papers for him. Thereupon Bartleby would tranquilly decline, and yet remain idle as before. Then the lawyer would give a great stare, and turn to me. And what could I say? At last I was made aware that all through the circle of my professional acquaintance a whisper of wonder was running round, having reference to the strange creature I kept at my office. This worried me very much. And as the idea came upon me of his possibly turning out a long-lived man, and keep occupying my chambers, and denying my authority; and perplexing my visitors; and scandalizing my professional reputation; and casting a general gloom over the premises; keeping soul and body together to the last upon his savings (for doubtless he spent but half a dime a day), and in the end perhaps outlive me, and claim possession of my office by right of his perpetual occupancy—as all these dark anticipations crowded upon me more and more, and my friends continually intruded their relentless remarks upon the apparition in my room, a great change was wrought in me. I resolved to gather all my faculties together and forever rid me of this intolerable incubus.

Ere revolving any complicated project, however, adapted to this end, I first simply suggested to Bartleby the propriety of his permanent departure. In a calm and serious tone, I commended the idea to his careful and mature consideration. But, having taken three days to meditate upon it, he apprised me that his original determination remained the same; in short, that he still preferred to abide with me.

What shall I do? I now said to myself, buttoning up my coat to the last button. What shall I do? what ought I to do? what does conscience say I *should* do with this man, or, rather, ghost. Rid myself of him, I must; go, he shall. But how? You will not thrust him, the poor, pale, passive mortal—you will not thrust such a helpless creature out of your door? you will not dishonor yourself by such cruelty? No, I will not, I cannot do that. Rather would I let him live and die here, and then mason up his remains in the wall. What, then, will you do? For all your coaxing, he will not budge. Bribes he leaves under your own paperweight on your table; in short, it is quite plain that he prefers to cling to you.

Then something severe, something unusual, must be done. What! surely you will not have him collared by a constable, and commit his innocent pallor to the common jail? And upon what ground could you procure such a thing to be done?—a vagrant, is he? What! he a vagrant, a wanderer, who refuses to budge? It is because he will *not* be a vagrant, then, that you seek to count him *as* a vagrant. That is too absurd. No visible means of support: there I have him. Wrong again: for indubitably he *does* support himself, and that is the only unanswerable proof that any man can show of his possessing the means so to do. No more, then. Since he will not quit me, I must quit him. I will change my offices; I will move elsewhere, and give him fair notice that if I find him on my new premises I will then proceed against him as a common trespasser.

Acting accordingly, next day I thus addressed him: "I find these chambers too far from the City Hall; the air is unwholesome. In a word, I propose to remove my offices next week, and shall no longer require your services. I tell you this now, in order that you may seek another place."

He made no reply, and nothing more was said.

On the appointed day I engaged carts and men, proceeded to my chambers, and, having but little furniture, everything was removed in a few hours. Throughout, the scrivener remained standing behind the screen, which I directed to be removed the last thing. It was withdrawn; and, being folded up like a huge folio, left him the motionless occupant of a naked room. I stood in the entry watching him a moment, while something from within me upbraided me.

I re-entered, with my hand in my pocket—and—and my heart in my mouth.

"Good-bye, Bartleby; I am going—good-bye; and God some way bless you; and take that," slipping something in his hand. But it dropped upon the floor, and then—strange to say—I tore myself from him whom I had so longed to be rid of.

Established in my new quarters, for a day or two I kept the door locked, and started at every footfall in the passages. When I returned to my rooms after any little absence, I would pause at the threshold for an instant and attentively listen ere applying my key. But these fears were needless. Bartleby never came nigh me.

I thought all was going well, when a perturbed-looking stranger visited me, inquiring whether I was the person who had recently occupied rooms at No. —— Wall Street.

Full of forebodings, I replied that I was.

"Then, sir," said the stranger, who proved a lawyer, "you are responsible for the man you left there. He refuses to do any copying; he refuses to do anything; he says he prefers not to; and he refuses to quit the premises."

"I am very sorry, sir," said I, with assumed tranquillity, but an inward tremor, "but, really, the man you allude to is nothing to me—he is no relation or apprentice of mine, that you should hold me responsible for him."

"In mercy's name, who is he?"

"I certainly cannot inform you. I know nothing about him. Formerly I employed him as a copyist; but he has done nothing for me now for some time past."

"I shall settle him, then—good morning, sir."

Several days passed, and I heard nothing more; and, though I often felt a charitable prompting to call at the place and see poor Bartleby, yet a certain squeamishness, of I know not what, withheld me.

All is over with him, by this time, thought I at last, when, through another week, no further intelligence reached me. But, coming to my room the day after, I found several persons waiting at my door in a high state of nervous excitement.

"That's the man—here he comes," cried the foremost one, whom I recognized as the lawyer who had previously called upon me alone.

"You must take him away, sir, at once," cried a portly person among them, advancing upon me, and whom I knew to be the landlord of No. —— Wall Street. "These gentlemen, my tenants, cannot stand it any longer; Mr. B——," pointing to the lawyer, "has turned him out of his room, and he now persists in haunting the building generally, sitting upon the banisters of the stairs by day, and sleeping in the entry by night. Everybody is concerned; clients are leaving the offices; some fears are entertained of a mob; something you must do, and that without delay."

Aghast at this torrent, I fell back before it, and would fain have locked myself in my new quarters. In vain I persisted that Bartleby was nothing to me—no more than to anyone else. In vain—I was the last person known to have anything to do with him, and they held me to the terrible account. Fearful, then, of being exposed in the papers (as one person present obscurely threatened), I considered the matter, and at length said that if the lawyer would give me a confidential interview with the scrivener, in his (the lawyer's) own room, I would, that afternoon, strive my best to rid them of the nuisance they complained of.

Going upstairs to my old haunt, there was Bartleby silently sitting upon the banister at the landing.

"What are you doing here, Bartleby?" said I.

"Sitting upon the banister," he mildly replied.

I motioned him into the lawyer's room, who then left us.

"Bartleby," said I, "are you aware that you are the cause of great tribulation to me, by persisting in occupying the entry after being dismissed from the office?"

No answer.

"Now one of two things must take place. Either you must do something, or something must be done to you. Now what sort of business would you like to engage in? Would you like to re-engage in copying for someone?"

"No; I would prefer not to make any change."

"Would you like a clerkship in a dry-goods store?"

"There is too much confinement about that. No, I would not like a clerkship; but I am not particular."

"Too much confinement," I cried; "why you keep yourself confined all the time!"

"I would prefer not to take a clerkship," he rejoined, as if to settle that little item at once.

"How would a bartender's business suit you? There is no trying of the eyesight in that."

"I would not like it at all; though, as I said before, I am not particular."

His unwonted wordiness inspirited me. I returned to the charge.

"Well, then, would you like to travel through the country collecting bills for the merchants? That would improve your health."

"No, I would prefer to be doing something else."

"How, then, would going as a companion to Europe, to entertain some young gentleman with your conversation—how would that suit you?"

"Not at all. It does not strike me that there is anything definite about that. I like to be stationary. But I am not particular."

"Stationary you shall be, then," I cried, now losing all patience, and, for the first time in all my exasperating connection with him, fairly flying into a passion. "If you do not go away from these premises before night, I shall feel bound—indeed, I *am* bound—to—to—to quit the premises myself!" I rather absurdly concluded, knowing not with what possible threat to try to frighten his immobility into compliance. Despairing of all further efforts, I was precipitately leaving him, when a final thought occurred to me—one which had not been wholly unindulged before.

"Bartleby," said I, in the kindest tone I could assume under such exciting circumstances, "will you go home with me now—not to my office, but my dwelling—and remain there till we can conclude upon some convenient arrangement for you at our leisure? Come, let us start now, right away."

"No; at present I would prefer not to make any change at all."

I answered nothing, but, effectually dodging everyone by the suddenness and rapidity of my flight, rushed from the building, ran up Wall Street towards Broadway, and, jumping into the first omnibus, was soon removed from pursuit. As soon as tranquillity returned, I distinctly perceived that I had now done all that I possibly could, both in respect to the demands of the landlord and his tenants, and with regard to my own desire and sense of duty, to benefit Bartleby, and shield him from rude persecution. I now strove to be entirely carefree and quiescent, and my conscience justified me in the attempt, though, indeed, it was not so successful as I could have wished. So fearful was I of being again hunted out by the incensed landlord and his exasperated tenants that, surrendering my business to Nippers for a few days, I drove about the upper part of the town and through the suburbs in my rockaway; crossed over to Jersey City and Hoboken, and paid fugitive visits to Manhattanville and Astoria. In fact, I almost lived in my rockaway for the time.

When again I entered my office, lo, a note from the landlord lay upon the desk. I opened it with trembling hands. It informed me that the writer had sent to the police, and had Bartleby removed to the Tombs as a vagrant. Moreover, since I knew more about him than anyone else, he wished me to appear at that place and make a suitable statement of the facts. These tidings had a conflicting effect upon me. At first I was indignant, but at last almost approved. The landlord's energetic, summary disposition had led him to adopt a procedure which I do not think I would have decided upon myself; and yet, as a last resort, under such peculiar circumstances, it seemed the only plan.

As I afterwards learned, the poor scrivener, when told that he must be conducted to the Tombs, offered not the slightest obstacle, but, in his pale, unmoving way, silently acquiesced.

Some of the compassionate and curious bystanders joined the party, and, headed by one of the constables arm in arm with Bartleby, the silent processsion filed its way through all the noise, and heat, and joy of the roaring thoroughfares at noon.

The same day I received the note, I went to the Tombs, or, to speak more properly, the Halls of Justice. Seeking the right officer, I stated the purpose of my call, and was informed that the individual I described was indeed within. I then assured the functionary that Bartleby was a perfectly honest man, and greatly to be compassionated, however unaccountably eccentric. I narrated all I knew, and closed by suggesting the idea of letting him remain in as indulgent confinement as possible till something less harsh might be done—though, indeed, I hardly knew what. At all events, if nothing else could be decided upon, the almshouse must receive him. I then begged to have an interview.

Being under no disgraceful charge, and quite serene and harmless in all his ways, they had permitted him freely to wander about the prison, and, especially, in the inclosed grass-platted yards thereof. And so I found him there, standing all alone in the quietest of the yards, his face towards a high wall, while all around, from the narrow slits of the jail windows, I thought I saw peering out upon him the eyes of murderers and thieves.

"Bartleby!"

"I know you," he said, without looking round—"and I want nothing to say to you."

"It was not I that brought you here, Bartleby," said I, keenly pained at his implied suspicion. "And, to you, this should not be so vile a place. Nothing reproachful attaches to you by being here. And see, it is not so sad a place as one might think. Look, there is the sky, and here is the grass."

"I know where I am," he replied, but would say nothing more, and so I left him.

As I entered the corridor again, a broad meatlike man in an apron accosted me, and, jerking his thumb over his shoulder, said—"Is that your friend?"

"Yes."

"Does he want to starve? If he does, let him live on the prison fare, that's all."

"Who are you?" asked I, not knowing what to make of such an unofficially speaking person in such a place.

"I am the grubman. Such gentlemen as have friends here hire me to provide them with something good to eat."

"Is this so?" said I, turning to the turnkey.

He said it was.

"Well, then," said I, slipping some silver into the grubman's hands (for so they called him), "I want you to give particular attention to my friend there; let him have the best dinner you can get. And you must be as polite to him as possible."

"Introduce me, will you?" said the grubman, looking at me with an expression which seemed to say he was all impatience for an opportunity to give a specimen of his breeding.

Thinking it would prove of benefit to the scrivener, I acquiesced, and, asking the grubman his name, went up with him to Bartleby.

"Bartleby, this is a friend; you will find him very useful to you."

"Your sarvant, sir, your sarvant," said the grubman, making a low salutation behind his apron. "Hope you find it pleasant here, sir; nice grounds—cool apartments—hope you'll stay with us some time—try to make it agreeable. What will you have for dinner today?"

"I prefer not to dine today," said Bartleby, turning away. "It would disagree with me; I am unused to dinners." So saying, he slowly moved to the other side of the inclosure and took up a position fronting the dead-wall.

"How's this?" said the grubman, addressing me with a stare of astonishment. "He's odd, ain't he?"

"I think he is a little deranged," said I, sadly.

"Deranged? deranged is it? Well, now, upon my word, I thought that friend of yourn was a gentleman forger; they are always pale and genteel-like, them forgers. I can't help pity 'em—can't help it, sir. Did you know Monroe Edwards?" he added, touchingly, and paused. Then, laying his hand piteously on my shoulder, sighed, "he died of consumption at Sing-Sing. So you weren't acquainted with Monroe?"

"No, I was never socially acquainted with any forgers. But I cannot stop longer. Look to my friend yonder. You will not lose by it. I will see you again."

Some few days after this, I again obtained admission to the Tombs, and went through the corridors in quest of Bartleby; but without finding him.

"I saw him coming from his cell not long ago," said a turnkey, "maybe he's gone to loiter in the yards."

So I went in that direction.

"Are you looking for the silent man?" said another turnkey, passing me. "Yonder he lies—sleeping in the yard there. 'Tis not twenty minutes since I saw him lie down."

The yard was entirely quiet. It was not accessible to the common prisoners. The surrounding walls, of amazing thickness, kept off all sounds behind them. The Egyptian character of the masonry weighed upon me with its gloom. But a soft imprisoned turf grew underfoot. The heart of the eternal pyramids, it seemed, wherein, by some strange magic, through the clefts, grass-seed, dropped by birds, had sprung.

Strangely huddled at the base of the wall, his knees drawn up and lying on his side, his head touching the cold stones, I saw the wasted Bartleby. But nothing stirred. I paused, then went close up to him, stooped over, and saw that his dim eyes were open; otherwise he seemed profoundly sleeping. Something prompted me to touch him. I felt his hand, when a tingling shiver ran up my arm and down my spine to my feet.

The round face of the grubman peered upon me now. "His dinner is ready. Won't he dine today, either? Or does he live without dining?"

"Lives without dining," said I, and closed the eyes.

"Eh!—He's asleep, ain't he?"

"With kings and counselors," murmured I.

There would seem little need for proceeding further in this history. Imagination will readily supply the meager recital of poor Bartleby's interment. But, ere parting with the reader, let me say that if this little narrative has sufficiently interested him to awaken curiosity as to who Bartleby was, and what manner of life he led prior to the present narrator's making his acquaintance, I can only reply that in such curiosity I fully share, but am wholly unable to gratify it. Yet here I hardly know whether I should divulge one little item of rumor which came to my ear a few months after the scrivener's decease. Upon what basis it rested, I could never ascertain, and hence how true it is I cannot now tell. But, inasmuch as this vague report has not been without a certain suggestive interest to me, however sad, it may prove the same with some others, and so I will briefly mention it. The report was this: that Bartleby had been a subordinate clerk in the Dead Letter Office at Washington, from which he had been suddenly removed by a change in the administration. When I think over this rumor, hardly can I express the emotions which seize me. Dead letters! does it not sound like dead men? Conceive a man by nature and misfortune prone to a pallid hopelessness, can any business seem more fitted to heighten it than that of continually handling these dead letters, and assorting them for the flames? For by the cartload they are annually burned. Sometimes from out the folded paper the pale clerk takes a ring—the finger it was meant for, perhaps, molders in the grave; a bank note sent in swiftest charity—he whom it would relieve nor eats nor hungers any more; pardon for those who died despairing; hope for those who died unhoping; good tidings for those who died stifled by unrelieved calamities. On errands of life, these letters speed to death.

Ah, Bartleby! Ah, humanity!

SAMUEL LANGHORNE CLEMENS (MARK TWAIN)

The Notorious Jumping Frog of Calaveras County

IN COMPLIANCE WITH THE request of a friend of mine, who wrote me from the East, I called on good-natured, garrulous old Simon Wheeler, and inquired after my friend's friend, Leonidas W. Smiley, as requested to do, and I hereunto append the result. I have a lurking suspicion that *Leonidas W.* Smiley is a myth; that my friend never knew such a personage; and that he only conjectured that if I asked old Wheeler about him, it would remind him of his infamous *Jim* Smiley, and he would go to work and bore me to death with some exasperating reminiscence of him as long and as tedious as it should be useless to me. If that was the design, it succeeded.

I found Simon Wheeler dozing comfortably by the barroom stove of the dilapidated tavern in the decayed mining camp of Angel's, and I noticed that he was fat and bald-headed, and had an expression of winning gentleness and simplicity upon his tranquil countenance. He roused up, and gave me good day. I told him that a friend of mine had commissioned me to make some inquiries about a cherished companion of his boyhood named *Leonidas W.* Smiley—*Rev. Leonidas W.* Smiley, a young minister of the Gospel, who he had heard was at one time a resident of Angel's Camp. I added that if Mr. Wheeler could tell me anything about this Rev. Leonidas W. Smiley, I would feel under many obligations to him.

Simon Wheeler backed me into a corner and blockaded me there with his chair, and then sat down and reeled off the monotonous narrative which follows this paragraph. He never smiled, he never frowned, he never changed his voice from the gentle-flowing key to which he tuned his initial sentence, he never betrayed the slightest suspicion of enthusiasm; but all through the interminable narrative there ran a vein of impressive earnestness and sincerity, which showed me plainly that, so far from his imagining that there was anything ridiculous or funny about his story, he regarded it as a really important matter, and admired its two heroes as men of transcendent genius in *finesse*. I let him go on in his own way, and never interrupted him once.

"Rev. Leonidas W. H'm, Reverend Le—well, there was a feller here once by the name of *Jim* Smiley, in the winter of '49—or maybe it was the spring of '50—I don't recollect exactly, somehow, though what makes me think it was one or the other is because I remember the big flume warn't finished when he first come to the camp; but anyway, he was the curiousest man about always betting on anything that turned up you ever see, if he could get anybody to bet on the other side; and if he couldn't he'd change sides. Any way that suited the other man would suit *him*—any way just so's he got a bet, *he* was satisfied. But still he was lucky, uncommon lucky; he most always come out winner. He was always ready and laying for a chance; there couldn't be no solit'ry thing mentioned but that feller'd offer to bet on it, and take ary side you please, as I was just telling you. If there was a horse-race, you'd find him flush or you'd find him busted at the end of it; if there was a dog-fight, he'd bet on it; if there was a cat-fight, he'd bet on it; if there was a chicken-fight, he'd bet on it; why, if there was two birds setting on a fence, he would bet you which one would fly first; or if there was a camp-meeting, he would be there reg'lar to bet on Parson Walker, which he judged to be the best exhorter about here, and so he was too, and a good man. If he even see a straddle-bug start to go anywheres, he would bet you how long it would take him to get to—to wherever he was going to, and if you took him up, he would foller that straddle-bug to Mexico but what he would find out where he was bound for and how long he was on the road. Lots of the boys here has seen that Smiley, and can tell you about him. Why, it never made no difference to *him*—he'd bet on *any* thing—the dangdest feller. Parson Walker's wife laid very sick once, for a good while, and it seemed as if they warn't going to save her; but one morning he come in, and Smiley up and asked him how she was, and he said she was considerable better—thank the Lord for his inf'nite mercy—and coming on so smart that with the blessing of Prov'dence she'd get well yet; and Smiley, before he thought, says, 'Well, I'll resk two-and-a-half she don't anyway.'

"Thish-yer Smiley had a mare—the boys called her the fifteen-minute nag, but that was only in fun, you know, because of course she was faster than that—and he used to win money on that horse, for all she was so slow and always had the asthma, or the distemper, or the consumption, or something of that kind. They used to give her two or three hundred yards' start, and then pass her under way; but always at the fag end of the race she'd get excited and desperate like, and come cavorting and straddling up, and scattering her legs around limber, sometimes in the air, and sometimes out to one side among the fences, and kicking up m-o-r-e dust and raising m-o-r-e racket with her coughing and sneezing and blowing her nose—and always fetch up at the stand just about a neck ahead, as near as you could cipher it down.

"And he had a little small bull-pup, that to look at him you'd think he warn't worth a cent but to set around and look ornery and lay for a chance to steal something. But as soon as money was up on him he was a different dog; his under-jaw'd begin to stick out like the fo'castle of a steamboat, and his teeth would uncover and shine like the furnaces. And a dog might tackle him and bully-rag him, and bite him, and throw him over his shoulder two or three times, and Andrew Jackson—which was the name of the pup—Andrew Jackson would never let on but what *he* was satisfied, and hadn't expected nothing else—and the bets being doubled and doubled on the other side all the time, till the money was all up; and then all of a sudden he would grab that other dog jest by the j'int of his hind leg and freeze to it—not chaw, you understand, but only just grip and hang on till they throwed up the sponge, if it was a year. Smiley always come out winner on that pup, till he harnessed a dog once that didn't have no hind legs, because they'd been sawed off in a circular saw, and when the thing had gone along far enough, and the money was all up, and he come to make a snatch for his pet holt, he see in a minute how he'd been imposed on, and how the other dog had him in the door, so to speak, and he 'peared surprised, and then he looked sorter discouraged-like, and didn't try no more to win the fight, and so he got shucked out bad. He give Smiley a look, as much as to say his heart was broke, and it was *his* fault, for putting up a dog that hadn't no hind legs for him to take holt of, which was his main dependence in a fight, and then he limped off a piece and laid down and died. It was a good pup, was that Andrew Jackson, and would have made a name for hisself if he'd lived, for the stuff was in him and he had genius—I know it, because he hadn't no opportunities to speak of, and it don't stand to reason that a dog could make such a fight as he could under them circumstances if he hadn't no talent. It always makes me feel sorry when I think of that last fight of his'n, and the way it turned out.

"Well, thish-yer Smiley had rat-tarriers, and chicken cocks, and tomcats and all them kind of things, till you couldn't rest, and you couldn't fetch nothing for him to bet on but he'd match you. He ketched a frog one day, and took him home, and said he cal'lated to educate him; and so he never done nothing for three months but set in his back yard and learn that frog to jump. And you bet you he *did* learn him, too. He'd give him a little punch behind, and the next minute you'd see that frog whirling in the air like a doughnut—see him turn one summerset, or maybe a couple, if he got a good start, and come down flat-footed and all right, like a cat. He got him up so in the matter of ketching flies, and kep' him in practice so constant, that he'd nail a fly every time as fur as he could see him. Smiley said all a frog wanted was education, and he could do 'most anything—and I believe him. Why, I've seen him set Dan'l Webster down here on this floor—Dan'l Webster was the name of the frog—and sing out, 'Flies, Dan'l, flies!' and quicker'n you could wink he'd spring straight up and snake a fly off'n the counter there, and flop down on the floor ag'in as solid as a gob of mud, and fall to scratching the side of his head with his hind foot as indifferent as if he hadn't no idea he'd been doin' any more'n any frog might do. You never see a frog so modest and straightfor'ard as he was, for all he was so gifted. And when it come to fair and square jumping on a dead level, he could get over more ground at one straddle than any animal of his breed you ever see. Jumping on a dead level was his strong suit, you understand; and when it come to that, Smiley would ante up money on him as long as he had a red. Smiley was monstrous proud of his frog, and well he might be, for fellers that had traveled and been everywheres all said he laid over any frog that ever *they* see.

"Well, Smiley kep' the beast in a little lattice box, and he used to fetch him down-town sometimes and lay for a bet. One day a feller—a stranger in the camp, he was—come acrost him with his box, and says:

" 'What might it be that you've got in the box?'

"And Smiley says, sorter indifferent-like, 'It might be a parrot, or it might be a canary, maybe, but it ain't—it's only just a frog.'

"And the feller took it, and looked at it careful, and turned it round this way and that, and says, 'H'm—so 'tis. Well, what's *he* good for?'

" 'Well,' Smiley says, easy and careless, 'he's good enough for *one* thing, I should judge—he can outjump any frog in Calaveras County.'

"The feller took the box again, and took another long, particular look, and give it back to Smiley, and says, very deliberate, 'Well,' he says, 'I don't see no p'ints about that frog that's any better'n any other frog.'

" 'Maybe you don't,' Smiley says. 'Maybe you understand frogs and maybe you don't understand 'em; maybe you've had experience, and maybe you ain't only a amature, as it were. Anyways, I've got *my* opinion, and I'll resk forty dollars that he can outjump any frog in Calaveras County.'

"And the feller studied a minute, and then says, kinder sad-like, 'Well, I'm only a stranger here, and I ain't got no frog; but if I had a frog, I'd bet you.'

"And then Smiley says, 'That's all right—that's all right—if you'll hold my box a minute, I'll go and get you a frog.' And so the feller took the box, and put up his forty dollars along with Smiley's, and set down to wait.

"So he set there a good while thinking and thinking to himself, and then he got the frog out and prized his mouth open and took a teaspoon and filled him full of quail-shot—filled him pretty near up to his chin—and set him on the floor. Smiley he went to the swamp and slopped around in the mud for a long time, and finally he ketched a frog, and fetched him in, and give him to this feller, and says:

" 'Now, if you're ready, set him alongside of Dan'l, with his fore paws just even with Dan'l's, and I'll give the word.' Then he says, 'One—two—three—*git!*' and him and the feller touched up the frogs from behind, and the new frog hopped off lively, but Dan'l give a heave, and hysted up his shoulders—so—like a Frenchman, but it warn't no use—he couldn't budge; he was planted as solid as a church, and he couldn't no more stir than if he was anchored out. Smiley was a good deal surprised, and he was disgusted too, but he didn't have no idea what the matter was, of course.

"The feller took the money and started away; and when he was going out at the door, he sorter jerked his thumb over his shoulder—so—at Dan'l, and says again, very deliberate, 'Well,' he says, 'I don't see no p'ints about that frog that's any better'n any other frog.'

"Smiley he stood scratching his head and looking down at Dan'l a long time, and at last he says, 'I do wonder what in the nation that frog throw'd off for—I wonder if there ain't something the matter with him—he 'pears to look mighty baggy, somehow.' And he ketched Dan'l by the nap of the neck, and hefted him, and says, 'Why blame my cats if he don't weigh five pound!' and turned him upside down and he belched out a double handful of shot. And then he see how it was, and he was the maddest man—he set the frog down and took out after the feller, but he never ketched him. And—"

[Here Simon Wheeler heard his name called from the front yard, and got up to see what was wanted.] And turning to me as he moved away, he said: "Just set where you are, stranger, and rest easy—I ain't going to be gone a second."

But, by your leave, I did not think that a continuation of the history of the enterprising vagabond *Jim* Smiley would be likely to afford me much information concerning the Rev. *Leonidas W.* Smiley, and so I started away.

At the door I met the sociable Wheeler returning, and he buttonholed me and recommenced:

"Well, thish-yer Smiley had a yaller one-eyed cow that didn't have no tail, only just a short stump like a bannanner, and——"

However, lacking both time and inclination, I did not wait to hear about the afflicted cow, but took my leave.

AMBROSE BIERCE

An Occurrence at Owl Creek Bridge

I

A MAN STOOD UPON a railroad bridge in northern Alabama, looking down into the swift water twenty feet below. The man's hands were behind his back, the wrists bound with a cord. A rope closely encircled his neck. It was attached to a stout cross-timber above his head and the slack fell to the level of his knees. Some loose boards laid upon the sleepers supporting the metals of the railway supplied a footing for him and his executioners—two private soldiers of the Federal army, directed by a sergeant who in civil life may have been a deputy sheriff. At a short remove upon the same temporary platform was an officer in the uniform of his rank, armed. He was a captain. A sentinel at each end of the bridge stood with his rifle in the position known as "support," that is to say, vertical in front of the left shoulder, the hammer resting on the forearm thrown straight across the chest—a formal and unnatural position, enforcing an erect carriage of the body. It did not appear to be the duty of these two men to know what was occurring at the centre of the bridge; they merely blockaded the two ends of the foot planking that traversed it.

Beyond one of the sentinels nobody was in sight; the railroad ran straight away into a forest for a hundred yards, then, curving, was lost to view. Doubtless there was an outpost farther along. The other bank of the stream was open ground—a gentle acclivity topped with a stockade of vertical tree trunks, loopholed for rifles, with a single embrasure through which protruded the muzzle of a brass cannon commanding the bridge. Midway of the slope between bridge and fort were the spectators—a single company of infantry in line, at "parade rest," the butts of the rifles on the ground, the barrels inclining slightly backward against the right shoulder, the hands crossed upon the stock. A lieutenant stood at the right of the line, the point of his sword upon the ground, his left hand resting upon his right. Excepting the group of four at the centre of the bridge, not a man moved. The company faced the bridge, staring stonily, motionless. The sentinels, facing the banks of the stream, might have been statues to adorn the bridge. The captain stood with folded arms, silent, observing the work of his subordinates, but making no sign. Death is a dignitary who when he comes announced is to be received with formal manifestations of respect, even by those most familiar with him. In the code of military etiquette silence and fixity are forms of deference.

The man who was engaged in being hanged was apparently about thirty-five years of age. He was a civilian, if one might judge from his habit, which was that of a planter. His features were good—a straight nose, firm mouth, broad forehead, from which his long, dark hair was combed straight back, falling behind his ears to the collar of his well-fitting frock-coat. He wore a mustache and pointed beard, but no whiskers; his eyes were large and dark gray, and had a kindly expression which one would hardly have expected in one whose neck was in the hemp. Evidently this was no vulgar assassin. The liberal military code makes provision for hanging many kinds of persons, and gentlemen are not excluded.

The preparations being complete, the two private soldiers stepped aside and each drew away the plank upon which he had been standing. The sergeant turned to the captain, saluted and placed himself immediately behind that officer, who in turn moved apart one pace. These movements left the condemned man and the sergeant standing on the two ends of the same plank, which spanned three of the cross-ties of the bridge. The end upon which the civilian stood almost, but not quite, reached a fourth. This plank had been held in place by the weight of the captain; it was now held by that of the sergeant. At a signal from the former the latter would step aside, the plank would tilt and the condemned man go down between two ties. The arrangement commended itself to his judgment as simple and effective. His face had not been covered nor his eyes bandaged. He looked a moment at his "unsteadfast footing," then let his gaze wander to the swirling water of the stream racing madly beneath his feet. A piece of dancing driftwood caught his attention and his eyes followed it down the current. How slowly it appeared to move! What a sluggish stream!

He closed his eyes in order to fix his last thoughts upon his wife and children. The water, touched to gold by the early sun, the brooding mists under the banks at some distance down the stream, the fort, the soldiers, the piece of drift—all had distracted him. And now he became conscious of a new disturbance. Striking through the thought of his dear ones was a sound which he could neither ignore nor understand, a sharp, distinct, metallic percussion like the stroke of a blacksmith's hammer upon the anvil; it had the same ringing quality. He wondered what it was, and whether immeasurably distant or near by—it seemed both. Its recurrence was regular, but as slow as the tolling of a death knell. He awaited each stroke with impatience and—he knew not why—apprehension. The intervals of silence grew progressively longer; the delays became maddening. With their greater infrequency the sounds increased in strength and sharpness. They hurt his ear like the thrust of a knife; he feared he would shriek. What he heard was the ticking of his watch.

He unclosed his eyes and saw again the water below him. "If I could free my hands," he thought, "I might throw off the noose and spring into the stream. By diving I could evade the bullets and, swimming vigorously, reach the bank, take to the woods and get away home. My home, thank God, is as yet outside their lines; my wife and little ones are still beyond the invader's farthest advance."

As these thoughts, which have here to be set down in words, were flashed into the doomed man's brain rather than evolved from it the captain nodded to the sergeant. The sergeant stepped aside.

II

Peyton Farquhar was a well-to-do planter, of an old and highly respected Alabama family. Being a slave owner and like other slave owners a politician he was naturally an original secessionist and ardently devoted to the Southern cause. Circumstances of an imperious nature, which it is unnecessary to relate here, had prevented him from taking service with the gallant army that had fought the disastrous campaigns ending with the fall of Corinth, and he chafed under the inglorious restraint, longing for the release of his energies, the larger life of the soldier, the opportunity for distinction. That opportunity, he felt, would come, as it comes to all in war time. Meanwhile he did what he could. No service was too humble for him to perform in aid of the South, no adventure too perilous for him to undertake if consistent with the character of a civilian who was at heart a soldier, and who in good faith and without too much qualification assented to at least a part of the frankly villainous dictum that all is fair in love and war.

One evening while Farquhar and his wife were sitting on a rustic bench near the entrance to his grounds, a gray-clad soldier rode up to the gate and asked for a drink of water. Mrs. Farquhar was only too happy to serve him with her own white hands. While she was fetching the water her husband approached the dusty horseman and inquired eagerly for news from the front.

"The Yanks are repairing the railroads," said the man, "and are getting ready for another advance. They have reached the Owl Creek bridge, put it in order and built a stockade on the north bank. The commandant has issued an order, which is posted everywhere, declaring that any civilian caught interfering with the railroad, its bridges, tunnels or trains will be summarily hanged. I saw the order."

"How far is it to the Owl Creek bridge?" Farquhar asked.

"About thirty miles."

"Is there no force on this side the creek?"

"Only a picket post half a mile out, on the railroad, and a single sentinel at this end of the bridge."

"Suppose a man—a civilian and student of hanging—should elude the picket post and perhaps get the better of the sentinel," said Farquhar, smiling, "what could he accomplish?"

The soldier reflected. "I was there a month ago," he replied. "I observed that the flood of last winter had lodged a great quantity of driftwood against the wooden pier at this end of the bridge. It is now dry and would burn like tow."

The lady had now brought the water, which the soldier drank. He thanked her ceremoniously, bowed to her husband and rode away. An hour later, after nightfall, he repassed the plantation, going northward in the direction from which he had come. He was a Federal scout.

III

As Peyton Farquhar fell straight downward through the bridge he lost consciousness and was as one already dead. From this state he was awakened—ages later, it seemed to him—by the pain of a sharp pressure upon his throat, followed by a sense of suffocation. Keen, poignant agonies seemed to shoot from his neck downward through every fibre of his body and limbs. These pains appeared to flash along well-defined lines of ramification and to beat with an inconceivably rapid periodicity. They seemed like streams of pulsating fire heating him to an intolerable temperature. As to his head, he was conscious of nothing but a feeling of fulness—of congestion. These sensations were unaccompanied by thought. The intellectual part of his nature was already effaced; he had power only to feel, and feeling was torment. He was conscious of motion. Encompassed in a luminous cloud, of which he was now merely the fiery heart, without material substance, he swung through unthinkable arcs of oscillation, like a vast pendulum. Then all at once, with terrible suddenness, the light about him shot upward with the noise of a loud plash; a frightful roaring was in his ears, and all was cold and dark. The power of thought was restored; he knew that the rope had broken and he had fallen into the stream. There was no additional strangulation; the noose about his neck was already suffocating him and kept the water from his lungs. To die of hanging at the bottom of a river!—the idea seemed to him ludicrous. He opened his eyes in the darkness and saw above him a gleam of light, but how distant, how inaccessible! He was still sinking, for the light became fainter and fainter until it was a mere glimmer. Then it began to grow and brighten, and he knew that he was rising toward the surface—knew it with reluctance, for he was now very comfortable. "To be hanged and drowned," he thought, "that is not so bad; but I do not wish to be shot. No; I will not be shot; that is not fair."

He was not conscious of an effort, but a sharp pain in his wrist apprised him that he was trying to free his hands. He gave the struggle his attention, as an idler might observe the feat of a juggler, without interest in the outcome. What splendid effort!—what magnificent, what superhuman strength! Ah, that was a fine endeavor! Bravo! The cord fell away; his arms parted and floated upward, the hands dimly seen on each side in the growing light. He watched them with a new interest as first one and then the other pounced upon the noose at his neck. They tore it away and thrust it fiercely aside, its undulations resembling those of a water-snake. "Put it back, put it back!" He thought he shouted these words to his hands, for the undoing of the noose had been succeeded by the direst pang that he had yet experienced. His neck ached horribly; his brain was on fire; his heart, which had been fluttering faintly, gave a great leap, trying to force itself out at his mouth. His whole body was racked and wrenched with an insupportable anguish! But his disobedient hands gave no heed to the command. They beat the water vigorously with quick, downward strokes, forcing him to the surface. He felt his head emerge; his eyes were blinded by the sunlight; his chest expanded convulsively, and with a supreme and crowning agony his lungs engulfed a great draught of air, which instantly he expelled in a shriek!

He was now in full possession of his physical senses. They were, indeed, preternaturally keen and alert. Something in the awful disturbance of his organic system had so exalted and refined them that they made record of things never before perceived. He felt the ripples upon his face and heard their separate sounds as they struck. He looked at the forest on the bank of the stream, saw the individual trees, the leaves and the veining of each leaf—saw the very insects upon them: the locusts, the brilliant-bodied flies, the gray spiders stretching their webs from twig to twig. He noted the prismatic colors in all the dewdrops upon a million blades of grass. The humming of the gnats that danced above the eddies of the stream, the beating of the dragon-flies' wings, the strokes of the water-spiders' legs, like oars which had lifted their boat—all these made audible music. A fish slid along beneath his eyes and he heard the rush of its body parting the water.

He had come to the surface facing down the stream; in a moment the visible world seemed to wheel slowly round, himself the pivotal point, and he saw the bridge, the fort, the soldiers upon the bridge, the captain, the sergeant, the two privates, his executioners. They were in silhouette against the blue sky. They shouted and gesticulated, pointing at him. The captain had drawn his pistol, but did not fire; the others were unarmed. Their movements were grotesque and horrible, their forms gigantic.

Suddenly he heard a sharp report and something struck the water smartly within a few inches of his head, spattering his face with spray. He heard a second report, and saw one of the sentinels with his rifle at his shoulder, a light cloud of blue smoke rising from the muzzle. The man in the water saw the eye of the man on the bridge gazing into his own through the sights of the rifle. He observed that it was a gray eye and remembered having read that gray eyes were keenest, and that all famous marksmen had them. Nevertheless, this one had missed.

A counter-swirl had caught Farquhar and turned him half round; he was again looking into the forest on the bank opposite the fort. The sound of a clear, high voice in a monotonous singsong now rang out behind him and came across the water with a distinctness that pierced and subdued all other sounds, even the beating of the ripples in his ears. Although no soldier, he had frequented camps enough to know the dread significance of that deliberate, drawling, aspirated chant; the lieutenant on shore was taking a part in the morning's work. How coldly and pitilessly—with what an even, calm intonation, presaging, and enforcing tranquility in the men—with what accurately measured intervals fell those cruel words:

"Attention company! . . . Shoulder arms! . . . Ready! . . . Aim! . . . Fire!"

Farquhar dived—dived as deeply as he could. The water roared in his ears like the voice of Niagara, yet he heard the dulled thunder of the volley and, rising again toward the surface, met shining bits of metal, singularly flattened, oscillating slowly downward. Some of them touched him on the face and hands, then fell away, continuing their descent. One lodged between his collar and neck; it was uncomfortably warm and he snatched it out.

As he rose to the surface, gasping for breath, he saw that he had been a long time under water; he was perceptibly farther down stream—nearer to safety. The soldiers had almost finished reloading; the metal ramrods flashed all at once in the sunshine as they were drawn from the barrels, turned in the air, and thrust into their sockets. The two sentinels fired again, independently and ineffectually.

The hunted man saw all this over his shoulder; he was now swimming vigorously with the current. His brain was as energetic as his arms and legs; he thought with the rapidity of lightning.

"The officer," he reasoned, "will not make that martinet's error a second time. It is as easy to dodge a volley as a single shot. He has probably already given the command to fire at will. God help me, I cannot dodge them all!"

An appalling plash within two yards of him was followed by a loud, rushing sound, *diminuendo,* which seemed to travel back through the air to the fort and died in an explosion which stirred the very river to its deeps! A rising sheet of water curved over him, fell down upon him, blinded him, strangled him! The cannon had taken a hand in the game. As he shook his head free from the commotion of the smitten water he heard the deflected shot humming through the air ahead, and in an instant it was cracking and smashing the branches in the forest beyond.

"They will not do that again," he thought; "the next time they will use a charge of grape. I must keep my eye upon the gun; the smoke will apprise me—the report arrives too late; it lags behind the missile. That is a good gun."

Suddenly he felt himself whirled round and round—spinning like a top. The water, the banks, the forests, the now distant bridge, fort and men—all were commingled and blurred. Objects were represented by their colors only; circular horizontal streaks of color—that was all he saw. He had been caught in a vortex and was being whirled on with a velocity of advance and gyration that made him giddy and sick. In a few moments he was flung upon the gravel at the foot of the left bank of the stream—the southern bank—and behind a projecting point which concealed him from his enemies. The sudden arrest of his motion, the abrasion of one of his hands on the gravel, restored him, and he wept with delight. He dug his fingers into the sand; threw it over himself in handfuls and audibly blessed it. It looked like diamonds, rubies, emeralds; he could think of nothing beautiful which it did not resemble. The trees upon the bank were giant garden plants; he noted a definite order in their arrangement, inhaled the fragrance of their blooms. A strange, roseate light shone through the spaces among their trunks and the wind made in their branches the music of æolian harps. He had no wish to perfect his escape—was content to remain in that enchanting spot until retaken.

A whiz and rattle of grapeshot among the branches high above his head roused him from his dream. The baffled cannoneer had fired him a random farewell. He sprang to his feet, rushed up the sloping bank, and plunged into the forest.

All that day he traveled, laying his course by the rounding sun. The forest seemed interminable; nowhere did he discover a break in it, not even a woodman's road. He had not known that he lived in so wild a region. There was something uncanny in the revelation.

By nightfall he was fatigued, footsore, famishing. The thought of his wife and children urged him on. At last he found a road which led him in what he knew to be the right direction. It was as wide and straight as a city street, yet it seemed untraveled. No fields bordered it, no dwelling anywhere. Not so much as the barking of a dog suggested human habitation. The black bodies of the trees formed a straight wall on both sides, terminating on the horizon in a point, like a diagram in a lesson in perspective. Overhead, as he looked up through this rift in the wood, shone great golden stars looking unfamiliar and grouped in strange constellations. He was sure they were arranged in some order which had a secret and malign significance. The wood on either side was full of singular noises, among which—once, twice, and again—he distinctly heard whispers in an unknown tongue.

His neck was in pain and lifting his hand to it he found it horribly swollen. He knew that it had a circle of black where the rope had bruised it. His eyes felt congested; he could no longer close them. His tongue was swollen with thirst; he relieved its fever by thrusting it forward from between his teeth into the cold air. How softly the turf had carpeted the untraveled avenue—he could no longer feel the roadway beneath his feet!

Doubtless, despite his suffering, he had fallen asleep while walking, for now he sees another scene—perhaps he has merely recovered from a delirium. He stands at the gate of his own home. All is as he left it, and all bright and beautiful in the morning sunshine. He must have traveled the entire night. As he pushes open the gate and passes up the wide white walk, he sees a flutter of female garments; his wife, looking fresh and cool and sweet, steps down from the veranda to meet him. At the bottom of the steps she stands waiting, with a smile of ineffable joy, an attitude of matchless grace and dignity. Ah, how beautiful she is! He springs forward with extended arms. As he is about to clasp her he feels a stunning blow upon the back of the neck; a blinding white light blazes all about him with a sound like the shock of a cannon—then all is darkness and silence!

Peyton Farquhar was dead; his body, with a broken neck, swung gently from side to side beneath the timbers of the Owl Creek bridge.

HENRY JAMES

My Friend Bingham

CONSCIOUS AS I AM of a deep aversion to stories of a painful nature, I have often asked myself whether, in the events here set forth, the element of pain is stronger than that of joy. An affirmative answer to this question would have stood as a veto upon the publication of my story, for it is my opinion that the literature of horrors needs no extension. Such an answer, however, I am unwilling to pronounce; while, on the other hand, I hesitate to assume the responsibility of a decided negative. I have therefore determined to leave the solution to the reader. I may add, that I am very sensible of the superficial manner in which I have handled my facts. I bore no other part in the accomplishment of these facts than that of a cordial observer; and it was impossible that, even with the best will in the world, I should fathom the emotions of the actors. Yet, as the very faintest reflection of human passions, under the pressure of fate, possesses an immortal interest, I am content to appeal to the reader's sympathy, and to assure him of my own fidelity.

Towards the close of summer, in my twenty-eighth year, I went down to the seaside to rest from a long term of work, and to enjoy, after several years of separation, a *tête-à-tête* with an intimate friend. My friend had just arrived from Europe, and we had agreed to spend my vacation together by the side of the sounding sea, and within easy reach of the city. On taking possession of our lodgings, we found that we should have no fellow-idlers, and we hailed joyously the prospect of the great marine solitudes which each of us declared that he found so abundantly peopled by the other. I hasten to impart to the reader the following facts in regard to the man whom I found so good a companion.

George Bingham had been born and bred among people for whom, as he grew to manhood, he learned to entertain a most generous contempt,—people in whom the hereditary possession of a large property—for he assured me that the facts stood in the relation of cause and effect—had extinguished all intelligent purpose and principle. I trust that I do not speak rhetorically when I describe in these terms the combined ignorance and vanity of my friend's progenitors. It was their fortune to make a splendid figure while they lived, and I feel little compunction in hinting at their poverty in certain human essentials. Bingham was no declaimer, and indeed no great talker; and it was only now and then, in an allusion to the past as the field of a wasted youth, that he expressed his profound resentment. I read this for the most part in the severe humility with which he regarded the future, and under cover of which he seemed to salute it as void at least (whatever other ills it might contain) of those domestic embarrassments which had been the bane of his first manhood. I have no doubt that much may be said, within limits, for the graces of that society against which my friend embodied so violent a reaction, and especially for its good-humor,—that home-keeping benevolence which accompanies a sense of material repletion. It is equally probable that to persons of a simple constitution these graces may wear a look of delightful and enduring mystery; but poor Bingham was no simpleton. He was a man of opinions numerous, delicate, and profound. When, with the lapse of his youth, he awoke to a presentiment of these opinions, and cast his first interrogative glance upon the world, he found that in his own little section of it he and his opinions were a piece of melancholy impertinence. Left, at twenty-three years of age, by his father's death, in possession of a handsome property, and absolute master of his actions, he had thrown himself blindly into the world. But, as he afterwards assured me, so superficial was his knowledge of the real world,—the world of labor and inquiry,—that he had found himself quite incapable of intelligent action. In this manner he had wasted a great deal of time. He had travelled much, however; and, being a keen observer of men and women, he had acquired a certain practical knowledge of human nature. Nevertheless, it was not till he was nearly thirty years old that he had begun to live for himself. "By myself," he explained, "I mean something else than this monstrous hereditary faculty for doing nothing and thinking of nothing." And he led me to believe, or I should rather say he allowed me to believe, that at this moment he had made a serious attempt to study. But upon this point he was not very explicit; for if he blushed equally for the manner in which he had slighted his opportunities, he blushed equally for the manner in which he had used them. It is my belief that he had but a limited capacity for study, and I am certain that to the end of his days there subsisted in his mind a very friendly relation between fancies and facts.

Bingham was *par excellence* a moralist, a man of sentiment. I know—he knew himself—that, in this busy Western world, this character represents no recognized avocation; but in the absence of such avocation, its exercise was nevertheless very dear to him. I protest that it was very dear to me, and that, at the end of a long morning devoted to my office-desk, I have often felt as if I had contributed less to the common cause than I have felt after moralizing—or, if you please, sentimentalizing—half an hour with my friend. He was an idler, assuredly; but his candor, his sagacity, his good taste, and, above all, a certain diffident enthusiasm which followed its objects with the exquisite trepidation of an unconfessed and despairing lover,—these things, and a hundred more, redeemed him from vulgarity. For three years before we came together, as I have intimated, my impressions of my friend had rested on his letters; and yet, from the first hour which we spent together, I felt that they had done him no wrong. We were genuine friends. I don't know that I can offer better proof of this than by saying that, as our old personal relations resumed their force, and the time-shrunken outlines of character filled themselves out, I greeted the reappearance of each familiar foible on Bingham's part quite as warmly as I did that of the less punctual virtue. Compared, indeed, with the comrade of earlier years, my actual companion was a well-seasoned man of the world; but with all his acquired humility and his disciplined *bonhomie*, he had failed to divest himself of a certain fastidiousness of mind, a certain formalism of manner, which are the token and the prerogative of one who has not been obliged to address himself to practical questions. The charm bestowed by these facts upon Bingham's conversation—a charm often vainly invoked in their absence—is explained by his honest indifference to their action, and his indisposition to turn them to account in the interest of the picturesque,—an advantage but too easy of conquest for a young man, rich, accomplished, and endowed with good looks and a good name. I may say, perhaps, that to a critical mind my friend's prime distinction would have been his very positive refusal to drape himself, after the current taste, with those brilliant stuffs which fortune had strewn at his feet.

Of course, a great deal of our talk bore upon Bingham's recent travels, adventures, and sensations. One of these last he handled very frankly, and treated me to a bit of genuine romance. He had been in love, and had been cruelly jilted, but had now grown able to view the matter with much of the impartial spirit of those French critics whose works were his favorite reading. His account of the young lady's character and motives would indeed have done credit to many a clever *feuilleton*. I was the less surprised, however, at his severely dispassionate tone, when, in retracing the process of his opinions, I discerned the traces—the ravages, I may almost say—of a solemn act of renunciation. Bingham had forsworn marriage. I made haste to assure him that I considered him quite too young for so austere a resolve.

"I can't help it," said he; "I feel a foreboding that I shall live and die alone."

"A foreboding?" said I. "What's a foreboding worth?"

"Well, then, rationally considered, my marriage is improbable."

"But it's not to be rationally considered," I objected. "It belongs to the province of sentiment."

"But you deny me sentiment. I fall back upon my foreboding."

"That's not sentiment,—it's superstition," I answered. "Your marrying will depend upon your falling in love; and your falling in love will certainly not depend upon yourself."

"Upon whom, then?"

"Upon some unknown fair one,—Miss A, B, or C."

"Well," said Bingham, submissively, "I wish she would make haste and reveal herself."

These remarks had been exchanged in the hollow of a cliff which sloped seaward, and where we had lazily stretched ourselves at length on the grass. The grass had grown very long and brown; and as we lay with our heads quite on a level with it, the view of the immediate beach and the gentle breakers was so completely obstructed by the rank, coarse herbage, that our prospect was reduced to a long, narrow band of deep blue ocean traversing its black fibres, and to the great vault of the sky. We had strolled out a couple of hours before, bearing each a borrowed shot-gun and accompanied by a friendly waterdog, somewhat languidly disposed towards the slaughter of wild ducks. We were neither of us genuine sportsmen, and it is certain that, on the whole, we meant very kindly to the ducks. It was at all events fated that on that day they should suffer but lightly at our hands. For the half-hour previous to the exchange of the remarks just cited, we had quite forgotten our real business; and, with our pieces lost in the grass beside us, and our dog, weary of inaction, wandering far beyond call, we looked like any straw-picking truants. At last Bingham rose to his feet, with the asseveration that it would never do for us to return empty-handed. "But, behold," he exclaimed, as he looked down across the breadth of the beach, "there is our friend of the cottage, with the sick little boy."

I brought myself into a sitting posture, and glanced over the cliff. Down near the edge of the water sat a young woman, tossing stones into it for the amusement of a child, who stood lustily crowing and clapping his hands. Her title to be called our friend lay in the fact, that on our way to the beach we had observed her issuing from a cottage hard by the hotel, leading by the hand a pale-faced little boy, muffled like an invalid. The hotel, as I have said, was all but deserted, and this young woman had been the first person to engage our idle observation. We had seen that, although plainly dressed, she was young, pretty, and modest; and, in the absence of heavier cares, these facts had sufficed to make her interesting. The question had arisen between us, whether she was a native of the shore, or a visitor like ourselves. Bingham inclined to the former view of the case, and I to the latter. There was, indeed, a certain lowliness in her aspect; but I had contended that it was by no means a rustic lowliness. Her dress was simple, but it was well made and well worn; and I noticed that, as she strolled along, leading her little boy, she cast upon sky and sea the lingering glance of one to whom, in their integrity, these were unfamiliar objects. She was the wife of some small tradesman, I argued, who had brought her child to the seaside by the physician's decree. But Bingham declared that it was utterly illogical to suppose her to be a mother of five years' motherhood; and that, for his part, he saw nothing in her appearance inconsistent with rural influences. The child was her nephew, the son of a married sister, and she a sentimental maiden aunt. Obviously the volume she had in her hand was Tennyson. In the absence on both sides of authentic data, of course the debate was not prolonged; and the subject of it had passed from our memories some time before we again met her on the beach. She soon became aware of our presence, however; and, with a natural sense of intrusion, we immediately resumed our walk. The last that I saw of her, as we rounded a turn in the cliff which concealed the backward prospect, was a sudden grasp of the child's arm, as if to withdraw him from the reach of a hastily advancing wave.

Half an hour's further walk led us to a point which we were not tempted to exceed. We shot between us some half a dozen birds; but as our dog, whose talents had been sadly misrepresented, proved very shy of the deep water, and succeeded in bringing no more than a couple of our victims to shore, we resolved to abstain from further destruction, and to return home quietly along the beach, upon which we had now descended.

"If we meet our young lady," said Bingham, "we can gallantly offer her our booty."

Some five minutes after he had uttered these words, a couple of great sea-gulls came flying landward over our heads, and, after a long gyration in mid-air, boldly settled themselves on the slope of the cliff at some three hundred yards in front of us, a point at which it projected almost into the waves. After a momentary halt, one of them rose again on his long pinions and soared away seaward; the other remained. He sat perched on a jutting boulder some fifteen feet high, sunning his fishy breast.

"I wonder if I could put a shot into him," said Bingham.

"Try," I answered; and, as he rapidly charged and levelled his piece, I remember idly repeating, while I looked at the great bird,

> "God save thee, ancient mariner,
> From the fiends that plague thee thus!
> Why look'st thou so? 'With my cross-bow
> I shot the albatross.'"

"He's going to rise," I added.

But Bingham had fired. The creature rose, indeed, half sluggishly, and yet with too hideous celerity. His movement drew from us a cry which was almost simultaneous with the report of Bingham's gun. I cannot express our relation to what followed it better than by saying that it exposed to our sight, beyond the space suddenly left vacant, the happy figure of the child from whom we had parted but an hour before. He stood with his little hands extended, and his face raised toward the retreating bird. Of the sickening sensation which assailed our common vision as we saw him throw back his hands to his head, and reel downwards our of sight, I can give no verbal account, nor of the rapidity with which we crossed the smooth interval of sand, and rounded the bluff.

The child's companion had scrambled up the rocky bank towards the low ledge from which he had fallen, and to which access was of course all too easy. She had sunk down upon the stones, and was wildly clasping the boy's body. I turned from this spectacle to my friend, as to an image of equal woe. Bingham, pale as death, bounded over the stones, and fell on his knees. The woman let him take the child out of her arms, and bent over, with her forehead on a rock, moaning. I have never seen helplessness so vividly embodied as in this momentary group.

"Did it strike his head?" cried Bingham. "What the devil was he doing up there?"

"I told him he'd get hurt," said the young woman, with harrowing simplicity. "To shoot straight at him!—He's killed!"

"Great heavens! Do you mean to say that I saw him?" roared Bingham. "How did I know he was there? Did you see us?"

The young woman shook her head. "Of course I didn't see you. I saw you with your guns before. Oh, he's killed!"

"He's not killed. It was mere duck shot. Don't talk such stuff.—My own poor little man!" cried George. "Charles, where *were* our eyes?"

"He wanted to catch the bird," moaned our companion. "Baby, my boy! open your eyes. Speak to your mother. For God's sake, get some help!"

She had put out her hands to take the child from Bingham, who had half angrily lifted him out of her reach. The senseless movement with which, as she disengaged him from Bingham's grasp, he sank into her arms, was clearly the senselessness of death. She burst into sobs. I went and examined the child.

"He *may* not be killed," I said, turning to Bingham; "keep your senses. It's not your fault. We *couldn't* see each other."

Bingham rose stupidly to his feet.

"She must be got home," I said.

"We must get a carriage. Will you go or stay?"

I saw that he had seen the truth. He looked about him with an expression of miserable impotence. "Poor little devil!" he said, hoarsely.

"Will you go for a carriage?" I repeated, taking his hand, "or will you stay?"

Our companion's sobs redoubled their violence.

"I'll stay," said he. "Bring some woman."

I started at a hard run. I left the beach behind me, passed the white cottage at whose garden gate two women were gossiping, and reached the hotel stable, where I had the good fortune to find a vehicle at my disposal. I drove straight back to the white cottage. One of the women had disappeared, and the other was lingering among her flowers,—a middle-aged, keen-eyed person. As I descended and hastily addressed her, I read in her rapid glance an anticipation of evil tidings.

"The young woman who stays with you—" I began.

"Yes," she said, "my second-cousin. Well?"

"She's in trouble. She wants you to come to her. Her little boy has hurt himself." I had time to see that I need fear no hysterics.

"Where did you leave her?" asked my companion.

"On the beach."

"What's the matter with the child?"

"He fell from a rock. There's no time to be lost." There was a certain antique rigidity about the woman which was at once irritating and reassuring. I was impelled both to quicken her apprehensions and to confide in her self-control. "For all I know, ma'am," said I, "the child is killed."

She gave me an angry stare. "For all you know!" she exclaimed. "Where were your wits? Were you afraid to look at him?"

"Yes, half afraid."

She glanced over the paling at my vehicle. "Am I to get into that?" she asked.

"If you will be so good."

She turned short about, and re-entered the house, where, as I stood out among the dahlias and the pinks, I heard a rapid opening and shutting of drawers. She shortly reappeared, equipped for driving; and, having locked the house door, and pocketed the key, came and faced me, where I stood ready to help her into the wagon.

"We'll stop for the doctor," she began.

"The doctor," said I, "is of no use."

A few moments of hard driving brought us to my starting-point. The tide had fallen perceptibly in my absence; and I remember receiving a strange impression of the irretrievable nature of the recent event from the sight of poor Bingham, standing down at the low-water-mark, and looking sea-ward with his hands in his pockets. The mother of his little victim still sat on the heap of stones where she had fallen, pressing her child to her breast. I helped my companion to descend, which she did with great deliberation. It is my belief that, as we drove along the beach, she derived from the expression of Bingham's figure, and from the patient aversion of his face, a suspicion of his relation to the opposite group. It was not till the elder woman had come within a few steps of her, that the younger became aware of her approach. I merely had time to catch the agonized appeal of her upward glance, and the broad compassion of the other's stooping movement, before I turned my back upon their encounter, and walked down towards my friend. The monotonous murmur of the waves had covered the sound of our wagon-wheels, and Bingham stood all unconscious of the coming of relief,—distilling I know not what divine relief from the simple beauty of sea and sky. I had laid my hand on his shoulder before he turned about. He looked towards the base of the cliff. I knew that a great effusion of feeling would occur in its natural order; but how should I help him across the interval?

"That's her cousin," I said at random. "She seems a very capable woman."

"The child is quite dead," said Bingham, for all answer. I was struck by the plainness of his statement. In the comparative freedom of my own thoughts I had failed to make allowance for the embarrassed movement of my friend's. It was not, therefore, until afterwards that I acknowledged he had thought to better purpose than I;

inasmuch as the very simplicity of his tone implied a positive acceptance (for the moment) of the dreadful fact which he uttered.

"The sooner they get home, the better," I said. It was evident that the elder of our companions had already embraced this conviction. She had lifted the child and placed him in the carriage, and she was now turning towards his mother and inviting her to ascend. Even at the distance at which I stood, the mingled firmness and tenderness of her gestures were clearly apparent. They seemed, moreover, to express a certain indifference to our movements, an independence of our further interference, which—fanciful as the assertion may look—was not untinged with irony. It was plain that, by whatever rapid process she had obtained it, she was already in possession of our story. "Thank God for strong-minded women!" I exclaimed;—and yet I could not repress a feeling that it behooved me, on behalf of my friend, to treat as an equal with the vulgar movement of antipathy which he was destined to encounter, and of which, in the irresistible sequence of events, the attitude of this good woman was an index.

We walked towards the carriage together. "I shall not come home directly," said Bingham; "but don't be alarmed about me."

I looked at my watch. "I give you two hours," I said, with all the authority of my affection.

The new-comer had placed herself on the back seat of the vehicle beside the sufferer, who on entering had again possessed herself of her child. As I went about to mount in front, Bingham came and stood by the wheel. I read his purpose in his face,—the desire to obtain from the woman he had wronged some recognition of his *human* character, some confession that she dimly distinguished him from a wild beast or a thunderbolt. One of her hands lay exposed, pressing together on her knee the lifeless little hands of her boy. Bingham removed his hat, and placed his right hand on that of the young woman. I saw that she started at his touch, and that he vehemently tightened his grasp.

"It's too soon to talk of forgiveness," said he, "for it's too soon for me to think intelligently of the wrong I have done you. God has brought us together in a very strange fashion."

The young woman raised her bowed head, and gave my friend, if not just the look he coveted, at least the most liberal glance at her command,—a look which, I fancy, helped him to face the immediate future. But these are matters too delicate to be put into words.

I spent the hours that elapsed before Bingham's return to the inn in gathering information about the occupants of the cottage. Impelled by that lively intuition of calamity which is natural to women, the housekeeper of the hotel, a person of evident kindliness and discretion, lost no time in winning my confidence. I was not unwilling that the tragic incident which had thus arrested our idleness should derive its earliest publicity from my own lips; and I was forcibly struck with the exquisite impartiality with which this homely creature bestowed her pity. Miss Horner, I learned, the mistress of the cottage, was the last representative of a most respectable family, native to the neighboring town. It had been for some years her practice to let lodgings during the summer. At the close of the present season she had invited her kinswoman, Mrs. Hicks, to spend the autumn with her. That this lady was the widow of a Baptist minister; that her husband had died some three years before; that she was very poor; that her child had been sickly, and that the care of his health had so impeded her exertions for a livelihood, that she had been intending to leave him with Miss Horner for the winter, and obtain a "situation" in town;—these facts were the salient points of the housekeeper's somewhat prolix recital.

The early autumn dusk had fallen when Bingham returned. He looked very tired. He had been walking for several hours, and, as I fancied, had grown in some degree familiar with his new responsibilities. He was very hungry, and made a vigorous attack upon his supper. I had been indisposed to eat, but the sight of his healthy appetite restored my own. I had grown weary of my thoughts, and I found something salutary in the apparent simplicity and rectitude of Bingham's state of mind.

"I find myself taking it very quietly," he said, in the course of his repast. "There is something so absolute in the nature of the calamity, that one is compelled to accept it. I don't see how I could endure to have mutilated the poor little mortal. To kill a human being is, after all, the least injury you can do him." He spoke these words deliberately, with his eyes on mine, and with an expression of perfect candor. But as he paused, and in spite of my perfect assent to their meaning, I could not help mentally reverting to the really tragic phase of the affair; and I suppose my features revealed to Bingham's scrutiny the process of my thoughts. His pale face flushed a burning crimson, his lips trembled. "Yes, my boy!" he cried; "that's where it's damnable." He buried his head in his hands, and burst into tears.

We had a long talk. At the end of it, we lit our cigars, and came out upon the deserted piazza. There was a lovely starlight, and, after a few turns in silence, Bingham left my side and strolled off towards a bend in the road, in the direction of the sea. I saw him stand motionless for a long time, and then I heard him call me. When I reached his side, I saw that he had been watching a light in the window of the white cottage. We heard the village bell in the distance striking nine.

"Charles," said Bingham, "suppose you go down there and make some offer of your services. God knows whom the poor creatures have to look to. She has had a couple of men thrust into her life. She must take the good with the bad."

I lingered a moment. "It's a difficult task," I said. "What shall I say?"

Bingham silently puffed his cigar. He stood with his arms folded, and his head thrown back, slowly measuring the starry sky. "I wish she could come our here and look at that sky," he said at last. "It's a sight for bereaved mothers. Somehow, my dear boy," he pursued, "I never felt less depressed in my life. It's none of my doing."

"It would hardly do for me to tell her that," said I.

"I don't know," said Bingham. "This isn't an occasion for the exchange of compliments. I'll tell you what you may tell her. I suppose they will have some funeral services within a day or two. Tell her that I should like very much to be present."

I set off for the cottage. Its mistress in person introduced me into the little parlor.

"Well, sir?" she said, in hard, dry accents.

"I've come," I answered, "to ask whether I can be of any assistance to Mrs. Hicks."

Miss Horner shook her head in a manner which deprived her negation of half its dignity. "What assistance is possible?" she asked.

"A man," said I, "may relieve a woman of certain cares—"

"O, men are a blessed set! You had better leave Mrs. Hicks to me."

"But will you at least tell me how she is,—if she has in any degree recovered herself?"

At this moment the door of the adjoining room was opened, and Mrs. Hicks stood on the threshold, bearing a lamp,—a graceful and pathetic figure. I now had occasion to observe that she was a woman of decided beauty. Her fair hair was drawn back into a single knot behind her head, and the lamplight deepened the pallor of her face and the darkness of her eyes. She wore a calico dressing-gown and a shawl.

"What do you wish?" she asked, in a voice clarified, if I may so express it, by long weeping.

"He wants to know whether he can be of any assistance," said the elder lady.

Mrs. Hicks glanced over her shoulder into the room she had left. "Would you like to look at the child?" she asked, in a whisper.

"Lucy!" cried Miss Horner.

I walked straight over to Mrs. Hicks, who turned and led the way to a little bed. My conductress raised her lamp aloft, and let the light fall gently on the little white-draped figure. Even the bandage about the child's head had not dispelled his short-lived prettiness. Heaven knows that to remain silent was easy enough; but Heaven knows, too, that to break the silence—and to break it as I broke it—was equally easy. "He must have been a very pretty child," I said.

"Yes, he was very pretty. He had black eyes. I don't know whether you noticed."

"No, I didn't notice," said I. "When is he to be buried?"

"The day after to-morrow. I am told that I shall be able to avoid an inquest."

"Mr. Bingham has attended to that," I said. And then I paused, revolving his petition.

But Mrs. Hicks anticipated it. "If you would like to be present at the funeral," she said, "you are welcome to come.—And so is your friend."

"Mr. Bingham bade me ask leave. There is a great deal that I should like to say to you for him," I added, "but I won't spoil it by trying. It's his own business."

The young woman looked at me with her deep, dark eyes. "I pity him from my heart," she said, pressing her hands to her breast. "I had rather have my sorrow than his."

"They are pretty much one sorrow," I answered. "I don't see that you can divide it. You are two to bear it. Bingham is a wise, good fellow," I went on. "I have shared a great many joys with him. In Heaven's name," I cried, "don't bear hard on him!"

"How can I bear hard?" she asked, opening her arms and letting them drop. The movement was so deeply expressive of weakness and loneliness, that, feeling all power to reply stifled in a rush of compassion, I silently made my exit.

On the following day, Bingham and I went up to town, and on the third day returned in time for the funeral. Besides the two ladies, there was no one present but ourselves and the village minister, who of course spoke as briefly as decency allowed. He had accompanied the ladies in a carriage to the graveyard, while Bingham and I had come on foot. As we turned away from the grave, I saw my friend approach Mrs. Hicks. They stood talking beside the freshly-turned earth, while the minister and I attended Miss Horner to the carriage. After she had seated herself, I lingered at the door, exchanging sober commonplaces with the reverend gentleman. At last Mrs. Hicks followed us, leaning on Bingham's arm.

"Margaret," she said, "Mr. Bingham and I are going to stay here awhile. Mr. Bingham will walk home with me. I'm *very* much obliged to you, Mr. Bland," she added, turning to the minister and extending her hand.

I bestowed upon my friend a glance which I felt to be half interrogative and half sympathetic. He gave me his hand, and answered the benediction by its pressure, while he answered the inquiry by his words. "If you are still disposed to go back to town this afternoon," he said, "you had better not wait for me. I may not have time to catch the boat."

I of course made no scruple of returning immediately to the city. Some ten days elapsed before I again saw Bingham; but I found my attention so deeply engrossed with work, that I scarcely measured the interval. At last, one morning, he came into my office.

"I take for granted," I said, "that you have not been all this time at B——."

"No; I've been on my travels. I came to town the day after you came. I found at my rooms a letter from a lawyer in Baltimore, proposing the sale of some of my property there, and I seized upon it as an excuse for making a journey to that city. I felt the need of movement, of action of some kind. But when I reached Baltimore, I didn't even go to see my correspondent. I pushed on to Washington, walked about for thirty-six hours, and came home."

He had placed his arm on my desk, and stood supporting his head on his hand, with a look of great physical exhaustion.

"You look very tired," said I.

"I haven't slept," said he. "I had such a talk with that woman!"

"I'm sorry that you should have felt the worse for it."

"I feel both the worse and the better. She talked about the child."

"It's well for her," said I, "that she was able to do it."

"She wasn't able, strictly speaking. She began calmly enough, but she very soon broke down."

"Did you see her again?"

"I called upon her the next day, to tell her that I was going to town, and to ask if I could be useful to her. But she seems to stand in perfect isolation. She assured me that she was in want of nothing."

"What sort of a woman does she seem to be, taking her in herself?"

"Bless your soul! I can't take her in herself!" cried Bingham, with some vehemence. "And yet, stay," he added; "she's a very pleasing woman."

"She's very pretty."

"Yes; she's very pretty. In years, she's little more than a young girl. In her ideas, she's one of 'the people.'"

"It seems to me," said I, "that the frankness of her conduct toward you is very much to her credit."

"It doesn't offend you, then?"

"Offend me? It gratifies me beyond measure."

"I think that, if you had seen her as I have seen her, it would interest you deeply. I'm at a loss to determine whether it's the result of great simplicity or great sagacity. Of course, it's absurd to suppose that, ten days ago, it could have been the result of anything but a beautiful impulse. I think that tomorrow I shall again go down to B——."

I allowed Bingham time to have made his visit and to have brought me an account of his further impressions; but as three days went by without his re-appearance, I called at his lodgings. He was still out of town. The fifth day, however, brought him again to my office.

"I've been at B—— constantly," he said, "and I've had several interviews with our friend."

"Well; how fares it?"

"It fares well. I'm forcibly struck with her good sense. In matters of mind—in matters of soul, I may say—she has the touch of an angel, or rather the touch of a woman. That's quite sufficient."

"Does she keep her composure?"

"Perfectly. You can imagine nothing simpler and less sentimental than her manner. She makes me forget myself most divinely. The child's death colors our talk; but it doesn't confine or obstruct it. You see she has her religion: she can afford to be natural."

Weary as my friend looked, and shaken by his sudden subjection to care, it yet seemed to me, as he pronounced these words, that his eye had borrowed a purer light and his voice a fresher tone. In short, where I discerned it, how I detected it, I know not; but I felt that he carried a secret. He sat poking with his walking-stick at a nail in the carpet, with his eyes dropped. I saw about his mouth the faint promise of a distant smile,—a smile which six months would bring to maturity.

"George," said I, "I have a fancy."

He looked up. "What is it?"

"You've lost your heart."

He stared a moment, with a sudden frown. "To whom?" he asked.

"To Mrs. Hicks."

With a frown, I say, but a frown that was as a smile to the effect of my rejoinder. He rose to his feet; all his color deserted his face and rushed to his eyes.

"I beg your pardon if I'm wrong," I said.

Bingham had turned again from pale to crimson. "Don't beg *my* pardon," he cried. "You may say what you please. Beg *hers!*" he added, bitterly.

I resented the charge of injustice. "I've done *her* no wrong!" I answered. "I haven't said," I went on with a certain gleeful sense that I was dealing with massive truths,—"I haven't said that she had lost her heart to you!"

"Good God, Charles!" cried Bingham, "what a horrid imagination you have!"

"I am not responsible for my imagination."

"Upon my soul, I hope *I*'m not!" cried Bingham, passionately. "I have enough without that."

"George," I said, after a moment's reflection, "if I thought I had insulted you, I would make amends. But I have said nothing to be ashamed of. I believe that I have hit the truth. Your emotion proves it. I spoke hastily; but you must admit that, having caught a glimpse of the truth, I couldn't stand indifferent to it."

"The truth! the truth! What truth?"

"Aren't you in love with Mrs. Hicks? Admit it like a man."

"Like a man! Like a brute. Haven't I done the woman wrong enough?"

"Quite enough, I hope."

"Haven't I turned her simple joys to bitterness?"

"I grant it."

"And now you want me to insult her by telling her that I love her?"

"I want you to tell her nothing. What you tell her is your own affair. Remember that, George. It's as little mine as it is the rest of the world's."

Bingham stood listening, with a contracted brow and his hand grasping his stick. He walked to the dusty office-window and halted a moment, watching the great human throng in the street. Then he turned and came towards me. Suddenly he stopped short. "God forgive me!" he cried; "I believe I do love her."

The fountains of my soul were stirred. "Combining my own hasty impressions of Mrs. Hicks with yours, George," I said, "the consummation seems to me exquisitely natural."

It was in these simple words that we celebrated the sacred fact. It seemed as if, by tacit agreement, the evolution of this fact was result enough for a single interview.

A few days after this interview, in the evening, I called at Bingham's lodgings. His servant informed me that my friend was out of town, although he was unable to indicate his whereabouts. But as I turned away from the door a hack drew up, and the object of my quest descended, equipped with a travelling-bag. I went down and greeted him under the gaslamp.

"Shall I go in with you?" I asked; "or shall I go my way?"

"You had better come in," said Bingham. "I have something to say.—I have been down to B——," he resumed, when the servant had left us alone in his sitting-room. His tone bore the least possible tinge of a confession; but of course it was not as a confessor that I listened.

"Well," said I, "how is our friend?"

"Our friend—" answered Bingham. "Will you have a cigar?"

"No, I thank you."

"Our friend— Ah, Charles, it's a long story."

"I sha'n't mind that, if it's an interesting one."

"To a certain extent it's a painful one. It's painful to come into collision with incurable vulgarity of feeling."

I was puzzled. "Has that been your fortune?" I asked.

"It has been my fortune to bring Mrs. Hicks into a great deal of trouble. The case, in three words, is this. Miss Horner has seen fit to resent, in no moderate terms, what she calls the 'extraordinary intimacy' existing between Mrs. Hicks and myself. Mrs. Hicks, as was perfectly natural, has resented her cousin's pretension to regulate her conduct. Her expression of this feeling has led to her expulsion from Miss Horner's house."

"Has she any other friend to turn to?"

"No one, except some relatives of her husband, who are very poor people, and of whom she wishes to ask no favors."

"Where has she placed herself?"

"She is in town. We came up together this afternoon. I went with her to some lodgings which she had formerly occupied, and which were fortunately vacant."

"I suppose it's not to be regretted that she has left B——. She breaks with sad associations."

"Yes; but she renews them too, on coming to town."

"How so?"

"Why, damn it," said Bingham, with a tremor in his voice, "the woman is utterly poor."

"Has she no resources whatever?"

"A hundred dollars a year, I believe,—worse than nothing."

"Has she any marketable talents or accomplishments?"

"I believe she is up to some pitiful needle-work or other. Such a woman! O horrible world!"

"Does *she* say so?" I asked.

"She? No indeed. She thinks it's all for the best. I suppose it is. But it seems but a bad best."

"I wonder," said I, after a pause, "whether I might see Mrs. Hicks. Do you think she would receive me?"

Bingham looked at me an instant keenly. "I suppose so," said he. "You can try."

"I shall go, not out of curiosity," I resumed, "but out of—"

"Out of what?"

"Well, in fine, I should like to see her again."

Bingham gave me Mrs. Hicks's address, and in the course of a few evenings I called upon her. I had abstained from bestowing a fine name upon the impulse which dictated this act; but I am nevertheless free to declare that kindliness and courtesy had a large part in it. Mrs. Hicks had taken up her residence in a plain, small house, in a decent by-street, where, upon presenting myself, I was ushered into a homely sitting-room (apparently her own), and left to await her coming. Her greeting was simple and cordial, and not untinged with a certain implication of gratitude. She had taken for granted, on my part, all possible sympathy and good-will; but as she had regarded me besides as a man of many cares, she had thought it improbable that we should meet again. It was no long time before I became conscious of that generous charm which Bingham had rigorously denominated her good-sense. Good-sense assuredly was there, but good-sense mated and prolific. Never had I seen, it seemed to me, as the moments elapsed, so exquisitely modest a use of such charming faculties,—an intelligence so sensible of its obligations and so indifferent to its privileges. It was obvious that she had been a woman of plain associations: her allusions were to homely facts, and her manner direct and unstudied; and yet, in spite of these limitations, it was equally obvious that she was a person to be neither patronized, dazzled, nor deluded. O the satisfaction which, in the course of that quiet dialogue, I took in this sweet infallibility! How it effaced her loneliness and poverty, and added dignity to her youth and beauty! It made her, potentially at least, a woman of the world. It was an anticipation of the self-possession, the wisdom, and perhaps even in some degree of the wit, which comes through the experience of society,—the result, on Mrs. Hicks's part, of I know not what hours of suffering, despondency, and self-dependence. With whatever intentions, therefore, I might have come before her, I should have found it impossible to address her as any other than an equal, and to regard her affliction as anything less than an absolute mystery. In fact, we hardly touched upon it; and it was only covertly that we alluded to Bingham's melancholy position. I will not deny that in a certain sense I regretted Mrs. Hicks's reserve. It is true that I had a very informal claim upon her confidence; but I had gone to her with a half-defined hope that this claim would be liberally interpreted. It was not even recognized; my vague intentions of counsel and assistance had lain undivined; and I departed with the impression that my social horizon had been considerably enlarged, but that my charity had by no means secured a pensioner.

Mrs. Hicks had given me permission to repeat my visit, and after the lapse of a fortnight I determined to do so. I had seen Bingham several times in the interval. He was of course much interested in my impressions of our friend; and I fancied that my admiration gave him even more pleasure than he allowed himself to express. On entering Mrs. Hicks's parlor a second time, I found him in person standing before the fireplace, and talking apparently with some vehemence to Mrs. Hicks, who sat listening on the sofa. Bingham turned impatiently to the door as I crossed the threshold, and Mrs. Hicks rose to welcome me with all due composure. I was nevertheless sensible that my entrance was ill-timed; yet a retreat was impossible. Bingham kept his place on the hearth-rug, and mechanically gave me his hand,—standing irresolute, as I thought, between annoyance and elation. The fact that I had interrupted a somewhat passionate interview was somehow so obvious, that, at the prompting of a very delicate feeling, Mrs. Hicks hastened to anticipate my apologies.

"Mr. Bingham was giving me a lecture," she said; and there was perhaps in her accent a faint suspicion of bitterness. "He will doubtless be glad of another auditor."

"No," said Bingham, "Charles is a better talker than listener. You shall have two lectures instead of one." He uttered this sally without even an attempt to smile.

"What is your subject?" said I. "Until I know that, I shall promise neither to talk nor to listen."

Bingham laid his hand on my arm. "He represents the world," he said, addressing our hostess. "You're afraid of the world. There, make your appeal."

Mrs. Hicks stood silent a moment, with a contracted brow and a look of pain on her face. Then she turned to me with a half-smile. "I don't believe you represent the world," she said; "you are too good."

"She flatters you," said Bingham. "You wish to corrupt him, Mrs. Hicks."

Mrs. Hicks glanced for an instant from my friend to myself. There burned in her eyes a far-searching light, which consecrated the faint irony of the smile which played about her lips. "O you men!" she said,—"you are so wise, so deep!" It was on Bingham that her eyes rested last; but after a pause, extending her hand, she transferred them to me. "Mr. Bingham," she pursued, "seems to wish you to be admitted to our counsels. There is every reason why his friends should be my friends. You will be interested to know that he has asked me to be his wife."

"Have you given him an answer?" I asked.

"He was pressing me for an answer when you came in. He conceives me to have a great fear of the judgments of men, and he was saying very hard things about them. But they have very little, after all, to do with the matter. The world may heed it, that Mr. Bingham should marry Mrs. Hicks, but it will care very little whether or no Mrs. Hicks marries Mr. Bingham. You are the world, for me," she cried with beautiful inconsequence, turning to her suitor; "I know no other." She put out her hands, and he took them.

I am at a loss to express the condensed force of these rapid words,—the amount of passion, of reflection, of experience, which they seemed to embody. They were the simple utterance of a solemn and intelligent choice; and, as such, the whole phalanx of the Best Society assembled in judgment could not have done less than salute them. What honest George Bingham said, what I said, is of little account. The proper conclusion of my story lies in the highly dramatic fact that out of the depths of her bereavement—out of her loneliness and her pity—this richly gifted woman had emerged, responsive to the passion of him who had wronged her all but as deeply as he loved her. The reader will decide, I think, that this catastrophe offers as little occasion for smiles as for tears. My narrative is a piece of genuine prose.

It was not until six months had elapsed that Bingham's marriage took place. It has been a truly happy one. Mrs. Bingham is now, in the fulness of her bloom, with a single exception, the most charming woman I know. I have often assured her—once too often, possibly—that, thanks to that invaluable good-sense of hers, she is also the happiest. She has made a devoted wife; but—and in occasional moments of insight it has seemed to me that this portion of her fate is a delicate tribute to a fantastic principle of equity—she has never again become a mother. In saying that she has made a devoted wife, it may seem that I have written Bingham's own later history. Yet as the friend of his younger days, the comrade of his *belle jeunesse*, the partaker of his dreams, I would fain give him a sentence apart. What shall it be? He is a truly incorruptible soul; he is a confirmed philosopher; he has grown quite stout.

HENRY JAMES

The Beast in the Jungle

I

WHAT DETERMINED THE SPEECH that startled him in the course of their encounter scarcely matters, being probably but some words spoken by himself quite without intention—spoken as they lingered and slowly moved together after their renewal of acquaintance. He had been conveyed by friends an hour or two before to the house at which she was staying; the party of visitors at the other house, of whom he was one, and thanks to whom it was his theory, as always, that he was lost in the crowd, had been invited over to luncheon. There had been after luncheon much dispersal, all in the interest of the original motive, a view of Weatherend itself and the fine things, intrinsic features, pictures, heirlooms, treasures of all the arts, that made the place almost famous; and the great rooms were so numerous that guests could wander at their will, hang back from the principal group and in cases where they took such matters with the last seriousness give themselves up to mysterious appreciations and measurements. There were persons to be observed, singly or in couples, bending toward objects in out-of-the-way corners with their hands on their knees and their heads nodding quite as with the emphasis of an excited sense of smell. When they were two they either mingled their sounds of ecstasy or melted into silences of even deeper import, so that there were aspects of the occasion that gave it for Marcher much the air of the "look round," previous to a sale highly advertised, that excites or quenches, as may be, the dream of acquisition. The dream of acquisition at Weatherend would have had to be wild indeed, and John Marcher found himself, among such suggestions, disconcerted almost equally by the presence of those who knew too much and by that of those who knew nothing. The great rooms caused so much poetry and history to press upon him that he needed some straying apart to feel in a proper relation with them, though this impulse was not, as happened, like the gloating of some of his companions, to be compared to the movements of a dog sniffing a cupboard. It had an issue promptly enough in a direction that was not to have been calculated.

It led, briefly, in the course of the October afternoon, to his closer meeting with May Bartram, whose face, a reminder, yet not quite a remembrance, as they sat much separated at a very long table, had begun merely by troubling him rather pleasantly. It affected him as the sequel of something of which he had lost the beginning. He knew it, and for the time quite welcomed it, as a continuation, but didn't know what it continued, which was an interest or an amusement the greater as he was also somehow aware—yet without a direct sign from her—that the young woman herself hadn't lost the thread. She hadn't lost it, but she wouldn't give it back to him, he saw, without some putting forth of his hand for it; and he not only saw that, but saw several things more, things odd enough in the light of the fact that at the moment some accident of grouping brought them face to face he was still merely fumbling with the idea that any contact between them in the past would have had no importance. If it had had no importance he scarcely knew why his actual impression of her should so seem to have so much; the answer to which, however, was that in such a life as they all appeared to be leading for the moment one could but take things as they came. He was satisfied, without in the least being able to say why, that this young lady might roughly have ranked in the house as a poor relation; satisfied also that she was not there on a brief visit, but was more or less a part of the establishment—almost a working, a remunerated part. Didn't she enjoy at periods a protection that she paid for by helping, among other services, to show the place and explain it, deal with the tiresome people, answer questions about the dates of the building, the styles of the furniture, the authorship of the pictures, the favourite haunts of the ghost? It wasn't that she looked as if you could have given her shillings—it was impossible to look less so. Yet when she finally drifted toward him, distinctly handsome, though ever so much older—older than when he had seen her before—it might have been as an effect of her guessing that he had, within the couple of hours, devoted more imagination to her than to all the others put together, and had thereby penetrated to a kind of truth that the others were too stupid for. She *was* there on harder terms than any one; she was there as a consequence of things suffered, one way and another, in the interval of years; and she remembered him very much as she was remembered—only a good deal better.

By the time they at last thus came to speech they were alone in one of the rooms—remarkable for a fine portrait over the chimney-place—out of which their friends had passed, and the charm of it was that even before they had spoken they had practically arranged with each other to stay behind for talk. The charm, happily, was in other things too—partly in there being scarce a spot at Weatherend without something to stay behind for. It was in the way the autumn day looked into the high windows as it waned; the way the red light, breaking at the close from under a low sombre sky, reached out in a long shaft and played over old wainscots, old tapestry, old gold, old colour. It was most of all perhaps in the way she came to him as if, since she had been turned on to deal with the simpler sort, he might, should he choose to keep the whole thing down, just take her mild attention for a part of her general business. As soon as he heard her voice, however, the gap was filled up and the missing link supplied; the slight irony he divined in her attitude lost its advantage. He almost jumped at it to get there before her. "I met you years and years ago in Rome. I remember all about it." She confessed to disappointment—she had been so sure he didn't; and to prove how well he did he began to pour forth the particular recollections that popped up as he called for them. Her face and her voice, all at his service now, worked the miracle—the impression operating like the torch of a lamplighter who touches into flame, one by one, a long row of gas-jets. Marcher flattered himself the illumination was brilliant, yet he was really still more pleased on her showing him, with amusement, that in his haste to make everything right he had got most things rather wrong. It hadn't been at Rome—it had been at Naples; and it hadn't been eight years before—it had been more nearly ten. She hadn't been, either, with her uncle and aunt, but with her mother and her brother; in addition to which it was not with the Pembles *he* had been, but with the Boyers, coming down in their company from Rome—a point on which she insisted, a little to his confusion, and as to which she had her evidence in hand. The Boyers she had known, but didn't know the Pembles, though she had heard of them, and it was the people he was with who had made them acquainted. The incident of the thunderstorm that had raged round them with such violence as to drive them for refuge into an excavation—this incident had not occurred at the Palace of the Caesars, but at Pompeii, on an occasion when they had been present there at an important find.

He accepted her amendments, he enjoyed her corrections, though the moral of them was, she pointed out, that he *really* didn't remember the least thing about her; and he only felt it as a drawback that when all was made strictly historic there didn't appear much of anything left. They lingered together still, she neglecting her office—for from the moment he was so clever she had no proper right to him—and both neglecting the house, just waiting as to see if a memory or two more wouldn't again breathe on them. It hadn't taken them many minutes, after all, to put down on the table, like the cards of a pack, those that constituted their respective hands; only what came out was that the pack was unfortunately not perfect—that the past, invoked, invited, encouraged, could give them, naturally, no more than it had. It had made them anciently meet—her at twenty, him at twenty-five; but nothing was so strange, they seemed to say to each other, as that, while so occupied, it hadn't done a little more for them. They looked at each other as with the feeling of an occasion missed; the present would have been so much better if the other, in the far distance, in the foreign land, hadn't been so stupidly meagre. There weren't apparently, all counted, more than a dozen little old things that had succeeded in coming to pass between them; trivialities of youth, simplicities of freshness, stupidities of ignorance, small possible germs, but too deeply buried—too deeply (didn't it seem?) to sprout after so many years. Marcher could only feel he ought to have rendered her some service—saved her from a capsized boat in the Bay or at least recovered her dressing-bag, filched from her cab in the streets of Naples by a lazzarone with a stiletto. Or it would have been nice if he could have been taken with fever all alone at his hotel, and she could have come to look after him, to write to his people, to drive him out in convalescence. *Then* they would be in possession of the something or other that their actual show seemed to lack. It yet somehow presented itself, this show, as too good to be spoiled; so that they were reduced for a few minutes more to wondering a little helplessly why—since they seemed to know a certain number of the same people—their reunion had been so long averted. They didn't use that name for it, but their delay from minute to minute to join the others was a kind of confession that they didn't quite want it to be a failure. Their attempted supposition of reasons for their not having met but showed how little they knew of each other. There came in fact a moment when Marcher felt a positive pang. It was vain to pretend she was an old friend, for all the communities were wanting, in spite of which it was as an old friend that he saw she would have suited him. He had new ones enough—was surrounded with them for instance on the stage of the other house; as a new one he probably wouldn't have so much as noticed her. He would have liked to invent something, get her to make-believe with him that some passage of a romantic or critical kind *had* originally occurred. He was really almost reaching out in imagination—as against time—for something that would do, and saying to himself that if it didn't come this sketch of a fresh start would show for quite awkwardly bungled. They would separate, and now for no second or no third chance. They would have tried and not succeeded. Then it was, just at the turn, as he afterwards made it out to himself, that, everything else failing, she herself decided to take up the case and, as it were, save the situation. He felt as soon as she spoke that she had been consciously keeping back what she said and hoping to get on without it; a scruple in her that immensely touched him when, by the end of three or four minutes more, he was able to measure it. What she brought out, at any rate, quite cleared the air and supplied the link—the link it was so odd he should frivolously have managed to lose.

"You know you told me something I've never forgotten and that again and again has made me think of you since; it was that tremendously hot day when we went to Sorrento, across the bay, for the breeze. What I allude to was what you said to me, on the way back, as we sat under the awning of the boat enjoying the cool. Have you forgotten?"

He had forgotten and was even more surprised than ashamed. But the great thing was that he saw in this no vulgar reminder of any "sweet" speech. The vanity of women had long memories, but she was making no claim on him of a compliment or a mistake. With another woman, a totally different one, he might have feared the recall possibly even of some imbecile "offer." So, in having to say that he had indeed forgotten, he was conscious rather of a loss than of a gain; he already saw an interest in the matter of her mention. "I try to think—but I give it up. Yet I remember the Sorrento day."

"I'm not very sure you do," May Bartram after a moment said; "and I'm not very sure I ought to want you to. It's dreadful to bring a person back at any time to what he was ten years before. If you've lived away from it," she smiled, "so much the better."

"Ah if *you* haven't why should I?" he asked.

"Lived away, you mean, from what I myself was?"

"From what *I* was. I was of course an ass," Marcher went on; "but I would rather know from you just the sort of ass I was than—from the moment you have something in your mind—not know anything."

Still, however, she hesitated. "But if you've completely ceased to be that sort—?"

"Why I can then all the more bear to know. Besides, perhaps I haven't."

"Perhaps. Yet if you haven't," she added, "I should suppose you'd remember. Not indeed that *I* in the least connect with my impression the invidious name you use. If I had only thought you foolish," she explained, "the thing I speak of wouldn't so have remained with me. It was about yourself." She waited as if it might come to him; but as, only meeting her eyes in wonder, he gave no sign, she burnt her ships. "Has it ever happened?"

Then it was that, while he continued to stare, a light broke for him and the blood slowly came to his face, which began to burn with recognition. "Do you mean I told you—?" But he faltered, lest what came to him shouldn't be right, lest he should only give himself away.

"It was something about yourself that it was natural one shouldn't forget—that is if one remembered you at all. That's why I ask you," she smiled, "if the thing you then spoke of has ever come to pass?"

Oh then he saw, but he was lost in wonder and found himself

embarrassed. This, he also saw, made her sorry for him, as if her allusion had been a mistake. It took him but a moment, however, to feel it hadn't been, much as it had been a surprise. After the first little shock of it her knowledge on the contrary began, even if rather strangely, to taste sweet to him. She was the only other person in the world then who would have it, and she had had it all these years, while the fact of his having so breathed his secret had unaccountably faded from him. No wonder they couldn't have met as if nothing had happened. "I judge," he finally said, "that I know what you mean. Only I had strangely enough lost any sense of having taken you so far into my confidence."

"Is it because you've taken so many others as well?"

"I've taken nobody. Not a creature since then."

"So that I'm the only person who knows?"

"The only person in the world."

"Well," she quickly replied, "I myself have never spoken. I've never, never repeated of you what you told me." She looked at him so that he perfectly believed her. Their eyes met over it in such a way that he was without a doubt. "And I never will."

She spoke with an earnestness that, as if almost excessive, put him at ease about her possible derision. Somehow the whole question was a new luxury to him—that is from the moment she was in possession. If she didn't take the sarcastic view she clearly took the sympathetic, and that was what he had had, in all the long time, from no one whomsoever. What he felt was that he couldn't at present have begun to tell her, and yet could profit perhaps exquisitely by the accident of having done so of old. "Please don't then. We're just right as it is."

"Oh I am," she laughed, "if you are!" To which she added: "Then you do still feel in the same way?"

It was impossible he shouldn't take to himself that she was really interested, though it all kept coming as perfect surprise. He had thought of himself so long as abominably alone, and lo he wasn't alone a bit. He hadn't been, it appeared, for an hour—since those moments on the Sorrento boat. It was *she* who had been, he seemed to see as he looked at her—she who had been made so by the graceless fact of his lapse of fidelity. To tell her what he had told her—what had it been but to ask something of her? something that she had given, in her charity, without his having, by a remembrance, by a return of the spirit, failing another encounter, so much as thanked her. What he had asked of her had been simply at first not to laugh at him. She had beautifully not done so for ten years, and she was not doing so now. So he had endless gratitude to make up. Only for that he must see just how he had figured to her. "What, exactly, was the account I gave—?"

"Of the way you did feel? Well, it was very simple. You said you had had from your earliest time, as the deepest thing within you, the sense of being kept for something rare and strange, possibly prodigious and terrible, that was sooner or later to happen to you, that you had in your bones the foreboding and the conviction of, and that would perhaps overwhelm you."

"Do you call that very simple?" John Marcher asked.

She thought a moment. "It was perhaps because I seemed, as you spoke, to understand it."

"You do understand it?" he eagerly asked.

Again she kept her kind eyes on him. "You still have the belief?"

"Oh!" he exclaimed helplessly. There was too much to say.

"Whatever it's to be," she clearly made out, "it hasn't yet come."

He shook his head in complete surrender now. "It hasn't yet come. Only, you know, it isn't anything I'm to *do,* to achieve in the world, to be distinguished or admired for. I'm not such an ass as *that.* It would be much better, no doubt, if I were."

"It's to be something you're merely to suffer?"

"Well, say to wait for—to have to meet, to face, to see suddenly break out in my life; possibly destroying all further consciousness, possibly annihilating me; possibly, on the other hand, only altering everything, striking at the root of all my world and leaving me to the consequences, however they shape themselves."

She took this in, but the light in her eyes continued for him not to be that of mockery. "Isn't what you describe perhaps but the expectation—or at any rate the sense of danger, familiar to so many people—of falling in love?"

John Marcher wondered. "Did you ask me that before?"

"No—I wasn't so free-and-easy then. But it's what strikes me now."

"Of course," he said after a moment, "it strikes you. Of course it strikes *me.* Of course what's in store for me may be no more than that. The only thing is," he went on, "that I think if it had been that I should by this time know."

"Do you mean because you've *been* in love?" And then as he but looked at her in silence: "You've been in love, and it hasn't meant such a cataclysm, hasn't proved the great affair?"

"Here I am, you see. It hasn't been overwhelming."

"Then it hasn't been love," said May Bartram.

"Well, I at least thought it was. I took it for that—I've taken it till now. It was agreeable, it was delightful, it was miserable," he explained. "But it wasn't strange. It wasn't what *my* affair's to be."

"You want something all to yourself—something that nobody else knows or *has* known?"

"It isn't a question of what I 'want'—God knows I don't want anything. It's only a question of the apprehension that haunts me—that I live with day by day."

He said this so lucidly and consistently that he could see it further impose itself. If she hadn't been interested before she'd have been interested now. "Is it a sense of coming violence?"

Evidently now too again he liked to talk of it. "I don't think of it as—when it does come—necessarily violent. I only think of it as natural and as of course above all unmistakeable. I think of it simply as *the* thing. *The* thing will of itself appear natural."

"Then how will it appear strange?"

Marcher bethought himself. "It won't—to *me.*"

"To whom then?"

"Well," he replied, smiling at last, "say to you."

"Oh then I'm to be present?"

"Why you *are* present—since you know."

"I see." She turned it over. "But I mean at the catastrophe."

At this, for a minute, their lightness gave way to their gravity; it was as if the long look they exchanged held them together. "It will only depend on yourself—if you'll watch with me."

"Are you afraid?" she asked.

"Don't leave me *now,*" he went on.

"Are you afraid?" she repeated.

"Do you think me simply out of my mind?" he pursued instead of answering. "Do I merely strike you as a harmless lunatic?"

"No," said May Bartram. "I understand you. I believe you."

"You mean you feel how my obsession—poor old thing!—may correspond to some possible reality?"

"To some possible reality."

"Then you *will* watch with me?"

She hesitated, then for the third time put her question. "Are you afraid?"

"Did I tell you I was—at Naples?"

"No, you said nothing about it."

"Then I don't know. And I should *like* to know," said John Marcher. "You'll tell me yourself whether you think so. If you'll watch with me you'll see."

"Very good then." They had been moving by this time across the room, and at the door, before passing out, they paused as for the full wind-up of their understanding. "I'll watch with you," said May Bartram.

II

The fact that she "knew"—knew and yet neither chaffed him nor betrayed him—had in a short time begun to constitute between them a goodly bond, which became more marked when, within the year that followed their afternoon at Weatherend, the opportunities for meeting multiplied. The event that thus promoted these occasions was the death of the ancient lady her great-aunt, under whose wing, since losing her mother, she had to such an extent found shelter, and who, though but the widowed mother of the new successor to the property, had succeeded—thanks to a high tone and a high temper—in not forfeiting the supreme position at the great house. The deposition of this personage arrived but with her death, which, followed by many changes, made in particular a difference for the young woman in whom Marcher's expert attention had recognised from the first a dependent with a pride that might ache though it didn't bristle. Nothing for a long time had made him easier than the thought that the aching must have been much soothed by Miss Bartram's now finding herself able to set up a small home in London. She had acquired property, to an amount that made that luxury just possible, under her aunt's extremely complicated will, and when the whole matter began to be straightened out, which indeed took time, she let him know that the happy issue was at last in view. He had seen her again before that day, both because she had more than once accompanied the ancient lady to town and because he had paid another visit to the friends who so conveniently made of Weatherend one of the charms of their own hospitality. These friends had taken him back there; he had achieved there again with Miss Bartram some quiet detachment; and he had in London succeeded in persuading her to more than one brief absence from her aunt. They went together, on these latter occasions, to the National Gallery and the South Kensington Museum, where, among vivid reminders, they talked of Italy at large—not now attempting to recover, as at first, the taste of their youth and their ignorance. That recovery, the first day at Weatherend, had served its purpose well, had given them quite enough; so that they were, to Marcher's sense, no longer hovering about the headwaters of their stream, but had felt their boat pushed sharply off and down the current.

They were literally afloat together; for our gentleman this was marked, quite as marked as that the fortunate cause of it was just the buried treasure of her knowledge. He had with his own hands dug up this little hoard, brought to light—that is to within reach of the dim day constituted by their discretions and privacies—the object of value the hiding-place of which he had, after putting it into the ground himself, so strangely, so long forgotten. The rare luck of having again just stumbled on the spot made him indifferent to any other question; he would doubtless have devoted more time to the odd accident of his lapse of memory if he hadn't been moved to devote so much to the sweetness, the comfort, as he felt, for the future, that this accident itself had helped to keep fresh. It had never entered into his plan that any one should "know," and mainly for the reason that it wasn't in him to tell any one. That would have been impossible, for nothing but the amusement of a cold world would have waited on it. Since, however, a mysterious fate had opened his mouth betimes, in spite of him, he would count that a compensation and profit by it to the utmost. That the right person *should* know tempered the asperity of his secret more even than his shyness had permitted him to imagine; and May Bartram was clearly right, because—well, because there she was. Her knowledge simply settled it; he would have been sure enough by this time had she been wrong. There was that in his situation, no doubt, that disposed him too much to see her as a mere confidant, taking all her light for him from the fact—the fact only—of her interest in his predicament; from her mercy, sympathy, seriousness, her consent not to regard him as the funniest of the funny. Aware, in fine, that her price for him was just in her giving him this constant sense of his being admirably spared, he was careful to remember that she had also a life of her own, with things that might happen to *her,* things that in friendship one should likewise take account of. Something fairly remarkable came to pass with him, for that matter, in this connexion—something represented by a certain passage of his consciousness, in the suddenest way, from one extreme to the other.

He had thought himself, so long as nobody knew, the most disinterested person in the world, carrying his concentrated burden, his perpetual suspense, ever so quietly, holding his tongue about it, giving others no glimpse of it nor of its effect upon his life, asking of them no allowance and only making on his side all those that were asked. He hadn't disturbed people with the queerness of their having to know a haunted man, though he had had moments of rather special temptation on hearing them say they were forsooth "unsettled." If they were as unsettled as he was—he who had never been settled for an hour in his life—they would know what it meant. Yet it wasn't, all the same, for him to make them, and he listened to them civilly enough. This was why he had such good—though possibly such rather colourless—manners; this was why, above all, he could regard himself, in a greedy world, as decently—as in fact perhaps even a little sublimely—unselfish. Our point is accordingly that he valued this character quite sufficiently to measure his present danger of letting it lapse, against which he promised himself to be much on his guard. He was quite ready, none the less, to be selfish just a little, since surely no more charming occasion for it had come to him. "Just a little," in a word, was just as much as Miss Bartram, taking one day with another, would let him. He never would be in the least coercive, and would keep well before him the lines on which consideration for her—the very highest—ought to proceed. He would thoroughly establish the heads under which her affairs, her requirements, her peculiarities—he went so far as to give them the latitude of that name—would come into their intercourse. All this naturally was a sign of how much he took the intercourse itself for granted. There was nothing more to be done about *that.* It simply existed; had sprung into being with her first penetrating question to him in the autumn light there at Weatherend. The real form it should have taken on the basis that stood out large was the form of their marrying. But the devil in this was that the very basis itself put marrying out of the question. His conviction, his apprehension, his obsession, in short, wasn't a privilege he could invite a woman to share; and that consequence of it was precisely what was the matter with him. Something or other lay in wait for him, amid the twists and the turns of the months and the years, like a crouching beast in the jungle. It signified little whether the crouching beast were destined to slay him or to be slain. The definite point was the inevitable spring of the creature; and the definite lesson from that was that a man of feeling didn't cause himself to be accompanied by a lady on a tiger-hunt. Such was the image under which he had ended by figuring his life.

They had at first, none the less, in the scattered hours spent together, made no allusion to that view of it; which was a sign he was handsomely alert to give that he didn't expect, that he in fact didn't care, always to be talking about it. Such a feature in one's outlook was really like a hump on one's back. The difference it made every minute of the day existed quite independently of discussion. One discussed of course *like* a hunchback, for there was always, if nothing else, the hunchback face. That remained, and she was watching him; but people watched best, as a general thing, in silence, so that such would be predominantly the manner of their vigil. Yet he didn't want, at the same time, to be tense and solemn; tense and solemn was what he imagined he too much showed for with other people. The thing to be, with the one person who knew, was easy and natural—to make the reference rather than be seeming to avoid it, to avoid it rather than be seeming to make it, and to keep it, in any case, familiar, facetious even, rather than pedantic and portentous. Some such consideration as the latter was doubtless in his mind for instance when he wrote pleasantly to Miss Bartram that perhaps the great thing he had so long felt as in the lap of the gods was no more than this circumstance, which touched him so nearly, of her acquiring a house in London. It was the first allusion they had yet again made, needing any other hitherto so little; but when she replied, after having given him the news, that she was by no means satisfied with such a trifle as the climax to so special a suspense, she almost set him wondering if she hadn't even a larger conception of singularity for him than he had for himself. He was at all events destined to become aware little by little, as time went by, that she was all the while looking at his life, judging it, measuring it, in the light of the thing she knew, which grew to be at last, with the consecration of the years, never mentioned between them save as "the real truth" about him. That had always been his own form of reference to it, but she adopted the form so quietly that, looking back at the end of a period, he knew there was no moment at which it was traceable that she had, as he might say, got inside his idea, or exchanged the attitude of beautifully indulging for that of still more beautifully believing him.

It was always open to him to accuse her of seeing him but as the most harmless of maniacs, and this, in the long run—since it covered so much ground—was his easiest description of their friendship. He had a screw loose for her, but she liked him in spite of it and was practically, against the rest of the world, his kind wise keeper, unremunerated but fairly amused and, in the absence of other near ties, not disreputably occupied. The rest of the world of course thought him queer, but she, she only, knew how, and above all why, queer; which was precisely what enabled her to dispose the concealing veil in the right folds. She took his gaiety from him—since it had to pass with them for gaiety—as she took everything else; but she certainly so far justified by her unerring touch his finer sense of the degree to which he had ended by convincing her. *She* at least never spoke of the secret of his life except as "the real truth about you," and she had in fact a wonderful way of making it seem, as such, the secret of her own life too. That was in fine how he so constantly felt her as allowing for him; he couldn't on the whole call it anything else. He allowed for himself, but she, exactly, allowed still more; partly because, better placed for a sight of the matter, she traced his unhappy perversion through reaches of its course into which he could scarce follow it. He knew how he felt, but, besides knowing that, she knew how he *looked* as well; he knew each of the things of importance he was insidiously kept from doing, but she could add up the amount they made, understand how much, with a lighter weight on his spirit, he might have done, and thereby establish how, clever as he was, he fell short. Above all she was in the secret of the difference between the forms he went through—those of his little office under Government, those of caring for his modest patrimony, for his library, for his garden in the country, for the people in London whose invitations he accepted and repaid—and the detachment that reigned beneath them and that made of all behaviour, all that could in the least be called behaviour, a long act of dissimulation. What it had come to was that he wore a mask painted with the social simper, out of the eye-holes of which there looked eyes of an expression not in the least matching the other features. This the stupid world, even after years, had never more than half-discovered. It was only May Bartram who had, and she achieved, by an art indescribable, the feat of at once—or perhaps it was only alternately—meeting the eyes from in front and mingling her own vision, as from over his shoulder, with their peep through the apertures.

So while they grew older together she did watch with him, and so she let this association give shape and colour to her own existence. Beneath *her* forms as well detachment had learned to sit, and behaviour had become for her, in the social sense, a false account of herself. There was but one account of her that would have been true all the while and that she could give straight to nobody, least of all to John Marcher. Her whole attitude was a virtual statement, but the perception of that only seemed called to take its place for him as one of the many things necessarily crowded out of his consciousness. If she had moreover, like himself, to make sacrifices to their real truth, it was to be granted that her compensation might have affected her as more prompt and more natural. They had long periods, in this London time, during which, when they were together, a stranger might have listened to them without in the least pricking up his ears; on the other hand the real truth was equally liable at any moment to rise to the surface, and the auditor would then have wondered indeed what they were talking about. They had from an early hour made up their mind that society was, luckily, unintelligent, and the margin allowed them by this had fairly become one of their commonplaces. Yet there were still moments when the situation turned almost fresh—usually under the effect of some expression drawn from herself. Her expressions doubtless repeated themselves, but her intervals were generous. "What saves us, you know, is that we answer so completely to so usual an appearance: that of the man and woman whose friendship has become such a daily habit—or almost—as to be at last indispensable." That for instance was a remark she had frequently enough had occasion to make, though she had given it at different times different developments. What we are especially concerned with is the turn it happened to take from her one afternoon when he had come to see her in honour of her birthday. This anniversary had fallen on a Sunday, at a season of thick fog and general outward gloom; but he had brought her his customary offering, having known her now long enough to have established a hundred small traditions. It was one of his proofs to himself, the present he made her on her birthday, that he hadn't sunk into real selfishness. It was mostly nothing more than a small trinket, but it was always fine of its kind, and he was regularly careful to pay for it more than he thought he could afford. "Our habit saves you at least, don't you see? because it makes you, after all, for the vulgar, indistinguishable from other men. What's the most inveterate mark of men in general? Why the capacity to spend endless time with dull women—to spend it I won't say without being bored, but without minding that they are, without being driven off at a tangent by it; which comes to the same thing. I'm your dull woman, a part of the daily bread for which you pray at church. That covers your tracks more than anything."

"And what covers yours?" asked Marcher, whom his dull woman could mostly to this extent amuse. "I see of course what you mean by your saving me, in this way and that, so far as other people are concerned—I've seen it all along. Only what is it that saves *you?* I often think, you know, of that."

She looked as if she sometimes thought of that too, but rather in a different way. "Where other people, you mean, are concerned?"

"Well, you're really so in with me, you know—as a sort of result of my being so in with yourself. I mean of my having such an immense regard for you, being so tremendously mindful of all you've done for me. I sometimes ask myself if it's quite fair. Fair I mean to have so involved and—since one may say it—interested you. I almost feel as if you hadn't really had time to do anything else."

"Anything else but be interested?" she asked. "Ah what else does one ever want to be? If I've been 'watching' with you, as we long ago agreed I was to do, watching's always in itself an absorption."

"Oh certainly," John Marcher said, "if you hadn't had your curiosity—! Only doesn't it sometimes come to you as time goes on that your curiosity isn't being particularly repaid?"

May Bartram had a pause. "Do you ask that, by any chance, because you feel at all that yours isn't? I mean because you have to wait so long."

Oh he understood what she meant! "For the thing to happen that never does happen? For the beast to jump out? No, I'm just where I was about it. It isn't a matter as to which I can *choose*, I can decide for a change. It isn't one as to which there *can* be a change. It's in the lap of the gods. One's in the hands of one's law—there one is. As to the form the law will take, the way it will operate, that's its own affair."

"Yes," Miss Bartram replied; "of course one's fate's coming, of course it *has* come in its own form and its own way, all the while. Only, you know, the form and the way in your case were to have been—well, something so exceptional and, as one may say, so particularly *your* own."

Something in this made him look at her with suspicion. "You say 'were to *have* been,' as if in your heart you had begun to doubt."

"Oh!" she vaguely protested.

"As if you believe," he went on, "that nothing will now take place."

She shook her head slowly but rather inscrutably. "You're far from my thought."

He continued to look at her. "What then is the matter with you?"

"Well," she said after another wait, "the matter with me is simply that I'm more sure than ever my curiosity, as you call it, will be but too well repaid."

They were frankly grave now; he had got up from his seat, had turned once more about the little drawing-room to which, year after year, he brought his inevitable topic; in which he had, as he might have said, tasted their intimate community with every sauce, where every object was as familiar to him as the things of his own house and the very carpets were worn with his fitful walk very much as the desks in old counting-houses are worn by the elbows of generations of clerks. The generations of his nervous moods had been at work there, and the place was the written history of his whole middle life. Under the impression of what his friend had just said he knew himself, for some reason, more aware of these things; which made him, after a moment, stop again before her. "Is it possibly that you've grown afraid?"

"Afraid?" He thought, as she repeated the word, that his question had made her, a little, change colour; so that, lest he should have touched on a truth, he explained very kindly: "You remember that that was what you asked *me* long ago—that first day at Weatherend."

"Oh yes, and you told me you didn't know—that I was to see for myself. We've said little about it since, even in so long a time."

"Precisely," Marcher interposed— "quite as if it were too delicate a matter for us to make free with. Quite as if we might find, on pressure, that I *am* afraid. For then," he said, "we shouldn't, should we? quite know what to do."

She had for the time no answer to this question. "There have been days when I thought you were. Only, of course," she added, "there have been days when we have thought almost anything."

"Everything. Oh!" Marcher softly groaned as with a gasp, half-spent, at the face, more uncovered just then than it had been for a long while, of the imagination always with them. It had always had its incalculable moments of glaring out, quite as with the very eyes of the very Beast, and, used as he was to them, they could still draw from him the tribute of a sigh that rose from the depths of his being. All they had thought, first and last, rolled over him; the past seemed to have been reduced to mere barren speculation. This in fact was what the place had just struck him as so full of—the simplification of everything but the state of suspense. That remained only by seeming to hang in the void surrounding it. Even his original fear, if fear it had been, had lost itself in the desert. "I judge, however," he continued, "that you see I'm not afraid now."

"What I see, as I make it out, is that you've achieved something almost unprecedented in the way of getting used to danger. Living with it so long and so closely you've lost your sense of it; you know it's there, but you're indifferent, and you cease even, as of old, to have to whistle in the dark. Considering what the danger is," May Bartram wound up, "I'm bound to say I don't think your attitude could well be surpassed."

John Marcher faintly smiled. "It's heroic?"

"Certainly—call it that."

It was what he would have liked indeed to call it. "I *am* then a man of courage?"

"That's what you were to show me."

He still, however, wondered. "But doesn't the man of courage know what he's afraid of—or *not* afraid of? I don't know *that,* you see. I don't focus it. I can't name it. I only know I'm exposed."

"Yes, but exposed—how shall I say?—so directly. So intimately. That's surely enough."

"Enough to make you feel then—as what we may call the end and the upshot of our watch—that I'm not afraid?"

"You're not afraid. But it isn't," she said, "the end of our watch. That is it isn't the end of yours. You've everything still to see."

"Then why haven't *you?*" he asked. He had had, all along, to-day, the sense of her keeping something back, and he still had it. As this was his first impression of that it quite made a date. The case was the more marked as she didn't at first answer; which in turn made him go on. "You know something I don't." Then his voice, for that of a man of courage, trembled a little. "You know what's to happen." Her silence, with the face she showed, was almost a confession—it made him sure. "You know, and you're afraid to tell me. It's so bad that you're afraid I'll find out."

All this might be true, for she did look as if, unexpectedly to her, he had crossed some mystic line that she had secretly drawn round her. Yet she might, after all, not have worried; and the real climax was that he himself, at all events, needn't. "You'll never find out."

III

It was all to have made, none the less, as I have said, a date; which came out in the fact that again and again, even after long intervals, other things that passed between them wore in relation to this hour but the character of recalls and results. Its immediate effect had been indeed rather to lighten insistence—almost to provoke a reaction; as if their topic had dropped by its own weight and as if moreover, for that matter, Marcher had been visited by one of his occasional warnings against egotism. He had kept up, he felt, and very decently on the whole, his consciousness of the importance of not being selfish, and it was true that he had never sinned in that direction without promptly enough trying to press the scales the other way. He often repaired his fault, the season permitting, by inviting his friend to accompany him to the opera: and it not infrequently thus happened that, to show he didn't wish her to have but one sort of food for her mind, he was the cause of her appearing there with him a dozen nights in the month. It even happened that, seeing her home at such times, he occasionally went in with her to finish, as he called it, the evening, and, the better to make his point, sat down to the frugal but always careful little supper that awaited his pleasure. His point was made, he thought, by his not eternally insisting with her on himself; made for instance, at such hours, when it befell that, her piano at hand and each of them familiar with it, they went over passages of the opera together. It chanced to be on one of these occasions, however, that he reminded her of her not having answered a certain question he had put to her during the talk that had taken place between them on her last birthday. "What is it that saves *you*?"—saved her, he meant, from that appearance of variation from the usual human type. If he had practically escaped remark, as she pretended, by doing, in the most important particular, what most men do—find the answer to life in patching up an alliance of a sort with a woman no better than himself—how had she escaped it, and how could the alliance, such as it was, since they must suppose it had been more or less noticed, have failed to make her rather positively talked about?

"I never said," May Bartram replied, "that it hadn't made me a good deal talked about."

"Ah well then you're not 'saved.'"

"It hasn't been a question for me. If you've had your woman I've had," she said, "my man."

"And you mean that makes you all right?"

Oh it was always as if there were so much to say! "I don't know why it shouldn't make me—humanly, which is what we're speaking of—as right as it makes you."

"I see," Marcher returned. "'Humanly,' no doubt, as showing that you're living for something. Not, that is, just for me and my secret."

May Bartram smiled. "I don't pretend it exactly shows that I'm not living for you. It's my intimacy with you that's in question."

He laughed as he saw what she meant. "Yes, but since, as you say, I'm only, so far as people make out, ordinary, you're—aren't you?—no more than ordinary either. You help me to pass for a man like another. So if I *am*, as I understand you, you're not compromised. Is that it?"

She had another of her waits, but she spoke clearly enough. "That's it. It's all that concerns me—to help you to pass for a man like another."

He was careful to acknowledge the remark handsomely. "How kind, how beautiful, you are to me! How shall I ever repay you?"

She had her last grave pause, as if there might be a choice of ways. But she chose. "By going on as you are."

It was into this going on as he was that they relapsed, and really for so long a time that the day inevitably came for a further sounding of their depths. These depths, constantly bridged over by a structure firm enough in spite of its lightness and of its occasional oscillation in the somewhat vertiginous air, invited on occasion, in the interest of their nerves, a dropping of the plummet and a measurement of the abyss. A difference had been made moreover, once for all, by the fact that she had all the while not appeared to feel the need of rebutting his charge of an idea within her that she didn't dare to express—a charge uttered just before one of the fullest of their later discussions ended. It had come up for him then that she "knew" something and that what she knew was bad—too bad to tell him. When he had spoken of it as visibly so bad that she was afraid he might find it out, her reply had left the matter too equivocal to be let alone and yet, for Marcher's special sensibility, almost too formidable again to touch. He circled about it at a distance that alternately narrowed and widened and that still wasn't much affected by the consciousness in him that there was nothing she could "know," after all, any better than he did. She had no source of knowledge he hadn't equally—except of course that she might have finer nerves. That was what women had where they were interested; they made out things, where people were concerned, that the people often couldn't have made out for themselves. Their nerves, their sensibility, their imagination, were conductors and revealers, and the beauty of May Bartram was in particular that she had given herself so to his case. He felt in these days what, oddly enough, he had never felt before, the growth of a dread of losing her by some catastrophe—some catastrophe that yet wouldn't at all be *the* catastrophe: partly because she had almost of a sudden begun to strike him as more useful to him than ever yet, and partly by reason of an appearance of uncertainty in her health, coincident and equally new. It was characteristic of the inner detachment he had hitherto so successfully cultivated and to which our whole account of him is a reference, it was characteristic that his complications, such as they were, had never yet seemed so as at this crisis to thicken about him, even to the point of making him ask himself if he were, by any chance, of a truth, within sight or sound, within touch or reach, within the immediate jurisdiction, of the thing that waited.

When the day came, as come it had to, that his friend confessed to him her fear of a deep disorder in her blood, he felt somehow the shadow of a change and the chill of a shock. He immediately began to imagine aggravations and disasters, and above all to think of her peril as the direct menace for himself of personal privation. This indeed gave him one of those partial recoveries of equanimity that were agreeable to him—it showed him that what was still first in his mind was the loss she herself might suffer. "What if she should have to die before knowing, before seeing—?" It would have been brutal, in the early stages of her trouble, to put that question to her; but it had immediately sounded for him to his own concern, and the possibility was what most made him sorry for her. If she did "know," moreover, in the sense of her having had some—what should he think?—mystical irresistible light, this would make the matter not better, but worse, inasmuch as her original adoption of his own curiosity had quite become the basis of her life. She had been living to see what would *be* to be seen, and it would quite lacerate her to have to give up before the accomplishment of the vision. These reflexions, as I say, quickened his generosity; yet, make them as he might, he saw himself, with the lapse of the period, more and more disconcerted. It lapsed for him with a strange steady sweep, and the oddest oddity was that it gave him, independently of the threat of much inconvenience, almost the only positive surprise his career, if career it could be called, had yet offered him. She kept the house as she had never done; he had to go to her to see her—she could meet him nowhere now, though there was scarce a corner of their loved old London in which she hadn't in the past, at one time or another, done so; and he found her always seated by her fire in the deep old-fashioned chair she was less and less able to leave. He had been struck one day, after an absence exceeding his usual measure, with her suddenly looking much older to him than he had ever thought of her being; then he recognised that the suddenness was all on his side—he had just simply and suddenly noticed. She looked older because inevitably, after so many years, she *was* old, or almost; which was of course true in still greater measure of her companion. If she was old, or almost, John Marcher assuredly was, and yet it was her showing of the lesson, not his own, that brought the truth home to him. His surprises began here; when once they had begun they multiplied; they came rather with a rush: it was as if, in the oddest way in the world, they had all been kept back, sown in a thick cluster, for the late afternoon of life, the time at which for people in general the unexpected has died out.

One of them was that he should have caught himself—for he *had* so done—*really* wondering if the great accident would take form now as nothing more than his being condemned to see this charming woman, this admirable friend, pass away from him. He had never so unreservedly qualified her as while confronted in thought with such a possibility; in spite of which there was small doubt for him that as an answer to his long riddle the mere effacement of even so fine a feature of his situation would be an abject anti-climax. It would represent, as connected with his past attitude, a drop of dignity under the shadow of which his existence could only become the most grotesque of failures. He had been far from holding it a failure—long as he had waited for the appearance that was to make it a success. He had waited for quite another thing, not for such a thing as that. The breath of his good faith came short, however, as he recognised how long he had waited, or how long at least his companion had. That she, at all events, might be recorded as having waited in vain—this affected him sharply, and all the more because of his at first having done little more than amuse himself with the idea. It grew more grave as the gravity of her condition grew, and the state of mind it produced in him, which he himself ended by watching as if it had been some definite disfigurement of his outer person, may pass for another of his surprises. This conjoined itself still with another, the really stupefying consciousness of a question that he would have allowed to shape itself had he dared. What did everything mean—what, that is, did *she* mean, she and her vain waiting and her probable death and the soundless admonition of it all—unless that, at this time of day, it was simply, it was overwhelmingly too late? He had never at any stage of his queer consciousness admitted the whisper of such a correction; he had never till within these last few months been so false to his conviction as not to hold that what was to come to him had time, whether *he* struck himself as having it or not. That at last, at last, he certainly hadn't it, to speak of, or had it but in the scantiest measure—such, soon enough, as things went with him, became the inference with which his old obsession had to reckon: and this it was not helped to do by the more and more confirmed appearance that the great vagueness casting the long shadow in which he had lived had, to attest itself, almost no margin left. Since it was in Time that he was to have met his fate, so it was in Time that his fate was to have acted; and as he waked up to the sense of no longer being young, which was exactly the sense of being stale, just as that, in turn, was the sense of being weak, he waked up to another matter beside. It all hung together; they were subject, he and the great vagueness, to an equal and indivisible law. When the possibilities themselves had accordingly turned stale, when the secret of the gods had grown faint, had perhaps even quite evaporated, that, and that only, was failure. It wouldn't have been failure to be bankrupt, dishonoured, pilloried, hanged; it was failure not to be anything. And so, in the dark valley into which his path had taken its unlooked-for twist, he wondered not a little as he groped. He didn't care what awful crash might overtake him, with what ignominy or what monstrosity he might yet be associated—since he wasn't after all too utterly old to suffer—if it would only be decently proportionate to the posture he had kept, all his life, in the threatened presence of it. He had but one desire left—that he shouldn't have been "sold."

IV

Then it was that, one afternoon, while the spring of the year was young and new she met all in her own way his frankest betrayal of these alarms. He had gone in late to see her, but evening hadn't settled and she was presented to him in that long fresh light of waning April days which affects us often with a sadness sharper than the greyest hours of autumn. The week had been warm, the spring was supposed to have begun early, and May Bartram sat, for the first time in the year, without a fire; a fact that, to Marcher's sense, gave the scene of which she formed part a smooth and ultimate look, an air of knowing, in its immaculate order and cold meaningless cheer, that it would never see a fire again. Her own aspect—he could scarce have said why—intensified this note. Almost as white as wax, with the marks and signs in her face as numerous and as fine as if they had been etched by a needle, with soft white draperies relieved by a faded green scarf on the delicate tone of which the years had further refined, she was the picture of a serene and exquisite but impenetrable sphinx, whose head, or indeed all whose person, might have been powdered with silver. She was a sphinx, yet with her white petals and green fronds she might have been a lily too—only an artificial lily, wonderfully imitated and constantly kept, without dust or stain, though not exempt from a slight droop and a complexity of faint creases, under some clear glass bell. The perfection of household care, of high polish and finish, always reigned in her rooms, but they now looked most as if everything had been wound up, tucked in, put away, so that she might sit with folded hands and with nothing more to do. She was "out of it," to Marcher's vision; her work was over; she communicated with him as across some gulf or from some island of rest that she had already reached, and it made him feel strangely abandoned. Was it—or rather wasn't it—that if for so long she had been watching with him the answer to their question must have swum into her ken and taken on its name, so that her occupation was verily gone? He had as much as charged her with this in saying to her, many months before, that she even then knew something she was keeping from him. It was a point he had never since ventured to press, vaguely fearing as he did that it might become a difference, perhaps a disagreement, between them. He had in this later time turned nervous, which was what he in all the other years had never been; and the oddity was that his nervousness should have waited till he had begun to doubt, should have held off so long as he was sure. There was something, it seemed to him, that the wrong word would bring down on his head, something that would so at least ease off his tension. But he wanted not to speak the wrong word; that would make everything ugly. He wanted the knowledge he lacked to drop on him, if drop it could, by its own august weight. If she was to forsake him it was surely for her to take leave. This was why he didn't directly ask her again what she knew; but it was also why, approaching the matter from another side, he said to her in the course of his visit: "What do you regard as the very worst that at this time of day *can* happen to me?"

He had asked her that in the past often enough; they had, with the odd irregular rhythm of their intensities and avoidances, exchanged ideas about it and then had seen the ideas washed away by cool intervals, washed like figures traced in sea-sand. It had ever been the mark of their talk that the oldest allusions in it required but a little dismissal and reaction to come out again, sounding for the hour as new. She could thus at present meet his enquiry quite freshly and patiently. "Oh yes, I've repeatedly thought, only it always seemed to me of old that I couldn't quite make up my mind. I thought of dreadful things, between which it was difficult to choose; and so must you have done."

"Rather! I feel now as if I had scarce done anything else. I appear to myself to have spent my life in thinking of nothing *but* dreadful things. A great many of them I've at different times named to you, but there were others I couldn't name."

"They were too, too dreadful?"

"Too, too dreadful—some of them."

She looked at him a minute, and there came to him as he met it an inconsequent sense that her eyes, when one got their full clearness, were still as beautiful as they had been in youth, only beautiful with a strange cold light—a light that somehow was a part of the effect, if it wasn't rather a part of the cause, of the pale hard sweetness of the season and the hour. "And yet," she said at last, "there are horrors we've mentioned."

It deepened the strangeness to see her, as such a figure in such a picture, talk of "horrors," but she was to do in a few minutes something stranger yet—though even of this he was to take the full measure but afterwards—and the note of it already trembled. It was, for the matter of that, one of the signs that her eyes were having again the high flicker of their prime. He had to admit, however, what she said. "Oh yes, there were times when we did go far." He caught himself in the act of speaking as if it all were over. Well, he wished it were; and the consummation depended for him clearly more and more on his friend.

But she had now a soft smile. "Oh far—!"

It was oddly ironic. "Do you mean you're prepared to go further?"

She was frail and ancient and charming as she continued to look at him, yet it was rather as if she had lost the thread. "Do you consider that we went far?"

"Why I thought it the point you were just making—that we *had* looked most things in the face."

"Including each other?" She still smiled. "But you're quite right. We've had together great imaginations, often great fears; but some of them have been unspoken."

"Then the worst—we haven't faced that. I *could* face it, I believe, if I knew what you think it. I feel," he explained, "as if I had lost my power to conceive such things." And he wondered if he looked as blank as he sounded. "It's spent."

"Then why do you assume," she asked, "that mine isn't?"

"Because you've given me signs to the contrary. It isn't a question for you of conceiving, imagining, comparing. It isn't a question now of choosing." At last he came out with it. "You know something I don't. You've shown me that before."

These last words had affected her, he made out in a moment, exceedingly, and she spoke with firmness. "I've shown you, my dear, nothing."

He shook his head. "You can't hide it."

"Oh, oh!" May Bartram sounded over what she couldn't hide. It was almost a smothered groan.

"You admitted it months ago, when I spoke of it to you as of something you were afraid I should find out. Your answer was that I couldn't, that I wouldn't, and I don't pretend I have. But you had something therefore in mind, and I now see how it must have been, how it still is, the possibility that, of all possibilities, has settled itself for you as the worst. This," he went on, "is why I appeal to you. I'm only afraid of ignorance to-day—I'm not afraid of knowledge." And then as for a while she said nothing: "What makes me sure is that I see in your face and feel here, in this air and amid these appearances, that you're out of it. You've done. You've had your experience. You leave me to my fate."

Well, she listened, motionless and white in her chair, as on a decision to be made, so that her manner was fairly an avowal, though still, with a small fine inner stiffness, an imperfect surrender. "It *would* be the worst," she finally let herself say. "I mean the thing I've never said."

It hushed him a moment. "More monstrous than all the monstrosities we've named?"

"More monstrous. Isn't that what you sufficiently express," she asked, "in calling it the worst?"

Marcher thought. "Assuredly—if you mean, as I do, something that includes all the loss and all the shame that are thinkable."

"It would if it *should* happen," said May Bartram. "What we're speaking of, remember, is only my idea."

"It's your belief," Marcher returned. "That's enough for me. I feel your beliefs are right. Therefore if, having this one, you give me no more light on it, you abandon me."

"No, no!" she repeated. "I'm with you—don't you see?—still." And as to make it more vivid to him she rose from her chair—a movement she seldom risked in these days—and showed herself, all draped and all soft, in her fairness and slimness. "I haven't forsaken you."

It was really, in its effort against weakness, a generous assurance, and had the success of the impulse not, happily, been great, it would have touched him to pain more than to pleasure. But the cold charm in her eyes had spread, as she hovered before him, to all the rest of her person, so that it was for the minute almost a recovery of youth. He couldn't pity her for that; he could only take her as she showed—as capable even yet of helping him. It was as if, at the same time, her light might at any instant go out; wherefore he must make the most of it. There passed before him with intensity the three or four things he wanted most to know; but the question that came of itself to his lips really covered the others. "Then tell me if I shall consciously suffer."

She promptly shook her head. "Never!"

It confirmed the authority he imputed to her, and it produced on him an extraordinary effect. "Well, what's better than that? Do you call that the worst?"

"You think nothing is better?" she asked.

She seemed to mean something so special that he again sharply wondered, though still with the dawn of a prospect of relief. "Why not, if one doesn't *know*?" After which, as their eyes, over his question, met in a silence, the dawn deepened and something to his purpose came prodigiously out of her very face. His own, as he took it in, suddenly flushed to the forehead, and he gasped with the force of a perception to which, on the instant, everything fitted. The sound of his gasp filled the air; then he became articulate. "I see—if I don't suffer!"

In her own look, however, was doubt. "You see what?"

"Why what you mean—what you've always meant."

She again shook her head. "What I mean isn't what I've always meant. It's different."

"It's something new?"

She hung back from it a little. "Something new. It's not what you think. I see what you think."

His divination drew breath then; only her correction might be wrong. "It isn't that I *am* a blockhead?" he asked between faintness and grimness. "It isn't that it's all a mistake?"

"A mistake?" she pityingly echoed. *That* possibility, for her, he saw, would be monstrous; and if she guaranteed him the immunity from pain it would accordingly not be what she had in mind. "Oh no," she declared; "it's nothing of that sort. You've been right."

Yet he couldn't help asking himself if she weren't, thus pressed, speaking but to save him. It seemed to him he should be most in a hole if his history should prove all a platitude. "Are you telling me the truth, so that I shan't have been a bigger idiot than I can bear to know? I *haven't* lived with a vain imagination, in the most besotted illusion? I haven't waited but to see the door shut in my face?"

She shook her head again. "However the case stands *that* isn't the truth. Whatever the reality, it *is* a reality. The door isn't shut. The door's open," said May Bartram.

"Then something's to come?"

She waited once again, always with her cold sweet eyes on him. "It's never too late." She had, with her gliding step, diminished the distance between them, and she stood nearer to him, close to him, a minute, as if still charged with the unspoken: Her movement might have been for some finer emphasis of what she was at once hesitating and deciding to say. He had been standing by the chimney-piece, fireless and sparely adorned, a small perfect old French clock and two morsels of rosy Dresden constituting all its furniture; and her hand grasped the shelf while she kept him waiting, grasped it a little as for support and encouragement. She only kept him waiting, however; that is he only waited. It had become suddenly, from her movement and attitude, beautiful and vivid to him that she had something more to give him; her wasted face delicately shone with it—it glittered almost as with the white lustre of silver in her expression. She was right, incontestably, for what he saw in her face was the truth, and strangely, without consequence, while their talk of it as dreadful was still in the air, she appeared to present it as inordinately soft. This, prompting bewilderment, made him but gape the more gratefully for her revelation, so that they continued for some minutes silent, her face shining at him, her contact imponderably pressing, and his stare all kind but all expectant. The end, none the less, was that what he had expected failed to come to him. Something else took place instead, which seemed to consist at first in the mere closing of her eyes. She gave way at the same instant to a slow fine shudder, and though he remained staring—though he stared in fact but the harder—turned off and regained her chair. It was the end of what she had been intending, but it left him thinking only of that.

"Well, you don't say—?"

She had touched in her passage a bell near the chimney and had sunk back strangely pale. "I'm afraid I'm too ill."

"Too ill to tell me?" It sprang up sharp to him, and almost to his lips, the fear she might die without giving him light. He checked himself in time from so expressing his question, but she answered as if she had heard the words.

"Don't you know—now?"

"'Now'—?" She had spoken as if some difference had been made within the moment. But her maid, quickly obedient to her bell, was already with them. "I know nothing." And he was afterwards to say to himself that he must have spoken with odious impatience, such an impatience as to show that, supremely disconcerted, he washed his hands of the whole question.

"Oh!" said May Bartram.

"Are you in pain?" he asked as the woman went to her.

"No," said May Bartram.

Her maid, who had put an arm round her as if to take her to her room, fixed on him eyes that appealingly contradicted her; in spite of which, however, he showed once more his mystification. "What then has happened?"

She was once more, with her companion's help, on her feet, and, feeling withdrawal imposed on him, he had blankly found his hat and gloves and had reached the door. Yet he waited for her answer. "What *was* to," she said.

V

He came back the next day, but she was then unable to see him, and as it was literally the first time this had occurred in the long stretch of their acquaintance he turned away, defeated and sore, almost angry—or feeling at least that such a break in their custom was really the beginning of the end—and wandered alone with his thoughts, especially with the one he was least able to keep down. She was dying and he would lose her; she was dying and his life would end. He stopped in the Park, into which he had passed, and stared before him at his recurrent doubt. Away from her the doubt pressed again; in her presence he had believed her, but as he felt his forlornness he threw himself into the explanation that, nearest at hand, had most of a miserable warmth for him and least of a cold torment. She had deceived him to save him—to put him off with something in which he should be able to rest. What could the thing that was to happen to him be, after all, but just this thing that had begun to happen? Her dying, her death, his consequent solitude—*that* was what he had figured as the Beast in the Jungle, that was what had been in the lap of the gods. He had had her word for it as he left her—what else on earth could she have meant? It wasn't a thing of a monstrous order; not a fate rare and distinguished; not a stroke of fortune that overwhelmed and immortalised; it had only the stamp of the common doom. But poor Marcher at this hour judged the common doom sufficient. It would serve his turn, and even as the consummation of infinite waiting he would bend his pride to accept it. He sat down on a bench in the twilight. He hadn't been a fool. Something had *been,* as she had said, to come. Before he rose indeed it had quite struck him that the final fact really matched with the long avenue through which he had had to reach it. As sharing his suspense and as giving herself all, giving her life, to bring it to an end, she had come with him every step of the way. He had lived by her aid, and to leave her behind would be cruelly, damnably to miss her. What could be more over-whelming than that?

Well, he was to know within the week, for though she kept him a while at bay, left him restless and wretched during a series of days on each of which he asked about her only again to have to turn away, she ended his trial by receiving him where she had always received him. Yet she had been brought out at some hazard into the presence of so many of the things that were, consciously, vainly, half their past, and there was scant service left in the gentleness of her mere desire, all too visible, to check his obsession and wind up his long trouble. That was clearly what she wanted; the one thing more, her own peace, while she could still put out her hand. He was so affected by her state that, once seated by her chair, he was moved to let everything go; it was she herself therefore who brought him back, took up again, before she dismissed him, her last word of the other time. She showed how she wished to leave their business in order. "I'm not sure you understood. You've nothing to wait for more. It *has* come."

Oh how he looked at her! "Really?"

"Really."

"The thing that, as you said, *was* to?"

"The thing that we began in our youth to watch for."

Face to face with her once more he believed her; it was a claim to which he had so abjectly little to oppose. "You mean that it has come as a positive definite occurrence, with a name and a date?"

"Positive. Definite. I don't know about the 'name,' but oh with a date!"

He found himself again too helplessly at sea. "But come in the night—come and passed me by?"

May Bartram had her strange faint smile. "Oh no, it hasn't passed you by!"

"But if I haven't been aware of it and it hasn't touched me—?"

"Ah your not being aware of it"—and she seemed to hesitate an instant to deal with this—"your not being aware of it is the strangeness *in* the strangeness. It's the wonder *of* the wonder." She spoke as with the softness almost of a sick child, yet now at last, at the end of all, with the perfect straightness of a sibyl. She visibly knew that she knew, and the effect on him was of something co-ordinate, in its high character, with the law that had ruled him. It was the true voice of the law; so on her lips would the law itself have sounded. "It *has* touched you," she went on. "It has done its office. It has made you all its own."

"So utterly without my knowing it?"

"So utterly without your knowing it." His hand, as he leaned to her, was on the arm of her chair, and, dimly smiling always now, she placed her own on it. "It's enough if *I* know it."

"Oh!" he confusedly breathed, as she herself of late so often had done.

"What I long ago said is true. You'll never know now, and I think you ought to be content. You've *had* it," said May Bartram.

"But had what?"

"Why what was to have marked you out. The proof of your law. It has acted. I'm too glad," she then bravely added, "to have been able to see what it's *not.*"

He continued to attach his eyes to her, and with the sense that it was all beyond him, and that *she* was too, he would still have sharply challenged her hadn't he so felt it an abuse of her weakness to do more than take devoutly what she gave him, take it hushed as to a revelation. If he did speak, it was out of the foreknowledge of his loneliness to come. "If you're glad of what it's 'not' it might then have been worse?"

She turned her eyes away, she looked straight before her; with which after a moment: "Well, you know our fears."

He wondered. "It's something then we never feared?"

On this slowly she turned to him. "Did we ever dream, with all our dreams, that we should sit and talk of it thus?"

He tried for a little to make out that they had; but it was as if their dreams, numberless enough, were in solution in some thick cold mist through which thought lost itself. "It might have been that we couldn't talk?"

"Well"—she did her best for him—"not from this side. This, you see," she said, "is the *other* side."

"I think," poor Marcher returned, "that all sides are the same to me." Then, however, as she gently shook her head in correction: "We mightn't, as it were, have got across—?"

"To where we are—no. We're *here*"—she made her weak emphasis.

"And much good does it do us!" was her friend's frank comment.

"It does us the good it can. It does us the good that *it* isn't here. It's past. It's behind," said May Bartram. "Before—" but her voice dropped.

He had got up, not to tire her, but it was hard to combat his yearning. She after all told him nothing but that his light had failed—which he knew well enough without her. "Before—?" he blankly echoed.

"Before, you see, it was always to *come.* That kept it present."

"Oh I don't care what comes now! Besides," Marcher added, "it seems to me I liked it better present, as you say, than I can like it absent with *your* absence."

"Oh mine!"—and her pale hands made light of it.

"With the absence of everything." He had a dreadful sense of standing there before her for—so far as anything but this proved, this bottomless drop was concerned—the last time of their life. It rested on him with a weight he felt he could scarce bear, and this weight it apparently was that still pressed out what remained in him of speakable protest. "I believe you; but I can't begin to pretend I understand. *Nothing,* for me, is past; nothing *will* pass till I pass myself, which I pray my stars may be as soon as possible. Say, however," he added, "that I've eaten my cake, as you contend, to the last crumb—how can the thing I've never felt at all be the thing I was marked out to feel?"

She met him perhaps less directly, but she met him unperturbed. "You take your 'feelings' for granted. You were to suffer your fate. That was not necessarily to know it."

"How in the world—when what is such knowledge but suffering?"

She looked up at him a while in silence. "No—you don't understand."

"I suffer," said John Marcher.

"Don't, don't!"

"How can I help at least *that*?"

"Don't!" May Bartram repeated.

She spoke it in a tone so special, in spite of her weakness, that he stared an instant—stared as if some light, hitherto hidden, had shimmered across his vision. Darkness again closed over it, but the gleam had already become for him an idea. "Because I haven't the right—?"

"Don't *know*—when you needn't," she mercifully urged. "You needn't—for we shouldn't."

"Shouldn't?" If he could but know what she meant!

"No—it's too much."

"Too much?" he still asked but, with a mystification that was the next moment of a sudden to give way. Her words, if they meant something, affected him in this light—the light also of her wasted face—as meaning *all,* and the sense of what knowledge had been for herself came over him with a rush which broke through into a question. "Is it of that then you're dying?"

She but watched him, gravely at first, as to see, with this, where he was, and she might have seen something or feared something that moved her sympathy. "I would live for you still—if I could." Her eyes closed for a little, as if, withdrawn into herself, she were for a last time trying. "But I can't!" she said as she raised them again to take leave of him.

She couldn't indeed, as but too promptly and sharply appeared, and he had no vision of her after this that was anything but darkness and doom. They had parted for ever in that strange talk; access to her chamber of pain, rigidly guarded, was almost wholly forbidden him; he was feeling now moreover, in the face of doctors, nurses, the two or three relatives attracted doubtless by the presumption of what she had to "leave," how few were the rights, as they were called in such cases, that he had to put forward, and how odd it might even seem that their intimacy shouldn't have given him more of them. The stupidest fourth cousin had more, even though she had been nothing in such a person's life. She had been a feature of features in *his,* for what else was it to have been so indispensable? Strange beyond saying were the ways of existence, baffling for him the anomaly of his lack, as he felt it to be, of producible claim. A woman might have been, as it were, everything to him, and it might yet present him in no connexion that any one seemed held to recognise. If this was the case in these closing weeks it was the case more sharply on the occasion of the last offices rendered, in the great grey London cemetery, to what had been mortal, to what had been precious, in his friend. The concourse at her grave was not numerous, but he saw himself treated as scarce more nearly concerned with it than if there had been a thousand others. He was in short from this moment face to face with the fact that he was to profit extraordinarily little by the interest May Bartram had taken in him. He couldn't quite have said what he expected, but he hadn't surely expected this approach to a double privation. Not only had her interest failed him, but he seemed to feel himself unattended—and for a reason he couldn't seize—by the distinction, the dignity, the propriety, if nothing else, of the man markedly bereaved. It was as if in the view of society he had not *been* markedly bereaved, as if there still failed some sign or proof of it, and as if none the less his character could never be affirmed nor the deficiency ever made up. There were moments as the weeks went by when he would have liked, by some almost aggressive act, to take his stand on the intimacy of his loss, in order that it *might* be questioned and his retort, to the relief of his spirit, so recorded; but the moments of an irritation more helpless followed fast on these, the moments during which, turning things over with a good conscience but with a bare horizon, he found himself wondering if he oughtn't to have begun, so to speak, further back.

He found himself wondering indeed at many things, and this last speculation had others to keep it company. What could he have done, after all, in her lifetime, without giving them both, as it were, away? He couldn't have made known she was watching him, for that would have published the superstition of the Beast. This was what closed his mouth now—now that the Jungle had been threshed to vacancy and that the Beast had stolen away. It sounded too foolish and too flat; the difference for him in this particular, the extinction in his life of the element of suspense, was such as in fact to surprise him. He could scarce have said what the effect resembled; the abrupt cessation, the positive prohibition, of music perhaps, more than anything else, in some place all adjusted and all accustomed to sonority and to attention. If he could at any rate have conceived lifting the veil from his image at some moment of the past (what had he done, after all, if not lift it to *her*?) so to do this to-day, to talk to people at large of the Jungle cleared and confide to them that he now felt it as safe, would have been not only to see them listen as to a goodwife's tale, but really to hear himself tell one. What it presently came to in truth was that poor Marcher waded through his beaten grass, where no life stirred, where no breath sounded, where no evil eye seemed to gleam from a possible lair, very much as if vaguely looking for the Beast, and still more as if acutely missing it. He walked about in an existence that had grown strangely more spacious and, stopping fitfully in places where the undergrowth of life struck him as closer, asked himself yearningly, wondered secretly and sorely, if it would have lurked here or there. It would have at all events *sprung;* what was at least complete was his belief in the truth itself of the assurance given him. The change from his old sense to his new was absolute and final: what was to happen *had* so absolutely and finally happened that he was as little able to know a fear for his future as to know a hope; so absent in short was any question of anything still to come. He was to live entirely with the other question, that of his unidentified past, that of his having to see his fortune impenetrably muffled and masked.

The torment of this vision became then his occupation; he couldn't perhaps have consented to live but for the possibility of guessing. She had told him, his friend, not to guess; she had forbidden him, so far as he might, to know, and she had even in a sort denied the power in him to learn: which were so many things precisely, to deprive him of rest. It wasn't that he wanted, he argued for fairness, that anything past and done should repeat itself; it was only that he shouldn't, as an anticlimax, have been taken sleeping so sound as not to be able to win back by an effort of thought the lost stuff of consciousness. He declared to himself at moments that he would either win it back or have done with consciousness for ever; he made this idea his one motive in fine, made it so much his passion that none other, to compare with it, seemed ever to have touched him. The lost stuff of consciousness became thus for him as a strayed or stolen child to an unappeasable father; he hunted it up and down very much as if he were knocking at doors and enquiring of the police. This was the spirit in which, inevitably, he set himself to travel; he started on a journey that was to be as long as he could make it; it danced before him that, as the other side of the globe couldn't possibly have less to say to him, it might, by a possibility of suggestion, have more. Before he quitted London, however, he made a pilgrimage to May Bartram's grave, took his way to it through the endless avenues of the grim suburban metropolis, sought it out in the wilderness of tombs, and, though he had come but for the renewal of the act of farewell, found himself, when he had at last stood by it, beguiled into long intensities. He stood for an hour, powerless to turn away and yet powerless to penetrate the darkness of death; fixing with his eyes her inscribed name and date, beating his forehead against the fact of the secret they kept, drawing his breath, while he waited, as if some sense would in pity of him rise from the stones. He kneeled on the stones, however, in vain; they kept what they concealed; and if the face of the tomb did become a face for him it was because her two names became a pair of eyes that didn't know him. He gave them a last long look, but no palest light broke.

VI

He stayed away, after this, for a year; he visited the depths of Asia, spending himself on scenes of romantic interest, of superlative sanctity; but what was present to him everywhere was that for a man who had known what *he* had known the world was vulgar and vain. The state of mind in which he had lived for so many years shone out to him, in reflexion, as a light that coloured and refined, a light beside which the glow of the East was garish cheap and thin. The terrible truth was that he had lost—with everything else—a distinction as well; the things he saw couldn't help being common when he had become common to look at them. He was simply now one of them himself—he was in the dust, without a peg for the sense of difference; and there were hours when, before the temples of gods and the sepulchres of kings, his spirit turned for nobleness of association to the barely discriminated slab in the London suburb. That had become for him, and more intensely with time and distance, his one witness of a past glory. It was all that was left to him for proof or pride, yet the past glories of Pharaohs were nothing to him as he thought of it. Small wonder then that he came back to it on the morrow of his return. He was drawn there this time as irresistibly as the other, yet with a confidence, almost, that was doubtless the effect of the many months that had elapsed. He had lived, in spite of himself, into his change of feeling, and in wandering over the earth had wandered, as might be said, from the circumference to the centre of his desert. He had settled to his safety and accepted perforce his extinction; figuring to himself, with some colour, in the likeness of certain little old men he remembered to have seen, of whom, all meagre and wizened as they might look, it was related that they had in their time fought twenty duels or been loved by ten princesses. They indeed had been wondrous for others while he was but wondrous for himself; which, however, was exactly the cause of his haste to renew the wonder by getting back, as he might put it, into his own presence. That had quickened his steps and checked his delay. If his visit was prompt it was because he had been separated so long from the part of himself that alone he now valued.

It's accordingly not false to say that he reached his goal with a certain elation and stood there again with a certain assurance. The creature beneath the sod *knew* of his rare experience, so that, strangely now, the place had lost for him its mere blankness of expression. It met him in mildness—not, as before, in mockery; it wore for him the air of conscious greeting that we find, after absence, in things that have closely belonged to us and which seem to confess of themselves to the connexion. The plot of ground, the graven tablet, the tended flowers affected him so as belonging to him that he resembled for the hour a contented landlord reviewing a piece of property. Whatever had happened—well, had happened. He had not come back this time with the vanity of that question, his former worrying "what, *what*?" now practically so spent. Yet he would none the less never again so cut himself off from the spot; he would come back to it every month, for if he did nothing else by its aid he at least held up his head. It thus grew for him, in the oddest way, a positive resource; he carried out his idea of periodical returns, which took their place at last among the most inveterate of his habits. What it all amounted to, oddly enough, was that in his finally so simplified world this garden of death gave him the few square feet of earth on which he could still most live. It was as if, being nothing anywhere else for any one, nothing even for himself, he were just everything here, and if not for a crowd of witnesses or indeed for any witness but John Marcher, then by clear right of the register that he could scan like an open page. The open page was the tomb of his friend, and *there* were the facts of the past, there the truth of his life, there the backward reaches in which he could lose himself. He did this from time to time with such effect that he seemed to wander through the old years with his hand in the arm of a companion who was, in the most extraordinary manner, his other, his younger self; and to wander, which was more extraordinary yet, round and round a third presence—not wandering she, but stationary, still, whose eyes, turning with his revolution, never ceased to follow him, and whose seat was his point, so to speak, of orientation. Thus in short he settled to live—feeding all on the sense that he once *had* lived, and dependent on it not alone for a support but for an identity.

It sufficed him in its way for months and the year elapsed; it would doubtless even have carried him further but for an accident, superficially slight, which moved him, quite in another direction, with a force beyond any of his impressions of Egypt or of India. It was a thing of the merest chance—the turn, as he afterwards felt, of a hair, though he was indeed to live to believe that if light hadn't come to him in this particular fashion it would still have come in another. He was to live to believe this, I say, though he was not to live, I may not less definitely mention, to do much else. We allow him at any rate the benefit of the conviction, struggling up for him at the end, that, whatever might have happened or not happened, he would have come round of himself to the light. The incident of an autumn day had put the match to the train laid from of old by his misery. With the light before him he knew that even of late his ache had only been smothered. It was strangely drugged, but it throbbed; at the touch it began to bleed. And the touch, in the event, was the face of a fellow mortal. This face, one grey afternoon when the leaves were thick in the alleys, looked into Marcher's own, at the cemetery, with an expression like the cut of a blade. He felt it, that is, so deep down that he winced at the steady thrust. The person who so mutely assaulted him was a figure he had noticed, on reaching his own goal, absorbed by a grave a short distance away, a grave apparently fresh, so that the emotion of the visitor would probably match it for frankness. This fact alone forbade further attention, though during the time he stayed he remained vaguely conscious of his neighbour, a middle-aged man apparently, in mourning, whose bowed back, among the clustered monuments and mortuary yews, was constantly presented. Marcher's theory that these were elements in contact with which he himself revived, had suffered, on this occasion, it may be granted, a marked, an excessive check. The autumn day was dire for him as none had recently been, and he rested with a heaviness he had not yet known on the low stone table that bore May Bartram's name. He rested without power to move, as if some spring in him, some spell vouchsafed, had suddenly been broken for ever. If he could have done that moment as he wanted he would simply have stretched himself on the slab that was ready to take him, treating it as a place prepared to receive his last sleep. What in all the wide world had he now to keep awake for? He stared before him with the question, and it was then that, as one of the cemetery walks passed near him, he caught the shock of the face.

His neighbour at the other grave had withdrawn, as he himself, with force enough in him, would have done by now, and was advancing along the path on his way to one of the gates. This brought him close, and his pace was slow, so that—and all the more as there was a kind of hunger in his look—the two men were for a minute directly confronted. Marcher knew him at once for one of the deeply stricken—a perception so sharp that nothing else in the picture comparatively lived, neither his dress, his age, nor his presumable character and class; nothing lived but the deep ravage of the features he showed. He *showed* them—that was the point; he was moved, as he passed, by some impulse that was either a signal for sympathy or, more possibly, a challenge to an opposed sorrow. He might already have been aware of our friend, might at some previous hour have noticed in him the smooth habit of the scene, with which the state of his own senses so scantly consorted, and might thereby have been stirred as by an overt discord. What Marcher was at all events conscious of was in the first place that the image of scarred passion presented to him was conscious too—of something that profaned the air; and in the second that, roused, startled, shocked, he was yet the next moment looking after it, as it went, with envy. The most extraordinary thing that had happened to him—though he had given that name to other matters as well—took place, after his immediate vague stare, as a consequence of this impression. The stranger passed, but the raw glare of his grief remained, making our friend wonder in pity what wrong, what wound it expressed, what injury not to be healed. What had the man *had,* to make him by the loss of it so bleed and yet live?

Something—and this reached him with a pang—that *he,* John Marcher, hadn't; the proof of which was precisely John Marcher's arid end. No passion had ever touched him, for this was what passion meant; he had survived and maundered and pined, but where had been *his* deep ravage? The extraordinary thing we speak of was the sudden rush of the result of this question. The sight that had just met his eyes named to him, as in letters of quick flame, something he had utterly, insanely missed, and what he had missed made these things a train of fire, made them mark themselves in an anguish of inward throbs. He had seen *outside* of his life, not learned it within, the way a woman was mourned when she had been loved for herself: such was the force of his conviction of the meaning of the stranger's face, which still flared for him as a smoky torch. It hadn't come to him, the knowledge, on the wings of experience; it had brushed him, jostled him, upset him, with the disrespect of chance, the insolence of accident. Now that the illumination had begun, however, it blazed to the zenith, and what he presently stood there gazing at was the sounded void of his life. He gazed, he drew breath, in pain; he turned in his dismay, and, turning, he had before him in sharper incision than ever the open page of his story. The name on the table smote him as the passage of his neighbour had done, and what it said to him, full in the face, was that *she* was what he had missed. This was the awful thought, the answer to all the past, the vision at the dread clearness of which he grew as cold as the stone beneath him. Everything fell together, confessed, explained, overwhelmed; leaving him most of all stupefied at the blindness he had cherished. The fate he had been marked for he had met with a vengeance—he had emptied the cup to the lees; he had been the man of his time, *the* man, to whom nothing on earth was to have happened. That was the rare stroke—that was his visitation. So he saw it, as we say, in pale horror, while the pieces fitted and fitted. So *she* had seen it while he didn't, and so she served at this hour to drive the truth home. It was the truth, vivid and monstrous, that all the while he had waited the wait was itself his portion. This the companion of his vigil had at a given moment made out, and she had then offered him the chance to baffle his doom. One's doom, however, was never baffled, and on the day she told him his own had come down she had seen him but stupidly stare at the escape she offered him.

The escape would have been to love her; then, *then* he would have lived. *She* had lived—who could say now with what passion?—since she had loved him for himself; whereas he had never thought of her (ah how it hugely glared at him!) but in the chill of his egotism and the light of her use. Her spoken words came back to him—the chain stretched and stretched. The Beast had lurked indeed, and the Beast, at its hour, had sprung; it had sprung in that twilight of the cold April when, pale, ill, wasted, but all beautiful, and perhaps even then recoverable, she had risen from her chair to stand before him and let him imaginably guess. It had sprung as he didn't guess; it had sprung as she hopelessly turned from him, and the mark, by the time he left her, had fallen where it *was* to fall. He had justified his fear and achieved his fate; he had failed, with the last exactitude, of all he was to fail of; and a moan now rose to his lips as he remembered she had prayed he mightn't know. This horror of waking—*this* was knowledge, knowledge under the breath of which the very tears in his eyes seemed to freeze. Through them, none the less, he tried to fix it and hold it; he kept it there before him so that he might feel the pain. That at least, belated and bitter, had something of the taste of life. But the bitterness suddenly sickened him, and it was as if, horribly, he saw, in the truth, in the cruelty of his image, what had been appointed and done. He saw the Jungle of his life and saw the lurking Beast; then, while he looked, perceived it, as by a stir of the air, rise, huge and hideous, for the leap that was to settle him. His eyes darkened—it was close; and, instinctively turning, in his hallucination, to avoid it, he flung himself, face down, on the tomb.

SARAH ORNE JEWETT

A White Heron

I

THE WOODS WERE ALREADY filled with shadows one June evening, just before eight o'clock, though a bright sunset still glimmered faintly among the trunks of the trees. A little girl was driving home her cow, a plodding, dilatory, provoking creature in her behavior, but a valued companion for all that. They were going away from the western light, and striking deep into the dark woods, but their feet were familiar with the path, and it was no matter whether their eyes could see it or not.

There was hardly a night the summer through when the old cow could be found waiting at the pasture bars; on the contrary, it was her greatest pleasure to hide herself away among the high huckleberry bushes, and though she wore a loud bell she had made the discovery that if one stood perfectly still it would not ring. So Sylvia had to hunt for her until she found her, and call Co'! Co'! with never an answering Moo, until her childish patience was quite spent. If the creature had not given good milk and plenty of it, the case would have seemed very different to her owners. Besides, Sylvia had all the time there was, and very little use to make of it. Sometimes in pleasant weather it was a consolation to look upon the cow's pranks as an intelligent attempt to play hide and seek, and as the child had no playmates she lent herself to this amusement with a good deal of zest. Though this chase had been so long that the wary animal herself had given an unusual signal of her whereabouts, Sylvia had only laughed when she came upon Mistress Moolly at the swamp-side, and urged her affectionately homeward with a twig of birch leaves. The old cow was not inclined to wander farther, she even turned in the right direction for once as they left the pasture, and stepped along the road at a good pace. She was quite ready to be milked now, and seldom stopped to browse. Sylvia wondered what her grandmother would say because they were so late. It was a great while since she had left home at half past five o'clock, but everybody knew the difficulty of making this errand a short one. Mrs. Tilley had chased the hornéd torment too many summer evenings herself to blame any one else for lingering, and was only thankful as she waited that she had Sylvia, nowadays, to give such valuable assistance. The good woman suspected that Sylvia loitered occasionally on her own account; there never was such a child for straying out-of-doors since the world was made! Everybody said that it was a good change for a little maid who had tried to grow for eight years in a crowded manufacturing town, but, as for Sylvia herself, it seemed as if she never had been alive at all before she came to live at the farm. She thought often with wistful compassion of a wretched dry geranium that belonged to a town neighbor.

"'Afraid of folks,'" old Mrs. Tilley said to herself, with a smile, after she had made the unlikely choice of Sylvia from her daughter's houseful of children, and was returning to the farm. "'Afraid of folks,' they said! I guess she won't be troubled no great with 'em up to the old place!" When they reached the door of the lonely house and stopped to unlock it, and the cat came to purr loudly, and rub against them, a deserted pussy, indeed, but fat with young robins, Sylvia whispered that this was a beautiful place to live in, and she never should wish to go home.

The companions followed the shady woodroad, the cow taking slow steps, and the child very fast ones. The cow stopped long at the brook to drink, as if the pasture were not half a swamp, and Sylvia stood still and waited, letting her bare feet cool themselves in the shoal water, while the great twilight moths struck softly against her. She waded on through the brook as the cow moved away, and listened to the thrushes with a heart that beat fast with pleasure. There was a stirring in the great boughs overhead. They were full of little birds and beasts that seemed to be wide-awake, and going about their world, or else saying good-night to each other in sleepy twitters. Sylvia herself felt sleepy as she walked along. However, it was not much farther to the house, and the air was soft and sweet. She was not often in the woods so late as this, and it made her feel as if she were a part of the gray shadows and the moving leaves. She was just thinking how long it seemed since she first came to the farm a year ago, and wondering if everything went on in the noisy town just the same as when she was there; the thought of the great red-faced boy who used to chase and frighten her made her hurry along the path to escape from the shadow of the trees.

Suddenly this little woods-girl is horror-stricken to hear a clear whistle not very far away. Not a bird's whistle, which would have a sort of friendliness, but a boy's whistle, determined, and somewhat aggressive. Sylvia left the cow to whatever sad fate might await her, and stepped discreetly aside into the bushes, but she was just too late. The enemy had discovered her, and called out in a very cheerful and persuasive tone, "Halloa, little girl, how far is it to the road?" and trembling Sylvia answered almost inaudibly, "A good ways."

She did not dare to look boldly at the tall young man, who carried a gun over his shoulder, but she came out of her bush and again followed the cow, while he walked alongside.

"I have been hunting for some birds," the stranger said kindly, "and I have lost my way, and need a friend very much. Don't be afraid," he added gallantly. "Speak up and tell me what your name is, and whether you think I can spend the night at your house, and go out gunning early in the morning."

Sylvia was more alarmed than before. Would not her grandmother consider her much to blame? But who could have foreseen such an accident as this? It did not appear to be her fault, and she hung her head as if the stem of it were broken, but managed to answer "Sylvy," with much effort when her companion again asked her name.

Mrs. Tilley was standing in the doorway when the trio came into view. The cow gave a loud moo by way of explanation.

"Yes, you'd better speak up for yourself, you old trial! Where'd she tuck herself away this time, Sylvy?" Sylvia kept an awed silence; she knew by instinct that her grandmother did not comprehend the gravity of the situation. She must be mistaking the stranger for one of the farmer-lads of the region.

The young man stood his gun beside the door, and dropped a

heavy game-bag beside it; then he bade Mrs. Tilley good-evening, and repeated his wayfarer's story, and asked if he could have a night's lodging.

"Put me anywhere you like," he said. "I must be off early in the morning, before day; but I am very hungry, indeed. You can give me some milk at any rate, that's plain."

"Dear sakes, yes," responded the hostess, whose long slumbering hospitality seemed to be easily awakened. "You might fare better if you went out on the main road a mile or so, but you're welcome to what we've got. I'll milk right off, and you make yourself at home. You can sleep on husks or feathers," she proffered graciously. "I raised them all myself. There's good pasturing for geese just below here towards the ma'sh. Now step round and set a plate for the gentleman, Sylvy!" and Sylvia promptly stepped. She was glad to have something to do, and she was hungry herself.

It was a surprise to find so clean and comfortable a little dwelling in this New England wilderness. The young man had known the horrors of its most primitive housekeeping, and the dreary squalor of that level of society which does not rebel at the companionship of hens. This was the best thrift of an old-fashioned farmstead, though on such a small scale it seemed like a hermitage. He listened eagerly to the old woman's quaint talk, he watched Sylvia's pale face and shining gray eyes with ever growing enthusiasm, and insisted that this was the best supper he had eaten for a month; then, afterward, the new-made friends sat down in the doorway together while the moon came up.

Soon it would be berry-time, and Sylvia was a great help at picking. The cow was a good milker, though a plaguy thing to keep track of, the hostess gossiped frankly, adding presently that she had buried four children, so that Sylvia's mother, and a son (who might be dead) in California were all the children she had left. "Dan, my boy, was a great hand to go gunning," she explained sadly. "I never wanted for pa'tridges or gray squer'ls while he was to home. He's been a great wand'rer, I expect, and he's no hand to write letters. There, I don't blame him, I'd ha' seen the world myself if it had been so I could.

"Sylvia takes after him," the grandmother continued affectionately, after a minute's pause. "There ain't a foot o' ground she don't know her way over, and the wild creatur's counts her one o' themselves. Squer'ls she'll tame to come an' feed right out o' her hands, and all sorts o' birds. Last winter she got the jay-birds to bangeing here, and I believe she'd 'a' scanted herself of her own meals to have plenty to throw out amongst 'em, if I hadn't kep' watch. Anything but crows, I tell her, I'm willin' to help support,—though Dan he went an' tamed one o' them that did seem to have reason same as folks. It was round here a good spell after he went away. Dan an' his father they didn't hitch,—but he never held up his head ag'in after Dan had dared him an' gone off."

The guest did not notice this hint of family sorrows in his eager interest in something else.

"So Sylvy knows all about birds, does she?" he exclaimed, as he looked round at the little girl who sat, very demure but increasingly sleepy, in the moonlight. "I am making a collection of birds myself. I have been at it ever since I was a boy." (Mrs. Tilley smiled.) "There are two or three very rare ones I have been hunting for these five years. I mean to get them on my own ground if they can be found."

"Do you cage 'em up?" asked Mrs. Tilley doubtfully, in response to this enthusiastic announcement.

"Oh, no, they're stuffed and preserved, dozens and dozens of them," said the ornithologist, "and I have shot or snared every one myself. I caught a glimpse of a white heron three miles from here on Saturday, and I have followed it in this direction. They have never been found in this district at all. The little white heron, it is," and he turned again to look at Sylvia with the hope of discovering that the rare bird was one of her acquaintances.

But Sylvia was watching a hop-toad in the narrow footpath.

"You would know the heron if you saw it," the stranger continued eagerly. "A queer tall white bird with soft feathers and long thin legs. And it would have a nest perhaps in the top of a high tree, made of sticks, something like a hawk's nest."

Sylvia's heart gave a wild beat; she knew that strange white bird, and had once stolen softly near where it stood in some bright green swamp grass, away over at the other side of the woods. There was an open place where the sunshine always seemed strangely yellow and hot, where tall, nodding rushes grew, and her grandmother had warned her that she might sink in the soft black mud underneath and never be heard of more. Not far beyond were the salt marshes and beyond those was the sea, the sea which Sylvia wondered and dreamed about, but never had looked upon, though its great voice could often be heard above the noise of the woods on stormy nights.

"I can't think of anything I should like so much as to find that heron's nest," the handsome stranger was saying. "I would give ten dollars to anybody who could show it to me," he added desperately, "and I mean to spend my whole vacation hunting for it if need be. Perhaps it was only migrating, or had been chased out of its own region by some bird of prey."

Mrs. Tilley gave amazed attention to all this, but Sylvia still watched the toad, not divining, as she might have done at some calmer time, that the creature wished to get to its hole under the doorstep, and was much hindered by the unusual spectators at that hour of the evening. No amount of thought, that night, could decide how many wished-for treasures the ten dollars, so lightly spoken of, would buy.

The next day the young sportsman hovered about the woods, and Sylvia kept him company, having lost her first fear of the friendly lad, who proved to be most kind and sympathetic. He told her many things about the birds and what they knew and where they lived and what they did with themselves. And he gave her a jack-knife, which she thought as great a treasure as if she were a desert-islander. All day long he did not once make her troubled or afraid except when he brought down some unsuspecting singing creature from its bough. Sylvia would have liked him vastly better without his gun; she could not understand why he killed the very birds he seemed to like so much. But as the day waned, Sylvia still watched the young man with loving admiration. She had never seen anybody so charming and delightful; the woman's heart, asleep in the child, was vaguely thrilled by a dream of love. Some premonition of that great power stirred and swayed these young foresters who traversed the solemn woodlands with soft-footed silent care. They stopped to listen to a bird's song; they pressed forward again eagerly, parting the branches,—speaking to each other rarely and in whispers; the young man going first and Sylvia following, fascinated, a few steps behind, with her gray eyes dark with excitement.

She grieved because the longed-for white heron was elusive, but she did not lead the guest, she only followed, and there was no such thing as speaking first. The sound of her own unquestioned voice would have terrified her,—it was hard enough to answer yes or no when there was need of that. At last evening began to fall, and they drove the cow home together, and Sylvia smiled with pleasure when they came to the place where she heard the whistle and was afraid only the night before.

II

Half a mile from home, at the farther edge of the woods, where the land was highest, a great pine-tree stood, the last of its generation. Whether it was left for a boundary mark, or for what reason, no one could say; the woodchoppers who had felled its mates were dead and gone long ago, and a whole forest of sturdy trees, pines and oaks and maples, had grown again. But the stately head of this old pine towered above them all and made a landmark for sea and shore miles and miles away. Sylvia knew it well. She had always believed that whoever climbed to the top of it could see the ocean; and the little girl had often laid her hand on the great rough trunk and looked up wistfully at those dark boughs that the wind always stirred, no matter how hot and still the air might be below. Now she thought of the tree with a new excitement, for why, if one climbed it at break of day, could not one see all the world, and easily discover whence the white heron flew, and mark the place, and find the hidden nest?

What a spirit of adventure, what wild ambition! What fancied triumph and delight and glory for the later morning when she could make known the secret! It was almost too real and too great for the childish heart to bear.

All night the door of the little house stood open, and the whippoorwills came and sang upon the very step. The young sportsman and his old hostess were sound asleep, but Sylvia's great design kept her broad awake and watching. She forgot to think of sleep. The short summer night seemed as long as the winter darkness, and at last when the whippoorwills ceased, and she was afraid the morning would after all come too soon, she stole out of the house and followed the pasture path through the woods, hastening toward the open ground beyond, listening with a sense of comfort and companionship to the drowsy twitter of a half-awakened bird, whose perch she had jarred in passing. Alas, if the great wave of human interest which flooded for the first time this dull little life should sweep away the satisfaction of an existence heart to heart with nature and the dumb life of the forest!

There was the huge tree asleep yet in the paling moonlight, and small and hopeful Sylvia began with utmost bravery to mount to the top of it, with tingling, eager blood coursing the channels of her whole frame, with her bare feet and fingers, that pinched and held like bird's claws to the monstrous ladder reaching up, up, almost to the sky itself. First she must mount the white oak tree that grew alongside, where she was almost lost among the dark branches and the green leaves heavy and wet with dew; a bird fluttered off its nest, and a red squirrel ran to and fro and scolded pettishly at the harmless housebreaker. Sylvia felt her way easily. She had often climbed there, and knew that higher still one of the oak's upper branches chafed against the pine trunk, just where its lower boughs were set close together. There, when she made the dangerous pass from one tree to the other, the great enterprise would really begin.

She crept out along the swaying oak limb at last, and took the daring step across into the old pine-tree. The way was harder than she thought; she must reach far and hold fast, the sharp dry twigs caught and held her and scratched her like angry talons, the pitch made her thin little fingers clumsy and stiff as she went round and round the tree's great stem, higher and higher upward. The sparrows and robins in the woods below were beginning to wake and twitter to the dawn, yet it seemed much lighter there aloft in the pine-tree, and the child knew that she must hurry if her project were to be of any use.

The tree seemed to lengthen itself out as she went up, and to reach farther and farther upward. It was like a great main-mast to the voyaging earth; it must truly have been amazed that morning through all its ponderous frame as it felt this determined spark of human spirit creeping and climbing from higher branch to branch. Who knows how steadily the least twigs held themselves to advantage this light, weak creature on her way! The old pine must have loved his new dependent. More than all the hawks, and bats, and moths, and even the sweet-voiced thrushes, was the brave, beating heart of the solitary gray-eyed child. And the tree stood still and held away the winds that June morning while the dawn grew bright in the east.

Sylvia's face was like a pale star, if one had seen it from the ground, when the last thorny bough was past, and she stood trembling and tired but wholly triumphant, high in the tree-top. Yes, there was the sea with the dawning sun making a golden dazzle over it, and toward that glorious east flew two hawks with slow-moving pinions. How low they looked in the air from that height when before one had only seen them far up, and dark against the blue sky. Their gay feathers were as soft as moths; they seemed only a little way from the tree, and Sylvia felt as if she too could go flying away among the clouds. Westward, the woodlands and farms reached miles and miles into the distance; here and there were church steeples, and white villages; truly it was a vast and awesome world.

The birds sang louder and louder. At last the sun came up bewilderingly bright. Sylvia could see the white sails of ships out at sea, and the clouds that were purple and rose-colored and yellow at first began to fade away. Where was the white heron's nest in the sea of green branches, and was this wonderful sight and pageant of the world the only reward for having climbed to such a giddy height? Now look down again, Sylvia, where the green marsh is set among the shining birches and dark hemlocks; there where you saw the white heron once you will see him again; look, look! a white spot of him like a single floating feather comes up from the dead hemlock and grows larger, and rises, and comes close at last, and goes by the landmark pine with steady sweep of wing and outstretched slender neck and crested head. And wait! wait! do not move a foot or a finger, little girl, do not send an arrow of light and consciousness from your two eager eyes, for the heron has perched on a pine bough not far beyond yours, and cries back to his mate on the nest, and plumes his feathers for the new day!

The child gives a long sigh a minute later when a company of shouting cat-birds comes also to the tree, and vexed by their fluttering and lawlessness the solemn heron goes away. She knows his secret now, the wild, light, slender bird that floats and wavers, and goes back like an arrow presently to his home in the green world beneath.

Then Sylvia, well satisfied, makes her perilous way down again, not daring to look far below the branch she stands on, ready to cry sometimes because her fingers ache and her lamed feet slip. Wondering over and over again what the stranger would say to her, and what he would think when she told him how to find his way straight to the heron's nest.

"Sylvy, Sylvy!" called the busy old grandmother again and again, but nobody answered, and the small husk bed was empty, and Sylvia had disappeared.

The guest waked from a dream, and remembering his day's pleasure hurried to dress himself that it might sooner begin. He was sure from the way the shy little girl looked once or twice yesterday that she had at least seen the white heron, and now she must really be persuaded to tell. Here she comes now, paler than ever, and her worn old frock is torn and tattered, and smeared with pine pitch. The grandmother and the sportsman stand in the door together and question her, and the splendid moment has come to speak of the dead hemlock-tree by the green marsh.

But Sylvia does not speak after all, though the old grandmother fretfully rebukes her, and the young man's kind appealing eyes are looking straight into her own. He can make them rich with money; he has promised it, and they are poor now. He is so well worth making happy, and he waits to hear the story she can tell.

No, she must keep silence! What is it that suddenly forbids her and makes her dumb? Has she been nine years growing, and now, when the great world for the first time puts out a hand to her, must she thrust it aside for a bird's sake? The murmur of the pine's green branches is in her ears, she remembers how the white heron came flying through the golden air and how they watched the sea and the morning together, and Sylvia cannot speak; she cannot tell the heron's secret and give its life away.

Dear loyalty, that suffered a sharp pang as the guest went away disappointed later in the day, that could have served and followed him and loved him as a dog loves! Many a night Sylvia heard the echo of his whistle haunting the pasture path as she came home with the loitering cow. She forgot even her sorrow at the sharp report of his gun and the piteous sight of thrushes and sparrows dropping silent to the ground, their songs hushed and their pretty feathers stained and wet with blood. Were the birds better friends than their hunter might have been,—who can tell? Whatever treasures were lost to her, woodlands and summertime, remember! Bring your gifts and graces and tell your secrets to this lonely country child!

SARAH ORNE JEWETT

The Flight of Betsey Lane

I

ONE WINDY MORNING IN May, three old women sat together near an open window in the shed chamber of Byfleet Poor-house. The wind was from the northwest, but their window faced the southeast, and they were only visited by an occasional pleasant waft of fresh air. They were close together, knee to knee, picking over a bushel of beans, and commanding a view of the dandelion-starred, green yard below, and of the winding, sandy road that led to the village, two miles away. Some captive bees were scolding among the cobwebs of the rafters overhead, or thumping against the upper panes of glass; two calves were bawling from the barnyard, where some of the men were at work loading a dump-cart and shouting as if every one were deaf. There was a cheerful feeling of activity, and even an air of comfort, about the Byfleet Poor-house. Almost every one was possessed of a most interesting past, though there was less to be said about the future. The inmates were by no means distressed or unhappy; many of them retired to this shelter only for the winter season, and would go out presently, some to begin such work as they could still do, others to live in their own small houses; old age had impoverished most of them by limiting their power of endurance; but far from lamenting the fact that they were town charges, they rather liked the change and excitement of a winter residence on the poor-farm. There was a sharp-faced, hard-worked young widow with seven children, who was an exception to the general level of society, because she deplored the change in her fortunes. The older women regarded her with suspicion, and were apt to talk about her in moments like this, when they happened to sit together at their work.

The three bean-pickers were dressed alike in stout brown ginghams, checked by a white line, and all wore great faded aprons of blue drilling, with sufficient pockets convenient to the right hand. Miss Peggy Bond was a very small, belligerent-looking person, who wore a huge pair of steel-bowed spectacles, holding her sharp chin well up in air, as if to supplement an inadequate nose. She was more than half blind, but the spectacles seemed to face upward instead of square ahead, as if their wearer were always on the sharp lookout for birds. Miss Bond had suffered much personal damage from time to time, because she never took heed where she planted her feet, and so was always tripping and stubbing her bruised way through the world. She had fallen down hatchways and cellarways, and stepped composedly into deep ditches and pasture brooks; but she was proud of stating that she was upsighted, and so was her father before her. At the poorhouse, where an unusual malady was considered a distinction, upsightedness was looked upon as a most honorable infirmity. Plain rheumatism, such as afflicted Aunt Lavina Dow, whose twisted hands found even this light work difficult and tiresome,—plain rheumatism was something of everyday occurrence, and nobody cared to hear about it. Poor Peggy was a meek and friendly soul, who never put herself forward; she was just like other folks, as she always loved to say, but Mrs. Lavina Dow was a different sort of person altogether, of great dignity and, occasionally, almost aggressive behavior. The time had been when she could do a good day's work with anybody: but for many years now she had not left the town-farm, being too badly crippled to work; she had no relations or friends to visit, but from an innate love of authority she could not submit to being one of those who are forgotten by the world. Mrs. Dow was the hostess and social lawgiver here, where she remembered every inmate and every item of interest for nearly forty years, besides an immense amount of town history and biography for three or four generations back.

She was the dear friend of the third woman, Betsey Lane; together they led thought and opinion—chiefly opinion—and held sway, not only over Byfleet Poor-farm, but also the selectmen and all others in authority. Betsey Lane had spent most of her life as aid-in-general to the respected household of old General Thornton. She had been much trusted and valued, and, at the breaking up of that once large and flourishing family, she had been left in good circumstances, what with legacies and her own comfortable savings; but by sad misfortune and lavish generosity everything had been scattered, and after much illness, which ended in a stiffened arm and more uncertainty, the good soul had sensibly decided that it was easier for the whole town to support her than for a part of it. She had always hoped to see something of the world before she died; she came of an adventurous, seafaring stock, but had never made a longer journey than to the towns of Danby and Northville, thirty miles away.

They were all old women; but Betsey Lane, who was sixty-nine, and looked much older, was the youngest. Peggy Bond was far on in the seventies, and Mrs. Dow was at least ten years older. She made a great secret of her years; and as she sometimes spoke of events prior to the Revolution with the assertion of having been an eye-witness, she naturally wore an air of vast antiquity. Her tales were an inexpressible delight to Betsey Lane, who felt younger by twenty years because her friend and comrade was so unconscious of chronological limitations.

The bushel basket of cranberry beans was within easy reach, and each of the pickers had filled her lap from it again and again. The shed chamber was not an unpleasant place in which to sit at work, with its traces of seed corn hanging from the brown cross-beams, its spare churns, and dusty loom, and rickety wool-wheels, and a few bits of old furniture. In one far corner was a wide board of dismal use and suggestion, and close beside it an old cradle. There was a battered chest of drawers where the keeper of the poor-house kept his garden-seeds, with the withered remains of three seed cucumbers ornamenting the top. Nothing beautiful could be discovered, nothing interesting, but there was something usable and homely about the place. It was the favorite and untroubled bower of the bean-pickers, to which they might retreat unmolested from the public apartments of this rustic institution.

Betsey Lane blew away the chaff from her handful of beans. The spring breeze blew the chaff back again, and sifted it over her face and shoulders. She rubbed it out of her eyes impatiently, and happened to notice old Peggy holding her own handful high, as if it were an oblation, and turning her queer, up-tilted head this way and that, to look at the beans sharply, as if she were first cousin to a hen.

"There, Miss Bond, 't is kind of botherin' work for you, ain't it?" Betsey inquired compassionately.

"I feel to enjoy it, anything that I can do my own way so," responded Peggy. "I like to do my part. Ain't that old Mis' Fales comin' up the road? It sounds like her step."

The others looked, but they were not farsighted, and for a moment Peggy had the advantage. Mrs. Fales was not a favorite.

"I hope she ain't comin' here to put up this spring. I guess she won't now, it's gettin' so late," said Betsey Lane. "She likes to go rovin' soon as the roads is settled."

"'T is Mis' Fales!" said Peggy Bond, listening with solemn anxiety. "There, do let's pray her by!"

"I guess she's headin' for her cousin's folks up Beech Hill way," said Betsey presently. "If she'd left her daughter's this mornin', she'd have got just about as far as this. I kind o' wish she had stepped in just to pass the time o' day, long's she wa'n't going to make no stop."

There was a silence as to further speech in the shed chamber; and even the calves were quiet in the barnyard. The men had all gone away to the field where corn-planting was going on. The beans clicked steadily into the wooden measure at the pickers' feet. Betsey Lane began to sing a hymn, and the others joined in as best they might, like autumnal crickets; their voices were sharp and cracked, with now and then a few low notes of plaintive tone. Betsey herself could sing pretty well, but the others could only make a kind of accompaniment. Their voices ceased altogether at the higher notes.

"Oh my! I wish I had the means to go to the Centennial," mourned Betsey Lane, stopping so suddenly that the others had to go on croaking and shrilling without her for a moment before they could stop. "It seems to me as if I can't die happy 'less I do," she added; "I ain't never seen nothin' of the world, an' here I be."

"What if you was as old as I be?" suggested Mrs. Dow pompously. "You've got time enough yet, Betsey; don't you go an' despair. I knowed of a woman that went clean round the world four times when she was past eighty, an' enjoyed herself real well. Her folks followed the sea; she had three sons an' a daughter married,—all shipmasters, and she'd been with her own husband when they was young. She was left a widder early, and fetched up her family herself,—a real stirrin', smart woman. After they'd got married off, an' settled, an' was doing well, she come to be lonesome; and first she tried to stick it out alone, but she wa'n't one that could; an' she got a notion she had n't nothin' before her but her last sickness, and she wa'n't a person that enjoyed havin' other folks do for her. So one on her boys—I guess 't was the oldest—said he was going to take her to sea; there was ample room, an' he was sailin' a good time o' year for the Cape o' Good Hope an' way up to some o' them tea-ports in the Chiny Seas. She was all high to go, but it made a sight o' talk at her age; an' the minister made it a subject o' prayer the last Sunday, and all the folks took a last leave; but she said to some she'd fetch 'em home something real pritty, and so did. An' then they come home t' other way, round the Horn, an' she done so well, an' was such a sight o' company, the other child'n was jealous, an' she promised she'd go a v'y'ge long o' each on 'em. She was as sprightly a person as ever I see; an' could speak well o' what she'd seen."

"Did she die to sea?" asked Peggy, with interest.

"No, she died to home between v'y'ges, or she'd gone to sea again. I was to her funeral. She liked her son George's ship the best; 't was the one she was going on to Callao. They said the men aboard all called her 'gran'ma'am,' an' she kep' 'em mended up, an' would go below and tend to 'em if they was sick. She might 'a' been alive an' enjoyin' of herself a good many years but for the kick of a cow; 't was a new cow out of a drove, a dreadful unruly beast."

Mrs. Dow stopped for breath, and reached down for a new supply of beans; her empty apron was gray with soft chaff. Betsey Lane, still pondering on the Centennial, began to sing another verse of her hymn, and again the old women joined her. At this moment some strangers came driving round into the yard from the front of the house. The turf was soft, and our friends did not hear the horses' steps. Their voices cracked and quavered; it was a funny little concert, and a lady in an open carriage just below listened with sympathy and amusement.

II

"Betsey! Betsey! Miss Lane!" a voice called eagerly at the foot of the stairs that led up from the shed. "Betsey! There's a lady here wants to see you right away."

Betsey was dazed with excitement, like a country child who knows the rare pleasure of being called out of school. "Lor', I ain't fit to go down, be I?" she faltered, looking anxiously at her friends; but Peggy was gazing even nearer to the zenith than usual, in her excited effort to see down into the yard, and Mrs. Dow only nodded somewhat jealously, and said that she guessed 't was nobody would do her any harm. She rose ponderously, while Betsey hesitated, being, as they would have said, all of a twitter. "It is a lady, certain," Mrs. Dow assured her; "'t ain't often there's a lady comes here."

"While there was any of Mis' Gen'ral Thornton's folks left, I wa'n't without visits from the gentry," said Betsey Lane, turning back proudly at the head of the stairs, with a touch of old-world pride and sense of high station. Then she disappeared, and closed the door behind her at the stair-foot with a decision quite unwelcome to the friends above.

"She need n't 'a' been so dreadful 'fraid anybody was goin' to listen. I guess we've got folks to ride an' see us, or had once, if we hain't now," said Miss Peggy Bond, plaintively.

"I expect 't was only the wind shoved it to," said Aunt Lavina. "Betsey is one that gits flustered easier than some. I wish 't was somebody to take her off an' give her a kind of a good time; she's young to settle down 'long of old folks like us. Betsey 's got a notion o' rovin' such as ain't my natur', but I should like to see her satisfied. She'd been a very understandin' person, if she had the advantages that some does."

"'T is so," said Peggy Bond, tilting her chin high. "I suppose you can't hear nothin' they're saying? I feel my hearin' ain't up to whar it was. I can hear things close to me well as ever; but there, hearin' ain't everything; 't ain't as if we lived where there was more goin' on to hear. Seems to me them folks is stoppin' a good while."

"They surely be," agreed Lavina Dow.

"I expect it's somethin' particular. There ain't none of the Thornton folks left, except one o' the gran'darters, an' I've often heard Betsey remark that she should never see her more, for she lives to London. Strange how folks feels contented in them strayaway places off to the ends of the airth."

The flies and bees were buzzing against the hot window-panes; the handfuls of beans were clicking into the brown wooden measure.

A bird came and perched on the window-sill, and then flitted away toward the blue sky. Below, in the yard, Betsey Lane stood talking with the lady. She had put her blue drilling apron over her head, and her face was shining with delight.

"Lor', dear," she said, for at least the third time, "I remember ye when I first see ye; an awful pritty baby you was, an' they all said you looked just like the old gen'ral. Be you goin' back to foreign parts right away?"

"Yes, I'm going back; you know that all my children are there. I wish I could take you with me for a visit," said the charming young guest. "I'm going to carry over some of the pictures and furniture from the old house; I didn't care half so much for them when I was younger as I do now. Perhaps next summer we shall all come over for a while. I should like to see my girls and boys playing under the pines."

"I wish you re'lly was livin' to the old place," said Betsey Lane. Her imagination was not swift; she needed time to think over all that was being told her, and she could not fancy the two strange houses across the sea. The old Thornton house was to her mind the most delightful and elegant in the world.

"Is there anything I can do for you?" asked Mrs. Strafford kindly,—"anything that I can do for you myself, before I go away? I shall be writing to you, and sending some pictures of the children, and you must let me know how you are getting on."

"Yes, there is one thing, darlin'. If you could stop in the village an' pick me out a pritty, little, small lookin'-glass, that I can keep for my own an' have to remember you by. 'T ain't that I want to set me above the rest o' the folks, but I was always used to havin' my own when I was to your grandma's. There's very nice folks here, some on 'em, and I'm better off than if I was able to keep house; but sence you ask me, that's the only thing I feel cropin' about. What be you goin' right back for? ain't you goin' to see the great fair to Pheladelphy, that everybody talks about?"

"No," said Mrs. Strafford, laughing at this eager and almost convicting question. "No; I'm going back next week. If I were, I believe that I should take you with me. Good-by, dear old Betsey; you make me feel as if I were a little girl again; you look just the same."

For full five minutes the old woman stood out in the sunshine, dazed with delight, and majestic with a sense of her own consequence. She held something tight in her hand, without thinking what it might be; but just as the friendly mistress of the poor-farm came out to hear the news, she tucked the roll of money into the bosom of her brown gingham dress. " 'T was my dear Mis' Katy Strafford," she turned to say proudly. "She come way over from London; she's been sick; they thought the voyage would do her good. She said most the first thing she had on her mind was to come an' find me, and see how I was, an' if I was comfortable; an' now she's goin' right back. She's got two splendid houses; an' said how she wished I was there to look after things,—she remembered I was always her gran'ma's right hand. Oh, it does so carry me back, to see her! Seems if all the rest on 'em must be there together to the old house. There, I must go right up an' tell Mis' Dow an' Peggy."

"Dinner 's all ready; I was just goin' to blow the horn for the menfolks," said the keeper's wife. "They'll be right down. I expect you've got along smart with them beans,—all three of you together;" but Betsey's mind roved so high and so far at that moment that no achievements of bean-picking could lure it back

III

The long table in the great kitchen soon gathered its company of waifs and strays,—creatures of improvidence and misfortune, and the irreparable victims of old age. The dinner was satisfactory, and there was not much delay for conversation. Peggy Bond and Mrs. Dow and Betsey Lane always sat together at one end, with an air of putting the rest of the company below the salt. Betsey was still flushed with excitement; in fact, she could not eat as much as usual, and she looked up from time to time expectantly, as if she were likely to be asked to speak of her guest; but everybody was hungry, and even Mrs. Dow broke in upon some attempted confidences by asking inopportunely for a second potato. There were nearly twenty at the table, counting the keeper and his wife and two children, noisy little persons who had come from school with the small flock belonging to the poor widow, who sat just opposite our friends. She finished her dinner before any one else, and pushed her chair back; she always helped with the housework,—a thin, sorry, bad-tempered-looking poor soul, whom grief had sharpened instead of softening. "I expect you feel too fine to set with common folks," she said enviously to Betsey.

"Here I be a-settin'," responded Betsey calmly. "I don' know's I behave more unbecomin' than usual." Betsey prided herself upon her good and proper manners; but the rest of the company, who would have liked to hear the bit of morning news, were now defrauded of that pleasure. The wrong note had been struck; there was a silence after the clatter of knives and plates, and one by one the cheerful town charges disappeared. The bean-picking had been finished, and there was a call for any of the women who felt like planting corn; so Peggy Bond, who could follow the line of hills pretty fairly, and Betsey herself, who was still equal to anybody at that work, and Mrs. Dow, all went out to the field together. Aunt Lavina labored slowly up the yard, carrying a light splint-bottomed kitchen chair and her knitting-work, and sat near the stone wall on a gentle rise, where she could see the pond and the green country, and exchange a word with her friends as they came and went up and down the rows. Betsey vouchsafed a word now and then about Mrs. Strafford, but you would have thought that she had been suddenly elevated to Mrs. Strafford's own cares and the responsibilities attending them, and had little in common with her old associates. Mrs. Dow and Peggy knew well that these high-feeling times never lasted long, and so they waited with as much patience as they could muster. They were by no means without that true tact which is only another word for unselfish sympathy.

The strip of corn land ran along the side of a great field; at the upper end of it was a field-corner thicket of young maples and walnut saplings, the children of a great nut-tree that marked the boundary. Once, when Betsey Lane found herself alone near this shelter at the end of her row, the other planters having lagged behind beyond the rising ground, she looked stealthily about, and then put her hand inside her gown, and for the first time took out the money that Mrs. Strafford had given her. She turned it over and over with an astonished look: there were new bank-bills for a hundred dollars. Betsey gave a funny little shrug of her shoulders, came out of the bushes, and took a step or two on the narrow edge of turf, as if she were going to dance; then she hastily tucked away her treasure, and stepped discreetly down into the soft harrowed and hoed land, and began to drop corn again, five kernels to a hill. She had seen the top of Peggy

Bond's head over the knoll, and now Peggy herself came entirely into view, gazing upward to the skies, and stumbling more or less, but counting the corn by touch and twisting her head about anxiously to gain advantage over her uncertain vision. Betsey made a friendly, inarticulate little sound as they passed; she was thinking that somebody said once that Peggy's eyesight might be remedied if she could go to Boston to the hospital; but that was so remote and impossible an undertaking that no one had ever taken the first step. Betsey Lane's brown old face suddenly worked with excitement, but in a moment more she regained her usual firm expression, and spoke carelessly to Peggy as she turned and came alongside.

The high spring wind of the morning had quite fallen; it was a lovely May afternoon. The woods about the field to the northward were full of birds, and the young leaves scarcely hid the solemn shapes of a company of crows that patiently attended the corn-planting. Two of the men had finished their hoeing, and were busy with the construction of a scarecrow; they knelt in the furrows, chuckling, and looking over some forlorn, discarded garments. It was a time-honored custom to make the scarecrow resemble one of the poor-house family; and this year they intended to have Mrs. Lavina Dow protect the field in effigy; last year it was the counterfeit of Betsey Lane who stood on guard, with an easily recognized quilted hood and the remains of a valued shawl that one of the calves had found airing on a fence and chewed to pieces. Behind the men was the foundation for this rustic attempt at statuary,—an upright stake and bar in the form of a cross. This stood on the highest part of the field; and as the men knelt near it, and the quaint figures of the corn-planters went and came, the scene gave a curious suggestion of foreign life. It was not like New England; the presence of the rude cross appealed strangely to the imagination.

IV

Life flowed so smoothly, for the most part, at the Byfleet Poor-farm, that nobody knew what to make, later in the summer, of a strange disappearance. All the elder inmates were familiar with illness and death, and the poor pomp of a town-pauper's funeral. The comings and goings and the various misfortunes of those who composed this strange family, related only through its disasters, hardly served for the excitement and talk of a single day. Now that the June days were at their longest, the old people were sure to wake earlier than ever; but one morning, to the astonishment of every one, Betsey Lane's bed was empty; the sheets and blankets, which were her own, and guarded with jealous care, were carefully folded and placed on a chair not too near the window, and Betsey had flown. Nobody had heard her go down the creaking stairs. The kitchen door was unlocked, and the old watch-dog lay on the step outside in the early sunshine, wagging his tail and looking wise, as if he were left on guard and meant to keep the fugitive's secret.

"Never knowed her to do nothin' afore 'thout talking it over a fortnight, and paradin' off when we could all see her," ventured a spiteful voice. "Guess we can wait till night to hear 'bout it."

Mrs. Dow looked sorrowful and shook her head. "Betsey had an aunt on her mother's side that went and drownded of herself; she was a pritty-appearing woman as ever you see."

"Perhaps she's gone to spend the day with Decker's folks," suggested Peggy Bond. "She always takes an extra early start; she was speakin' lately o' going up their way;" but Mrs. Dow shook her head with a most melancholy look. "I'm impressed that something 's befell her," she insisted. "I heard her a-groanin' in her sleep. I was wakeful the forepart o' the night,—'t is very unusual with me, too."

"'T wa'n't like Betsey not to leave us any word," said the other old friend, with more resentment than melancholy. They sat together almost in silence that morning in the shed chamber. Mrs. Dow was sorting and cutting rags, and Peggy braided them into long ropes, to be made into mats at a later date. If they had only known where Betsey Lane had gone, they might have talked about it until dinner-time at noon; but failing this new subject, they could take no interest in any of their old ones. Out in the field the corn was well up, and the men were hoeing. It was a hot morning in the shed chamber, and the woolen rags were dusty and hot to handle.

V

Byfleet people knew each other well, and when this mysteriously absent person did not return to the town-farm at the end of a week, public interest became much excited; and presently it was ascertained that Betsey Lane was neither making a visit to her friends the Deckers on Birch Hill, nor to any nearer acquaintances; in fact, she had disappeared altogether from her wonted haunts. Nobody remembered to have seen her pass, hers had been such an early flitting; and when somebody thought of her having gone away by train, he was laughed at for forgetting that the earliest morning train from South Byfleet, the nearest station, did not start until long after eight o'clock; and if Betsey had designed to be one of the passengers, she would have started along the road at seven, and been seen and known of all women. There was not a kitchen in that part of Byfleet that did not have windows toward the road. Conversation rarely left the level of the neighborhood gossip: to see Betsey Lane, in her best clothes, at that hour in the morning, would have been the signal for much exercise of imagination; but as day after day went by without news, the curiosity of those who knew her best turned slowly into fear, and at last Peggy Bond again gave utterance to the belief that Betsey had either gone out in the early morning and put an end to her life, or that she had gone to the Centennial. Some of the people at table were moved to loud laughter,—it was at supper-time on a Sunday night,—but others listened with great interest.

"She never'd put on her good clothes to drownd herself," said the widow. "She might have thought 't was good as takin' 'em with her, though. Old folks has wandered off an' got lost in the woods afore now."

Mrs. Dow and Peggy resented this impertinent remark, but deigned to take no notice of the speaker. "She would n't have wore her best clothes to the Centennial, would she?" mildly inquired Peggy, bobbing her head toward the ceiling. "'T would be a shame to spoil your best things in such a place. An' I don't know of her havin' any money; there's the end o' that."

"You're bad as old Mis' Bland, that used to live neighbor to our folks," said one of the old men. "She was dreadful precise; an' she so begretched to wear a good alapaca dress that was left to her, that it hung in a press forty year, an' baited the moths at last."

"I often seen Mis' Bland a-goin' in to meetin' when I was a young girl," said Peggy Bond approvingly. "She was a good-appearin' woman, an' she left property."

"Wish she'd left it to me, then," said the poor soul opposite, glancing at her pathetic row of children: but it was not good manners at the farm to deplore one's situation, and Mrs. Dow and Peggy only frowned. "Where do you suppose Betsey can be?" said Mrs. Dow, for the twentieth time. "She did n't have no money. I know she ain't gone far, if it's so that she's yet alive. She's b'en real pinched all the spring."

"Perhaps that lady that come one day give her some," the keeper's wife suggested mildly.

"Then Betsey would have told me," said Mrs. Dow, with injured dignity.

VI

On the morning of her disappearance, Betsey rose even before the pewee and the English sparrow, and dressed herself quietly, though with trembling hands, and stole out of the kitchen door like a plunderless thief. The old dog licked her hand and looked at her anxiously; the tortoise-shell cat rubbed against her best gown, and trotted away up the yard, then she turned anxiously and came after the old woman, following faithfully until she had to be driven back. Betsey was used to long country excursions afoot. She dearly loved the early morning; and finding that there was no dew to trouble her, she began to follow pasture paths and short cuts across the fields, surprising here and there a flock of sleepy sheep, or a startled calf that rustled out from the bushes. The birds were pecking their breakfast from bush and turf; and hardly any of the wild inhabitants of that rural world were enough alarmed by her presence to do more than flutter away if they chanced to be in her path. She stepped along, light-footed and eager as a girl, dressed in her neat old straw bonnet and black gown, and carrying a few belongings in her best bundle-handkerchief, one that her only brother had brought home from the East Indies fifty years before. There was an old crow perched as sentinel on a small, dead pine-tree, where he could warn friends who were pulling up the sprouted corn in a field close by; but he only gave a contemptuous caw as the adventurer appeared, and she shook her bundle at him in revenge, and laughed to see him so clumsy as he tried to keep his footing on the twigs.

"Yes, I be," she assured him. "I'm a-goin' to Pheladelphy, to the Centennial, same 's other folks. I'd jest as soon tell ye 's not, old crow;" and Betsey laughed aloud in pleased content with herself and her daring, as she walked along. She had only two miles to go to the station at South Byfleet, and she felt for the money now and then, and found it safe enough. She took great pride in the success of her escape, and especially in the long concealment of her wealth. Not a night had passed since Mrs. Strafford's visit that she had not slept with the roll of money under her pillow by night, and buttoned safe inside her dress by day. She knew that everybody would offer advice and even commands about the spending or saving of it; and she brooked no interference.

The last mile of the foot-path to South Byfleet was along the railway track; and Betsey began to feel in haste, though it was still nearly two hours to train time. She looked anxiously forward and back along the rails every few minutes, for fear of being run over; and at last she caught sight of an engine that was apparently coming toward her, and took flight into the woods before she could gather courage to follow the path again. The freight train proved to be at a standstill, waiting at a turnout; and some of the men were straying about, eating their early breakfast comfortably in this time of leisure. As the old woman came up to them, she stopped too, for a moment of rest and conversation.

"Where be ye goin'?" she asked pleasantly; and they told her. It was to the town where she had to change cars and take the great through train; a point of geography which she had learned from evening talks between the men at the farm.

"What 'll ye carry me there for?"

"We don't run no passenger cars," said one of the young fellows, laughing. "What makes you in such a hurry?"

"I'm startin' for Pheladelphy, an' it's a gre't ways to go."

"So 't is; but you're consid'able early, if you're makin' for the eight-forty train. See here! you have n't got a needle an' thread 'long of you in that bundle, have you? If you'll sew me on a couple o' buttons, I'll give ye a free ride. I'm in a sight o' distress, an' none o' the fellows is provided with as much as a bent pin."

"You poor boy! I'll have you seen to, in half a minute. I'm troubled with a stiff arm, but I'll do the best I can."

The obliging Betsey seated herself stiffly on the slope of the embankment, and found her thread and needle with utmost haste. Two of the train-men stood by and watched the careful stitches, and even offered her a place as spare brakeman, so that they might keep her near; and Betsey took the offer with considerable seriousness, only thinking it necessary to assure them that she was getting most too old to be out in all weathers. An express went by like an earthquake, and she was presently hoisted on board an empty box-car by two of her new and flattering acquaintances, and found herself before noon at the end of the first stage of her journey, without having spent a cent, and furnished with any amount of thrifty advice. One of the young men, being compassionate of her unprotected state as a traveler, advised her to find out the widow of an uncle of his in Philadelphia, saying despairingly that he could n't tell her just how to find the house; but Miss Betsey Lane said that she had an English tongue in her head, and should be sure to find whatever she was looking for. This unexpected incident of the freight train was the reason why everybody about the South Byfleet station insisted that no such person had taken passage by the regular train that same morning, and why there were those who persuaded themselves that Miss Betsey Lane was probably lying at the bottom of the poor-farm pond.

VII

"Land sakes!" said Miss Betsey Lane, as she watched a Turkish person parading by in his red fez, "I call the Centennial somethin' like the day o' judgment! I wish I was goin' to stop a month, but I dare say 't would be the death o' my poor old bones."

She was leaning against the barrier of a patent pop-corn establishment, which had given her a sudden reminder of home, and of the winter nights when the sharp-kerneled little red and yellow ears were brought out, and Old Uncle Eph Flanders sat by the kitchen stove, and solemnly filled a great wooden chopping-tray for the refreshment of the company. She had wandered and loitered and looked until her eyes and head had grown numb and unreceptive; but it is only unimaginative persons who can be really astonished. The imagination can always outrun the possible and actual sights and sounds of the world; and this plain old body from Byfleet rarely found anything rich and splendid enough to surprise her. She saw the wonders of the West and the splendors of the East with equal calmness and satisfaction; she had always known that there was an amazing world outside the boundaries of Byfleet. There was a piece of paper in her pocket on which was marked, in her clumsy handwriting, "If Betsey Lane should meet with accident, notify the selectmen of Byfleet"; but having made this slight provision for the future, she had thrown herself boldly into the sea of strangers, and then had made the joyful discovery that friends were to be found at every turn.

There was something delightfully companionable about Betsey; she had a way of suddenly looking up over her big spectacles with a reassuring and expectant smile, as if you were going to speak to her, and you generally did. She must have found out where hundreds of people came from, and whom they had left at home, and what they thought of the great show, as she sat on a bench to rest, or leaned over the railings where free luncheons were afforded by the makers of hot waffles and molasses candy and fried potatoes; and there was not a night when she did not return to her lodgings with a pocket crammed with samples of spool cotton and nobody knows what. She had already collected small presents for almost everybody she knew at home, and she was such a pleasant, beaming old country body, so unmistakably appreciative and interested, that nobody ever thought of wishing that she would move on. Nearly all the busy people of the Exhibition called her either Aunty or Grandma at once, and made little pleasures for her as best they could. She was a delightful contrast to the indifferent, stupid crowd that drifted along, with eyes fixed at the same level, and seeing, even on that level, nothing for fifty feet at a time. "What be you making here, dear?" Betsey Lane would ask joyfully, and the most perfunctory guardian hastened to explain. She squandered money as she had never had the pleasure of doing before, and this hastened the day when she must return to Byfleet. She was always inquiring if there were any spectacle-sellers at hand, and received occasional directions; but it was a difficult place for her to find her way about in, and the very last day of her stay arrived before she found an exhibitor of the desired sort, an oculist and instrument-maker.

"I called to get some specs for a friend that's upsighted," she gravely informed the salesman, to his extreme amusement. "She's dreadful troubled, and jerks her head up like a hen a-drinkin'. She's got a blur a-growin' an' spreadin', an' sometimes she can see out to one side on't, and more times she can't."

"Cataracts," said a middle-aged gentleman at her side; and Betsey Lane turned to regard him with approval and curiosity.

" 'T is Miss Peggy Bond I was mentioning, of Byfleet Poor-farm," she explained. "I count on gettin' some glasses to relieve her trouble, if there's any to be found."

"Glasses won't do her any good," said the stranger. "Suppose you come and sit down on this bench, and tell me all about it. First, where is Byfleet?" and Betsey gave the directions at length.

"I thought so," said the surgeon. "How old is this friend of yours?"

Betsey cleared her throat decisively, and smoothed her gown over her knees as if it were an apron; then she turned to take a good look at her new acquaintance as they sat on the rustic bench together. "Who be you, sir, I should like to know?" she asked, in a friendly tone.

"My name's Dunster."

"I take it you're a doctor," continued Betsey, as if they had overtaken each other walking from Byfleet to South Byfleet on a summer morning.

"I'm a doctor; part of one at least," said he. "I know more or less about eyes; and I spend my summers down on the shore at the mouth of your river; some day I'll come up and look at this person. How old is she?"

"Peggy Bond is one that never tells her age; 't ain't come quite up to where she'll begin to brag of it, you see," explained Betsey reluctantly; "but I know her to be nigh to seventy-six, one way or t' other. Her an' Mrs. Mary Ann Chick was same year's child'n, and Peggy knows I know it, an' two or three times when we've be'n in the buryin'-ground where Mary Ann lays an' has her dates right on her headstone, I could n't bring Peggy to take no sort o' notice. I will say she makes, at times, a convenience of being upsighted. But there, I feel for her,—everybody does; it keeps her stubbin' an' trippin' against everything, beakin' and gazin' up the way she has to."

"Yes, yes," said the doctor, whose eyes were twinkling. "I'll come and look after her, with your town doctor, this summer,—some time in the last of July or first of August."

"You'll find occupation," said Betsey, not without an air of patronage. "Most of us to the Byfleet Farm has got our ails, now I tell ye. You ain't got no bitters that'll take a dozen years right off an ol' lady's shoulders?"

The busy man smiled pleasantly, and shook his head as he went away. "Dunster," said Betsey to herself, soberly committing the new name to her sound memory. "Yes, I must n't forget to speak of him to the doctor, as he directed. I do' know now as Peggy would vally herself quite so much accordin' to, if she had her eyes fixed same as other folks. I expect there would n't been a smarter woman in town, though, if she'd had a proper chance. Now I've done what I set to do for her, I do believe, an' 't wa'n't glasses, neither. I'll git her a pritty little shawl with that money I laid aside. Peggy Bond ain't got a pritty shawl. I always wanted to have a real good time, an' now I'm havin' it."

VIII

Two or three days later, two pathetic figures might have been seen crossing the slopes of the poor-farm field, toward the low shores of Byfield pond. It was early in the morning, and the stubble of the lately mown grass was wet with rain and hindering to old feet. Peggy Bond was more blundering and liable to stray in the wrong direction than usual; it was one of the days when she could hardly see at all. Aunt Lavina Dow was unusually clumsy of movement, and stiff in the joints; she had not been so far from the house for three years. The morning breeze filled the gathers of her wide gingham skirt, and aggravated the size of her unwieldy figure. She supported herself with a stick, and trusted beside to the fragile support of Peggy's arm. They were talking together in whispers.

"Oh, my sakes!" exclaimed Peggy, moving her small head from side to side. "Hear you wheeze, Mis' Dow! This may be the death o' you; there, do go slow! You set here on the side-hill, an' le' me go try if I can see."

"It needs more eyesight than you've got," said Mrs. Dow, panting between the words. "Oh! to think how spry I was in my young days, an' here I be now, the full of a door, an' all my complaints so aggravated by my size. 'T is hard! 't is hard! but I'm a-doin' of all this for pore Betsey's sake. I know they've all laughed, but I look to see her ris' to the top o' the pond this day,—'t is just nine days since she departed; an' say what they may, I know she hove herself in. It run in her family; Betsey had an aunt that done just so, an' she ain't be'n like herself, a-broodin' an' hivin' away alone, an' nothin' to say to you an' me that was always sich good company all together. Somethin' sprung her mind, now I tell ye, Mis' Bond."

"I feel to hope we sha'n't find her, I must say," faltered Peggy. It was plain that Mrs. Dow was the captain of this doleful expedition. "I guess she ain't never thought o' drowndin' of herself, Mis' Dow; she's gone off a-visitin' way over to the other side o' South Byfleet; some thinks she's gone to the Centennial even now!"

"She had n't no proper means, I tell ye," wheezed Mrs. Dow indignantly; "an' if you prefer that others should find her floatin' to the top this day, instid of us that's her best friends, you can step back to the house."

They walked on in aggrieved silence. Peggy Bond trembled with excitement, but her companion's firm grasp never wavered, and so they came to the narrow, gravelly margin and stood still. Peggy tried in vain to see the glittering water and the pondlilies that starred it; she knew that they must be there; once, years ago, she had caught fleeting glimpses of them, and she never forgot what she had once seen. The clear blue sky overhead, the dark pine-woods beyond the pond, were all clearly pictured in her mind. "Can't you see nothin'?" she faltered; "I believe I'm wuss 'n upsighted this day. I'm going to be blind."

"No," said Lavina Dow solemnly; "no, there ain't nothin' whatever, Peggy. I hope to mercy she ain't"—

"Why, whoever'd expected to find you 'way out here!" exclaimed a brisk and cheerful voice. There stood Betsey Lane herself, close behind them, having just emerged from a thicket of alders that grew close by. She was following the short way homeward from the railroad.

"Why, what's the matter, Mis' Dow? You ain't overdoin', be ye? an' Peggy's all of a flutter. What in the name o' natur' ails ye?"

"There ain't nothin' the matter, as I knows on," responded the leader of this fruitless expedition. "We only thought we'd take a stroll this pleasant mornin'," she added, with sublime self-possession. "Where 've you be'n, Betsey Lane?"

"To Pheladelphy, ma'am," said Betsey, looking quite young and gay, and wearing a townish and unfamiliar air that upheld her words. "All ought to go that can; why, you feel's if you'd be'n all round the world. I guess I've got enough to think of and tell ye for the rest o' my days. I've always wanted to go somewheres. I wish you'd be'n there, I do so. I've talked with folks from Chiny an' the back o' Pennsylvany: and I see folks way from Australy that 'peared as well as anybody; an' I see how they made spool cotton, an' sights o' other things; an' I spoke with a doctor that lives down to the beach in the summer, an' he offered to come up 'long in the first of August, an' see what he can do for Peggy's eyesight. There was di'monds there as big as pigeon's eggs; an' I met with Mis' Abby Fletcher from South Byfleet depot; an' there was hogs there that weighed risin' thirteen hunderd"—

"I want to know," said Mrs. Lavina Dow and Peggy Bond, together.

"Well, 't was a great exper'ence for a person," added Lavina, turning ponderously, in spite of herself, to give a last wistful look at the smiling waters of the pond.

"I don't know how soon I be goin' to settle down," proclaimed the rustic sister of Sindbad. "What's for the good o' one's for the good of all. You just wait till we're setting together up in the old shed chamber! You know, my dear Mis' Katy Strafford give me a han'some present o' money that day she come to see me; and I'd be'n a-dreamin' by night an' day o' seein' that Centennial; and when I come to think on 't I felt sure somebody ought to go from this neighborhood, if 't was only for the good o' the rest; and I thought I'd better be the one. I wa'n't goin' to ask the selec'men neither. I've come back with one-thirty-five in money, and I see everything there, an' I fetched ye all a little somethin'; but I'm full o' dust now, an' pretty nigh beat out. I never see a place more friendly than Pheladelphy; but 't ain't natural to a Byfleet person to be always walkin' on a level. There, now, Peggy, you take my bundle-handkercher and the basket, and let Mis' Dow sag on to me. I'll git her along twice as easy."

With this the small elderly company set forth triumphant toward the poor-house, across the wide green field.

MARY E. WILKINS FREEMAN

A New England Nun

IT WAS LATE IN the afternoon, and the light was waning. There was a difference in the look of the tree shadows out in the yard. Somewhere in the distance cows were lowing and a little bell was tinkling; now and then a farm-wagon tilted by, and the dust flew; some blue-shirted laborers with shovels over their shoulders plodded past; little swarms of flies were dancing up and down before the peoples' faces in the soft air. There seemed to be a gentle stir arising over everything for the mere sake of subsidence—a very premonition of rest and hush and night.

This soft diurnal commotion was over Louisa Ellis also. She had been peacefully sewing at her sitting-room window all the afternoon. Now she quilted her needle carefully into her work, which she folded precisely, and laid in a basket with her thimble and thread and scissors. Louisa Ellis could not remember that ever in her life she had mislaid one of these little feminine appurtenances, which had become, from long use and constant association, a very part of her personality.

Louisa tied a green apron round her waist, and got out a flat straw hat with a green ribbon. Then she went into the garden with a little blue crockery bowl, to pick some currants for her tea. After the currants were picked she sat on the back door-step and stemmed them, collecting the stems carefully in her apron, and afterwards throwing them into the hen-coop. She looked sharply at the grass beside the step to see if any had fallen there.

Louisa was slow and still in her movements; it took her a long time to prepare her tea; but when ready it was set forth with as much grace as if she had been a veritable guest to her own self. The little square table stood exactly in the centre of the kitchen, and was covered with a starched linen cloth whose border pattern of flowers glistened. Louisa had a damask napkin on her tea-tray, where were arranged a cut-glass tumbler full of teaspoons, a silver cream-pitcher, a china sugar-bowl, and one pink china cup and saucer. Louisa used china every day—something which none of her neighbors did. They whispered about it among themselves. Their daily tables were laid with common crockery, their sets of best china stayed in the parlor closet, and Louisa Ellis was no richer nor better bred than they. Still she would use the china. She had for her supper a glass dish full of sugared currants, a plate of little cakes, and one of light white biscuits. Also a leaf or two of lettuce, which she cut up daintily. Louisa was very fond of lettuce, which she raised to perfection in her little garden. She ate quite heartily, though in a delicate, pecking way; it seemed almost surprising that any considerable bulk of the food should vanish.

After tea she filled a plate with nicely baked thin corn-cakes, and carried them out into the back-yard.

"Cæsar!" she called. "Cæsar! Cæsar!"

There was a little rush, and the clank of a chain, and a large yellow-and-white dog appeared at the door of his tiny hut, which was half hidden among the tall grasses and flowers. Louisa patted him and gave him the corn-cakes. Then she returned to the house and washed the tea-things, polishing the china carefully. The twilight had deepened; the chorus of the frogs floated in at the open window wonderfully loud and shrill, and once in a while a long sharp drone from a tree-toad pierced it. Louisa took off her green gingham apron, disclosing a shorter one of pink and white print. She lighted her lamp, and sat down again with her sewing.

In about half an hour Joe Dagget came. She heard his heavy step on the walk, and rose and took off her pink-and-white apron. Under that was still another—white linen with a little cambric edging on the bottom; that was Louisa's company apron. She never wore it without her calico sewing apron over it unless she had a guest. She had barely folded the pink and white one with methodical haste and laid it in a table-drawer when the door opened and Joe Dagget entered.

He seemed to fill up the whole room. A little yellow canary that had been asleep in his green cage at the south window woke up and fluttered wildly, beating his little yellow wings against the wires. He always did so when Joe Dagget came into the room.

"Good-evening," said Louisa. She extended her hand with a kind of solemn cordiality.

"Good-evening, Louisa," returned the man, in a loud voice.

She placed a chair for him, and they sat facing each other, with the table between them. He sat bolt-upright, toeing out his heavy feet squarely, glancing with a good-humored uneasiness around the room. She sat gently erect, folding her slender hands in her white-linen lap.

"Been a pleasant day," remarked Dagget.

"Real pleasant," Louisa assented, softly. "Have you been haying?" she asked, after a little while.

"Yes, I've been haying all day, down in the ten-acre lot. Pretty hot work."

"It must be."

"Yes, it's pretty hot work in the sun."

"Is your mother well to-day?"

"Yes, mother's pretty well."

"I suppose Lily Dyer's with her now?"

Dagget colored. "Yes, she's with her," he answered, slowly.

He was not very young, but there was a boyish look about his large face. Louisa was not quite as old as he, her face was fairer and smoother, but she gave people the impression of being older.

"I suppose she's a good deal of help to your mother," she said, further.

"I guess she is; I don't know how mother'd get along without her," said Dagget, with a sort of embarrassed warmth.

"She looks like a real capable girl. She's pretty-looking too," remarked Louisa.

"Yes, she is pretty fair looking."

Presently Dagget began fingering the books on the table. There was a square red autograph album, and a Young Lady's Gift-Book which had belonged to Louisa's mother. He took them up one after the other and opened them; then laid them down again, the album on the Gift-Book.

Louisa kept eying them with mild uneasiness. Finally she rose and changed the position of the books, putting the album underneath. That was the way they had been arranged in the first place.

Dagget gave an awkward little laugh. "Now what difference did it make which book was on top?" said he.

Louisa looked at him with a deprecating smile. "I always keep them that way," murmured she.

"You do beat everything," said Dagget, trying to laugh again. His large face was flushed.

He remained about an hour longer, then rose to take leave. Going out, he stumbled over a rug, and trying to recover himself, hit Louisa's work-basket on the table, and knocked it on the floor.

He looked at Louisa, then at the rolling spools; he ducked himself awkwardly toward them, but she stopped him. "Never mind," said she; "I'll pick them up after you're gone."

She spoke with a mild stiffness. Either she was a little disturbed, or his nervousness affected her, and made her seem constrained in her effort to reassure him.

When Joe Dagget was outside he drew in the sweet evening air with a sigh, and felt much as an innocent and perfectly well-intentioned bear might after his exit from a china shop.

Louisa, on her part, felt much as the kind-hearted, long-suffering owner of the china shop might have done after the exit of the bear.

She tied on the pink, then the green apron, picked up all the scattered treasures and replaced them in her work-basket, and straightened the rug. Then she set the lamp on the floor, and began sharply examining the carpet. She even rubbed her fingers over it, and looked at them.

"He's tracked in a good deal of dust," she murmured. "I thought he must have."

Louisa got a dust-pan and brush, and swept Joe Dagget's track carefully.

If he could have known it, it would have increased his perplexity and uneasiness, although it would not have disturbed his loyalty in the least. He came twice a week to see Louisa Ellis, and every time, sitting there in her delicately sweet room, he felt as if surrounded by a hedge of lace. He was afraid to stir lest he should put a clumsy foot or hand through the fairy web, and he had always the consciousness that Louisa was watching fearfully lest he should.

Still the lace and Louisa commanded perforce his perfect respect and patience and loyalty. They were to be married in a month, after a singular courtship which had lasted for a matter of fifteen years. For fourteen out of the fifteen years the two had not once seen each other, and they had seldom exchanged letters. Joe had been all those years in Australia, where he had gone to make his fortune, and where he had stayed until he made it. He would have stayed fifty years if it had taken so long, and come home feeble and tottering, or never come home at all, to marry Louisa.

But the fortune had been made in the fourteen years, and he had come home now to marry the woman who had been patiently and unquestioningly waiting for him all that time.

Shortly after they were engaged he had announced to Louisa his determination to strike out into new fields, and secure a competency before they should be married. She had listened and assented with the sweet serenity which never failed her, not even when her lover set forth on that long and uncertain journey. Joe, buoyed up as he was by his sturdy determination, broke down a little at the last, but Louisa kissed him with a mild blush, and said good-by.

"It won't be for long," poor Joe had said, huskily; but it was for fourteen years.

In that length of time much had happened. Louisa's mother and brother had died, and she was all alone in the world. But greatest happening of all—a subtle happening which both were too simple to understand—Louisa's feet had turned into a path, smooth maybe under a calm, serene sky, but so straight and unswerving that it could only meet a check at her grave, and so narrow that there was no room for any one at her side.

Louisa's first emotion when Joe Dagget came home (he had not apprised her of his coming) was consternation, although she would not admit it to herself, and he never dreamed of it. Fifteen years ago she had been in love with him—at least she considered herself to be. Just at that time, gently acquiescing with and falling into the natural drift of girlhood, she had seen marriage ahead as a reasonable feature and a probable desirability of life. She had listened with calm docility to her mother's views upon the subject. Her mother was remarkable for her cool sense and sweet, even temperament. She talked wisely to her daughter when Joe Dagget presented himself, and Louisa accepted him with no hesitation. He was the first lover she had ever had.

She had been faithful to him all these years. She had never dreamed of the possibility of marrying any one else. Her life, especially for the last seven years, had been full of a pleasant peace, she had never felt discontented nor impatient over her lover's absence; still she had always looked forward to his return and their marriage as the inevitable conclusion of things. However, she had fallen into a way of placing it so far in the future that it was almost equal to placing it over the boundaries of another life.

When Joe came she had been expecting him, and expecting to be married for fourteen years, but she was as much surprised and taken aback as if she had never thought of it.

Joe's consternation came later. He eyed Louisa with an instant confirmation of his old admiration. She had changed but little. She still kept her pretty manner and soft grace, and was, he considered, every whit as attractive as ever. As for himself, his stent was done; he had turned his face away from fortune-seeking, and the old winds of romance whistled as loud and sweet as ever through his ears. All the song which he had been wont to hear in them was Louisa; he had for a long time a loyal belief that he heard it still, but finally it seemed to him that although the winds sang always that one song, it had another name. But for Louisa the wind had never more than murmured; now it had gone down, and everything was still. She listened for a little while with half-wistful attention; then she turned quietly away and went to work on her wedding clothes.

Joe had made some extensive and quite magnificent alterations in his house. It was the old homestead; the newly-married couple would live there, for Joe could not desert his mother, who refused to leave her old home. So Louisa must leave hers. Every morning, rising and going about among her neat maidenly possessions, she felt as one looking her last upon the faces of dear friends. It was true that in a measure she could take them with her, but, robbed of their old environments, they would appear in such new guises that they would almost cease to be themselves. Then there were some peculiar features of her happy solitary life which she would probably be obliged to relinquish altogether. Sterner tasks than these graceful but half-needless ones would probably devolve upon her. There would be a large house to care for; there would be company to entertain; there would be Joe's rigorous and feeble old mother to wait upon; and it would be contrary to all thrifty village traditions for her to keep more than one servant. Louisa had a little still, and she used to occupy herself pleasantly in summer weather with distilling the sweet and aromatic essences from roses and peppermint and spearmint. By-and-by her still must be laid away. Her store of essences was already considerable, and there would be no time for her to distil for the mere pleasure of it. Then Joe's mother would think it foolishness; she had already hinted her opinion in the matter. Louisa dearly loved to sew a linen seam, not always for use, but for the simple, mild pleasure which she took in it. She would have been loath to confess how more than once she had ripped a seam for the mere delight of sewing it together again. Sitting at her window during long sweet afternoons, drawing her needle gently through the dainty fabric, she was peace itself. But there was small chance of such foolish comfort in the future. Joe's mother, domineering, shrewd old matron that she was even in her old age, and very likely even Joe himself, with his honest masculine rudeness, would laugh and frown down all these pretty but senseless old maiden ways.

Louisa had almost the enthusiasm of an artist over the mere order and cleanliness of her solitary home. She had throbs of genuine triumph at the sight of the window-panes which she had polished until they shone like jewels. She gloated gently over her orderly bureau-drawers, with their exquisitely folded contents redolent with lavender and sweet clover and very purity. Could she be sure of the endurance of even this? She had visions, so startling that she half repudiated them as indelicate, of coarse masculine belongings strewn about in endless litter; of dust and disorder arising necessarily from a coarse masculine presence in the midst of all this delicate harmony.

Among her forebodings of disturbance, not the least was with regard to Cæsar. Cæsar was a veritable hermit of a dog. For the greater part of his life he had dwelt in his secluded hut, shut out from the society of his kind and all innocent canine joys. Never had Cæsar since his early youth watched at a woodchuck's hole; never had he known the delights of a stray bone at a neighbor's kitchen door. And it was all on account of a sin committed when hardly out of his puppyhood. No one knew the possible depth of remorse of which this mild-visaged, altogether innocent-looking old dog might be capable; but whether or not he had encountered remorse, he had encountered a full measure of righteous retribution. Old Cæsar seldom lifted up his voice in a growl or a bark; he was fat and sleepy; there were yellow rings which looked like spectacles around his dim old eyes; but there was a neighbor who bore on his hand the imprint of several of Cæsar's sharp white youthful teeth, and for that he had lived at the end of a chain, all alone in a little hut, for fourteen years. The neighbor, who was choleric and smarting with the pain of his wound, had demanded either Cæsar's death or complete ostracism. So Louisa's brother, to whom the dog had belonged, had built him his little kennel and tied him up. It was now fourteen years since, in a flood of youthful spirits, he had inflicted that memorable bite, and with the exception of short excursions, always at the end of the chain, under the strict guardianship of his master or Louisa, the old dog had remained a close prisoner. It is doubtful if, with his limited ambition, he took much pride in the fact, but it is certain that he was possessed of considerable cheap fame. He was regarded by all the children in the village and by many adults as a very monster of ferocity. St. George's dragon could hardly have surpassed in evil repute Louisa Ellis's old yellow dog. Mothers charged their children with solemn emphasis not to go too near to him, and the children listened and believed greedily, with a fascinated appetite for terror, and ran by Louisa's house stealthily, with many sidelong and backward glances at the terrible dog. If perchance he sounded a hoarse bark, there was a panic. Wayfarers chancing into Louisa's yard eyed him with respect, and inquired if the chain were stout. Cæsar at large might have seemed a very ordinary dog, and excited no comment whatever; chained, his reputation overshadowed him, so that he lost his own proper outlines and looked darkly vague and enormous. Joe Dagget, however, with his good-humored sense and shrewdness, saw him as he was. He strode valiantly up to him and patted him on the head, in spite of Louisa's soft clamor of warning, and even attempted to set him loose. Louisa grew so alarmed that he desisted, but kept announcing his opinion in the matter quite forcibly at intervals. "There ain't a better-natured dog in town," he would say, "and it's down-right cruel to keep him tied up there. Some day I'm going to take him out."

Louisa had very little hope that he would not, one of these days, when their interests and possessions should be more completely fused in one. She pictured to herself Cæsar on the rampage through the quiet and unguarded village. She saw innocent children bleeding in his path. She was herself very fond of the old dog, because he had belonged to her dead brother, and he was always very gentle with her; still she had great faith in his ferocity. She always warned people not to go too near him. She fed him on ascetic fare of corn-mush and cakes, and never fired his dangerous temper with heating and sanguinary diet of flesh and bones. Louisa looked at the old dog munching his simple fare, and thought of her approaching marriage and trembled. Still no anticipation of disorder and confusion in lieu of sweet peace and harmony, no forebodings of Cæsar on the rampage, no wild fluttering of her little yellow canary, were sufficient to turn her a hair's-breadth. Joe Dagget had been fond of her and working for her all these years. It was not for her, whatever came to pass, to prove untrue and break his heart. She put the exquisite little stitches into her wedding-garments, and the time went on until it was only a week before her wedding day. It was a Tuesday evening, and the wedding was to be a week from Wednesday.

There was a full moon that night. About nine o'clock Louisa strolled down the road a little way. There were harvest-fields on either hand, bordered by low stone walls. Luxuriant clumps of bushes grew beside the wall, and trees—wild cherry and old apple-trees—at intervals. Presently Louisa sat down on the wall and looked about her with mildly sorrowful reflectiveness. Tall shrubs of blueberry and meadow-sweet, all woven together and tangled with blackberry vines and horsebriers, shut her in on either side. She had a little clear space between them. Opposite her, on the other side of the road, was a spreading tree; the moon shone between its boughs, and the leaves twinkled like silver. The road was bespread with a beautiful shifting dapple of silver and shadow; the air was full of a mysterious sweetness. "I wonder if it's wild grapes?" murmured Louisa. She sat there some time. She was just thinking of rising, when she heard footsteps and low voices, and remained quiet. It was a lonely place, and she felt a little timid. She thought she would keep still in the shadow and let the persons, whoever they might be, pass her.

But just before they reached her the voices ceased, and the footsteps. She understood that their owners had also found seats upon the stone wall. She was wondering if she could not steal away unobserved, when the voice broke the stillness. It was Joe Dagget's. She sat still and listened.

The voice was announced by a loud sigh, which was as familiar as itself. "Well," said Dagget, "you've made up your mind, then, I suppose?"

"Yes," returned another voice; "I'm going day after to-morrow."

"That's Lily Dyer," thought Louisa to herself. The voice embodied itself in her mind. She saw a girl tall and full-figured, with a firm, fair face, looking fairer and firmer in the moonlight, her strong yellow hair braided in a close knot. A girl full of a calm rustic strength and bloom, with a masterful way which might have be-seemed a princess. Lily Dyer was a favorite with the village folk; she had just the qualities to arouse the admiration. She was good and handsome and smart. Louisa had often heard her praises sounded.

"Well," said Joe Dagget, "I ain't got a word to say."

"I don't know what you could say," returned Lily Dyer.

"Not a word to say," repeated Joe, drawing out the words heavily. Then there was a silence. "I ain't sorry," he began at last, "that that happened yesterday—that we kind of let on how we felt to each other. I guess it's just as well we knew. Of course I can't do anything any different. I'm going right on an' get married next week. I ain't going back on a woman that's waited for me fourteen years, an' break her heart."

"If you should jilt her to-morrow, I wouldn't have you," spoke up the girl, with sudden vehemence.

"Well, I ain't going to give you the chance," said he; "but I don't believe you would, either."

"You'd see I wouldn't. Honor's honor, an' right's right. An' I'd never think anything of any man that went against 'em for me or any other girl; you'd find that out, Joe Dagget."

"Well, you'll find out fast enough that I ain't going against 'em for you or any other girl," returned he. Their voices sounded almost as if they were angry with each other. Louisa was listening eagerly.

"I'm sorry you feel as if you must go away," said Joe, "but I don't know but it's best."

"Of course it's best. I hope you and I have got common-sense."

"Well, I suppose you're right." Suddenly Joe's voice got an undertone of tenderness. "Say, Lily," said he, "I'll get along well enough myself, but I can't bear to think— You don't suppose you're going to fret much over it?"

"I guess you'll find out I sha'n't fret much over a married man."

"Well, I hope you won't—I hope you won't, Lily. God knows I do. And—I hope—one of these days—you'll—come across somebody else—"

"I don't see any reason why I shouldn't." Suddenly her tone changed. She spoke in a sweet, clear voice, so loud that she could have been heard across the street. "No, Joe Dagget," said she, "I'll never marry any other man as long as I live. I've got good sense, an' I ain't going to break my heart nor make a fool of myself; but I'm never going to be married, you can be sure of that. I ain't that sort of a girl to feel this way twice."

Louisa heard an exclamation and a soft commotion behind the bushes; then Lily spoke again—the voice sounded as if she had risen. "This must be put a stop to," said she. "We've stayed here long enough. I'm going home."

Louisa sat there in a daze, listening to their retreating steps. After a while she got up and slunk softly home herself. The next day she did her housework methodically; that was as much a matter of course as breathing; but she did not sew on her wedding-clothes. She sat at her window and meditated. In the evening Joe came. Louisa Ellis had never known that she had any diplomacy in her, but when she came to look for it that night she found it, although meek of its kind, among her little feminine weapons. Even now she could hardly believe that she had heard aright, and that she would not do Joe a terrible injury should she break her troth-plight. She wanted to sound him without betraying too soon her own inclinations in the matter. She did it successfully, and they finally came to an understanding; but it was a difficult thing, for he was as afraid of betraying himself as she.

She never mentioned Lily Dyer. She simply said that while she had no cause of complaint against him, she had lived so long in one way that she shrank from making a change.

"Well, I never shrank, Louisa," said Dagget. "I'm going to be honest enough to say that I think maybe it's better this way; but if you'd wanted to keep on, I'd have stuck to you till my dying day. I hope you know that."

"Yes, I do," said she.

That night she and Joe parted more tenderly than they had done for a long time. Standing in the door, holding each other's hands, a last great wave of regretful memory swept over them.

"Well, this ain't the way we've thought it was all going to end, is it, Louisa?" said Joe.

She shook her head. There was a little quiver on her placid face.

"You let me know if there's ever anything I can do for you," said he. "I ain't ever going to forget you, Louisa." Then he kissed her, and went down the path.

Louisa, all alone by herself that night, wept a little, she hardly knew why; but the next morning, on waking, she felt like a queen who, after fearing lest her domain be wrested away from her, sees it firmly insured in her possession.

Now the tall weeds and grasses might cluster around Cæsar's little hermit hut, the snow might fall on its roof year in and year out, but he never would go on a rampage through the unguarded village. Now the little canary might turn itself into a peaceful yellow ball night after night, and have no need to wake and flutter with wild terror against its bars. Louisa could sew linen seams, and distil roses, and dust and polish and fold away in lavender, as long as she listed. That afternoon she sat with her needle-work at the window, and felt fairly steeped in peace. Lily Dyer, tall and erect and blooming, went past; but she felt no qualm. If Louisa Ellis had sold her birthright she did not know it, the taste of the pottage was so delicious, and had been her sole satisfaction for so long. Serenity and placid narrowness had become to her as the birthright itself. She gazed ahead through a long reach of future days strung together like pearls in a rosary, every one like the others, and all smooth and flawless and innocent, and her heart went up in thankfulness. Outside was the fervid summer afternoon; the air was filled with the sounds of the busy harvest of men and birds and bees; there were halloos, metallic clatterings, sweet calls, and long hummings. Louisa sat, prayerfully numbering her days, like an uncloistered nun.

MARY E. WILKINS FREEMAN

The Revolt of "Mother"

"FATHER!"

"What is it?"

"What are them men diggin' over there in the field for?"

There was a sudden dropping and enlarging of the lower part of the old man's face, as if some heavy weight had settled therein; he shut his mouth tight, and went on harnessing the great bay mare. He hustled the collar on to her neck with a jerk.

"Father!"

The old man slapped the saddle upon the mare's back.

"Look here, father, I want to know what them men are diggin' over in the field for, an' I'm goin' to know."

"I wish you'd go into the house, mother, an' 'tend to your own affairs," the old man said then. He ran his words together, and his speech was almost as inarticulate as a growl.

But the woman understood; it was her most native tongue. "I ain't goin' into the house till you tell me what them men are doin' over there in the field," said she.

Then she stood waiting. She was a small woman, short and straight-waisted like a child in her brown cotton gown. Her forehead was mild and benevolent between the smooth curves of gray hair; there were meek downward lines about her nose and mouth; but her eyes, fixed upon the old man, looked as if the meekness had been the result of her own will, never of the will of another.

They were in the barn, standing before the wide open doors. The spring air, full of the smell of growing grass and unseen blossoms, came in their faces. The deep yard in front was littered with farm wagons and piles of wood; on the edges, close to the fence and the house, the grass was a vivid green, and there were some dandelions.

The old man glanced doggedly at his wife as he tightened the last buckles on the harness. She looked as immovable to him as one of the rocks in his pasture-land, bound to the earth with generations of blackberry vines. He slapped the reins over the horse, and started forth from the barn.

"*Father!*" said she.

The old man pulled up. "What is it?"

"I want to know what them men are diggin' over there in that field for."

"They're diggin' a cellar, I s'pose, if you've got to know."

"A cellar for what?"

"A barn."

"A barn? You ain't goin' to build a barn over there where we was goin' to have a house, father?"

The old man said not another word. He hurried the horse into the farm wagon, and clattered out of the yard, jouncing as sturdily on his seat as a boy.

The woman stood a moment looking after him, then she went out of the barn across a corner of the yard to the house. The house, standing at right angles with the great barn and a long reach of sheds and out-buildings, was infinitesimal compared with them. It was scarcely as commodious for people as the little boxes under the barn eaves were for doves.

A pretty girl's face, pink and delicate as a flower, was looking out of one of the house windows. She was watching three men who were digging over in the field which bounded the yard near the road line. She turned quietly when the woman entered.

"What are they digging for, mother?" said she. "Did he tell you?"

"They're diggin' for—a cellar for a new barn."

"Oh, mother, he ain't going to build another barn?"

"That's what he says."

A boy stood before the kitchen glass combing his hair. He combed slowly and painstakingly, arranging his brown hair in a smooth hillock over his forehead. He did not seem to pay any attention to the conversation.

"Sammy, did you know father was going to build a new barn?" asked the girl.

The boy combed assiduously.

"Sammy!"

He turned, and showed a face like his father's under his smooth crest of hair. "Yes, I s'pose I did," he said, reluctantly.

"How long have you known it?" asked his mother.

" 'Bout three months, I guess."

"Why didn't you tell of it?"

"Didn't think 'twould do no good."

"I don't see what father wants another barn for," said the girl, in her sweet, slow voice. She turned again to the window, and stared out at the digging men in the field. Her tender, sweet face was full of a gentle distress. Her forehead was as bald and innocent as a baby's, with the light hair strained back from it in a row of curl-papers. She was quite large, but her soft curves did not look as if they covered muscles.

Her mother looked sternly at the boy. "Is he goin' to buy more cows?" said she.

The boy did not reply; he was tying his shoes.

"Sammy, I want you to tell me if he's goin' to buy more cows."

"I s'pose he is."

"How many?"

"Four, I guess."

His mother said nothing more. She went into the pantry, and there was a clatter of dishes. The boy got his cap from a nail behind the door, took an old arithmetic from the shelf, and started for school. He was lightly built, but clumsy. He went out of the yard with a curious spring in the hips, that made his loose home-made jacket tilt up in the rear.

The girl went to the sink, and began to wash the dishes that were piled up there. Her mother came promptly out of the pantry, and shoved her aside. "You wipe 'em," said she; "I'll wash. There's a good many this mornin'."

The mother plunged her hands vigorously into the water, the girl wiped the plates slowly and dreamily. "Mother," said she, "don't you think it's too bad father's going to build that new barn, much as we need a decent house to live in?"

Her mother scrubbed a dish fiercely. "You ain't found out yet we're women-folks, Nanny Penn," said she. "You ain't seen enough of men-folks yet to. One of these days you'll find it out, an' then you'll know that we know only what men-folks think we do, so far as any use of it goes, an' how we'd ought to reckon men-folks in with Providence, an' not complain of what they do any more than we do of the weather."

"I don't care; I don't believe George is anything like that, anyhow," said Nanny. Her delicate face flushed pink, her lips pouted softly, as if she were going to cry.

"You wait an' see. I guess George Eastman ain't no better than other men. You hadn't ought to judge father, though. He can't help it, 'cause he don't look at things jest the way we do. An' we've been pretty comfortable here, after all. The roof don't leak—ain't never but once—that's one thing. Father's kept it shingled right up."

"I do wish we had a parlor."

"I guess it won't hurt George Eastman any to come to see you in a nice clean kitchen. I guess a good many girls don't have as good a place as this. Nobody's ever heard me complain."

"I ain't complained either, mother."

"Well, I don't think you'd better, a good father an' a good home as you've got. S'pose your father made you go out an' work for your livin'? Lots of girls have to that ain't no stronger an' better able to than you be."

Sarah Penn washed the frying-pan with a conclusive air. She scrubbed the outside of it as faithfully as the inside. She was a masterly keeper of her box of a house. Her one living-room never seemed to have in it any of the dust which the friction of life with inanimate matter produces. She swept, and there seemed to be no dirt to go before the broom; she cleaned, and one could see no difference. She was like an artist so perfect that he has apparently no art. To-day she got out a mixing bowl and a board, and rolled some pies, and there was no more flour upon her than upon her daughter who was doing finer work. Nanny was to be married in the fall, and she was sewing on some white cambric and embroidery. She sewed industriously while her mother cooked, her soft milk-white hands and wrists showed whiter than her delicate work.

"We must have the stove moved out in the shed before long," said Mrs. Penn. "Talk about not havin' things, it's been a real blessin' to be able to put a stove up in that shed in hot weather. Father did one good thing when he fixed that stove-pipe out there."

Sarah Penn's face as she rolled her pies had that expression of meek vigor which might have characterized one of the New Testament saints. She was making mince-pies. Her husband, Adoniram Penn, liked them better than any other kind. She baked twice a week. Adoniram often liked a piece of pie between meals. She hurried this morning. It had been later than usual when she began, and she wanted to have a pie baked for dinner. However deep a resentment she might be forced to hold against her husband, she would never fail in sedulous attention to his wants.

Nobility of character manifests itself at loop-holes when it is not provided with large doors. Sarah Penn's showed itself to-day in flaky dishes of pastry. So she made the pies faithfully, while across the table she could see, when she glanced up from her work, the sight that rankled in her patient and steadfast soul—the digging of the cellar of the new barn in the place where Adoniram forty years ago had promised her their new house should stand.

The pies were done for dinner. Adoniram and Sammy were home a few minutes after twelve o'clock. The dinner was eaten with serious haste. There was never much conversation at the table in the Penn family. Adoniram asked a blessing, and they ate promptly, then rose up and went about their work.

Sammy went back to school, taking soft sly lopes out of the yard like a rabbit. He wanted a game of marbles before school, and feared his father would give him some chores to do. Adoniram hastened to the door and called after him, but he was out of sight.

"I don't see what you let him go for, mother," said he. "I wanted him to help me unload that wood."

Adoniram went to work out in the yard unloading wood from the wagon. Sarah put away the dinner dishes, while Nanny took down her curl-papers and changed her dress. She was going down to the store to buy some more embroidery and thread.

When Nanny was gone, Mrs. Penn went to the door. "Father!" she called.

"Well, what is it!"

"I want to see you jest a minute, father."

"I can't leave this wood nohow. I've got to git it unloaded an' go for a load of gravel afore two o'clock. Sammy had ought to helped me. You hadn't ought to let him go to school so early."

"I want to see you jest a minute."

"I tell ye I can't, nohow, mother."

"Father, you come here." Sarah Penn stood in the door like a queen; she held her head as if it bore a crown; there was that patience which makes authority royal in her voice. Adoniram went.

Mrs. Penn led the way into the kitchen, and pointed to a chair. "Sit down, father," said she; "I've got somethin' I want to say to you."

He sat down heavily; his face was quite stolid, but he looked at her with restive eyes. "Well, what is it, mother?"

"I want to know what you're buildin' that new barn for, father?"

"I ain't got nothin' to say about it."

"It can't be you think you need another barn?"

"I tell ye I ain't got nothin' to say about it, mother; an' I ain't goin' to say nothin'."

"Be you goin' to buy more cows?"

Adoniram did not reply; he shut his mouth tight.

"I know you be, as well as I want to. Now, father, look here"—Sarah Penn had not sat down; she stood before her husband in the humble fashion of a Scripture woman—"I'm goin' to talk real plain to you; I never have sence I married you, but I'm goin' to now. I ain't never complained, an' I ain't goin' to complain now, but I'm goin' to talk plain. You see this room here, father; you look at it well. You see there ain't no carpet on the floor, an' you see the paper is all dirty, an' droppin' off the walls. We ain't had no new paper on it for ten year, an' then I put it on myself, an' it didn't cost but ninepence a roll. You see this room, father; it's all the one I've had to work in an' eat in an' sit in sence we was married. There ain't another woman in the whole town whose husband ain't got half the means you have but what's got better. It's all the room Nanny's got to have her company in; an' there ain't one of her mates but what's got better, an' their fathers not so able as hers is. It's all the room she'll have to be married in. What would you have thought, father, if we had had our weddin' in a room no better than this? I was married in my mother's parlor, with a carpet on the floor, an' stuffed furniture, an' a mahogany card-table, An' this is all the room my daughter will have to be married in. Look here, father!"

Sarah Penn went across the room as though it were a tragic stage. She flung open a door and disclosed a tiny bedroom, only large enough for a bed and bureau, with a path between. "There, father," said she—"there's all the room I've had to sleep in forty year. All my children were born there—the two that died, an' the two that's livin'. I was sick with a fever there."

She stepped to another door and opened it. It led into the small, ill-lighted pantry. "Here," said she, "is all the buttery I've got—every place I've got for my dishes, to set away my victuals in, an' to keep my milk-pans in. Father, I've been takin' care of the milk of six cows in this place, an' now you're goin' to build a new barn, an' keep more cows, an' give me more to do in it."

She threw open another door. A narrow crooked flight of stairs wound upward from it. "There, father," said she, "I want you to look at the stairs that go up to them two unfinished chambers that are all the places our son an' daughter have had to sleep in all their lives. There ain't a prettier girl in town nor a more ladylike one than Nanny, an' that's the place she has to sleep in. It ain't so good as your horse's stall; it ain't so warm an' tight."

Sarah Penn went back and stood before her husband. "Now, father," said she, "I want to know if you think you're doin' right an' accordin' to what you profess. Here, when we was married, forty year ago, you promised me faithful that we should have a new house built in that lot over in the field before the year was out. You said you had money enough, an' you wouldn't ask me to live in no such place as this. It is forty year now, an' you've been makin' more money, an' I've been savin' of it for you ever since, an' you ain't built no house yet. You've built sheds an' cow-houses an' one new barn, an' now you're goin' to build another. Father, I want to know if you think it's right. You're lodgin' your dumb beasts better than you are your own flesh an' blood. I want to know if you think it's right."

"I ain't got nothin' to say."

"You can't say nothin' without ownin' it ain't right, father. An' there's another thing—I ain't complained; I've got along forty year, an' I s'pose I should forty more, if it wa'n't for that—if we don't have another house. Nanny she can't live with us after she's married. She'll have to go somewheres else to live away from us, an' it don't seem as if I could have it so, noways, father. She wa'n't ever strong. She's got considerable color, but there wa'n't never any backbone to her. I've always took the heft of everything off her, an' she ain't fit to keep house an' do everything herself. She'll be all worn out inside of a year. Think of her doin' all the washin' an' ironin' an' bakin' with them soft white hands an' arms, an' sweepin'! I can't have it so, noways, father."

Mrs. Penn's face was burning; her mild eyes gleamed. She had pleaded her little cause like a Webster; she had ranged from severity to pathos; but her opponent employed that obstinate silence which makes eloquence futile with mocking echoes. Adoniram arose clumsily.

"Father, ain't you got nothin' to say?" said Mrs. Penn.

"I've got to go off after that load of gravel. I can't stan' here talkin' all day."

"Father, won't you think it over, an' have a house built there instead of a barn?"

"I ain't got nothin' to say."

Adoniram shuffled out. Mrs. Penn went into her bedroom. When she came out, her eyes were red. She had a roll of unbleached cotton cloth. She spread it out on the kitchen table, and began cutting out some shirts for her husband. The men over in the field had a team to help them this afternoon; she could hear their halloos. She had a scanty pattern for the shirts; she had to plan and piece the sleeves.

Nanny came home with her embroidery, and sat down with her needlework. She had taken down her curl-papers, and there was a soft roll of fair hair like an aureole over her forehead; her face was as delicately fine and clear as porcelain. Suddenly she looked up, and the tender red flamed all over her face and neck. "Mother," said she.

"What say?"

"I've been thinking—I don't see how we're goin' to have any—wedding in this room. I'd be ashamed to have his folks come if we didn't have anybody else."

"Mebbe we can have some new paper before then; I can put it on. I guess you won't have no call to be ashamed of your belongin's."

"We might have the wedding in the new barn," said Nanny, with gentle pettishness. "Why, mother, what makes you look so?"

Mrs. Penn had started, and was staring at her with a curious expression. She turned again to her work, and spread out a pattern carefully on the cloth. "Nothin'," said she.

Presently Adoniram clattered out of the yard in his two-wheeled dump cart, standing as proudly upright as a Roman charioteer. Mrs. Penn opened the door and stood there a minute looking out; the halloos of the men sounded louder.

It seemed to her all through the spring months that she heard nothing but the halloos and the noises of saws and hammers. The new barn grew fast. It was a fine edifice for this little village. Men came on pleasant Sundays, in their meeting suits and clean shirt bosoms, and stood around it admiringly. Mrs. Penn did not speak of it, and Adoniram did not mention it to her, although sometimes, upon a return from inspecting it, he bore himself with injured dignity.

"It's a strange thing how your mother feels about the new barn," he said, confidentially, to Sammy one day.

Sammy only grunted after an odd fashion for a boy; he had learned it from his father.

The barn was all completed ready for use by the third week in July. Adoniram had planned to move his stock in on Wednesday; on Tuesday he received a letter which changed his plans. He came in with it early in the morning. "Sammy's been to the post-office," said he, "an' I've got a letter from Hiram." Hiram was Mrs. Penn's brother, who lived in Vermont.

"Well," said Mrs. Penn, "what does he say about the folks?"

"I guess they're all right. He says he thinks if I come up country right off there's a chance to buy jest the kind of a horse I want." He stared reflectively out of the window at the new barn.

Mrs. Penn was making pies. She went on clapping the rolling-pin into the crust, although she was very pale, and her heart beat loudly.

"I dun' know but what I'd better go," said Adoniram. "I hate to go off jest now, right in the midst of hayin', but the ten-acre lot's cut, an' I guess Rufus an' the others can git along without me three or four days. I can't get a horse round here to suit me, nohow, an' I've got to have another for all that wood-haulin' in the fall. I told Hiram to watch out, an' if he got wind of a good horse to let me know. I guess I'd better go."

"I'll get out your clean shirt an' collar," said Mrs. Penn calmly.

She laid out Adoniram's Sunday suit and his clean clothes on the bed in the little bedroom. She got his shaving-water and razor ready. At last she buttoned on his collar and fastened his black cravat.

Adoniram never wore his collar and cravat except on extra occasions. He held his head high, with a rasped dignity. When he was all ready, with his coat and hat brushed, and a lunch of pie and cheese in a paper bag, he hesitated on the threshold of the door. He looked at his wife, and his manner was defiantly apologetic. "*If* them cows come to-day, Sammy can drive 'em into the new barn," said he; "an' when they bring the hay up, they can pitch it in there."

"Well," replied Mrs. Penn.

Adoniram set his shaven face ahead and started. When he had cleared the door-step, he turned and looked back with a kind of nervous solemnity. "I shall be back by Saturday if nothin' happens," said he.

"Do be careful, father," returned his wife.

She stood in the door with Nanny at her elbow and watched him out of sight. Her eyes had a strange, doubtful expression in them; her peaceful forehead was contracted. She went in, and about her baking again. Nanny sat sewing. Her wedding-day was drawing nearer, and she was getting pale and thin with her steady sewing. Her mother kept glancing at her.

"Have you got that pain in your side this mornin'?" she asked.

"A little."

Mrs. Penn's face, as she worked, changed, her perplexed forehead smoothed, her eyes were steady, her lips firmly set. She formed a maxim for herself, although incoherently with her unlettered thoughts. "Unsolicited opportunities are the guide-posts of the Lord to the new roads of life," she repeated in effect, and she made up her mind to her course of action.

"S'posin' I *had* wrote to Hiram," she muttered once, when she was in the pantry—"s'posin' I had wrote, an' asked him if he knew of any horse? But I didn't, an' father's goin' wa'n't none of my doin'. It looks like a providence." Her voice rang out quite loud at the last.

"What you talkin' about, mother?" called Nanny.

"Nothin'."

Mrs. Penn hurried her baking; at eleven o'clock it was all done. The load of hay from the west field came slowly down the cart track, and drew up at the new barn. Mrs. Penn ran out. "Stop!" she screamed—"stop!"

The men stopped and looked; Sammy upreared from the top of the load, and stared at his mother.

"Stop!" she cried out again. "Don't you put the hay in that barn; put it in the old one."

"Why, he said to put it in here," returned one of the haymakers, wonderingly. He was a young man, a neighbor's son, whom Adoniram hired by the year to help on the farm.

"Don't you put the hay in the new barn; there's room enough in the old one, ain't there?" said Mrs. Penn.

"Room enough," returned the hired man, in his thick, rustic tones. "Didn't need the new barn, nohow, far as room's concerned. Well, I s'pose he changed his mind." He took hold of the horses' bridles.

Mrs. Penn went back to the house. Soon the kitchen windows were darkened, and a fragrance like warm honey came into the room.

Nanny laid down her work. "I thought father wanted them to put the hay into the new barn?" she said, wonderingly.

"It's all right," replied her mother.

Sammy slid down from the load of hay, and came in to see if dinner was ready.

"I ain't goin' to get a regular dinner to-day, as long as father's gone," said his mother. "I've let the fire go out. You can have some bread an' milk an' pie. I thought we could get along." She set out some bowls of milk, some bread, and a pie on the kitchen table. "You'd better eat your dinner now," said she. "You might jest as well get through with it. I want you to help me afterward."

Nanny and Sammy stared at each other. There was something strange in their mother's manner. Mrs. Penn did not eat anything herself. She went into the pantry, and they heard her moving dishes while they ate. Presently she came out with a pile of plates. She got the clothes-basket out of the shed, and packed them in it. Nanny and Sammy watched. She brought out cups and saucers, and put them in with the plates.

"What you goin' to do, mother?" inquired Nanny, in a timid voice. A sense of something unusual made her tremble, as if it were a ghost. Sammy rolled his eyes over his pie.

"You'll see what I'm goin' to do," replied Mrs. Penn. "If you're through, Nanny, I want you to go up-stairs an' pack up your things; an' I want you, Sammy, to help me take down the bed in the bedroom."

"Oh, mother, what for?" gasped Nanny.

"You'll see."

During the next few hours a feat was performed by this simple, pious New England mother which was equal in its way to Wolfe's storming of the Heights of Abraham. It took no more genius and audacity of bravery for Wolfe to cheer his wondering soldiers up those steep precipices, under the sleeping eyes of the enemy, than for Sarah Penn, at the head of her children, to move all their little household goods into the new barn while her husband was away.

Nanny and Sammy followed their mother's instructions without a murmur; indeed, they were overawed. There is a certain uncanny and superhuman quality about all such purely original undertakings as their mother's was to them. Nanny went back and forth with her light loads, and Sammy tugged with sober energy.

At five o'clock in the afternoon the little house in which the Penns had lived for forty years had emptied itself into the new barn.

Every builder builds somewhat for unknown purposes, and is in a measure a prophet. The architect of Adoniram Penn's barn, while he designed it for the comfort of four-footed animals, had planned better than he knew for the comfort of humans. Sarah Penn saw at a glance its possibilities. Those great box-stalls, with quilts hung before them, would make better bedrooms than the one she had occupied for forty years, and there was a tight carriage-room. The harness-room, with its chimney and shelves, would make a kitchen of her dreams. The great middle space would make a parlor, by-and-by, fit for a palace. Up stairs there was as much room as down. With partitions and windows, what a house would there be! Sarah looked at the row of stanchions before the allotted space for cows, and reflected that she would have her front entry there.

At six o'clock the stove was up in the harness-room, the kettle was boiling, and the table set for tea. It looked almost as home-like as the abandoned house across the yard had ever done. The young hired man milked, and Sarah directed him calmly to bring the milk to the new barn. He came gaping, dropping little blots of foam from the brimming pails on the grass. Before the next morning he had spread the story of Adoniram Penn's wife moving into the new barn all over the little village. Men assembled in the store and talked it over, women with shawls over their heads scuttled into each other's houses before their work was done. Any deviation from the ordinary course of life in this quiet town was enough to stop all progress in it. Everybody paused to look at the staid, independent figure on the side track. There was a difference of opinion with regard to her. Some held her to be insane; some, of a lawless and rebellious spirit.

Friday the minister went to see her. It was in the forenoon, and she was at the barn door shelling pease for dinner. She looked up and returned his salutation with dignity, then she went on with her work. She did not invite him in. The saintly expression of her face remained fixed, but there was an angry flush over it.

The minister stood awkwardly before her, and talked. She handled the pease as if they were bullets. At last she looked up, and her eyes showed the spirit that her meek front had covered for a lifetime.

"There ain't no use talkin', Mr. Hersey," said she. "I've thought it all over an' over, an' I believe I'm doin' what's right. I've made it the subject of prayer, an' it's betwixt me an' the Lord an' Adoniram. There ain't no call for nobody else to worry about it."

"Well, of course, if you have brought it to the Lord in prayer, and feel satisfied that you are doing right, Mrs. Penn," said the minister, helplessly. His thin gray-bearded face was pathetic. He was a sickly man; his youthful confidence had cooled; he had to scourge himself up to some of his pastoral duties as relentlessly as a Catholic ascetic, and then he was prostrated by the smart.

"I think it's right jest as much as I think it was right for our forefathers to come over from the old country 'cause they didn't have what belonged to 'em," said Mrs. Penn. She arose. The barn threshold might have been Plymouth Rock from her bearing. "I don't doubt you mean well, Mr. Hersey," said she, "but there are things people hadn't ought to interfere with. I've been a member of the church for over forty year. I've got my own mind an' my own feet, an' I'm goin' to think my own thoughts an' go my own ways, an' nobody but the Lord is goin' to dictate to me unless I've a mind to have him. Won't you come in an' set down? How is Mis' Hersey?"

"She is well, I thank you," replied the minister. He added some more perplexed apologetic remarks; then he retreated.

He could expound the intricacies of every character study in the Scriptures, he was competent to grasp the Pilgrim Fathers and all historical innovators, but Sarah Penn was beyond him. He could deal with primal cases, but parallel ones worsted him. But, after all, although it was aside from his province, he wondered more how Adoniram Penn would deal with his wife than how the Lord would. Everybody shared the wonder. When Adoniram's four new cows arrived, Sarah ordered three to be put in the old barn, the other in the house shed where the cooking-stove had stood. That added to the excitement. It was whispered that all four cows were domiciled in the house.

Towards sunset on Saturday, when Adoniram was expected home, there was a knot of men in the road near the new barn. The hired man had milked, but he still hung around the premises. Sarah Penn had supper all ready. There were brown-bread and baked beans and a custard pie; it was the supper that Adoniram loved on a Saturday night. She had on a clean calico, and she bore herself imperturbably. Nanny and Sammy kept close at her heels. Their eyes were large, and Nanny was full of nervous tremors. Still there was to them more pleasant excitement than anything else. An inborn confidence in their mother over their father asserted itself.

Sammy looked out of the harness-room window. "There he is," he announced, in an awed whisper. He and Nanny peeped around the casing. Mrs. Penn kept on about her work. The children watched Adoniram leave the new horse standing in the drive while he went to the house door. It was fastened. Then he went around to the shed. That door was seldom locked, even when the family was away. The thought how her father would be confronted by the cow flashed upon Nanny. There was a hysterical sob in her throat. Adoniram emerged from the shed and stood looking about in a dazed fashion. His lips moved; he was saying something, but they could not hear what it was. The hired man was peeping around a corner of the old barn, but nobody saw him.

Adoniram took the new horse by the bridle and led him across the yard to the new barn. Nanny and Sammy slunk close to their mother. The barn doors rolled back, and there stood Adoniram, with the long mild face of the great Canadian farm horse looking over his shoulder.

Nanny kept behind her mother, but Sammy stepped suddenly forward, and stood in front of her.

Adoniram stared at the group. "What on airth you all down here for?" said he. "What's the matter over to the house?"

"We've come here to live, father," said Sammy. His shrill voice quavered out bravely.

"What"—Adoniram sniffed—"what is it smells like cookin?" said he. He stepped forward and looked in the open door of the harness-room. Then he turned to his wife. His old bristling face was pale and frightened. "What on airth does this mean, mother?" he gasped.

"You come in here, father," said Sarah. She led the way into the harness-room and shut the door. "Now, father," said she, "you needn't be scared. I ain't crazy. There ain't nothin' to be upset over. But we've come here to live, an' we're goin' to live here. We've got jest as good a right here as new horses an' cows. The house wa'n't fit for us to live in any longer, an' I made up my mind I wa'n't goin' to stay there. I've done my duty by you forty year, an' I'm goin' to do it now; but I'm goin' to live here. You've got to put in some windows and partitions; an' you'll have to buy some furniture."

"Why, mother!" the old man gasped.

"You'd better take your coat off an' get washed—there's the wash-basin—an' then we'll have supper."

"Why, mother!"

Sammy went past the window, leading the new horse to the old barn. The old man saw him, and shook his head speechlessly. He tried to take off his coat, but his arms seemed to lack the power. His wife helped him. She poured some water into the tin basin, and put in a piece of soap. She got the comb and brush, and smoothed his thin gray hair after he had washed. Then she put the beans, hot bread, and tea on the table. Sammy came in, and the family drew up. Adoniram sat looking dazedly at his plate, and they waited.

"Ain't you goin' to ask a blessin', father?" said Sarah.

And the old man bent his head and mumbled.

All through the meal he stopped eating at intervals, and stared furtively at his wife; but he ate well. The home food tasted good to him, and his old frame was too sturdily healthy to be affected by his mind. But after supper he went out, and sat down on the step of the smaller door at the right of the barn, through which he had meant his Jerseys to pass in stately file, but which Sarah designed for her front house door, and he leaned his head on his hands.

After the supper dishes were cleared away and the milk-pans washed, Sarah went out to him. The twilight was deepening. There was a clear green glow in the sky. Before them stretched the smooth level of field; in the distance was a cluster of hay-stacks like the huts of a village; the air was very cool and calm and sweet. The landscape might have been an ideal one of peace.

Sarah bent over and touched her husband on one of his thin, sinewy shoulders. "Father!"

The old man's shoulders heaved: he was weeping.

"Why, don't do so, father," said Sarah.

"I'll—put up the—partitions, an'—everything you—want, mother."

Sarah put her apron up to her face; she was overcome by her own triumph.

Adoniram was like a fortress whose walls had no active resistance, and went down the instant the right besieging tools were used. "Why, mother," he said, hoarsely, "I hadn't no idee you was so set on't as all this comes to."

CHARLES W. CHESNUTT

The Wife of His Youth

I

Mr. Ryder was going to give a ball. There were several reasons why this was an opportune time for such an event.

Mr. Ryder might aptly be called the dean of the Blue Veins. The original Blue Veins were a little society of colored persons organized in a certain Northern city shortly after the war. Its purpose was to establish and maintain correct social standards among a people whose social condition presented almost unlimited room for improvement. By accident, combined perhaps with some natural affinity, the society consisted of individuals who were, generally speaking, more white than black. Some envious outsider made the suggestion that no one was eligible for membership who was not white enough to show blue veins. The suggestion was readily adopted by those who were not of the favored few, and since that time the society, though possessing a longer and more pretentious name, had been known far and wide as the "Blue Vein Society," and its members as the "Blue Veins."

The Blue Veins did not allow that any such requirement existed for admission to their circle, but, on the contrary, declared that character and culture were the only things considered; and that if most of their members were light-colored, it was because such persons, as a rule, had had better opportunities to qualify themselves for membership. Opinions differed, too, as to the usefulness of the society. There were those who had been known to assail it violently as a glaring example of the very prejudice from which the colored race had suffered most; and later, when such critics had succeeded in getting on the inside, they had been heard to maintain with zeal and earnestness that the society was a lifeboat, an anchor, a bulwark and a shield,—a pillar of cloud by day and of fire by night, to guide their people through the social wilderness. Another alleged prerequisite for Blue Vein membership was that of free birth; and while there was really no such requirement, it is doubtless true that very few of the members would have been unable to meet it if there had been. If there were one or two of the older members who had come up from the South and from slavery, their history presented enough romantic circumstances to rob their servile origin of its grosser aspects.

While there were no such tests of eligibility, it is true that the Blue Veins had their notions on these subjects, and that not all of them were equally liberal in regard to the things they collectively disclaimed. Mr. Ryder was one of the most conservative. Though he had not been among the founders of the society, but had come in some years later, his genius for social leadership was such that he had speedily become its recognized adviser and head, the custodian of its standards, and the preserver of its traditions. He shaped its social policy, was active in providing for its entertainment, and when the interest fell off, as it sometimes did, he fanned the embers until they burst again into a cheerful flame.

There were still other reasons for his popularity. While he was not as white as some of the Blue Veins, his appearance was such as to confer distinction upon them. His features were of a refined type, his hair was almost straight; he was always neatly dressed; his manners were irreproachable, and his morals above suspicion. He had come to Groveland a young man, and obtaining employment in the office of a railroad company as messenger had in time worked himself up to the position of stationery clerk, having charge of the distribution of the office supplies for the whole company. Although the lack of early training had hindered the orderly development of a naturally fine mind, it had not prevented him from doing a great deal of reading or from forming decidedly literary tastes. Poetry was his passion. He could repeat whole pages of the great English poets; and if his pronunciation was sometimes faulty, his eye, his voice, his gestures, would respond to the changing sentiment with a precision that revealed a poetic soul and disarmed criticism. He was economical, and had saved money; he owned and occupied a very comfortable house on a respectable street. His residence was handsomely furnished, containing among other things a good library, especially rich in poetry, a piano, and some choice engravings. He generally shared his house with some young couple, who looked after his wants and were company for him; for Mr. Ryder was a single man. In the early days of his connection with the Blue Veins he had been regarded as quite a catch, and young ladies and their mothers had manoeuvred with much ingenuity to capture him. Not, however, until Mrs. Molly Dixon visited Groveland had any woman ever made him wish to change his condition to that of a married man.

Mrs. Dixon had come to Groveland from Washington in the spring, and before the summer was over she had won Mr. Ryder's heart. She possessed many attractive qualities. She was much younger than he; in fact, he was old enough to have been her father, though no one knew exactly how old he was. She was whiter than he, and better educated. She had moved in the best colored society of the country, at Washington, and had taught in the schools of that city. Such a superior person had been eagerly welcomed to the Blue Vein Society, and had taken a leading part in its activities. Mr. Ryder had at first been attracted by her charms of person, for she was very good looking and not over twenty-five; then by her refined manners and the vivacity of her wit. Her husband had been a government clerk, and at his death had left a considerable life insurance. She was visiting friends in Groveland, and, finding the town and the people to her liking, had prolonged her stay indefinitely. She had not seemed displeased at Mr. Ryder's attentions, but on the contrary had given him every proper encouragement; indeed, a younger and less cautious man would long since have spoken. But he had made up his mind, and had only to determine the time when he would ask her to be his wife. He decided to give a ball in her honor, and at some time during the evening of the ball to offer her his heart and hand. He had no special fears about the outcome, but, with a little touch of romance, he wanted the surroundings to be in harmony with his own feelings when he should have received the answer he expected.

Mr. Ryder resolved that this ball should mark an epoch in the social history of Groveland. He knew, of course,—no one could know better,—the entertainments that had taken place in past years, and what must be done to surpass them. His ball must be worthy of the lady in whose honor it was to be given, and must, by the quality of its guests, set an example for the future. He had observed of late a growing liberality, almost a laxity, in social matters, even among members of his own set, and had several times been forced to meet in a social way persons whose complexions and callings in life were hardly up to the standard which he considered proper for the society to maintain. He had a theory of his own.

"I have no race prejudice," he would say, "but we people of mixed blood are ground between the upper and the nether millstone. Our fate lies between absorption by the white race and extinction in the black. The one doesn't want us yet, but may take us in time. The other would welcome us, but it would be for us a backward step. 'With malice towards none, with charity for all,' we must do the best we can for ourselves and those who are to follow us. Self-preservation is the first law of nature."

His ball would serve by its exclusiveness to counteract leveling tendencies, and his marriage with Mrs. Dixon would help to further the upward process of absorption he had been wishing and waiting for.

II

The ball was to take place on Friday night. The house had been put in order, the carpets covered with canvas, the halls and stairs decorated with palms and potted plants; and in the afternoon Mr. Ryder sat on his front porch, which the shade of a vine running up over a wire netting made a cool and pleasant lounging place. He expected to respond to the toast "The Ladies" at the supper, and from a volume of Tennyson—his favorite poet—was fortifying himself with apt quotations. The volume was open at "A Dream of Fair Women." His eyes fell on these lines, and he read them aloud to judge better of their effect:—

> "At length I saw a lady within call,
> Stiller than chisell'd marble, standing there;
> A daughter of the gods, divinely tall,
> And most divinely fair."

He marked the verse, and turning the page read the stanza beginning,—

"O sweet pale Margaret,
O rare pale Margaret."

He weighed the passage a moment, and decided that it would not do. Mrs. Dixon was the palest lady he expected at the ball, and she was of a rather ruddy complexion, and of lively disposition and buxom build. So he ran over the leaves until his eye rested on the description of Queen Guinevere:—

"She seem'd a part of joyous Spring;
A gown of grass-green silk she wore,
Buckled with golden clasps before;
A light-green tuft of plumes she bore
Closed in a golden ring.
* * * * * *
"She look'd so lovely, as she sway'd
The rein with dainty finger-tips,
A man had given all other bliss,
And all his worldly worth for this,
To waste his whole heart in one kiss
Upon her perfect lips."

As Mr. Ryder murmured these words audibly, with an appreciative thrill, he heard the latch of his gate click, and a light footfall sounding on the steps. He turned his head, and saw a woman standing before his door.

She was a little woman, not five feet tall, and proportioned to her height. Although she stood erect, and looked around her with very bright and restless eyes, she seemed quite old; for her face was crossed and recrossed with a hundred wrinkles, and around the edges of her bonnet could be seen protruding here and there a tuft of short gray wool. She wore a blue calico gown of ancient cut, a little red shawl fastened around her shoulders with an old-fashioned brass brooch, and a large bonnet profusely ornamented with faded red and yellow artificial flowers. And she was very black,—so black that her toothless gums, revealed when she opened her mouth to speak, were not red, but blue. She looked like a bit of the old plantation life, summoned up from the past by the wave of a magician's wand, as the poet's fancy had called into being the gracious shapes of which Mr. Ryder had just been reading.

He rose from his chair and came over to where she stood.

"Good-afternoon, madam," he said.

"Good-evenin', suh," she answered, ducking suddenly with a quaint curtsy. Her voice was shrill and piping, but softened somewhat by age. "Is dis yere whar Mistuh Ryduh lib, suh?" she asked, looking around her doubtfully, and glancing into the open windows, through which some of the preparations for the evening were visible.

"Yes," he replied, with an air of kindly patronage, unconsciously flattered by her manner, "I am Mr. Ryder. Did you want to see me?"

"Yas, suh, ef I ain't 'sturbin' of you too much."

"Not at all. Have a seat over here behind the vine, where it is cool. What can I do for you?"

"'Scuse me, suh," she continued, when she had sat down on the edge of a chair, "'scuse me, suh, I's lookin' for my husban'. I heerd you wuz a big man an' had libbed heah a long time, an' I 'lowed you wouldn't min' ef I'd come roun' an' ax you ef you'd ever heerd of a merlatter man by de name er Sam Taylor 'quirin' roun' in de chu'ches ermongs' de people fer his wife 'Liza Jane?"

Mr. Ryder seemed to think for a moment.

"There used to be many such cases right after the war," he said, "but it has been so long that I have forgotten them. There are very few now. But tell me your story, and it may refresh my memory."

She sat back farther in her chair so as to be more comfortable, and folded her withered hands in her lap.

"My name's 'Liza," she began, "'Liza Jane. W'en I wuz young I us'ter b'long ter Marse Bob Smif, down in ole Missoura. I wuz bawn down dere. W'en I wuz a gal I wuz married ter a man named Jim. But Jim died, an' after dat I married a merlatter man named Sam Taylor. Sam wuz freebawn, but his mammy and daddy died, an' de w'ite folks 'prenticed him ter my marster fer ter work fer 'im 'tel he wuz growed up. Sam worked in de fiel', an' I wuz de cook. One day Ma'y Ann, ole miss's maid, came rushin' out ter de kitchen, an' says she, ''Liza Jane, ole marse gwine sell yo' Sam down de ribber.'

"'Go way f'm yere,' says I; 'my husban''s free!'

"'Don' make no diff'ence. I heerd ole marse tell ole miss he wuz gwine take yo' Sam 'way wid 'im ter-morrow, fer he needed money, an' he knowed whar he could git a t'ousan' dollars fer Sam an' no questions axed.'

"W'en Sam come home f'm de fiel' dat night, I tole him 'bout ole marse gwine steal 'im, an' Sam run erway. His time wuz mos' up, an' he swo' dat w'en he wuz twenty-one he would come back an' he'p me run erway, er else save up de money ter buy my freedom. An' I know he'd 'a' done it, fer he thought a heap er me, Sam did. But w'en he come back he did n' fin' me, fer I wuz n' dere. Ole marse had heerd dat I warned Sam, so he had me whip' an' sol' down de ribber.

"Den de wah broke out, an' w'en it wuz ober de cullud folks wuz scattered. I went back ter de ole home; but Sam wuz n' dere, an' I could n' l'arn nuffin' 'bout 'im. But I knowed he'd be'n dere to look fer me an' had n' foun' me, an' had gone erway ter hunt fer me.

"I's be'n lookin' fer 'im eber sence," she added simply, as though twenty-five years were but a couple of weeks, "an' I knows he's be'n lookin' fer me. Fer he sot a heap er sto' by me, Sam did, an' I know he's be'n huntin' fer me all dese years,—'less'n he's be'n sick er sump'n, so he could n' work, er out'n his head, so he could n' 'member his promise. I went back down de ribber, fer I 'lowed he'd gone down dere lookin' fer me. I's be'n ter Noo Orleens, an' Atlanty, an' Charleston, an' Richmon'; an' w'en I'd be'n all ober de Souf I come ter de Norf. Fer I knows I'll fin' 'im some er dese days," she added softly, "er he'll fin' me, an' den we'll bofe be as happy in freedom as we wuz in de ole days befo' de wah." A smile stole over her withered countenance as she paused a moment, and her bright eyes softened into a far-away look.

This was the substance of the old woman's story. She had wandered a little here and there. Mr. Ryder was looking at her curiously when she finished.

"How have you lived all these years?" he asked.

"Cookin', suh. I's a good cook. Does you know anybody w'at needs a good cook, suh? I's stoppin' wid a cullud fam'ly roun' de corner yonder 'tel I kin git a place."

"Do you really expect to find your husband? He may be dead long ago."

She shook her head emphatically. "Oh no, he ain' dead. De signs an' de tokens tells me. I dremp three nights runnin' on'y dis las' week dat I foun' him."

"He may have married another woman. Your slave marriage would not have prevented him, for you never lived with him after the war, and without that your marriage doesn't count."

"Would n' make no diff'ence wid Sam. He would n' marry no yuther 'ooman 'tel he foun' out 'bout me. I knows it," she added. "Sump'n 's be'n tellin' me all dese years dat I's gwine fin' Sam 'fo' I dies."

"Perhaps he's outgrown you, and climbed up in the world where he wouldn't care to have you find him."

"No, indeed, suh," she replied, "Sam ain' dat kin' er man. He wuz good ter me, Sam wuz, but he wuz n' much good ter nobody e'se, fer he wuz one er de triflin'es' han's on de plantation. I 'spec's ter haf ter suppo't 'im, w'en I fin' 'im, fer he nebber would work 'less'n he had ter. But den he wuz free, an' he did n' git no pay fer his work, an' I don' blame 'im much. Mebbe he's done better sence he run erway, but I ain' 'spectin' much."

"You may have passed him on the street a hundred times during the twenty-five years, and not have known him; time works great changes."

She smiled incredulously. "I'd know 'im 'mongs' a hund'ed men. Fer dey wuz n' no yuther merlatter man like my man Sam, an' I could n' be mistook. I's toted his picture roun' wid me twenty-five years."

"May I see it?" asked Mr. Ryder. "It might help me to remember whether I have seen the original."

As she drew a small parcel from her bosom he saw that it was fastened to a string that went around her neck. Removing several wrappers, she brought to light an old-fashioned daguerreotype in a black case. He looked long and intently at the portrait. It was faded with time, but the features were still distinct, and it was easy to see what manner of man it had represented.

He closed the case, and with a slow movement handed it back to her.

"I don't know of any man in town who goes by that name," he said, "nor have I heard of any one making such inquiries. But if you will leave me your address, I will give the matter some attention, and if I find out anything I will let you know."

She gave him the number of a house in the neighborhood, and went away, after thanking him warmly.

He wrote the address on the fly-leaf of the volume of Tennyson, and, when she had gone, rose to his feet and stood looking after her curiously. As she walked down the street with mincing step, he saw several persons whom she passed turn and look back at her with a smile of kindly amusement. When she had turned the corner, he went upstairs to his bedroom, and stood for a long time before the mirror of his dressing-case, gazing thoughtfully at the reflection of his own face.

III

At eight o'clock the ballroom was a blaze of light and the guests had begun to assemble; for there was a literary programme and some routine business of the society to be gone through with before the dancing. A black servant in evening dress waited at the door and directed the guests to the dressing-rooms.

The occasion was long memorable among the colored people of the city; not alone for the dress and display, but for the high average of intelligence and culture that distinguished the gathering as a whole. There were a number of school-teachers, several young doctors, three or four lawyers, some professional singers, an editor, a lieutenant in the United States army spending his furlough in the city, and others in various polite callings; these were colored, though most of them would not have attracted even a casual glance because of any marked difference from white people. Most of the ladies were in evening costume, and dress coats and dancing pumps were the rule among the men. A band of string music, stationed in an alcove behind a row of palms, played popular airs while the guests were gathering.

The dancing began at half past nine. At eleven o'clock supper was served. Mr. Ryder had left the ballroom some little time before the intermission, but reappeared at the supper-table. The spread was worthy of the occasion, and the guests did full justice to it. When the coffee had been served, the toast-master, Mr. Solomon Sadler, rapped for order. He made a brief introductory speech, complimenting host and guests, and then presented in their order the toasts of the evening. They were responded to with a very fair display of after-dinner wit.

"The last toast," said the toast-master, when he reached the end of the list, "is one which must appeal to us all. There is no one of us of the sterner sex who is not at some time dependent upon woman,—in infancy for protection, in manhood for companionship, in old age for care and comforting. Our good host has been trying to live alone, but the fair faces I see around me to-night prove that he too is largely dependent upon the gentler sex for most that makes life worth living,—the society and love of friends,—and rumor is at fault if he does not soon yield entire subjection to one of them. Mr. Ryder will now respond to the toast,—The Ladies."

There was a pensive look in Mr. Ryder's eyes as he took the floor and adjusted his eyeglasses. He began by speaking of woman as the gift of Heaven to man, and after some general observations on the relations of the sexes he said: "But perhaps the quality which most distinguishes woman is her fidelity and devotion to those she loves. History is full of examples, but has recorded none more striking than one which only to-day came under my notice."

He then related, simply but effectively, the story told by his visitor of the afternoon. He gave it in the same soft dialect, which came readily to his lips, while the company listened attentively and sympathetically. For the story had awakened a responsive thrill in many hearts. There were some present who had seen, and others who had heard their fathers and grandfathers tell, the wrongs and sufferings of this past generation, and all of them still felt, in their darker moments, the shadow hanging over them. Mr. Ryder went on:—

"Such devotion and confidence are rare even among women. There are many who would have searched a year, some who would have waited five years, a few who might have hoped ten years; but for twenty-five years this woman has retained her affection for and her faith in a man she has not seen or heard of in all that time.

"She came to me to-day in the hope that I might be able to help her find this long-lost husband. And when she was gone I gave my fancy rein, and imagined a case I will put to you.

"Suppose that this husband, soon after his escape, had learned that his wife had been sold away, and that such inquiries as he could make brought no information of her whereabouts. Suppose that he was young, and she much older than he; that he was light, and she was black; that their marriage was a slave marriage, and legally binding only if they chose to make it so after the war. Suppose, too, that he made his way to the North, as some of us have done, and there, where he had larger opportunities, had improved them, and had in the course of all these years grown to be as different from the ignorant boy who ran away from fear of slavery as the day is from the night. Suppose, even, that he had qualified himself, by industry, by thrift, and by study, to win the friendship and be considered worthy the society of such people as these I see around me to-night, gracing my board and filling my heart with gladness; for I am old enough to remember the day when such a gathering would not have been possible in this land. Suppose, too, that, as the years went by, this man's memory of the past grew more and more indistinct, until at last it was rarely, except in his dreams, that any image of this bygone period rose before his mind. And then suppose that accident should bring to his knowledge the fact that the wife of his youth, the wife he had left behind him,—not one who had walked by his side and kept pace with him in his upward struggle, but one upon whom advancing years and a laborious life had set their mark,—was alive and seeking him, but that he was absolutely safe from recognition or discovery, unless he chose to reveal himself. My friends, what would the man do? I will presume that he was one who loved honor, and tried to deal justly with all men. I will even carry the case further, and suppose that perhaps he had set his heart upon another, whom he had hoped to call his own. What would he do, or rather what ought he to do, in such a crisis of a lifetime?

"It seemed to me that he might hesitate, and I imagined that I was an old friend, a near friend, and that he had come to me for advice; and I argued the case with him. I tried to discuss it impartially. After we had looked upon the matter from every point of view, I said to him, in words that we all know:—

> 'This above all: to thine own self be true,
> And it must follow, as the night the day,
> Thou canst not then be false to any man.'

Then, finally, I put the question to him, 'Shall you acknowledge her?'

"And now, ladies and gentlemen, friends and companions, I ask you, what should he have done?"

There was something in Mr. Ryder's voice that stirred the hearts of those who sat around him. It suggested more than mere sympathy with an imaginary situation; it seemed rather in the nature of a personal appeal. It was observed, too, that his look rested more especially upon Mrs. Dixon, with a mingled expression of renunciation and inquiry.

She had listened, with parted lips and streaming eyes. She was the first to speak: "He should have acknowledged her."

"Yes," they all echoed, "he should have acknowledged her."

"My friends and companions," responded Mr. Ryder, "I thank you, one and all. It is the answer I expected, for I knew your hearts."

He turned and walked toward the closed door of an adjoining room, while every eye followed him in wondering curiosity. He came back in a moment, leading by the hand his visitor of the afternoon, who stood startled and trembling at the sudden plunge into this scene of brilliant gayety. She was neatly dressed in gray, and wore the white cap of an elderly woman.

"Ladies and gentlemen," he said, "this is the woman, and I am the man, whose story I have told you. Permit me to introduce to you the wife of my youth."

CHARLES W. CHESNUTT

The Passing of Grandison

I

When it is said that it was done to please a woman, there ought perhaps to be enough said to explain anything; for what a man will not do to please a woman is yet to be discovered. Nevertheless, it might be well to state a few preliminary facts to make it clear why young Dick Owens tried to run one of his father's negro men off to Canada.

In the early fifties, when the growth of anti-slavery sentiment and the constant drain of fugitive slaves into the North had so alarmed the slaveholders of the border States as to lead to the passage of the Fugitive Slave Law, a young white man from Ohio, moved by compassion for the sufferings of a certain bondman who happened to have a "hard master," essayed to help the slave to freedom. The attempt was discovered and frustrated; the abductor was tried and convicted for slave-stealing, and sentenced to a term of imprisonment in the penitentiary. His death, after the expiration of only a small part of the sentence, from cholera contracted while nursing stricken fellow prisoners, lent to the case a melancholy interest that made it famous in anti-slavery annals.

Dick Owens had attended the trial. He was a youth of about twenty-two, intelligent, handsome, and amiable, but extremely indolent, in a graceful and gentlemanly way; or, as old Judge Fenderson put it more than once, he was lazy as the Devil,—a mere figure of speech, of course, and not one that did justice to the Enemy of Mankind. When asked why he never did anything serious, Dick would good-naturedly reply, with a well-modulated drawl, that he didn't have to. His father was rich; there was but one other child, an unmarried daughter, who because of poor health would probably never marry, and Dick was therefore heir presumptive to a large estate. Wealth or social position he did not need to seek, for he was born to both. Charity Lomax had shamed him into studying law, but notwithstanding an hour or so a day spent at old Judge Fenderson's office, he did not make remarkable headway in his legal studies.

"What Dick needs," said the judge, who was fond of tropes, as became a scholar, and of horses, as was befitting a Kentuckian, "is the whip of necessity, or the spur of ambition. If he had either, he would soon need the snaffle to hold him back."

But all Dick required, in fact, to prompt him to the most remarkable thing he accomplished before he was twenty-five, was a mere suggestion from Charity Lomax. The story was never really known to but two persons until after the war, when it came out because it was a good story and there was no particular reason for its concealment.

Young Owens had attended the trial of this slave-stealer, or martyr,—either or both,—and, when it was over, had gone to call on Charity Lomax, and, while they sat on the veranda after sundown, had told her all about the trial. He was a good talker, as his career in later years disclosed, and described the proceedings very graphically.

"I confess," he admitted, "that while my principles were against the prisoner, my sympathies were on his side. It appeared that he was of good family, and that he had an old father and mother, respectable people, dependent upon him for support and comfort in their declining years. He had been led into the matter by pity for a negro whose master ought to have been run out of the county long ago for abusing his slaves. If it had been merely a question of old Sam Briggs's negro, nobody would have cared anything about it. But father and the rest of them stood on the principle of the thing, and told the judge so, and the fellow was sentenced to three years in the penitentiary."

Miss Lomax had listened with lively interest.

"I've always hated old Sam Briggs," she said emphatically, "ever since the time he broke a negro's leg with a piece of cordwood. When I hear of a cruel deed it makes the Quaker blood that came from my grandmother assert itself. Personally I wish that all Sam Briggs's negroes would run away. As for the young man, I regard him as a hero. He dared something for humanity. I could love a man who would take such chances for the sake of others."

"Could you love me, Charity, if I did something heroic?"

"You never will, Dick. You're too lazy for any use. You'll never do anything harder than playing cards or fox-hunting."

"Oh, come now, sweetheart! I've been courting you for a year, and it's the hardest work imaginable. Are you never going to love me?" he pleaded.

His hand sought hers, but she drew it back beyond his reach.

"I'll never love you, Dick Owens, until you have done something. When that time comes, I'll think about it."

"But it takes so long to do anything worth mentioning, and I don't want to wait. One must read two years to become a lawyer, and work five more to make a reputation. We shall both be gray by then."

"Oh, I don't know," she rejoined. "It doesn't require a lifetime for a man to prove that he is a man. This one did something, or at least tried to."

"Well, I'm willing to attempt as much as any other man. What do you want me to do, sweetheart? Give me a test."

"Oh, dear me!" said Charity, "I don't care what you *do*, so you do *something*. Really, come to think of it, why should I care whether you do anything or not?"

"I'm sure I don't know why you should, Charity," rejoined Dick humbly, "for I'm aware that I'm not worthy of it."

"Except that I do hate," she added, relenting slightly, "to see a really clever man so utterly lazy and good for nothing."

"Thank you, my dear; a word of praise from you has sharpened my wits already. I have an idea! Will you love me if *I* run a negro off to Canada?"

"What nonsense!" said Charity scornfully. "You must be losing your wits. Steal another man's slave, indeed, while your father owns a hundred!"

"Oh, there'll be no trouble about that," responded Dick lightly; "I'll run off one of the old man's; we've got too many anyway. It may not be quite as difficult as the other man found it, but it will be just as unlawful, and will demonstrate what I am capable of."

"Seeing's believing," replied Charity. "Of course, what you are talking about now is merely absurd. I'm going away for three weeks, to visit my aunt in Tennessee. If you're able to tell me, when I return, that you've done something to prove your quality, I'll—well, you may come and tell me about it."

II

Young Owens got up about nine o'clock next morning, and while making his toilet put some questions to his personal attendant, a rather bright looking young mulatto of about his own age.

"Tom," said Dick.

"Yas, Mars Dick," responded the servant.

"I'm going on a trip North. Would you like to go with me?"

Now, if there was anything that Tom would have liked to make, it was a trip North. It was something he had long contemplated in the abstract, but had never been able to muster up sufficient courage to attempt in the concrete. He was prudent enough, however, to dissemble his feelings.

"I wouldn't min' it, Mars Dick, ez long ez you'd take keer er me an' fetch me home all right."

Tom's eyes belied his words, however, and his young master felt well assured that Tom needed only a good opportunity to make him run away. Having a comfortable home, and a dismal prospect in case of failure, Tom was not likely to take any desperate chances; but young Owens was satisfied that in a free State but little persuasion would be required to lead Tom astray. With a very logical and characteristic desire to gain his end with the least necessary expenditure of effort, he decided to take Tom with him, if his father did not object.

Colonel Owens had left the house when Dick went to breakfast, so Dick did not see his father till luncheon.

"Father," he remarked casually to the colonel, over the fried chicken, "I'm feeling a trifle run down. I imagine my health would be improved somewhat by a little travel and change of scene."

"Why don't you take a trip North?" suggested his father. The colonel added to paternal affection a considerable respect for his son as the heir of a large estate. He himself had been "raised" in comparative poverty, and had laid the foundations of his fortune by hard work; and while he despised the ladder by which he had climbed, he could not entirely forget it, and unconsciously manifested, in his intercourse with his son, some of the poor man's deference toward the wealthy and well-born.

"I think I'll adopt your suggestion, sir," replied the son, "and run up to New York; and after I've been there awhile I may go on to Boston for a week or so. I've never been there, you know."

"There are some matters you can talk over with my factor in New York," rejoined the colonel, "and while you are up there among the Yankees, I hope you'll keep your eyes and ears open to find out what the rascally abolitionists are saying and doing. They're becoming altogether too active for our comfort, and entirely too many ungrateful niggers are running away. I hope the conviction of that fellow yesterday may discourage the rest of the breed. I'd just like to catch any one trying to run off one of my darkeys. He'd get short shrift; I don't think any Court would have a chance to try him."

"They are a pestiferous lot," assented Dick, "and dangerous to our institutions. But say, father, if I go North I shall want to take Tom with me."

Now, the colonel, while a very indulgent father, had pronounced views on the subject of negroes, having studied them, as he often said, for a great many years, and, as he asserted oftener still, understanding them perfectly. It is scarcely worth while to say, either, that he valued more highly than if he had inherited them the slaves he had toiled and schemed for.

"I don't think it safe to take Tom up North," he declared, with promptness and decision. "He's a good enough boy, but too smart to trust among those low-down abolitionists. I strongly suspect him of having learned to read, though I can't imagine how. I saw him with a newspaper the other day, and while he pretended to be looking at a woodcut, I'm almost sure he was reading the paper. I think it by no means safe to take him."

Dick did not insist, because he knew it was useless. The colonel would have obliged his son in any other matter, but his negroes were the outward and visible sign of his wealth and station, and therefore sacred to him.

"Whom do you think it safe to take?" asked Dick. "I suppose I'll have to have a body-servant."

"What's the matter with Grandison?" suggested the colonel. "He's handy enough, and I reckon we can trust him. He's too fond of good eating, to risk losing his regular meals; besides, he's sweet on your mother's maid, Betty, and I've promised to let 'em get married before long. I'll have Grandison up, and we'll talk to him. Here, you boy Jack," called the colonel to a yellow youth in the next room who was catching flies and pulling their wings off to pass the time, "go down to the barn and tell Grandison to come here.

"Grandison," said the colonel, when the negro stood before him, hat in hand.

"Yas, marster."

"Haven't I always treated you right?"

"Yas, marster."

"Haven't you always got all you wanted to eat?"

"Yas, marster."

"And as much whiskey and tobacco as was good for you, Grandison?"

"Y-a-s, marster."

"I should just like to know, Grandison, whether you don't think yourself a great deal better off than those poor free negroes down by the plank road, with no kind master to look after them and no mistress to give them medicine when they're sick and—and"—

"Well, I sh'd jes' reckon I is better off, suh, dan dem lowdown free niggers, suh! Ef anybody ax 'em who dey b'long ter, dey has ter say nobody, er e'se lie erbout it. Anybody ax me who I b'longs ter, I ain' got no 'casion ter be shame' ter tell 'em, no, suh, 'deed I ain', suh!"

The colonel was beaming. This was true gratitude, and his feudal heart thrilled at such appreciative homage. What cold-blooded, heartless monsters they were who would break up this blissful relationship of kindly protection on the one hand, of wise subordination and loyal dependence on the other! The colonel always became indignant at the mere thought of such wickedness.

"Grandison," the colonel continued, "your young master Dick is going North for a few weeks, and I am thinking of letting him take you along. I shall send you on this trip, Grandison, in order that you may take care of your young master. He will need some one to wait on him, and no one can ever do it so well as one of the boys brought up with him on the old plantation. I am going to trust him in your hands, and I'm sure you'll do your duty faithfully, and bring him back home safe and sound—to old Kentucky."

Grandison grinned. "Oh yas, marster, I'll take keer er young Mars Dick."

"I want to warn you, though, Grandison," continued the colonel impressively, "against these cussed abolitionists, who try to entice servants from their comfortable homes and their indulgent masters, from the blue skies, the green fields, and the warm sunlight of their southern home, and send them away off yonder to Canada, a dreary country, where the woods are full of wildcats and wolves and bears, where the snow lies up to the eaves of the houses for six months of the year, and the cold is so severe that it freezes your breath and curdles your blood; and where, when runaway niggers get sick and can't work, they are turned out to starve and die, unloved and uncared for. I reckon, Grandison, that you have too much sense to permit yourself to be led astray by any such foolish and wicked people."

"'Deed, suh, I would n' low none er dem cussed, lowdown abolitioners ter come nigh me, suh. I'd—I'd—would I be 'lowed ter hit 'em, suh?"

"Certainly, Grandison," replied the colonel, chuckling, "hit 'em as hard as you can. I reckon they'd rather like it. Begad, I believe they would! It would serve 'em right to be hit by a nigger!"

"Er ef I didn't hit 'em, suh," continued Grandison reflectively, "I'd tell Mars Dick, en *he'd* fix 'em. He'd smash de face off'n 'em, suh, I jes' knows he would."

"Oh yes, Grandison, your young master will protect you. You need fear no harm while he is near."

"Dey won't try ter steal me, will dey, marster?" asked the negro, with sudden alarm.

"I don't know, Grandison," replied the colonel, lighting a fresh cigar. "They're a desperate set of lunatics, and there's no telling what they may resort to. But if you stick close to your young master, and remember always that he is your best friend, and understands your real needs, and has your true interests at heart, and if you will be careful to avoid strangers who try to talk to you, you'll stand a fair chance of getting back to your home and your friends. And if you please your master Dick, he'll buy you a present, and a string of beads for Betty to wear when you and she get married in the fall."

"Thanky, marster, thanky, suh," replied Grandison, oozing gratitude at every pore; "you is a good marster, to be sho', suh; yas, 'deed you is. You kin jes' bet me and Mars Dick gwine git 'long jes' lack I wuz own boy ter Mars Dick. En it won't be my fault ef he don' want me fer his boy all de time, w'en we come back home ag'in."

"All right, Grandison, you may go now. You needn't work any more to-day, and here's a piece of tobacco for you off my own plug."

"Thanky, marster, thanky, marster! You is de bes' marster any nigger ever had in dis worl'." And Grandison bowed and scraped and disappeared round the corner, his jaws closing around a large section of the colonel's best tobacco.

"You may take Grandison," said the colonel to his son. "I allow he's abolitionist-proof."

III

Richard Owens, Esq., and servant, from Kentucky, registered at the fashionable New York hostelry for Southerners in those days, a hotel where an atmosphere congenial to Southern institutions was sedulously maintained. But there were negro waiters in the dining-room, and mulatto bell-boys, and Dick had no doubt that Grandison, with the native gregariousness and garrulousness of his race, would foregather and palaver with them sooner or later, and Dick hoped that they would speedily inoculate him with the virus of freedom. For it was not Dick's intention to say anything to his servant about his plan to free him, for obvious reasons. To mention one of them, if Grandison should go away, and by legal process be recaptured, his young master's part in the matter would doubtless become known, which would be embarrassing to Dick, to say the least. If, on the other hand, he should merely give Grandison sufficient latitude, he had no doubt he would eventually lose him. For while not exactly skeptical about Grandison's perfervid loyalty, Dick had been a somewhat keen observer of human nature, in his own indolent way, and based his expectations upon the force of the example and argument that his servant could scarcely fail to encounter. Grandison should have a fair chance to become free by his own initiative; if it should become necessary to adopt other measures to get rid of him, it would be time enough to act when the necessity arose; and Dick Owens was not the youth to take needless trouble.

The young master renewed some acquaintances and made others, and spent a week or two very pleasantly in the best society of the metropolis, easily accessible to a wealthy, well-bred young Southerner, with proper introductions. Young women smiled on him, and young men of convivial habits pressed their hospitalities; but the memory of Charity's sweet, strong face and clear blue eyes made him proof against the blandishments of the one sex and the persuasions of the other. Meanwhile he kept Grandison supplied with pocket-money, and left him mainly to his own devices. Every night when Dick came in he hoped he might have to wait upon himself, and every morning he looked forward with pleasure to the prospect of making his toilet unaided. His hopes, however, were doomed to disappointment, for every night when he came in Grandison was on hand with a bootjack, and a nightcap mixed for his young master as the colonel had taught him to mix it, and every morning Grandison appeared with his master's boots blacked and his clothes brushed, and laid his linen out for the day.

"Grandison," said Dick one morning, after finishing his toilet, "this is the chance of your life to go around among your own people and see how they live. Have you met any of them?"

"Yas, suh, I's seen some of 'em. But I don' keer nuffin fer 'em, suh. Dey 're diffe'nt f'm de niggers down ou' way. Dey 'lows dey 're free, but dey ain' got sense 'nuff ter know dey ain' half as well off as dey would be down Souf, whar dey'd be 'preciated."

When two weeks had passed without any apparent effect of evil example upon Grandison, Dick resolved to go on to Boston, where he thought the atmosphere might prove more favorable to his ends. After he had been at the Revere House for a day or two without losing Grandison, he decided upon slightly different tactics.

Having ascertained from a city directory the addresses of several well-known abolitionists, he wrote them each a letter something like this:—

> DEAR FRIEND AND BROTHER:—
>
> A wicked slaveholder from Kentucky, stopping at the Revere House, has dared to insult the liberty-loving people of Boston by bringing his slave into their midst. Shall this be tolerated? Or shall steps be taken in the name of liberty to rescue a fellow-man from bondage? For obvious reasons I can only sign myself,
>
> A FRIEND OF HUMANITY.

That his letter might have an opportunity to prove effective, Dick made it a point to send Grandison away from the hotel on various errands. On one of these occasions Dick watched him for quite a distance down the street. Grandison had scarcely left the hotel when a long-haired, sharp-featured man came out behind him, followed him, soon overtook him, and kept along beside him until they turned the next corner. Dick's hopes were roused by this spectacle, but sank correspondingly when Grandison returned to the hotel. As Grandison said nothing about the encounter, Dick hoped there might be some self-consciousness behind this unexpected reticence, the results of which might develop later on.

But Grandison was on hand again when his master came back to the hotel at night, and was in attendance again in the morning, with hot water, to assist at his master's toilet. Dick sent him on further errands from day to day, and upon one occasion came squarely up to him—inadvertently of course—while Grandison was engaged in conversation with a young white man in clerical garb. When Grandison saw Dick approaching, he edged away from the preacher and hastened toward his master, with a very evident expression of relief upon his countenance.

"Mars Dick," he said, "dese yer abolitioners is jes' pesterin' de life out er me tryin' ter git me ter run away. I don' pay no 'tention ter 'em, but dey riles me so sometimes dat I'm feared I'll hit some of 'em some er dese days, an' dat mought git me inter trouble. I ain' said nuffin' ter you 'bout it, Mars Dick, fer I did n' wanter 'sturb yo' min'; but I don' like it, suh; no, suh, I don'! Is we gwine back home 'fo' long, Mars Dick?"

"We'll be going back soon enough," replied Dick somewhat shortly, while he inwardly cursed the stupidity of a slave who could be free and would not, and registered a secret vow that if he were unable to get rid of Grandison without assassinating him, and were therefore compelled to take him back to Kentucky, he would see that Grandison got a taste of an article of slavery that would make him regret his wasted opportunities. Meanwhile he determined to tempt his servant yet more strongly.

"Grandison," he said next morning, "I'm going away for a day or two, but I shall leave you here. I shall lock up a hundred dollars in this drawer and give you the key. If you need any of it, use it and enjoy yourself,—spend it all if you like,—for this is probably the last chance you'll have for some time to be in a free State, and you'd better enjoy your liberty while you may."

When he came back a couple of days later and found the faithful Grandison at his post, and the hundred dollars intact, Dick felt seriously annoyed. His vexation was increased by the fact that he could not express his feelings adequately. He did not even scold Grandison; how could he, indeed, find fault with one who so sensibly recognized his true place in the economy of civilization, and kept it with such touching fidelity?

"I can't say a thing to him," groaned Dick. "He deserves a leather medal, made out of his own hide tanned. I reckon I'll write to father and let him know what a model servant he has given me."

He wrote his father a letter which made the colonel swell with pride and pleasure. "I really think," the colonel observed to one of his friends, "that Dick ought to have the nigger interviewed by the Boston papers, so that they may see how contented and happy our darkeys really are."

Dick also wrote a long letter to Charity Lomax, in which he said, among many other things, that if she knew how hard he was working, and under what difficulties, to accomplish something serious for her sake, she would no longer keep him in suspense, but overwhelm him with love and admiration.

Having thus exhausted without result the more obvious methods of getting rid of Grandison, and diplomacy having also proved a failure, Dick was forced to consider more radical measures. Of course he might run away himself, and abandon Grandison, but this would be merely to leave him in the United States, where he was still a slave, and where, with his notions of loyalty, he would speedily be reclaimed. It was necessary, in order to accomplish the purpose of his trip to the North, to leave Grandison permanently in Canada, where he would be legally free.

"I might extend my trip to Canada," he reflected, "but that would be too palpable. I have it! I'll visit Niagara Falls on the way home, and lose him on the Canada side. When he once realizes that he is actually free, I'll warrant that he'll stay."

So the next day saw them westward bound, and in due course of time, by the somewhat slow conveyances of the period, they found themselves at Niagara. Dick walked and drove about the Falls for several days, taking Grandison along with him on most occasions. One morning they stood on the Canadian side, watching the wild whirl of the waters below them.

"Grandison," said Dick, raising his voice above the roar of the cataract, "do you know where you are now?"

"I's wid you, Mars Dick; dat's all I keers."

"You are now in Canada, Grandison, where your people go when they run away from their masters. If you wished, Grandison, you might walk away from me this very minute, and I could not lay my hand upon you to take you back."

Grandison looked around uneasily.

"Let's go back ober de ribber, Mars Dick. I's feared I'll lose you ovuh heah, an' den I won' hab no marster, an' won't nebber be able to git back home no mo'."

Discouraged, but not yet hopeless, Dick said, a few minutes later,—

"Grandison, I'm going up the road a bit, to the inn over yonder. You stay here until I return. I'll not be gone a great while."

Grandison's eyes opened wide and he looked somewhat fearful.

"Is dey any er dem dadblasted abolitioners roun' heah, Mars Dick?"

"I don't imagine that there are," replied his master, hoping there might be. "But I'm not afraid of *your* running away, Grandison. I only wish I were," he added to himself.

Dick walked leisurely down the road to where the whitewashed inn, built of stone, with true British solidity, loomed up through the trees by the roadside. Arrived there he ordered a glass of ale and a sandwich, and took a seat at a table by a window, from which he could see Grandison in the distance. For a while he hoped that the seed he had sown might have fallen on fertile ground, and that Grandison, relieved from the restraining power of a master's eye, and finding himself in a free country, might get up and walk away; but the hope was vain, for Grandison remained faithfully at his post, awaiting his master's return. He had seated himself on a broad flat stone, and, turning his eyes away from the grand and awe-inspiring spectacle that lay close at hand, was looking anxiously toward the inn where his master sat cursing his ill-timed fidelity.

By and by a girl came into the room to serve his order, and Dick very naturally glanced at her; and as she was young and pretty and remained in attendance, it was some minutes before he looked for Grandison. When he did so his faithful servant had disappeared.

To pay his reckoning and go away without the change was a matter quickly accomplished. Retracing his footsteps toward the Falls, he saw, to his great disgust, as he approached the spot where he had left Grandison, the familiar form of his servant stretched out on the ground, his face to the sun, his mouth open, sleeping the time away, oblivious alike to the grandeur of the scenery, the thunderous roar of the cataract, or the insidious voice of sentiment.

"Grandison," soliloquized his master, as he stood gazing down at his ebony encumbrance, "I do not deserve to be an American citizen; I ought not to have the advantages I possess over you; and I certainly am not worthy of Charity Lomax, if I am not smart enough to get rid of you. I have an idea! You shall yet be free, and I will be the instrument of your deliverance. Sleep on, faithful and affectionate servitor, and dream of the blue grass and the bright skies of old Kentucky, for it is only in your dreams that you will ever see them again!"

Dick retraced his footsteps towards the inn. The young woman chanced to look out of the window and saw the handsome young gentleman she had waited on a few minutes before, standing in the road a short distance away, apparently engaged in earnest conversation with a colored man employed as hostler for the inn. She thought she saw something pass from the white man to the other, but at that moment her duties called her away from the window, and when she looked out again the young gentleman had disappeared, and the hostler, with two other young men of the neighborhood, one white and one colored, were walking rapidly towards the Falls.

IV

Dick made the journey homeward alone, and as rapidly as the conveyances of the day would permit. As he drew near home his conduct in going back without Grandison took on a more serious aspect than it had borne at any previous time, and although he had prepared the colonel by a letter sent several days ahead, there was still the prospect of a bad quarter of an hour with him; not, indeed, that his father would upbraid him, but he was likely to make searching inquiries. And notwithstanding the vein of quiet recklessness that had carried Dick through his preposterous scheme, he was a very poor liar, having rarely had occasion or inclination to tell anything but the truth. Any reluctance to meet his father was more than offset, however, by a stronger force drawing him homeward, for Charity Lomax must long since have returned from her visit to her aunt in Tennessee.

Dick got off easier than he had expected. He told a straight story, and a truthful one, so far as it went.

The colonel raged at first, but rage soon subsided into anger, and anger moderated into annoyance, and annoyance into a sort of garrulous sense of injury. The colonel thought he had been hardly used; he had trusted this negro, and he had broken faith. Yet, after all, he did not blame Grandison so much as he did the abolitionists, who were undoubtedly at the bottom of it.

As for Charity Lomax, Dick told her, privately of course, that he had run his father's man, Grandison, off to Canada, and left him there.

"Oh, Dick," she had said with shuddering alarm, "what have you done? If they knew it they'd send you to the penitentiary, like they did that Yankee."

"But they don't know it," he had replied seriously; adding, with an injured tone, "you don't seem to appreciate my heroism like you did that of the Yankee; perhaps it's because I wasn't caught and sent to the penitentiary. I thought you wanted me to do it."

"Why, Dick Owens!" she exclaimed. "You know I never dreamed of any such outrageous proceeding.

"But I presume I'll have to marry you," she concluded, after some insistence on Dick's part, "if only to take care of you. You are too reckless for anything; and a man who goes chasing all over the North, being entertained by New York and Boston society and having negroes to throw away, needs some one to look after him."

"It's a most remarkable thing," replied Dick fervently, "that your views correspond exactly with my profoundest convictions. It proves beyond question that we were made for one another."

They were married three weeks later. As each of them had just returned from a journey, they spent their honeymoon at home.

A week after the wedding they were seated, one afternoon, on the piazza of the colonel's house, where Dick had taken his bride, when a negro from the yard ran down the lane and threw open the big gate for the colonel's buggy to enter. The colonel was not alone. Beside him, ragged and travel-stained, bowed with weariness, and upon his face a haggard look that told of hardship and privation, sat the lost Grandison.

The colonel alighted at the steps.

"Take the lines, Tom," he said to the man who had opened the gate, "and drive round to the barn. Help Grandison down,—poor devil, he's so stiff he can hardly move!—and get a tub of water and wash him and rub him down, and feed him, and give him a big drink of whiskey, and then let him come round and see his young master and his new mistress."

The colonel's face wore an expression compounded of joy and indignation,—joy at the restoration of a valuable piece of property; indignation for reasons he proceeded to state.

"It's astounding, the depths of depravity the human heart is capable of! I was coming along the road three miles away, when I heard some one call me from the roadside. I pulled up the mare, and who should come out of the woods but Grandison. The poor nigger could hardly crawl along, with the help of a broken limb. I was never more astonished in my life. You could have knocked me down with a feather. He seemed pretty far gone,—he could hardly talk above a whisper,—and I had to give him a mouthful of whiskey to brace him up so he could tell his story. It's just as I thought from the beginning, Dick; Grandison had no notion of running away; he knew when he was well off, and where his friends were. All the persuasions of abolition liars and runaway niggers did not move him. But the desperation of those fanatics knew no bounds; their guilty consciences gave them no rest. They got the notion somehow that Grandison belonged to a nigger-catcher, and had been brought North as a spy to help capture ungrateful runaway servants. They actually kidnaped him—just think of it!—and gagged him and bound him and threw him rudely into a wagon, and carried him into the gloomy depths of a Canadian forest, and locked him in a lonely hut, and fed him on bread and water for three weeks. One of the scoundrels wanted to kill him, and persuaded the others that it ought to be done; but they got to quarreling about how they should do it, and before they had their minds made up Grandison escaped, and, keeping his back steadily to the North Star, made his way, after suffering incredible hardships, back to the old plantation, back to his master, his friends, and his home. Why, it's as good as one of Scott's novels! Mr. Simms or some other one of our Southern authors ought to write it up."

"Don't you think, sir," suggested Dick, who had calmly smoked his cigar throughout the colonel's animated recital, "that that kidnaping yarn sounds a little improbable? Isn't there some more likely explanation?"

"Nonsense, Dick; it's the gospel truth! Those infernal abolitionists are capable of anything—everything! Just think of their locking the poor, faithful nigger up, beating him, kicking him, depriving him of his liberty, keeping him on bread and water for three long, lonesome weeks, and he all the time pining for the old plantation!"

There were almost tears in the colonel's eyes at the picture of Grandison's sufferings that he conjured up. Dick still professed to be slightly skeptical, and met Charity's severely questioning eye with bland unconsciousness.

The colonel killed the fatted calf for Grandison, and for two or three weeks the returned wanderer's life was a slave's dream of pleasure. His fame spread throughout the county, and the colonel gave him a permanent place among the house servants, where he could always have him conveniently at hand to relate his adventures to admiring visitors.

About three weeks after Grandison's return the colonel's faith in sable humanity was rudely shaken, and its foundations almost broken up. He came near losing his belief in the fidelity of the negro to his master,—the servile virtue most highly prized and most sedulously cultivated by the colonel and his kind. One Monday morning Grandison was missing. And not only Grandison, but his wife, Betty the maid; his mother, aunt Eunice; his father, uncle Ike; his brothers, Tom and John, and his little sister Elsie, were likewise absent from the plantation; and a hurried search and inquiry in the neighborhood resulted in no information as to their whereabouts. So much valuable property could not be lost without an effort to recover it, and the wholesale nature of the transaction carried consternation to the hearts of those whose ledgers were chiefly bound in black. Extremely energetic measures were taken by the colonel and his friends. The fugitives were traced, and followed from point to point, on their northward run through Ohio. Several times the hunters were close upon their heels, but the magnitude of the escaping party begot unusual vigilance on the part of those who sympathized with the fugitives, and strangely enough, the underground railroad seemed to have had its tracks cleared and signals set for this particular train. Once, twice, the colonel though he had them, but they slipped through his fingers.

One last glimpse he caught of his vanishing property, as he stood, accompanied by a United States marshal, on a wharf at a port on the south shore of Lake Erie. On the stern of a small steamboat which was receding rapidly from the wharf, with her nose pointing toward Canada, there stood a group of familiar dark faces, and the look they cast backward was not one of longing for the fleshpots of Egypt. The colonel saw Grandison point him out to one of the crew of the vessel, who waved his hand derisively toward the colonel. The latter shook his fist impotently—and the incident was closed.

CHARLOTTE PERKINS GILMAN

The Yellow Wall-Paper

It is very seldom that mere ordinary people like John and myself secure ancestral halls for the summer.

A colonial mansion, a hereditary estate, I would say a haunted house, and reach the height of romantic felicity—but that would be asking too much of fate!

Still I will proudly declare that there is something queer about it.

Else, why should it be let so cheaply? And why have stood so long untenanted?

John laughs at me, of course, but one expects that in marriage.

John is practical in the extreme. He has no patience with faith, an intense horror of superstition, and he scoffs openly at any talk of things not to be felt and seen and put down in figures.

John is a physician, and *perhaps*—(I would not say it to a living soul, of course, but this is dead paper and a great relief to my mind—) *perhaps* that is one reason I do not get well faster.

You see he does not believe I am sick!

And what can one do?

If a physician of high standing, and one's own husband, assures friends and relatives that there is really nothing the matter with one but temporary nervous depression—a slight hysterical tendency—what is one to do?

My brother is also a physician, and also of high standing, and he says the same thing.

So I take phosphates or phosphites—whichever it is, and tonics, and journeys, and air, and exercise, and am absolutely forbidden to "work" until I am well again.

Personally, I disagree with their ideas.

Personally, I believe that congenial work, with excitement and change, would do me good.

But what is one to do?

I did write for a while in spite of them; but it *does* exhaust me a good deal—having to be so sly about it, or else meet with heavy opposition.

I sometimes fancy that in my condition if I had less opposition and more society and stimulus—but John says the very worst thing I can do is to think about my condition, and I confess it always makes me feel bad.

So I will let it alone and talk about the house.

The most beautiful place! It is quite alone, standing well back from the road, quite three miles from the village. It makes me think of English places that you read about, for there are hedges and walls and gates that lock, and lots of separate little houses for the gardeners and people.

There is a *delicious* garden! I never saw such a garden—large and shady, full of box-bordered paths, and lined with long grape-covered arbors with seats under them.

There were greenhouses, too, but they are all broken now.

There was some legal trouble, I believe, something about the heirs and co-heirs; anyhow, the place has been empty for years.

That spoils my ghostliness, I am afraid, but I don't care—there is something strange about the house—I can feel it.

I even said so to John one moonlight evening, but he said what I felt was a *draught,* and shut the window.

I get unreasonably angry with John sometimes. I'm sure I never used to be so sensitive. I think it is due to this nervous condition.

But John says if I feel so, I shall neglect proper self-control; so I take pains to control myself—before him, at least, and that makes me very tired.

I don't like our room a bit. I wanted one downstairs that opened on the piazza and had roses all over the window, and such pretty old-fashioned chintz hangings! but John would not hear of it.

He said there was only one window and not room for two beds, and no near room for him if he took another.

He is very careful and loving, and hardly lets me stir without special direction.

I have a schedule prescription for each hour in the day; he takes all care from me, and so I feel basely ungrateful not to value it more.

He said we came here solely on my account, that I was to have perfect rest and all the air I could get. "Your exercise depends on your strength, my dear," said he, "and your food somewhat on your appetite; but air you can absorb all the time." So we took the nursery at the top of the house.

It is a big, airy room, the whole floor nearly, with windows that look all ways, and air and sunshine galore. It was nursery first and then playroom and gymnasium, I should judge; for the windows are barred for little children, and there are rings and things in the walls.

The paint and paper look as if a boys' school had used it. It is stripped off—the paper—in great patches all around the head of my bed, about as far as I can reach, and in a great place on the other side of the room low down. I never saw a worse paper in my life.

One of those sprawling flamboyant patterns committing every artistic sin.

It is dull enough to confuse the eye in following, pronounced enough to constantly irritate and provoke study, and when you follow the lame uncertain curves for a little distance they suddenly commit suicide—plunge off at outrageous angles, destroy themselves in unheard of contradictions.

The color is repellant, almost revolting: a smouldering unclean yellow, strangely faded by the slow-turning sunlight.

It is a dull yet lurid orange in some places, a sickly sulphur tint in others.

No wonder the children hated it! I should hate it myself if I had to live in this room long.

There comes John, and I must put this away,—he hates to have me write a word.

* * * * * *

We have been here two weeks, and I haven't felt like writing before, since that first day.

I am sitting by the window now, up in this atrocious nursery, and there is nothing to hinder my writing as much as I please, save lack of strength.

John is away all day, and even some nights when his cases are serious.

I am glad my case is not serious!

But these nervous troubles are dreadfully depressing.

John does not know how much I really suffer. He knows there is no *reason* to suffer, and that satisfies him.

Of course it is only nervousness. It does weigh on me so not to do my duty in any way!

I meant to be such a help to John, such a real rest and comfort, and here I am a comparative burden already!

Nobody would believe what an effort it is to do what little I am able,—to dress and entertain, and order things.

It is fortunate Mary is so good with the baby. Such a dear baby!

And yet I *cannot* be with him, it makes me so nervous.

I suppose John never was nervous in his life. He laughs at me so about this wall-paper!

At first he meant to repaper the room, but afterwards he said that I was letting it get the better of me, and that nothing was worse for a nervous patient than to give way to such fancies.

He said that after the wall-paper was changed it would be the heavy bedstead, and then the barred windows, and then that gate at the head of the stairs, and so on.

"You know the place is doing you good," he said, "and really, dear, I don't care to renovate the house just for a three months' rental."

"Then do let us go downstairs," I said, "there are such pretty rooms there."

Then he took me in his arms and called me a blessed little goose, and said he would go down cellar, if I wished, and have it white-washed into the bargain.

But he is right enough about the beds and windows and things.

It is an airy and comfortable room as any one need wish, and, of course, I would not be so silly as to make him uncomfortable just for a whim.

I'm really getting quite fond of the big room, all but that horrid paper.

Out of one window I can see the garden, those mysterious deep-shaded arbors, the riotous old fashioned flowers, and bushes and gnarly trees.

Out of another I get a lovely view of the bay and a little private wharf belonging to the estate. There is a beautiful shaded lane that runs down there from the house. I always fancy I see people walking in these numerous paths and arbors, but John has cautioned me not to give way to fancy in the least. He says that with my imaginative power and habit of story-making, a nervous weakness like mine is sure to lead to all manner of excited fancies and that I ought to use my will and good sense to check the tendency. So I try.

I think sometimes that if I were only well enough to write a little it would relieve the press of ideas and rest me.

But I find I get pretty tired when I try.

It is so discouraging not to have any advice and companionship about my work. When I get really well, John says we will ask Cousin Henry and Julia down for a long visit; but he says he would as soon put fireworks in my pillow-case as to let me have those stimulating people about now.

I wish I could get well faster.

But I must not think about that. This paper looks to me as if it *knew* what a vicious influence it had!

There is a recurrent spot where the pattern lolls like a broken neck and two bulbous eyes stare at you upside down.

I get positively angry with the impertinence of it and the everlastingness. Up and down and sideways they crawl, and those absurd, unblinking eyes are everywhere. There is one place where two breadths didn't match, and the eyes go all up and down the line, one a little higher than the other.

I never saw so much expression in an inanimate thing before, and we all know how much expression they have! I used to lie awake as a child and get more entertainment and terror out of blank walls and plain furniture than most children could find in a toy-store.

I remember what a kindly wink the knobs of our big, old bureau used to have, and there was one chair that always seemed like a strong friend.

I used to feel that if any of the other things looked too fierce I could always hop into that chair and be safe.

The furniture in this room is no worse than inharmonious, however, for we had to bring it all from downstairs. I suppose when this was used as a playroom they had to take the nursery things out, and no wonder! I never saw such ravages as the children have made here.

The wall-paper, as I said before, is torn off in spots, and it sticketh closer than a brother—they must have had perseverance as well as hatred.

Then the floor is scratched and gouged and splintered, the plaster itself is dug out here and there, and this great heavy bed which is all we found in the room, looks as if it had been through the wars.

But I don't mind it a bit—only the paper.

There comes John's sister. Such a dear girl as she is, and so careful of me! I must not let her find me writing.

She is a perfect and enthusiastic housekeeper, and hopes for no better profession. I verily believe she thinks it is the writing which made me sick!

But I can write when she is out, and see her a long way off from these windows.

There is one that commands the road, a lovely shaded winding road, and one that just looks off over the country. A lovely country, too, full of great elms and velvet meadows.

This wallpaper has a kind of sub-pattern in a different shade, a particularly irritating one, for you can only see it in certain lights, and not clearly then.

But in the places where it isn't faded and where the sun is just so—I can see a strange, provoking, formless sort of figure, that seems to skulk about behind that silly and conspicuous front design.

There's sister on the stairs!

* * * * * *

Well, the Fourth of July is over! The people are all gone and I am tired out. John thought it might do me good to see a little company, so we just had mother and Nellie and the children down for a week.

Of course I didn't do a thing. Jennie sees to everything now.

But it tired me all the same.

John says if I don't pick up faster he shall send me to Weir Mitchell in the fall.

But I don't want to go there at all. I had a friend who was in his hands once, and she says he is just like John and my brother, only more so!

Besides, it is such an undertaking to go so far.

I don't feel as if it was worth while to turn my hand over for anything, and I'm getting dreadfully fretful and querulous.

I cry at nothing, and cry most of the time.

Of course I don't when John is here, or anybody else, but when I am alone.

And I am alone a good deal just now. John is kept in town very often by serious cases, and Jennie is good and lets me alone when I want her to.

So I walk a little in the garden or down that lovely lane, sit on the porch under the roses, and lie down up here a good deal.

I'm getting really fond of the room in spite of the wallpaper. Perhaps *because* of the wallpaper.

It dwells in my mind so!

I lie here on this great immovable bed—it is nailed down, I believe—and follow that pattern about by the hour. It is as good as gymnastics, I assure you. I start, we'll say, at the bottom, down in the corner over there where it has not been touched, and I determine for the thousandth time that I *will* follow that pointless pattern to some sort of a conclusion.

I know a little of the principle of design, and I know this thing was not arranged on any laws of radiation, or alternation, or repetition, or symmetry, or anything else that I ever heard of.

It is repeated, of course, by the breadths, but not otherwise.

Looked at in one way each breadth stands alone, the bloated curves and flourishes—a kind of "debased Romanesque" with *delirium tremens*—go waddling up and down in isolated columns of fatuity.

But, on the other hand, they connect diagonally, and the sprawling outlines run off in great slanting waves of optic horror, like a lot of wallowing seaweeds in full chase.

The whole thing goes horizontally, too, at least it seems so, and I exhaust myself in trying to distinguish the order of its going in that direction.

They have used a horizontal breadth for a frieze, and that adds wonderfully to the confusion.

There is one end of the room where it is almost intact, and there, when the crosslights fade and the low sun shines directly upon it, I can almost fancy radiation after all,—the interminable grotesques seem to form around a common centre and rush off in headlong plunges of equal distraction.

It makes me tired to follow it. I will take a nap I guess.

* * * * * *

I don't know why I should write this.

I don't want to.

I don't feel able.

And I know John would think it absurd. But I *must* say what I feel and think in some way—it is such a relief!

But the effort is getting to be greater than the relief.

Half the time now I am awfully lazy, and lie down ever so much.

John says I mustn't lose my strength, and has me take cod liver oil and lots of tonics and things, to say nothing of ale and wine and rare meat.

Dear John! He loves me very dearly, and hates to have me sick. I tried to have a real earnest reasonable talk with him the other day, and tell him how I wish he would let me go and make a visit to Cousin Henry and Julia.

But he said I wasn't able to go, nor able to stand it after I got there; and I did not make out a very good case for myself, for I was crying before I had finished.

It is getting to be a great effort for me to think straight. Just this nervous weakness I suppose.

And dear John gathered me up in his arms, and just carried me upstairs and laid me on the bed, and sat by me and read to me till it tired my head.

He said I was his darling and his comfort and all he had, and that I must take care of myself for his sake, and keep well.

He says no one but myself can help me out of it, that I must use my will and self-control and not let any silly fancies run away with me.

There's one comfort, the baby is well and happy, and does not have to occupy this nursery with the horrid wallpaper.

If we had not used it, that blessed child would have! What a fortunate escape! Why, I wouldn't have a child of mine, an impressionable little thing, live in such a room for worlds.

I never thought of it before, but it is lucky that John kept me here after all, I can stand it so much easier than a baby, you see.

Of course I never mention it to them any more—I am too wise,—but I keep watch of it all the same.

There are things in that paper that nobody knows but me, or ever will.

Behind that outside pattern the dim shapes get clearer every day.

It is always the same shape, only very numerous.

And it is like a woman stooping down and creeping about behind that pattern. I don't like it a bit. I wonder—I begin to think—I wish John would take me away from here!

* * * * * *

It is so hard to talk with John about my case, because he is so wise, and because he loves me so.

But I tried it last night.

It was moonlight. The moon shines in all around just as the sun does.

I hate to see it sometimes, it creeps so slowly, and always comes in by one window or another.

John was asleep and I hated to waken him, so I kept still and watched the moonlight on that undulating wallpaper till I felt creepy.

The faint figure behind seemed to shake the pattern, just as if she wanted to get out.

I got up softly and went to feel and see if the paper *did* move, and when I came back John was awake.

"What is it, little girl?" he said. "Don't go walking about like that—you'll get cold."

I thought it was a good time to talk, so I told him that I really was not gaining here, and that I wished he would take me away.

"Why, darling!" said he, "our lease will be up in three weeks, and I can't see how to leave before.

"The repairs are not done at home, and I cannot possibly leave town just now. Of course if you were in any danger, I could and would, but you really are better, dear, whether you can see it or not. I am a doctor, dear, and I know. You are gaining flesh and color, your appetite is better, I feel really much easier about you."

"I don't weigh a bit more," said I, "nor as much; and my appetite may be better in the evening when you are here, but it is worse in the morning when you are away!"

"Bless her little heart!" said he with a big hug, "she shall be as sick as she pleases! But now let's improve the shining hours by going to sleep, and talk about it in the morning!"

"And you won't go away?" I asked gloomily.

"Why, how can I, dear? It is only three weeks more and then we will take a nice little trip of a few days while Jennie is getting the house ready. Really dear you are better!"

"Better in body perhaps—" I began, and stopped short, for he sat up straight and looked at me with such a stern, reproachful look that I could not say another word.

"My darling," said he, "I beg of you, for my sake and for our child's sake, as well as for your own, that you will never for one instant let that idea enter your mind! There is nothing so dangerous, so fascinating, to a temperament like yours. It is a false and foolish fancy. Can you not trust me as a physician when I tell you so?"

So of course I said no more on that score, and we went to sleep before long. He thought I was asleep first, but I wasn't, and lay there for hours trying to decide whether that front pattern and the back pattern really did move together or separately.

* * * * * *

On a pattern like this, by daylight, there is a lack of sequence, a defiance of law, that is a constant irritant to a normal mind.

The color is hideous enough, and unreliable enough, and infuriating enough, but the pattern is torturing.

You think you have mastered it, but just as you get well underway in following, it turns a back-somersault and there you are. It slaps you in the face, knocks you down, and tramples upon you. It is like a bad dream.

The outside pattern is a florid arabesque, reminding one of a fungus. If you can imagine a toadstool in joints, an interminable string of toadstools, budding and sprouting in endless convolutions—why, that is something like it.

That is, sometimes!

There is one marked peculiarity about this paper, a thing nobody seems to notice but myself, and that is that it changes as the light changes.

When the sun shoots in through the east window—I always watch for that first long, straight ray—it changes so quickly that I never can quite believe it.

That is why I watch it always.

By moonlight—the moon shines in all night when there is a moon—I wouldn't know it was the same paper.

At night in any kind of light, in twilight, candlelight, lamplight, and worst of all by moonlight, it becomes bars! The outside pattern I mean, and the woman behind it is as plain as can be.

I didn't realize for a long time what the thing was that showed behind, that dim sub-pattern, but now I am quite sure it is a woman.

By daylight she is subdued, quiet. I fancy it is the pattern that keeps her so still. It is so puzzling. It keeps me quiet by the hour.

I lie down ever so much now. John says it is good for me, and to sleep all I can.

Indeed he started the habit by making me lie down for an hour after each meal.

It is a very bad habit I am convinced, for you see I don't sleep.

And that cultivates deceit, for I don't tell them I'm awake—O no!

The fact is I am getting a little afraid of John.

He seems very queer sometimes, and even Jennie has an inexplicable look.

It strikes me occasionally, just as a scientific hypothesis,—that perhaps it is the paper!

I have watched John when he did not know I was looking, and come into the room suddenly on the most innocent excuses, and I've caught him several times *looking at the paper*! And Jennie too. I caught Jennie with her hand on it once.

She didn't know I was in the room, and when I asked her in a quiet, a very quiet voice, with the most restrained manner possible, what she was doing with the paper—she turned around as if she had been caught stealing, and looked quite angry—asked me why I should frighten her so!

Then she said that the paper stained everything it touched, that she had found yellow smooches on all my clothes and John's, and she wished we would be more careful!

Did not that sound innocent? But I know she was studying that pattern, and I am determined that nobody shall find it out but myself!

* * * * * *

Life is very much more exciting now than it used to be. You see I have something more to expect, to look forward to, to watch. I really do eat better, and am more quiet than I was.

John is so pleased to see me improve! He laughed a little the other day, and said I seemed to be flourishing in spite of my wall-paper.

I turned it off with a laugh. I had no intention of telling him it was *because* of the wall-paper—he would make fun of me. He might even want to take me away.

I don't want to leave now until I have found it out. There is a week more, and I think that will be enough.

* * * * * *

I'm feeling ever so much better! I don't sleep much at night, for it is so interesting to watch developments; but I sleep a good deal in the daytime.

In the daytime it is tiresome and perplexing.

There are always new shoots on the fungus, and new shades of yellow all over it. I cannot keep count of them, though I have tried conscientiously.

It is the strangest yellow, that wall-paper! It makes me think of all the yellow things I ever saw—not beautiful ones like buttercups, but old foul, bad yellow things.

But there is something else about that paper—the smell! I noticed it the moment we came into the room, but with so much air and sun it was not bad. Now we have had a week of fog and rain, and whether the windows are open or not, the smell is here.

It creeps all over the house.

I find it hovering in the dining-room, skulking in the parlor, hiding in the hall, lying in wait for me on the stairs.

It gets into my hair.

Even when I go to ride, if I turn my head suddenly and surprise it—there is that smell!

Such a peculiar odor, too! I have spent hours in trying to analyze it, to find what it smelled like.

It is not bad—at first, and very gentle, but quite the subtlest, most enduring odor I ever met.

In this damp weather it is awful, I wake up in the night and find it hanging over me.

It used to disturb me at first. I thought seriously of burning the house—to reach the smell.

But now I am used to it. The only thing I can think of that it is like is the *color* of the paper! A yellow smell.

There is a very funny mark on this wall, low down, near the mop-board. A streak that runs round the room. It goes behind every piece of furniture, except the bed, a long, straight, even *smooch,* as if it had been rubbed over and over.

I wonder how it was done and who did it, and what they did it for. Round and round and round—round and round and round—it makes me dizzy!

* * * * * *

I really have discovered something at last.

Through watching so much at night, when it changes so, I have finally found out.

The front pattern *does* move—and no wonder! The woman behind shakes it!

Sometimes I think there are a great many women behind, and sometimes only one, and she crawls around fast, and her crawling shakes it all over.

Then in the very bright spots she keeps still, and in the very shady spots she just takes hold of the bars and shakes them hard.

And she is all the time trying to climb through. But nobody could climb through that pattern—it strangles so; I think that is why it has so many heads.

They get through, and then the pattern strangles them off and turns them upside down, and makes their eyes white!

If those heads were covered or taken off it would not be half so bad.

* * * * * *

I think that woman gets out in the daytime!

And I'll tell you why—privately—I've seen her!

I can see her out of every one of my windows!

It is the same woman, I know, for she is always creeping, and most women do not creep by daylight.

I see her in that long shaded lane, creeping up and down. I see her in those dark grape arbors, creeping all around the garden.

I see her on that long road under the trees, creeping along, and when a carriage comes she hides under the blackberry vines.

I don't blame her a bit. It must be very humiliating to be caught creeping by daylight!

I always lock the door when I creep by daylight. I can't do it at night, for I know John would suspect something at once.

And John is so queer now, that I don't want to irritate him. I wish he would take another room! Besides, I don't want anybody to get that woman out at night but myself.

I often wonder if I could see her out of all the windows at once.

But, turn as fast as I can, I can only see out of one at one time.

And though I always see her, she *may* be able to creep faster than I can turn!

I have watched her sometimes away off in the open country, creeping as fast as a cloud shadow in a high wind.

* * * * * *

If only that top pattern could be gotten off from the under one! I mean to try it, little by little.

I have found out another funny thing, but I shan't tell it this time! It does not do to trust people too much.

There are only two more days to get this paper off, and I believe John is beginning to notice. I don't like the look in his eyes.

And I heard him ask Jennie a lot of professional questions about me. She had a very good report to give.

She said I slept a good deal in the daytime.

John knows I don't sleep very well at night, for all I'm so quiet!

He asked me all sorts of questions, too, and pretended to be very loving and kind.

As if I couldn't see through him!

Still, I don't wonder he acts so, sleeping under this paper for three months.

It only interests me, but I feel sure John and Jennie are secretly affected by it.

* * * * * *

Hurrah! This is the last day, but it is enough. John to stay in town over night, and won't be out until this evening.

Jennie wanted to sleep with me—the sly thing! but I told her I should undoubtedly rest better for a night all alone.

That was clever, for really I wasn't alone a bit! As soon as it was moonlight and that poor thing began to crawl and shake the pattern, I got up and ran to help her.

I pulled and she shook, I shook and she pulled, and before morning we had peeled off yards of that paper.

A strip about as high as my head and half around the room.

And then when the sun came and that awful pattern began to laugh at me, I declared I would finish it to-day!

We go away to-morrow, and they are moving all my furniture down again to leave things as they were before.

Jennie looked at the wall in amazement, but I told her merrily that I did it out of pure spite at the vicious thing.

She laughed and said she wouldn't mind doing it herself, but I must not get tired.

How she betrayed herself that time!

But I am here, and no person touches this paper but me,—not *alive*!

She tried to get me out of the room—it was too patent! But I said it was so quiet and empty and clean now that I believed I would lie down again and sleep all I could; and not to wake me even for dinner—I would call when I woke.

So now she is gone, and the servants are gone, and the things are gone, and there is nothing left but that great bedstead nailed down, with the canvas mattress we found on it.

We shall sleep downstairs to-night, and take the boat home to-morrow.

I quite enjoy the room, now it is bare again.

How those children did tear about here!

This bedstead is fairly gnawed!

But I must get to work.

I have locked the door and thrown the key down into the front path.

I don't want to go out, and I don't want to have anybody come in, till John comes.

I want to astonish him.

I've got a rope up here that even Jennie did not find. If that woman does get out, and tries to get away, I can tie her!

But I forgot I could not reach far without anything to stand on!

This bed will *not* move!

I tried to lift and push it until I was lame, and then I got so angry I bit off a little piece at one corner—but it hurt my teeth.

Then I peeled off all the paper I could reach standing on the floor. It sticks horribly and the pattern just enjoys it! All those strangled heads and bulbous eyes and waddling fungus growths just shriek with derision!

I am getting angry enough to do something desperate. To jump out of the window would be admirable exercise, but the bars are too strong even to try.

Besides I wouldn't do it. Of course not. I know well enough that a step like that is improper and might be misconstrued.

I don't like to *look* out of the windows even—there are so many of those creeping women, and they creep so fast.

I wonder if they all come out of that wall-paper as I did?

But I am securely fastened now by my well-hidden rope—you don't get *me* out in the road there!

I suppose I shall have to get back behind the pattern when it comes night, and that is hard!

It is so pleasant to be out in this great room and creep around as I please!

I don't want to go outside. I won't, even if Jennie asks me to.

For outside you have to creep on the ground, and everything is green instead of yellow.

But here I can creep smoothly on the floor, and my shoulder just fits in that long smooch around the wall, so I cannot lose my way.

Why there's John at the door!

It is no use, young man, you can't open it!

How he does call and pound!

Now he's crying for an axe.

It would be a shame to break down that beautiful door!

"John dear!" said I in the gentlest voice, "the key is down by the front steps, under a plantain leaf!"

That silenced him for a few moments.

Then he said—very quietly indeed, "Open the door, my darling!"

"I can't," said I. "The key is down by the front door under a plantain leaf!"

And then I said it again, several times, very gently and slowly, and said it so often that he had to go and see, and he got it of course, and came in. He stopped short by the door.

"What is the matter?" he cried. "For God's sake, what are you doing!"

I kept on creeping just the same, but I looked at him over my shoulder.

"I've got out at last," said I, "in spite of you and Jane! And I've pulled off most of the paper, so you can't put me back!"

Now why should that man have fainted? But he did, and right across my path by the wall, so that I had to creep over him every time!

WILLIAM SYDNEY PORTER (O. HENRY)

The Gift of the Magi

ONE DOLLAR AND EIGHTY-SEVEN cents. That was all. And sixty cents of it was in pennies. Pennies saved one and two at a time by bulldozing the grocer and the vegetable man and the butcher until one's cheeks burned with the silent imputation of parsimony that such close dealing implied. Three times Della counted it. One dollar and eighty-seven cents. And the next day would be Christmas.

There was clearly nothing to do but flop down on the shabby little couch and howl. So Della did it. Which instigates the moral reflection that life is made up of sobs, sniffles, and smiles, with sniffles predominating.

While the mistress of the home is gradually subsiding from the first stage to the second, take a look at the home. A furnished flat at $8 per week. It did not exactly beggar description, but it certainly had that word on the lookout for the mendicancy squad.

In the vestibule below was a letter-box into which no letter would go, and an electric button from which no mortal finger could coax a ring. Also appertaining thereunto was a card bearing the name "Mr. James Dillingham Young."

The "Dillingham" had been flung to the breeze during a former period of prosperity when its possessor was being paid $30 per week. Now, when the income was shrunk to $20, the letters of "Dillingham" looked blurred, as though they were thinking seriously of contracting to a modest and unassuming D. But whenever Mr. James Dillingham Young came home and reached his flat above he was called "Jim" and greatly hugged by Mrs. James Dillingham Young, already introduced to you as Della. Which is all very good.

Della finished her cry and attended to her cheeks with the powder rag. She stood by the window and looked out dully at a gray cat walking a gray fence in a gray backyard. Tomorrow would be Christmas Day, and she had only $1.87 with which to buy Jim a present. She had been saving every penny she could for months, with this result. Twenty dollars a week doesn't go far. Expenses had been greater than she had calculated. They always are. Only $1.87 to buy a present for Jim. Her Jim. Many a happy hour she had spent planning for something nice for him. Something fine and rare and sterling—something just a little bit near to being worthy of the honor of being owned by Jim.

There was a pier-glass between the windows of the room. Perhaps you have seen a pier-glass in an $8 flat. A very thin and very agile person may, by observing his reflection in a rapid sequence of longitudinal strips, obtain a fairly accurate conception of his looks. Della, being slender, had mastered the art.

Suddenly she whirled from the window and stood before the glass. Her eyes were shining brilliantly, but her face had lost its color within twenty seconds. Rapidly she pulled down her hair and let it fall to its full length.

Now, there were two possessions of the James Dillingham Youngs in which they both took a mighty pride. One was Jim's gold watch that had been his father's and his grandfather's. The other was Della's hair. Had the Queen of Sheba lived in the flat across the airshaft, Della would have let her hair hang out the window some day to dry just to depreciate Her Majesty's jewels and gifts. Had King Solomon been the janitor, with all his treasures piled up in the basement, Jim would have pulled out his watch every time he passed, just to see him pluck at his beard from envy.

So now Della's beautiful hair fell about her rippling and shining like a cascade of brown waters. It reached below her knee and made itself almost a garment for her. And then she did it up again nervously and quickly. Once she faltered for a minute and stood still while a tear or two splashed on the worn red carpet.

On went her old brown jacket; on went her old brown hat. With a whirl of skirts and with the brilliant sparkle still in her eyes, she fluttered out the door and down the stairs to the street.

Where she stopped the sign read: "Mme. Sofronie. Hair Goods

of All Kinds." One flight up Della ran, and collected herself, panting. Madame, large, too white, chilly, hardly looked the "Sofronie."

"Will you buy my hair?" asked Della.

"I buy hair," said Madame. "Take yer hat off and let's have a sight at the looks of it."

Down rippled the brown cascade.

"Twenty dollars," said Madame, lifting the mass with a practised hand.

"Give it to me quick," said Della.

Oh, and the next two hours tripped by on rosy wings. Forget the hashed metaphor. She was ransacking the stores for Jim's present.

She found it at last. It surely had been made for Jim and no one else. There was no other like it in any of the stores, and she had turned all of them inside out. It was a platinum fob chain simple and chaste in design, properly proclaiming its value by substance alone and not by meretricious ornamentation—as all good things should do. It was even worthy of The Watch. As soon as she saw it she knew that it must be Jim's. It was like him. Quietness and value—the description applied to both. Twenty-one dollars they took from her for it, and she hurried home with the 87 cents. With that chain on his watch Jim might be properly anxious about the time in any company. Grand as the watch was, he sometimes looked at it on the sly on account of the old leather strap that he used in place of a chain.

When Della reached home her intoxication gave way a little to prudence and reason. She got out her curling irons and lighted the gas and went to work repairing the ravages made by generosity added to love. Which is always a tremendous task, dear friends—a mammoth task.

Within forty minutes her head was covered with tiny, close-lying curls that made her look wonderfully like a truant schoolboy. She looked at her reflection in the mirror long, carefully, and critically.

"If Jim doesn't kill me," she said to herself, "before he takes a second look at me, he'll say I look like a Coney Island chorus girl. But what could I do—oh! what could I do with a dollar and eighty-seven cents?"

At 7 o'clock the coffee was made and the frying-pan was on the back of the stove hot and ready to cook the chops.

Jim was never late. Della doubled the fob chain in her hand and sat on the corner of the table near the door that he always entered. Then she heard his step on the stair away down on the first flight, and she turned white for just a moment. She had a habit of saying little silent prayers about the simplest everyday things, and now she whispered: "Please God, make him think I am still pretty."

The door opened and Jim stepped in and closed it. He looked thin and very serious. Poor fellow, he was only twenty-two—and to be burdened with a family! He needed a new overcoat and he was without gloves.

Jim stopped inside the door, as immovable as a setter at the scent of quail. His eyes were fixed upon Della, and there was an expression in them that she could not read, and it terrified her. It was not anger, nor surprise, nor disapproval, nor horror, nor any of the sentiments that she had been prepared for. He simply stared at her fixedly with that peculiar expression on his face.

Della wriggled off the table and went for him.

"Jim, darling," she cried, "don't look at me that way. I had my hair cut off and sold it because I couldn't have lived through Christmas without giving you a present. It'll grow out again—you won't mind, will you? I just had to do it. My hair grows awfully fast. Say 'Merry Christmas!' Jim, and let's be happy. You don't know what a nice—what a beautiful, nice gift I've got for you."

"You've cut off your hair?" asked Jim, laboriously, as if he had not arrived at that patent fact yet even after the hardest mental labor.

"Cut it off and sold it," said Della. "Don't you like me just as well, anyhow? I'm me without my hair, ain't I?"

Jim looked about the room curiously.

"You say your hair is gone?" he said, with an air almost of idiocy.

"You needn't look for it," said Della. "It's sold, I tell you—sold and gone, too. It's Christmas Eve, boy. Be good to me, for it went for you. Maybe the hairs of my head were numbered," she went on with a sudden serious sweetness, "but nobody could ever count my love for you. Shall I put the chops on, Jim?"

Out of his trance Jim seemed quickly to wake. He enfolded his Della. For ten seconds let us regard with discreet scrutiny some inconsequential object in the other direction. Eight dollars a week or a million a year—what is the difference? A mathematician or a wit would give you the wrong answer. The magi brought valuable gifts, but that was not among them. This dark assertion will be illuminated later on.

Jim drew a package from his overcoat pocket and threw it upon the table.

"Don't make any mistake, Dell," he said, "about me. I don't think there's anything in the way of a haircut or a shave or a shampoo that could make me like my girl any less. But if you'll unwrap that package you may see why you had me going a while at first."

White fingers and nimble tore at the string and paper. And then an ecstatic scream of joy; and then, alas! a quick feminine change to hysterical tears and wails, necessitating the immediate employment of all the comforting powers of the lord of the flat.

For there lay The Combs—the set of combs, side and back, that Della had worshipped for long in a Broadway window. Beautiful combs, pure tortoise shell, with jewelled rims—just the shade to wear in the beautiful vanished hair. They were expensive combs, she knew, and her heart had simply craved and yearned over them without the least hope of possession. And now, they were hers, but the tresses that should have adorned the coveted adornments were gone.

But she hugged them to her bosom, and at length she was able to look up with dim eyes and a smile and say: "My hair grows so fast, Jim!"

And then Della leaped up like a little singed cat and cried, "Oh, oh!"

Jim had not yet seen his beautiful present. She held it out to him eagerly upon her open palm. The dull precious metal seemed to flash with a reflection of her bright and ardent spirit.

"Isn't it a dandy, Jim? I hunted all over town to find it. You'll have to look at the time a hundred times a day now. Give me your watch. I want to see how it looks on it."

Instead of obeying, Jim tumbled down on the couch and put his hands under the back of his head and smiled.

"Dell," said he, "let's put our Christmas presents away and keep 'em a while. They're too nice to use just at present. I sold the watch to get the money to buy your combs. And now suppose you put the chops on."

The magi, as you know, were wise men—wonderfully wise men—who brought gifts to the Babe in the manger. They invented the art of giving Christmas presents. Being wise, their gifts were no doubt wise ones, possibly bearing the privilege of exchange in case of duplication. And here I have lamely related to you the uneventful chronicle of two foolish children in a flat who most unwisely sacrificed for each other the greatest treasures of their house. But in a last word to the wise of these days let it be said that of all who give gifts these two were the wisest. Of all who give and receive gifts, such as they are wisest. Everywhere they are wisest. They are the magi.

WILLIAM SYDNEY PORTER (O. HENRY)

The Ransom of Red Chief

It looked like a good thing: but wait till I tell you. We were down South, in Alabama—Bill Driscoll and myself—when this kidnapping idea struck us. It was, as Bill afterward expressed it, "during a moment of temporary mental apparition"; but we didn't find that out till later.

There was a town down there, as flat as a flannel-cake, and called Summit, of course. It contained inhabitants of as undeleterious and self-satisfied a class of peasantry as ever clustered around a Maypole.

Bill and me had a joint capital of about six hundred dollars, and we needed just two thousand dollars more to pull off a fraudulent town-lot scheme in Western Illinois with. We talked it over on the front steps of the hotel. Philoprogenitiveness, says we, is strong in semi-rural communities; therefore, and for other reasons, a kidnapping project ought to do better there than in the radius of newspapers that send reporters out in plain clothes to stir up talk about such things. We knew that Summit couldn't get after us with anything stronger than constables and, maybe, some lackadaisical bloodhounds and a diatribe or two in the *Weekly Farmers' Budget*. So, it looked good.

We selected for our victim the only child of a prominent citizen named Ebenezer Dorset. The father was respectable and tight, a mortgage fancier and a stern, upright collection-plate passer and forecloser. The kid was a boy of ten, with bas-relief freckles, and hair the colour of the cover of the magazine you buy at the news-stand when you want to catch a train. Bill and me figured that Ebenezer would melt down for a ransom of two thousand dollars to a cent. But wait till I tell you.

About two miles from Summit was a little mountain, covered with a dense cedar brake. On the rear elevation of this mountain was a cave. There we stored provisions.

One evening after sundown, we drove in a buggy past old Dorset's house. The kid was in the street, throwing rocks at a kitten on the opposite fence.

"Hey, little boy!" says Bill, "would you like to have a bag of candy and a nice ride?"

The boy catches Bill neatly in the eye with a piece of brick.

"That will cost the old man an extra five hundred dollars," says Bill, climbing over the wheel.

That boy put up a fight like a welter-weight cinnamon bear; but, at last, we got him down in the bottom of the buggy and drove away. We took him up to the cave, and I hitched the horse in the cedar brake. After dark I drove the buggy to the little village, three miles away, where we had hired it, and walked back to the mountain.

Bill was pasting court-plaster over the scratches and bruises on his features. There was a fire burning behind the big rock at the entrance of the cave, and the boy was watching a pot of boiling coffee, with two buzzard tail-feathers stuck in his red hair. He points a stick at me when I come up, and says:

"Ha! cursed paleface, do you dare to enter the camp of Red Chief, the terror of the plains?"

"He's all right now," says Bill, rolling up his trousers and examining some bruises on his shins. "We're playing Indian. We're making Buffalo Bill's show look like magic-lantern views of Palestine in the town hall. I'm Old Hank, the Trapper, Red Chief's captive, and I'm to be scalped at daybreak. By Geronimo! that kid can kick hard."

Yes, sir, that boy seemed to be having the time of his life. The fun of camping out in a cave had made him forget that he was a captive himself. He immediately christened me Snake-eye, the Spy, and announced that, when his braves returned from the warpath, I was to be broiled at the stake at the rising of the sun.

Then we had supper; and he filled his mouth full of bacon and bread and gravy, and began to talk. He made a during-dinner speech something like this:

"I like this fine. I never camped out before; but I had a pet 'possum once, and I was nine last birthday. I hate to go to school. Rats ate up sixteen of Jimmy Talbot's aunt's speckled hen's eggs. Are there any real Indians in these woods? I want some more gravy. Does the trees moving make the wind blow? We had five puppies. What makes your nose so red, Hank? My father has lots of money. Are the stars hot? I whipped Ed Walker twice, Saturday. I don't like girls. You dassent catch toads unless with a string. Do oxen make any noise? Why are oranges round? Have you got beds to sleep on in this cave? Amos Murray has got six toes. A parrot can talk, but a monkey or a fish can't. How many does it take to make twelve?"

Every few minutes he would remember that he was a pesky redskin, and pick up his stick rifle and tiptoe to the mouth of the cave to rubber for the scouts of the hated paleface. Now and then he would let out a war-whoop that made Old Hank the Trapper shiver. That boy had Bill terrorized from the start.

"Red Chief," says I to the kid, "would you like to go home?"

"Aw, what for?" says he. "I don't have any fun at home. I hate to go to school. I like to camp out. You won't take me back home again, Snake-eye, will you?"

"Not right away," says I. "We'll stay here in the cave a while."

"All right!" says he. "That'll be fine. I never had such fun in all my life."

We went to bed about eleven o'clock. We spread down some wide blankets and quilts and put Red Chief between us. We weren't afraid he'd run away. He kept us awake for three hours, jumping up and reaching for his rifle and screeching: "Hist! pard," in mine and Bill's ears, as the fancied crackle of a twig or the rustle of a leaf revealed to his young imagination the stealthy approach of the outlaw band. At last, I fell into a troubled sleep, and dreamed that I had been kidnapped and chained to a tree by a ferocious pirate with red hair.

Just at daybreak, I was awakened by a series of awful screams from Bill. They weren't yells, or howls, or shouts, or whoops, or yawps, such as you'd expect from a manly set of vocal organs—they were simply indecent, terrifying, humiliating screams, such as women emit when they see ghosts or caterpillars. It's an awful thing to hear a strong, desperate, fat man scream incontinently in a cave at daybreak.

I jumped up to see what the matter was. Red Chief was sitting on Bill's chest, with one hand twined in Bill's hair. In the other he had the sharp case-knife we used for slicing bacon; and he was industriously and realistically trying to take Bill's scalp, according to the sentence that had been pronounced upon him the evening before.

I got the knife away from the kid and made him lie down again. But, from that moment, Bill's spirit was broken. He laid down on his side of the bed, but he never closed an eye again in sleep as long as that boy was with us. I dozed off for a while, but along toward sun-up I remembered that Red Chief had said I was to be burned at the stake at the rising of the sun. I wasn't nervous or afraid; but I sat up and lit my pipe and leaned against a rock.

"What you getting up so soon for, Sam?" asked Bill.

"Me?" says I. "Oh, I got a kind of a pain in my shoulder. I thought sitting up would rest it."

"You're a liar!" says Bill. "You're afraid. You was to be burned at sunrise, and you was afraid he'd do it. And he would, too, if he could find a match. Ain't it awful, Sam? Do you think anybody will pay out money to get a little imp like that back home?"

"Sure," said I. "A rowdy kid like that is just the kind that parents dote on. Now, you and the Chief get up and cook breakfast, while I go up on the top of this mountain and reconnoitre."

I went up on the peak of the little mountain and ran my eye over the contiguous vicinity. Over toward Summit I expected to see the sturdy yeomanry of the village armed with scythes and pitchforks beating the countryside for the dastardly kidnappers. But what I saw was a peaceful landscape dotted with one man ploughing with a dun mule. Nobody was dragging the creek; no couriers dashed hither and yon, bringing tidings of no news to the distracted parents. There was a sylvan attitude of somnolent sleepiness pervading that section of the external outward surface of Alabama that lay exposed to my view. "Perhaps," says I to myself, "it has not yet been discovered that the wolves have borne away the tender lambkin from the fold. Heaven help the wolves!" says I, and I went down the mountain to breakfast.

When I got to the cave I found Bill backed up against the side of it, breathing hard, and the boy threatening to smash him with a rock half as big as a cocoanut.

"He put a red-hot boiled potato down my back," explained Bill, "and then mashed it with his foot; and I boxed his ears. Have you got a gun about you, Sam?"

I took the rock away from the boy and kind of patched up the argument. "I'll fix you," says the kid to Bill. "No man ever yet struck the Red Chief but what he got paid for it. You better beware!"

After breakfast the kid takes a piece of leather with strings wrapped around it out of his pocket and goes outside the cave unwinding it.

"What's he up to now?" says Bill, anxiously. "You don't think he'll run away, do you, Sam?"

"No fear of it," says I. "He don't seem to be much of a home body. But we've got to fix up some plan about the ransom. There don't seem to be much excitement around Summit on account of his disappearance; but maybe they haven't realized yet that he's gone. His folks may think he's spending the night with Aunt Jane or one of the neighbours. Anyhow, he'll be missed to-day. To-night we must get a message to his father demanding the two thousand dollars for his return."

Just then we heard a kind of war-whoop, such as David might have emitted when he knocked out the champion Goliath. It was a sling that Red Chief had pulled out of his pocket, and he was whirling it around his head.

I dodged, and heard a heavy thud and a kind of a sigh from Bill, like a horse gives out when you take his saddle off. A niggerhead rock the size of an egg had caught Bill just behind his left ear. He loosened himself all over and fell in the fire across the frying pan of hot water for washing the dishes. I dragged him out and poured cold water on his head for half an hour.

By and by, Bill sits up and feels behind his ear and says: "Sam, do you know who my favourite Biblical character is?"

"Take it easy," says I. "You'll come to your senses presently."

"King Herod," says he. "You won't go away and leave me here alone, will you, Sam?"

I went out and caught that boy and shook him until his freckles rattled.

"If you don't behave," says I, "I'll take you straight home. Now, are you going to be good, or not?"

"I was only funning," says he sullenly. "I didn't mean to hurt Old Hank. But what did he hit me for? I'll behave, Snake-eye, if you won't send me home, and if you'll let me play the Black Scout to-day."

"I don't know the game," says I. "That's for you and Mr. Bill to decide. He's your playmate for the day. I'm going away for a while, on business. Now, you come in and make friends with him and say you are sorry for hurting him, or home you go, at once."

I made him and Bill shake hands, and then I took Bill aside and told him I was going to Poplar Cove, a little village three miles from the cave, and find out what I could about how the kidnapping had been regarded in Summit. Also, I thought it best to send a peremptory letter to old man Dorset that day, demanding the ransom and dictating how it should be paid.

"You know, Sam," says Bill, "I've stood by you without batting an eye in earthquakes, fire and flood—in poker games, dynamite outrages, police raids, train robberies and cyclones. I never lost my nerve yet till we kidnapped that two-legged skyrocket of a kid. He's got me going. You won't leave me long with him, will you, Sam?"

"I'll be back some time this afternoon," says I. "You must keep the boy amused and quiet till I return. And now we'll write the letter to old Dorset."

Bill and I got paper and pencil and worked on the letter while Red Chief, with a blanket wrapped around him, strutted up and down, guarding the mouth of the cave. Bill begged me tearfully to make the ransom fifteen hundred dollars instead of two thousand. "I ain't attempting," says he, "to decry the celebrated moral aspect of parental affection, but we're dealing with humans, and it ain't human for anybody to give up two thousand dollars for that forty-pound chunk of freckled wildcat. I'm willing to take a chance at fifteen hundred dollars. You can charge the difference up to me."

So, to relieve Bill, I acceded, and we collaborated a letter that ran this way:

Ebenezer Dorset, Esq.:

We have your boy concealed in a place far from Summit. It is useless for you or the most skilful detectives to attempt to find him. Absolutely, the only terms on which you can have him restored to you are these: We demand fifteen hundred dollars in large bills for his return: the money to be left at midnight to-night at the same spot and in the same box as your reply—as hereinafter described. If you agree to these terms, send your answer in writing by a solitary messenger to-night at half-past eight o'clock. After crossing Owl Creek, on the road to Poplar Cove, there are three large trees about a hundred yards apart, close to the fence of the wheat field on the right-hand side. At the bottom of the fence-post, opposite the third tree, will be found a small pasteboard box.

The messenger will place the answer in this box and return immediately to Summit.

If you attempt any treachery or fail to comply with our demand as stated, you will never see your boy again.

If you pay the money as demanded, he will be returned to you safe and well within three hours. These terms are final, and if you do not accede to them no further communication will be attempted.

Two Desperate Men.

I addressed this letter to Dorset, and put it in my pocket. As I was about to start, the kid comes up to me and says:

"Aw, Snake-eye, you said I could play the Black Scout while you was gone."

"Play it, of course," says I. "Mr. Bill will play with you. What kind of a game is it?"

"I'm the Black Scout," says Red Chief, "and I have to ride to the stockade to warn the settlers that the Indians are coming. I'm tired of playing Indian myself. I want to be the Black Scout."

"All right," says I. "It sounds harmless to me. I guess Mr. Bill will help you foil the pesky savages."

"What am I to do?" asks Bill, looking at the kid suspiciously.

"You are the hoss," says Black Scout. "Get down on your hands and knees. How can I ride to the stockade without a hoss?"

"You'd better keep him interested," said I, "till we get the scheme going. Loosen up."

Bill gets down on his all fours, and a look comes in his eye like a rabbit's when you catch it in a trap.

"How far is it to the stockade, kid?" he asks, in a husky manner of voice.

"Ninety miles," says the Black Scout. "And you have to hump yourself to get there on time. Whoa, now!"

The Black Scout jumps on Bill's back and digs his heels in his side.

"For Heaven's sake," says Bill, "hurry back, Sam, as soon as you can. I wish we hadn't made the ransom more than a thousand. Say, you quit kicking me or I'll get up and warm you good."

I walked over to Poplar Cove and sat around the post-office and store, talking with the chawbacons that came in to trade. One whiskerando says that he hears Summit is all upset on account of Elder Ebenezer Dorset's boy having been lost or stolen. That was all I wanted to know. I bought some smoking tobacco, referred casually to the price of black-eyed peas, posted my letter surreptitiously and came away. The postmaster said the mail-carrier would come by in an hour to take the mail on to Summit.

When I got back to the cave Bill and the boy were not to be found. I explored the vicinity of the cave, and risked a yodel or two, but there was no response.

So I lighted my pipe and sat down on a mossy bank to await developments.

In about half an hour I heard the bushes rustle, and Bill wabbled out into the little glade in front of the cave. Behind him was the kid, stepping softly like a scout, with a broad grin on his face. Bill stopped, took off his hat and wiped his face with a red handkerchief. The kid stopped about eight feet behind him.

"Sam," says Bill, "I suppose you'll think I'm a renegade, but I couldn't help it. I'm a grown person with masculine proclivities and habits of self-defense, but there is a time when all systems of egotism and predominance fail. The boy is gone. I have sent him home. All is off. There was martyrs in old times," goes on Bill, "that suffered death rather than give up the particular graft they enjoyed. None of 'em ever was subjugated to such supernatural tortures as I have been. I tried to be faithful to our articles of depredation; but there came a limit."

"What's the trouble, Bill?" I asks him.

"I was rode," says Bill, "the ninety miles to the stockade, not barring an inch. Then, when the settlers was rescued, I was given oats. Sand ain't a palatable substitute. And then, for an hour I had to try to explain to him why there was nothin' in holes, how a road can run both ways and what makes the grass green. I tell you, Sam, a human can only stand so much. I takes him by the neck of his clothes and drags him down the mountain. On the way he kicks my legs black-and-blue from the knees down; and I've got to have two or three bites on my thumb and hand cauterized.

"But he's gone"—continues Bill—"gone home. I showed him the road to Summit and kicked him about eight feet nearer there at one kick. I'm sorry we lose the ransom; but it was either that or Bill Driscoll to the madhouse."

Bill is puffing and blowing, but there is a look of ineffable peace and growing content on his rose-pink features.

"Bill," says I, "there isn't any heart disease in your family, is there?"

"No," says Bill, "nothing chronic except malaria and accidents. Why?"

"Then you might turn around," says I, "and have a look behind you."

Bill turns and sees the boy, and loses his complexion and sits down plump on the ground and begins to pluck aimlessly at grass and little sticks. For an hour I was afraid of his mind. And then I told him that my scheme was to put the whole job through immediately and that we would get the ransom and be off with it by midnight if old Dorset fell in with our proposition. So Bill braced up enough to give the kid a weak sort of a smile and a promise to play the Russian in a Japanese war with him as soon as he felt a little better.

I had a scheme for collecting that ransom without danger of being caught by counterplots that ought to commend itself to professional kidnappers. The tree under which the answer was to be left—and the money later on—was close to the road fence with big, bare fields on all sides. If a gang of constables should be watching for any one to come for the note they could see him a long way off crossing the fields or in the road. But no, sirree! At half-past eight I was up in that tree as well hidden as a tree toad, waiting for the messenger to arrive.

Exactly on time, a half-grown boy rides up the road on a bicycle, locates the pasteboard box at the foot of the fence-post, slips a folded piece of paper into it and pedals away again back toward Summit.

I waited an hour and then concluded the thing was square. I slid down the tree, got the note, slipped along the fence till I struck the woods, and was back at the cave in another half an hour. I opened the note, got near the lantern and read it to Bill. It was written with a pen in a crabbed hand, and the sum and substance of it was this:

Two Desperate Men.

Gentlemen: I received your letter to-day by post, in regard to the ransom you ask for the return of my son. I think you are a little high in your demands, and I hereby make you a counter-proposition, which I am inclined to believe you will accept. You bring Johnny home and pay me two hundred and fifty dollars in cash, and I agree to take him off your hands. You had better come at night, for the neighbours believe he is lost, and I couldn't be responsible for what they would do to anybody they saw bringing him back.

Very respectfully,
EBENEZER DORSET.

"Great pirates of Penzance!" says I; "of all the impudent——"

But I glanced at Bill, and hesitated. He had the most appealing look in his eyes I ever saw on the face of a dumb or a talking brute.

"Sam," says he, "what's two hundred and fifty dollars, after all? We've got the money. One more night of this kid will send me to a bed in Bedlam. Besides being a thorough gentleman, I think Mr. Dorset is a spendthrift for making us such a liberal offer. You ain't going to let the chance go, are you?"

"Tell you the truth, Bill," says I, "this little he ewe lamb has somewhat got on my nerves too. We'll take him home, pay the ransom and make our get-away."

We took him home that night. We got him to go by telling him that his father had bought a silver-mounted rifle and a pair of moccasins for him, and we were going to hunt bears the next day.

It was just twelve o'clock when we knocked at Ebenezer's front door. Just at the moment when I should have been abstracting the fifteen hundred dollars from the box under the tree, according to the original proposition, Bill was counting out two hundred and fifty dollars into Dorset's hand.

When the kid found out we were going to leave him at home he started up a howl like a calliope and fastened himself as tight as a leech to Bill's leg. His father peeled him away gradually, like a porous plaster.

"How long can you hold him?" asks Bill.

"I'm not as strong as I used to be," says old Dorset, "but I think I can promise you ten minutes."

"Enough," says Bill. "In ten minutes I shall cross the Central, Southern and Middle Western States, and be legging it trippingly for the Canadian border."

And, as dark as it was, and as fat as Bill was, and as good a runner as I am, he was a good mile and a half out of Summit before I could catch up with him.

EDITH WHARTON

The Other Two

WAYTHORN, ON THE DRAWING-ROOM hearth, waited for his wife to come down to dinner.

It was their first night under his own roof, and he was surprised at his thrill of boyish agitation. He was not so old, to be sure—his glass gave him little more than the five-and-thirty years to which his wife confessed—but he had fancied himself already in the temperate zone; yet here he was listening for her step with a tender sense of all it symbolized, with some old trail of verse about the garlanded nuptial door-posts floating through his enjoyment of the pleasant room and the good dinner just beyond it.

They had been hastily recalled from their honeymoon by the illness of Lily Haskett, the child of Mrs. Waythorn's first marriage. The little girl, at Waythorn's desire, had been transferred to his house on the day of her mother's wedding, and the doctor, on their arrival, broke the news that she was ill with typhoid, but declared that all the symptoms were favorable. Lily could show twelve years of unblemished health, and the case promised to be a light one. The nurse spoke as reassuringly, and after a moment of alarm Mrs. Waythorn had adjusted herself to the situation. She was very fond of Lily—her affection for the child had perhaps been her decisive charm in Waythorn's eyes—but she had the perfectly balanced nerves which her little girl had inherited, and no woman ever wasted less tissue in unproductive worry. Waythorn was therefore quite prepared to see her come in presently, a little late because of a last look at Lily, but as serene and well-appointed as if her good-night kiss had been laid on the brow of health. Her composure was restful to him; it acted as ballast to his somewhat unstable sensibilities. As he pictured her bending over the child's bed he thought how soothing her presence must be in illness: her very step would prognosticate recovery.

His own life had been a gray one, from temperament rather than circumstance, and he had been drawn to her by the unperturbed gaiety which kept her fresh and elastic at an age when most women's activities are growing either slack or febrile. He knew what was said about her; for, popular as she was, there had always been a faint undercurrent of detraction. When she had appeared in New York, nine or ten years earlier, as the pretty Mrs. Haskett whom Gus Varick had unearthed somewhere—was it in Pittsburgh or Utica?—society, while promptly accepting her, had reserved the right to cast a doubt on its own indiscrimination. Inquiry, however, established her undoubted connection with a socially reigning family, and explained her recent divorce as the natural result of a runaway match at seventeen; and as nothing was known of Mr. Haskett it was easy to believe the worst of him.

Alice Haskett's remarriage with Gus Varick was a passport to the set whose recognition she coveted, and for a few years the Varicks were the most popular couple in town. Unfortunately the alliance was brief and stormy, and this time the husband had his champions. Still, even Varick's stanchest supporters admitted that he was not meant for matrimony, and Mrs. Varick's grievances were of a nature to bear the inspection of the New York courts. A New York divorce is in itself a diploma of virtue, and in the semi-widowhood of this second separation Mrs. Varick took on an air of sancity, and was allowed to confide her wrongs to some of the most scrupulous ears in town. But when it was known that she was to marry Waythorn there was a momentary reaction. Her best friends would have preferred to see her remain in the rôle of the injured wife, which was as becoming to her as crape to a rosy complexion. True, a decent time had elapsed, and it was not even suggested that Waythorn had supplanted his predecessor. People shook their heads over him, however, and one grudging friend, to whom he affirmed that he took the step with his eyes open, replied oracularly: "Yes—and with your ears shut."

Waythorn could afford to smile at these innuendoes. In the Wall Street phrase, he had "discounted" them. He knew that society has not yet adapted itself to the consequences of divorce, and that till the adaptation takes place every woman who uses the freedom the law accords her must be her own social justification. Waythorn had an amused confidence in his wife's ability to justify herself. His expectations were fulfilled, and before the wedding took place Alice Varick's group had rallied openly to her support. She took it all imperturbably; she had a way of surmounting obstacles without seeming to be aware of them, and Waythorn looked back with wonder at the trivialities over which he had worn his nerves thin. He had the sense of having found refuge in a richer, warmer nature than his own, and his satisfaction, at the moment, was humorously summed up in the thought that his wife, when she had done all she could for Lily, would not be ashamed to come down and enjoy a good dinner.

The anticipation of such enjoyment was not, however, the sentiment expressed by Mrs. Waythorn's charming face when she presently joined him. Though she had put on her most engaging teagown she had neglected to assume the smile that went with it, and Waythorn thought he had never seen her look so nearly worried.

"What is it?" he asked. "Is anything wrong with Lily?"

"No; I've just been in and she's still sleeping." Mrs. Waythorn hesitated. "But something tiresome has happened."

He had taken her two hands, and now perceived that he was crushing a paper between them.

"This letter?"

"Yes—Mr. Haskett has written—I mean his lawyer has written."

Waythorn felt himself flush uncomfortably. He dropped his wife's hands.

"What about?"

"About seeing Lily. You know the courts—"

"Yes, yes," he interrupted nervously.

Nothing was known about Haskett in New York. He was vaguely supposed to have remained in the outer darkness from which his wife had been rescued, and Waythorn was one of the few who were aware that he had given up his business in Utica and followed her to New York in order to be near his little girl. In the days of his wooing, Waythorn had often met Lily on the doorstep, rosy and smiling, on her way "to see papa."

"I am so sorry," Mrs. Waythorn murmured.

He roused himself. "What does he want?"

"He wants to see her. You know she goes to him once a week."

"Well—he doesn't expect her to go to him now, does he?"

"No—he has heard of her illness; but he expects to come here."

"Here?"

Mrs. Waythorn reddened under his gaze. They looked away from each other.

"I'm afraid he has the right. . . . You'll see. . . ." She made a proffer of the letter.

Waythorn moved away with a gesture of refusal. He stood staring about the softly lighted room, which a moment before had seemed so full of bridal intimacy.

"I'm so sorry," she repeated. "If Lily could have been moved—"

"That's out of the question," he returned impatiently.

"I suppose so."

Her lip was beginning to tremble, and he felt himself a brute.

"He must come, of course," he said. "When is—his day?"

"I'm afraid—tomorrow."

"Very well. Send a note in the morning."

The butler entered to announce dinner.

Waythorn turned to his wife. "Come—you must be tired. It's beastly, but try to forget about it," he said, drawing her hand through his arm.

"You're so good, dear. I'll try," she whispered back.

Her face cleared at once, and as she looked at him across the flowers, between the rosy candle-shades, he saw her lips waver back into a smile.

"How pretty everything is!" she sighed luxuriously.

He turned to the butler. "The champagne at once, please. Mrs. Waythorn is tired."

In a moment or two their eyes met above the sparkling glasses. Her own were quite clear and untroubled: he saw that she had obeyed his injunction and forgotten.

II

Waythorn, the next morning, went down town earlier than usual. Haskett was not likely to come till the afternoon, but the instinct of flight drove him forth. He meant to stay away all day—he had thoughts of dining at his club. As his door closed behind him he reflected that before he opened it again it would have admitted another man who had as much right to enter it as himself, and the thought filled him with a physical repugnance.

He caught the "elevated" at the employees' hour, and found himself crushed between two layers of pendulous humanity. At Eighth Street the man facing him wriggled out, and another took his place. Waythorn glanced up and saw that it was Gus Varick. The men were so close together that it was impossible to ignore the smile of recognition on Varick's handsome overblown face. And after all—why not? They had always been on good terms, and Varick had been divorced before Waythorn's attentions to his wife began. The two exchanged a word on the perennial grievance of the congested trains, and when a seat at their side was miraculously left empty the instinct of self-preservation made Waythorn slip into it after Varick.

The latter drew the stout man's breath of relief. "Lord—I was beginning to feel like a pressed flower." He leaned back, looking unconcernedly at Waythorn. "Sorry to hear that Sellers is knocked out again."

"Sellers?" echoed Waythorn, starting at his partner's name.

Varick looked surprised. "You didn't know he was laid up with the gout?"

"No, I've been away—I only got back last night." Waythorn felt himself reddening in anticipation of the other's smile.

"Ah—yes; to be sure. And Sellers' attack came on two days ago. I'm afraid he's pretty bad. Very awkward for me, as it happens, because he was just putting through a rather important thing for me."

"Ah?" Waythorn wondered vaguely since when Varick had been dealing in "important things." Hitherto he had dabbled only in the shallow pools of speculation, with which Waythorn's office did not usually concern itself.

It occurred to him that Varick might be talking at random, to relieve the strain of their propinquity. That strain was becoming momentarily more apparent to Waythorn, and when, at Cortlandt Street, he caught sight of an acquaintance and had a sudden vision of the picture he and Varick must present to an initiated eye, he jumped up with a muttered excuse.

"I hope you'll find Sellers better," said Varick civilly, and he stammered back: "If I can be of any use to you—" and let the departing crowd sweep him to the platform.

At his office he heard that Sellers was in fact ill with the gout, and would probably not be able to leave the house for some weeks.

"I'm sorry it should have happened so, Mr. Waythorn," the senior clerk said with affable significance. "Mr. Sellers was very much upset at the idea of giving you such a lot of extra work just now."

"Oh, that's no matter," said Waythorn hastily. He secretly welcomed the pressure of additional business, and was glad to think that, when the day's work was over, he would have to call at his partner's on the way home.

He was late for luncheon, and turned in at the nearest restaurant instead of going to his club. The place was full and the waiter hurried him to the back of the room to capture the only vacant table. In the cloud of cigar-smoke Waythorn did not at once distinguish his neighbors; but presently, looking about him, he saw Varick seated a few feet off. This time, luckily, they were too far apart for conversation, and Varick who faced another way, had probably not even seen him; but there was an irony in their renewed nearness.

Varick was said to be fond of good living, and as Waythorn sat dispatching his hurried luncheon he looked across half enviously at the other's leisurely degustation of his meal. When Waythorn first saw him he had been helping himself with critical deliberation to a bit of Camembert at the ideal point of liquefaction, and now, the cheese removed, he was just pouring his *café double* from its little two-storied earthern pot. He poured slowly, his ruddy profile bent above the task, and one beringed white hand steadying the lid of the coffee-pot; then he stretched his other hand to the decanter of cognac at his elbow, filled a liqueur-glass, took a tentative sip, and poured the brandy into his coffee-cup.

Waythorn watched him in a kind of fascination. What was he thinking of—only the flavor of the coffee and the liqueur? Had the morning's meeting left no more trace in his thoughts than on his face? Had his wife so completely passed out of his life that even this odd encounter with her present husband, within a week after her remarriage, was no more than an incident in his day? And as Waythorn mused, another idea struck him: had Haskett ever met Varick as Varick and he had just met? The recollection of Hasket perturbed him, and he rose and left the restaurant, taking a circuitous way out to escape the placid irony of Varick's nod.

It was after seven when Waythorn reached home. He thought the footman who opened the door looked at him oddly.

"How is Miss Lily?" he asked in haste.

"Doing very well, sir. A gentleman—"

"Tell Barlow to put off dinner for half an hour," Waythorn cut him off, hurrying upstairs.

He went straight to his room and dressed without seeing his wife. When he reached the drawing-room she was there, fresh and radiant. Lily's day had been good; the doctor was not coming back that evening.

At dinner Waythorn told her of Sellers' illness and of the resulting complications. She listened sympathetically, adjuring him not to let himself be overworked, and asking vague feminine questions about the routine of the office. Then she gave him the chronicle of Lily's day; quoted the nurse and doctor, and told him who had called to inquire. He had never seen her more serene and unruffled. It stuck him, with a curious pang, that she was very happy in being with him, so happy that she found a childish pleasure in rehearsing the trivial incidents of her day.

After dinner they went to the library, and the servant put the coffee and liqueurs on a low table before her and left the room. She looked singularly soft and girlish in her rosy pale dress, against the dark leather of one of his bachelor armchairs. A day earlier the contrast would have charmed him.

He turned away now, choosing a cigar with affected deliberation.

"Did Haskett come?" he asked, with his back to her.

"Oh, yes—he came."

"You didn't see him, of course?"

She hesitated a moment. "I let the nurse see him."

That was all. There was nothing more to ask. He swung round toward her, applying a match to his cigar. Well, the thing was over for a week, at any rate. He would try not to think of it. She looked up at him, a trifle rosier than usual, with a smile in her eyes.

"Ready for your coffee, dear?"

He leaned against the mantelpiece, watching her as she lifted the coffee-pot. The lamplight struck a gleam from her bracelets and tipped her soft hair with brightness. How light and slender she was, and how each gesture flowed into the next! She seemed a creature all compact of harmonies. As the thought of Haskett receded, Waythorn felt himself yielding again to the joy of possessorship. They were his, those white hands with their flitting motions, his the light haze of hair, the lips and eyes. . . .

She set down the coffee-pot, and reached for the decanter of cognac, measured off a liqueur-glass and poured it into his cup.

Waythorn uttered a sudden exclamation.

"What is the matter?" she said, startled.

"Nothing; only—I don't take cognac in my coffee."

"Oh, how stupid of me," she cried.

Their eyes met, and she blushed a sudden agonized red.

III

Ten days later, Mr. Sellers, still house-bound, asked Waythorn to call on his way down town.

The senior partner, with his swaddled foot propped up by the fire, greeted his associate with an air of embarrassment.

"I'm sorry, my dear fellow; I've got to ask you to do an awkward thing for me."

Waythorn waited, and the other went on, after a pause apparently given to the arrangement of his phrases: "The fact is, when I was knocked out I had just gone into a rather complicated piece of business for—Gus Varick."

"Well?" said Waythorn, with an attempt to put him at his ease.

"Well—it's this way: Varick came to me the day before my attack. He had evidently had an inside tip from somebody, and had made about a hundred thousand. He came to me for advice, and I suggested his going in with Vanderlyn."

"Oh, the deuce!" Waythorn exclaimed. He saw in a flash what had happened. The investment was an alluring one, but required negotiation. He listened quietly while Sellers put the case before him, and, the statement ended, he said: "You think I ought to see Varick?"

"I'm afraid I can't as yet. The doctor is obdurate. And this thing can't wait. I hate to ask you, but no one else in the office knows the ins and outs of it."

Waythorn stood silent. He did not care a farthing for the success of Varick's venture, but the honor of the office was to be considered, and he could hardly refuse to oblige his partner.

"Very well," he said, "I'll do it."

That afternoon, apprised by telephone, Varick called at the office. Waythorn, waiting in his private room, wondered what the others thought of it. The newspapers, at the time of Mrs. Waythorn's marriage, had acquainted their readers with every detail of her previous matrimonial ventures, and Waythorn could fancy the clerks smiling behind Varick's back as he was ushered in.

Varick bore himself admirably. He was easy without being undignified, and Waythorn was conscious of cutting a much less impressive figure. Varick had no experience of business, and the talk prolonged itself for nearly an hour while Waythorn set forth with scrupulous precision the details of the proposed transaction.

"I'm awfully obliged to you," Varick said as he rose. "The fact is I'm not used to having much money to look after, and I don't want to make an ass of myself—" He smiled, and Waythorn could not help noticing that there was something pleasant about his smile. "It feels uncommonly queer to have enough cash to pay one's bills. I'd have sold my soul for it a few years ago!"

Waythorn winced at the allusion. He had heard it rumored that a lack of funds had been one of the determining causes of the Varick separation, but it did not occur to him that Varick's words were intentional. It seemed more likely that the desire to keep clear of embarrassing topics had fatally drawn him into one. Waythorn did not wish to be outdone in civility.

"We'll do the best we can for you," he said. "I think this is a good thing you're in."

"Oh, I'm sure it's immense. It's awfully good of you—" Varick broke off, embarrassed. "I suppose the thing's settled now—but if—"

"If anything happens before Sellers is about, I'll see you again," said Waythorn quietly. He was glad, in the end, to appear the more self-possessed of the two.

The course of Lily's illness ran smooth, and as the days passed Waythorn grew used to the idea of Haskett's weekly visit. The first time the day came round, he stayed out late, and questioned his wife as to the visit on his return. She replied at once that Haskett had merely seen the nurse downstairs, as the doctor did not wish anyone in the child's sickroom till after the crisis.

The following week, Waythorn was again conscious of the recurrence of the day, but had forgotten it by the time he came home to dinner. The crisis of the disease came a few days later, with a rapid decline of fever, and the little girl was pronounced out of danger. In the rejoicing which ensued the thought of Haskett passed out of Waythorn's mind, and one afternoon, letting himself into the house with a latch-key, he went straight to his library without noticing a shabby hat and umbrella in the hall.

In the library he found a small effaced-looking man with a thinnish gray beard sitting on the edge of a chair. The stranger might have been a piano-tuner, or one of those mysteriously efficient persons who are summoned in emergencies to adjust some detail of the domestic machinery. He blinked at Waythorn through a pair of gold-rimmed spectacles and said mildly: "Mr. Waythorn, I presume? I am Lily's father."

Waythorn flushed. "Oh—" he stammered uncomfortably. He broke off, disliking to appear rude. Inwardly he was trying to adjust the actual Haskett to the image of him projected by his wife's reminiscences. Waythorn had been allowed to infer that Alice's first husband was a brute.

"I am sorry to intrude," said Haskett, with his over-the-counter politeness.

"Don't mention it," returned Waythorn, collecting himself. "I suppose the nurse has been told?"

"I presume so. I can wait," said Haskett. He had a resigned way of speaking, as though life had worn down his natural powers of resistance.

Waythorn stood on the threshold, nervously pulling off his gloves.

"I'm sorry you've been detained. I will send for the nurse," he said; and as he opened the door he added with an effort: "I'm glad we can give you a good report of Lily." He winced as the *we* slipped out, but Haskett seemed not to notice it.

"Thank you, Mr. Waythorn. It's been an anxious time for me."

"Ah, well, that's past. Soon she'll be able to go to you." Waythorn nodded and passed out.

In his own room he flung himself down with a groan. He hated the womanish sensibility which made him suffer so acutely for the grotesque chances of life. He had known when he married that his wife's former husbands were both living, and that amid the multiplied contacts of modern existence there were a thousand chances to one that he would run against one or the other, yet he found himself as much disturbed by his brief encounter with Haskett as though the law had not obligingly removed all difficulties in the way of their meeting.

Waythorn sprang up and began to pace the room nervously. He had not suffered half as much from his two meetings with Varick. It was Haskett's presence in his own house that made the situation so intolerable. He stood still, hearing steps in the passage.

"This way, please," he heard the nurse say. Haskett was being taken upstairs, then: not a corner of the house but was open to him. Waythorn dropped into another chair, staring vaguely ahead of him. On his dressing-table stood a photograph of Alice, taken when he had first known her. She was Alice Varick then—how fine and exquisite he had thought her! Those were Varick's pearls about her neck. At Waythorn's instance they had been returned before her marriage. Had Haskett ever given her any trinkets—and what had become of them, Waythorn wondered? He realized suddenly that he knew very little of Haskett's past or present situation; but from the man's appearance and manner of speech he could reconstruct with curious precision the surroundings of Alice's first marriage. And it startled him to think that she had, in the background of her life, a phase of existence so different from anything with which he had connected her. Varick, whatever his faults, was a gentleman, in the conventional, traditional sense of the term: the sense which at that moment seemed, oddly enough, to have most meaning to Waythorn. He and Varick had the same social habits, spoke the same language, understood the same allusions. But this other man . . . it was grotesquely uppermost in Waythorn's mind that Haskett had worn a made-up tie attached with an elastic. Why should that ridiculous detail symbolize the whole man? Waythorn was exasperated by his own paltriness, but the fact of the tie expanded, forced itself on him, became as it were the key to Alice's past. He could see her, as Mrs. Haskett, sitting in a "front parlor" furnished in plush, with a pianola, and a copy of *Ben Hur* on the center-table. He could see her going to the theater with Haskett—or perhaps even to a "Church Sociable"—she in a "picture hat" and Haskett in a black frockcoat, a little creased, with the made-up tie on an elastic. On the way home they would stop and look at the illuminated shop windows, lingering over the photographs of New York actresses. On Sunday afternoons Haskett would take her for a walk, pushing Lily ahead of them in a white enameled perambulator, and Waythorn had a vision of the people they would stop and talk to. He could fancy how pretty Alice must have looked, in a dress adroitly constructed from the hints of a New York fashion-paper, and how she must have looked down on the other women, chafing at her life, and secretly feeling that she belonged in a bigger place.

For the moment his foremost thought was one of wonder at the way in which she had shed the phase of existence which her marriage with Haskett implied. It was as if her whole aspect, every gesture, every inflection, every allusion, were a studied negation of that period of her life. If she had denied being married to Haskett she could hardly have stood more convicted of duplicity than in this obliteration of the self which had been his wife.

Waythorn started up, checking himself in the analysis of her motives. What right had he to create a fantastic effigy of her and then pass judgment on it? She had spoken vaguely of her first marriage as unhappy, had hinted, with becoming reticence, that Haskett had brought havoc among her young illusions. . . . It was a pity for Waythorn's peace of mind that Haskett's very inoffensiveness shed a new light on the nature of those illusions. A man would rather think that his wife has been brutalized by her first husband than that the process has been reversed.

IV

"Mr. Waythorn, I don't like that French governess of Lily's."

Haskett, subdued and apologetic, stood before Waythorn in the library, revolving his shabby hat in his hand.

Waythorn, surprised in his armchair over the evening paper, stared back perplexedly at his visitor.

"You'll excuse my asking to see you," Haskett continued. "But this is my last visit, and I thought if I could have a word with you it would be a better way than writing to Mrs. Waythorn's lawyer."

Waythorn rose uneasily. He did not like the French governess either; but that was irrelevant.

"I am not so sure of that," he returned stiffly; "but since you wish it I will give your message to—my wife." He always hesitated over the possessive pronoun in addressing Haskett.

The latter sighed. "I don't know as that will help much. She didn't like it when I spoke to her."

Waythorn turned red. "When did you see her?" he asked.

"Not since the first day I came to see Lily—right after she was taken sick. I remarked to her then that I didn't like the governess."

Waythorn made no answer. He remembered distinctly that, after that first visit, he had asked his wife if she had seen Haskett. She had lied to him then, but she had respected his wishes since; and the incident cast a curious light on her character. He was sure she would not have seen Haskett that first day if she had divined that Waythorn would object, and the fact that she did not divine it was almost as disagreeable to the latter as the discovery that she had lied to him.

"I don't like the woman," Haskett was repeating with mild persistency. "She ain't straight, Mr. Waythorn—she'll teach the child to be underhand. I've noticed a change in Lily—she's too anxious to please—and she don't always tell the truth. She used to be the straightest child, Mr. Waythorn—" He broke off, his voice a little thick. "Not but what I want her to have a stylish education," he ended.

Waythorn was touched. "I'm sorry, Mr. Haskett; but frankly, I don't quite see what I can do."

Haskett hesitated. Then he laid his hat on the table, and advanced to the hearth-rug, on which Waythorn was standing. There was nothing aggressive in his manner, but he had the solemnity of a timid man resolved on a decisive measure.

"There's just one thing you can do, Mr. Waythorn," he said. "You can remind Mrs. Waythorn that, by the decree of the courts, I am entitled to have a voice in Lily's bringing up." He paused, and went on more deprecatingly: "I'm not the kind to talk about enforcing my rights, Mr. Waythorn. I don't know as I think a man is entitled to rights he hasn't known how to hold on to; but this business of the child is different. I've never let go there—and I never mean to."

The scene left Waythorn deeply shaken. Shamefacedly, in indirect ways, he had been finding out about Haskett; and all that he had learned was favorable. The little man, in order to be near his daughter, had sold out his share in a profitable business in Utica, and accepted a modest clerkship in a New York manufacturing house. He boarded in a shabby street and had few acquaintances. His passion for Lily filled his life. Waythorn felt that this exploration of Haskett was like groping about with a dark-lantern in his wife's past; but he saw now that there were recesses his lantern had not explored. He had never inquired into the exact circumstances of his wife's first matrimonial rupture. On the surface all had been fair. It was she who had obtained the divorce, and the court had given her the child. But Waythorn knew how many ambiguities such a verdict might cover. The mere fact that Haskett retained a right over his daughter implied an unsuspected compromise. Waythorn was an idealist. He always refused to recognize unpleasant contingencies till he found himself confronted with them, and then he saw them followed by a spectral train of consequences. His next days were thus haunted, and he determined to try to lay the ghosts by conjuring them up in his wife's presence.

When he repeated Haskett's request a flame of anger passed over her face; but she subdued it instantly and spoke with a slight quiver of outraged motherhood.

"It is very ungentlemanly of him," she said.

The word grated on Waythorn. "That is neither here nor there. It's a bare question of rights."

She murmured: "It's not as if he could ever be a help to Lily—"

Waythorn flushed. This was even less to his taste. "The question is," he repeated, "what authority has he over her?"

She looked downward, twisting herself a little in her seat. "I am willing to see him—I thought you objected," she faltered.

In a flash he understood that she knew the extent of Haskett's claims. Perhaps it was not the first time she had resisted them.

"My objecting has nothing to do with it," he said coldly; "if Haskett has a right to be consulted you must consult him."

She burst into tears, and he saw that she expected him to regard her as a victim.

Haskett did not abuse his rights. Waythorn had felt miserably sure that he would not. But the governess was dismissed, and from time to time the little man demanded an interview with Alice. After the first outburst she accepted the situation with her usual adaptability. Haskett had once reminded Waythorn of the piano-tuner, and Mrs. Waythorn, after a month or two, appeared to class him with that domestic familiar. Waythorn could not but respect the father's tenacity. At first he had tried to cultivate the suspicion that Haskett might be "up to" something, that he had an object in securing a foothold in the house. But in his heart Waythorn was sure of Haskett's single-mindedness; he even guessed in the latter a mild contempt for such advantages as his relation with the Waythorns might offer. Haskett's sincerity of purpose made him invulnerable, and his successor had to accept him as a lien on the property.

Mr. Sellers was sent to Europe to recover from his gout, and Varick's affairs hung on Waythorn's hands. The negotiations were prolonged and complicated; they necessitated frequent conferences between the two men, and the interests of the firm forbade Waythorn's suggesting that his client should transfer his business to another office.

Varick appeared well in the transaction. In moments of relaxation his coarse streak appeared, and Waythorn dreaded his geniality; but in the office he was concise and clear-headed, with a flattering deference to Waythorn's judgment. Their business relations being so affably established, it would have been absurd for the two men to ignore each other in society. The first time they met in a drawing-room, Varick took up their intercourse in the same easy key, and his hostess's grateful glance obliged Waythorn to respond to it. After that they ran across each other frequently, and one evening at a ball Waythorn, wandering through the remoter rooms, came upon Varick seated beside his wife. She colored a little, and faltered in what she was saying; but Varick nodded to Waythorn without rising, and the latter strolled on.

In the carriage, on the way home, he broke out nervously; "I didn't know you spoke to Varick."

Her voice trembled a little. "It's the first time—he happened to be standing near me; I didn't know what to do. It's so awkward, meeting everywhere—and he said you had been very kind about some business."

"That's different," said Waythorn.

She paused a moment. "I'll do just as you wish," she returned pliantly. "I thought it would be less awkward to speak to him when we meet."

Her pliancy was beginning to sicken him. Had she really no will of her own—no theory about her relation to these men? She had accepted Haskett—did she mean to accept Varick? It was "less awkward," as she had said, and her instinct was to evade difficulties or to circumvent them. With sudden vividness Waythorn saw how the instinct had developed. She was "as easy as an old shoe"—a shoe that too many feet had worn. Her elasticity was the result of tension in too many different directions. Alice Haskett—Alice Varick—Alice Waythorn—she had been each in turn, and had left hanging to each name a little of her privacy, a little of her personality, a little of the inmost self where the unknown god abides.

"Yes—it's better to speak to Varick," said Waythorn wearily.

V

The winter wore on, and society took advantage of the Waythorn's acceptance of Varick. Harassed hostesses were grateful to them for bridging over a social difficulty, and Mrs. Waythorn was held up as a miracle of good taste. Some experimental spirits could not resist the diversion of throwing Varick and his former wife together, and there were those who thought he found a zest in the propinquity. But Mrs. Waythorn's conduct remained irreproachable. She neither avoided Varick nor sought him out. Even Waythorn could not but admit that she had discovered the solution of the newest social problem.

He had married her without giving much thought to that problem. He had fancied that a woman can shed her past like a man. But now he saw Alice was bound to hers both by the circumstances which forced her into continued relation with it, and by the traces it had left on her nature. With grim irony Waythorn compared himself to a member of a syndicate. He held so many shares in his wife's personality and his predecessors were his partners in the business. If there had been any element of passion in the transaction he would have felt less deteriorated by it. The fact that Alice took her change of husbands like a change of weather reduced the situation to mediocrity. He could have forgiven her for blunders, for excesses; for resisting Haskett, for yielding to Varick; for anything but her acquiescence and her tact. She reminded him of a juggler tossing knives; but the knives were blunt and she knew they would never cut her.

And then, gradually, habit formed a protecting surface for his sensibilities. If he paid for each day's comfort with the small change of his illusions, he grew daily to value the comfort more and set less store upon the coin. He had drifted into a dulling propinquity with Haskett and Varick and he took refuge in the cheap revenge of satirizing the situation. He even began to reckon up the advantages which accrued from it, to ask himself it it were not better to own a third of a wife who knew how to make a man happy than a whole one who had lacked opportunity to acquire the art. For it *was* an art, and made up, like all others, of concessions, eliminations and embellishments; of lights judiciously thrown and shadows skillfully softened. His wife knew exactly how to manage the lights, and he knew exactly to what training she owed her skill. He even tried to trace the source of his obligations, to discriminate between the influences which had combined to produce his domestic happiness: he perceived that Haskett's commonness had made Alice worship good breeding, while Varick's liberal construction of the marriage bond had taught her to value the conjugal virtues; so that he was directly indebted to his predecessors for the devotion which made his life easy if not inspiring.

From this phase he passed into that of complete acceptance. He ceased to satirize himself because time dulled the irony of the situation and the joke lost its humor with its sting. Even the sight of Haskett's hat on the hall table had ceased to touch the springs of epigram. The hat was often seen there now, for it had been decided that it was better for Lily's father to visit her than for the little girl to go to his boarding-house. Waythorn, having acquiesced in this arrangement, had been surprised to find how little difference it made. Haskett was never obtrusive, and the few visitors who met him on the stairs were unaware of his identity. Waythorn did not know how often he saw Alice, but with himself Haskett was seldom in contact.

One afternoon, however, he learned on entering that Lily's father was waiting to see him. In the library he found Haskett occupying a chair in his usual provisional way. Waythorn always felt grateful to him for not leaning back.

"I hope you'll excuse me, Mr. Waythorn," he said rising. "I wanted to see Mrs. Waythorn about Lily, and your man asked me to wait here till she came in."

"Of course," said Waythorn, remembering that a sudden leak had that morning given over the drawing-room to the plumbers.

He opened his cigar-case and held it out to his visitor, and Haskett's acceptance seemed to mark a fresh stage in their intercourse. The spring evening was chilly, and Waythorn invited his guest to draw up his chair to the fire. He meant to find an excuse to leave Haskett in a moment; but he was tired and cold, and after all the little man no longer jarred on him.

The two were enclosed in the intimacy of their blended cigar-smoke when the door opened and Varick walked into the room. Waythorn rose abruptly. It was the first time that Varick had come to the house, and the surprise of seeing him, combined with the singular inopportuneness of his arrival, gave a new edge to Waythorn's blunted sensibilities. He stared at his visitor without speaking.

Varick seemed too preoccupied to notice his host's embarrassment.

"My dear fellow," he exclaimed in his most expansive tone, "I must apologize for tumbling in on you in this way, but I was too late to catch you down town, and so I thought—"

He stopped short, catching sight of Haskett, and his sanguine color deepened to a flush which spread vividly under his scant blond hair. But in a moment he recovered himself and nodded slightly. Haskett returned the bow in silence, and Waythorn was still groping for speech when the footman came in carrying a tea-table.

The intrusion offered a welcome vent to Waythorn's nerves. "What the deuce are you bringing this here for?" he said sharply.

"I beg your pardon, sir, but the plumbers are still in the drawing-room, and Mrs. Waythorn said she would have tea in the library." The footman's perfectly respectful tone implied a reflection on Waythorn's reasonableness.

"Oh, very well," said the latter resignedly, and the footman proceeded to open the folding tea-table and set out its complicated appointments. While this interminable process continued the three men stood motionless, watching it with a fascinated stare, till Waythorn, to break the silence, said to Varick: "Won't you have a cigar?"

He held out the case he had just tendered to Haskett, and Varick helped himself with a smile. Waythorn looked about for a match, and finding none, proffered a light from his own cigar. Haskett, in the background, held his ground mildly, examining his cigar-tip now and then, and stepping forward at the right moment to knock its ashes into the fire.

The footman at last withdrew, and Varick immediately began: "If I could just say half a word to you about this business—"

"Certainly," stammered Waythorn; "in the dining-room—"

But as he placed his hand on the door it opened from without, and his wife appeared on the threshold.

She came in fresh and smiling, in her street dress and hat, shedding a fragrance from the boa which she loosened in advancing.

"Shall we have tea in here, dear?" she began; and then she caught sight of Varick. Her smile deepened, veiling a slight tremor of surprise.

"Why, how do you do?" she said with a distinct note of pleasure.

As she shook hands with Varick she saw Haskett standing behind him. Her smile faded for a moment, but she recalled it quickly, with a scarcely perceptible side-glance at Waythorn.

"How do you do, Mr. Haskett?" she said, and shook hands with him a shade less cordially.

The three men stood awkwardly before her, till Varick, always the most self-possessed, dashed into an explanatory phrase.

"We—I had to see Waythorn a moment on business," he stammered, brick-red from chin to nape.

Haskett stepped forward with his air of mild obstinacy. "I am sorry to intrude; but you appointed five o'clock—" he directed his resigned glance to the time-piece on the mantel.

She swept aside their embarrassment with a charming gesture of hospitality.

"I'm sorry—I'm always late; but the afternoon was so lovely." She stood drawing off her gloves, propitiatory and graceful, diffusing about her a sense of ease and familiarity in which the situation lost its grotesqueness. "But before talking business," she added brightly, "I'm sure everyone wants a cup of tea."

She dropped into her low chair by the tea-table, and the two visitors, as if drawn by her smile, advanced to receive the cups she held out.

She glanced about for Waythorn, and he took the third cup with a laugh.

STEPHEN CRANE

The Open Boat

A Tale Intended to Be After the Fact:
Being the Experience of Four Men from
the Sunk Steamer *Commodore*

I

NONE OF THEM KNEW the color of the sky. Their eyes glanced level, and were fastened upon the waves that swept toward them. These waves were of the hue of slate, save for the tops, which were of foaming white, and all of the men knew the colors of the sea. The horizon narrowed and widened, and dipped and rose, and at all times its edge was jagged with waves that seemed thrust up in points like rocks.

Many a man ought to have a bathtub larger than the boat which here rode upon the sea. These waves were most wrongfully and barbarously abrupt and tall, and each froth-top was a problem in small-boat navigation.

The cook squatted in the bottom, and looked with both eyes at the six inches of gunwale which separated him from the ocean. His sleeves were rolled over his fat forearms, and the two flaps of his unbuttoned vest dangled as he bent to bail out the boat. Often he said, "Gawd! that was a narrow clip." As he remarked it he invariably gazed eastward over the broken sea.

The oiler, steering with one of the two oars in the boat, sometimes raised himself suddenly to keep clear of water that swirled in over the stern. It was a thin little oar, and it seemed often ready to snap.

The correspondent, pulling at the other oar, watched the waves and wondered why he was there.

The injured captain, lying in the bow, was at this time buried in that profound dejection and indifference which comes, temporarily at least, to even the bravest and most enduring when, willy-nilly, the firm fails, the army loses, the ship goes down. The mind of a master of a vessel is rooted deep in the timbers of her, though he command for a day or a decade; and this captain had on him the stern impression of a scene in the grays of dawn of seven turned faces, and later a stump of a topmast with a white ball on it, that slashed to and fro at the waves, went low and lower, and down. Thereafter there was something strange in his voice. Although steady, it was deep with mourning, and of a quality beyond oration or tears.

"Keep 'er a little more south, Billie," he said.

"A little more south, sir," said the oiler in the stern.

A seat in this boat was not unlike a seat upon a bucking broncho, and by the same token a broncho is not much smaller. The craft pranced and reared and plunged like an animal. As each wave came, and she rose for it, she seemed like a horse making at a fence outrageously high. The manner of her scramble over these walls of water is a mystic thing, and, moreover, at the top of them were ordinarily these problems in white water, the foam racing down from the summit of each wave requiring a new leap, and a leap from the air. Then, after scornfully bumping a crest, she would slide and race and splash down a long incline, and arrive bobbing and nodding in front of the next menace.

A singular disadvantage of the sea lies in the fact that after successfully surmounting one wave you discover that there is another behind it just as important and just as nervously anxious to do something effective in the way of swamping boats. In a ten-foot dinghy one can get an idea of the resources of the sea in the line of waves that is not probable to the average experience, which is never at sea in a dinghy. As each slaty wall of water approached, it shut all else from the view of the men in the boat, and it was not difficult to imagine that this particular wave was the final outburst of the ocean, the last effort of the grim water. There was a terrible grace in the move of the waves, and they came in silence, save for the snarling of the crests.

In the wan light the faces of the men must have been gray. Their eyes must have glinted in strange ways as they gazed steadily astern. Viewed from a balcony, the whole thing would doubtless have been weirdly picturesque. But the men in the boat had no time to see it, and if they had had leisure, there were other things to occupy their minds. The sun swung steadily up the sky, and they knew it was broad day because the color of the sea changed from slate to emerald green streaked with amber lights, and the foam was like tumbling snow. The process of the breaking day was unknown to them. They were aware only of this effect upon the color of the waves that rolled toward them.

In disjointed sentences the cook and the correspondent argued as to the difference between a life-saving station and a house of refuge. The cook had said: "There's a house of refuge just north of the Mosquito Inlet Light, and as soon as they see us they'll come off in their boat and pick us up."

"As soon as who see us?" said the correspondent.

"The crew," said the cook.

"Houses of refuge don't have crews," said the correspondent. "As I understand them, they are only places where clothes and grub are stored for the benefit of shipwrecked people. They don't carry crews."

"Oh, yes, they do," said the cook.

"No, they don't," said the correspondent.

"Well we're not there yet, anyhow," said the oiler, in the stern.

"Well," said the cook, "perhaps it's not a house of refuge that I'm thinking of as being near Mosquito Inlet Light; perhaps it's a life-saving station."

"We're not there yet," said the oiler in the stern.

II

As the boat bounced from the top of each wave the wind tore through the hair of the hatless men, and as the craft plopped her stern down again the spray slashed past them. The crest of each of these waves was a hill, from the top of which the men surveyed for a moment a broad tumultuous expanse, shining and wind-riven. It was probably splendid, it was probably glorious, this play of the free sea, wild with lights of emerald and white and amber.

"Bully good thing it's an on-shore wind," said the cook. "If not, where would we be? Wouldn't have a show."

"That's right," said the correspondent.

The busy oiler nodded his assent.

Then the captain, in the bow, chuckled in a way that expressed humor, contempt, tragedy, all in one. "Do you think we've got much of a show now, boys?" said he.

Whereupon the three were silent, save for a trifle of hemming and hawing. To express any particular optimism at this time they felt to be childish and stupid, but they all doubtless possessed this sense of the situation in their minds. A young man thinks doggedly at such times. On the other hand, the ethics of their condition was decidedly against any open suggestion of hopelessness. So they were silent.

"Oh, well," said the captain, soothing his children, "we'll get ashore all right."

But there was that in his tone which made them think; so the oiler quoth, "Yes, if this wind holds."

The cook was bailing. "Yes! if we don't catch hell in the surf."

Canton-flannel gulls flew near and far. Sometimes they sat down on the sea, near patches of brown seaweed that rolled over the waves with a movement like carpets on a line in a gale. The birds sat comfortably in groups, and they were envied by some in the dinghy, for the wrath of the sea was no more to them than it was to a covey of prairie chickens a thousand miles inland. Often they came very close and stared at the men with black bead-like eyes. At these times they were uncanny and sinister in their unblinking scrutiny, and the men hooted angrily at them, telling them to be gone. One came, and evidently decided to alight on the top of the captain's head. The bird flew parallel to the boat and did not circle, but made short sidelong jumps in the air in chicken-fashion. His black eyes were wistfully fixed upon the captain's head. "Ugly brute," said the oiler to the bird. "You look as if you were made with a jack-knife." The cook and the correspondent swore darkly at the creature. The captain naturally wished to knock it away with the end of the heavy painter, but he did not dare do it, because anything resembling an emphatic gesture would have capsized this freighted boat; and so, with his open hand, the captain gently and carefully waved the gull away. After it had been discouraged from the pursuit the captain breathed easier on account of his hair, and others breathed easier because the bird struck their minds at this time as being somehow gruesome and ominous.

In the meantime the oiler and the correspondent rowed. They sat together in the same seat, and each rowed an oar. Then the oiler took both oars; then the correspondent took both oars; then the oiler; then the correspondent. They rowed and they rowed. The very ticklish part of the business was when the time came for the reclining one in the stern to take his turn at the oars. By the very last star of truth, it is easier to steal eggs from under a hen than it was to change seats in the dinghy. First the man in the stern slid his hand along the thwart and moved with care, as if he were of Sèvres. Then the man in the rowing-seat slid his hand along the other thwart. It was all done with the most extraordinary care. As the two sidled past each other, the whole party kept watchful eyes on the coming wave, and the captain cried: "Look out, now! Steady, there!"

The brown mats of seaweed that appeared from time to time were like islands, bits of earth. They were traveling, apparently, neither one way nor the other. They were, to all intents, stationary. They informed the men in the boat that it was making progress slowly toward the land.

The captain, rearing cautiously in the bow after the dinghy soared on a great swell, said that he had seen the lighthouse at Mosquito Inlet. Presently the cook remarked that he had seen it. The correspondent was at the oars then, and for some reason he too wished to look at the lighthouse; but his back was toward the far shore, and the waves were important, and for some time he could not seize an opportunity to turn his head. But at last there came a wave more gentle than the others, and when at the crest of it he swiftly scoured the western horizon.

"See it?" said the captain.

"No," said the correspondent, slowly; "I didn't see anything."

"Look again," said the captain. He pointed. "It's exactly in that direction."

At the top of another wave the correspondent did as he was bid, and this time his eyes chanced on a small, still thing on the edge of the swaying horizon. It was precisely like the point of a pin. It took an anxious eye to find a lighthouse so tiny.

"Think we'll make it, Captain?"

"If this wind holds and the boat don't swamp, we can't do much else," said the captain.

The little boat, lifted by each towering sea and splashed viciously by the crests, made progress that in the absence of seaweed was not apparent to those in her. She seemed just a wee thing wallowing, miraculously top up, at the mercy of five oceans. Occasionally a great spread of water, like white flames, swarmed into her.

"Bail her, cook," said the captain, serenely.

"All right, Captain," said the cheerful cook.

III

It would be difficult to describe the subtle brotherhood of men that was here established on the seas. No one said that it was so. No one mentioned it. But it dwelt in the boat, and each man felt it warm him. They were a captain, an oiler, a cook, and a correspondent, and they were friends—friends in a more curiously iron-bound degree than may be common. The hurt captain, lying against the water-jar in the bow, spoke always in a low voice and calmly; but he could never command a more ready and swiftly obedient crew than the motley three of the dinghy. It was more than a mere recognition of what was best for the common safety. There was surely in it a quality that was personal and heart-felt. And after this devotion to the commander of the boat, there was this comradeship, that the correspondent, for instance, who had been taught to be cynical of men, knew even at the time was the best experience of his life. But no one said that it was so. No one mentioned it.

"I wish we had a sail," remarked the captain. "We might try my overcoat on the end of an oar, and give you two boys a chance to rest." So the cook and correspondent held the mast and spread wide the overcoat; the oiler steered; and the little boat made good way with her new rig. Sometimes the oiler had to scull sharply to keep a sea from breaking into the boat, but otherwise sailing was a success.

Meanwhile the lighthouse had been growing slowly larger. It had now almost assumed color, and appeared like a little gray shadow on the sky. The man at the oars could not be prevented from turning his head rather often to try for a glimpse of this little gray shadow.

At last, from the top of each wave, the men in the tossing boat could see land. Even as the lighthouse was an upright shadow on the sky, this land seemed but a long black shadow on the sea. It certainly was thinner than paper. "We must be about opposite New Smyrna," said the cook, who had coasted this shore often in schooners. "Captain, by the way, I believe they abandoned that life-saving station there about a year ago."

"Did they?" said the captain.

The wind slowly died away. The cook and the correspondent were not now obliged to slave in order to hold high the oar. But the waves continued their old impetuous swooping at the dinghy, and the little craft, no longer under way, struggled woundily over them. The oiler or the correspondent took the oars again.

Shipwrecks are apropos of nothing. If men could only train for them and have them occur when the men had reached pink condition there would be less drowning at sea. Of the four in the dinghy none had slept any time worth mentioning for two days and two nights previous to embarking in the dinghy, and in the excitement of clambering about the deck of a foundering ship they had also forgotten to eat heartily.

For these reasons, and for others, neither the oiler nor the correspondent was fond of rowing at this time. The correspondent wondered ingenuously how in the name of all that was sane could there be people who thought it amusing to row a boat. It was not an amusement; it was a diabolical punishment, and even a genius of mental aberrations could never conclude that it was anything but a horror to the muscles and a crime against the back. He mentioned to the boat in general how the amusement of rowing struck him, and the weary-faced oiler smiled in full sympathy. Previously to the foundering, by the way, the oiler had worked a double watch in the engine-room of the ship.

"Take her easy now, boys," said the captain. "Don't spend yourselves. If we have to run a surf you'll need all your strength, because we'll sure have to swim for it. Take your time."

Slowly the land arose from the sea. From a black line it became a line of black and a line of white—trees and sand. Finally the captain said that he could make out a house on the shore. "That's the house of refuge, sure," said the cook. "They'll see us before long, and come out after us."

The distant lighthouse reared high. "The keeper ought to be able to make us out now, if he's looking through a glass," said the captain. "He'll notify the life-saving people."

"None of those other boats could have got ashore to give word of this wreck," said the oiler, in a low voice, "else the life-boat would be out hunting us."

Slowly and beautifully the land loomed out of the sea. The wind came again. It had veered from the north-east to the south-east. Finally a new sound struck the ears of the men in the boat. It was the low thunder of the surf on the shore. "We'll never be able to make the lighthouse now," said the captain. "Swing her head a little more north, Billie."

"A little more north, sir," said the oiler.

Whereupon the little boat turned her nose once more down the wind, and all but the oarsman watched the shore grow. Under the influence of this expansion doubt and direful apprehension were leaving the minds of the men. The management of the boat was still most absorbing, but it could not prevent a quiet cheerfulness. In an hour, perhaps, they would be ashore.

Their backbones had become thoroughly used to balancing in the boat, and they now rode this wild colt of a dinghy like circus men. The correspondent thought that he had been drenched to the skin, but happening to feel in the top pocket of his coat, he found therein eight cigars. Four of them were soaked with sea-water; four were perfectly scatheless. After a search, somebody produced three dry matches; and thereupon the four waifs rode impudently in their little boat and, with an assurance of an impending rescue shining in their eyes, puffed at the big cigars, and judged well and ill of all men. Everybody took a drink of water.

IV

"Cook," remarked the captain, "there don't seem to be any signs of life about your house of refuge."

"No," replied the cook. "Funny they don't see us!"

A broad stretch of lowly coast lay before the eyes of the men. It was of low dunes topped with dark vegetation. The roar of the surf was plain, and sometimes they could see the white lip of a wave as it spun up the beach. A tiny house was blocked out black upon the sky. Southward, the slim lighthouse lifted its little gray length.

Tide, wind, and waves were swinging the dinghy northward. "Funny they don't see us," said the men.

The surf's roar was here dulled, but its tone was nevertheless thunderous and mighty. As the boat swam over the great rollers the men sat listening to this roar. "We'll swamp sure," said everybody.

It is fair to say here that there was not a life-saving station within twenty miles in either direction; but the men did not know this fact, and in consequence they made dark and opprobrious remarks concerning the eyesight of the nation's life-savers. Four scowling men sat in the dinghy and surpassed records in the invention of epithets.

"Funny they don't see us."

The light-heartedness of a former time had completely faded. To their sharpened minds it was easy to conjure pictures of all kinds of incompetency and blindness and, indeed, cowardice. There was the shore of the populous land, and it was bitter and bitter to them that from it came no sign.

"Well," said the captain, ultimately, "I suppose we'll have to make a try for ourselves. If we stay out here too long, we'll none of us have strength left to swim after the boat swamps."

And so the oiler, who was at the oars, turned the boat straight for shore. There was a sudden tightening of muscles. There was some thinking.

"If we don't all get ashore," said the captain— "if we don't all get ashore, I suppose you fellows know where to send news of my finish?"

They then briefly exchanged some addresses and admonitions. As for the reflections of the men, there was a great deal of rage in them. Perchance they might be formulated thus: "If I am going to be drowned—if I am going to be drowned—if I am going to be drowned, why, in the name of the seven mad gods who rule the sea, was I allowed to come thus far and contemplate sand and trees? Was I brought here merely to have my nose dragged away as I was about to nibble the sacred cheese of life? It is preposterous. If this old ninny-woman, Fate, cannot do better than this, she should be deprived of the management of men's fortunes. She is an old hen who knows not her intention. If she has decided to drown me, why did she not do it in the beginning and save me all this trouble? The whole affair is absurd.—But no; she cannot mean to drown me. She dare not drown me. She cannot drown me. Not after all this work." Afterward the man might have had an impulse to shake his fist at the clouds. "Just you drown me, now, and then hear what I call you!"

The billows that came at this time were more formidable. They seemed always just about to break and roll over the little boat in a turmoil of foam. There was a preparatory and long growl in the speech of them. No mind unused to the sea would have concluded that the dinghy could ascend these sheer heights in time. The shore was still afar. The oiler was a wily surfman. "Boys," he said swiftly, "she won't live three minutes more, and we're too far out to swim. Shall I take her to sea again, Captain?"

"Yes; go ahead!" said the captain.

This oiler, by a series of quick miracles and fast and steady oarsmanship, turned the boat in the middle of the surf and took her safely to sea again.

There was a considerable silence as the boat bumped over the furrowed sea to deeper water. Then somebody in gloom spoke: "Well, anyhow, they must have seen us from the shore by now."

The gulls went in slanting flight up the wind toward the gray, desolate east. A squall, marked by dingy clouds and clouds brick-red like smoke from a burning building, appeared from the south-east.

"What do you think of those life-saving people? Ain't they peaches?"

"Funny they haven't seen us."

"Maybe they think we're out here for sport! Maybe they think we're fishin'. Maybe they think we're damned fools."

It was a long afternoon. A changed tide tried to force them southward, but wind and wave said northward. Far ahead, where coast-line, sea, and sky formed their mighty angle, there were little dots which seemed to indicate a city on the shore.

"St. Augustine?"

The captain shook his head. "Too near Mosquito Inlet."

And the oiler rowed, and then the correspondent rowed; then the oiler rowed. It was a weary business. The human back can become the seat of more aches and pains than are registered in books for the composite anatomy of a regiment. It is a limited area, but it can become the theater of innumerable muscular conflicts, tangles, wrenches, knots, and other comforts.

"Did you ever like to row, Billie?" asked the correspondent.

"No," said the oiler; "hang it!"

When one exchanged the rowing-seat for a place in the bottom of the boat, he suffered a bodily depression that caused him to be careless of everything save an obligation to wiggle one finger. There was cold sea-water swashing to and fro in the boat, and he lay in it. His head, pillowed on a thwart, was within an inch of the swirl of a wave-crest, and sometimes a particularly obstreperous sea came inboard and drenched him once more. But these matters did not annoy him. It is almost certain that if the boat had capsized he would have tumbled comfortably out upon the ocean as if he felt sure that it was a great soft mattress.

"Look! There's a man on the shore!"

"Where?"

"There! See 'im? See 'im?"

"Yes, sure! He's walking along."

"Now he's stopped. Look! He's facing us!"

"He's waving at us!"

"So he is! By thunder!"

"Ah, now we're all right! Now we're all right! There'll be a boat out here for us in half an hour."

"He's going on. He's running. He's going up to that house there."

The remote beach seemed lower than the sea, and it required a searching glance to discern the little black figure. The captain saw a floating stick, and they rowed to it. A bath towel was by some weird chance in the boat, and, tying this on the stick, the captain waved it. The oarsman did not dare turn his head, so he was obliged to ask questions.

"What's he doing now?"

"He's standing still again. He's looking, I think.—There he goes again—toward the house.—Now he's stopped again."

"Is he waving at us?"

"No, not now; he was, though."

"Look! There comes another man!"

"He's running."

"Look at him go, would you!"

"Why, he's on a bicycle. Now he's met the other man. They're both waving at us. Look!"

"There comes something up the beach."

"What the devil is that thing?"

"Why, it looks like a boat."

"Why, certainly, it's a boat."

"No; it's on wheels."

"Yes, so it is. Well, that must be the life-boat. They drag them along shore on a wagon."

"That's the life-boat, sure."

"No, by God, it's—it's an omnibus."

"I tell you it's a life-boat."

"It is not! It's an omnibus. I can see it plain. See? One of these big hotel omnibuses."

"By thunder, you're right. It's an omnibus, sure as fate. What do you suppose they are doing with an omnibus? Maybe they are going around collecting the life-crew, hey?"

"That's it, likely. Look! There's a fellow waving a little black flag. He's standing on the steps of the omnibus. There come those other two fellows. Now they're all talking together. Look at the fellow with the flag. Maybe he ain't waving it!"

"That ain't a flag, is it? That's his coat. Why, certainly, that's his coat."

"So it is; it's his coat. He's taken it off and is waving it around his head. But would you look at him swing it!"

"Oh, say, there isn't any life-saving station there. That's just a winter-resort hotel omnibus that has brought over some of the boarders to see us drown."

"What's that idiot with the coat mean? What's he signaling, anyhow?"

"It looks as if he were trying to tell us to go north. There must be a life-saving station up there."

"No; he thinks we're fishing. Just giving us a merry hand. See? Ah, there, Willie!"

"Well, I wish I could make something out of those signals. What do you suppose he means?"

"He don't mean anything; he's just playing."

"Well, if he'd just signal us to try the surf again, or to go to sea and wait, or go north, or go south, or go to hell, there would be some reason in it. But look at him! He just stands there and keeps his coat revolving like a wheel. The ass!"

"There come more people."

"Now there's quite a mob. Look! Isn't that a boat?"

"Where? Oh, I see where you mean. No, that's no boat."

"That fellow is still waving his coat."

"He must think we like to see him do that. Why don't he quit it? It don't mean anything."

"I don't know. I think he is trying to make us go north. It must be that there's a life-saving station there somewhere."

"Say, he ain't tired yet. Look at 'im wave!"

"Wonder how long he can keep that up. He's been revolving his coat ever since he caught sight of us. He's an idiot. Why aren't they getting men to bring a boat out? A fishing-boat—one of those big yawls—could come out here all right. Why don't he do something?"

"Oh, it's all right now."

"They'll have a boat out here for us in less than no time, now that they've seen us."

A faint yellow tone came into the sky over the low land. The shadows on the sea slowly deepened. The wind bore coldness with it, and the men began to shiver.

"Holy smoke!" said one, allowing his voice to express his impious mood, "if we keep on monkeying out here! If we've got to flounder out here all night!"

"Oh, we'll never have to stay here all night! Don't you worry. They've seen us now, and it won't be long before they'll come chasing out after us."

The shore grew dusky. The man waving a coat blended gradually into this gloom, and it swallowed in the same manner the omnibus and the group of people. The spray, when it dashed uproariously over the side, made the voyagers shrink and swear like men who were being branded.

"I'd like to catch the chump who waved the coat. I feel like socking him one, just for luck."

"Why? What did he do?"

"Oh, nothing, but then he seemed so damned cheerful."

In the meantime the oiler rowed, and then the correspondent

rowed, and then the oiler rowed. Gray-faced and bowed forward, they mechanically, turn by turn, plied the leaden oars. The form of the lighthouse had vanished from the southern horizon, but finally a pale star appeared, just lifting from the sea. The streaked saffron in the west passed before the all-merging darkness, and the sea to the east was black. The land had vanished, and was expressed only by the low and drear thunder of the surf.

"If I am going to be drowned—if I am going to be drowned—if I am going to be drowned, why, in the name of the seven mad gods who rule the sea, was I allowed to come thus far and contemplate sand and trees? Was I brought here merely to have my nose dragged away as I was about to nibble the sacred cheese of life?"

The patient captain, drooped over the water-jar, was sometimes obliged to speak to the oarsman.

"Keep her head up! Keep her head up!"

"Keep her head up, sir." The voices were weary and low.

This was surely a quiet evening. All save the oarsman lay heavily and listlessly in the boat's bottom. As for him, his eyes were just capable of noting the tall black waves that swept forward in a most sinister silence, save for an occasional subdued growl of a crest.

The cook's head was on a thwart, and he looked without interest at the water under his nose. He was deep in other scenes. Finally he spoke. "Billie," he murmured, dreamfully, "what kind of pie do you like best?"

V

"Pie!" said the oiler and the correspondent, agitatedly. "Don't talk about those things, blast you!"

"Well," said the cook, "I was just thinking about ham sandwiches and—"

A night on the sea in an open boat is a long night. As darkness settled finally, the shine of the light, lifting from the sea in the south, changed to full gold. On the northern horizon a new light appeared, a small bluish gleam on the edge of the waters. These two lights were the furniture of the world. Otherwise there was nothing but waves.

Two men huddled in the stern, and distances were so magnificent in the dinghy that the rower was enabled to keep his feet partly warm by thrusting them under his companions. Their legs indeed extended far under the rowing-seat until they touched the feet of the captain forward. Sometimes, despite the efforts of the tired oarsman, a wave came piling into the boat, an icy wave of the night, and the chilling water soaked them anew. They would twist their bodies for a moment and groan, and sleep the dead sleep once more, while the water in the boat gurgled about them as the craft rocked.

The plan of the oiler and the correspondent was for one to row until he lost the ability, and then arouse the other from his sea-water couch in the bottom of the boat.

The oiler plied the oars until his head drooped forward and the overpowering sleep blinded him; and he rowed yet afterward. Then he touched a man in the bottom of the boat, and called his name. "Will you spell me for a little while?" he said, meekly.

"Sure, Billie," said the correspondent, awaking and dragging himself to a sitting position. They exchanged places carefully, and the oiler, cuddling down in the sea-water at the cook's side, seemed to go to sleep instantly.

The particular violence of the sea had ceased. The waves came without snarling. The obligation of the man at the oars was to keep the boat headed so that the tilt of the rollers would not capsize her, and to preserve her from filling when the crests rushed past. The black waves were silent and hard to be seen in the darkness. Often one was almost upon the boat before the oarsman was aware.

In a low voice the correspondent addressed the captain. He was not sure that the captain was awake, although this iron man seemed to be always awake. "Captain, shall I keep her making for that light north, sir?"

The same steady voice answered him. "Yes. Keep it about two points off the port bow."

The cook had tied a life-belt around himself in order to get even the warmth which this clumsy cork contrivance could donate, and he seemed almost stove-like when a rower, whose teeth invariably chattered wildly as soon as he ceased his labor, dropped down to sleep.

The correspondent, as he rowed, looked down at the two men sleeping underfoot. The cook's arm was around the oiler's shoulders, and, with their fragmentary clothing and haggard faces, they were the babes of the sea—a grotesque rendering of the old babes in the wood.

Later he must have grown stupid at his work, for suddenly there was a growling of water, and a crest came with a roar and a swash into the boat, and it was a wonder that it did not set the cook afloat in his life-belt. The cook continued to sleep, but the oiler sat up, blinking his eyes and shaking with the new cold.

"Oh, I'm awful sorry, Billie," said the correspondent, contritely.

"That's all right, old boy," said the oiler, and lay down again and was asleep.

Presently it seemed that even the captain dozed, and the correspondent thought that he was the one man afloat on all the oceans. The wind had a voice as it came over the waves, and it was sadder than the end.

There was a long, loud swishing astern of the boat, and a gleaming trail of phosphorescence, like blue flame, was furrowed on the black waters. It might have been made by a monstrous knife.

Then there came a stillness, while the correspondent breathed with open mouth and looked at the sea.

Suddenly there was another swish and another long flash of bluish light, and this time it was alongside the boat, and might almost have been reached with an oar. The correspondent saw an enormous fin speed like a shadow through the water, hurling the crystalline spray and leaving the long glowing trail.

The correspondent looked over his shoulder at the captain. His face was hidden, and he seemed to be asleep. He looked at the babes of the sea. They certainly were asleep. So, being bereft of sympathy, he leaned a little way to one side and swore softly into the sea.

But the thing did not then leave the vicinity of the boat. Ahead or astern, on one side or the other, at intervals long or short, fled the long sparkling streak, and there was to be heard the *whirroo* of the dark fin. The speed and power of the thing was greatly to be admired. It cut the water like a gigantic and keen projectile.

The presence of this biding thing did not affect the man with the same horror that it would if he had been a picnicker. He simply looked at the sea dully and swore in an undertone.

Nevertheless, it is true that he did not wish to be alone with the thing. He wished one of his companions to awake by chance and keep him company with it. But the captain hung motionless over the water-jar, and the oiler and the cook in the bottom of the boat were plunged in slumber.

VI

"If I am going to be drowned—if I am going to be drowned—if I am going to be drowned, why, in the name of the seven mad gods who rule the sea, was I allowed to come thus far and contemplate sand and trees?"

During this dismal night, it may be remarked that a man would conclude that it was really the intention of the seven mad gods to drown him, despite the abominable injustice of it. For it was certainly an abominable injustice to drown a man who had worked so hard, so hard. The man felt it would be a crime most unnatural. Other people had drowned at sea since galleys swarmed with painted sails, but still—

When it occurs to a man that nature does not regard him as important, and that she feels she would not maim the universe by disposing of him, he at first wishes to throw bricks at the temple, and he hates deeply the fact that there are no bricks and no temples. Any visible expression of nature would surely be pelleted with his jeers.

Then, if there be no tangible thing to hoot, he feels, perhaps, the desire to confront a personification and indulge in pleas, bowed to one knee, and with hands supplicant, saying, "Yes, but I love myself."

A high cold star on a winter's night is the word he feels that she says to him. Thereafter he knows the pathos of his situation.

The men in the dinghy had not discussed these matters, but each had, no doubt, reflected upon them in silence and according to his mind. There was seldom any expression upon their faces save the general one of complete weariness. Speech was devoted to the business of the boat.

To chime the notes of his emotion, a verse mysteriously entered the correspondent's head. He had even forgotten that he had forgotten this verse, but it suddenly was in his mind.

A soldier of the Legion lay dying in Algiers;
There was lack of woman's nursing, there was
dearth of woman's tears;
But a comrade stood beside him, and he took that
comrade's hand,
And he said, "I never more shall see my own, my
native land."

In his childhood the correspondent had been made acquainted with the fact that a soldier of the Legion lay dying in Algiers, but he had never regarded the fact as important. Myriads of his school-fellows had informed him of the soldier's plight, but the dinning had naturally ended by making him perfectly indifferent. He had never considered it his affair that a soldier of the Legion lay dying in Algiers, nor had it appeared to him as a matter for sorrow. It was less to him than the breaking of a pencil's point.

Now, however, it quaintly came to him as a human, living thing. It was no longer merely a picture of a few throes in the breast of a poet, meanwhile drinking tea and warming his feet at the grate; it was an actuality—stern, mournful, and fine.

The correspondent plainly saw the soldier. He lay on the sand with his feet out straight and still. While his pale left hand was upon his chest in an attempt to thwart the going of his life, the blood came between his fingers. In the far Algerian distance, a city of low square forms was set against a sky that was faint with the last sunset hues. The correspondent, plying the oars and dreaming of the slow and slower movements of the lips of the soldier, was moved by a profound and perfectly impersonal comprehension. He was sorry for the soldier of the Legion who lay dying in Algiers.

The thing which had followed the boat and waited had evidently grown bored at the delay. There was no longer to be heard the slash of the cutwater, and there was no longer the flame of the long trail. The light in the north still glimmered, but it was apparently no nearer to the boat. Sometimes the boom of the surf rang in the correspondent's ears, and he turned the craft seaward then and rowed harder. Southward, some one had evidently built a watch-fire on the beach. It was too low and too far to be seen, but it made a shimmering, roseate reflection upon the bluff in back of it, and this could be discerned from the boat. The wind came stronger, and sometimes a wave suddenly raged out like a mountain cat, and there was to be seen the sheen and sparkle of a broken crest.

The captain, in the bow, moved on his water-jar and sat erect. "Pretty long night," he observed to the correspondent. He looked at the shore. "Those life-saving people take their time."

"Did you see that shark playing around?"

"Yes, I saw him. He was a big fellow, all right."

"Wish I had known you were awake."

Later the correspondent spoke into the bottom of the boat. "Billie!" There was a slow and gradual disentanglement. "Billie, will you spell me?"

"Sure," said the oiler.

As soon as the correspondent touched the cold, comfortable sea-water in the bottom of the boat and had huddled close to the cook's life-belt he was deep in sleep, despite the fact that his teeth played all the popular airs. This sleep was so good to him that it was but a moment before he heard a voice call his name in a tone that demonstrated the last stages of exhaustion. "Will you spell me?"

"Sure, Billie."

The light in the north had mysteriously vanished, but the correspondent took his course from the wide-awake captain.

Later in the night they took the boat farther out to sea, and the captain directed the cook to take one oar at the stern and keep the boat facing the seas. He was to call out if he should hear the thunder of the surf. This plan enabled the oiler and the correspondent to get respite together. "We'll give those boys a chance to get into shape again," said the captain. They curled down and, after a few preliminary chatterings and trembles, slept once more the dead sleep. Neither knew they had bequeathed to the cook the company of another shark, or perhaps the same shark.

As the boat caroused on the waves, spray occasionally bumped over the side and gave them a fresh soaking, but this had no power to break their repose. The ominous slash of the wind and the water affected them as it would have affected mummies.

"Boys," said the cook, with the notes of every reluctance in his voice, "she's drifted in pretty close. I guess one of you had better take her to sea again." The correspondent, aroused, heard the crash of the toppled crests.

As he was rowing, the captain gave him some whisky-and-water, and this steadied the chills out of him. "If I ever get ashore, and anybody shows me even a photograph of an oar—"

At last there was a short conversation.

"Billie!—Billie, will you spell me?"

"Sure," said the oiler.

VII

When the correspondent again opened his eyes, the sea and the sky were each of the gray hue of the dawning. Later, carmine and gold was painted upon the waters. The morning appeared finally, in its splendor, with a sky of pure blue, and the sunlight flamed on the tips of the waves.

On the distant dunes were set many little black cottages, and a tall white windmill reared above them. No man, nor dog, nor bicycle appeared on the beach. The cottages might have formed a deserted village.

The voyagers scanned the shore. A conference was held in the boat. "Well," said the captain, "if no help is coming, we might better try a run through the surf right away. If we stay out here much longer we will be too weak to do anything for ourselves at all." The others silently acquiesced in this reasoning. The boat was headed for the beach. The correspondent wondered if none ever ascended the tall wind-tower, and if then they never looked seaward. This tower was a giant, standing with its back to the plight of the ants. It represented in a degree, to the correspondent, the serenity of nature amid the struggles of the individual—nature in the wind, and nature in the vision of men. She did not seem cruel to him then, nor beneficent, nor treacherous, nor wise. But she was indifferent, flatly indifferent. It is, perhaps, plausible that a man in this situation, impressed with the unconcern of the universe, should see the innumerable flaws of his life, and have them taste wickedly in his mind, and wish for another chance. A distinction between right and wrong seems absurdly clear to him, then, in this new ignorance of the grave-edge, and he understands that if he were given another opportunity he would mend his conduct and his words, and be better and brighter during an introduction or at a tea.

"Now, boys," said the captain, "she is going to swamp sure. All we can do is to work her in as far as possible, and then when she swamps, pile out and scramble for the beach. Keep cool now, and don't jump until she swamps sure."

The oiler took the oars. Over his shoulders he scanned the surf. "Captain," he said, "I think I'd better bring her about and keep her head-on to the seas and back her in."

"All right, Billie," said the captain. "Back her in." The oiler swung the boat then, and, seated in the stern, the cook and the correspondent were obliged to look over their shoulders to contemplate the lonely and indifferent shore.

The monstrous inshore rollers heaved the boat high until the men were again enabled to see the white sheets of water scudding up the slanted beach. "We won't get in very close," said the captain. Each time a man could wrest his attention from the rollers, he turned his glance toward the shore, and in the expression of the eyes during this contemplation there was a singular quality. The correspondent, observing the others, knew that they were not afraid, but the full meaning of their glances was shrouded.

As for himself, he was too tired to grapple fundamentally with the fact. He tried to coerce his mind into thinking of it, but the mind was dominated at this time by the muscles, and the muscles said they did not care. It merely occurred to him that if he should drown it would be a shame.

There were no hurried words, no pallor, no plain agitation. The men simply looked at the shore. "Now, remember to get well clear of the boat when you jump," said the captain.

Seaward the crest of a roller suddenly fell with a thunderous crash, and the long white comber came roaring down upon the boat.

"Steady now," said the captain. The men were silent. They turned their eyes from the shore to the comber and waited. The boat slid up the incline, leaped at the furious top, bounced over it, and swung down the long back of the wave. Some water had been shipped, and the cook bailed it out.

But the next crest crashed also. The tumbling, boiling flood of white water caught the boat and whirled it almost perpendicular.

Water swarmed in from all sides. The correspondent had his hands on the gunwale at this time, and when the water entered at that place he swiftly withdrew his fingers, as if he objected to wetting them.

The little boat, drunken with this weight of water, reeled and snuggled deeper into the sea.

"Bail her out, cook! Bail her out!" said the captain.

"All right, Captain," said the cook.

"Now, boys, the next one will do for us sure," said the oiler. "Mind to jump clear of the boat."

The third wave moved forward, huge, furious, implacable. It fairly swallowed the dinghy, and almost simultaneously the men tumbled into the sea. A piece of life-belt had lain in the bottom of the boat, and as the correspondent went overboard he held this to his chest with his left hand.

The January water was icy, and he reflected immediately that it was colder than he had expected to find it off the coast of Florida. This appeared to his dazed mind as a fact important enough to be noted at the time. The coldness of the water was sad; it was tragic. This fact was somehow mixed and confused with his opinion of his own situation, so that it seemed almost a proper reason for tears. The water was cold.

When he came to the surface he was conscious of little but the noisy water. Afterward he saw his companions in the sea. The oiler was ahead in the race. He was swimming strongly and rapidly. Off to the correspondent's left, the cook's great white and corked back bulged out of the water; and in the rear the captain was hanging with his one good hand to the keel of the overturned dinghy.

There is a certain immovable quality to a shore, and the correspondent wondered at it amid the confusion of the sea.

It seemed also very attractive; but the correspondent knew that it was a long journey, and he paddled leisurely. The piece of life-preserver lay under him, and sometimes he whirled down the incline of a wave as if he were on a hand-sled.

But finally he arrived at a place in the sea where travel was beset with difficulty. He did not pause swimming to inquire what manner of current had caught him, but there his progress ceased. The shore was set before him like a bit of scenery on a stage, and he looked at it and understood with his eyes each detail of it.

As the cook passed, much farther to the left, the captain was calling to him, "Turn over on your back, cook! Turn over on your back and use the oar."

"All right, sir." The cook turned on his back, and, paddling with an oar, went ahead as if he were a canoe.

Presently the boat also passed to the left of the correspondent, with the captain clinging with one hand to the keel. He would have appeared like a man raising himself to look over a board fence if it were not for the extraordinary gymnastics of the boat. The correspondent marveled that the captain could still hold to it.

They passed on nearer to shore—the oiler, the cook, the captain—and following them went the water-jar, bouncing gaily over the seas.

The correspondent remained in the grip of this strange new enemy—a current. The shore, with its white slope of sand and its green bluff topped with little silent cottages, was spread like a picture before him. It was very near to him then, but he was impressed as one who, in a gallery, looks at a scene from Brittany or Algiers.

He thought: "I am going to drown? Can it be possible? Can it be possible? Can it be possible?" Perhaps an individual must consider his own death to be the final phenomenon of nature.

But later a wave perhaps whirled him out of this small deadly current, for he found suddenly that he could again make progress toward the shore. Later still he was aware that the captain, clinging with one hand to the keel of the dinghy, had his face turned away from the shore and toward him, and was calling his name. "Come to the boat! Come to the boat!"

In his struggle to reach the captain and the boat, he reflected that when one gets properly wearied drowning must really be a comfortable arrangement—a cessation of hostilities accompanied by a large degree of relief; and he was glad of it, for the main thing in his mind for some moments had been horror of the temporary agony. He did not wish to be hurt.

Presently he saw a man running along the shore. He was undressing with most remarkable speed. Coat, trousers, shirt, everything flew magically off him.

"Come to the boat!" called the captain.

"All right, Captain." As the correspondent paddled, he saw the captain let himself down to bottom and leave the boat. Then the correspondent performed his one little marvel of the voyage. A large wave caught him and flung him with ease and supreme speed completely over the boat and far beyond it. It struck him even then as an event in gymnastics and a true miracle of the sea. An overturned boat in the surf is not a plaything to a swimming man.

The correspondent arrived in water that reached only to his waist, but his condition did not enable him to stand for more than a moment. Each wave knocked him into a heap, and the undertow pulled at him.

Then he saw the man who had been running and undressing, and undressing and running, come bounding into the water. He dragged ashore the cook, and then waded toward the captain; but the captain waved him away and sent him to the correspondent. He was naked—naked as a tree in winter; but a halo was about his head, and he shone like a saint. He gave a strong pull, and a long drag, and a bully heave at the correspondent's hand. The correspondent, schooled in the minor formulae, said, "Thanks, old man." But suddenly the man cried, "What's that?" He pointed a swift finger. The correspondent said, "Go."

In the shallows, face downward, lay the oiler. His forehead touched sand that was periodically, between each wave, clear of the sea.

The correspondent did not know all that transpired afterward. When he achieved safe ground he fell, striking the sand with each particular part of his body. It was as if he had dropped from a roof, but the thud was grateful to him.

It seemed that instantly the beach was populated with men with blankets, clothes, and flasks, and women with coffee-pots and all the remedies sacred to their minds. The welcome of the land to the men from the sea was warm and generous; but a still and dripping shape was carried slowly up the beach, and the land's welcome for it could only be the different and sinister hospitality of the grave.

When it came night, the white waves paced to and fro in the moonlight, and the wind brought the sound of the great sea's voice to the men on the shore, and they felt that they could then be interpreters.

STEPHEN CRANE

The Blue Hotel

I

THE PALACE HOTEL AT Fort Romper was painted a light blue, a shade that is on the legs of a kind of heron, causing the bird to declare its position against any background. The Palace Hotel, then, was always screaming and howling in a way that made the dazzling winter landscape of Nebraska seem only a gray swampish hush. It stood alone on the prairie, and when the snow was falling the town two hundred yards away was not visible. But when the traveler alighted at the railway station he was obliged to pass the Palace Hotel before he could come upon the company of low clapboard houses which composed Fort Romper, and it was not to be thought that any traveler could pass the Palace Hotel without looking at it. Pat Scully, the proprietor, had proved himself a master of strategy when he chose his paints. It is true that on clear days, when the great transcontinental expresses, long lines of swaying Pullmans, swept through Fort Romper, passengers were overcome at the sight, and the cult that knows the brown-reds and the subdivisions of the dark greens of the East expressed shame, pity, horror, in a laugh. But to the citizens of this prairie town and to the people who would naturally stop there, Pat Scully had performed a feat. With this opulence and splendor, these creeds, classes, egotisms, that streamed through Romper on the rails day after day, they had no color in common.

As if the displayed delights of such a blue hotel were not sufficiently enticing, it was Scully's habit to go every morning and evening to meet the leisurely trains that stopped at Romper and work his seductions upon any man that he might see wavering, gripsack in hand.

One morning, when a snow-crusted engine dragged its long string of freight cars and its one passenger coach to the station, Scully performed the marvel of catching three men. One was a shaky and quick-eyed Swede, with a great shining cheap valise; one was a tall bronzed cowboy, who was on his way to a ranch near the Dakota line; one was a little silent man from the East, who didn't look it, and didn't announce it. Scully practically made them prisoners. He was so nimble and merry and kindly that each probably felt it would be the height of brutality to try to escape. They trudged off over the creaking board sidewalks in the wake of the eager little Irishman. He wore a heavy fur cap squeezed tightly down on his head. It caused his two red ears to stick out stiffly, as if they were made of tin.

At last, Scully, elaborately, with boisterous hospitality, conducted them through the portals of the blue hotel. The room which they entered was small. It seemed to be merely a proper temple for an enormous stove, which, in the center, was humming with godlike violence. At various points on its surface the iron had become luminous and glowed yellow from the heat. Beside the stove Scully's son Johnnie was playing High-Five with an old farmer who had whiskers both gray and sandy. They were quarreling. Frequently the old farmer turned his face toward a box of sawdust—colored brown from tobacco juice—that was behind the stove, and spat with an air of great impatience and irritation. With a loud flourish of words Scully destroyed the game of cards, and bustled his son upstairs with part of the baggage of the new guests. He himself conducted them to three basins of the coldest water in the world. The cowboy and the Easterner burnished themselves fiery red with this water, until it seemed to be some kind of metal-polish. The Swede, however, merely dipped his fingers gingerly and with trepidation. It was notable that throughout this series of small ceremonies the three travelers were made to feel that Scully was very benevolent. He was conferring great favors upon them. He handed the towel from one to another with an air of philanthropic impulse.

Afterward they went to the first room, and, sitting about the stove, listened to Scully's officious clamor at his daughters, who were preparing the midday meal. They reflected in the silence of experienced men who tread carefully amid new people. Nevertheless, the old farmer, stationary, invincible in his chair near the warmest part of the stove, turned his face from the sawdust-box frequently and addressed a glowing commonplace to the strangers. Usually he was answered in short but adequate sentences by either the cowboy or the Easterner. The Swede said nothing. He seemed to be occupied in making furtive estimates of each man in the room. One might have thought that he had the sense of silly suspicion which comes to guilt. He resembled a badly frightened man.

Later, at dinner, he spoke a little, addressing his conversation entirely to Scully. He volunteered that he had come from New York, where for ten years he had worked as a tailor. These facts seemed to strike Scully as fascinating, and afterward he volunteered that he had lived at Romper for fourteen years. The Swede asked about the crops and the price of labor. He seemed barely to listen to Scully's extended replies. His eyes continued to rove from man to man.

Finally, with a laugh and a wink, he said that some of these Western communities were very dangerous; and after his statement he straightened his legs under the table, tilted his head, and laughed again, loudly. It was plain that the demonstration had no meaning to the others. They looked at him wondering and in silence.

II

As the men trooped heavily back into the front room, the two little windows presented views of a turmoiling sea of snow. The huge arms of the wind were making attempts—mighty, circular, futile—to embrace the flakes as they sped. A gate-post like a still man with a blanched face stood aghast amid this profligate fury. In a hearty voice Scully announced the presence of a blizzard. The guests of the blue hotel, lighting their pipes, assented with grunts of lazy masculine contentment. No island of the sea could be exempt in the degree of this little room with its humming stove. Johnnie, son of Scully, in a tone which defined his opinion of his ability as a card-player, challenged the old farmer of both gray and sandy whiskers to a game of High-Five. The farmer agreed with a contemptuous and bitter scoff. They sat close to the stove, and squared their knees under a wide board. The cowboy and the Easterner watched the game with interest. The Swede remained near the window, aloof, but with a countenance that showed signs of an inexplicable excitement.

The play of Johnnie and the gray-beard was suddenly ended by another quarrel. The old man arose while casting a look of heated scorn at his adversary. He slowly buttoned his coat, and then stalked with fabulous dignity from the room. In the discreet silence of all the other men the Swede laughed. His laughter rang somehow childish. Men by this time had begun to look at him askance, as if they wished to inquire what ailed him.

A new game was formed jocosely. The cowboy volunteered to become the partner of Johnnie, and they all then turned to ask the Swede to throw in his lot with the little Easterner. He asked some questions about the game, and, learning that it wore many names, and that he had played it when it was under an alias, he accepted the invitation. He strode toward the men nervously, as if he expected to be assaulted. Finally, seated, he gazed from face to face and laughed shrilly. This laugh was so strange that the Easterner looked up quickly, the cowboy sat intent and with his mouth open, and Johnnie paused, holding the cards with still fingers.

Afterward there was a short silence. Then Johnnie said, "Well, let's get at it. Come on now!" They pulled their chairs forward until their knees were bunched under the board. They began to play, and their interest in the game caused the others to forget the manner of the Swede.

The cowboy was a board-whacker. Each time that he held superior cards he whanged them, one by one, with exceeding force, down upon the improvised table, and took the tricks with a glowing air of prowess and pride that sent thrills of indignation into the hearts of his opponents. A game with a board-whacker in it is sure to become intense. The countenances of the Easterner and the Swede were miserable whenever the cowboy thundered down his aces and kings, while Johnnie, his eyes gleaming with joy, chuckled and chuckled.

Because of the absorbing play none considered the strange ways of the Swede. They paid strict heed to the game. Finally, during a lull caused by a new deal, the Swede suddenly addressed Johnnie: "I suppose there have been a good many men killed in this room." The jaws of the others dropped and they looked at him.

"What in hell are you talking about?" said Johnnie.

The Swede laughed again his blatant laugh, full of a kind of false courage and defiance. "Oh, you know what I mean all right," he answered.

"I'm a liar if I do!" Johnnie protested. The card was halted, and the men stared at the Swede. Johnnie evidently felt that as the son of the proprietor he should make a direct inquiry. "Now, what might you be drivin' at, mister?" he asked. The Swede winked at him. It was a wink full of cunning. His fingers shook on the edge of the board. "Oh, maybe you think I have been to nowheres. Maybe you think I'm a tenderfoot?"

"I don't know nothin' about you," answered Johnnie, "and I don't give a damn where you've been. All I got to say is that I don't know what you're driving at. There hain't never been nobody killed in this room."

The cowboy, who had been steadily gazing at the Swede, then spoke: "What's wrong with you, mister?"

Apparently it seemed to the Swede that he was formidably menaced. He shivered and turned white near the corners of his mouth. He sent an appealing glance in the direction of the little Easterner. During these moments he did not forget to wear his air of advanced pot-valor. "They say they don't know what I mean," he remarked mockingly to the Easterner.

The latter answered after prolonged and cautious reflection. "I don't understand you," he said, impassively.

The Swede made a movement then which announced that he thought he had encountered treachery from the only quarter where he had expected sympathy, if not help. "Oh, I see you are all against me. I see—"

The cowboy was in a state of deep stupefaction. "Say," he cried, as he tumbled the deck violently down upon the board, "say, what are you gittin' at, hey?"

The Swede sprang up with the celerity of a man escaping from a snake on the floor. "I don't want to fight!" he shouted. "I don't want to fight!"

The cowboy stretched his long legs indolently and deliberately. His hands were in his pockets. He spat into the sawdust-box. "Well, who the hell thought you did?" he inquired.

The Swede backed rapidly toward a corner of the room. His hands were out protectingly in front of his chest, but he was making an obvious struggle to control his fright. "Gentlemen," he quavered, "I suppose I am going to be killed before I can leave this house! I suppose I am going to be killed before I can leave this house!" In his eyes was the dying-swan look. Through the windows could be seen the snow turning blue in the shadow of dusk. The wind tore at the house, and some loose thing beat regularly against the clapboards like a spirit tapping.

A door opened, and Scully himself entered. He paused in surprise as he noted the tragic attitude of the Swede. Then he said, "What's the matter here?"

The Swede answered him swiftly and eagerly: "These men are going to kill me."

"Kill you!" ejaculated Scully. "Kill you! What are you talkin'?"

The Swede made the gesture of a martyr.

Scully wheeled sternly upon his son. "What is this, Johnnie?"

The lad had grown sullen. "Damned if I know," he answered. "I can't make no sense to it." He began to shuffle the cards, fluttering them together with an angry snap. "He says a good many men have been killed in this room, or something like that. And he says he's goin' to be killed here too. I don't know what ails him. He's crazy, I shouldn't wonder."

Scully then looked for explanation to the cowboy, but the cowboy simply shrugged his shoulders.

"Kill you?" said Scully again to the Swede. "Kill you? Man, you're off your nut."

"Oh, I know," burst out the Swede. "I know what will happen. Yes, I'm crazy—yes. Yes, of course, I'm crazy—yes. But I know one thing—" There was a sort of sweat of misery and terror upon his face. "I know I won't get out of here alive."

The cowboy drew a deep breath, as if his mind was passing into the last stages of dissolution. "Well, I'm doggoned," he whispered to himself.

Scully wheeled suddenly and faced his son. "You've been troublin' this man!"

Johnnie's voice was loud with its burden of grievance. "Why, good Gawd, I ain't done nothin' to 'im."

The Swede broke in. "Gentlemen, do not disturb yourselves.

I will leave this house. I will go away, because"—he accused them dramatically with his glance—"because I do not want to be killed."

Scully was furious with his son. "Will you tell me what is the matter, you young devil? What's the matter, anyhow? Speak out!"

"Blame it!" cried Johnnie in despair, "don't I tell you I don't know? He—he says we want to kill him, and that's all I know. I can't tell what ails him."

The Swede continued to repeat: "Never mind, Mr. Scully; never mind. I will leave this house. I will go away, because I do not wish to be killed. Yes, of course, I am crazy—yes. But I know one thing! I will go away. I will leave this house. Never mind, Mr. Scully; never mind. I will go away."

"You will not go 'way," said Scully. "You will not go 'way until I hear the reason of this business. If anybody has troubled you I will take care of him. This is my house. You are under my roof, and I will not allow any peaceable man to be troubled here." He cast a terrible eye upon Johnnie, the cowboy, and the Easterner.

"Never mind, Mr. Scully; never mind. I will go away. I do not wish to be killed." The Swede moved toward the door which opened upon the stairs. It was evidently his intention to go at once for his baggage.

"No, no," shouted Scully peremptorily; but the white-faced man slid by him and disappeared. "Now," said Scully severely, "what does this mane?"

Johnnie and the cowboy cried together: "Why, we didn't do nothin' to 'im!"

Scully's eyes were cold. "No," he said, "you didn't?"

Johnnie swore a deep oath. "Why, this is the wildest loon I ever see. We didn't do nothin' at all. We were just sittin' here playin' cards, and he—"

The father suddenly spoke to the Easterner. "Mr. Blanc," he asked, "what has these boys been doin'?"

The Easterner reflected again. "I didn't see anything wrong at all," he said at last, slowly.

Scully began to howl. "But what does it mane?" He stared ferociously at his son. "I have a mind to lather you for this, me boy."

Johnnie was frantic. "Well, what have I done?" he bawled at his father.

III

"I think you are tongue-tied," said Scully finally to his son, the cowboy, and the Easterner; and at the end of this scornful sentence he left the room.

Upstairs the Swede was swiftly fastening the straps of his great valise. Once his back happened to be half turned toward the door, and, hearing a noise there, he wheeled and sprang up, uttering a loud cry. Scully's wrinkled visage showed grimly in the light of the small lamp he carried. This yellow effulgence, streaming upward, colored only his prominent features, and left his eyes, for instance, in mysterious shadow. He resembled a murderer.

"Man! man!" he exclaimed, "have you gone daffy?"

"Oh, no! Oh, no!" rejoined the other. "There are people in this world who know pretty nearly as much as you do—understand?"

For a moment they stood gazing at each other. Upon the Swede's deathly pale cheeks were two spots brightly crimson and sharply edged, as if they had been carefully painted. Scully placed the light on the table and sat himself on the edge of the bed. He spoke ruminatively. "By cracky, I never heard of such a thing in my life. It's a complete muddle. I can't, for the soul of me, think how you ever got this idea into your head." Presently he lifted his eyes and asked: "And did you sure think they were going to kill you?"

The Swede scanned the old man as if he wished to see into his mind. "I did," he said at last. He obviously suspected that this answer might precipitate an outbreak. As he pulled on a strap his whole arm shook, the elbow wavering like a bit of paper.

Scully banged his hand impressively on the footboard of the bed. "Why, man, we're goin' to have a line of ilictric street-cars in this town next spring."

"'A line of electric street-cars,'" repeated the Swede, stupidly.

"And," said Scully, "there's a new railroad goin' to be built down from Broken Arm to here. Not to mintion the four churches and the smashin' big brick schoolhouse. Then there's the big factory, too. Why, in two years Romper'll be a met-tro-*pol*-is."

Having finished the preparation of his baggage, the Swede straightened himself. "Mr. Scully," he said, with sudden hardihood, "how much do I owe you?"

"You don't owe me anythin'," said the old man, angrily.

"Yes, I do," retorted the Swede. He took seventy-five cents from his pocket and tendered it to Scully; but the latter snapped his fingers in disdainful refusal. However, it happened that they both stood gazing in a strange fashion at three silver pieces on the Swede's open palm.

"I'll not take your money," said Scully at last. "Not after what's been goin' on here." Then a plan seemed to strike him. "Here," he cried, picking up his lamp and moving toward the door. "Here! Come with me a minute."

"No," said the Swede, in overwhelming alarm.

"Yes," urged the old man. "Come on! I want you to come and see a picter—just across the hall—in my room."

The Swede must have concluded that his hour was come. His jaw dropped and his teeth showed like a dead man's. He ultimately followed Scully across the corridor, but he had the step of one hung in chains.

Scully flashed the light high on the wall of his own chamber. There was revealed a ridiculous photograph of a little girl. She was leaning against a balustrade of gorgeous decoration, and the formidable bang to her hair was prominent. The figure was as graceful as an upright sled-stake, and, withal, it was of the hue of lead. "There," said Scully, tenderly, "that's the picter of my little girl that died. Her name was Carrie. She had the purtiest hair you ever saw! I was that fond of her, she—"

Turning then, he saw that the Swede was not contemplating the picture at all, but, instead, was keeping keen watch on the gloom in the rear.

"Look, man!" cried Scully, heartily. "That's the picter of my little gal that died. Her name was Carrie. And then here's the picter of my oldest boy, Michael. He's a lawyer in Lincoln, an' doin' well. I gave that boy a grand eddication, and I'm glad for it now. He's a fine boy. Look at 'im now. Ain't he bold as blazes, him there in Lincoln, an honored an' respicted gintleman! An honored and respicted gintleman," concluded Scully with a flourish. And, so saying, he smote the Swede jovially on the back.

The Swede faintly smiled.

"Now," said the old man, "there's only one more thing." He

dropped suddenly to the floor and thrust his head beneath the bed. The Swede could hear his muffled voice. "I'd keep it under me piller if it wasn't for that boy Johnnie. Then there's the old woman— Where is it now? I never put it twice in the same place. Ah, now come out with you!"

Presently he backed clumsily from under the bed, dragging with him an old coat rolled into a bundle. "I've fetched him," he muttered. Kneeling on the floor, he unrolled the coat and extracted from its heart a large yellow-brown whisky-bottle.

His first maneuver was to hold the bottle up to the light. Reassured, apparently, that nobody had been tampering with it, he thrust it with a generous movement toward the Swede.

The weak-kneed Swede was about to eagerly clutch this element of strength, but he suddenly jerked his hand away and cast a look of horror upon Scully.

"Drink," said the old man affectionately. He had risen to his feet, and now stood facing the Swede.

There was a silence. Then again Scully again: "Drink!"

The Swede laughed wildly. He grabbed the bottle, put it to his mouth; and as his lips curled absurdly around the opening and his throat worked, he kept his glance, burning with hatred, upon the old man's face.

IV

After the departure of Scully the three men, with the cardboard still upon their knees, preserved for a long time an astounded silence. Then Johnnie said: "That's the dod-dangedest Swede I ever see."

"He ain't no Swede," said the cowboy scornfully.

"Well, what is he then?" cried Johnnie. "What is he then?"

"It's my opinion," replied the cowboy deliberately, "he's some kind of a Dutchman." It was a venerable custom of the country to entitle as Swedes all light-haired men who spoke with a heavy tongue. In consequence the idea of the cowboy was not without its daring. "Yes, sir," he repeated. "It's my opinion this feller is some kind of a Dutchman."

"Well, he says he's a Swede, anyhow," muttered Johnnie, sulkily. He turned to the Easterner: "What do you think, Mr. Blanc?"

"Oh, I don't know," replied the Easterner.

"Well, what do you think makes him act that way?" asked the cowboy.

"Why, he's frightened." The Easterner knocked his pipe against a rim of the stove. "He's clear frightened out of his boots."

"What at?" cried Johnnie and the cowboy together.

The Easterner reflected over his answer.

"What at?" cried the others again.

"Oh, I don't know, but it seems to me this man has been reading dime novels, and he thinks he's right out in the middle of it—the shootin' and stabbin' and all."

"But," said the cowboy, deeply scandalized, "this ain't Wyoming, ner none of them places. This is Nebrasker."

"Yes," added Johnnie, "an' why don't he wait till he gits *out West*?"

The traveled Easterner laughed. "It isn't different there even—not in these days. But he thinks he's right in the middle of hell."

Johnnie and the cowboy mused long.

"It's awful funny," remarked Johnnie at last.

"Yes," said the cowboy. "This is a queer game. I hope we don't git snowed in, because then we'd have to stand this here man bein' around with us all the time. That wouldn't be no good."

"I wish pop would throw him out," said Johnnie.

Presently they heard a loud stamping on the stairs, accompanied by ringing jokes in the voice of old Scully, and laughter, evidently from the Swede. The men around the stove stared vacantly at each other. "Gosh!" said the cowboy. The door flew open, and old Scully, flushed and anecdotal, came into the room. He was jabbering at the Swede, who followed him, laughing bravely. It was the entry of two roisterers from a banquet hall.

"Come now," said Scully sharply to the three seated men, "move up and give us a chance at the stove." The cowboy and the Easterner obediently sidled their chairs to make room for the new-comers. Johnnie, however, simply arranged himself in a more indolent attitude, and then remained motionless.

"Come! Git over, there," said Scully.

"Plenty of room on the other side of the stove," said Johnnie.

"Do you think we want to sit in the draught?" roared the father.

But the Swede here interposed with a grandeur of confidence.

"No, no. Let the boy sit where he likes," he cried in a bullying voice to the father.

"All right! All right!" said Scully, deferentially. The cowboy and the Easterner exchanged glances of wonder.

The five chairs were formed in a crescent about one side of the stove. The Swede began to talk; he talked arrogantly, profanely, angrily. Johnnie, the cowboy, and the Easterner maintained a morose silence, while old Scully appeared to be receptive and eager, breaking in constantly with sympathetic ejaculations.

Finally the Swede announced that he was thirsty. He moved in his chair, and said that he would go for a drink of water.

"I'll git it for you," cried Scully at once.

"No," said the Swede, contemptuously. "I'll get it for myself." He arose and stalked with the air of an owner off into the executive parts of the hotel.

As soon as the Swede was out of hearing Scully sprang to his feet and whispered intensely to the others: "Upstairs he thought I was tryin' to poison 'im."

"Say," said Johnnie, "this makes me sick. Why don't you throw 'im out in the snow?"

"Why, he's all right now," declared Scully. "It was only that he was from the East, and he thought this was a tough place. That's all. He's all right now."

The cowboy looked with admiration upon the Easterner. "You were straight," he said. "You were on to that there Dutchman."

"Well," said Johnnie to his father, "he may be all right now, but I don't see it. Other time he was scared, but now he's too fresh."

Scully's speech was always a combination of Irish brogue and idiom, Western twang and idiom, and scraps of curiously formal diction taken from the story-books and newspapers. He now hurled a strange mass of language at the head of his son. "What do I keep? What do I keep? What do I keep?" he demanded, in a voice of thunder. He slapped his knee impressively, to indicate that he himself was going to make reply, and that all should heed. "I keep a hotel," he shouted. "A hotel, do you mind? A guest under my roof has sacred privileges. He is to be intimidated by none. Not one word shall he hear that would prijudice him in favor of goin' away. I'll not have it. There's no place in this here town where they can say they iver took in a guest of mine because he was afraid to stay here." He wheeled suddenly upon the cowboy and the Easterner. "Am I right?"

"Yes, Mr. Scully," said the cowboy, "I think you're right."

"Yes, Mr. Scully," said the Easterner, "I think you're right."

V

At six-o'clock supper, the Swede fizzed like a fire-wheel. He sometimes seemed on the point of bursting into riotous song, and in all his madness he was encouraged by old Scully. The Easterner was encased in reserve; the cowboy sat in wide-mouthed amazement, forgetting to eat, while Johnnie wrathily demolished great plates of food. The daughters of the house, when they were obliged to replenish the biscuits, approached as warily as Indians, and, having succeeded in their purpose, fled with ill-concealed trepidation. The Swede domineered the whole feast, and he gave it the appearance of a cruel bacchanal. He seemed to have grown suddenly taller; he gazed, brutally disdainful, into every face. His voice rang through the room. Once when he jabbed out harpoon-fashion with his fork to pinion a biscuit, the weapon nearly impaled the hand of the Easterner, which had been stretched quietly out for the same biscuit.

After supper, as the men filed toward the other room, the Swede smote Scully ruthlessly on the shoulder. "Well, old boy, that was a good, square meal." Johnnie looked hopefully at his father; he knew that shoulder was tender from an old fall; and, indeed, it appeared for a moment as if Scully was going to flame out over the matter, but in the end he smiled a sickly smile and remained silent. The others understood from his manner that he was admitting his responsibility for the Swede's new view-point.

Johnnie, however, addressed his parent in an aside. "Why don't you license somebody to kick you downstairs?" Scully scowled darkly by way of reply.

When they were gathered about the stove, the Swede insisted on another game of High-Five. Scully gently deprecated the plan at first, but the Swede turned a wolfish glare upon him. The old man subsided, and the Swede canvassed the others. In his tone there was always a great threat. The cowboy and the Easterner both remarked indifferently that they would play. Scully said that he would presently have to go to meet the 6:58 train, and so the Swede turned menacingly upon Johnnie. For a moment their glances crossed like blades, and then Johnnie smiled and said, "Yes, I'll play."

They formed a square, with the little board on their knees. The Easterner and the Swede were again partners. As the play went on, it was noticeable that the cowboy was not board-whacking as usual. Meanwhile, Scully, near the lamp, had put on his spectacles and, with an appearance curiously like an old priest, was reading a newspaper. In time he went out to meet the 6:58 train, and, despite his precautions, a gust of polar wind whirled into the room as he opened the door. Besides scattering the cards, it chilled the players to the marrow. The Swede cursed frightfully. When Scully returned, his entrance disturbed a cosy and friendly scene. The Swede again cursed. But presently they were once more intent, their heads bent forward and their hands moving swiftly. The Swede had adopted the fashion of board-whacking.

Scully took up his paper and for a long time remained immersed in matters which were extraordinarily remote from him. The lamp burned badly, and once he stopped to adjust the wick. The newspaper, as he turned from page to page, rustled with a slow and comfortable sound. Then suddenly he heard three terrible words: "You are cheatin'!"

Such scenes often prove that there can be little of dramatic import in environment. Any room can present a tragic front; any room can be comic. This little den was now hideous as a torture-chamber. The new faces of the men themselves had changed it upon the instant. The Swede held a huge fist in front of Johnnie's face, while the latter looked steadily over it into the blazing orbs of his accuser. The Easterner had grown pallid; the cowboy's jaw had dropped in that expression of bovine amazement which was one of his important mannerisms. After the three words, the first sound in the room was made by Scully's paper as it floated forgotten to his feet. His spectacles had also fallen from his nose, but by a clutch he had saved them in air. His hand, grasping the spectacles, now remained poised awkwardly and near his shoulder. He stared at the card-players.

Probably the silence was while a second elapsed. Then, if the floor had been suddenly twitched out from under the men they could not have moved quicker. The five had projected themselves headlong toward a common point. It happened that Johnnie, in rising to hurl himself upon the Swede, had stumbled slightly because of his curiously instinctive care for the cards and the board. The loss of the moment allowed time for the arrival of Scully, and also allowed the cowboy time to give the Swede a great push which sent him staggering back. The men found tongue together, and hoarse shouts of rage, appeal, or fear burst from every throat. The cowboy pushed and jostled feverishly at the Swede, and the Easterner and Scully clung wildly to Johnnie; but through the smoky air, above the swaying bodies of the peace-compellers, the eyes of the two warriors ever sought each other in glances of challenge that were at once hot and steely.

Of course the board had been overturned, and now the whole company of cards was scattered over the floor, where the boots of the men trampled the fat and painted kings and queens as they gazed with their silly eyes at the war that was waging above them.

Scully's voice was dominating the yells. "Stop now! Stop, I say! Stop, now—"

Johnnie, as he struggled to burst through the rank formed by Scully and the Easterner, was crying, "Well, he says I cheated! He says I cheated! I won't allow no man to say I cheated! If he says I cheated, he's a——!"

The cowboy was telling the Swede, "Quit, now! Quit, d'ye hear—"

The screams of the Swede never ceased: "He did cheat! I saw him! I saw him—"

As for the Easterner, he was importuning in a voice that was not heeded: "Wait a moment, can't you? Oh, wait a moment. What's the good of a fight over a game of cards? Wait a moment—"

In this tumult no complete sentences were clear. "Cheat"—"Quit"—"He says"—these fragments pierced the uproar and rang out sharply. It was remarkable that, whereas Scully undoubtedly made the most noise, he was the least heard of any of the riotous band.

Then suddenly there was a great cessation. It was as if each man had paused for breath; and although the room was still lighted with the anger of men, it could be seen that there was no danger of immediate conflict, and at once Johnnie, shouldering his way forward, almost succeeded in confronting the Swede. "What did you say I cheated for? What did you say I cheated for? I don't cheat, and I won't let no man say I do!"

The Swede said, "I saw you! I saw you!"

"Well," cried Johnnie, "I'll fight any man what says I cheat!"

"No, you won't," said the cowboy. "Not here."

"Ah, be still, can't you?" said Scully, coming between them.

The quiet was sufficient to allow the Easterner's voice to be heard. He was repeating, "Oh, wait a moment, can't you? What's the good of a fight over a game of cards? Wait a moment!"

Johnnie, his red face appearing above his father's shoulder, hailed the Swede again. "Did you say I cheated?"

The Swede showed his teeth. "Yes."

"Then," said Johnnie, "we must fight."

"Yes, fight," roared the Swede. He was like a demoniac. "Yes, fight! I'll show you what kind of a man I am! I'll show you who you want to fight! Maybe you think I can't fight! Maybe you think I can't! I'll show you, you skin, you card-sharp! Yes, you cheated! You cheated! You cheated!"

"Well, let's go at it, then, mister," said Johnnie, coolly.

The cowboy's brow was beaded with sweat from his efforts in intercepting all sorts of raids. He turned in despair to Scully. "What are you goin' to do now?"

A change had come over the Celtic visage of the old man. He now seemed all eagerness; his eyes glowed.

"We'll let them fight," he answered, stalwartly. "I can't put up with it any longer. I've stood this damned Swede till I'm sick. We'll let them fight."

VI

The men prepared to go out of doors. The Easterner was so nervous that he had great difficulty in getting his arms into the sleeves of his new leather coat. As the cowboy drew his fur cap down over his ears his hands trembled. In fact, Johnnie and old Scully were the only ones who displayed no agitation. These preliminaries were conducted without words.

Scully threw open the door. "Well, come on," he said. Instantly a terrific wind caused the flame of the lamp to struggle at its wick, while a puff of black smoke sprang from the chimney-top. The stove was in mid-current of the blast, and its voice swelled to equal the roar of the storm. Some of the scarred and bedabbled cards were caught up from the floor and dashed helplessly against the farther wall. The men lowered their heads and plunged into the tempest as into a sea.

No snow was falling, but great whirls and clouds of flakes, swept up from the ground by the frantic winds, were streaming southward with the speed of bullets. The covered land was blue with the sheen of an unearthly satin, and there was no other hue save where, at the low, black railway station—which seemed incredibly distant—one light gleamed like a tiny jewel. As the men floundered into a thigh-deep drift, it was known that the Swede was bawling out something. Scully went to him, put a hand on his shoulder, and projected an ear. "What's that you say?" he shouted.

"I say," bawled the Swede again, "I won't stand much show against this gang. I know you'll all pitch on me."

Scully smote him reproachfully on the arm. "Tut, man!" he yelled. The wind tore the words from Scully's lips and scattered them far alee.

"You are all a gang of—" boomed the Swede, but the storm also seized the remainder of this sentence.

Immediately turning their backs upon the wind, the men had swung around a corner to the sheltered side of the hotel. It was the function of the little house to preserve here, amid this great devastation of snow, an irregular V-shape of heavily encrusted grass, which crackled beneath the feet. One could imagine the great drifts piled against the windward side. When the party reached the comparative peace of this spot it was found that the Swede was still bellowing.

"Oh, I know what kind of a thing this is! I know you'll all pitch on me. I can't lick you all!"

Scully turned upon him panther-fashion. "You'll not have to whip all of us. You'll have to whip my son Johnnie. An' the man what troubles you durin' that time will have me to dale with."

The arrangements were swiftly made. The two men faced each other, obedient to the harsh commands of Scully, whose face, in the subtly luminous gloom, could be seen set in the austere impersonal lines that are pictured on the countenances of the Roman veterans.

The Easterner's teeth were chattering, and he was hopping up and down like a mechanical toy. The cowboy stood rock-like.

The contestants had not stripped off any clothing. Each was in his ordinary attire. Their fists were up, and they eyed each other in a calm that had the elements of leonine cruelty in it.

During this pause, the Easterner's mind, like a film, took lasting impressions of three men—the iron-nerved master of the ceremony; the Swede, pale, motionless, terrible; and Johnnie, serene yet ferocious, brutish yet heroic. The entire prelude had in it a tragedy greater than the tragedy of action, and this aspect was accentuated by the long, mellow cry of the blizzard, as it sped the tumbling and wailing flakes into the black abyss of the south.

"Now!" said Scully.

The two combatants leaped forward and crashed together like bullocks. There was heard the cushioned sound of blows, and of a curse squeezing out from between the tight teeth of one.

As for the spectators, the Easterner's pent-up breath exploded from him with a pop of relief, absolute relief from the tension of the preliminaries. The cowboy bounded into the air with a yowl. Scully was immovable as from supreme amazement and fear at the fury of the fight which he himself had permitted and arranged.

For a time the encounter in the darkness was such a perplexity of flying arms that it presented no more detail than would a swiftly revolving wheel. Occasionally a face, as if illumined by a flash of light, would shine out, ghastly and marked with pink spots. A moment later, the men might have been known as shadows, if it were not for the involuntary utterance of oaths that came from them in whispers.

Suddenly a holocaust of warlike desire caught the cowboy, and he bolted forward with the speed of a broncho. "Go it, Johnnie! go it! Kill him! Kill him!"

Scully confronted him. "Kape back," he said; and by his glance the cowboy could tell that this man was Johnnie's father.

To the Easterner there was a monotony of unchangeable fighting that was an abomination. This confused mingling was eternal to his sense, which was concentrated in a longing for the end, the priceless end. Once the fighters lurched near him, and as he scrambled hastily backward he heard them breathe like men on the rack.

"Kill him, Johnnie! Kill him! Kill him! Kill him!" The cowboy's face was contorted like one of those agony masks in museums.

"Keep still," said Scully, icily.

Then there was a sudden loud grunt, incomplete, cut short, and Johnnie's body swung away from the Swede and fell with sickening heaviness to the grass. The cowboy was barely in time to prevent the mad Swede from flinging himself upon his prone adversary. "No, you don't," said the cowboy, interposing an arm. "Wait a second."

Scully was at his son's side. "Johnnie! Johnnie, me boy!" His voice had a quality of melancholy tenderness. "Johnnie! Can you go on with it?" He looked anxiously down into the bloody, pulpy face of his son.

There was a moment of silence, and then Johnnie answered in his ordinary voice, "Yes, I—it—yes."

Assisted by his father he struggled to his feet. "Wait a bit now till you git your wind," said the old man.

A few paces away the cowboy was lecturing the Swede. "No, you don't! Wait a second!"

The Easterner was plucking at Scully's sleeve. "Oh, this is enough," he pleaded. "This is enough! Let it go as it stands. This is enough!"

"Bill," said Scully, "git out of the road." The cowboy stepped aside. "Now." The combatants were actuated by a new caution as they advanced toward collision. They glared at each other, and then the Swede aimed a lightning blow that carried with it his entire weight. Johnnie was evidently half stupid from weakness, but he miraculously dodged, and his fist sent the overbalanced Swede sprawling.

The cowboy, Scully, and the Easterner burst into a cheer that was like a chorus of triumphant soldiery, but before its conclusion the Swede had scuffed agilely to his feet and come in berserk abandon at his foe. There was another perplexity of flying arms, and Johnnie's body again swung away and fell, even as a bundle might fall from a roof. The Swede instantly staggered to a little wind-waved tree and leaned upon it, breathing like an engine, while his savage and flame-lit eyes roamed from face to face as the men bent over Johnnie. There was a splendor of isolation in his situation at this time which the Easterner felt once when, lifting his eyes from the man on the ground, he beheld that mysterious and lonely figure, waiting.

"Are you any good yet, Johnnie?" asked Scully in a broken voice.

The son gasped and opened his eyes languidly. After a moment he answered, "No—I ain't—any good—any—more." Then from shame and bodily ill, he began to weep, the tears furrowing down through the blood-stains on his face. "He was too—too—too heavy for me."

Scully straightened and addressed the waiting figure. "Stranger," he said, evenly, "it's all up with our side." Then his voice changed into that vibrant huskiness which is commonly the tone of the most simple and deadly announcements. "Johnnie is whipped."

Without replying, the victor moved off on the route to the front door of the hotel.

The cowboy was formulating new and unspellable blasphemies. The Easterner was startled to find that they were out in a wind that seemed to come direct from the shadowed arctic floes. He heard again the wail of the snow as it was flung to its grave in the south. He knew now that all this time the cold had been sinking into him deeper and deeper, and he wondered that he had not perished. He felt indifferent to the condition of the vanquished man.

"Johnnie, can you walk?" asked Scully.

"Did I hurt—hurt him any?" asked the son.

"Can you walk, boy? Can you walk?"

Johnnie's voice was suddenly strong. There was a robust impatience in it. "I asked you whether I hurt him any!"

"Yes, yes, Johnnie," answered the cowboy, consolingly; "he's hurt a good deal."

They raised him from the ground, and as soon as he was on his feet he went tottering off, rebuffing all attempts at assistance. When the party rounded the corner they were fairly blinded by the pelting of the snow. It burned their faces like fire. The cowboy carried Johnnie through the drift to the door. As they entered, some cards again rose from the floor and beat against the wall.

The Easterner rushed to the stove. He was so profoundly chilled that he almost dared to embrace the glowing iron. The Swede was not in the room. Johnnie sank into a chair and, folding his arms on his knees, buried his face in them. Scully, warming one foot and then the other at a rim of the stove, muttered to himself with Celtic mournfulness. The cowboy had removed his fur cap, and with a dazed and rueful air he was running one hand through his tousled locks. From overhead they could hear the creaking of boards, as the Swede tramped here and there in his room.

The sad quiet was broken by the sudden flinging open of a door that led toward the kitchen. It was instantly followed by an inrush of women. They precipitated themselves upon Johnnie amid a chorus of lamentation. Before they carried their prey off to the kitchen, there to be bathed and harangued with that mixture of sympathy and abuse which is a feat of their sex, the mother straightened herself and fixed old Scully with an eye of stern reproach. "Shame be upon you, Patrick Scully!" she cried. "Your own son, too. Shame be upon you!"

"There, now! Be quiet, now!" said the old man, weakly.

"Shame be upon you, Patrick Scully!" The girls, rallying to this slogan, sniffed disdainfully in the direction of those trembling accomplices, the cowboy and the Easterner. Presently they bore Johnnie away, and left the three men to dismal reflection.

VII

"I'd like to fight this here Dutchman myself," said the cowboy, breaking a long silence.

Scully wagged his head sadly. "No, that wouldn't do. It wouldn't be right. It wouldn't be right."

"Well, why wouldn't it?" argued the cowboy. "I don't see no harm in it."

"No," answered Scully, with mournful heroism. "It wouldn't be right. It was Johnnie's fight, and now we mustn't whip the man just because he whipped Johnnie."

"Yes, that's true enough," said the cowboy; "but—he better not get fresh with me, because I couldn't stand no more of it."

"You'll not say a word to him," commanded Scully, and even then they heard the tread of the Swede on the stairs. His entrance was made theatric. He swept the door back with a bang and swaggered to the middle of the room. No one looked at him. "Well," he cried, insolently, at Scully, "I s'pose you'll tell me now how much I owe you?"

The old man remained stolid. "You don't owe me nothin'."

"Huh!" said the Swede, "huh! Don't owe 'im nothin'."

The cowboy addressed the Swede. "Stranger, I don't see how you come to be so gay around here."

Old Scully was instantly alert. "Stop!" he shouted, holding his hand forth, fingers upward. "Bill, you shut up!"

The cowboy spat carelessly into the sawdust-box. "I didn't say a word, did I?" he asked.

"Mr. Scully," called the Swede, "how much do I owe you?" It was seen that he was attired for departure, and that he had his valise in his hand.

"You don't owe me nothin'," repeated Scully in the same imperturbable way.

"Huh!" said the Swede. "I guess you're right. I guess if it was any way at all, you'd owe me somethin'. That's what I guess." He turned to the cowboy. "'Kill him! Kill him! Kill him!'" he mimicked, and then guffawed victoriously.

"'Kill him!'" He was convulsed with ironical humor.

But he might have been jeering the dead. The three men were immovable and silent, staring with glassy eyes at the stove.

The Swede opened the door and passed into the storm, giving one derisive glance backward at the still group.

As soon as the door was closed, Scully and the cowboy leaped to their feet and began to curse. They trampled to and fro, waving their arms and smashing into the air with their fists. "Oh, but that was a hard minute!" wailed Scully. "That was a hard minute! Him there leerin' and scoffin'! One bang at his nose was worth forty dollars to me that minute! How did you stand it, Bill?"

"How did I stand it?" cried the cowboy in a quivering voice. "How did I stand it? Oh!"

The old man burst into sudden brogue. "I'd loike to take that Swade," he wailed, "and hould 'im down on a shtone flure and bate 'im to a jelly wid a shtick!"

The cowboy groaned in sympathy. "I'd like to git him by the neck and ha-ammer him"—he brought his hand down on a chair with a noise like a pistol-shot—"hammer that there Dutchman until he couldn't tell himself from a dead coyote!"

"I'd bate 'im until he—"

"I'd show *him* some things—"

And then together they raised a yearning, fanatic cry—"Oh-o-oh! if we only could—"

"Yes!"

"Yes!"

"And then I'd—"

"O-o-oh!"

VIII

The Swede, tightly gripping his valise, tacked across the face of the storm as if he carried sails. He was following a line of little naked, grasping trees which, he knew, must mark the way of the road. His face, fresh from the pounding of Johnnie's fists, felt more pleasure than pain in the wind and the driving snow. A number of square shapes loomed upon him finally, and he knew them as the houses of the main body of the town. He found a street and made travel along it, leaning heavily upon the wind whenever, at a corner, a terrific blast caught him.

He might have been in a deserted village. We picture the world as thick with conquering and elated humanity, but here, with the bugles of the tempest pealing, it was hard to imagine a peopled earth. One viewed the existence of man then as a marvel, and conceded a glamour of wonder to these lice which were caused to cling to a whirling, fire-smitten, ice-locked, disease-stricken, space-lost bulb. The conceit of man was explained by this storm to be the very engine of life. One was a coxcomb not to die in it. However, the Swede found a saloon.

In front of it an indomitable red light was burning, and the snowflakes were made blood-color as they flew through the circumscribed territory of the lamp's shining. The Swede pushed open the door of the saloon and entered. A sanded expanse was before him, and at the end of it four men sat about a table drinking. Down one side of the room extended a radiant bar, and its guardian was leaning upon his elbows listening to the talk of the men at the table. The Swede dropped his valise upon the floor and, smiling fraternally upon the barkeeper, said, "Gimme some whisky, will you?" The man placed a bottle, a whisky-glass and a glass of ice-thick water upon the bar. The Swede poured himself an abnormal portion of whisky and drank it in three gulps. "Pretty bad night," remarked the bartender, indifferently. He was making the pretension of blindness which is usually a distinction of his class; but it could have been seen that he was furtively studying the half-erased blood-stains on the face of the Swede. "Bad night," he said again.

"Oh, it's good enough for me," replied the Swede, hardily, as he poured himself some more whisky. The barkeeper took his coin and maneuvered it through its reception by the highly nickeled cash-machine. A bell rang; a card labelled "20 cts." had appeared.

"No," continued the Swede, "this isn't too bad weather. It's good enough for me."

"So?" murmured the barkeeper, languidly.

The copious drams made the Swede's eyes swim, and he breathed a trifle heavier. "Yes, I like this weather. I like it. It suits me." It was apparently his design to impart a deep significance to these words.

"So?" murmured the bartender again. He turned to gaze dreamily at the scroll-like birds and bird-like scrolls which had been drawn with soap upon the mirrors in back of the bar.

"Well, I guess I'll take another drink," said the Swede, presently. "Have something?"

"No, thanks; I'm not drinkin'," answered the bartender. Afterward he asked, "How did you hurt your face?"

The Swede immediately began to boast loudly. "Why, in a fight. I thumped the soul out of a man down here at Scully's hotel."

The interest of the four men at the table was at last aroused.

"Who was it?" said one.

"Johnnie Scully," blustered the Swede. "Son of the man what runs it. He will be pretty near dead for some weeks, I can tell you. I made a nice thing of him, I did. He couldn't get up. They carried him in the house. Have a drink?"

Instantly the men in some subtle way encased themselves in reserve. "No, thanks," said one. The group was of curious formation. Two were prominent local business men; one was the district attorney; and one was a professional gambler of the kind known as "square." But a scrutiny of the group would not have enabled an observer to pick the gambler from the men of more reputable pursuits. He was, in fact, a man so delicate in manner, when among people of fair class, and so judicious in his choice of victims, that in the strictly masculine part of the town's life he had come to be explicitly trusted and admired. People called him a thoroughbred. The fear and contempt with which his craft was regarded were undoubtedly the reason why his quiet dignity shone conspicuous above the quiet dignity of men who might be merely hatters, billiard-markers, or grocery clerks. Beyond an occasional unwary traveler who came by rail, this gambler was supposed to prey solely upon reckless and senile farmers, who, when flush with good crops, drove into town in all the pride and confidence of an absolutely invulnerable stupidity. Hearing at times in circuitous fashion of the despoilment of such a farmer, the important men of Romper invariably laughed in contempt of the victim, and if they thought of the wolf at all, it was with a kind of pride at the knowledge that he would never dare think of attacking their wisdom and courage. Besides, it was popular that this gambler had a real wife and two real children in a neat cottage in a suburb, where he led an exemplary home life; and when any one even suggested a discrepancy in his character, the crowd immediately vociferated descriptions of this virtuous family circle. Then men who led exemplary home lives, and men who did not lead exemplary home lives, all subsided in a bunch, remarking that there was nothing more to be said.

However, when a restriction was placed upon him—as, for instance, when a strong clique of members of the new Pollywog Club refused to permit him, even as a spectator, to appear in the rooms of the organization—the candor and gentleness with which he accepted the judgment disarmed many of his foes and made his friends more desperately partisan. He invariably distinguished between himself and a respectable Romper man so quickly and frankly that his manner actually appeared to be a continual broadcast compliment.

And one must not forget to declare the fundamental fact of his entire position in Romper. It is irrefutable that in all affairs outside his business, in all matters that occur eternally and commonly between man and man, this thieving card-player was so generous, so just, so moral, that, in a contest he could have put to flight the consciences of nine tenths of the citizens of Romper.

And so it happened that he was seated in this saloon with the two prominent local merchants and the district attorney.

The Swede continued to drink raw whisky, meanwhile babbling at the barkeeper and trying to induce him to indulge in potations. "Come on. Have a drink. Come on. What—no? Well, have a little one, then. By gawd, I've whipped a man to-night, and I want to celebrate. I whipped him good, too. Gentlemen," the Swede cried to the men at the table, "have a drink?"

"Ssh!" said the barkeeper.

The group at the table, although furtively attentive, had been pretending to be deep in talk, but now a man lifted his eyes toward the Swede and said, shortly, "Thanks. We don't want any more."

At this reply the Swede ruffled out his chest like a rooster. "Well," he exploded, "it seems I can't get anybody to drink with me in this town. Seems so, don't it? Well!"

"Ssh!" said the barkeeper.

"Say," snarled the Swede, "don't you try to shut me up. I won't have it. I'm a gentleman, and I want people to drink with me. And I want 'em to drink with me now. *Now*—do you understand?" He rapped the bar with his knuckles.

Years of experience had calloused the bartender. He merely grew sulky. "I hear you," he answered.

"Well," cried the Swede, "listen hard then. See those men over there? Well, they're going to drink with me, and don't you forget it. Now you watch."

"Hi!" yelled the barkeeper, "this won't do!"

"Why won't it?" demanded the Swede. He stalked over to the table, and by chance laid his hand upon the shoulder of the gambler. "How about this?" he asked wrathfully. "I asked you to drink with me."

The gambler simply twisted his head and spoke over his shoulder. "My friend, I don't know you."

"Oh, hell!" answered the Swede, "come and have a drink."

"Now, my boy," advised the gambler, kindly, "take your hand off my shoulder and go 'way and mind your own business." He was a little, slim man, and it seemed strange to hear him use this tone of heroic patronage to the burly Swede. The other men at the table said nothing.

"What! You won't drink with me, you little dude? I'll make you, then! I'll make you!" The Swede had grasped the gambler frenziedly at the throat, and was dragging him from his chair. The other men sprang up. The barkeeper dashed around the corner of his bar. There was a great tumult, and then was seen a long blade in the hand of the gambler. It shot forward, and a human body, this citadel of virtue, wisdom, power, was pierced as easily as if it had been a melon. The Swede fell with a cry of supreme astonishment.

The prominent merchants and the district attorney must have at once tumbled out of the place backward. The bartender found himself hanging limply to the arm of a chair and gazing into the eyes of a murderer.

"Henry," said the latter, as he wiped his knife on one of the towels that hung beneath the bar rail, "you tell 'em where to find me. I'll be home, waiting for 'em." Then he vanished. A moment afterward the barkeeper was in the street dinning through the storm for help and, moreover, companionship.

The corpse of the Swede, alone in the saloon, had its eyes fixed upon a dreadful legend that dwelt atop the cash-machine: "This registers the amount of your purchase."

IX

Months later, the cowboy was frying pork over the stove of a little ranch near the Dakota line, when there was a quick thud of hoofs outside, and presently the Easterner entered with the letters and the papers.

"Well," said the Easterner at once, "the chap that killed the Swede has got three years. Wasn't much, was it?"

"He has? Three years?" The cowboy poised his pan of pork, while he ruminated upon the news. "Three years. That ain't much."

"No. It was a light sentence," replied the Easterner as he unbuckled his spurs. "Seems there was a good deal of sympathy for him in Romper."

"If the bartender had been any good," observed the cowboy, thoughtfully, "he would have gone in and cracked that there Dutchman on the head with a bottle in the beginnin' of it and stopped all this here murderin'."

"Yes, a thousand things might have happened," said the Easterner, tartly.

The cowboy returned his pan of pork to the fire, but his philosophy continued. "It's funny, ain't it? If he hadn't said Johnnie was cheatin' he'd be alive this minute. He was an awful fool. Game played for fun, too. Not for money. I believe he was crazy."

"I feel sorry for that gambler," said the Easterner.

"Oh, so do I," said the cowboy. "He don't deserve none of it for killin' who he did."

"The Swede might not have been killed if everything had been square."

"Might not have been killed?" exclaimed the cowboy. "Everythin' square? Why, when he said that Johnnie was cheatin' and acted like such a jackass? And then in the saloon he fairly walked up to git hurt?" With these arguments the cowboy browbeat the Easterner and reduced him to rage.

"You're a fool!" cried the Easterner, viciously. "You're a bigger jackass than the Swede by a million majority. Now let me tell you one thing. Let me tell you something. Listen! Johnnie *was* cheating!"

"'Johnnie,'" said the cowboy, blankly. There was a minute of silence, and then he said, robustly, "Why, no. The game was only for fun."

"Fun or not," said the Easterner, "Johnnie was cheating. I saw him. I know it. I saw him. And I refused to stand up and be a man. I let the Swede fight it out alone. And you—you were simply puffing around the place and wanting to fight. And then old Scully himself! We are all in it! This poor gambler isn't even a noun. He is kind of an adverb. Every sin is the result of a collaboration. We, five of us, have collaborated in the murder of this Swede. Usually there are from a dozen to forty women really involved in every murder, but in this case it seems to be only five men—you, I, Johnnie, old Scully; and that fool of an unfortunate gambler came merely as a culmination, the apex of a human movement, and gets all the punishment."

The cowboy, injured and rebellious, cried out blindly into this fog of mysterious theory: "Well, I didn't do anythin', did I?"

JACK LONDON

To Build a Fire

Day had broken cold and gray, exceedingly cold and gray, when the man turned aside from the main Yukon trail and climbed the high earth-bank, where a dim and little-travelled trail led eastward through the fat spruce timberland. It was a steep bank, and he paused for breath at the top, excusing the act to himself by looking at his watch. It was nine o'clock. There was no sun nor hint of sun, though there was not a cloud in the sky. It was a clear day, and yet there seemed an intangible pall over the face of things, a subtle gloom that made the day dark, and that was due to the absence of sun. This fact did not worry the man. He was used to the lack of sun. It had been days since he had seen the sun, and he knew that a few more days must pass before that cheerful orb, due south, would just peep above the sky-line and dip immediately from view.

The man flung a look back along the way he had come. The Yukon lay a mile wide and hidden under three feet of ice. On top of this ice were as many feet of snow. It was all pure white, rolling in gentle undulations where the ice-jams of the freeze-up had formed. North and south, as far as his eye could see, it was unbroken white, save for a dark hair-line that curved and twisted from around the spruce-covered island to the south, and that curved and twisted away into the north, where it disappeared behind another spruce-covered island. This dark hair-line was the trail—the main trail—that led south five hundred miles to the Chilcoot Pass, Dyea, and salt water; and that led north seventy miles to Dawson, and still on to the north a thousand miles to Nulato, and finally to St. Michael on Bering Sea, a thousand miles and half a thousand more.

But all this—the mysterious, far-reaching hair-line trail, the absence of sun from the sky, the tremendous cold, and the strangeness and weirdness of it all—made no impression on the man. It was not because he was long used to it. He was a newcomer in the land, a *chechaquo*, and this was his first winter. The trouble with him was that he was without imagination. He was quick and alert in the things of life, but only in the things, and not in the significances. Fifty degrees below zero meant eighty-odd degrees of frost. Such fact impressed him as being cold and uncomfortable, and that was all. It did not lead him to meditate upon his frailty as a creature of temperature, and upon man's frailty in general, able only to live within certain narrow limits of heat and cold; and from there on it did not lead him to the conjectural field of immortality and man's place in the universe. Fifty degrees below zero stood for a bite of frost that hurt and that must be guarded against by the use of mittens, ear-flaps, warm moccasins, and thick socks. Fifty degrees below zero was to him just precisely fifty degrees below zero. That there should be anything more to it than that was a thought that never entered his head.

As he turned to go on, he spat speculatively. There was a sharp, explosive crackle that startled him. He spat again. And again, in the air, before it could fall to the snow, the spittle crackled. He knew that at fifty below spittle crackled on the snow, but this spittle had crackled in the air. Undoubtedly it was colder than fifty below—how much colder he did not know. But the temperature did not matter. He was bound for the old claim on the left fork of Henderson Creek, where the boys were already. They had come over across the divide from the Indian Creek country, while he had come the roundabout way to take a look at the possibilities of getting out logs in the spring from the islands in the Yukon. He would be in to camp by six o'clock; a bit after dark, it was true, but the boys would be there, a fire would be going, and a hot supper would be ready. As for lunch, he pressed his hand against the protruding bundle under his jacket. It was also under his shirt, wrapped up in a handkerchief and lying against the naked skin. It was the only way to keep the biscuits from freezing. He smiled agreeably to himself as he thought of those biscuits, each cut open and sopped in bacon grease, and each enclosing a generous slice of fried bacon.

He plunged in among the big spruce trees. The trail was faint. A foot of snow had fallen since the last sled had passed over, and he was glad he was without a sled, travelling light. In fact, he carried nothing but the lunch wrapped in the handkerchief. He was surprised, however, at the cold. It certainly was cold, he concluded, as he rubbed his numb nose and cheek-bones with his mittened hand. He was a warm-whiskered man, but the hair on his face did not protect the high cheek-bones and the eager nose that thrust itself aggressively into the frosty air.

At the man's heels trotted a dog, a big native husky, the proper wolf-dog, gray-coated and without any visible or temperamental difference from its brother, the wild wolf. The animal was depressed by the tremendous cold. It knew that it was no time for travelling. Its instinct told it a truer tale than was told to the man by the man's judgment. In reality, it was not merely colder than fifty below zero; it was colder than sixty below, than seventy below. It was seventy-five below zero. Since the freezing-point is thirty-two above zero, it meant that one hundred and seven degrees of frost obtained. The dog did not know anything about thermometers. Possibly in its brain there was no sharp consciousness of a condition of very cold such as was in the man's brain. But the brute had its instinct. It experienced a vague but menacing apprehension that subdued it and made it slink along at the man's heels, and that made it question eagerly every unwonted movement of the man as if expecting him to go into camp or to seek shelter somewhere and build a fire. The dog had learned fire, and it wanted fire, or else to burrow under the snow and cuddle its warmth away from the air.

The frozen moisture of its breathing had settled on its fur in a fine powder of frost, and especially were its jowls, muzzle, and eyelashes whitened by its crystalled breath. The man's red beard and mustache were likewise frosted, but more solidly, the deposit taking the form of ice and increasing with every warm, moist breath he exhaled. Also, the man was chewing tobacco, and the muzzle of ice held his lips so rigidly that he was unable to clear his chin when he expelled the juice. The result was that a crystal beard of the color and solidity of amber was increasing its length on his chin. If he fell down it would shatter itself, like glass, into brittle fragments. But he did not mind the appendage. It was the penalty all tobacco-chewers paid in that country, and he had been out before in two cold snaps. They had not been so cold as this, he knew, but by the spirit thermometer at Sixty Mile he knew they had been registered at fifty below and at fifty-five.

He held on through the level stretch of woods for several miles, crossed a wide flat of nigger-heads, and dropped down a bank to the frozen bed of a small stream. This was Henderson Creek, and he knew he was ten miles from the forks. He looked at his watch. It was ten o'clock. He was making four miles an hour, and he calculated that he would arrive at the forks at half-past twelve. He decided to celebrate that event by eating his lunch there.

The dog dropped in again at his heels, with a tail drooping discouragement, as the man swung along the creek-bed. The furrow of the old sled-trail was plainly visible, but a dozen inches of snow covered the marks of the last runners. In a month no man had come up or down that silent creek. The man held steadily on. He was not much given to thinking, and just then particularly he had nothing to think about save that he would eat lunch at the forks and that at six o'clock he would be in camp with the boys. There was nobody to talk to; and, had there been, speech would have been impossible because of the ice-muzzle on his mouth. So he continued monotonously to chew tobacco and to increase the length of his amber beard.

Once in a while the thought reiterated itself that it was very cold and that he had never experienced such cold. As he walked along he rubbed his cheek-bones and nose with the back of his mittened hand. He did this automatically, now and again changing hands. But rub as he would, the instant he stopped his cheek-bones went numb, and the following instant the end of his nose went numb. He was sure to frost his cheeks; he knew that, and experienced a pang of regret that he had not devised a nose-strap of the sort Bud wore in cold snaps. Such a strap passed across the cheeks, as well, and saved them. But it didn't matter much, after all. What were frosted cheeks? A bit painful, that was all; they were never serious.

Empty as the man's mind was of thoughts, he was keenly observant, and he noticed the changes in the creek, the curves and bends and timber-jams, and always he sharply noted where he placed his feet. Once, coming around a bend, he shied abruptly, like a startled horse, curved away from the place where he had been walking, and retreated several paces back along the trail. The creek he knew was frozen clear to the bottom,—no creek could contain water in that arctic winter,—but he knew also that there were springs that bubbled out from the hillsides and ran along under the snow and on top the ice of the creek. He knew that the coldest snaps never froze these springs, and he knew likewise their danger. They were traps. They hid pools of water under the snow that might be three inches deep, or three feet. Sometimes a skin of ice half an inch thick covered them, and in turn was covered by the snow. Sometimes there were alternate layers of water and ice-skin, so that when one broke through he kept on breaking through for a while, sometimes wetting himself to the waist.

That was why he had shied in such panic. He had felt the give under his feet and heard the crackle of a snow-hidden ice-skin. And to get his feet wet in such a temperature meant trouble and danger. At the very least it meant delay, for he would be forced to stop and build a fire, and under its protection to bare his feet while he dried his socks and moccasins. He stood and studied the creek-bed and its banks, and decided that the flow of water came from the right. He reflected awhile, rubbing his nose and cheeks, then skirted to the left, stepping gingerly and testing the footing for each step. Once clear of the danger, he took a fresh chew of tobacco and swung along at his four-mile gait.

In the course of the next two hours he came upon several similar traps. Usually the snow above the hidden pools had a sunken, candied appearance that advertised the danger. Once again, however, he had a close call; and once, suspecting danger, he compelled the dog to go on in front. The dog did not want to go. It hung back until the man shoved it forward, and then it went quickly across the white, unbroken surface. Suddenly it broke through, floundered to one side, and got away to firmer footing. It had wet its forefeet and legs, and almost immediately the water that clung to it turned to ice. It made quick efforts to lick the ice off its legs, then dropped down in the snow and began to bite out the ice that had formed between the toes. This was a matter of instinct. To permit the ice to remain would mean sore feet. It did not know this. It merely obeyed the mysterious prompting that arose from the deep crypts of its being.

But the man knew, having achieved a judgment on the subject, and he removed the mitten from his right hand and helped tear out the ice-particles. He did not expose his fingers more than a minute, and was astonished at the swift numbness that smote them. It certainly was cold. He pulled on the mitten hastily, and beat the hand savagely across his chest.

At twelve o'clock the day was at its brightest. Yet the sun was too far south on its winter journey to clear the horizon. The bulge of the earth intervened between it and Henderson Creek, where the man walked under a clear sky at noon and cast no shadow. At half-past twelve, to the minute, he arrived at the forks of the creek. He was pleased at the speed he had made. If he kept it up, he would certainly be with the boys by six. He unbuttoned his jacket and shirt and drew forth his lunch. The action consumed no more than a quarter of a minute, yet in that brief moment the numbness laid hold of the exposed fingers. He did not put the mitten on, but, instead, struck the fingers a dozen sharp smashes against his leg. Then he sat down on a snow-covered log to eat. The sting that followed upon the striking of his fingers against his leg ceased so quickly that he was startled. He had had no chance to take a bite of biscuit. He struck the fingers repeatedly and returned them to the mitten, baring the other hand for the purpose of eating. He tried to take a mouthful, but the ice-muzzle prevented. He had forgotten to build a fire and thaw out. He chuckled at his foolishness, and as he chuckled he noted the numbness creeping into the exposed fingers. Also, he noted that the stinging which had first come to his toes when he sat down was already passing away. He wondered whether the toes were warm or numb. He moved them inside the moccasins and decided that they were numb.

He pulled the mitten on hurriedly and stood up. He was a bit frightened. He stamped up and down until the stinging returned into the feet. It certainly was cold, was his thought. That man from Sulphur Creek had spoken the truth when telling how cold it sometimes got in the country. And he had laughed at him at the time! That showed one must not be too sure of things. There was no mistake about it, it *was* cold. He strode up and down, stamping his feet and threshing his arms, until reassured by the returning warmth. Then he got out matches and proceeded to make a fire. From the undergrowth, where high water of the previous spring had lodged a supply of seasoned twigs, he got his fire-wood. Working carefully from a small beginning, he soon had a roaring fire, over which he thawed the ice from his face and in the protection of which he ate his biscuits. For the moment the cold of space was outwitted. The dog took satisfaction in the fire, stretching out close enough for warmth and far enough away to escape being singed.

When the man had finished, he filled his pipe and took his comfortable time over a smoke. Then he pulled on his mittens, settled the ear-flaps of his cap firmly about his ears, and took the creek trail up the left fork. The dog was disappointed and yearned back toward the fire. This man did not know cold. Possibly all the generations of his ancestry had been ignorant of cold, of real cold, of cold one hundred and seven degrees below freezing-point. But the dog knew; all its ancestry knew, and it had inherited the knowledge. And it knew that it was not good to walk abroad in such fearful cold. It was the time to lie snug in a hole in the snow and wait for a curtain of cloud to be drawn across the face of outer space whence this cold came. On the other hand, there was no keen intimacy between the dog and the man. The one was the toil-slave of the other, and the only caresses it had ever received were the caresses of the whip-lash and of harsh and menacing throat-sounds that threatened the whip-lash. So the dog made no effort to communicate its apprehension to the man. It was not concerned in the welfare of the man; it was for its own sake that it yearned back toward the fire. But the man whistled, and spoke to it with the sound of whip-lashes, and the dog swung in at the man's heels and followed after.

The man took a chew of tobacco and proceeded to start a new amber beard. Also, his moist breath quickly powdered with white his mustache, eyebrows, and lashes. There did not seem to be so many springs on the left fork of the Henderson, and for half an hour the man saw no signs of any. And then it happened. At a place where there were no signs, where the soft, unbroken snow seemed to advertise solidity beneath, the man broke through. It was not deep. He wet himself halfway to the knees before he floundered out to the firm crust.

He was angry, and cursed his luck aloud. He had hoped to get into camp with the boys at six o'clock, and this would delay him an hour, for he would have to build a fire and dry out his foot-gear. This was imperative at that low temperature—he knew that much; and he turned aside to the bank, which he climbed. On top, tangled in the underbrush about the trunks of several small spruce trees, was a high-water deposit of dry fire-wood—sticks and twigs, principally, but also larger portions of seasoned branches and fine, dry, last-year's grasses. He threw down several large pieces on top of the snow. This served for a foundation and prevented the young flame from drowning itself in the snow it otherwise would melt. The flame he got by touching a match to a small shred of birch-bark that he took from his pocket. This burned even more readily than paper. Placing it on the foundation, he fed the young flame with wisps of dry grass and with the tiniest dry twigs.

He worked slowly and carefully, keenly aware of his danger. Gradually, as the flame grew stronger, he increased the size of the twigs with which he fed it. He squatted in the snow, pulling the twigs out from their entanglement in the brush and feeding directly to the flame. He knew there must be no failure. When it is seventy-five below zero, a man must not fail in his first attempt to build a fire—that is, if his feet are wet. If his feet are dry, and he fails, he can run along the trail for half a mile and restore his circulation. But the circulation of wet and freezing feet cannot be restored by running when it is seventy-five below. No matter how fast he runs, the wet feet will freeze the harder.

All this the man knew. The old-timer on Sulphur Creek had told him about it the previous fall, and now he was appreciating the advice. Already all sensation had gone out of his feet. To build the fire he had been forced to remove his mittens, and the fingers had quickly gone numb. His pace of four miles an hour had kept his heart pumping blood to the surface of his body and to all the extremities. But the instant he stopped, the action of the pump eased down. The cold of space smote the unprotected tip of the planet, and he, being on that unprotected tip, received the full force of the blow. The blood of his body recoiled before it. The blood was alive, like the dog, and like the dog it wanted to hide away and cover itself up from the fearful cold. So long as he walked four miles an hour, he pumped that blood, willy-nilly, to the surface; but now it ebbed away and sank down into the recesses of his body. The extremities were the first to feel its absence. His wet feet froze the faster, and his exposed fingers numbed the faster, though they had not yet begun to freeze. Nose and cheeks were already freezing, while the skin of all his body chilled as it lost its blood.

But he was safe. Toes and nose and cheeks would be only touched by the frost, for the fire was beginning to burn with strength. He was feeding it with twigs the size of his finger. In another minute he would be able to feed it with branches the size of his wrist, and then he could remove his wet foot-gear, and, while it dried, he could keep his naked feet warm by the fire, rubbing them at first, of course, with snow. The fire was a success. He was safe. He remembered the advice of the old-timer on Sulphur Creek, and smiled. The old-timer had been very serious in laying down the law that no man must travel alone in the Klondike after fifty below. Well, here he was; he had had the accident; he was alone; and he had saved himself. Those old-timers were rather womanish, some of them, he thought. All a man had to do was to keep his head, and he was all right. Any man who was a man could travel alone. But it was surprising, the rapidity with which his cheeks and nose were freezing. And he had not thought his fingers could go lifeless in so short a time. Lifeless they were, for he could scarcely make them move together to grip a twig, and they seemed remote from his body and from him. When he touched a twig, he had to look and see whether or not he had hold of it. The wires were pretty well down between him and his finger-ends.

All of which counted for little. There was the fire, snapping and crackling and promising life with every dancing flame. He started to untie his moccasins. They were coated with ice; the thick German socks were like sheaths of iron halfway to the knees; and the moccasin strings were like rods of steel all twisted and knotted as by some conflagration. For a moment he tugged with his numb fingers, then, realizing the folly of it, he drew his sheath-knife.

But before he could cut the strings, it happened. It was his own fault or, rather, his mistake. He should not have built the fire under the spruce tree. He should have built it in the open. But it had been easier to pull the twigs from the brush and drop them directly on the fire. Now the tree under which he had done this carried a weight of snow on its boughs. No wind had blown for weeks, and each bough was fully freighted. Each time he had pulled a twig he had communicated a slight agitation to the tree—an imperceptible agitation, so far as he was concerned, but an agitation sufficient to bring about the disaster. High up in the tree one bough capsized its load of snow. This fell on the boughs beneath, capsizing them. This process continued, spreading out and involving the whole tree. It grew like an avalanche, and it descended without warning upon the man and the fire, and the fire was blotted out! Where it had burned was a mantle of fresh and disordered snow.

The man was shocked. It was as though he had just heard his own sentence of death. For a moment he sat and stared at the spot where the fire had been. Then he grew very calm. Perhaps the old-timer on Sulphur Creek was right. If he had only had a trail-mate he would have been in no danger now. The trail-mate could have built the fire. Well, it was up to him to build the fire over again, and this second time there must be no failure. Even if he succeeded, he would most likely lose some toes. His feet must be badly frozen by now, and there would be some time before the second fire was ready.

Such were his thoughts, but he did not sit and think them. He was busy all the time they were passing through his mind. He made a new foundation for a fire, this time in the open, where no treacherous tree could blot it out. Next, he gathered dry grasses and tiny twigs from the high-water flotsam. He could not bring his fingers together to pull them out, but he was able to gather them by the handful. In this way he got many rotten twigs and bits of green moss that were undesirable, but it was the best he could do. He worked methodically, even collecting an armful of the larger branches to be used later when the fire gathered strength. And all the while the dog sat and watched him, a certain yearning wistfulness in its eyes, for it looked upon him as the fire-provider, and the fire was slow in coming.

When all was ready, the man reached in his pocket for a second piece of birch-bark. He knew the bark was there, and, though he could not feel it with his fingers, he could hear its crisp rustling as he fumbled for it. Try as he would, he could not clutch hold of it. And all the time, in his consciousness, was the knowledge that each instant his feet were freezing. This thought tended to put him in a panic, but he fought against it and kept calm. He pulled on his mittens with his teeth, and threshed his arms back and forth, beating his hands with all his might against his sides. He did this sitting down, and he stood up to do it; and all the while the dog sat in the snow, its wolf-brush of a tail curled around warmly over its forefeet, its sharp wolf-ears pricked forward intently as it watched the man. And the man, as he beat and threshed with his arms and hands, felt a great surge of envy as he regarded the creature that was warm and secure in its natural covering.

After a time he was aware of the first far-away signals of sensation in his beaten fingers. The faint tingling grew stronger till it evolved into a stinging ache that was excruciating, but which the man hailed with satisfaction. He stripped the mitten from his right hand and fetched forth the birch-bark. The exposed fingers were quickly going numb again. Next he brought out his bunch of sulphur matches. But the tremendous cold had already driven the life out of his fingers. In his effort to separate one match from the others, the whole bunch fell in the snow. He tried to pick it out of the snow, but failed. The dead fingers could neither touch nor clutch. He was very careful. He drove the thought of his freezing feet, and nose, and cheeks, out of his mind, devoting his whole soul to the matches. He watched, using the sense of vision in place of that of touch, and when he saw his fingers on each side the bunch, he closed them—that is, he willed to close them, for the wires were down, and the fingers did not obey. He pulled the mitten on the right hand, and beat it fiercely against his knee. Then, with both mittened hands, he scooped the bunch of matches, along with much snow, into his lap. Yet he was no better off.

After some manipulation he managed to get the bunch between the heels of his mittened hands. In this fashion he carried it to his mouth. The ice crackled and snapped when by a violent effort he opened his mouth. He drew the lower jaw in, curled the upper lip out of the way, and scraped the bunch with his upper teeth in order to separate a match. He succeeded in getting one, which he dropped on his lap. He was no better off. He could not pick it up. Then he devised a way. He picked it up in his teeth and scratched it on his leg. Twenty times he scratched before he succeeded in lighting it. As it flamed he held it with his teeth to the birch-bark. But the burning brimstone went up his nostrils and into his lungs, causing him to cough spasmodically. The match fell into the snow and went out.

The old-timer on Sulphur Creek was right, he thought in the moment of controlled despair that ensued: after fifty below, a man should travel with a partner. He beat his hands, but failed in exciting any sensation. Suddenly he bared both hands, removing the mittens with his teeth. He caught the whole bunch between the heels of his hands. His arm-muscles not being frozen enabled him to press the hand-heels tightly against the matches. Then he scratched the bunch along his leg. It flared into flame, seventy sulphur matches at once! There was no wind to blow them out. He kept his head to one side to escape the strangling fumes, and held the blazing bunch to the birch-bark. As he so held it, he became aware of sensation in his hand. His flesh was burning. He could smell it. Deep down below the surface he could feel it. The sensation developed into pain that grew acute. And still he endured it, holding the flame of the matches clumsily to the bark that would not light readily because his own burning hands were in the way, absorbing most of the flame.

At last, when he could endure no more, he jerked his hands apart. The blazing matches fell sizzling into the snow, but the birch-bark was alight. He began laying dry grasses and the tiniest twigs on the flame. He could not pick and choose, for he had to lift the fuel between the heels of his hands. Small pieces of rotten wood and green moss clung to the twigs, and he bit them off as well as he could with his teeth. He cherished the flame carefully and awkwardly. It meant life, and it must not perish. The withdrawal of blood from the surface of his body now made him begin to shiver, and he grew more awkward. A large piece of green moss fell squarely on the little fire. He tried to poke it out with his fingers, but his shivering frame made him poke too far, and he disrupted the nucleus of the little fire, the burning grasses and tiny twigs separating and scattering. He tried to poke them together again, but in spite of the tenseness of the effort, his shivering got away with him, and the twigs were hopelessly scattered. Each twig gushed a puff of smoke and went out. The fire-provider had failed. As he looked apathetically about him, his eyes chanced on the dog, sitting across the ruins of the fire from him, in the snow, making restless, hunching movements, slightly lifting one forefoot and then the other, shifting its weight back and forth on them with wistful eagerness.

The sight of the dog put a wild idea into his head. He remembered the tale of the man, caught in a blizzard, who killed a steer and crawled inside the carcass, and so was saved. He would kill the dog and bury his hands in the warm body until the numbness went out of them. Then he could build another fire. He spoke to the dog, calling it to him; but in his voice was a strange note of fear that frightened the animal, who had never known the man to speak in such way before. Something was the matter, and its suspicious nature sensed danger—it knew not what danger, but somewhere, somehow, in its brain arose an apprehension of the man. It flattened its ears down at the sound of the man's voice, and its restless, hunching movements and the liftings and shiftings of its forefeet became more pronounced; but it would not come to the man. He got on his hands and knees and crawled toward the dog. This unusual posture again excited suspicion, and the animal sidled mincingly away.

The man sat up in the snow for a moment and struggled for calmness. Then he pulled on his mittens, by means of his teeth, and got upon his feet. He glanced down at first in order to assure himself that he was really standing up, for the absence of sensation in his feet left him unrelated to the earth. His erect position in itself started to drive the webs of suspicion from the dog's mind; and when he spoke peremptorily, with the sound of whip-lashes in his voice, the dog rendered its customary allegiance and came to him. As it came within reaching distance, the man lost his control. His arms flashed out to the dog, and he experienced genuine surprise when he discovered that his hands could not clutch, that there was neither bend nor feeling in the fingers. He had forgotten for the moment that they were frozen and that they were freezing more and more. All this happened quickly, and before the animal could get away, he encircled its body with his arms. He sat down in the snow, and in this fashion held the dog, while it snarled and whined and struggled.

But it was all he could do, hold its body encircled in his arms and sit there. He realized that he could not kill the dog. There was no way to do it. With his helpless hands he could neither draw nor hold his sheath-knife nor throttle the animal. He released it, and it plunged wildly away, with tail between its legs, and still snarling. It halted forty feet away and surveyed him curiously, with ears sharply pricked forward. The man looked down at his hands in order to locate them, and found them hanging on the ends of his arms. It struck him as curious that one should have to use his eyes in order to find out where his hands were. He began threshing his arms back and forth, beating the mittened hands against his sides. He did this for five minutes, violently, and his heart pumped enough blood up to the surface to put a stop to his shivering. But no sensation was aroused in the hands. He had an impression that they hung like weights on the ends of his arms, but when he tried to run the impression down, he could not find it.

A certain fear of death, dull and oppressive, came to him. This fear quickly became poignant as he realized that it was no longer a mere matter of freezing his fingers and toes, or of losing his hands and feet, but that it was a matter of life and death with the chances against him. This threw him into a panic, and he turned and ran up the creek-bed along the old, dim trail. The dog joined in behind and kept up with him. He ran blindly, without intention, in fear such as he had never known in his life. Slowly, as he ploughed and floundered through the snow, he began to see things again,—the banks of the creek, the old timber-jams, the leafless aspens, and the sky. The running made him feel better. He did not shiver. Maybe, if he ran on, his feet would thaw out; and, anyway, if he ran far enough, he would reach camp and the boys. Without doubt he would lose some fingers and toes and some of his face; but the boys would take care of him, and save the rest of him when he got there. And at the same time there was another thought in his mind that said he would never get to the camp and the boys; that it was too many miles away, that the freezing had too great a start on him, and that he would soon be stiff and dead. This thought he kept in the background and refused to consider. Sometimes it pushed itself forward and demanded to be heard, but he thrust it back and strove to think of other things.

It struck him as curious that he could run at all on feet so frozen that he could not feel them when they struck the earth and took the weight of his body. He seemed to himself to skim along above the surface, and to have no connection with the earth. Somewhere he had once seen a winged Mercury, and he wondered if Mercury felt as he felt when skimming over the earth.

His theory of running until he reached camp and the boys had one flaw in it: he lacked the endurance. Several times he stumbled, and finally he tottered, crumpled up, and fell. When he tried to rise, he failed. He must sit and rest, he decided, and next time he would merely walk and keep on going. As he sat and regained his breath, he noted that he was feeling quite warm and comfortable. He was not shivering, and it even seemed that a warm glow had come to his chest and trunk. And yet, when he touched his nose or cheeks, there was no sensation. Running would not thaw them out. Nor would it thaw out his hands and feet. Then the thought came to him that the frozen portions of his body must be extending. He tried to keep this thought down, to forget it, to think of something else; he was aware of the panicky feeling that it caused, and he was afraid of the panic. But the thought asserted itself, and persisted, until it produced a vision of his body totally frozen. This was too much, and he made another wild run along the trail. Once he slowed down to a walk, but the thought of the freezing extending itself made him run again.

And all the time the dog ran with him, at his heels. When he fell down a second time, it curled its tail over its forefeet and sat in front of him, facing him, curiously eager and intent. The warmth and security of the animal angered him, and he cursed it till it flattened down its ears appeasingly. This time the shivering came more quickly upon the man. He was losing in his battle with the frost. It was creeping into his body from all sides. The thought of it drove him on, but he ran no more than a hundred feet, when he staggered and pitched headlong. It was his last panic. When he had recovered his breath and control, he sat up and entertained in his mind the conception of meeting death with dignity. However, the conception did not come to him in such terms. His idea of it was that he had been making a fool of himself, running around like a chicken with its head cut off—such was the simile that occurred to him. Well, he was bound to freeze anyway, and he might as well take it decently. With this new-found peace of mind came the first glimmerings of drowsiness. A good idea, he thought, to sleep off to death. It was like taking an anæsthetic. Freezing was not so bad as people thought. There were lots worse ways to die.

He pictured the boys finding his body next day. Suddenly he found himself with them, coming along the trail and looking for himself. And, still with them, he came around a turn in the trail and found himself lying in the snow. He did not belong with himself any more, for even then he was out of himself, standing with the boys and looking at himself in the snow. It certainly was cold, was his thought. When he got back to the States he could tell the folks what real cold was. He drifted on from this to a vision of the old-timer on Sulphur Creek. He could see him quite clearly, warm and comfortable, and smoking a pipe.

"You were right, old hoss; you were right," the man mumbled to the old-timer of Sulphur Creek.

Then the man drowsed off into what seemed to him the most comfortable and satisfying sleep he had ever known. The dog sat facing him and waiting. The brief day drew to a close in a long, slow twilight. There were no signs of a fire to be made, and, besides, never in the dog's experience had it known a man to sit like that in the snow and make no fire. As the twilight drew on, its eager yearning for the fire mastered it, and with a great lifting and shifting of forefeet, it whined softly, then flattened its ears down in anticipation of being chidden by the man. But the man remained silent. Later, the dog whined loudly. And still later it crept close to the man and caught the scent of death. This made the animal bristle and back away. A little longer it delayed, howling under the stars that leaped and danced and shone brightly in the cold sky. Then it turned and trotted up the trail in the direction of the camp it knew, where were the other food-providers and fire-providers.

SHERWOOD ANDERSON

Hands

UPON THE HALF DECAYED veranda of a small frame house that stood near the edge of a ravine near the town of Winesburg, Ohio, a fat little old man walked nervously up and down. Across a long field that had been seeded for clover but that had produced only a dense crop of yellow mustard weeds, he could see the public highway along which went a wagon filled with berry pickers returning from the fields. The berry pickers, youths and maidens, laughed and shouted boisterously. A boy clad in a blue shirt leaped from the wagon and attempted to drag after him one of the maidens, who screamed and protested shrilly. The feet of the boy in the road kicked up a cloud of dust that floated across the face of the departing sun. Over the long field came a thin girlish voice. "Oh, you Wing Biddlebaum, comb your hair, it's falling into your eyes," commanded the voice to the man, who was bald and whose nervous little hands fiddled about the bare white forehead as though arranging a mass of tangled locks.

Wing Biddlebaum, forever frightened and beset by a ghostly band of doubts did not think of himself as in any way a part of the life of the town where he had lived for twenty years. Among all the people of Winesburg but one had come close to him. With George Willard, son of Tom Willard, the proprietor of the New Willard House, he had formed something like a friendship. George Willard was the reporter on the *Winesburg Eagle* and sometimes in the evenings he walked out along the highway to Wing Biddlebaum's house. Now as the old man walked up and down on the veranda, his hands moving nervously about, he was hoping that George Willard would come and spend the evening with him. After the wagon containing the berry pickers had passed, he went across the field through the tall mustard weeds and climbing a rail fence peered anxiously along the road to the town. For a moment he stood thus, rubbing his hands together and looking up and down the road, and then, fear overcoming him, ran back to walk again upon the porch on his own house.

In the presence of George Willard, Wing Biddlebaum, who for twenty years had been the town mystery, lost something of his timidity, and his shadowy personality, submerged in a sea of doubts, came forth to look at the world. With the young reporter at his side, he ventured in the light of day into Main Street or strode up and down on the rickety front porch of his own house, talking excitedly. The voice that had been low and trembling became shrill and loud. The bent figure straightened. With a kind of wriggle, like a fish returned to the brook by the fisherman, Biddlebaum the silent began to talk, striving to put into words the ideas that had been accumulated by his mind during long years of silence.

Wing Biddlebaum talked much with his hands. The slender expressive fingers, forever active, forever striving to conceal themselves in his pockets or behind his back, came forth and became the piston rods of his machinery of expression.

The story of Wing Biddlebaum is a story of hands. Their restless activity, like unto the beating of the wings of an imprisoned bird, had given him his name. Some obscure poet of the town had thought of it. The hands alarmed their owner. He wanted to keep them hidden away and looked with amazement at the quiet inexpressive hands of other men who worked beside him in the fields, or passed, driving sleepy teams on country roads.

When he talked to George Willard, Wing Biddlebaum closed his fists and beat with them upon a table or on the walls of his house. The action made him more comfortable. If the desire to talk came to him when the two were walking in the fields, he sought out a stump or the top board of a fence and with his hands pounding busily talked with renewed ease.

The story of Wing Biddlebaum's hands is worth a book in itself. Sympathetically set forth it would tap many strange, beautiful qualities in obscure men. It is a job for a poet. In Winesburg the hands had attracted attention merely because of their activity. With them

Wing Biddlebaum had picked as high as a hundred and forty quarts of strawberries in a day. They became his distinguishing feature, the source of his fame. Also they made more grotesque an already grotesque and elusive individuality. Winesburg was proud of the hands of Wing Biddlebaum in the same spirit in which it was proud of Banker White's new stone house and Wesley Moyer's bay stallion, Tony Tip, that had won the two-fifteen trot at the fall races in Cleveland.

As for George Willard, he had many times wanted to ask about the hands. At times an almost overwhelming curiosity had taken hold of him. He felt that there must be a reason for their strange activity and their inclination to keep hidden away and only a growing respect for Wing Biddlebaum kept him from blurting out the questions that were often in his mind.

Once he had been on the point of asking. The two were walking in the fields on a summer afternoon and had stopped to sit upon a grassy bank. All afternoon Wing Biddlebaum had talked as one inspired. By a fence he had stopped and beating like a giant woodpecker upon the top board had shouted at George Willard, condemning his tendency to be too much influenced by the people about him. "You are destroying yourself," he cried. "You have the inclination to be alone and to dream and you are afraid of dreams. You want to be like others in town here. You hear them talk and you try to imitate them."

On the grassy bank Wing Biddlebaum had tried again to drive his point home. His voice became soft and reminiscent, and with a sigh of contentment he launched into a long rambling talk, speaking as one lost in a dream.

Out of the dream Wing Biddlebaum made a picture for George Willard. In the picture men lived again in a kind of pastoral golden age. Across a green open country came clean-limbed young men, some afoot, some mounted upon horses. In crowds the young men came to gather about the feet of an old man who sat beneath a tree in a tiny garden and who talked to them.

Wing Biddlebaum became wholly inspired. For once he forgot the hands. Slowly they stole forth and lay upon George Willard's shoulders. Something new and bold came into the voice that talked. "You must try to forget all you have learned," said the old man. "You must begin to dream. From this time on you must shut your ears to the roaring of the voices."

Pausing in his speech, Wing Biddlebaum looked long and earnestly at George Willard. His eyes glowed. Again he raised the hands to caress the boy and then a look of horror swept over his face.

With a convulsive movement of his body, Wing Biddlebaum sprang to his feet and thrust his hands deep into his trousers pockets. Tears came to his eyes. "I must be getting along home. I can talk no more with you," he said nervously.

Without looking back, the old man had hurried down the hillside and across a meadow, leaving George Willard perplexed and frightened upon the grassy slope. With a shiver of dread the boy arose and went along the road toward town. "I'll not ask him about his hands," he thought, touched by the memory of the terror he had seen in the man's eyes. "There's something wrong, but I don't want to know what it is. His hands have something to do with his fear of me and of everyone."

And George Willard was right. Let us look briefly into the story of the hands. Perhaps our talking of them will arouse the poet who will tell the hidden wonder story of the influence for which the hands were but fluttering pennants of promise.

In his youth Wing Biddlebaum had been a school teacher in a town in Pennsylvania. He was not then known as Wing Biddlebaum, but went by the less euphonic name of Adolph Myers. As Adolph Myers he was much loved by the boys of his school.

Adolph Myers was meant by nature to be a teacher of youth. He was one of those rare, little-understood men who rule by a power so gentle that it passes as a lovable weakness. In their feeling for the boys under their charge such men are not unlike the finer sort of women in their love of men.

And yet that is but crudely stated. It needs the poet there. With the boys of his school, Adolph Myers had walked in the evening or had sat talking until dusk upon the schoolhouse steps lost in a kind of dream. Here and there went his hands, caressing the shoulders of the boys, playing about the tousled heads. As he talked his voice became soft and musical. There was a caress in that also. In a way the voice and the hands, the stroking of the shoulders and the touching of the hair were a part of the schoolmaster's effort to carry a dream into the young minds. By the caress that was in his fingers he expressed himself. He was one of those men in whom the force that creates life is diffused, not centralized. Under the caress of his hands doubt and disbelief went out of the minds of the boys and they began also to dream.

And then the tragedy. A half-witted boy of the school became enamored of the young master. In his bed at night he imagined unspeakable things and in the morning went forth to tell his dreams as facts. Strange, hideous accusations fell from his loose-hung lips. Through the Pennsylvania town went a shiver. Hidden, shadowy doubts that had been in men's minds concerning Adolph Myers were galvanized into beliefs.

The tragedy did not linger. Trembling lads were jerked out of bed and questioned. "He put his arms about me," said one. "His fingers were always playing in my hair," said another.

One afternoon a man of the town, Henry Bradford, who kept a saloon, came to the schoolhouse door. Calling Adolph Myers into the school yard he began to beat him with his fists. As his hard knuckles beat down into the frightened face of the schoolmaster, his wrath became more and more terrible. Screaming with dismay, the children ran here and there like disturbed insects. "I'll teach you to put your hands on my boy, you beast," roared the saloon keeper, who, tired of beating the master, had begun to kick him about the yard.

Adolph Myers was driven from the Pennsylvania town in the night. With lanterns in their hands a dozen men came to the door of the house where he lived alone and commanded that he dress and come forth. It was raining and one of the men had a rope in his hands. They had intended to hang the schoolmaster, but something in his figure, so small, white, and pitiful, touched their hearts and they let him escape. As he ran away into the darkness they repented of their weakness and ran after him, swearing and throwing sticks and great balls of soft mud at the figure that screamed and ran faster and faster into the darkness.

For twenty years Adolph Myers had lived alone in Winesburg. He was but forty but looked sixty-five. The name of Biddlebaum he got from a box of goods seen at a freight station as he hurried through an eastern Ohio town. He had an aunt in Winesburg, a black-toothed old woman who raised chickens, and with her he lived until she died. He had been ill for a year after the experience in Pennsylvania, and after his recovery worked as a day laborer in the fields, going timidly about and striving to conceal his hands. Although he did not understand what had happened he felt that the hands must be to blame. Again and again the fathers of the boys had talked of the hands. "Keep your hands to yourself," the saloon keeper had roared, dancing with fury in the schoolhouse yard.

Upon the veranda of his house by the ravine, Wing Biddlebaum continued to walk up and down until the sun had disappeared and the road beyond the field was lost in the grey shadows. Going into his house he cut slices of bread and spread honey upon them. When the rumble of the evening train that took away the express cars loaded with the day's harvest of berries had passed and restored the silence of the summer night, he went again to walk upon the veranda. In the darkness he could not see the hands and they became quiet. Although he still hungered for the presence of the boy, who was the medium through which he expressed his love of man, the hunger became again a part of his loneliness and his waiting. Lighting a lamp, Wing Biddlebaum washed the few dishes soiled by his simple meal and, setting up a folding cot by the screen door that led to the porch, prepared to undress for the night. A few stray white bread crumbs lay on the cleanly washed floor by the table; putting the lamp upon a low stool he began to pick up the crumbs, carrying them to his mouth one by one with unbelievable rapidity. In the dense blotch of light beneath the table, the kneeling figure looked like a priest engaged in some service of his church. The nervous expressive fingers, flashing in and out of the light, might well have been mistaken for the fingers of the devotee going swiftly through decade after decade of his rosary.

SHERWOOD ANDERSON

The Untold Lie

Ray Pearson and Hal Winters were farm hands employed on a farm three miles north of Winesburg. On Saturday afternoons they came into town and wandered about through the streets with other fellows from the country.

Ray was a quiet, rather nervous man of perhaps fifty with a brown beard and shoulders rounded by too much and too hard labor. In his nature he was as unlike Hal Winters as two men can be unlike.

Ray was an altogether serious man and had a little sharp-featured wife who had also a sharp voice. The two, with half a dozen thin-legged children, lived in a tumble-down frame house beside a creek at the back end of the Wills farm where Ray was employed.

Hal Winters, his fellow employee, was a young fellow. He was not of the Ned Winters family, who were very respectable people in Winesburg, but was one of the three sons of the old man called Windpeter Winters who had a sawmill near Unionville, six miles away, and who was looked upon by everyone in Winesburg as a confirmed old reprobate.

People from the part of Northern Ohio in which Winesburg lies will remember old Windpeter by his unusual and tragic death. He got drunk one evening in town and started to drive home to Unionville along the railroad tracks. Henry Brattenburg, the butcher, who lived out that way, stopped him at the edge of the town and told him he was sure to meet the down train but Windpeter slashed at him with his whip and drove on. When the train struck and killed him and his two horses a farmer and his wife who were driving home along a nearby road saw the accident. They said that old

Windpeter stood up on the seat of his wagon, raving and swearing at the onrushing locomotive, and that he fairly screamed with delight when the team, maddened by his incessant slashing at them, rushed straight ahead to certain death. Boys like young George Willard and Seth Richmond will remember the incident quite vividly because, although everyone in our town said that the old man would go straight to hell and that the community was better off without him, they had a secret conviction that he knew what he was doing and admired his foolish courage. Most boys have seasons of wishing they could die gloriously instead of just being grocery clerks and going on with their humdrum lives.

But this is not the story of Windpeter Winters nor yet of his son Hal who worked on the Wills farm with Ray Pearson. It is Ray's story. It will, however, be necessary to talk a little of young Hal so that you will get into the spirit of it.

Hal was a bad one. Everyone said that. There were three of the Winters boys in that family, John, Hal, and Edward, all broad-shouldered big fellows like old Windpeter himself and all fighters and woman-chasers and generally all-around bad ones.

Hal was the worst of the lot and always up to some devilment. He once stole a load of boards from his father's mill and sold them in Winesburg. With the money he bought himself a suit of cheap, flashy clothes. Then he got drunk and when his father came raving into town to find him, they met and fought with their fists on Main Street and were arrested and put into jail together.

Hal went to work on the Wills farm because there was a country school teacher out that way who had taken his fancy. He was only twenty-two then but had already been in two or three of what were spoken of in Winesburg as "women scrapes." Everyone who heard of his infatuation for the school teacher was sure it would turn out badly. "He'll only get her into trouble, you'll see," was the word that went around.

And so these two men, Ray and Hal, were at work in a field on a day in the late October. They were husking corn and occasionally something was said and they laughed. Then came silence. Ray, who was the more sensitive and always minded things more, had chapped hands and they hurt. He put them into his coat pockets and looked away across the fields. He was in a sad, distracted mood and was affected by the beauty of the country. If you knew the Winesburg country in the fall and how the low hills are all splashed with yellows and reds you would understand his feeling. He began to think of the time, long ago when he was a young fellow living with his father, then a baker in Winesburg, and how on such days he had wandered away into the woods to gather nuts, hunt rabbits, or just to loaf about and smoke his pipe. His marriage had come about through one of his days of wandering. He had induced a girl who waited on trade in his father's shop to go with him and something had happened. He was thinking of that afternoon and how it had affected his whole life when a spirit of protest awoke in him. He had forgotten about Hal and muttered words. "Tricked by Gad, that's what I was, tricked by life and made a fool of," he said in a low voice.

As though understanding his thoughts, Hal Winters spoke up. "Well, has it been worth while? What about it, eh? What about marriage and all that?" he asked and then laughed. Hal tried to keep on laughing but he too was in an earnest mood. He began to talk earnestly. "Has a fellow got to do it?" he asked. "Has he got to be harnessed up and driven through life like a horse?"

Hal didn't wait for an answer but sprang to his feet and began to walk back and forth between the corn shocks. He was getting more and more excited. Bending down suddenly he picked up an ear of the yellow corn and threw it at the fence. "I've got Nell Gunther in trouble," he said. "I'm telling you, but you keep your mouth shut."

Ray Pearson arose and stood staring. He was almost a foot shorter than Hal, and when the younger man came and put his two hands on the older man's shoulders they made a picture. There they stood in the big empty field with the quiet corn shocks standing in rows behind them and the red and yellow hills in the distance, and from being just two indifferent workmen they had become all alive to each other. Hal sensed it and because that was his way he laughed. "Well, old daddy," he said awkwardly, "come on, advise me. I've got Nell in trouble. Perhaps you've been in the same fix yourself. I know what everyone would say is the right thing to do, but what do you say? Shall I marry and settle down? Shall I put myself into the harness to be worn out like an old horse? You know me, Ray. There can't anyone break me but I can break myself. Shall I do it or shall I tell Nell to go to the devil? Come on, you tell me. Whatever you say, Ray, I'll do."

Ray couldn't answer. He shook Hal's hands loose and turning walked straight away toward the barn. He was a sensitive man and there were tears in his eyes. He knew there was only one thing to say to Hal Winters, son of old Windpeter Winters, only one thing that all his own training and all the beliefs of the people he knew would approve, but for his life he couldn't say what he knew he should say.

At half-past four that afternoon Ray was puttering about the barnyard when his wife came up the lane along the creek and called him. After the talk with Hal he hadn't returned to the cornfield but worked about the barn. He had already done the evening chores and had seen Hal, dressed and ready for a roistering night in town, come out of the farmhouse and go into the road. Along the path to his own house he trudged behind his wife, looking at the ground and thinking. He couldn't make out what was wrong. Every time he raised his eyes and saw the beauty of the country in the failing light he wanted to do something he had never done before, shout or scream or hit his wife with his fists or something equally unexpected and terrifying. Along the path he went scratching his head and trying to make it out. He looked hard at his wife's back but she seemed all right.

She only wanted him to go into town for groceries and as soon as she had told him what she wanted began to scold. "You're always puttering," she said. "Now I want you to hustle. There isn't anything in the house for supper and you've got to get to town and back in a hurry."

Ray went into his own house and took an overcoat from a hook back of the door. It was torn about the pockets and the collar was shiny. His wife went into the bedroom and presently came out with a soiled cloth in one hand and three silver dollars in the other. Somewhere in the house a child wept bitterly and a dog that had been sleeping by the stove arose and yawned. Again the wife scolded. "The children will cry and cry. Why are you always puttering?" she asked.

Ray went out of the house and climbed the fence into a field. It was just growing dark and the scene that lay before him was lovely. All the low hills were washed with color and even the little clusters of bushes in the corners of the fences were alive with beauty. The whole world seemed to Ray Pearson to have become alive with something just as he and Hal had suddenly become alive when they stood in the corn field staring into each other's eyes.

The beauty of the country about Winesburg was too much for Ray on that fall evening. That is all there was to it. He could not stand it. Of a sudden he forgot all about being a quiet old farm hand and throwing off the torn overcoat began to run across the field. As he ran he shouted a protest against his life, against all life, against everything that makes life ugly. "There was no promise made," he cried into the empty spaces that lay about him. "I didn't promise my Minnie anything and Hal hasn't made any promise to Nell. I know he hasn't. She went into the woods with him because she wanted to go. What he wanted she wanted. Why should I pay? Why should Hal pay? Why should anyone pay? I don't want Hal to become old and worn out. I'll tell him. I won't let it go on. I'll catch Hal before he gets to town and I'll tell him."

Ray ran clumsily and once he stumbled and fell down. "I must catch Hal and tell him," he kept thinking, and although his breath came in gasps he kept running harder and harder. As he ran he thought of things that hadn't come into his mind for years—how at the time he married he had planned to go west to his uncle in Portland, Oregon—how he hadn't wanted to be a farm hand, but had thought when he got out West he would go to sea and be a sailor or get a job on a ranch and ride a horse into Western towns, shouting and laughing and waking the people in the houses with his wild cries. Then as he ran he remembered his children and in fancy felt their hands clutching at him. All of his thoughts of himself were involved with the thoughts of Hal and he thought the children were clutching at the younger man also. "They are the accidents of life, Hal," he cried. "They are not mine or yours. I had nothing to do with them."

Darkness began to spread over the fields as Ray Pearson ran on and on. His breath came in little sobs. When he came to the fence at the edge of the road and confronted Hal Winters, all dressed up and smoking a pipe as he walked jauntily along, he could not have told what he thought or what he wanted.

Ray Pearson lost his nerve and this is really the end of the story of what happened to him. It was almost dark when he got to the fence and he put his hands on the top bar and stood staring. Hal

Winters jumped a ditch and coming up close to Ray put his hands into his pockets and laughed. He seemed to have lost his own sense of what had happened in the corn field and when he put up a strong hand and took hold of the lapel of Ray's coat he shook the old man as he might have shaken a dog that had misbehaved.

"You came to tell me, eh?" he said. "Well, never mind telling me anything. I'm not a coward and I've already made up my mind." He laughed again and jumped back across the ditch. "Nell ain't no fool," he said. "She didn't ask me to marry her. I want to marry her. I want to settle down and have kids."

Ray Pearson also laughed. He felt like laughing at himself and all the world.

As the form of Hal Winters disappeared in the dusk that lay over the road that led to Winesburg, he turned and walked slowly back across the fields to where he had left his torn overcoat. As he went some memory of pleasant evenings spent with the thin-legged children in the tumble-down house by the creek must have come into his mind, for he muttered words. "It's just as well. Whatever I told him would have been a lie," he said softly, and then his form also disappeared into the darkness of the fields.

WILLA CATHER

Paul's Case

IT WAS PAUL'S AFTERNOON to appear before the faculty of the Pittsburgh High School to account for his various misdemeanors. He had been suspended a week ago, and his father had called at the Principal's office and confessed his perplexity about his son. Paul entered the faculty room suave and smiling. His clothes were a trifle outgrown, and the tan velvet on the collar of his open overcoat was frayed and worn; but for all that there was something of the dandy about him, and he wore an opal pin in his neatly knotted black four-in-hand, and a red carnation in his buttonhole. This latter adornment the faculty somehow felt was not properly significant of the contrite spirit befitting a boy under the ban of suspension.

Paul was tall for his age and very thin, with high, cramped shoulders and a narrow chest. His eyes were remarkable for a certain hysterical brilliancy, and he continually used them in a conscious, theatrical sort of way, peculiarly offensive in a boy. The pupils were abnormally large, as though he were addicted to belladonna, but there was a glassy glitter about them which that drug does not produce.

When questioned by the Principal as to why he was there, Paul stated, politely enough, that he wanted to come back to school. This was a lie, but Paul was quite accustomed to lying; found it, indeed, indispensable for overcoming friction. His teachers were asked to state their respective charges against him, which they did with such a rancor and aggrievedness as evinced that this was not a usual case. Disorder and impertinence were among the offenses named, yet each of his instructors felt that it was scarcely possible to put into words the real cause of the trouble, which lay in a sort of hysterically defiant manner of the boy's; in the contempt which they all knew he felt for them, and which he seemingly made not the least effort to conceal. Once, when he had been making a synopsis of a paragraph at the blackboard, his English teacher had stepped to his side and attempted to guide his hand. Paul had started back with a shudder and thrust his hands violently behind him. The astonished woman could scarcely have been more hurt and embarrassed had he struck at her. The insult was so involuntary and definitely personal as to be unforgettable. In one way and another, he had made all his teachers, men and women alike, conscious of the same feeling of physical aversion. In one class he habitually sat with his hand shading his eyes; in another he always looked out of the window during the recitation; in another he made a running commentary on the lecture, with humorous intent.

His teachers felt this afternoon that his whole attitude was symbolized by his shrug and his flippantly red carnation flower, and they fell upon him without mercy, his English teacher leading the pack. He stood through it smiling, his pale lips parted over his white teeth. (His lips were continually twitching, and he had a habit of raising his eyebrows that was contemptuous and irritating to the last degree.) Older boys than Paul had broken down and shed tears under the ordeal, but his set smile did not once desert him, and his only sign of discomfort was the nervous trembling of the fingers that toyed with the buttons of his overcoat, and an occasional jerking of the other hand which held his hat. Paul was always smiling, always glancing about him, seeming to feel that people might be watching him and trying to detect something. This conscious expression, since it was as far as possible from boyish mirthfulness, was usually attributed to insolence or "smartness."

As the inquisition proceeded, one of his instructors repeated an impertinent remark of the boy's, and the Principal asked him whether he thought that a courteous speech to make to a woman. Paul shrugged his shoulder slightly and his eyebrows twitched.

"I don't know," he replied. "I didn't mean to be polite or impolite, either. I guess it's a sort of way I have, of saying things regardless."

The Principal asked him whether he didn't think that a way it would be well to get rid of. Paul grinned and said he guessed so. When he was told that he could go, he bowed gracefully and went out. His bow was like a repetition of the scandalous red carnation.

His teachers were in despair, and his drawing master voiced the feeling of them all when he declared there was something about the boy which none of them understood. He added: "I don't really believe that smile of his comes altogether from insolence; there's something sort of haunted about it. The boy is not strong, for one thing. There is something wrong about the fellow."

The drawing master had come to realize that, in looking at Paul, one saw only his white teeth and the forced animation of his eyes. One warm afternoon the boy had gone to sleep at his drawing board, and his master had noted with amazement what a white, blue-veined face it was; drawn and wrinkled like an old man's about the eyes, the lips twitching even in his sleep.

His teachers left the building dissatisfied and unhappy, humiliated to have felt so vindictive toward a mere boy, to have uttered this feeling in cutting terms, and to have set each other on, as it were, in the gruesome game of intemperate reproach. One of them remembered having seen a miserable street cat set at bay by a ring of tormentors.

As for Paul, he ran down the hill whistling the Soldiers' Chorus from *Faust,* looking wildly behind him now and then to see whether some of his teachers were not there to witness his light-heartedness. As it was now late in the afternoon and Paul was on duty that evening as usher at Carnegie Hall, he decided that he would not go home to supper.

When he reached the concert hall the doors were not yet open. It was chilly outside, and he decided to go up into the picture gallery—always deserted at this hour—where there were some of Raffelli's gay studies of Paris streets and an airy blue Venetian scene or two that always exhilarated him. He was delighted to find no one in the gallery but the old guard, who sat in the corner, a newspaper on his knee, a black patch over one eye and the other closed. Paul possessed himself of the place and walked confidently up and down, whistling under his breath. After a while he sat down before a blue Rico and lost himself. When he bethought him to look at his watch, it was after seven o'clock, and he rose with a start and ran downstairs, making a face at Augustus Cæsar, peering out from the cast-room, and an evil gesture at the Venus of Milo as he passed her on the stairway.

When Paul reached the ushers' dressing-room half a dozen boys were there already, and he began excitedly to tumble into his uniform. It was one of the few that at all approached fitting, and Paul thought it very becoming—though he knew the tight, straight coat accentuated his narrow chest, about which he was exceedingly sensitive. He was always excited while he dressed, twangling all over to the tuning of the strings and the preliminary flourishes of the horns in the music-room; but tonight he seemed quite beside himself, and he teased and plagued the boys until, telling him that he was crazy, they put him down on the floor and sat on him.

Somewhat calmed by his suppression, Paul dashed out to the front of the house to seat the early comers. He was a model usher. Gracious and smiling he ran up and down the aisles. Nothing was too much trouble for him; he carried messages and brought programs as though it were his greatest pleasure in life, and all the people in his section thought him a charming boy, feeling that he remembered and admired them. As the house filled, he grew more and more vivacious and animated, and the color came to his cheeks and lips. It was very much as though this were a great reception and Paul were the host. Just as the musicians came out to take their places, his English teacher arrived with checks for the seats which a prominent manufacturer had taken for the season. She betrayed some embarrassment when she handed Paul the tickets, and a *hauteur* which subsequently made her feel very foolish. Paul was startled for a moment, and had the feeling of wanting to put her out; what business had she here among all these fine people and gay colors? He looked her over and decided that she was not appropriately dressed and must be a fool to sit downstairs in such togs. The tickets had probably been sent her out of kindness, he reflected, as he put down a seat for her, and she had about as much right to sit there as he had.

When the symphony began Paul sank into one of the rear seats with a long sigh of relief, and lost himself as he had done before the Rico. It was not that symphonies, as such, meant anything in particular to Paul, but the first sigh of the instruments seemed to free some hilarious spirit within him; something that struggled there like the Genius in the bottle found by the Arab fisherman. He felt a sudden zest of life; the lights danced before his eyes and the concert hall blazed into unimaginable splendor. When the soprano soloist came on, Paul forgot even the nastiness of his teacher's being there, and gave himself up to the peculiar intoxication such personages always had for him. The soloist chanced to be a German woman, by no means in her first youth, and the mother of many children; but she wore a satin gown and a tiara, and she had that indefinable air of achievement, that world-shine upon her, which always blinded Paul to any possible defects.

After a concert was over, Paul was often irritable and wretched until he got to sleep—and tonight he was even more than usually restless. He had the feeling of not being able to let down; of its being impossible to give up this delicious excitement which was the only thing that could be called living at all. During the last number he withdrew and, after hastily changing his clothes in the dressing-room, slipped out to the side door where the singer's carriage stood. Here he began pacing rapidly up and down the walk, waiting to see her come out.

Over yonder the Schenley, in its vacant stretch, loomed big and square through the fine rain, the windows of its twelve stories glowing like those of a lighted cardboard house under a Christmas tree. All the actors and singers of any importance stayed there when they were in the city, and a number of the big manufacturers of the place lived there in the winter. Paul had often hung about the hotel, watching the people go in and out, longing to enter and leave schoolmasters and dull care behind him forever.

At last the singer came out, accompanied by the conductor, who helped her into her carriage and closed the door with a cordial *auf wiedersehen*—which set Paul to wondering whether she were not an old sweetheart of his. Paul followed the carriage over to the hotel, walking so rapidly as not to be far from the entrance when the singer alighted and disappeared behind the swinging glass doors which were opened by a Negro in a tall hat and a long coat. In the moment that the door was ajar, it seemed to Paul that he, too, entered. He seemed to feel himself go after her up the steps, into the warm, lighted building, into an exotic, a tropical world of shiny, glistening surfaces and basking ease. He reflected upon the mysterious dishes that were brought into the dining room, the green bottles in buckets of ice, as he had seen them in the supper party pictures of the Sunday supplement. A quick gust of wind brought the rain down with sudden vehemence, and Paul was startled to find that he was still outside in the slush of the gravel driveway; that his boots were letting in the water and his scanty overcoat was clinging wet about him; that the lights in front of the concert hall were out, and that the rain was driving in sheets between him and the orange glow of the windows above him. There it was, what he wanted—tangibly before him, like the fairy world of a Christmas pantomime; as the rain beat in his face, Paul wondered whether he were destined always to shiver in the black night outside, looking up at it.

He turned and walked reluctantly toward the car tracks. The end had to come some time; his father in his night-clothes at the top of the stairs, explanations that did not explain, hastily improvised fictions that were forever tripping him up, his upstairs room and its horrible yellow wallpaper, the creaking bureau with the greasy plush collarbox, and over his painted wooden bed the pictures of George Washington and John Calvin, and the framed motto, "Feed my Lambs," which had been worked in red worsted by his mother, whom Paul could not remember.

Half an hour later, Paul alighted from the Negley Avenue car and went slowly down one of the side streets off the main thoroughfare. It was a highly respectable street, where all the houses were exactly alike, and where business men of moderate means begot and reared large families of children, all of whom went to Sabbath-school and learned the shorter catechism, and were interested in arithmetic; all of whom were as exactly alike as their homes, and of a piece with the monotony in which they lived. Paul never went up Cordelia Street without a shudder of loathing. His home was next to the house of the Cumberland minister. He approached it tonight with the nerveless sense of defeat, the hopeless feeling of sinking back forever into ugliness and commonness that he had always had when he came home. The moment he turned into Cordelia Street he felt the waters close above his head. After each of these orgies of living, he experienced all the physical depression which follows a debauch; the loathing of respectable beds, of common food, of a house permeated by kitchen odors; a shuddering repulsion for the flavorless, colorless mass of everyday existence; a morbid desire for cool things and soft lights and fresh flowers.

The nearer he approached the house, the more absolutely unequal Paul felt to the sight of it all; his ugly sleeping chamber; the cold bathroom with the grimy zinc tub, the cracked mirror, the dripping spigots; his father, at the top of the stairs, his hairy legs sticking out from his nightshirt, his feet thrust into carpet slippers. He was so much later than usual that there would certainly be inquiries and reproaches. Paul stopped short before the door. He felt that he could not be accosted by his father tonight; that he could not toss again on that miserable bed. He would not go in. He would tell his father that he had no carfare, and it was raining so hard he had gone home with one of the boys and stayed all night.

Meanwhile, he was wet and cold. He went around to the back of the house and tried one of the basement windows, found it open, raised it cautiously, and scrambled down the cellar wall to the floor. There he stood, holding his breath, terrified by the noise he had made; but the floor above him was silent, and there was no creak on the stairs. He found a soap-box, and carried it over to the soft ring of light that streamed from the furnace door, and sat down. He was horribly afraid of rats, so he did not try to sleep, but sat looking distrustfully at the dark, still terrified lest he might have awakened his father. In such reactions, after one of the experiences which made days and nights out of the dreary blanks of the calendar, when his senses were deadened, Paul's head was always singularly clear. Suppose his father had heard him getting in at the window and had come down and shot him for a burglar? Then, again, suppose his father had come down, pistol in hand, and he had cried out in time to save himself, and his father had been horrified to think how nearly he had killed him? Then, again, suppose a day should come when his father would remember that night, and wish there had been no warning cry to stay his hand? With this last supposition Paul entertained himself until daybreak.

The following Sunday was fine; the sodden November chill was broken by the last flash of autumnal summer. In the morning Paul had to go to church and Sabbath-school, as always. On seasonable Sunday afternoons the burghers of Cordelia Street usually sat out on their front "stoops," and talked to their neighbors on the next stoop, or called to those across the street in neighborly fashion. The men sat placidly on gay cushions placed upon the steps that led down to the sidewalk, while the women, in their Sunday "waists," sat in rockers on the cramped porches, pretending to be greatly at their ease. The children played in the streets; there were so many of them that the place resembled the recreation grounds of a kindergarten. The men on the steps—all in their shirt sleeves, their vests unbuttoned—sat with their legs well apart, their stomachs comfortably protruding, and talked of the prices of things, or told anecdotes of the sagacity of their various chiefs and overlords. They occasionally looked over the multitude of squabbling children, listened affectionately to their high-pitched, nasal voices, smiling to see their own proclivities reproduced in their offspring, and interspersed their legends of the iron kings with remarks about their sons' progress at school, their grades in arithmetic, and the amounts they had saved in their toy banks. On this last Sunday of November, Paul sat all the afternoon on the lowest step of his "stoop," staring into the street, while his sisters, in their rockers, were talking to the minister's daughters next door about how many shirtwaists they had made in the last week, and how many waffles someone had eaten at the last church supper. When the weather was warm, and his father was in a particularly jovial frame of mind, the girls made lemonade, which was always brought out in a red-glass pitcher, ornamented with forget-me-nots in blue enamel. This the girls thought very fine, and the neighbors joked about the suspicious color of the pitcher.

Today Paul's father, on the top step, was talking to a young man who shifted a restless baby from knee to knee. He happened to be the young man who was daily held up to Paul as a model, and after whom it was his father's dearest hope that he would pattern. This young man was of a ruddy complexion, with a compressed, red mouth, and faded near-sighted eyes, over which he wore thick spectacles, with gold bows that curved about his ears. He was clerk to one of the magnates of a great steel corporation, and was looked upon in Cordelia Street as a young man with a future. There was a story that, some five years ago—he was now barely twenty-six—he had been a trifle "dissipated," but in order to curb his appetites and save the loss of time and strength that a sowing of wild oats might have entailed, he had taken his chief's advice, oft reiterated to his employees, and at twenty-one had married the first woman whom he could persuade to share his fortunes. She happened to be an angular school mistress, much older than he, who also wore thick glasses, and who had now borne him four children, all near-sighted, like herself.

The young man was relating how his chief, now cruising in the Mediterranean, kept in touch with all the details of the business, arranging his office hours on his yacht just as though he were at home, and "knocking off work enough to keep two stenographers busy." His father told, in turn, the plan his corporation was considering, of putting in an electric railway plant at Cairo. Paul snapped his teeth; he had an awful apprehension that they might spoil it all before he got there. Yet he rather liked to hear these legends of the iron kings, that were told and retold on Sundays and holidays; these stories of palaces in Venice, yachts on the Mediterranean, and high play at Monte Carlo appealed to his fancy, and he was interested in the triumphs of cash boys who had become famous, though he had no mind for the cash-boy stage.

After supper was over, and he had helped to dry the dishes, Paul nervously asked his father whether he could go to George's to get some help in his geometry, and still more nervously asked for carfare. This latter request he had to repeat, as his father, on principle, did not like to hear requests for money, whether much or little. He asked Paul whether he could not go to some boy who lived nearer, and told him that he ought not to leave his school work until Sunday; but he gave him the dime. He was not a poor man, but he had a worthy ambition to come up in the world. His only reason for allowing Paul to usher was that he thought a boy ought to be earning a little.

Paul bounded upstairs, scrubbed the greasy odor of the dishwater from his hands with the ill-smelling soap he hated, and then shook over his fingers a few drops of violet water from the bottle he kept hidden in his drawer. He left the house with his geometry conspicuously under his arm, and the moment he got out of Cordelia Street and boarded a downtown car, he shook off the lethargy of two deadening days, and began to live again.

The leading juvenile of the permanent stock company which played at one of the downtown theaters was an acquaintance of Paul's, and the boy had been invited to drop in at the Sunday night rehearsals whenever he could. For more than a year Paul had spent every available moment loitering about Charley Edwards's dressing-room. He had won a place among Edwards's following not only because the young actor, who could not afford to employ a dresser, often found him useful, but because he recognized in Paul something akin to what churchmen termed "vocation."

It was at the theater and at Carnegie Hall that Paul really lived; the rest was but a sleep and a forgetting. This was Paul's fairy tale, and it had for him all the allurement of a secret love. The moment he inhaled the gassy, painty, dusty odor behind the scenes, he breathed like a prisoner set free, and felt within him the possibility of doing or saying splendid, brilliant things. The moment the cracked orchestra beat out the overture from *Martha,* or jerked at the serenade from *Rigoletto,* all stupid and ugly things slid from him, and his senses were deliciously, yet delicately fired.

Perhaps it was because, in Paul's world, the natural nearly always wore the guise of ugliness, that a certain element of artificiality seemed to him necessary in beauty. Perhaps it was because his experience of life elsewhere was so full of Sabbath-school picnics, petty economies, wholesome advice as to how to succeed in life, and the unescapable odors of cooking, that he found this existence so alluring, these smartly-clad men and women so attractive, that he was so moved by these starry apple orchards that bloomed perennially under the limelight.

It would be difficult to put it strongly enough how convincingly the stage entrance of that theater was for Paul the actual portal of Romance. Certainly none of the company ever suspected it, least of all Charley Edwards. It was very like the old stories that used to float about London of fabulously rich Jews, who had subterranean halls, with palms, and fountains, and soft lamps and richly apparelled women who never saw the disenchanting light of London day. So, in the midst of that smoke-palled city, enamored of figures and grimy toil, Paul had his secret temple, his wishing-carpet, his bit of blue-and-white Mediterranean shore bathed in perpetual sunshine.

Several of Paul's teachers had a theory that his imagination had been perverted by garish fiction; but the truth was, he scarcely ever read at all. The books at home were not such as would either tempt or corrupt a youthful mind, and as for reading the novels that some of his friends urged upon him—well, he got what he wanted much more quickly from music; any sort of music, from an orchestra to a barrel organ. He needed only the spark, the indescribable thrill that made his imagination master of his senses, and he could make plots and pictures enough of his own. It was equally true that he was not stage-struck—not, at any rate, in the usual acceptation of that expression. He had no desire to become an actor, any more than he had to become a musician. He felt no necessity to do any of these things; what he wanted was to see, to be in the atmosphere, float on the wave of it, to be carried out, blue league after blue league, away from everything.

After a night behind the scenes, Paul found the schoolroom more than ever repulsive; the bare floors and naked walls; the prosy men who never wore frock coats, or violets in their buttonholes; the women with their dull gowns, shrill voices, and pitiful seriousness about prepositions that govern the dative. He could not bear to have the other pupils think, for a moment, that he took these people seriously; he must convey to them that he considered it all trivial, and was there only by way of a joke, anyway. He had autograph pictures of all the members of the stock company which he showed his classmates, telling them the most incredible stories of his familiarity with these people, of his acquaintance with the soloists who came to Carnegie Hall, his suppers with them and the flowers he sent them. When these stories lost their effect, and his audience grew listless, he would bid all the boys good-by, announcing that he was going to travel for a while; going to Naples, to California, to Egypt. Then, next Monday, he would slip back, conscious and nervously smiling, his sister was ill, and he would have to defer his voyage until spring.

Matters went steadily worse with Paul at school. In the itch to let his instructors know how heartily he despised them, and how thoroughly he was appreciated elsewhere, he mentioned once or twice that he had no time to fool with theorems; adding—with a twitch of the eyebrows and a touch of that nervous bravado which so perplexed them—that he was helping the people down at the stock company; they were old friends of his.

The upshot of the matter was that the Principal went to Paul's father, and Paul was taken out of school and put to work. The manager at Carnegie Hall was told to get another usher in his stead; the door-keeper at the theater was warned not to admit him to the house; and Charley Edwards remorsefully promised the boy's father not to see him again.

The members of the stock company were vastly amused when some of Paul's stories reached them—especially the women. They were hard-working women, most of them supporting indolent husbands or brothers, and they laughed rather bitterly at having stirred the boy to such fervid and florid inventions. They agreed with the faculty and with his father, that Paul's was a bad case.

The east-bound train was plowing through a January snowstorm; the dull dawn was beginning to show gray when the engine whistled a mile out of Newark. Paul started up from the seat where he had lain curled in uneasy slumber, rubbed the breath-misted window glass with his hand, and peered out. The snow was whirling in curling eddies above the white bottom lands, and the drifts lay already deep in the fields and along the fences, while here and there the long dead grass and dried weed stalks protruded black above it. Lights shone from the scattered houses, and a gang of laborers who stood beside the track waved their lanterns.

Paul had slept very little, and he felt grimy and uncomfortable. He had made the all-night journey in a day coach because he was afraid if he took a Pullman he might be seen by some Pittsburgh business man who had noticed him in Denny & Carson's office. When the whistle woke him, he clutched quickly at his breast pocket, glancing about him with an uncertain smile. But the little, clay-bespattered Italians were still sleeping, the slatternly women across the aisle were in open-mouthed oblivion, and even the crumby, crying babies were for the nonce stilled. Paul settled back to struggle with his impatience as best he could.

When he arrived at the Jersey City station, he hurried through his breakfast, manifestly ill at ease and keeping a sharp eye about him. After he reached the Twenty-third Street station, he consulted a cabman, and had himself driven to a men's furnishing establishment which was just opening for the day. He spent upward of two hours there, buying with endless reconsidering and great care. His new street suit he put on in the fitting-room; the frock coat and dress clothes he had bundled into the cab with his new shirts. Then he drove to a hatter's and a shoe house. His next errand was at Tiffany's, where he selected silver-mounted brushes and a scarf-pin.

He would not wait to have his silver marked, he said. Lastly, he stopped at a trunk shop on Broadway, and had his purchases packed into various traveling bags.

It was a little after one o'clock when he drove up to the Waldorf, and, after settling with the cabman, went into the office. He registered from Washington; said his mother and father had been abroad, and that he had come down to await the arrival of their steamer. He told his story plausibly and had no trouble, since he offered to pay for them in advance, in engaging his rooms; a sleeping-room, sitting room and bath.

Not once, but a hundred times Paul had planned this entry into New York. He had gone over every detail of it with Charley Edwards, and in his scrap book at home there were pages of description about New York hotels, cut from the Sunday papers.

When he was shown to his sitting room on the eighth floor, he saw at a glance that everything was as it should be; there was but one detail in his mental picture that the place did not realize, so he rang for the bell boy and sent him down for flowers. He moved about nervously until the boy returned, putting away his new linen and fingering it delightedly as he did so. When the flowers came, he put them hastily into water, and then tumbled into a hot bath. Presently he came out of his white bathroom, resplendent in his new silk underwear, and playing with the tassels of his red robe. The snow was whirling so fiercely outside his windows that he could scarcely see across the street; but within, the air was deliciously soft and fragrant. He put the violets and jonquils on the tabouret beside the couch, and threw himself down with a long sigh, covering himself with a Roman blanket. He was thoroughly tired; he had been in such haste, he had stood up to such a strain, covered so much ground in the last twenty-four hours, that he wanted to think how it had all come about. Lulled by the sound of the wind, the warm air, and the cool fragrance of the flowers, he sank into deep, drowsy retrospection.

It had been wonderfully simple; when they had shut him out of the theater and concert hall, when they had taken away his bone, the whole thing was virtually determined. The rest was a mere matter of opportunity. The only thing that at all surprised him was his own courage—for he realized well enough that he had always been tormented by fear, a sort of apprehensive dread that, of late years, as the meshes of the lies he had told closed about him, had been pulling the muscles of his body tighter and tighter. Until now, he could not remember a time when he had not been dreading something. Even when he was a little boy, it was always there—behind him, or before, or on either side. There had always been the shadowed corner, the dark place into which he dared not look, but from which something seemed always to be watching him—and Paul had done things that were not pretty to watch, he knew.

But now he had a curious sense of relief, as though he had at last thrown down the gauntlet to the thing in the corner.

Yet it was but a day since he had been sulking in the traces; but yesterday afternoon that he had been sent to the bank with Denny & Carson's deposit, as usual—but this time he was instructed to leave the book to be balanced. There was above two thousand dollars in checks, and nearly a thousand in the bank notes which he had taken from the book and quietly transferred to his pocket. At the bank he had made out a new deposit slip. His nerves had been steady enough to permit of his returning to the office, where he had finished his work and asked for a full day's holiday tomorrow, Saturday, giving a perfectly reasonable pretext. The bank book, he knew, would not be returned before Monday or Tuesday, and his father would be out of town for the next week. From the time he slipped the bank notes into his pocket until he boarded the night train for New York, he had not known a moment's hesitation.

How astonishingly easy it had all been; here he was, the thing done; and this time there would be no awakening, no figure at the top of the stairs. He watched the snowflakes whirling by his window until he fell asleep.

When he awoke, it was four o'clock in the afternoon. He bounded up with a start; one of his precious days gone already! He spent nearly an hour in dressing, watching every stage of his toilet carefully in the mirror. Everything was quite perfect; he was exactly the kind of boy he had always wanted to be.

When he went downstairs, Paul took a carriage and drove up Fifth Avenue toward the Park. The snow had somewhat abated; carriages and tradesmen's wagons were hurrying soundlessly to and fro in the winter twilight; boys in woolen mufflers were shoveling off the doorsteps; the avenue stages made fine spots of color against the white street. Here and there on the corners whole flower gardens blooming behind glass windows, against which the snowflakes stuck and melted; violets, roses, carnations, lilies of the valley—somehow vastly more lovely and alluring that they blossomed thus unnaturally in the snow. The Park itself was a wonderful stage winter-piece.

When he returned, the pause of the twilight had ceased, and the tune of the streets had changed. The snow was falling faster, lights streamed from the hotels that reared their many stories fearlessly up into the storm, defying the raging Atlantic winds. A long, black stream of carriages poured down the avenue, intersected here and there by other streams, tending horizontally. There were a score of cabs about the entrance of his hotel, and his driver had to wait. Boys in livery were running in and out of the awning stretched across the sidewalk, up and down the red velvet carpet laid from the door to the street. Above, about, within it all, was the rumble and roar, the hurry and toss of thousands of human beings as hot for pleasure as himself, and on every side of him towered the glaring affirmation of the omnipotence of wealth.

The boy set his teeth and drew his shoulders together in a spasm of realization; the plot of all dramas, the text of all romances, the nerve-stuff of all sensations was whirling about him like the snowflakes. He burnt like a faggot in a tempest.

When Paul came down to dinner, the music of the orchestra floated up the elevator shaft to greet him. As he stepped into the thronged corridor, he sank back into one of the chairs against the wall to get his breath. The lights, the chatter, the perfumes, the bewildering medley of color—he had, for a moment, the feeling of not being able to stand it. But only for a moment; these were his own people, he told himself. He went slowly about the corridors, through the writing-rooms, smoking-rooms, reception-rooms, as though he were exploring the chambers of an enchanted palace, built and peopled for him alone.

When he reached the dining room he sat down at a table near a window. The flowers, the white linen, the many-colored wine glasses, the gay toilettes of the women, the low popping of corks, the undulating repetitions of the *Blue Danube* from the orchestra, all flooded Paul's dream with bewildering radiance. When the roseate tinge of his champagne was added—that cold, precious, bubbling stuff that creamed and foamed in his glass—Paul wondered that there were honest men in the world at all. This was what all the world was fighting for, he reflected; this was what all the struggle was about. He doubted the reality of his past. Had he ever known a place called Cordelia Street, a place where fagged-looking business men boarded the early car? Mere rivets in a machine they seemed to Paul—sickening men, with combings of children's hair always hanging to their coats, and the smell of cooking in their clothes. Cordelia Street—Ah, that belonged to another time and country! Had he not always been thus, had he not sat here night after night, from as far back as he could remember, looking pensively over just such shimmering textures, and slowly twirling the stem of a glass like this one between his thumb and middle finger? He rather thought he had.

He was not in the least abashed or lonely. He had no especial desire to meet or to know any of these people; all he demanded was the right to look on and conjecture, to watch the pageant. The mere stage properties were all he contended for. Nor was he lonely later in the evening, in his loge at the Opera. He was entirely rid of his nervous misgivings, of his forced aggressiveness, of the imperative desire to show himself different from his surroundings. He felt now that his surroundings explained him. Nobody questioned the purple; he had only to wear it passively. He had only to glance down at his dress coat to reassure himself that here it would he impossible for anyone to humiliate him.

He found it hard to leave his beautiful sitting room to go to bed that night, and sat long watching the raging storm from his turret window. When he went to sleep, it was with the lights turned on in his bedroom; partly because of his old timidity, and partly so that, if he should wake in the night, there would be no wretched moment of doubt, no horrible suspicion of yellow wallpaper, or of Washington and Calvin above his bed.

On Sunday morning the city was practically snow-bound. Paul breakfasted late, and in the afternoon he fell in with a wild San Francisco boy, a freshman at Yale, who said he had run down for a "little flyer" over Sunday. The young man offered to show Paul the night side of the town, and the two boys went off together after dinner, not returning to the hotel until seven o'clock the next morning. They had started out in the confiding warmth of a champagne friendship, but their parting in the elevator was singularly cool. The freshman pulled himself together to make his train, and Paul went to bed. He awoke at two o'clock in the afternoon, very thirsty and dizzy, and rang for ice water, coffee and the Pittsburgh papers.

On the part of the hotel management, Paul excited no suspicion. There was this to be said for him, that he wore his spoils with dignity and in no way made himself conspicuous. His chief greediness lay in his ears and eyes, and his excesses were not offensive ones. His dearest pleasures were the gray winter twilights in his sitting room; his quiet enjoyment of his flowers, his clothes, his wide divan, his cigarette and his sense of power. He could not remember a time when he had felt so at peace with himself. The mere release from the necessity of petty lying, lying every day and every day, restored his self-respect. He had never lied for pleasure, even at school; but to make himself noticed and admired, to assert his difference from other Cordelia Street boys; and he felt a good deal more manly, more honest, even, now that he had no need for boastful pretensions, now that he could, as his actor friends used to say, "dress the part." It was characteristic that remorse did not occur to him. His golden days went by without a shadow, and he made each as perfect as he could.

On the eighth day after his arrival in New York, he found the whole affair exploited in the Pittsburgh papers, exploited with a wealth of detail which indicated that local news of a sensational nature was at a low ebb. The firm of Denny & Carson announced that the boy's father had refunded the full amount of his theft, and that they had no intention of prosecuting. The Cumberland minister had been interviewed, and expressed his hope of yet reclaiming the motherless lad, and Paul's Sabbath-school teacher declared that she would spare no effort to that end. The rumor had reached Pittsburgh that the boy had been seen in a New York hotel, and his father had gone East to find him and bring him home.

Paul had just come in to dress for dinner; he sank into a chair, weak in the knees, and clasped his head in his hands. It was to be worse than jail, even; the tepid waters of Cordelia Street were to close over him finally and forever. The gray monotony stretched before him in hopeless, unrelieved years; Sabbath-school, Young People's Meeting, the yellow-papered room, the damp dish-towels; it all rushed back upon him with sickening vividness. He had the old feeling that the orchestra had suddenly stopped, the sinking sensation that the play was over. The sweat broke out on his face, and he sprang to his feet, looked about him with his white, conscious smile, and winked at himself in the mirror. With something of the childish belief in miracles with which he had so often gone to class, all his lessons unlearned, Paul dressed and dashed whistling down the corridor to the elevator.

He had no sooner entered the dining room and caught the measure of the music, than his remembrance was lightened by his old elastic power of claiming the moment, mounting with it, and finding it all sufficient. The glare and glitter about him, the mere scenic accessories had again, and for the last time, their old potency. He would show himself that he was game, he would finish the thing splendidly. He doubted, more than ever, the existence of Cordelia Street, and for the first time he drank his wine recklessly. Was he not, after all, one of these fortunate beings? Was he not still himself, and in his own place? He drummed a nervous accompaniment to the music and looked about him, telling himself over and over that it had paid.

He reflected drowsily, to the swell of the violin and the chill sweetness of his wine, that he might have done it more wisely. He might have caught an outbound steamer and been well out of their clutches before now. But the other side of the world had seemed too far away and too uncertain then; he could not have waited for it; his need had been too sharp. If he had to choose over again, he would do the same thing tomorrow. He looked affectionately about the dining room, now gilded with a soft mist. Ah, it had paid indeed!

Paul was awakened next morning by a painful throbbing in his head and feet. He had thrown himself across the bed without undressing, and had slept with his shoes on. His limbs and hands were lead heavy, and his tongue and throat were parched. There came upon him one of those fateful attacks of clear-headedness that never occurred except when he was physically exhausted and his nerves hung loose. He lay still and closed his eyes and let the tide of realities wash over him.

His father was in New York; "stopping at some joint or other," he told himself. The memory of successive summers on the front stoop fell upon him like a weight of black water. He had not a hundred dollars left; and he knew now, more than ever, that money was everything, the wall that stood between all he loathed and all he wanted. The thing was winding itself up; he had thought of that on his first glorious day in New York, and had even provided a way to snap the thread. It lay on his dressing-table now; he had got it out last night when he came blindly up from dinner—but the shiny metal hurt his eyes, and he disliked the look of it, anyway.

He rose and moved about with a painful effort, succumbing now and again to attacks of nausea. It was the old depression exaggerated; all the world had become Cordelia Street. Yet somehow he was not afraid of anything, was absolutely calm; perhaps because he had looked into the dark corner at last, and knew. It was bad enough, what he saw there; but somehow not so bad as his long fear of it had been. He saw everything clearly now. He had a feeling that he had made the best of it, that he had lived the sort of life he was meant to live, and for half an hour he sat staring at the revolver point. But he told himself that was not the way, so he went downstairs and took a cab to the ferry.

When Paul arrived at Newark, he got off the train and took another cab, directing the driver to follow the Pennsylvania tracks out of the town. The snow lay heavy on the roadways and had drifted deep in the open fields. Only here and there the dead grass or dried weed stalks projected, singularly black, above it. Once well into the country, Paul dismissed the carriage and walked, floundering along the tracks, his mind a medley of irrelevant things. He seemed to hold in his brain an actual picture of everything he had seen that morning. He remembered every feature of both his drivers, the toothless old woman from whom he had bought the red flowers in his coat, the agent from whom he had got his ticket, and all of his fellow-passengers on the ferry. His mind, unable to cope with vital matters near at hand, worked feverishly and deftly at sorting and grouping these images. They made for him a part of the ugliness of the world, of the ache in his head, and the bitter burning on his tongue. He stooped and put a handful of snow into his mouth as he walked, but that, too, seemed hot. When he reached a little hillside, where the tracks ran through a cut some twenty feet below him, he stopped and sat down.

The carnations in his coat were drooping with the cold, he noticed; all their red glory over. It occurred to him that all the flowers he had seen in the show windows that first night must have gone the same way, long before this. It was only one splendid breath they had, in spite of their brave mockery at the winter outside the glass. It was a losing game in the end, it seemed, this revolt against the homilies by which the world is run. Paul took one of the blossoms carefully from his coat and scooped a little hole in the snow, where he covered it up. Then he dozed a while, from his weak condition, seeming insensible to the cold.

The sound of an approaching train woke him, and he started to his feet, remembering only his resolution, and afraid lest he should be too late. He stood watching the approaching locomotive, his teeth chattering, his lips drawn away from them in a frightened smile; once or twice he glanced nervously sidewise, as though he were being watched. When the right moment came, he jumped. As he fell, the folly of his haste occurred to him with merciless clearness, the vastness of what he had left undone. There flashed through his brain, clearer than ever before, the blue of Adriatic water, the yellow of Algerian sands.

He felt something strike his chest—his body was being thrown swiftly through the air, on and on, immeasurably far and fast, while his limbs gently relaxed. Then, because the picture-making mechanism was crushed, the disturbing visions flashed into black, and Paul dropped back into the immense design of things.

F. SCOTT FITZGERALD

Bernice Bobs Her Hair

AFTER DARK ON SATURDAY night one could stand on the first tee of the golf-course and see the country-club windows as a yellow expanse over a very black and wavy ocean. The waves of this ocean, so to speak, were the heads of many curious caddies, a few of the more ingenious chauffeurs, the golf professional's deaf sister—and there were usually several stray, diffident waves who might have rolled inside had they so desired. This was the gallery.

The balcony was inside. It consisted of the circle of wicker chairs that lined the wall of the combination clubroom and ballroom. At these Saturday-night dances it was largely feminine; a great babel of middle-aged ladies with sharp eyes and icy hearts behind lorgnettes and large bosoms. The main function of the balcony was critical. It occasionally showed grudging admiration, but never approval, for it is well known among ladies over thirty-five that when the younger set dance in the summer-time it is with the very worst intentions in the world, and if they are not bombarded with stony eyes stray couples will dance weird barbaric interludes in the corners, and the more popular, more dangerous, girls will sometimes be kissed in the parked limousines of unsuspecting dowagers.

But, after all, this critical circle is not close enough to the stage to see the actors' faces and catch the subtler byplay. It can only frown and lean, ask questions and make satisfactory deductions from its set of postulates, such as the one which states that every young man with a large income leads the life of a hunted partridge. It never really appreciates the drama of the shifting, semicruel world of adolescence. No; boxes, orchestra-circle, principals, and chorus are represented by the medley of faces and voices that sway to the plaintive African rhythm of Dyer's dance orchestra.

From sixteen-year-old Otis Ormonde, who has two more years at Hill School, to G. Reece Stoddard, over whose bureau at home hangs a Harvard law diploma; from little Madeleine Hogue, whose hair still feels strange and uncomfortable on top of her head, to Bessie MacRae, who has been the life of the party a little too long—more than ten years—the medley is not only the centre of the stage but contains the only people capable of getting an unobstructed view of it.

With a flourish and a bang the music stops. The couples exchange artificial, effortless smiles, facetiously repeat "*la*-de-*da-da* dum-*dum*," and then the clatter of young feminine voices soars over the burst of clapping.

A few disappointed stags caught in midfloor as they had been about to cut in subsided listlessly back to the walls, because this was not like the riotous Christmas dances—these summer hops were considered just pleasantly warm and exciting, where even the younger marrieds rose and performed ancient waltzes and terrifying fox trots to the tolerant amusement of their younger brothers and sisters.

Warren McIntyre, who casually attended Yale, being one of the unfortunate stags, felt in his dinner-coat pocket for a cigarette and strolled out onto the wide, semidark veranda, where couples were scattered at tables, filling the lantern-hung night with vague words and hazy laughter. He nodded here and there at the less absorbed and as he passed each couple some half-forgotten fragment of a story played in his mind, for it was not a large city and every one was Who's Who to every one else's past. There, for example, were Jim Strain and Ethel Demorest, who had been privately engaged for three years. Every one knew that as soon as Jim managed to hold a job for more than two months she would marry him. Yet how bored they both looked, and how wearily Ethel regarded Jim sometimes, as if she wondered why she had trained the vines of her affection on such a wind-shaken poplar.

Warren was nineteen and rather pitying with those of his friends who hadn't gone East to college. But, like most boys, he bragged tremendously about the girls of his city when he was away from it.

There was Genevieve Ormonde, who regularly made the rounds of dances, house-parties, and football games at Princeton, Yale, Williams, and Cornell; there was black-eyed Roberta Dillon, who was quite as famous to her own generation as Hiram Johnson or Ty Cobb; and, of course, there was Marjorie Harvey, who besides having a fairylike face and a dazzling, bewildering tongue was already justly celebrated for having turned five cart-wheels in succession during the past pump-and-slipper dance at New Haven.

Warren, who had grown up across the street from Marjorie, had long been "crazy about her." Sometimes she seemed to reciprocate his feeling with a faint gratitude, but she had tried him by her infallible test and informed him gravely that she did not love him. Her test was that when she was away from him she forgot him and had affairs with other boys. Warren found this discouraging, especially as Marjorie had been making little trips all summer, and for the first two or three days after each arrival home he saw great heaps of mail on the Harveys' hall table addressed to her in various masculine handwritings. To make matters worse, all during the month of August she had been visited by her cousin Bernice from Eau Claire, and it seemed impossible to see her alone. It was always necessary to hunt round and find some one to take care of Bernice. As August waned this was becoming more and more difficult.

Much as Warren worshipped Marjorie, he had to admit that Cousin Bernice was sorta dopeless. She was pretty, with dark hair and high color, but she was no fun on a party. Every Saturday night he danced a long arduous duty dance with her to please Marjorie, but he had never been anything but bored in her company.

"Warren"—a soft voice at his elbow broke in upon his thoughts, and he turned to see Marjorie, flushed and radiant as usual. She laid a hand on his shoulder and a glow settled almost imperceptibly over him.

"Warren," she whispered, "do something for me—dance with Bernice. She's been stuck with little Otis Ormonde for almost an hour."

Warren's glow faded.

"Why—sure," he answered half-heartedly.

"You don't mind, do you? I'll see that you don't get stuck."

"'Sall right."

Marjorie smiled—that smile that was thanks enough.

"You're an angel, and I'm obliged loads."

With a sigh the angel glanced round the veranda, but Bernice and Otis were not in sight. He wandered back inside, and there in front of the women's dressing-room he found Otis in the centre of a group of young men who were convulsed with laughter. Otis was brandishing a piece of timber he had picked up, and discoursing volubly.

"She's gone in to fix her hair," he announced wildly. "I'm waiting to dance another hour with her."

Their laughter was renewed.

"Why don't some of you cut in?" cried Otis resentfully. "She likes more variety."

"Why, Otis," suggested a friend, "you've just barely got used to her."

"Why the two-by-four, Otis?" inquired Warren, smiling.

"The two-by-four? Oh, this? This is a club. When she comes out I'll hit her on the head and knock her in again."

Warren collapsed on a settee and howled with glee.

"Never mind, Otis," he articulated finally. "I'm relieving you this time."

Otis simulated a sudden fainting attack and handed the stick to Warren.

"If you need it, old man," he said hoarsely.

No matter how beautiful or brilliant a girl may be, the reputation of not being frequently cut in on makes her position at a dance unfortunate. Perhaps boys prefer her company to that of the butterflies with whom they dance a dozen times an evening, but youth in this jazz-nourished generation is temperamentally restless, and the idea of fox-trotting more than one full fox trot with the same girl is distasteful, not to say odious. When it comes to several dances and the intermissions between she can be quite sure that a young man, once relieved, will never tread on her wayward toes again.

Warren danced the next full dance with Bernice, and finally, thankful for the intermission, he led her to a table on the veranda. There was a moment's silence while she did unimpressive things with her fan.

"It's hotter here than in Eau Claire," she said.

Warren stifled a sigh and nodded. It might be for all he knew or cared. He wondered idly whether she was a poor conversationalist because she got no attention or got no attention because she was a poor conversationalist.

"You going to be here much longer?" he asked, and then turned rather red. She might suspect his reasons for asking.

"Another week," she answered, and stared at him as if to lunge at his next remark when it left his lips.

Warren fidgeted. Then with a sudden charitable impulse he decided to try part of his line on her. He turned and looked at her eyes.

"You've got an awfully kissable mouth," he began quietly.

This was a remark that he sometimes made to girls at college proms when they were talking in just such half dark as this. Bernice distinctly jumped. She turned an ungraceful red and became clumsy with her fan. No one had ever made such a remark to her before.

"Fresh!"—the word had slipped out before she realized it, and she bit her lip. Too late she decided to be amused, and offered him a flustered smile.

Warren was annoyed. Though not accustomed to have that remark taken seriously, still it usually provoked a laugh or a paragraph of sentimental banter. And he hated to be called fresh, except in a joking way. His charitable impulse died and he switched the topic.

"Jim Strain and Ethel Demorest sitting out as usual," he commented.

This was more in Bernice's line, but a faint regret mingled with her relief as the subject changed. Men did not talk to her about kissable mouths, but she knew that they talked in some such way to other girls.

"Oh, yes," she said, and laughed. "I hear they've been mooning round for years without a red penny. Isn't it silly?"

Warren's disgust increased. Jim Strain was a close friend of his brother's, and anyway he considered it bad form to sneer at people for not having money. But Bernice had had no intention of sneering. She was merely nervous.

II

When Marjorie and Bernice reached home at half after midnight they said good night at the top of the stairs. Though cousins, they were not intimates. As a matter of fact Marjorie had no female intimates—she considered girls stupid. Bernice on the contrary all through this parent-arranged visit had rather longed to exchange those confidences flavored with giggles and tears that she considered an indispensable factor in all feminine intercourse. But in this respect she found Marjorie rather cold; felt somehow the same difficulty in talking to her that she had in talking to men. Marjorie never giggled, was never frightened, seldom embarrassed, and in fact had very few of the qualities which Bernice considered appropriately and blessedly feminine.

As Bernice busied herself with tooth-brush and paste this night she wondered for the hundredth time why she never had any attention when she was away from home. That her family were the wealthiest in Eau Claire; that her mother entertained tremendously, gave little dinners for her daughter before all dances and bought her a car of her own to drive round in, never occurred to her as factors in her home-town social success. Like most girls she had been brought up on the warm milk prepared by Annie Fellows Johnston and on novels in which the female was beloved because of certain mysterious womanly qualities, always mentioned but never displayed.

Bernice felt a vague pain that she was not at present engaged in being popular. She did not know that had it not been for Marjorie's campaigning she would have danced the entire evening with one man; but she knew that even in Eau Claire other girls with less position and less pulchritude were given a much bigger rush. She attributed this to something subtly unscrupulous in those girls. It had never worried her, and if it had her mother would have assured her that the other girls cheapened themselves and that men really respected girls like Bernice.

She turned out the light in her bathroom, and on an impulse decided to go in and chat for a moment with her aunt Josephine, whose light was still on. Her soft slippers bore her noiselessly down the carpeted hall, but hearing voices inside she stopped near the partly opened door. Then she caught her own name, and without any definite intention of eavesdropping lingered—and the thread of the conversation going on inside pierced her consciousness sharply as if it had been drawn through with a needle.

"She's absolutely hopeless!" It was Marjorie's voice. "Oh, I know what you're going to say! So many people have told you how pretty and sweet she is, and how she can cook! What of it? She has a bum time. Men don't like her."

"What's a little cheap popularity?"

Mrs. Harvey sounded annoyed.

"It's everything when you're eighteen," said Marjorie emphatically. "I've done my best. I've been polite and I've made men dance with her, but they just won't stand being bored. When I think of that goregous coloring wasted on such a ninny, and think what Martha Carey could do with it—oh!"

"There's no courtesy these days."

Mrs. Harvey's voice implied that modern situations were too much for her. When she was a girl all young ladies who belonged to nice families had glorious times.

"Well," said Marjorie, "no girl can permanently bolster up a lame-duck visitor, because these days it's every girl for herself. I've even tried to drop her hints about clothes and things, and she's been furious—given me the funniest looks. She's sensitive enough to know she's not getting away with much, but I'll bet she consoles herself by thinking that she's very virtuous and that I'm too gay and fickle and will come to a bad end. All unpopular girls think that way. Sour grapes! Sarah Hopkins refers to Genevieve and Roberta and me as gardenia girls! I'll bet she'd give ten years of her life and her European education to be a gardenia girl and have three or four men in love with her and be cut in on every few feet at dances."

"It seems to me," interrupted Mrs. Harvey rather wearily, "that you ought to be able to do something for Bernice. I know she's not very vivacious."

Marjorie groaned.

"Vivacious! Good grief! I've never heard her say anything to a boy except that it's hot or the floor's crowded or that she's going to school in New York next year. Sometimes she asks them what kind of car they have and tells them the kind she has. Thrilling!"

There was a short silence, and then Mrs. Harvey took up her refrain:

"All I know is that other girls not half so sweet and attractive get partners. Martha Carey, for instance, is stout and loud, and her mother is distinctly common. Roberta Dillon is so thin this year that she looks as though Arizona were the place for her. She's dancing herself to death."

"But, mother," objected Marjorie impatiently, "Martha is cheerful and awfully witty and an awfully slick girl, and Roberta's a marvellous dancer. She's been popular for ages!"

Mrs. Harvey yawned.

"I think it's that crazy Indian blood in Bernice," continued Marjorie. "Maybe she's a reversion to type. Indian women all just sat round and never said anything."

"Go to bed, you silly child," laughed Mrs. Harvey. "I wouldn't have told you that if I'd thought you were going to remember it. And I think most of your ideas are perfectly idiotic," she finished sleepily.

There was another silence, while Marjorie considered whether or not convincing her mother was worth the trouble. People over forty can seldom be permanently convinced of anything. At eighteen our convictions are hills from which we look; at forty-five they are caves in which we hide.

Having decided this, Marjorie said good night. When she came out into the hall it was quite empty.

III

While Marjorie was breakfasting late next day Bernice came into the room with a rather formal good morning, sat down opposite, stared intently over and slightly moistened her lips.

"What's on your mind?" inquired Marjorie, rather puzzled.

Bernice paused before she threw her hand-grenade.

"I heard what you said about me to your mother last night."

Marjorie was startled, but she showed only a faintly heightened color and her voice was quite even when she spoke.

"Where were you?"

"In the hall. I didn't mean to listen—at first."

After an involuntary look of contempt Marjorie dropped her eyes and became very interested in balancing a stray corn-flake on her finger.

"I guess I'd better go back to Eau Claire—if I'm such a nuisance." Bernice's lower lip was trembling violently and she continued on a wavering note: "I've tried to be nice, and—and I've been first neglected and then insulted. No one ever visited me and got such treatment."

Marjorie was silent.

"But I'm in the way, I see. I'm a drag on you. Your friends don't like me." She paused, and then remembered another one of her grievances. "Of course I was furious last week when you tried to hint to me that that dress was unbecoming. Don't you think I know how to dress myself?"

"No," murmured Marjorie less than half-aloud.

"What?"

"I didn't hint anything," said Marjorie succinctly. "I said, as I remember, that it was better to wear a becoming dress three times straight than to alternate it with two frights."

"Do you think that was a very nice thing to say?"

"I wasn't trying to be nice." Then after a pause: "When do you want to go?"

Bernice drew in her breath sharply.

"Oh!" It was a little half-cry.

Marjorie looked up in surprise.

"Didn't you say you were going?"

"Yes, but——"

"Oh, you were only bluffing!"

They stared at each other across the breakfast-table for a moment. Misty waves were passing before Bernice's eyes, while Marjorie's face wore that rather hard expression that she used when slightly intoxicated undergraduates were making love to her.

"So you were bluffing," she repeated as if it were what she might have expected.

Bernice admitted it by bursting into tears. Marjorie's eyes showed boredom.

"You're my cousin," sobbed Bernice. "I'm v-v-visiting you. I was to stay a month, and if I go home my mother will know and she'll wah-wonder——"

Marjorie waited until the shower of broken words collapsed into little sniffles.

"I'll give you my month's allowance," she said coldly, "and you can spend this last week anywhere you want. There's a very nice hotel——"

Bernice's sobs rose to a flute note, and rising of a sudden she fled from the room.

An hour later, while Marjorie was in the library absorbed in composing one of those non-committal, marvellously elusive letters that only a young girl can write, Bernice reappeared, very red-eyed and consciously calm. She cast no glance at Marjorie but took a book at random from the shelf and sat down as if to read. Marjorie seemed absorbed in her letter and continued writing. When the clock showed noon Bernice closed her book with a snap.

"I suppose I'd better get my railroad ticket."

This was not the beginning of the speech she had rehearsed upstairs, but as Marjorie was not getting her cues—wasn't urging her to be reasonable; it's all a mistake—it was the best opening she could muster.

"Just wait till I finish this letter," said Marjorie without looking round. "I want to get it off in the next mail."

After another minute, during which her pen scratched busily, she turned round and relaxed with an air of "at your service." Again Bernice had to speak.

"Do you want me to go home?"

"Well," said Marjorie, considering, "I suppose if you're not having a good time you'd better go. No use being miserable."

"Don't you think common kindness——"

"Oh, please don't quote 'Little Women'!" cried Marjorie impatiently. "That's out of style."

"You think so?"

"Heavens, yes! What modern girl could live like those inane females?"

"They were the models for our mothers."

Marjorie laughed.

"Yes, they were—not! Besides, our mothers were all very well in their way, but they know very little about their daughters' problems."

Bernice drew herself up.

"Please don't talk about my mother."

Marjorie laughed.

"I don't think I mentioned her."

Bernice felt that she was being led away from her subject.

"Do you think you've treated me very well?"

"I've done my best. You're rather hard material to work with."

The lids of Bernice's eyes reddened.

"I think you're hard and selfish, and you haven't a feminine quality in you."

"Oh, my Lord!" cried Marjorie in desperation. "You little nut! Girls like you are responsible for all the tiresome colorless marriages; all those ghastly inefficiencies that pass as feminine qualities. What a blow it must be when a man with imagination marries the beautiful bundle of clothes that he's been building ideals round, and finds that she's just a weak, whining, cowardly mass of affectations!"

Bernice's mouth had slipped half open.

"The womanly woman!" continued Marjorie. "Her whole early life is occupied in whining criticisms of girls like me who really do have a good time."

Bernice's jaw descended farther as Marjorie's voice rose.

"There's some excuse for an ugly girl whining. If I'd been irretrievably ugly I'd never have forgiven my parents for bringing me into the world. But you're starting life without any handicap—" Marjorie's little fist clinched. "If you expect me to weep with you you'll be disappointed. Go or stay, just as you like." And picking up her letters she left the room.

Bernice claimed a headache and failed to appear at luncheon. They had a matinée date for the afternoon, but the headache persisting, Marjorie made explanations to a not very downcast boy. But when she returned late in the afternoon she found Bernice with a strangely set face waiting for her in her bedroom.

"I've decided," began Bernice without preliminaries, "that maybe you're right about things—possibly not. But if you'll tell me why your friends aren't—aren't interested in me I'll see if I can do what you want me to"

Marjorie was at the mirror shaking down her hair.

"Do you mean it?"

"Yes."

"Without reservations? Will you do exactly what I say?"

"Well, I——"

"Well nothing! Will you do exactly as I say?"

"If they're sensible things."

"They're not! You're no case for sensible things."

"Are you going to make—to recommend——"

"Yes, everything. If I tell you to take boxing lessons you'll have to do it. Write home and tell your mother you're going to stay another two weeks."

"If you'll tell me——"

"All right—I'll just give you a few examples now. First, you have no ease of manner. Why? Because you're never sure about your personal appearance. When a girl feels that she's perfectly groomed and dressed she can forget that part of her. That's charm. The more parts of yourself you can afford to forget the more charm you have."

"Don't I look all right?"

"No; for instance, you never take care of your eyebrows. They're black and lustrous, but by leaving them straggly they're a blemish. They'd be beautiful if you'd take care of them in one-tenth the time you take doing nothing. You're going to brush them so that they'll grow straight."

Bernice raised the brows in question.

"Do you mean to say that men notice eyebrows?"

"Yes—subconsciously. And when you go home you ought to have your teeth straightened a little. It's almost imperceptible, still——"

"But I thought," interrupted Bernice in bewilderment, "that you despised little dainty feminine things like that."

"I hate dainty minds," answered Marjorie. "But a girl has to be dainty in person. If she looks like a million dollars she can talk about Russia, ping-pong, or the League of Nations and get away with it."

"What else?"

"Oh, I'm just beginning! There's your dancing."

"Don't I dance all right?"

"No, you don't—you lean on a man; yes, you do—ever so slightly. I noticed it when we were dancing together yesterday. And you dance standing up straight instead of bending over a little. Probably some old lady on the side-line once told you that you looked so dignified that way. But except with a very small girl it's much harder on the man, and he's the one that counts."

"Go on." Bernice's brain was reeling.

"Well, you've got to learn to be nice to men who are sad birds. You look as if you'd been insulted whenever you're thrown with any except the most popular boys. Why, Bernice, I'm cut in on every few feet—and who does most of it? Why, those very sad birds. No girl can afford to neglect them. They're the big part of any crowd. Young boys too shy to talk are the very best conversational practice. Clumsy boys are the best dancing practice. If you can follow them and yet look graceful you can follow a baby tank across a barb-wire skyscraper."

Bernice sighed profoundly, but Marjorie was not through.

"If you go to a dance and really amuse, say, three sad birds that dance with you; if you talk so well to them that they forget they're stuck with you, you've done something. They'll come back next time, and gradually so many sad birds will dance with you that the attractive boys will see there's no danger of being stuck—then they'll dance with you."

"Yes," agreed Bernice faintly. "I think I begin to see."

"And finally," concluded Marjorie, "poise and charm will just come. You'll wake up some morning knowing you've attained it, and men will know it too."

Bernice rose.

"It's been awfully kind of you—but nobody's ever talked to me like this before, and I feel sort of startled."

Marjorie made no answer but gazed pensively at her own image in the mirror.

"You're a peach to help me," continued Bernice.

Still Marjorie did not answer, and Bernice thought she had seemed too grateful.

"I know you don't like sentiment," she said timidly.

Marjorie turned to her quickly.

"Oh, I wasn't thinking about that. I was considering whether we hadn't better bob your hair."

Bernice collapsed backward upon the bed.

IV

On the following Wednesday evening there was a dinner-dance at the country club. When the guests strolled in Bernice found her place-card with a slight feeling of irritation. Though at her right sat G. Reece Stoddard, a most desirable and distinguished young bachelor, the all-important left held only Charley Paulson. Charley lacked height, beauty, and social shrewdness, and in her new enlightenment Bernice decided that his only qualification to be her partner was that he had never been stuck with her. But this feeling of irritation left with the last of the soup-plates, and Marjorie's specific instruction came to her. Swallowing her pride she turned to Charley Paulson and plunged.

"Do you think I ought to bob my hair, Mr. Charley Paulson?"

Charley looked up in surprise.

"Why?"

"Because I'm considering it. It's such a sure and easy way of attracting attention."

Charley smiled pleasantly. He could not know this had been rehearsed. He replied that he didn't know much about bobbed hair. But Bernice was there to tell him.

"I want to be a society vampire, you see," she announced coolly, and went on to inform him that bobbed hair was the necessary prelude. She added that she wanted to ask his advice, because she had heard he was so critical about girls.

Charley, who knew as much about the psychology of women as he did of the mental states of Buddhist contemplatives, felt vaguely flattered.

"So I've decided," she continued, her voice rising slightly, "that early next week I'm going down to the Sevier Hotel barber-shop, sit in the first chair, and get my hair bobbed." She faltered, noticing that the people near her had paused in their conversation and were listening; but after a confused second Marjorie's coaching told, and she finished her paragraph to the vicinity at large. "Of course I'm charging admission, but if you'll all come down and encourage me I'll issue passes for the inside seats."

There was a ripple of appreciative laughter, and under cover of it G. Reece Stoddard leaned over quickly and said close to her ear: "I'll take a box right now."

She met his eyes and smiled as if he had said something surpassingly brilliant.

"Do you believe in bobbed hair?" asked G. Reece in the same undertone.

"I think it's unmoral," affirmed Bernice gravely. "But, of course, you've either got to amuse people or feed 'em or shock 'em." Marjorie had culled this from Oscar Wilde. It was greeted with a ripple of laughter from the men and a series of quick, intent looks from the girls. And then as though she had said nothing of wit or moment Bernice turned again to Charley and spoke confidentially in his ear.

"I want to ask you your opinion of several people. I imagine you're a wonderful judge of character."

Charley thrilled faintly—paid her a subtle compliment by overturning her water.

Two hours later, while Warren McIntyre was standing passively in the stag line abstractedly watching the dancers and wondering whither and with whom Marjorie had disappeared, an unrelated perception began to creep slowly upon him—a perception that Bernice, cousin to Marjorie, had been cut in on several times in the past five minutes. He closed his eyes, opened them and looked again. Several minutes back she had been dancing with a visiting boy, a matter easily accounted for; a visiting boy would know no better. But now she was dancing with some one else, and there was Charley Paulson headed for her with enthusiastic determination in his eye. Funny—Charley seldom danced with more than three girls an evening.

Warren was distinctly surprised when—the exchange having been effected—the man relieved proved to be none other than G. Reece Stoddard himself. And G. Reece seemed not at all jubilant at being relieved. Next time Bernice danced near, Warren regarded her intently. Yes, she was pretty, distinctly pretty; and to-night her face seemed really vivacious. She had that look that no woman, however histrionically proficient, can successfully counterfeit—she looked as if she were having a good time. He liked the way she had her hair arranged, wondered if it was brilliantine that made it glisten so. And that dress was becoming—a dark red that set off her shadowy eyes and high coloring. He remembered that he had thought her pretty when she first came to town, before he had realized that she was dull. Too bad she was dull—dull girls unbearable—certainly pretty though.

His thoughts zigzagged back to Marjorie. This disappearance would be like other disappearances. When she reappeared he would demand where she had been—would be told emphatically that it was none of his business. What a pity she was so sure of him! She basked in the knowledge that no other girl in town interested him; she defied him to fall in love with Genevieve or Roberta.

Warren sighed. The way to Marjorie's affections was a labyrinth indeed. He looked up. Bernice was again dancing with the visiting boy. Half unconsciously he took a step out from the stag line in her direction, and hesitated. Then he said to himself that it was charity. He walked toward her—collided suddenly with G. Reece Stoddard.

"Pardon me," said Warren.

But G. Reece had not stopped to apologize. He had again cut in on Bernice.

That night at one o'clock Marjorie, with one hand on the electric-light switch in the hall, turned to take a last look at Bernice's sparkling eyes.

"So it worked?"

"Oh, Marjorie, yes!" cried Bernice.

"I saw you were having a gay time."

"I did! The only trouble was that about midnight I ran short of talk. I had to repeat myself—with different men of course. I hope they won't compare notes."

"Men don't," said Marjorie, yawning, "and it wouldn't matter if they did—they'd think you were even trickier."

She snapped out the light, and as they started up the stairs Bernice grasped the banister thankfully. For the first time in her life she had been danced tired.

"You see," said Marjorie at the top of the stairs, "one man sees another man cut in and he thinks there must be something there. Well, we'll fix up some new stuff to-morrow. Good night."

"Good night."

As Bernice took down her hair she passed the evening before her in review. She had followed instructions exactly. Even when Charley Paulson cut in for the eighth time she had simulated delight and had apparently been both interested and flattered. She had not talked about the weather or Eau Claire or automobiles or her school, but had confined her conversation to me, you, and us.

But a few minutes before she fell asleep a rebellious thought was churning drowsily in her brain—after all, it was she who had done it. Marjorie, to be sure, had given her her conversation, but then Marjorie got much of her conversation out of things she read. Bernice had bought the red dress, though she had never valued it highly before Marjorie dug it out of her trunk—and her own voice had said the words, her own lips had smiled, her own feet had danced. Marjorie nice girl—vain, though—nice evening—nice boys—like Warren—Warren—Warren—what's-his-name—Warren——

She fell asleep.

V

To Bernice the next week was a revelation. With the feeling that people really enjoyed looking at her and listening to her came the foundation of self-confidence. Of course there were numerous mistakes at first. She did not know, for instance, that Draycott Deyo was studying for the ministry; she was unaware that he had cut in on her because he thought she was a quiet, reserved girl. Had she known these things she would not have treated him to the line which began "Hello, Shell Shock!" and continued with the bathtub story—"It takes a frightful lot of energy to fix my hair in the summer—there's so much of it—so I always fix it first and powder my face and put on my hat; then I get into the bathtub, and dress afterward. Don't you think that's the best plan?"

Though Draycott Deyo was in the throes of difficulties concerning baptism by immersion and might possibly have seen a connection, it must be admitted that he did not. He considered feminine bathing an immoral subject, and gave her some of his ideas on the depravity of modern society.

But to offset that unfortunate occurrence Bernice had several signal successes to her credit. Little Otis Ormonde pleaded off from a trip East and elected instead to follow her with a puppylike devotion, to the amusement of his crowd and to the irritation of G. Reece Stoddard, several of whose afternoon calls Otis completely ruined by the disgusting tenderness of the glances he bent on Bernice. He even told her the story of the two-by-four and the dressing-room to show her how frightfully mistaken he and every one else had been in their first judgment of her. Bernice laughed off that incident with a slight sinking sensation.

Of all Bernice's conversation perhaps the best known and most universally approved was the line about the bobbing of her hair.

"Oh, Bernice, when you goin' to get the hair bobbed?"

"Day after to-morrow maybe," she would reply, laughing. "Will you come and see me? Because I'm counting on you, you know."

"Will we? You know! But you better hurry up."

Bernice, whose tonsorial intentions were strictly dishonorable, would laugh again.

"Pretty soon now. You'd be surprised."

But perhaps the most significant symbol of her success was the gray car of the hypercritical Warren McIntyre, parked daily in front of the Harvey house. At first the parlor-maid was distinctly startled when he asked for Bernice instead of Marjorie; after a week of it she told the cook that Miss Bernice had gotta holda Miss Marjorie's best fella.

And Miss Bernice had. Perhaps it began with Warren's desire to rouse jealousy in Marjorie; perhaps it was the familiar though unrecognized strain of Marjorie in Bernice's conversation; perhaps it was both of these and something of sincere attraction besides. But somehow the collective mind of the younger set knew within a week that Marjorie's most reliable beau had made an amazing face-about and was giving an indisputable rush to Marjorie's guest. The question of the moment was how Marjorie would take it. Warren called Bernice on the 'phone twice a day, sent her notes, and they were frequently seen together in his roadster, obviously engrossed in one of those tense, significant conversations as to whether or not he was sincere.

Marjorie on being twitted only laughed. She said she was mighty glad that Warren had at last found some one who appreciated him. So the younger set laughed, too, and guessed that Marjorie didn't care and let it go at that.

One afternoon when there were only three days left of her visit Bernice was waiting in the hall for Warren, with whom she was going to a bridge party. She was in rather a blissful mood, and when Marjorie—also bound for the party—appeared beside her and began casually to adjust her hat in the mirror, Bernice was utterly unprepared for anything in the nature of a clash. Marjorie did her work very coldly and succinctly in three sentences.

"You may as well get Warren out of your head," she said coldly.

"What?" Bernice was utterly astounded.

"You may as well stop making a fool of yourself over Warren McIntyre. He doesn't care a snap of his fingers about you."

For a tense moment they regarded each other—Marjorie scornful, aloof; Bernice astounded, half-angry, half-afraid. Then two cars drove up in front of the house and there was a riotous honking. Both of them gasped faintly, turned, and side by side hurried out.

All through the bridge party Bernice strove in vain to master a rising uneasiness. She had offended Marjorie, the sphinx of sphinxes. With the most wholesome and innocent intentions in the world she had stolen Marjorie's property. She felt suddenly and horribly guilty. After the bridge game, when they sat in an informal circle and the conversation became general, the storm gradually broke. Little Otis Ormonde inadvertently precipitated it.

"When you going back to kindergarten, Otis?" some one had asked.

"Me? Day Bernice gets her hair bobbed."

"Then your education's over," said Marjorie quickly. "That's only a bluff of hers. I should think you'd have realized."

"That a fact?" demanded Otis, giving Bernice a reproachful glance.

Bernice's ears burned as she tried to think up an effectual come-back. In the face of this direct attack her imagination was paralyzed.

"There's a lot of bluffs in the world," continued Marjorie quite pleasantly. "I should think you'd be young enough to know that, Otis."

"Well," said Otis, "maybe so. But gee! With a line like Bernice's——"

"Really?" yawned Marjorie. "What's her latest bon mot?"

No one seemed to know. In fact, Bernice, having trifled with her muse's beau, had said nothing memorable of late.

"Was that really all a line?" asked Roberta curiously.

Bernice hesitated. She felt that wit in some form was demanded of her, but under her cousin's suddenly frigid eyes she was completely incapacitated.

"I don't know," she stalled.

"Splush!" said Marjorie. "Admit it!"

Bernice saw that Warren's eyes had left a ukulele he had been tinkering with and were fixed on her questioningly.

"Oh, I don't know!" she repeated steadily. Her cheeks were glowing.

"Splush!" remarked Marjorie again.

"Come through, Bernice," urged Otis. "Tell her where to get off."

Bernice looked round again—she seemed unable to get away from Warren's eyes.

"I like bobbed hair," she said hurriedly, as if he had asked her a question, "and I intend to bob mine."

"When?" demanded Marjorie.

"Any time."

"No time like the present," suggested Roberta.

Otis jumped to his feet.

"Good stuff!" he cried. "We'll have a summer bobbing party. Sevier Hotel barber-shop, I think you said."

In an instant all were on their feet. Bernice's heart throbbed violently.

"What?" she gasped.

Out of the group came Marjorie's voice, very clear and contemptuous.

"Don't worry—she'll back out!"

"Come on, Bernice!" cried Otis, starting toward the door.

Four eyes—Warren's and Marjorie's—stared at her, challenged her, defied her. For another second she wavered wildly.

"All right," she said swiftly, "I don't care if I do."

An eternity of minutes later, riding down-town through the late afternoon beside Warren, the others following in Roberta's car close behind, Bernice had all the sensations of Marie Antoinette bound for the guillotine in a tumbrel. Vaguely she wondered why she did not cry out that it was all a mistake. It was all she could do to keep from clutching her hair with both hands to protect it from the suddenly hostile world. Yet she did neither. Even the thought of her mother was no deterrent now. This was the test supreme of her sportsmanship; her right to walk unchallenged in the starry heaven of popular girls.

Warren was moodily silent, and when they came to the hotel he drew up at the curb and nodded to Bernice to precede him out. Roberta's car emptied a laughing crowd into the shop, which presented two bold plate-glass windows to the street.

Bernice stood on the curb and looked at the sign, Sevier Barber-Shop. It was a guillotine indeed, and the hangman was the first barber, who, attired in a white coat and smoking a cigarette, leaned nonchalantly against the first chair. He must have heard of her; he must have been waiting all week, smoking eternal cigarettes beside that portentous, too-often-mentioned first chair. Would they blindfold her? No, but they would tie a white cloth round her neck lest any of her blood—nonsense—hair—should get on her clothes.

"All right, Bernice," said Warren quickly.

With her chin in the air she crossed the sidewalk, pushed open the swinging screen-door, and giving not a glance to the uproarious, riotous row that occupied the waiting bench, went up to the first barber.

"I want you to bob my hair."

The first barber's mouth slid somewhat open. His cigarette dropped to the floor.

"Huh?"

"My hair—bob it!"

Refusing further preliminaries, Bernice took her seat on high. A man in the chair next to her turned on his side and gave her a glance, half lather, half amazement. One barber started and spoiled little Willy Schuneman's monthly haircut. Mr. O'Reilly in the last chair grunted and swore musically in ancient Gaelic as a razor bit into his cheek. Two bootblacks became wide-eyed and rushed for her feet. No, Bernice didn't care for a shine.

Outside a passer-by stopped and stared; a couple joined him; half a dozen small boys' noses sprang into life, flattened against the glass; and snatches of conversation borne on the summer breeze drifted in through the screen-door.

"Lookada long hair on a kid!"

"Where'd yuh get 'at stuff? 'At's a bearded lady he just finished shavin'."

But Bernice saw nothing, heard nothing. Her only living sense told her that this man in the white coat had removed one tortoise-shell comb and then another; that his fingers were fumbling clumsily with unfamiliar hairpins; that this hair, this wonderful hair of hers, was going—she would never again feel its long voluptuous pull as it hung in a dark-brown glory down her back. For a second she was near breaking down, and then the picture before her swam mechanically into her vision—Marjorie's mouth curling in a faint ironic smile as if to say:

"Give up and get down! You tried to buck me and I called your bluff. You see you haven't got a prayer."

And some last energy rose up in Bernice, for she clinched her hands under the white cloth, and there was a curious narrowing of her eyes that Marjorie remarked on to some one long afterward.

Twenty minutes later the barber swung her round to face the mirror, and she flinched at the full extent of the damage that had been wrought. Her hair was not curly, and now it lay in lank lifeless blocks on both sides of her suddenly pale face. It was ugly as sin—she had known it would be ugly as sin. Her face's chief charm had been a Madonna-like simplicity. Now that was gone and she was—well, frightfully mediocre—not stagy; only ridiculous, like a Greenwich Villager who had left her spectacles at home.

As she climbed down from the chair she tried to smile—failed miserably. She saw two of the girls exchange glances; noticed Marjorie's mouth curved in attenuated mockery—and that Warren's eyes were suddenly very cold.

"You see"—her words fell into an awkward pause—"I've done it."

"Yes, you've—done it," admitted Warren.

"Do you like it?"

There was a half-hearted "Sure" from two or three voices, another awkward pause, and then Marjorie turned swiftly and with serpentlike intensity to Warren.

"Would you mind running me down to the cleaners?" she asked. "I've simply got to get a dress there before supper. Roberta's driving right home and she can take the others."

Warren stared abstractedly at some infinite speck out the window. Then for an instant his eyes rested coldly on Bernice before they turned to Marjorie.

"Be glad to," he said slowly.

VI

Bernice did not fully realize the outrageous trap that had been set for her until she met her aunt's amazed glance just before dinner.

"Why, Bernice!"

"I've bobbed it, Aunt Josephine."

"Why, child!"

"Do you like it?"

"Why, Ber-nice!"

"I suppose I've shocked you."

"No, but what'll Mrs. Deyo think to-morrow night? Bernice, you should have waited until after the Deyos' dance—you should have waited if you wanted to do that."

"It was sudden, Aunt Josephine. Anyway, why does it matter to Mrs. Deyo particularly?"

"Why, child," cried Mrs. Harvey, "in her paper on 'The Foibles of the Younger Generation' that she read at the last meeting of the Thursday Club she devoted fifteen minutes to bobbed hair. It's her pet abomination. And the dance is for you and Marjorie!"

"I'm sorry."

"Oh, Bernice, what'll your mother say? She'll think I let you do it."

"I'm sorry."

Dinner was an agony. She had made a hasty attempt with a curling-iron, and burned her finger and much hair. She could see that her aunt was both worried and grieved, and her uncle kept saying, "Well, I'll be darned!" over and over in a hurt and faintly hostile tone. And Marjorie sat very quietly, intrenched behind a faint smile, a faintly mocking smile.

Somehow she got through the evening. Three boys called; Marjorie disappeared with one of them, and Bernice made a listless unsuccessful attempt to entertain the two others—sighed thankfully as she climbed the stairs to her room at half past ten. What a day!

When she had undressed for the night the door opened and Marjorie came in.

"Bernice," she said, "I'm awfully sorry about the Deyo dance. I'll give you my word of honor I'd forgotten all about it."

" 'Sall right," said Bernice shortly. Standing before the mirror she passed her comb slowly through her short hair.

"I'll take you down-town to-morrow," continued Marjorie, "and the hairdresser'll fix it so you'll look slick. I didn't imagine you'd go through with it. I'm really mighty sorry."

"Oh, 'sall right!"

"Still it's your last night, so I suppose it won't matter much."

Then Bernice winced as Marjorie tossed her own hair over her shoulders and began to twist it slowly into two long blond braids until in her cream-colored negligée she looked like a delicate painting of some Saxon princess. Fascinated, Bernice watched the braids grow. Heavy and luxurious they were, moving under the supple fingers like restive snakes—and to Bernice remained this relic and the curling-iron and a to-morrow full of eyes. She could see G. Reece Stoddard, who liked her, assuming his Harvard manner and telling his dinner partner that Bernice shouldn't have been allowed to go to the movies so much; she could see Draycott Deyo exchanging glances with his mother and then being conscientiously charitable to her. But then perhaps by to-morrow Mrs. Deyo would have heard the news; would send round an icy little note requesting that she fail to appear—and behind her back they would all laugh and know that Marjorie had made a fool of her; that her chance at beauty had been sacrificed to the jealous whim of a selfish girl. She sat down suddenly before the mirror, biting the inside of her cheek.

"I like it," she said with an effort. "I think it'll be becoming."

Marjorie smiled.

"It looks all right. For heaven's sake, don't let it worry you!"

"I won't."

"Good night, Bernice."

But as the door closed something snapped within Bernice. She sprang dynamically to her feet, clinching her hands, then swiftly and noiselessly crossed over to her bed and from underneath it dragged out her suitcase. Into it she tossed toilet articles and a change of clothing. Then she turned to her trunk and quickly dumped in two drawerfuls of lingerie and summer dresses. She moved quietly, but with deadly efficiency, and in three-quarters of an hour her trunk was locked and strapped and she was fully dressed in a becoming new travelling suit that Marjorie had helped her pick out.

Sitting down at her desk she wrote a short note to Mrs. Harvey, in which she briefly outlined her reasons for going. She sealed it, addressed it, and laid it on her pillow. She glanced at her watch. The train left at one, and she knew that if she walked down to the Marborough Hotel two blocks away she could easily get a taxicab.

Suddenly she drew in her breath sharply and an expression flashed into her eyes that a practised character reader might have connected vaguely with the set look she had worn in the barber's chair—somehow a development of it. It was quite a new look for Bernice—and it carried consequences.

She went stealthily to the bureau, picked up an article that lay there, and turning out all the lights stood quietly until her eyes became accustomed to the darkness. Softly she pushed open the door to Marjorie's room. She heard the quiet, even breathing of an untroubled conscience asleep.

She was by the bedside now, very deliberate and calm. She acted swiftly. Bending over she found one of the braids of Marjorie's hair, followed it up with her hand to the point nearest the head, and then holding it a little slack so that the sleeper would feel no pull, she reached down with the shears and severed it. With the pigtail in her hand she held her breath. Marjorie had muttered something in her sleep. Bernice deftly amputated the other braid, paused for an instant, and then flitted swiftly and silently back to her own room.

Down-stairs she opened the big front door, closed it carefully behind her, and feeling oddly happy and exuberant stepped off the porch into the moonlight, swinging her heavy grip like a shopping-bag. After a minute's brisk walk she discovered that her left hand still held the two blond braids. She laughed unexpectedly—had to shut her mouth hard to keep from emitting an absolute peal. She was passing Warren's house now, and on the impulse she set down her baggage, and swinging the braids like pieces of rope flung them at the wooden porch, where they landed with a slight thud. She laughed again, no longer restraining herself.

"Huh!" she giggled wildly. "Scalp the selfish thing!"

Then picking up her suitcase she set off at a half-run down the moonlit street.

F. SCOTT FITZGERALD

Winter Dreams

SOME OF THE CADDIES were poor as sin and lived in one-room houses with a neurasthenic cow in the front yard, but Dexter Green's father owned the second best grocery-store in Black Bear—the best one was "The Hub," patronized by the wealthy people from Sherry Island—and Dexter caddied only for pocket-money.

In the fall when the days became crisp and gray, and the long Minnesota winter shut down like the white lid of a box, Dexter's skis moved over the snow that hid the fairways of the golf course. At these times the country gave him a feeling of profound melancholy—it offended him that the links should lie in enforced fallowness, haunted by ragged sparrows for the long season. It was dreary, too, that on the tees where the gay colors fluttered in summer there were now only the desolate sand-boxes knee-deep in crusted ice. When he crossed the hills the wind blew cold as misery, and if the sun was out he tramped with his eyes squinted up against the hard dimensionless glare.

In April the winter ceased abruptly. The snow ran down into Black Bear Lake scarcely tarrying for the early golfers to brave the season with red and black balls. Without elation, without an interval of moist glory, the cold was gone.

Dexter knew that there was something dismal about this Northern spring, just as he knew there was something gorgeous about the fall. Fall made him clinch his hands and tremble and repeat idiotic sentences to himself, and make brisk abrupt gestures of command to imaginary audiences and armies. October filled him with hope which November raised to a sort of ecstatic triumph, and in this mood the fleeting brilliant impressions of the summer at Sherry

Island were ready grist to his mill. He became a golf champion and defeated Mr. T. A. Hedrick in a marvellous match played a hundred times over the fairways of his imagination, a match each detail of which he changed about untiringly—sometimes he won with almost laughable ease, sometimes he came up magnificently from behind. Again, stepping from a Pierce-Arrow automobile, like Mr. Mortimer Jones, he strolled frigidly into the lounge of the Sherry Island Golf Club—or perhaps, surrounded by an admiring crowd, he gave an exhibition of fancy diving from the spring-board of the club raft. . . . Among those who watched him in open-mouthed wonder was Mr. Mortimer Jones.

And one day it came to pass that Mr. Jones—himself and not his ghost—came up to Dexter with tears in his eyes and said that Dexter was the —— best caddy in the club, and wouldn't he decide not to quit if Mr. Jones made it worth his while, because every other —— caddy in the club lost one ball a hole for him—regularly——

"No, sir," said Dexter decisively, "I don't want to caddy any more." Then, after a pause: "I'm too old."

"You're not more than fourteen. Why the devil did you decide just this morning that you wanted to quit? You promised that next week you'd go over to the State tournament with me."

"I decided I was too old."

Dexter handed in his "A Class" badge, collected what money was due him from the caddy master, and walked home to Black Bear Village.

"The best —— caddy I ever saw," shouted Mr. Mortimer Jones over a drink that afternoon. "Never lost a ball! Willing! Intelligent! Quiet! Honest! Grateful!"

The little girl who had done this was eleven—beautifully ugly as little girls are apt to be who are destined after a few years to be inexpressibly lovely and bring no end of misery to a great number of men. The spark, however, was perceptible. There was a general ungodliness in the way her lips twisted down at the corners when she smiled, and in the—Heaven help us!—in the almost passionate quality of her eyes. Vitality is born early in such women. It was utterly in evidence now, shining through her thin frame in a sort of glow.

She had come eagerly out on to the course at nine o'clock with a white linen nurse and five small new golf-clubs in a white canvas bag which the nurse was carrying. When Dexter first saw her she was standing by the caddy house, rather ill at ease and trying to conceal the fact by engaging her nurse in an obviously unnatural conversation graced by startling and irrelevant grimaces from herself.

"Well, it's certainly a nice day, Hilda," Dexter heard her say. She drew down the corners of her mouth, smiled, and glanced furtively around, her eyes in transit falling for an instant on Dexter.

Then to the nurse:

"Well, I guess there aren't very many people out here this morning, are there?"

The smile again—radiant, blatantly artificial—convincing.

"I don't know what we're supposed to do now," said the nurse looking nowhere in particular.

"Oh, that's all right. I'll fix it up."

Dexter stood perfectly still, his mouth slightly ajar. He knew that if he moved forward a step his stare would be in her line of vision—if he moved backward he would lose his full view of her face. For a moment he had not realized how young she was. Now he remembered having seen her several times the year before—in bloomers.

Suddenly, involuntarily, he laughed, a short abrupt laugh—then, startled by himself, he turned and began to walk quickly away.

"Boy!"

Dexter stopped.

"Boy——"

Beyond question he was addressed. Not only that, but he was treated to that absurd smile, that preposterous smile—the memory of which at least a dozen men were to carry into middle age.

"Boy, do you know where the golf teacher is?"

"He's giving a lesson."

"Well, do you know where the caddy-master is?"

"He isn't here yet this morning."

"Oh." For a moment this baffled her. She stood alternately on her right and left foot.

"We'd like to get a caddy," said the nurse. "Mrs. Mortimer Jones sent us out to play golf, and we don't know how without we get a caddy."

Here she was stopped by an ominous glance from Miss Jones, followed immediately by the smile.

"There aren't any caddies here except me," said Dexter to the nurse, "and I got to stay here in charge until the caddy-master gets here."

"Oh."

Miss Jones and her retinue now withdrew, and at a proper distance from Dexter became involved in a heated conversation, which was concluded by Miss Jones taking one of the clubs and hitting it on the ground with violence. For further emphasis she raised it again and was about to bring it down smartly upon the nurse's bosom, when the nurse seized the club and twisted it from her hands.

"You damn little mean old *thing*!" cried Miss Jones wildly.

Another argument ensued. Realizing that the elements of comedy were implied in the scene, Dexter several times began to laugh, but each time restrained the laugh before it reached audibility. He could not resist the monstrous conviction that the little girl was justified in beating the nurse.

The situation was resolved by the fortuitous appearance of the caddy-master, who was appealed to immediately by the nurse.

"Miss Jones is to have a little caddy, and this one says he can't go."

"Mr. McKenna said I was to wait here till you came," said Dexter quickly.

"Well, he's here now." Miss Jones smiled cheerfully at the caddy-master. Then she dropped her bag and set off at a haughty mince toward the first tee.

"Well?" The caddy-master turned to Dexter. "What you standing there like a dummy for? Go pick up the young lady's clubs."

"I don't think I'll go out to-day," said Dexter.

"You don't——"

"I think I'll quit."

The enormity of his decision frightened him. He was a favorite caddy, and the thirty dollars a month he earned through the summer were not to be made elsewhere around the lake. But he had received a strong emotional shock, and his perturbation required a violent and immediate outlet.

It is not so simple as that, either. As so frequently would be the case in the future, Dexter was unconsciously dictated to by his winter dreams.

II

Now, of course, the quality and the seasonability of these winter dreams varied, but the stuff of them remained. They persuaded Dexter several years later to pass up a business course at the State university—his father, prospering now, would have paid his way—for the precarious advantage of attending an older and more famous university in the East, where he was bothered by his scanty funds. But do not get the impression, because his winter dreams happened to be concerned at first with musings on the rich, that there was anything merely snobbish in the boy. He wanted not association with glittering things and glittering people—he wanted the glittering things themselves. Often he reached out for the best without knowing why he wanted it—and sometimes he ran up against the mysterious denials and prohibitions in which life indulges. It is with one of those denials and not with his career as a whole that this story deals.

He made money. It was rather amazing. After college he went to the city from which Black Bear Lake draws its wealthy patrons. When he was only twenty-three and had been there not quite two years, there were already people who liked to say: "Now *there's* a boy—" All about him rich men's sons were peddling bonds precariously, or investing patrimonies precariously, or plodding through the two dozen volumes of the "George Washington Commercial Course," but Dexter borrowed a thousand dollars on his college degree and his confident mouth, and bought a partnership in a laundry.

It was a small laundry when he went into it, but Dexter made a specialty of learning how the English washed fine woolen golf-stockings without shrinking them, and within a year he was catering to the trade that wore knickerbockers. Men were insisting that their Shetland hose and sweaters go to his laundry, just as they had insisted on a caddy who could find golf-balls. A little later he was doing their wives' lingerie as well—and running five branches in different parts of the city. Before he was twenty-seven he owned the largest string of laundries in his section of the country. It was then that he sold out and went to New York. But the part of his story that concerns us goes back to the days when he was making his first big success.

When he was twenty-three Mr. Hart—one of the gray-haired men who liked to say "Now there's a boy"—gave him a guest card to the Sherry Island Golf Club for a week-end. So he signed his name one day on the register, and that afternoon played golf in a foursome with Mr. Hart and Mr. Sandwood and Mr. T. A. Hedrick. He did not consider it necessary to remark that he had once carried Mr. Hart's bag over this same links, and that he knew every trap and gully with his eyes shut—but he found himself glancing at the four caddies who trailed them, trying to catch a gleam or gesture that would remind him of himself, that would lessen the gap which lay between his present and his past.

It was a curious day, slashed abruptly with fleeting, familiar impressions. One minute he had the sense of being a trespasser—in the next he was impressed by the tremendous superiority he felt toward Mr. T. A. Hedrick, who was a bore and not even a good golfer any more.

Then, because of a ball Mr. Hart lost near the fifteenth green, an enormous thing happened. While they were searching the stiff grasses of the rough there was a clear call of "Fore!" from behind a hill in their rear. And as they all turned abruptly from their search a bright new ball sliced abruptly over the hill and caught Mr. T. A. Hedrick in the abdomen.

"By Gad!" cried Mr. T. A. Hedrick, "they ought to put some of these crazy women off the course. It's getting to be outrageous."

A head and a voice came up together over the hill:

"Do you mind if we go through?"

"You hit me in the stomach!" declared Mr. Hedrick wildly.

"Did I?" The girl approached the group of men. "I'm sorry. I yelled 'Fore!'"

Her glance fell casually on each of the men—then scanned the fairway for her ball.

"Did I bounce into the rough?"

It was impossible to determine whether this question was ingenuous or malicious. In a moment, however, she left no doubt, for as her partner came up over the hill she called cheerfully:

"Here I am! I'd have gone on the green except that I hit something."

As she took her stance for a short mashie shot, Dexter looked at her closely. She wore a blue gingham dress, rimmed at throat and shoulders with a white edging that accentuated her tan. The quality of exaggeration, of thinness, which had made her passionate eyes and down-turning mouth absurd at eleven, was gone now. She was arrestingly beautiful. The color in her cheeks was centred like the color in a picture—it was not a "high" color, but a sort of fluctuating and feverish warmth, so shaded that it seemed at any moment it would recede and disappear. This color and the mobility of her mouth gave a continual impression of flux, of intense life, of passionate vitality—balanced only partially by the sad luxury of her eyes.

She swung her mashie impatiently and without interest, pitching the ball into a sand-pit on the other side of the green. With a quick, insincere smile and a careless "Thank you!" she went on after it.

"That Judy Jones!" remarked Mr. Hedrick on the next tee, as they waited—some moments—for her to play on ahead. "All she needs is to be turned up and spanked for six months and then to be married off to an old-fashioned cavalry captain."

"My God, she's good-looking!" said Mr. Sandwood, who was just over thirty.

"Good-looking!" cried Mr. Hedrick contemptuously, "she always looks as if she wanted to be kissed! Turning those big cow-eyes on every calf in town!"

It was doubtful if Mr. Hedrick intended a reference to the maternal instinct.

"She'd play pretty good golf if she'd try," said Mr. Sandwood.

"She has no form," said Mr. Hedrick solemnly.

"She has a nice figure," said Mr. Sandwood.

"Better thank the Lord she doesn't drive a swifter ball," said Mr. Hart, winking at Dexter.

Later in the afternoon the sun went down with a riotous swirl of gold and varying blues and scarlets, and left the dry, rustling night of Western summer. Dexter watched from the veranda of the Golf Club, watched the even overlap of the waters in the little wind, silver molasses under the harvest-moon. Then the moon held a finger to her lips and the lake became a clear pool, pale and quiet. Dexter put on his bathing-suit and swam out to the farthest raft, where he stretched dripping on the wet canvas of the springboard.

There was a fish jumping and a star shining and the lights around the lake were gleaming. Over on a dark peninsula a piano was playing the songs of last summer and of summers before that—songs from "Chin-Chin" and "The Count of Luxemburg" and "The Chocolate Soldier"—and because the sound of a piano over a stretch of water had always seemed beautiful to Dexter he lay perfectly quiet and listened.

The tune the piano was playing at that moment had been gay and new five years before when Dexter was a sophomore at college. They had played it at a prom once when he could not afford the luxury of proms, and he had stood outside the gymnasium and listened. The sound of the tune precipitated in him a sort of ecstasy and it was with that ecstasy he viewed what happened to him now. It was a mood of intense appreciation, a sense that, for once, he was magnificently attuned to life and that everything about him was radiating a brightness and a glamour he might never know again.

A low, pale oblong detached itself suddenly from the darkness of the Island, spitting forth the reverberated sound of a racing motor-boat. Two white streamers of cleft water rolled themselves out behind it and almost immediately the boat was beside him, drowning out the hot tinkle of the piano in the drone of its spray. Dexter raising himself on his arms was aware of a figure standing at the wheel, of two dark eyes regarding him over the lengthening space of water—then the boat had gone by and was sweeping in an immense and purposeless circle of spray round and round in the middle of the lake. With equal eccentricity one of the circles flattened out and headed back toward the raft.

"Who's that?" she called, shutting off her motor. She was so near now that Dexter could see her bathing-suit, which consisted apparently of pink rompers.

The nose of the boat bumped the raft, and as the latter tilted rakishly he was precipitated toward her. With different degrees of interest they recognized each other.

"Aren't you one of those men we played through this afternoon?" she demanded.

He was.

"Well, do you know how to drive a motor-boat? Because if you do I wish you'd drive this one so I can ride on the surf-board behind. My name is Judy Jones"—she favored him with an absurd smirk—rather, what tried to be a smirk, for, twist her mouth as she might, it was not grotesque, it was merely beautiful—"and I live in a house over there on the Island, and in that house there is a man waiting for me. When he drove up at the door I drove out of the dock because he says I'm his ideal."

There was a fish jumping and a star shining and the lights around the lake were gleaming. Dexter sat beside Judy Jones and she explained how her boat was driven. Then she was in the water, swimming to the floating surf-board with a sinuous crawl. Watching her was without effort to the eye, watching a branch waving or a seagull flying. Her arms, burned to butternut, moved sinuously among the dull platinum ripples, elbow appearing first, casting the forearm back with a cadence of falling water, then reaching out and down, stabbing a path ahead.

They moved out into the lake; turning, Dexter saw that she was kneeling on the low rear of the now uptilted surf-board.

"Go faster," she called, "fast as it'll go."

Obediently he jammed the lever forward and the white spray mounted at the bow. When he looked around again the girl was standing up on the rushing board, her arms spread wide, her eyes lifted toward the moon.

"It's awful cold," she shouted. "What's your name?"

He told her.

"Well, why don't you come to dinner to-morrow night?"

His heart turned over like the fly-wheel of the boat, and, for the second time, her casual whim gave a new direction to his life.

III

Next evening while he waited for her to come down-stairs, Dexter peopled the soft deep summer room and the sun-porch that opened from it with the men who had already loved Judy Jones. He knew the sort of men they were—the men who when he first went to college had entered from the great prep schools with graceful clothes and the deep tan of healthy summers. He had seen that, in one sense, he was better than these men. He was newer and stronger. Yet in acknowledging to himself that he wished his children to be like them he was admitting that he was but the rough, strong stuff from which they eternally sprang.

When the time had come for him to wear good clothes, he had known who were the best tailors in America, and the best tailors in America had made him the suit he wore this evening. He had acquired that particular reserve peculiar to his university, that set it off from other universities. He recognized the value to him of such a mannerism and he had adopted it; he knew that to be careless in dress and manner required more confidence than to be careful. But carelessness was for his children. His mother's name had been Krimerlich. She was a Bohemian of the peasant class and she had talked broken English to the end of her days. Her son must keep to the set patterns.

At a little after seven Judy Jones came down-stairs. She wore a blue silk afternoon dress, and he was disappointed at first that she had not put on something more elaborate. This feeling was accentuated when, after a brief greeting, she went to the door of a butler's pantry and pushing it open called: "You can serve dinner, Martha." He had rather expected that a butler would announce dinner, that there would be a cocktail. Then he put these thoughts behind him as they sat down side by side on a lounge and looked at each other.

"Father and mother won't be here," she said thoughtfully.

He remembered the last time he had seen her father, and he was glad the parents were not to be here to-night—they might wonder who he was. He had been born in Keeble, a Minnesota village fifty miles farther north, and he always gave Keeble as his home instead of Black Bear Village. Country towns were well enough to come from if they weren't inconveniently in sight and used as footstools by fashionable lakes.

They talked of his university, which she had visited frequently during the past two years, and of the near-by city which supplied Sherry Island with its patrons, and whither Dexter would return next day to his prospering laundries.

During dinner she slipped into a moody depression which gave Dexter a feeling of uneasiness. Whatever petulance she uttered in her throaty voice worried him. Whatever she smiled at—at him, at a chicken liver, at nothing—it disturbed him that her smile could have no root in mirth, or even in amusement. When the scarlet corners of her lips curved down, it was less a smile than an invitation to a kiss.

Then, after dinner, she led him out on the dark sun-porch and deliberately changed the atmosphere.

"Do you mind if I weep a little?" she said.

"I'm afraid I'm boring you," he responded quickly.

"You're not. I like you. But I've just had a terrible afternoon. There was a man I cared about, and this afternoon he told me out of a clear sky that he was poor as a church-mouse. He'd never even hinted it before. Does this sound horribly mundane?"

"Perhaps he was afraid to tell you."

"Suppose he was," she answered. "He didn't start right. You see, if I'd thought of him as poor—well, I've been mad about loads of poor men, and fully intended to marry them all. But in this case, I hadn't thought of him that way, and my interest in him wasn't strong enough to survive the shock. As if a girl calmly informed her fiancé that she was a widow. He might not object to widows, but——

"Let's start right," she interrupted herself suddenly. "Who are you, anyhow?"

For a moment Dexter hesitated. Then:

"I'm nobody," he announced. "My career is largely a matter of futures."

"Are you poor?"

"No," he said frankly, "I'm probably making more money than any man my age in the Northwest. I know that's an obnoxious remark, but you advised me to start right."

There was a pause. Then she smiled and the corners of her mouth drooped and an almost imperceptible sway brought her closer to him, looking up into his eyes. A lump rose in Dexter's throat, and he waited breathless for the experiment, facing the unpredictable compound that would form mysteriously from the elements of their lips. Then he saw—she communicated her excitement to him, lavishly, deeply, with kisses that were not a promise but a fulfilment. They aroused in him not hunger demanding renewal but surfeit that would demand more surfeit . . . kisses that were like charity, creating want by holding back nothing at all.

It did not take him many hours to decide that he had wanted Judy Jones ever since he was a proud, desirous little boy.

IV

It began like that—and continued, with varying shades of intensity, on such a note right up to the dénouement. Dexter surrendered a part of himself to the most direct and unprincipled personality with which he had ever come in contact. Whatever Judy wanted, she went after with the full pressure of her charm. There was no divergence of method, no jockeying for position or premeditation of effects—there was a very little mental side to any of her affairs. She simply made men conscious to the highest degree of her physical loveliness. Dexter had no desire to change her. Her deficiencies were knit up with a passionate energy that transcended and justified them.

When, as Judy's head lay against his shoulder that first night, she whispered, "I don't know what's the matter with me. Last night I thought I was in love with a man and to-night I think I'm in love with you——"—it seemed to him a beautiful and romantic thing to say. It was the exquisite excitability that for the moment he controlled and owned. But a week later he was compelled to view this same quality in a different light. She took him in her roadster to a picnic supper, and after supper she disappeared, likewise in her roadster, with another man. Dexter became enormously upset and was scarcely able to be decently civil to the other people present. When she assured him that she had not kissed the other man, he knew she was lying—yet he was glad that she had taken the trouble to lie to him.

He was, as he found before the summer ended, one of a varying dozen who circulated about her. Each of them had at one time been favored above all others—about half of them still basked in the solace of occasional sentimental revivals. Whenever one showed signs of dropping out through long neglect, she granted him a brief honeyed hour, which encouraged him to tag along for a year or so longer. Judy made these forays upon the helpless and defeated without malice, indeed half unconscious that there was anything mischievous in what she did.

When a new man came to town every one dropped out—dates were automatically cancelled.

The helpless part of trying to do anything about it was that she did it all herself. She was not a girl who could be "won" in the kinetic sense—she was proof against cleverness, she was proof against charm; if any of these assailed her too strongly she would immediately resolve the affair to a physical basis, and under the magic of her physical splendor the strong as well as the brilliant played her game and not their own. She was entertained only by the gratification of her desires and by the direct exercise of her own charm. Perhaps from so much youthful love, so many youthful lovers, she had come, in self-defense, to nourish herself wholly from within.

Succeeding Dexter's first exhilaration came restlessness and dissatisfaction. The helpless ecstasy of losing himself in her was opiate rather than tonic. It was fortunate for his work during the winter that those moments of ecstasy came infrequently. Early in their acquaintance it had seemed for a while that there was a deep and spontaneous mutual attraction—that first August, for example—three days of long evenings on her dusky veranda, of strange wan kisses through the late afternoon, in shadowy alcoves or behind the protecting trellises of the garden arbors, of mornings when she was fresh as a dream and almost shy at meeting him in the clarity of the rising day. There was all the ecstasy of an engagement about it, sharpened by his realization that there was no engagement. It was during those three days that, for the first time, he had asked her to marry him. She said "maybe some day," she said "kiss me," she said "I'd like to marry you," she said "I love you"—she said—nothing.

The three days were interrupted by the arrival of a New York man who visited at her house for half September. To Dexter's agony, rumor engaged them. The man was the son of the president of a great trust company. But at the end of a month it was reported that Judy was yawning. At a dance one night she sat all evening in a motor-boat with a local beau, while the New Yorker searched the club for her frantically. She told the local beau that she was bored with her visitor, and two days later he left. She was seen with him at the station, and it was reported that he looked very mournful indeed.

On this note the summer ended. Dexter was twenty-four, and he found himself increasingly in a position to do as he wished. He joined two clubs in the city and lived at one of them. Though he was by no means an integral part of the stag-lines at these clubs, he managed to be on hand at dances where Judy Jones was likely to appear.

He could have gone out socially as much as he liked—he was an eligible young man, now, and popular with down-town fathers. His confessed devotion to Judy Jones had rather solidified his position. But he had no social aspirations and rather despised the dancing men who were always on tap for the Thursday or Saturday parties and who filled in at dinners with the younger married set. Already he was playing with the idea of going East to New York. He wanted to take Judy Jones with him. No disillusion as to the world in which she had grown up could cure his illusion as to her desirability.

Remember that—for only in the light of it can what he did for her be understood.

Eighteen months after he first met Judy Jones he became engaged to another girl. Her name was Irene Scheerer, and her father was one of the men who had always believed in Dexter. Irene was light-haired and sweet and honorable, and a little stout, and she had two suitors whom she pleasantly relinquished when Dexter formally asked her to marry him.

Summer, fall, winter, spring, another summer, another fall—so much he had given of his active life to the incorrigible lips of Judy Jones. She had treated him with interest, with encouragement, with malice, with indifference, with contempt. She had inflicted on him the innumerable little slights and indignities possible in such a case—as if in revenge for having ever cared for him at all. She had beckoned him and yawned at him and beckoned him again and he had responded often with bitterness and narrowed eyes. She had brought him ecstatic happiness and intolerable agony of spirit. She had caused him untold inconvenience and not a little trouble. She had insulted him, and she had ridden over him, and she had played his interest in her against his interest in his work—for fun. She had done everything to him except to criticise him—this she had not done—it seemed to him only because it might have sullied the utter indifference she manifested and sincerely felt toward him.

When autumn had come and gone again it occurred to him that he could not have Judy Jones. He had to beat this into his mind but he convinced himself at last. He lay awake at night for a while and argued it over. He told himself the trouble and the pain she had caused him, he enumerated her glaring deficiencies as a wife. Then he said to himself that he loved her, and after a while he fell asleep.

For a week, lest he imagined her husky voice over the telephone or her eyes opposite him at lunch, he worked hard and late, and at night he went to his office and plotted out his years.

At the end of a week he went to a dance and cut in on her once. For almost the first time since they had met he did not ask her to sit out with him or tell her that she was lovely. It hurt him that she did not miss these things—that was all. He was not jealous when he saw that there was a new man to-night. He had been hardened against jealousy long before.

He stayed late at the dance. He sat for an hour with Irene Scheerer and talked about books and about music. He knew very little about either. But he was beginning to be master of his own time now, and he had a rather priggish notion that he—the young and already fabulously successful Dexter Green—should know more about such things.

That was in October, when he was twenty-five. In January, Dexter and Irene became engaged. It was to be announced in June, and they were to be married three months later.

The Minnesota winter prolonged itself interminably, and it was almost May when the winds came soft and the snow ran down into Black Bear Lake at last. For the first time in over a year Dexter was enjoying a certain tranquillity of spirit. Judy Jones had been in Florida, and afterward in Hot Springs, and somewhere she had been engaged, and somewhere she had broken it off. At first, when Dexter had definitely given her up, it had made him sad that people still linked them together and asked for news of her, but when he began to be placed at dinner next to Irene Scheerer people didn't ask him about her any more—they told him about her. He ceased to be an authority on her.

May at last. Dexter walked the streets at night when the darkness was damp as rain, wondering that so soon, with so little done, so much of ecstasy had gone from him. May one year back had been marked by Judy's poignant, unforgivable, yet forgiven turbulence—it had been one of those rare times when he fancied she had grown to care for him. That old penny's worth of happiness he had spent for this bushel of content. He knew that Irene would be no more than a curtain spread behind him, a hand moving among gleaming tea-cups, a voice calling to children . . . fire and loveliness were gone, the magic of nights and the wonder of the varying hours and seasons . . . slender lips, down-turning, dropping to his lips and bearing him up into a heaven of eyes. . . . The thing was deep in him. He was too strong and alive for it to die lightly.

In the middle of May when the weather balanced for a few days on the thin bridge that led to deep summer he turned in one night at Irene's house. Their engagement was to be announced in a week now—no one would be surprised at it. And to-night they would sit together on the lounge at the University Club and look on for an hour at the dancers. It gave him a sense of solidity to go with her—she was so sturdily popular, so intensely "great."

He mounted the steps of the brownstone house and stepped inside.

"Irene," he called.

Mrs. Scheerer came out of the living-room to meet him.

"Dexter," she said, "Irene's gone up-stairs with a splitting headache. She wanted to go with you but I made her go to bed."

"Nothing serious, I——"

"Oh, no. She's going to play golf with you in the morning. You can spare her for just one night, can't you, Dexter?"

Her smile was kind. She and Dexter liked each other. In the living-room he talked for a moment before he said good-night.

Returning to the University Club, where he had rooms, he stood in the doorway for a moment and watched the dancers. He leaned against the door-post, nodded at a man or two—yawned.

"Hello, darling."

The familiar voice at his elbow startled him. Judy Jones had left a man and crossed the room to him—Judy Jones, a slender enamelled doll in cloth of gold: gold in a band at her head, gold in two slipper points at her dress's hem. The fragile glow of her face seemed to blossom as she smiled at him. A breeze of warmth and light blew through the room. His hands in the pockets of his dinner-jacket tightened spasmodically. He was filled with a sudden excitement.

"When did you get back?" he asked casually.

"Come here and I'll tell you about it."

She turned and he followed her. She had been away—he could have wept at the wonder of her return. She had passed through enchanted streets, doing things that were like provocative music. All mysterious happenings, all fresh and quickening hopes, had gone away with her, come back with her now.

She turned in the doorway.

"Have you a car here? If you haven't, I have."

"I have a coupé."

In then, with a rustle of golden cloth. He slammed the door. Into so many cars she had stepped—like this—like that—her back against the leather, so—her elbow resting on the door—waiting. She would have been soiled long since had there been anything to soil her—except herself—but this was her own self outpouring.

With an effort he forced himself to start the car and back into the street. This was nothing, he must remember. She had done this before, and he had put her behind him, as he would have crossed a bad account from his books.

He drove slowly down-town and, affecting abstraction, traversed the deserted streets of the business section, peopled here and there where a movie was giving out its crowd or where consumptive or pugilistic youth lounged in front of pool halls. The clink of glasses and the slap of hands on the bars issued from saloons, cloisters of glazed glass and dirty yellow light.

She was watching him closely and the silence was embarrassing, yet in this crisis he could find no casual word with which to profane the hour. At a convenient turning he began to zigzag back toward the University Club.

"Have you missed me?" she asked suddenly.

"Everybody missed you."

He wondered if she knew of Irene Scheerer. She had been back only a day—her absence had been almost contemporaneous with his engagement.

"What a remark!" Judy laughed sadly—without sadness. She looked at him searchingly. He became absorbed in the dashboard.

"You're handsomer than you used to be," she said thoughtfully. "Dexter, you have the most rememberable eyes."

He could have laughed at this, but he did not laugh. It was the sort of thing that was said to sophomores. Yet it stabbed at him.

"I'm awfully tired of everything, darling." She called every one darling, endowing the endearment with careless, individual comraderie. "I wish you'd marry me."

The directness of this confused him. He should have told her now that he was going to marry another girl, but he could not tell her. He could as easily have sworn that he had never loved her.

"I think we'd get along," she continued, on the same note, "unless probably you've forgotten me and fallen in love with another girl."

Her confidence was obviously enormous. She had said, in effect, that she found such a thing impossible to believe, that if it were true he had merely committed a childish indiscretion—and probably to show off. She would forgive him, because it was not a matter of any moment but rather something to be brushed aside lightly.

"Of course you could never love anybody but me," she continued, "I like the way you love me. Oh, Dexter, have you forgotten last year?"

"No, I haven't forgotten."

"Neither have I!"

Was she sincerely moved—or was she carried along by the wave of her own acting?

"I wish we could be like that again," she said, and he forced himself to answer:

"I don't think we can."

"I suppose not. . . . I hear you're giving Irene Scheerer a violent rush."

There was not the faintest emphasis on the name, yet Dexter was suddenly ashamed.

"Oh, take me home," cried Judy suddenly; "I don't want to go back to that idiotic dance—with those children."

Then, as he turned up the street that led to the residence district, Judy began to cry quietly to herself. He had never seen her cry before.

The dark street lightened, the dwellings of the rich loomed up around them, he stopped his coupé in front of the great white bulk of the Mortimer Joneses' house, somnolent, gorgeous, drenched with the splendor of the damp moonlight. Its solidity startled him. The strong walls, the steel of the girders, the breadth and beam and pomp of it were there only to bring out the contrast with the young beauty beside him. It was sturdy to accentuate her slightness—as if to show what a breeze could be generated by a butterfly's wing.

He sat perfectly quiet, his nerves in wild clamor, afraid that if he moved he would find her irresistibly in his arms. Two tears had rolled down her wet face and trembled on her upper lip.

"I'm more beautiful than anybody else," she said brokenly, "why can't I be happy?" Her moist eyes tore at his stability—her mouth turned slowly downward with an exquisite sadness: "I'd like to marry you if you'll have me, Dexter. I suppose you think I'm not worth having, but I'll be so beautiful for you, Dexter."

A million phrases of anger, pride, passion, hatred, tenderness fought on his lips. Then a perfect wave of emotion washed over him, carrying off with it a sediment of wisdom, of convention, of doubt, of honor. This was his girl who was speaking, his own, his beautiful, his pride.

"Won't you come in?" He heard her draw in her breath sharply.

Waiting.

"All right," his voice was trembling, "I'll come in."

V

It was strange that neither when it was over nor a long time afterward did he regret that night. Looking at it from the perspective of ten years, the fact that Judy's flare for him endured just one month seemed of little importance. Nor did it matter that by his yielding he subjected himself to a deeper agony in the end and gave serious hurt to Irene Scheerer and to Irene's parents, who had befriended him. There was nothing sufficiently pictorial about Irene's grief to stamp itself on his mind.

Dexter was at bottom hard-minded. The attitude of the city on his action was of no importance to him, not because he was going to leave the city, but because any outside attitude on the situation seemed superficial. He was completely indifferent to popular opinion. Nor, when he had seen that it was no use, that he did not possess in himself the power to move fundamentally or to hold Judy Jones, did he bear any malice toward her. He loved her, and he would love her until the day he was too old for loving—but he could not have her. So he tasted the deep pain that is reserved only for the strong, just as he had tasted for a little while the deep happiness.

Even the ultimate falsity of the grounds upon which Judy terminated the engagement that she did not want to "take him away" from Irene—Judy, who had wanted nothing else—did not revolt him. He was beyond any revulsion or any amusement.

He went East in February with the intention of selling out his laundries and settling in New York—but the war came to America in March and changed his plans. He returned to the West, handed over the management of the business to his partner, and went into the first officers' training-camp in late April. He was one of those young thousands who greeted the war with a certain amount of relief, welcoming the liberation from webs of tangled emotion.

VI

This story is not his biography, remember, although things creep into it which have nothing to do with those dreams he had when he was young. We are almost done with them and with him now. There is only one more incident to be related here, and it happens seven years farther on.

It took place in New York, where he had done well—so well that there were no barriers too high for him. He was thirty-two years old, and, except for one flying trip immediately after the war, he had not been West in seven years. A man named Devlin from Detroit came into his office to see him in a business way, and then and there this incident occurred, and closed out, so to speak, this particular side of his life.

"So you're from the Middle West," said the man Devlin with careless curiosity. "That's funny—I thought men like you were probably born and raised on Wall Street. You know—wife of one of my best friends in Detroit came from your city. I was an usher at the wedding."

Dexter waited with no apprehension of what was coming.

"Judy Simms," said Devlin with no particular interest; "Judy Jones she was once."

"Yes, I knew her." A dull impatience spread over him. He had heard, of course, that she was married—perhaps deliberately he had heard no more.

"Awfully nice girl," brooded Devlin meaninglessly, "I'm sort of sorry for her."

"Why?" Something in Dexter was alert, receptive, at once.

"Oh, Lud Simms has gone to pieces in a way. I don't mean he ill-uses her, but he drinks and runs around——"

"Doesn't she run around?"

"No. Stays at home with her kids."

"Oh."

"She's a little too old for him," said Devlin.

"Too old!" cried Dexter. "Why, man, she's only twenty-seven."

He was possessed with a wild notion of rushing out into the streets and taking a train to Detroit. He rose to his feet spasmodically.

"I guess you're busy," Devlin apologized quickly. "I didn't realize——"

"No, I'm not busy," said Dexter, steadying his voice. "I'm not busy at all. Not busy at all. Did you say she was—twenty-seven? No, I said she was twenty-seven."

"Yes, you did," agreed Devlin dryly.

"Go on, then. Go on."

"What do you mean?"

"About Judy Jones."

Devlin looked at him helplessly.

"Well, that's—I told you all there is to it. He treats her like the devil. Oh, they're not going to get divorced or anything. When he's particularly outrageous she forgives him. In fact, I'm inclined to think she loves him. She was a pretty girl when she first came to Detroit."

A pretty girl! The phrase struck Dexter as ludicrous.

"Isn't she—a pretty girl, any more?"

"Oh, she's all right."

"Look here," said Dexter, sitting down suddenly. "I don't understand. You say she was a 'pretty girl' and now you say she's 'all right.' I don't understand what you mean—Judy Jones wasn't a pretty girl, at all. She was a great beauty. Why, I knew her, I knew her. She was——"

Devlin laughed pleasantly.

"I'm not trying to start a row," he said. "I think Judy's a nice girl and I like her. I can't understand how a man like Lud Simms could fall madly in love with her, but he did." Then he added: "Most of the women like her."

Dexter looked closely at Devlin, thinking wildly that there must be a reason for this, some insensitivity in the man or some private malice.

"Lots of women fade just like *that*," Devlin snapped his fingers. "You must have seen it happen. Perhaps I've forgotten how pretty she was at her wedding. I've seen her so much since then, you see. She has nice eyes."

A sort of dullness settled down upon Dexter. For the first time in his life he felt like getting very drunk. He knew that he was laughing loudly at something Devlin had said, but he did not know what it was or why it was funny. When, in a few minutes, Devlin went he lay down on his lounge and looked out the window at the New York sky-line into which the sun was sinking in dull lovely shades of pink and gold.

He had thought that having nothing else to lose he was invulnerable at last—but he knew that he had just lost something more, as surely as if he had married Judy Jones and seen her fade away before his eyes.

The dream was gone. Something had been taken from him. In a sort of panic he pushed the palms of his hands into his eyes and tried to bring up a picture of the waters lapping on Sherry Island and the moonlit veranda, and gingham on the golf-links and the dry sun and the gold color of her neck's soft down. And her mouth damp to his kisses and her eyes plaintive with melancholy and her freshness like new fine linen in the morning. Why, these things were no longer in the world! They had existed and they existed no longer.

For the first time in years the tears were streaming down his face. But they were for himself now. He did not care about mouth and eyes and moving hands. He wanted to care, and he could not care. For he had gone away and he could never go back any more. The gates were closed, the sun was gone down, and there was no beauty but the gray beauty of steel that withstands all time. Even the grief he could have borne was left behind in the country of illusion, of youth, of the richness of life, where his winter dreams had flourished.

"Long ago," he said, "long ago, there was something in me, but now that thing is gone. Now that thing is gone, that thing is gone. I cannot cry. I cannot care. That thing will come back no more."

ERNEST HEMINGWAY

The End of Something

IN THE OLD DAYS Hortons Bay was a lumbering town. No one who lived in it was out of sound of the big saws in the mill by the lake. Then one year there were no more logs to make lumber. The lumber schooners came into the bay and were loaded with the cut of the mill that stood stacked in the yard. All the piles of lumber were carried away. The big mill building had all its machinery that was removable taken out and hoisted on board one of the schooners by the men who had worked in the mill. The schooner moved out of the bay toward the open lake carrying the two great saws, the travelling carriage that hurled the logs against the revolving, circular saws and all the rollers, wheels, belts and iron piled on a hull-deep load of lumber. Its open hold covered with canvas and lashed tight, the sails of the schooner filled and it moved out into the open lake, carrying with it everything that had made the mill a mill and Hortons Bay a town.

The one-story bunk houses, the eating-house, the company store, the mill offices, and the big mill itself stood deserted in the acres of sawdust that covered the swampy meadow by the shore of the bay.

Ten years later there was nothing of the mill left except the broken white limestone of its foundations showing through the swampy second growth as Nick and Marjorie rowed along the shore. They were trolling along the edge of the channel-bank where the bottom dropped off suddenly from sandy shallows to twelve feet of dark water. They were trolling on their way to the point to set night lines for rainbow trout.

"There's our old ruin, Nick," Marjorie said.

Nick, rowing, looked at the white stone in the green trees.

"There it is," he said.

"Can you remember when it was a mill?" Marjorie asked.

"I can just remember," Nick said.

"It seems more like a castle," Marjorie said.

Nick said nothing. They rowed on out of sight of the mill, following the shore line. Then Nick cut across the bay.

"They aren't striking," he said.

"No," Marjorie said. She was intent on the rod all the time they trolled, even when she talked. She loved to fish. She loved to fish with Nick.

Close beside the boat a big trout broke the surface of the water. Nick pulled hard on one oar so the boat would turn and the bait spinning far behind would pass where the trout was feeding. As the trout's back came up out of the water the minnows jumped wildly. They sprinkled the surface like a handful of shot thrown into the water. Another trout broke water, feeding on the other side of the boat.

"They're feeding," Marjorie said.

"But they won't strike," Nick said.

He rowed the boat around to troll past both the feeding fish, then headed it for the point. Marjorie did not reel in until the boat touched the shore.

They pulled the boat up the beach and Nick lifted out a pail of live perch. The perch swam in the water in the pail. Nick caught three of them with his hands and cut their heads off and skinned them while Marjorie chased with her hands in the bucket, finally caught a perch, cut its head off and skinned it. Nick looked at her fish.

"You don't want to take the ventral fin out," he said. "It'll be all right for bait but it's better with the ventral fin in."

He hooked each of the skinned perch through the tail. There were two hooks attached to a leader on each rod. Then Marjorie rowed the boat out over the channel-bank, holding the line in her teeth, and looking toward Nick, who stood on the shore holding the rod and letting the line run out from the reel.

"That's about right," he called.

"Should I let it drop?" Marjorie called back, holding the line in her hand.

"Sure. Let it go." Marjorie dropped the line overboard and watched the baits go down through the water.

She came in with the boat and ran the second line out the same way. Each time Nick set a heavy slab of driftwood across the butt of the rod to hold it solid and propped it up at an angle with a small slab. He reeled in the slack line so the line ran taut out to where the bait rested on the sandy floor of the channel and set the click on the reel. When a trout, feeding on the bottom, took the bait it would run with it, taking line out of the reel in a rush and making the reel sing with the click on.

Marjorie rowed up the point a little way so she would not disturb the line. She pulled hard on the oars and the boat went way up the beach. Little waves came in with it. Marjorie stepped out of the boat and Nick pulled the boat high up the beach.

"What's the matter, Nick?" Marjorie asked.

"I don't know," Nick said, getting wood for a fire.

They made a fire with driftwood. Marjorie went to the boat and brought a blanket. The evening breeze blew the smoke toward the point, so Marjorie spread the blanket out between the fire and the lake.

Marjorie sat on the blanket with her back to the fire and waited for Nick. He came over and sat down beside her on the blanket. In back of them was the close second-growth timber of the point and in front was the bay with the mouth of Hortons Creek. It was not quite dark. The fire-light went as far as the water. They could both see the two steel rods at an angle over the dark water. The fire glinted on the reels.

Marjorie unpacked the basket of supper.

"I don't feel like eating," said Nick.

"Come on and eat, Nick."

"All right."

They ate without talking, and watched the two rods and the fire-light in the water.

"There's going to be a moon tonight," said Nick. He looked across the bay to the hills that were beginning to sharpen against the sky. Beyond the hills he knew the moon was coming up.

"I know it," Marjorie said happily.

"You know everything," Nick said.

"Oh, Nick, please cut it out! Please, please don't be that way!"

"I can't help it," Nick said. "You do. You know everything. That's the trouble. You know you do."

Marjorie did not say anything.

"I've taught you everything. You know you do. What don't you know, anyway?"

"Oh, shut up," Marjorie said. "There comes the moon."

They sat on the blanket without touching each other and watched the moon rise.

"You don't have to talk silly," Marjorie said. "What's really the matter?"

"I don't know."

"Of course you know."

"No I don't."

"Go on and say it."

Nick looked on at the moon, coming up over the hills.

"It isn't fun any more."

He was afraid to look at Marjorie. Then he looked at her. She sat there with her back toward him. He looked at her back. "It isn't fun any more. Not any of it."

She didn't say anything. He went on. "I feel as though everything was gone to hell inside of me. I don't know, Marge. I don't know what to say."

He looked on at her back.

"Isn't love any fun?" Marjorie said.

"No," Nick said. Marjorie stood up. Nick sat there his head in his hands.

"I'm going to take the boat," Marjorie called to him. "You can walk back around the point."

"All right," Nick said. "I'll push the boat off for you."

"You don't need to," she said. She was afloat in the boat on the water with the moonlight on it. Nick went back and lay down with his face in the blanket by the fire. He could hear Marjorie rowing on the water.

He lay there for a long time. He lay there while he heard Bill come into the clearing walking around through the woods. He felt Bill coming up to the fire. Bill didn't touch him, either.

"Did she go all right?" Bill said.

"Yes," Nick said, lying, his face on the blanket.

"Have a scene?"

"No, there wasn't any scene."

"How do you feel?"

"Oh, go away, Bill! Go away for a while."

Bill selected a sandwich from the lunch basket and walked over to have a look at the rods.

AFTERWORDS: TWO CLASSIC ESSAYS ON THE SHORT STORY

REVIEW OF "TWICE-TOLD TALES" BY EDGAR ALLAN POE*

WE SAID A FEW hurried words about Mr. Hawthorne in our last number, with the design of speaking more fully in the present. We are still, however, pressed for room, and must necessarily discuss his volumes more briefly and more at random than their high merits deserve.

The book professes to be a collection of *tales*, yet is, in two respects, misnamed. These pieces are now in their third republication, and, of course, are thrice-told. Moreover, they are by no means *all* tales, either in the ordinary or in the legitimate understanding of the term. Many of them are pure essays; for example, "Sights from a Steeple," "Sunday at Home," "Little Annie's Ramble," "A Rill from the Town Pump," "The Toll-Gatherer's Day," "The Haunted Mind," "The Sister Years," "Snow-Flakes," "Night Sketches," and "Foot-Prints on the Sea-Shore." We mention these matters chiefly on account of their discrepancy with that marked precision and finish by which the body of the work is distinguished.

Of the essays just named, we must be content to speak in brief. They are each and all beautiful, without being characterised by the polish and adaptation so visible in the tales proper. A painter would at once note their leading or predominant feature, and style it *repose*. There is no attempt at effect. All is quiet, thoughtful, subdued. Yet this repose may exist simultaneously with high originality of thought; and Mr. Hawthorne has demonstrated the fact. At every

*The review originally appeared in *Graham's Magazine* (May 1842).

turn we meet with novel combinations; yet these combinations never surpass the limits of the quiet. We are soothed as we read; and withal is a calm astonishment that ideas so apparently obvious have never occurred or been presented to us before. Herein our author differs materially from Lamb or Hunt or Hazlitt—who, with vivid originality of manner and expression, have less of the true novelty of thought than is generally supposed, and whose originality, at best, has an uneasy and meretricious quaintness, replete with startling effects unfounded in nature, and inducing trains of reflection which lead to no satisfactory result. The Essays of Hawthorne have much of the character of Irving, with more of originality, and less of finish; while, compared with the Spectator, they have a vast superiority at all points. The Spectator, Mr. Irving, and Mr. Hawthorne have in common that tranquil and subdued manner which we have chosen to denominate *repose*; but, in the case of the two former, this repose is attained rather by the absence of novel combination, or of originality, than otherwise, and consists chiefly in the calm, quiet, unostentatious expression of common-place thoughts, in an unambitious, unadulterated Saxon. In them, by strong effort, we are made to conceive the absence of all. In the essays before us the absence of effort is too obvious to be mistaken, and a strong under-current of *suggestion* runs continuously beneath the upper stream of the tranquil thesis. In short; these effusions of Mr. Hawthorne are the product of a truly imaginative intellect, restrained, and in some measure repressed, by fastidiousness of taste, by constitutional melancholy and by indolence.

But it is of his tales that we desire principally to speak. The tale proper, in our opinion, affords unquestionably the fairest field for the exercise of the loftiest talent, which can be afforded by the wide domains of mere prose. Were we bidden to say how the highest genius could be most advantageously employed for the best display of its own powers, we should answer, without hesitation—in the composition of a rhymed poem, not to exceed in length what might be perused in an hour. Within this limit alone can the highest order of true poetry exist. We need only here say, upon this topic, that, in almost all classes of composition, the unity of effect or impression is a point of the greatest importance. It is clear, moreover, that this unity cannot be thoroughly preserved in productions whose perusal cannot be completed at one sitting. We may continue the reading of a prose composition, from the very nature of prose itself, much longer than we can persevere, to any good purpose, in the perusal of a poem. This latter, if truly fulfilling the demands of the poetic sentiment, induces an exaltation of the soul which cannot be long sustained. All high excitements are necessarily transient. Thus a long poem is a paradox. And, without unity of impression, the deepest effects cannot be brought about. Epics were the offspring of an imperfect sense of Art, and their reign is no more. A poem *too* brief may produce a vivid, but never an intense or enduring impression. Without a certain continuity of effort—without a certain duration or repetition of purpose—the soul is never deeply moved. There must be the dropping of the water upon the rock. De Beranger has wrought brilliant things—pungent and spirit-stirring—but, like all immassive bodies, they lack *momentum,* and thus fail to satisfy the Poetic Sentiment. They sparkle and excite, but, from want of continuity, fail deeply to impress. Extreme brevity will degenerate into epigrammatism; but the sin of extreme length is even more unpardonable. *In medio tutissimus ibis.*

Were we called upon, however, to designate that class of composition which, next to such a poem as we have suggested, should best fulfil the demands of high genius—should offer it the most advantageous field of exertion—we should unhesitatingly speak of the prose tale, as Mr. Hawthorne has here exemplified it. We allude to the short prose narrative, requiring from a half-hour to one or two hours in its perusal. The ordinary novel is objectionable, from its length, for reasons already stated in substance. As it cannot be read at one sitting, it deprives itself, of course, of the immense force derivable from *totality*. Worldly interests intervening during the pauses of perusal, modify, annul, or counteract, in a greater or less degree, the impressions of the book. But simple cessation in reading, would, of itself, be sufficient to destroy the true unity. In the brief tale, however, the author is enabled to carry out the fullness of his intention, be it what it may. During the hour of perusal the soul of the reader is at the writer's control. There are no external or extrinsic influences—resulting from weariness or interruption.

A skilful literary artist has constructed a tale. If wise, he has not fashioned his thoughts to accommodate his incidents; but having conceived, with deliberate care, a certain unique or single *effect* to be wrought out, he then invents such incidents—he then combines such events as may best aid him in establishing this preconceived effect. If his very initial sentence tend not to the outbringing of this effect, then he has failed in his first step. In the whole composition there should be no word written, of which the tendency, direct or indirect, is not to the one preestablished design. And by such means, with such care and skill, a picture is at length painted which leaves in the mind of him who contemplates it with a kindred art, a sense of the fullest satisfaction. The idea of the tale has been presented unblemished, because undisturbed; and this is an end unattainable by the novel. Undue brevity is just as exceptionable here as in the poem; but undue length is yet more to be avoided.

We have said that the tale has a point of superiority even over the poem. In fact, while the *rhythm* of this latter is an essential aid in the development of the poet's highest idea—the idea of the Beautiful—the artificialities of this rhythm are an inseparable bar to the development of all points of thought or expression which have their basis in *Truth*. But Truth is often, and in very great degree, the aim of the tale. Some of the finest tales are tales of ratiocination. Thus the field of this species of composition, if not in so elevated a region on the mountain of Mind, is a table-land of far vaster extent than the domain of the mere poem. Its products are never so rich, but infinitely more numerous, and more appreciable by the mass of mankind. The writer of the prose tale, in short, may bring to his theme a vast variety of modes or inflections of thought and expression—(the ratiocinative, for example, the sarcastic, or the humorous) which are not only antagonistical to the nature of the poem, but absolutely forbidden by one of its most peculiar and indispensable adjuncts; we allude, of course, to rhythm. It may be added here, *par parenthèse,* that the author who aims at the purely beautiful in a prose tale is laboring at great disadvantage. For Beauty can be better treated in a poem. Not so with terror, or passion, or horror, or a multitude of such other points. And here it will be seen how full of prejudice are the usual animadversions against those *tales of effect,* many fine examples of which were found in the earlier numbers of Blackwood. The impressions produced were wrought in a legitimate sphere of action, and constituted a legitimate although sometimes an exaggerated interest. They were relished by every man of genius; although there were found many men of genius who condemned them without just ground. The true critic will but demand that the design intended be accomplished, to the fullest extent, by the means most advantageously applicable.

We have very few American tales of real merit—we may say, indeed, none, with the exception of "The Tales of a Traveller" of Washington Irving, and these "Twice-Told Tales" of Mr. Hawthorne. Some of the pieces of Mr. John Neal abound in vigor and originality; but in general, his compositions of this class are excessively diffuse, extravagant, and indicative of an imperfect sentiment of Art. Articles at random are, now and then, met with in our periodicals which might be advantageously compared with the best effusions of the British Magazines; but, upon the whole, we are far behind our progenitors in this department of literature.

Of Mr. Hawthorne's Tales we would say, emphatically, that they belong to the highest region of Art—an Art subservient to genius of a very lofty order. We had supposed, with good reason for so supposing, that he had been thrust into his present position by one of the impudent *cliques* which beset our literature, and whose pretensions it is our full purpose to expose at the earliest opportunity; but we have been most agreeably mistaken. We know of few compositions which the critic can more honestly commend than these "Twice-Told Tales." As Americans, we feel proud of the book.

Mr. Hawthorne's distinctive trait is invention, creation, imagination, originality—a trait which, in the literature of fiction, is positively worth all the rest. But the nature of originality, so far as regards its manifestation in letters, is but imperfectly understood. The inventive or original mind as frequently displays itself in novelty of *tone* as in novelty of matter. Mr. Hawthorne is original at *all* points.

It would be a matter of some difficulty to designate the best of these tales; we repeat that, without exception, they are beautiful. "Wakefield" is remarkable for the skill with which an old idea—a well-known incident—is worked up or discussed. A man of whims conceives the purpose of quitting his wife and residing *incognito,* for twenty years, in her immediate neighborhood. Something of this kind actually happened in London. The force of Mr. Hawthorne's tale lies in the analysis of the motives which must or might have impelled the husband to such folly, in the first instance, with the possible causes of his perseverance. Upon this thesis a sketch of singular power has been constructed.

"The Wedding Knell" is full of the boldest imagination—an imagination fully controlled by taste. The most captious critic could find no flaw in this production.

"The Minister's Black Veil" is a masterly composition of which the sole defect is that to the rabble its exquisite skill will be *caviare*. The *obvious* meaning of this article will be found to smother its insinuated one. The *moral* put into the mouth of the dying minister will be supposed to convey the *true* import of the narrative; and that a crime of dark dye (having reference to the "young lady"), has been committed, is a point which only minds congenial with that of the author will perceive.

"Mr. Higginbotham's Catastrophe" is vividly original and managed most dexterously.

"Dr. Heidegger's Experiment" is exceedingly well imagined, and executed with surpassing ability. The artist breathes in every line of it.

"The White Old Maid" is objectionable, even more than the "Minister's Black Veil," on the score of its mysticism. Even with the thoughtful and analytic, there will be much trouble in penetrating its entire import.

"The Hollow of the Three Hills," we would quote in full, had we space;—not as evincing higher talent than any of the other pieces, but as affording an excellent example of the author's peculiar ability. The subject is commonplace. A witch subjects the Distant and the Past to the view of a mourner. It has been the fashion to describe, in such cases, a mirror in which the images of the absent appear; or a cloud of smoke is made to arise, and thence the figures are gradually unfolded. Mr. Hawthorne has wonderfully heightened his effect by making the ear, in place of the eye, the medium by which the fantasy is conveyed. The head of the mourner is enveloped in the cloak of the witch, and within its magic folds there arise sounds which have an all-sufficient intelligence. Throughout this article also, the artist is conspicuous—not more in positive than in negative merits. Not only is all done that should be done, but (what perhaps is an end with more difficulty attained) there is nothing done which should not be. Every word *tells*, and there is not a word that does *not* tell. . . .

In the way of objection we have scarcely a word to say of these tales. There is, perhaps, a somewhat too general or prevalent *tone*—a tone of melancholy and mysticism. The subjects are insufficiently varied. There is not so much of *versatility* evinced as we might well be warranted in expecting from the high powers of Mr. Hawthorne. But beyond these trivial exceptions we have really none to make. The style is purity itself. Force abounds. High imagination gleams from every page. Mr. Hawthorne is a man of the truest genius. We only regret that the limits of our Magazine will not permit us to pay him that full tribute of commendation, which, under other circumstances, we should be so eager to pay.

THE PHILOSOPHY OF THE SHORT-STORY*
BY BRANDER MATTHEWS

II

THE DIFFERENCE BETWEEN A Novel and a Novelet is one of length only: a Novelet is a brief Novel. But the difference between a Novel and a Short-story is a difference of kind. A true Short-story is something other and something more than a mere story which is short. A true Short-story differs from the Novel chiefly in its essential unity of impression. In a far more exact and precise use of the word, a Short-story has unity as a Novel cannot have it. Often, it may be noted by the way, the Short-story fulfils the three false unities of the French classic drama: it shows one action, in one place, on one day. A Short-story deals with a single character, a single event, a single emotion, or the series of emotions called forth by a single situation. Poe's paradox that a poem cannot greatly exceed a hundred lines in length under penalty of ceasing to be one poem and breaking into a string of poems, may serve to suggest the precise difference between the Short-story and the Novel. The Short-story is the single effect, complete and self-contained, while the Novel is of necessity broken into a series of episodes. Thus the Short-story has, what the Novel cannot have, the effect of "totality," as Poe called it, the unity of impression.

Of a truth the Short-story is not only not a chapter out of a Novel, or an incident or an episode extracted from a longer tale, but at its best it impresses the reader with the belief that it would be spoiled if it were made larger, or if it were incorporated into a more elaborate work. The

---

*From *The Philosophy of the Short-Story,* by Brander Matthews (New York: Longmans, Green and Co., 1901).

difference in spirit and in form between the Lyric and the Epic is scarcely greater than the difference between the Short-story and the Novel; and the "Raven" and "How we brought the good news from Ghent to Aix" are not more unlike the "Lady of the Lake" and "Paradise Lost," in form and in spirit, than the "Luck of Roaring Camp," and the "Man without a Country," two typical Short-stories, are unlike "Vanity Fair" and the "Heart of Midlothian," two typical Novels.

Another great difference between the Short-story and the Novel lies in the fact that the Novel, nowadays at least, must be a love-tale, while the Short-story need not deal with love at all. Although there are to be found by diligent search a few Novels which are not love-tales—and of course "Robinson Crusoe" is the example that swims at once into recollection—yet the immense majority of Novels have the tender passion either as the motive power of their machinery or as the pivot on which their plots turn. Although "Vanity Fair" was a Novel without a hero, nearly every other Novel has a hero and a heroine; and the novelist, however unwillingly, must concern himself in their love-affairs. . . .

While the Novel cannot get on easily without love, the Short-story can. Since love seems to be almost the only thing which will give interest to a long story, the writer of Novels has to get love into his tales as best he may, even when the subject rebels and when he himself is too old to take any delight in the mating of John and Joan. But the Short-story, being brief, does not need a love-interest to hold its parts together, and the writer of Short-stories has thus a greater freedom; he may do as he pleases; from him a love-tale is not expected.

But other things are required of a writer of Short-stories which are not required of a writer of Novels. The novelist may take his time; he has abundant room to turn about. The writer of Short-stories must be concise, and compression, a vigorous compression, is essential. For him, more than for any one else, the half is more than the whole. Again, the novelist may be commonplace, he may bend his best energies to the photographic reproduction of the actual; if he show us a cross-section of real life we are content; but the writer of Short-stories must have originality and ingenuity. If to compression, originality, and ingenuity he add also a touch of fantasy, so much the better.

In fact, it may be said that no one has ever succeeded as a writer of Short-stories who had not ingenuity, originality, and compression;

and that most of those who have succeeded in this line had also the touch of fantasy. But there are not a few successful novelists lacking, not only in fantasy and compression, but also in ingenuity and originality; they had other qualities, no doubt, but these they had not. If an example must be given, the name of Anthony Trollope will occur to all. Fantasy was a thing he abhorred; compression he knew not; and originality and ingenuity can be conceded to him only by a strong stretch of the ordinary meaning of the words. Other qualities he had in plenty, but not these. And, not having them, he was not a writer of Short-stories. Judging from his essay on Hawthorne, one may even go so far as to say that Trollope did not know a good Short-story when he saw it.

I have written "Short-stories" with a capital S and a hyphen because I wished to emphasize the distinction between the Short-story and the story which is merely short. The Short-story is a high and difficult department of fiction. The story which is short can be written by anybody who can write at all; and it may be good, bad, or indifferent; but at its best it is wholly unlike the Short-story. In "An Editor's Tales" Trollope has given us excellent specimens of the story which is short; and the narratives which make up this book are amusing enough and clever enough, but they are wanting in the individuality and in the completeness of the genuine Short-story. Like the brief tales to be seen in the British monthly magazines and in the Sunday editions of American newspapers into which they are copied, they are, for the most part, either merely amplified anecdotes or else incidents which might have been used in a Novel just as well as not.

Now, it cannot be said too emphatically that the genuine Short-story abhors the idea of the Novel. It neither can be conceived as part of a Novel, nor can it be elaborated and expanded so as to form a Novel. A good Short-story is no more the synopsis of a Novel than it is an episode from a Novel. A slight Novel, or a Novel cut down, is a Novelet: it is not a Short-story. Mr. Howells's "Their Wedding Journey" and Miss Howard's "One Summer" are Novelets,—little Novels. Mr. Anstey's "Vice Versa," Mr. Besant's "Case of Mr. Lucraft," Hugh Conway's "Called Back," Mr. Julian Hawthorne's "Archibald Malmaison," and Mr. Stevenson's "Strange Case of Dr. Jekyll and Mr. Hyde" are Short-stories in conception although they are without the compression which the Short-story requires. . . .

III

It is to be noted as a curious coincidence that there is no exact word in English to designate either *vers de société* or the Short-story, and yet in no language are there better *vers de société* or Short-stories than in English. It may be remarked also that there is a certain likeness between *vers de société* and Short-stories: for one thing, both seem easy to write and are hard. And the typical qualifications of each may apply with almost equal force to the other: *vers de société* should reveal compression, ingenuity, and originality, and Short-stories should have brevity and brilliancy. In no class of writing are neatness of construction and polish of execution more needed than in the writing of *vers de société* and of Short-stories. The writer of Short-stories must have the sense of form, which has well been called "the highest and last attribute of a creative writer." The construction must always be logical, adequate, harmonious.

Here is a weak spot in Mr. W. H. Bishop's "One of the Thirty Pieces," the fundamental idea of which—that fatality awaits every successive possessor of every one of the coins once paid to Judas for his betrayal of Jesus—has genuine strength, not fully developed in the story. But other of Mr. Bishop's stories—the "Battle of Bunkerloo," for instance—are admirable in all ways, conception and execution having an even excellence. Again, Hugh Conway's "Daughter of the Stars" is a Short-story which fails from sheer deficiency of style: here is one of the very finest Short-story ideas—the startling and fascinating fantasy that by sheer force of will a man might have been able to draw down from the depths of the sky a lovely astral maid to share his finite human life—ever given to any mortal, but the handling is at best barely sufficient. To do justice to the conception would tax the execution of a poet. We could merely wonder what the tale would have been had it occurred to Hawthorne, to Poe, or to Theophile Gautier. An idea logically developed by one possessing the sense of form and the gift of style is what we look for in the Short-story.

But, although the sense of form and the gift of style are essential to the writing of a good Short-story, they are secondary to the idea, to the conception, to the subject. Those who hold, with a certain American novelist, that it is no matter what you have to say, but only how you say it, need not attempt the Short-story; for the Short-story, far more than the Novel even, demands a subject. The Short-story is nothing if there is no story to tell;—one might almost say that a Short-story is nothing if it has no plot,—except that "plot" may suggest to some readers a complication and an elaboration which are not really needful. But a plan—if this word is less liable to misconception than "plot"—a plan a Short-story must have, while it would be easy to cite Novels of eminence which are wholly amorphous—for example, "Tristram Shandy."

Whatever its length, the Novel, so Mr. Henry James told us not long ago, "is, in its broadest definition, a personal impression of life." The most powerful force in French fiction today is M. Emile Zola, chiefly known in America and England, I fear me greatly, by the dirt which masks and degrades the real beauty and firm strength not seldom concealed in his novels; and M. Emile Zola declares that the novelist of the future will not concern himself with the artistic evolution of a plot: he will take *une histoire quelconque,* any kind of a story, and make it serve his purpose,—which is to give elaborate pictures of life in all its most minute details.

It is needless to say that the acceptance of these stories is a negation of the Short-story. Important as are form and style, the subject of the Short-story is of more importance yet. What you have to tell is of greater interest than how you tell it. . . . As a Short-story need not be a love-story, it is of no consequence at all whether they marry or die; but a Short-story in which nothing happens at all is an absolute impossibility.

Perhaps the difference between a Short-story and a Sketch can best be indicated by saying that, while a Sketch may be still-life, in a Short-story something always happens. A Sketch may be an outline of character, or even a picture of a mood of mind, but in a Short-story there must be something done, there must be an action. Yet the distinction, like that between the Novel and the Romance, is no longer of vital importance. In the preface to the "House of the Seven Gables," Hawthorne sets forth the difference between the Novel and the Romance, and claims for himself the privileges of the romancer. Mr. Henry James fails to see this difference. The fact is, that the Short-story and the Sketch, the Novel and the Romance, melt and merge one into the other, and no man may mete the boundaries of each, though their extremes lie far apart. With the more complete understanding of the principle of development and evolution in literary art, as in physical nature, we see the futility of a strict and rigid classification into precisely defined genera and species. All that is needful for us to remark now is that the Short-story has limitless possibilities: it may be as realistic as the most prosaic novel, or as fantastic as the most ethereal romance.

VII

The Short-story should not be void or without form, but its form may be whatever the author please. He has an absolute liberty of choice. It may be a personal narrative, like Poe's "Descent into the Maelstrom" or Mr. Hale's "My Double, and how he Undid me"; it may be impersonal, like Mr. Frederick B. Perkins's "Devil-Puzzlers" or Colonel J. W. De Forest's "Brigade Commander"; it may be a conundrum, like Mr. Stockton's insoluble query, the "Lady or the Tiger?"; it may be "A Bundle of Letters," like Mr. Henry James's story, or "A Letter and a Paragraph," like Mr. Bunner's; it may be a medley of letters and telegrams and narrative, like Mr. Aldrich's "Margery Daw"; it may be cast in any one of these forms, or in a combination of all of them, or in a wholly new form, if haply such may yet be found by diligent search. Whatever its form, it should have symmetry of design. If it have also wit or humour, pathos or poetry, and especially a distinct and unmistakable flavour of individuality, so much the better. But the chief requisites are compression, originality, ingenuity, and now and again a touch of fantasy. Sometimes we may detect in a writer of Short-stories a tendency toward the over-elaboration of ingenuity, toward the exhibition of ingenuity for its own sake, as in a Chinese puzzle. But mere cleverness is incompatible with greatness, and to commend a writer as "very clever" is not to give him high praise. From this fault of super-subtlety, women are free for the most part. They are more likely than men to rely on broad human emotion, and their tendency in error is toward the morbid analysis of a high-strung moral situation.

VIII

The more carefully we study the history of fiction the more clearly we perceive that the Novel and the Short-story are essentially different—that the difference between them is not one of mere length only, but fundamental. The Short-story seeks one set of effects in its own way, and the Novel seeks a wholly distinct set of effects in a wholly distinct way. We are led also to the conclusion that the Short-story—in spite of the fact that in our language it has no name of its own—is one of the few sharply defined literary forms. It is a *genre,* as M. Brunetière terms it, a species, as a naturalist might call it, as individual as the Lyric itself and as various. It is as distinct an entity as the Epic, as Tragedy, as Comedy. Now the Novel is not a form of the same sharply defined individuality; it is—or at least it may be—anything. It is the child of the Epic and the heir of the Drama; but it is a hybrid. And one of the foremost of living American novelists, who happens also to be one of the most acute and sympathetic of American critics, has told me that he was often distracted by the knowledge of this fact even while he was engaged in writing a novel.

In the history of literature the Short-story was developed long before the Novel, which indeed is but a creature of yesterday, and which was not really established in popular esteem as a worthy rival of the drama until after the widespread success of the Waverley Novels in the early years of the nineteenth century. The Short-story also seems much easier of accomplishment than the Novel, if only because it is briefer. And yet the list of the masters of the Short-story is far less crowded than the list of the masters of the longer form. There are a score or more very great novelists recorded in the history of fiction; but there are scarcely more than half a score Short-story writers of an equal eminence.

From Chaucer and Boccaccio we must spring across the centuries until we come to Hawthorne and Poe almost without finding another name that insists upon enrolment. In these five hundred years there were great novelists not a few, but there was no great writer of Short-stories. A little later than Hawthorne and Poe, and indeed almost contemporaneous with them, are Mérimée and Turgenef, whose title to be recorded there is none to dispute. Now at the end of the nineteenth century we find two more that no competent critic would dare to omit,—Guy de Maupassant and Rudyard Kipling.

BIOGRAPHICAL SKETCHES OF THE AUTHORS

SHERWOOD ANDERSON, born in 1876 in Camden, Ohio, left a successful business career, as well as his wife and children, to pursue his writing. *Winesburg, Ohio* (1919), a collection of interrelated short stories and sketches that combine portrayals of small-town life and explorations of the characters' inner lives, established the author as one of the great short-story writers of the twentieth century. His unadorned, almost spoken prose style influenced Ernest Hemingway and William Faulkner, as well as such later masters as Raymond Carver.

AMBROSE BIERCE, born in 1842 in Meigs County, Ohio, fought in the American Civil War, then went to work as a newspaperman, eventually writing as a satirist for William Randolph Hearst at the San Francisco *Examiner*. He was part of a literary circle that included Bret Harte and Mark Twain, and his numerous short stories and Civil War tales, collected in *In the Midst of Life* and other volumes, gave voice to the author's fiercely bitter cynicism. After an estrangement from his socialite wife and the deaths of his two sons, Bierce became increasingly disillusioned with life. In 1913 he crossed the border into Mexico and was never heard from again.

WILLA CATHER, born in 1873 in Virginia, moved with her family to Red Cloud, Nebraska, when she was ten years old. She began her publishing career at *Home Monthly* magazine in Pittsburgh and moved to New York City in 1906, where she worked for *McClure's Magazine* as a writer and eventually as the managing editor. Considered one of the great figures of early-twentieth-century American literature, Cather eventually followed the advice of a friend, writer Sarah Orne Jewett, and devoted herself to writing fiction.

She drew much of her inspiration from life in the Midwest and wrote several novels of the prairies, one of the best known of which is *O Pioneers!* (1913). She continued to write well into her later years and died in New York City in 1947.

CHARLES W. CHESNUTT, born in 1858 in Cleveland, Ohio, was the first African-American writer of fiction to be widely recognized. He spent most of his youth and young adulthood in North Carolina, and his knowledge of black culture in the South shaped all of his stories and novels. Chesnutt moved north to Cleveland to pursue a writing career, and in his most prolific period—between 1885 and 1905—he published more than fifty short stories and essays. His "The Goophered Grapevine" (1887) was the first story by a black writer to be accepted by *Atlantic Monthly* magazine. Chesnutt's collection *The Wife of His Youth and Other Stories of the Color Line* (1899) is considered a masterpiece for its unflinching realism in portraying slavery and the black experience during the American Reconstruction era.

SAMUEL LANGHORNE CLEMENS (MARK TWAIN), born in 1835, grew up in Hannibal, Missouri, a small town on the Mississippi River. Twain settled into writing after stints as a printer, newspaperman, gold panner, and riverboat pilot. He enjoyed his first success with *The Celebrated Jumping Frog of Calaveras County and Other Sketches* (1867), a collection of humorous writings that is rich in the mastery of American vernacular and biting satire—Twain's hallmarks. Though Twain traveled widely and settled in Connecticut, where he died in 1910, his best-known works are the novels drawn from his youth on the Mississippi, *The Adventures of Tom Sawyer* and *The Adventures of Huckleberry Finn*.

STEPHEN CRANE was born in 1871. In his short, brilliant career, he produced six novels, two collections of poetry, and more than 100 stories, works marked by keen psychological realism and precise observation. For *Maggie: A Girl of the Streets* (1893) Crane shadowed a New York prostitute for weeks, and in *The Red Badge of Courage* (1895) he drew on his own intuition and emotional insights to create a story of a young recruit's experiences during one key battle; the work is often cited as the first modern novel. Crane and his companion, Cora

Stewart, settled in England, where they socialized with such literary figures as Henry James, Joseph Conrad, and Ford Maddox Ford. Crane died of severe hemorrhaging of the lungs on June 5, 1900, five months before his twenty-ninth birthday.

F. SCOTT FITZGERALD, born in 1896, is best known for *The Great Gatsby* (1925), which has been called the greatest American novel of the twentieth century—as well as for his ill-fated marriage to Zelda Fitzgerald, the couple's high-flying lifestyle, and his alcoholism. After the publication and success of his first novel, *This Side of Paradise* (1920), Fitzgerald had his pick of high-paying magazines willing to publish his stories, such as "Bernice Bobs Her Hair" and "The Diamond as Big as the Ritz." All told, Fitzgerald had written some 160 magazine stories by the time he died of a heart attack at age forty-five, and in them and his novels he captured the essence of American society, which he found both addictively charming and repulsively base.

MARY E. WILKINS FREEMAN, born in 1852, spent an impoverished childhood in Brattleboro, Vermont, and other New England villages, which she would later immortalize in her sketches of conventional life, frustration, and steadfast morality. Freeman began writing stories and poems for children but quickly achieved success with her literature for adults. Throughout her literary career, Freeman published a dozen volumes of short stories, but her first two—*A Humble Romance and Other Stories* (1887) and *A New England Nun, and Other Stories* (1891)—remain the most popular.

CHARLOTTE PERKINS GILMAN, born in 1860, was a descendant of the Beechers, the prominent New England family, but was raised in poverty in and around Hartford, Connecticut. After marrying the artist Charles Walter Stetson and giving birth to a daughter, she fell into a deep depression. When she emerged from it several years later, she began lecturing and writing stories, poetry, and social essays concerning labor, ethics, and nineteenth-century womanhood. Her semi-autobiographical story "The Yellow Wall-Paper" became an essential tract of the women's movement, and her most famous work, *Women and Economics*, earned her international acclaim. Gilman committed suicide in 1935 while battling breast cancer.

NATHANIEL HAWTHORNE, born in Salem, Massachusetts, in 1804, was profoundly influenced by his family's New England Puritanism. Although he decided early on to rely "for support upon my pen" and counted among his admirers Herman Melville, Ralph Waldo Emerson, and Henry David Thoreau, Hawthorne was forced to support his wife and children by working at the custom houses in Boston and Salem and as U.S. consul to Liverpool, England. In his short stories and the now-classic novel *The Scarlet Letter* (1850), he explored recurrent themes of sin, guilt, and punishment.

ERNEST HEMINGWAY, born in 1899, is widely regarded as America's preeminent stylist of the twentieth century. He began his career as a journalist and went to Europe as an ambulance driver in World War I. In the 1920s he settled into life in Paris among the so-called Lost Generation—a group that included F. Scott Fitzgerald, John Dos Passos, and other great writers. He soon had success with the 1925 publication of *In Our Time*, one of his many collections of short stories; the next year he published *The Sun Also Rises*, the first of his critically acclaimed novels, which are now classics. Hemingway was awarded the Nobel Prize for Literature in 1954. He died of self-inflicted shotgun wounds in 1961.

HENRY JAMES, born into a wealthy family in New York City in 1843, spent his childhood in the United States and Europe. He began writing stories, reviews, and articles for magazines soon after dropping out of Harvard Law School. He frequently traveled to Europe and in 1876 settled permanently in London. In novels such as *Daisy Miller*, *The Wings of the Dove*, and *The Ambassadors*, he considered the differences between European and American culture. James is cited as one of literature's great stylists; because of both his ability to reveal his characters' inner lives and his complex style, characterized by lengthy sentences, he is sometimes said to have foreshadowed the "stream of consciousness" mode of writing. By the time of his death in1916, he had written twenty novels, 112 stories, and twelve plays, as well as volumes of travel writing and literary journalism and criticism.

SARAH ORNE JEWETT, born in 1849 in South Berwick, Maine, is one of America's most celebrated regional writers. She often accompanied her physician father on his rounds to visit farmers and fishermen; when she began to write, she portrayed these people and the landscapes of Maine with great precision. *Deephaven* (1877), a collection of sketches about life in a New England town, was published to great acclaim, but her best-known work is *The Country of the Pointed Firs* (1896), interrelated stories about life in a coastal town in Maine. Her career ended abruptly when she was severely injured in a carriage accident in 1902; she died seven years later.

JACK LONDON was born in 1876 in San Francisco. Largely self-educated, he worked as a newspaper delivery boy, cannery worker, and seaman aboard a sealing vessel and joined the Klondike Gold Rush in 1897. London returned to California and began writing newspaper articles on the Russo-Japanese war and the Mexican Revolution, as well as short stories; within two decades he had published forty-seven books. By 1913 he was the highest-paid writer in the world. His best-known works, *The Call of the Wild* and *White Fang*, draw heavily on his Yukon experience and reflect themes common to his work: fascination with Charles Darwin's notion of the survival of the fittest, avoidance of sentimentality, and commitment to presenting injustice and brutality. A hard liver and heavy drinker, London died of uremia and renal colic in 1916.

HERMAN MELVILLE was born in New York City in 1819. After working at several jobs to help support his mother and siblings, he sailed as a hand aboard the *Acushnet*, a whaling vessel bound for the South Seas; he spent time in the Marquesas Islands, Tahiti, and Hawaii. These foreign adventures provided material for Melville's first two novels, *Typee* (1846) and *Omoo* (1847), which met with success, as well as for *Moby-Dick* (1851), which was not well received. Tormented by this and other failures, Melville eventually gave up writing as a profession and for nineteen years held a job as a customs inspector at New York harbor. It was not until the "Melville revival" of the 1920s—some thirty years after his death in 1891—that *Moby-Dick* earned for the author the status of one of American literature's great masters.

EDGAR ALLAN POE was born in 1809, in Boston, the son of two actors. After an education in England and a brief stint at West Point, he began publishing prose and poetry and working as an editor. His "Murders in the Rue Morgue" is considered the first detective story, "The Fall of the House of Usher" established him as a writer of supernatural horror stories, and his poem "The Raven" brought him widespread fame. Despite these successes, Poe struggled with alcoholism and financial insolvency; he died after a drinking binge in 1849.

WILLIAM SYDNEY PORTER (O. HENRY) was born in 1862 in Greensboro, North Carolina. As a young man he went to Texas, where he worked as a ranch hand, newspaper reporter, and bank teller. Charged with embezzlement, Porter spent three years in prison and began to publish stories under the pseudonym "O. Henry." He drew from his experiences, writing about tramps and millionaires, shopgirls and Southern aristocrats, cops, thieves, cowboys, and con men, in stories that often have a surprise twist, or "snapper"—Porter's trademark ending. After his release from prison, Porter moved to New York, where his popularity soared; he wrote a story a week for the Sunday New York *World* and sold pieces to other magazines as well. By the time of his death, of tuberculosis and alcoholism at age forty-seven, O. Henry's full-blown literary career had lasted only ten years, but he had published hundreds of stories that continue to appeal to a worldwide audience.

EDITH WHARTON was born Edith Newbold Jones in 1862, into such wealth and privilege that her family inspired the phrase "keeping up with the Joneses." Her first major novel, *The House of Mirth*, was published in 1905 and enjoyed considerable literary success. *Ethan Frome* appeared six years later, solidifying Wharton's reputation as an important novelist; throughout her career she would publish many other novels and collections of short fiction. She earned the Pulitzer Prize for Fiction in 1921 for her novel *The Age of Innocence*—the first time the award had been won by a woman. Although Wharton settled in Europe, she continued to write about American customs and manners and often associated with such American writers as Henry James, F. Scott Fitzgerald, Sinclair Lewis, and Jack London. She died in France in 1937.

FOR FURTHER READING

Anderson, Sherwood. *Certain Things Last: The Selected Short Stories of Sherwood Anderson.* Edited by Charles E. Modlin. New York: Four Walls Eight Windows, 1992.

———. *Winesburg, Ohio.* Introduction by Malcolm Cowley. New York: Viking Press, 1960.

Bierce, Ambrose. *The Complete Short Stories of Ambrose Bierce.* Edited by Ernest Jerome Hopkins. Garden City, NY: Doubleday, 1970.

Cather, Willa. *Collected Short Fiction, 1892–1912.* Edited by Virginia Faulkner; introduction by Mildred R. Bennett. Lincoln: University of Nebraska Press, 1970.

———. *The Troll Garden.* New York: McClure, Phillips, 1905.

Chesnutt, Charles W. *Stories, Novels, and Essays.* New York: Library of America, 2002.

Crane, Stephen. *Complete Short Stories and Sketches of Stephen Crane.* Edited by Thomas A. Gullason. Garden City, NY: Doubleday, 1963.

Fitzgerald, F. Scott. *The Stories of F. Scott Fitzgerald.* Introduction by Malcolm Cowley. New York: Charles Scribner's Sons, 1951.

Freeman, Mary E. Wilkins. *A New England Nun, and Other Stories.* New York: Harper and Brothers, 1891.

———. *Selected Stories of Mary E. Wilkins Freeman.* Edited by Marjorie Pryse. New York: W. W. Norton, 1983.

Gilman, Charlotte Perkins. *The Yellow Wall-paper and Selected Stories of Charlotte Perkins Gilman.* Edited by Denise D. Knight. Newark: University of Delaware Press, 1994.

Hawthorne, Nathaniel. *Hawthorne's Short Stories.* Edited by Newton Arvin. New York: Alfred A. Knopf, 1946.

———. *Mosses from an Old Manse.* Boston: Houghton Mifflin, 1883.

Hemingway, Ernest. *The Complete Short Stories of Ernest Hemingway.* New York: Scribner's, 1987.

———. *In Our Time.* New York: Charles Scribner's Sons, 1930.

Henry, O. *The Complete Works of O. Henry.* With a Foreword by Harry Hansen. Garden City, NY: Doubleday, 1953.

James, Henry. *The Complete Tales of Henry James.* Edited by Leon Edel. Philadelphia: Lippincott, 1962–1964.

Jewett, Sarah Orne. *The Country of the Pointed Firs, and Other Stories.* Selected and arranged, with a preface, by Willa Cather. Garden City, NY: Doubleday, 1954.

London, Jack. *The Complete Short Stories of Jack London.* Edited by Earle Labor, Robert C. Leitz III, and I. Milo Shepard. Stanford, CA: Stanford University Press, 1993.

Melville, Herman. *Complete Shorter Fiction by Herman Melville.* Introduction by John Updike. New York: Alfred A. Knopf, 1997.

———. *Piazza Tales.* Edited by Egbert S. Oliver. New York: Hendricks House, 1948.

Poe, Edgar Allan. *Complete Stories and Poems.* Garden City, NY: Doubleday, 1966.

Twain, Mark. *The Complete Short Stories of Mark Twain Now Collected for the First Time.* Edited by Charles Neider. Garden City, NY: Doubleday, 1957.

Wharton, Edith. *Collected Stories, 1891–1910.* New York: Library of America, 2001.

———. *Collected Stories, 1911–1937.* New York: Library of America, 2001.

Other Works Cited in the Introduction

Hemingway, Ernest. *Green Hills of Africa.* New York: Charles Scribner's Sons, 1935.

James, Henry. *Hawthorne.* New York: Harper and Brothers, 1879.

———. *The Notebooks of Henry James.* Edited by F. O. Matthiessen and Kenneth B. Murdock. New York: Oxford University Press, 1947.

———. *The Art of the Novel: Critical Prefaces by Henry James.* New York: Charles Scribner's Sons, 1934.

Melville, Herman. "Hawthorne and His Mosses." *Literary World* (August 17–24, 1850).

Poe, Edgar Allan. "Review of *Twice-Told Tales.*" *Graham's Magazine* (May 1842).